SOUL KEEPER

"N good," he said, his words coming out as a strained whisper. "N good, Devin. Get up on your feet. Get up, damn it, get up or y u'll die."

It eemed both his mind and body were just fine with that sec d option. His vision darkened. He braced his weight on his arm and heaved with each individual breath.

Sh ld have turned back, he thought. *Should have . . . I should . . . An   a, take me into your arms . . .*

A rumbling noise pushed through his clouded mind and bro ght his gaze up to the mountain. Devin didn't understand, and e was too tired to try. The boulders were rising before him, sno   rolling off arms and legs. They rose as his mind dropped lo   a d unconsciousness blessedly took him from the pain.

SOUL KEEPER

DAVID DALGLISH

www.orbitbooks.net

ORBIT

First published in Great Britain in 2019 by Orbit

3 5 7 9 10 8 6 4 2

Copyright © 2019 by David Dalglish

Map copyright © 2019 by Tim Paul

Excerpt from *The Thousand Deaths of Ardor Benn* by Tyler Whitesides
Copyright © 2018 by Tyler Whitesides

The moral right of the author has been asserted.

A CIP catalogue record for this book
is available from the British Library.

ISBN 978-0-356-51158-0

Printed and bound in Great Britain by
Clays Ltd, Elcograf S.p.A

Papers used by Orbit are from well-managed forests
and other responsible sources.

Orbit
An imprint of
Little, Brown Book Group
Carmelite House
50 Victoria Embankment
London EC4Y 0DZ

An Hachette UK Company
www.hachette.co.uk

www.orbitbooks.net

For Devin,
A great kid who left us far too soon

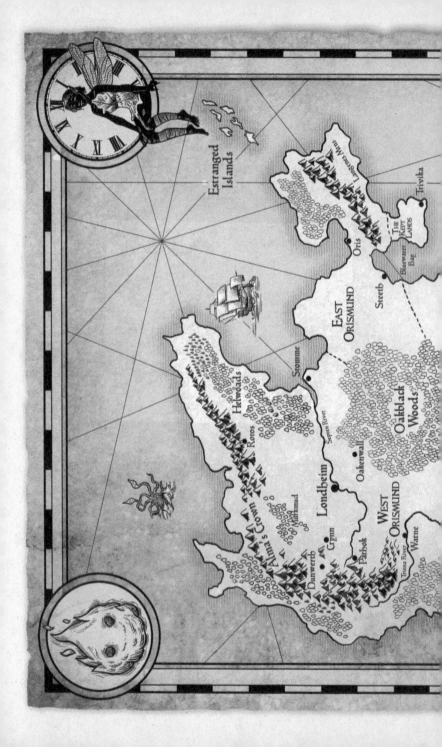

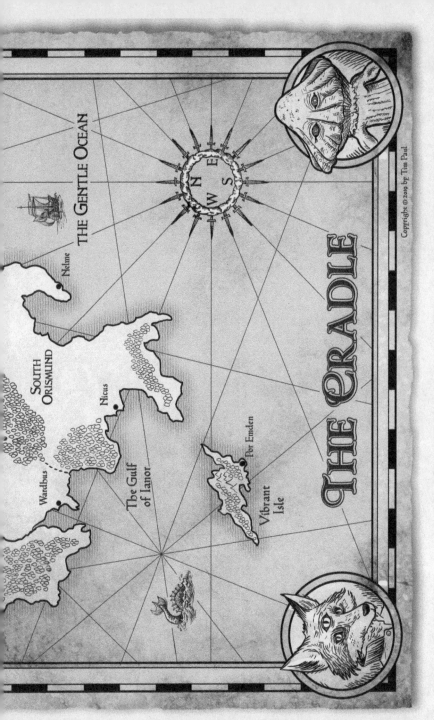

THE GENTLE OCEAN

SOUTH
ORISMUND

Nelme

Nicus

Wardbus

The Gulf
of Ianor

Por Emden

Vibrant
Isle

THE CRADLE

N
W   E
S

Copyright © 2019 by Tim Paul

CHAPTER 1

The reaping hour approached. Devin Eveson stood with the town mayor in a circle of pines, an unlit pyre between them. Starlight twinkled off the snow on the branches. The moon's glow created a ghostly skyline of the surrounding mountains.

"I hope your presence means Milly's soul finds rest," Mayor Jonathan said as he huddled in his worn brown coat. His pale skin was weathered and his head shaved, but his beard was still a lively black despite his age. "For thirty reapings I never did bury a body, but these last few? It seems the Three Sisters have grown fickle. Or perhaps they have abandoned us completely."

A young girl lay upon the pyre before Devin, seven or eight years old at most. All but her face was covered with a pale green blanket. Snow settled atop her raven hair, granting her a soft crown. It saddened Devin to see a child taken so young. Whatever disease was ravaging Dunwerth was a cruel and vicious one. Black welts covered the dark skin of her neck, and if he pulled the blanket away, he'd find dozens more across her body.

Do you hear my voice, Milly? he spoke inside his mind. *Heed my prayer, and enter the arms of the Sisters. Find safety. Find peace.*

"The Sisters have not abandoned us," Devin said to Jonathan. "When faith is tested, it either grows stronger or breaks entirely. We must not give up on the Sisters, lest they give up on us."

He used his feet to clear away snow from where he would kneel and pray. His heavy leather coat and padded gray trousers would protect him from the cold, but he'd rather not have his knees soak through.

"Maybe so," Jonathan said. "But since the plague hit our village I've had to bury the last five, not burn. Never needed a Soulkeeper to help me perform the ritual, not once until this mess began."

"And souls used to traverse to the heavens without any intercession necessary at all. The world changes, however slowly, and so we must change with it."

Dunwerth was not alone in its steady increase in burials. Village elders and town mayors used to be sufficient for the ritual, but now all across the Cradle, the need for skilled Soulkeepers grew. Anwyn, caretaker of the dead, seemed less and less inclined to guide souls to her bosom, forcing people to bury the bodies in the hope that their souls might return on their own some future night.

Devin recited the ritual prayer, taking great care with every syllable. He thanked Alma for the granting of life, Lyra for caring for Milly during her few short years, and last Anwyn for taking her soul into the heavens for an eternity of bliss. That finished, he scooped a handful of snow and then pressed it upon Milly's face, slowly covering everything above the neck. Mud from ocean waters was used on the east coast, rich black prairie soil in the southern grasslands, but here in the mountains, the snow would be her pyre mask.

Once it was finished Devin pulled the burnt leather glove off his right hand and carefully drew a triangle upon the mask and then a circle around the downward point. Each side represented one of the Sisters and their connections to the others, while the bottom circle was both sun and moon, life beginning and ending at the same place in the heavens. Devin clasped his hands behind his back, bowed his head, and waited.

The moon rose higher. Not a cloud marred the beautiful field of stars. In their light, at the base of the lonely mountain range that was Alma's Crown, in a circle of trees at the edge of the Dunwerth Forest, the two waited for Milly's soul to ascend.

Devin immediately felt the presence of the reaping hour upon its arrival. The world tensed, the animals hushed, the night fowl grew quiet and alert. Devin held his breath, his jaw clenched tightly as he stared at the symbol he'd drawn upon Milly's forehead. His hand drifted to the pendant hidden underneath his shirt, a silver moon inscribed into the downward point of a triangle. The symbol of Anwyn, goddess of the dusk, the caretaker of souls, and the gentle hands waiting at the end of all things. The symbol of the Soulkeepers.

"By Alma, we are born," Devin whispered into the silence. "By Lyra, we are guided. By Anwyn, we are returned. Beloved Sisters, take her home."

A soft blue light swelled from Milly's forehead, shining as a translucent pillar reaching all the way to the stars themselves. The triangular symbol brightened, and a little orb of swirling light rose from her forehead and ascended the blue pillar. Devin's every muscle relaxed. The soul had separated cleanly from the body. The risk was over.

Though the Mindkeepers of the Keeping Church debated a soul's true makeup, Devin had never wondered. In that brilliant white light he saw memories, emotions, flickering faces of loved ones. What else could the soul be but all the person had once been? The orb rose upward, slowly at first, then faster and faster as the blue pillar of light lifted it heavenward. By the time it vanished from view, the beam had faded and the reaping hour had passed. Owls resumed hooting, and in the distance, Devin heard a chorus of wolves crying to the moon.

"Thank Anwyn for that," Jonathan said, scratching at his beard. "I wasn't sure I could handle another burial."

If the soul had remained within the body Devin would have buried it beneath the ground to offer Milly another chance, every quiet unwatched night, to break free of her mortal prison and ascend to the heavens. Now that the soul had parted, the body was an empty shell, cast off no differently than a snake shedding its skin. Devin removed the cap to the oilskin hanging from his belt and began splashing it across the pyre's thin, dry wood. He put the skin away once it was emptied and pulled two flint stones from a pouch belted to the small of his back.

Three quick strikes and the sparks lit the oil. Triangular stones created the pyre's outline, with thick, braced logs propping up the body atop a bed of thick kindling. It'd taken over an hour to build the pyre so that it would safely burn throughout the night. Come spring, life would sprout anew from the ash shaped in the symbol of the Three Sisters.

"A fine job, Soulkeeper," Jonathan said, patting him on the back. "But I fear you'll have many more rituals to perform if you can't spare us from this plague. The rest wait in my home. Come see the extent of our misery."

"Home" was a wood cabin in the heart of quiet little Dunwerth. Devin had visited many such villages across the western frontier, and he preferred their aura of kinship to the guarded hustle of the great cities. The air was quiet, the moon settling lazily above the white-capped mountains. A thin layer of snow crunched underneath Devin's feet as they walked the main road. He pulled his coat tighter about him and crossed his arms. His position as a Soulkeeper had sent him all throughout West Orismund, but this was a place of firsts. Dunwerth, tucked deep into the mountains of Alma's Crown, was the westernmost village in the nation, as well as the highest in elevation. It certainly felt it. The air moved thin in his throat, his lungs never quite full. As for the cold, it mocked his layers of clothing as it relentlessly assaulted his skin.

"I'm sorry we couldn't give you a better greeting," Jonathan said. He stopped before the door to his home and fumbled for a key. "We take pride in our hospitality. It's a poor host who asks you to perform a reaping ritual upon your arrival instead of warming your feet by a fire."

"I did not come for hospitality. I came to help you in your time of need." Devin smiled at the older man. "Though I'll admit sitting by a fire sounds divine right about now."

Jonathan inserted his key and turned it with a satisfying click of iron.

"I wish that you could."

Candles lit the wide main room of the home, and a healthy blaze burned in the fireplace. A long couch was pushed to one wall, a padded rocking chair against the other, each to make room for the six men and women sleeping on the floor. In the firelight Devin easily saw the dark splotches seeping into their blankets. Two children shared the couch; a third curled up like a cat in the seat of the chair. She was softly crying.

"Sisters help us all," Devin whispered. A smell of rotting fruit permeated the air, intermixed with sweat and piss. Occasionally one of the villagers coughed in their sleep, and it was painful to hear.

"I have a single guest room," Jonathan said. "Three more are in there. That's where I've put those who still possess the strength to walk."

"I see you're back," a woman said. Devin turned to greet her. She stood in the hallway leading toward what appeared to be a kitchen. Her curly hair was pulled back from her face in a bun, her brown eyes bloodshot from exhaustion. She held a large basin of water with several cloths soaking in it. "How did . . . you know. The ritual. Did it go well?"

"Milly's body is ash and her soul is in a place of light and happiness," Devin answered.

"That's good to hear," the woman said. She scooted past the two of them and put the basin on a small end table. "Milly was a precious girl, and she deserved a much happier life than what the Sisters gave her."

"Theresa's been helping me with the sick," Jonathan said as the woman wrung out one of the cloths. "We'd have lost more lives already if not for her care."

"I'm only delaying what's certain," Theresa said, shaking her head. "I'm glad you've come, Soulkeeper. Only the Goddesses can spare us from this cruelty."

Theresa gently washed the face of the nearest sleeping man, focusing on the weeping black welts. Devin slipped past her to where the crying girl lay in her chair. She was the youngest victim he had seen so far, even younger than Milly. Her face was buried into her pillow and her blanket bunched at her shoulders. She heard his footsteps and turned, her tear-filled eyes a beautiful almond color. Devin furrowed his brow upon realizing that the girl's skin bore no sign of the black welts.

"Milly's sister," Theresa explained. "Her name's Arleen. She's not ill but we thought it best she not be alone."

"Do you not fear contagion?" Devin asked quietly.

"Of course we do, but no other home will take her. They're all convinced she'll spread the illness that claimed her aunt and sister."

Devin understood their fear but still felt it cruel. He knelt so that he and Arleen were at the same height, pulled off his hat, and set it on his knee. The girl watched him closely, as if fearing he might bite.

"Hello, Arleen," Devin whispered.

"Hello," she said. Her eyes lingered on the triangle-and-moon pendant hanging from his neck. "Are you a Soulkeeper?"

"I am," Devin said. "How did you know?"

The girl pointed at his Anwyn pendant.

"Jonathan's told me stories. He said one Soulkeeper could fight off an entire village."

Devin smiled softly.

"Your mayor exaggerates, little one."

"So you don't fight bad people?"

"Most of the time villages request my aid when they need herbal medicine, legal judgments, a wedding sermon, or a large number of reaping rituals performed. But if a village is in danger, then yes, I'll fight the bad people. I try to use my words before I use my sword and pistol, though."

"Are there bad guys here?"

"No bad guys, just some sick people I hope to make better."

The girl sank underneath her blanket. Devin could see the exhaustion weighing heavily on her eyes, and his heart went out to her.

"I have trouble sleeping when I'm sad," he offered. "Are you having trouble sleeping, too?"

"I'm trying not to be sad or cry," Arleen whispered. "Aunt Theresa says I need to be strong."

It hurt to hear a child who looked maybe six years old say such a thing.

"Even the strong cry," Devin said. He reached into one of several pockets of his thick coat and pulled out a small dried root, which he held before her so she might see. "While you cry, try to remember everything good about Milly, all right? Her smile. Her laugh. The times you played together. And when you can't cry anymore, will you do something for me? Will you chew this root?"

"Will it make me sleepy?"

"It will," Devin said.

She took the root in hand, then swept it underneath her blankets.

"I'll try," she whispered.

"I ask for nothing more."

He pulled her blanket higher over her as she curled deeper into the chair, her bleary eyes squeezing shut. A mournful shiver ran through his chest. So far the girl showed no signs of the sickness. So far . . .

Jonathan's hand settled on his shoulder.

"Lyra's love graces your touch, Soulkeeper. We are blessed that the Keeping Church chose you for our request. Please, follow me. We must speak plainly."

Jonathan's room was beyond the kitchen, a tiny square crammed full of books on desks and shelves. The bed was an incidental thing in the corner. Two lit candles slowly burned in their holders.

"I know of three more infected staying with their families

instead of here," the mayor said as he settled onto the edge of his bed. "They claim they'll give better care than I can, and they may well be right."

"This disease," Devin asked. "Is it always fatal?"

"Without exception," Jonathan said. The words left his tongue like lead. "Have you ever witnessed anything like this, Soulkeeper?"

Devin knew a hundred recipes to dry, chop, boil, and grind herbs and flowers to heal a variety of ailments, and just as many prayers to accompany the cures. But this dark rot spreading throughout the body?

"Never this extreme," Devin said. "I know of nothing that will fight it. The best I can do is ease their pain."

Jonathan ran both hands over his bald head.

"I thought as much. Truth be told, Soulkeeper, I did not expect that you could help these people when I summoned you."

Devin kept his tone calm despite his sudden annoyance. Petitioning the Keeping Church for a Soulkeeper was a serious affair. There were always more in need than there were Soulkeepers to give it, and lying on a petition could result in criminal charges depending on how grievous the lie.

"I have helped many places beset by illness and disease," Devin said. "How could you be so certain I would be of no help here?"

"Because it's happened before," the mayor said. "Years ago, when my grandfather was mayor. No plant or flower helped then, and I expect none will help now."

Devin's anger grew.

"I have sworn upon my life to bring aid to Dunwerth in its time of need," he said. "If I am not here to administer to the sick, then pray tell, what am I here for?"

Jonathan rose from the bed, pulled a book off a shelf, and offered it to Devin. A page was marked by a long loose cloth, and he opened to it and glanced over the loose, sloppy handwriting in the dim candlelight.

> I know my story will earn no belief, so I write this in secret, to be judged only after my death. I'll care not your opinions once in Anwyn's hands. Call me a fool if you wish, but I witnessed the impossible. I knelt before living stone and demanded its blood. I saw its face. I heard it speak its name like a woken god.
>
> Arothk. The only cure to pock-black disease.

"That is my grandfather's journal," Jonathan said when Devin glanced up with a sour expression on his face. "He was a good man, and a good mayor. He told no wild tales, and he was known throughout his life as a man of honesty."

"A faery tale?" Devin said, snapping the book shut. "I traveled all this way from Londheim to help you find a *faery tale*?"

Jonathan's face flushed bright red.

"You insult my grandfather," he said. "This is no faery tale. It is real, and it saved the lives of each and every person who had succumbed to the disease. Keep reading. He passed through the forest to the bald mountain, and at its base he met with Arothk, a creature of stone that gave of its own blood to cure the darkness."

"Enough," Devin said. "Why not send someone else? One of your hunters could have made the trip and back a dozen times before my arrival."

"Because we need your skill with those," Jonathan said. He pointed to the long, thin blade sheathed against Devin's left thigh and the hammerlock pistol holstered against his right. "Twice I have sent hunters into the woods, and neither time did they return. That forest is a cursed place now; anyone who steps inside can sense it. Help us, Soulkeeper. People I love and care about are *dying*. I may be desperate, but only because the solution is before me and I lack the strength to reach it. This is not some trumped-up tale told around a campfire. This is real."

Devin opened the book again, glancing over several more lines. It started with the goddess Lyra visiting the grandfather in a dream and ordering him to travel through the nearby forest to the base of the bald mountain. She'd told him that a creature from a time before mankind would await him there. From it, he would receive his cure.

"Jonathan, please, listen to me," he said. "The Sisters created the Cradle for *us*. Humans. They did not create monsters or faeries or whatever this Arothk creature supposedly is. We are their children, their *only* children. Whatever stories you've heard are not true, they were never true, and I will not risk my life and the lives of those here because of the ravings of a dead man's journal."

The mayor fell silent. Devin didn't blame him. In many ways, he'd just pronounced a death sentence for much of the village.

"I will do what I can to ease the burdens of the ill," he said, putting up a callous front. "For your sake, I'll not report your real request to the church."

"Your herbs and bandages are like pissing on a wildfire," Jonathan said. "At least you'll be here for the reaping rituals. Anwyn knows there will be a lot of them."

Devin slammed the journal down upon the desk.

"Do not belittle my coming here," he said. "I swore an oath

to aid Dunwerth and its villagers, and I did not take it lightly. I would put your lives above my own, yet what options do you give me, Jonathan? Forget silly tales in hidden journals. What would you have me do?"

"There is but one thing I would have you do, and you lack any faith or trust in me to do it."

It hurt having a man so desperate and afraid look upon him, judge him, and find him wanting. Devin rubbed his eyes as his mind whirled. Forget the stories of this Arothk creature. What was the truth hidden in the faery tale? If he pried away the fanciful retelling of dreams and ancient creatures granting cures, what might be left to explain the events that occurred?

"Your grandfather went to this…bald mountain, and he came back with a cure for the same disease you're suffering from now," Devin asked. "Is that correct?"

"More or less."

These people were clearly in need. Every fiber in his body wished to help them in some way. He could ease their pain with roots and herbs, but that was like massaging the shoulders of a man awaiting the fall of the executioner's axe. It wasn't a cure. Worse, he couldn't shake the nagging fear of what would happen if the disease spread from this little remote village to some of the larger towns, or Goddesses forbid, Londheim itself. The need for a cure would be dire…

"Let me rest for a few hours," he said. "My journey here was long."

"So you'll go?" Jonathan asked. Cautious optimism bubbled into his voice.

"I will go, but not to spill blood from a stone. Some weed or mushroom saved your people years ago, and I pray Lyra guides me to it now. As for your forest, I have no fear of lingering ghosts. Souls reside in the hands of Anwyn, Mayor, and she does not lose track."

Jonathan's dire smile gave him chills.

"You dismiss much," he said. "Keep your heart and mind open, Soulkeeper. Here in Alma's Crown we have learned to trust what you in the east dismiss as children's tales. We are the edge of the known world, and you soon walk into lands beyond. Tread carefully."

CHAPTER 2

Devin knelt before the forest's edge, his tricorn hat in his hands and his head bowed in prayer.

"Lyra, guide my steps this night as you do all nights," he whispered. "Protect the life Alma gave me, and should I fall, deliver me swiftly into Anwyn's embrace."

The howl of a distant wolf punctuated the end of his prayer. Devin pulled his hat low over his face and reclaimed the torch he'd staked into the ground. He took in a deep breath and then let it out slowly, the niggling fears and warnings of Dunwerth's mayor exiting with it.

"A forest like all others," he said. His gaze lingered on the enormous mountain looming over the pines. "All right, maybe not *quite* like all others."

The first mile was an easy one. The ground was flat, the snow thin, and the trees evenly spaced. Devin much preferred the pine forests of the west to the Helwoads that grew north of Stomme, his hometown. Those forests were unruly messes of brush and

pits, the trees themselves of wildly varying heights and separation, as if the oaks and elms jostled each other in a gluttonous
competition for the sun. Not here. Here, even the wild felt organized into straight lines.

Devin held his torch high and enjoyed the quiet of the forest
after the stress of the reaping ritual and visiting the plague-
ridden of Dunwerth. Hardships would return, and he would
burden himself when they did, but for now he refilled his heart
and mind with the tranquility.

The third mile was when the forest turned dark.

"Who is there?" he asked aloud, quickly turning about. Nothing
but snow and tree trunks softly lit by his torch, but he was certain
of being watched. Hearing his voice break the quiet only unsettled
him further. His footfalls crunching the top layer of snow were like
shattering stone.

"If Jonathan sent you to aid me, please come forth," he told
the night. "I gladly welcome the company."

Glinting blue eyes watched him from the corner of his
vision. He spun, saw nothing. Every hair stood on end. Again,
just beyond his line of sight, he saw blue eyes. Little phantoms,
just watching, always vanishing the moment he turned. Devin
pushed on through the forest, keeping his focus straight ahead as
the incline steadily sharpened. It was only a trick of the night, he
told himself. His torch's light reflecting off the snow, combining
with the moonlight…

Devin halted several minutes later and closed his eyes.

"Anwyn, send me your grace," he whispered in prayer. Trick
or not, he needed to calm down. So far nothing but a little glint
of light had him unnerved, that and the warnings of an old man
who'd never left his little frontier town of Dunwerth.

An earsplitting howl broke his prayer. It was close, and many more howls responded in answer.

Devin jammed the base of his torch into the ground and dropped to one knee while drawing his hammerlock pistol from its holster. He cocked the hammer halfway, exposing an opening into the barrel. His left hand pulled a flamestone out from a belt pouch, and pushed the heavy red orb through the opening and into the barrel. Cocking the hammer all the way back slid a metal shield across the opening, protecting against the possibility of an early discharge. He pulled a lead shot wrapped in thin cloth from a second pouch while simultaneously sliding the ramrod out from its sheath underneath the barrel. Two quick pumps and the pistol was loaded.

It took him all of seven seconds to perform the maneuver, but those seven felt like an eternity. Devin left the torch positioned in the snow and drew his sword as a pack of wolves emerged from the woods and circled around him. Devin kept perfectly still, his pistol ready in his left hand, his sword in the right. By his count there were six, and he scanned them in an attempt to locate their pack leader.

"Forgive my trespassing into your domain," Devin said. He kept his voice firm and his arms away from his body, which stretched his heavy coat and made him appear larger. His eyes never met theirs. He didn't wish to issue them a challenge, only convince the creatures that he would be no easy prey.

"Leave me be. Take your hunt elsewhere."

Devin slowly rotated, ensuring that no wolf stayed out of sight for long. They should have been snarling and nipping at his legs to scare him into fleeing...only they weren't. The six held their places, their teeth bared, their eyes watching him with frightening intelligence. Such strange behavior worried him more than any howl they could have made. Locating the biggest of the wolves, Devin pointed his pistol at its head and hoped the black-and-gray beast was their pack leader.

"I said be gone!" Devin shouted. Still they remained, unafraid.

You leave me no choice, he thought sadly. Wolves were majestic creatures, and he'd refused all offers to wear one of their pelts during his many travels about the western lands. But if anything would scare them off, it'd be the noise and power of his hammerlock. Taking aim between the pack leader's eyes, he squeezed the trigger.

The hammer snapped forward, the sharp spike on its front piercing the flamestone in half. The power within the orb exploded the instant it broke, ejecting fire and shot with a thunderous roar. His target never made a noise. The bullet caved in the front of its skull, dropping it dead instantly. The recoil pulled his aim to the sky, and Devin held the pistol above his head as smoke wafted from the muzzle.

None of the other wolves moved. The blast's echo gave the night its only sound. Their yellow eyes looked to his, and Devin swore he saw a uniquely human emotion in them: hate.

What in the void is happening here? he wondered.

Devin half-cocked the hammer with exaggeratedly slow movements, hoping not to provoke the wolves. The moment it clicked, the wolves growled in unison. Devin holstered his pistol under their watchful gaze. There would be no chance to reload.

"More of you will die," Devin said, his firm voice belying the growing unease in his breast. "Leave, now, all of you! Go!"

One of the remaining five finally broke from their position, but not to flee. The wolf trotted over to the downed corpse of their pack leader, nuzzled against the wound, and then turned

Devin's way. Blood smeared across its face like war paint. Human intelligence sparkled in its yellow eyes.

"Hunt," it growled.

The five wolves lunged, nearly catching Devin flatfooted from the shock of hearing that singular word. He rolled to his right at the last moment, his sword braced against his left shoulder. The wolf overshot, its lower body landing awkwardly atop Devin's roll. The sword sliced into its belly, spilling blood and intestines across his coat. Devin exploded back to his feet, his left arm flinging the wolf's body at the others to stall their attack. A second leapt ahead, its jaws wide. Devin jammed the tip of his sword straight down its throat, letting the creature kill itself as its weight slammed against him. He held in a scream as the creature's sharp claws scratched at his chest, his blood mixing with the blood of wolves.

The remaining three held back, suddenly wary of his sword. Devin took the moment to yank the torch free from the snow and wield it in his left hand. He batted the fire at them. Instead of backing away from the flame, they steadily circled, waiting for the right moment to attack with cold, calculated patience.

Fear clouds your mind, he told himself as he watched their pacing. *It didn't speak. Wolves don't* speak.

Devin sensed the wolf at his rear leaping for his back. He spun, his torch up and his sword slashing. His timing was off by the slightest amount, and his blade caught near the hilt in the wolf's ribs. Its body slammed into his, carrying them to the ground. Only the position of his torch saved him, the fire scraping across the beast's left eye. It snapped for his neck, missing and latching onto his shoulder instead. Each tug of its jaws was a scattershot of pain throughout his body. Devin ripped his sword free and then sawed at the wolf's underbelly, a mad race to rip the creature apart before it did likewise to him.

Its death came suddenly and without warning. Devin gasped as the wolf's weight collapsed atop him, but there was a blood-soaked silver lining: The dead beast offered a moment's protection against the other two wolves. They nipped and dove at him, seeking openings. Devin pushed the carcass up while rolling. His head curled into the chest of the dead wolf so they could only tear at his back. One leapt atop him, teeth sinking into the nape of his neck. Another went lower, closing its teeth about Devin's ankle. Devin twisted again, his sword swiping through the air.

The blood-masked wolf released upon seeing the attack and hopped up and away, but not quickly enough. Devin's sword sliced across its left front paw, cleaving it off at the joint. It whimpered and collapsed onto one side. Devin was given no reprieve. He was on his back now, exposed, and the other wolf took every advantage it could. The beast jumped atop his chest, its hungry mouth biting.

Teeth clasped about his face, pulling and tugging with an iron grip. Devin couldn't see, his eyes clenched shut out of reflex. He could barely think at all. Instinct ruled his actions, his left hand grabbing at the wolf's head, his right stabbing viciously. His sword cut open its throat once, twice, three times. Its jaw clenched tighter as the wolf's muscles seized in death. Only with an excruciating shriek of pain did Devin finally pull the beast free.

Devin rose on unsteady feet. Blood flowed down the left side of his face like a torrent. He met eyes with the final wolf, who limped closer. Its breathing grew more strained with every passing moment.

"Leave," Devin told it, his own breathing heavy. "I won't chase. You die for nothing."

The wolf's tongue licked at the blood across its face. It spoke again; this time it lacked anger or fury. Just tired, gravelly resignation.

"Hunt."

It rushed him on three legs, and despite its wounds the beast was still terrifying as it bared its teeth and snarled. Devin sidestepped the attack and then dropped his elbow upon the wolf's back. It crumpled onto its side, and Devin jammed his sword underneath its jaw and into the base of its skull. The creature died instantly. Strange as it seemed, Devin was glad. He didn't wish the wolf to suffer any more than it already had.

He wished he could say the same for himself. Devin collapsed amid the bodies, his mind reeling with shock. Jonathan had warned him. A dangerous, foul place he'd described the forest.

"Dangerous," Devin said as he grimaced, the bite marks across his chest, arms, and back burning like fire. Even talking hurt. "No kidding, Jonathan. No fucking kidding." He painfully pushed himself to his feet. "I hope you're still watching, Sisters, though at this point I think it's just for your own amusement."

He removed the glove from his left hand and gingerly touched the bite on his face. A large flap of skin hung loose beneath his eye, and even worse, his finger touched not flesh but bone. No amount of coin could have convinced him to look in a mirror.

"You're one ugly son of a bitch," Devin said as he slid his glove back on. Blood trickled across his lips. The stench and taste of it overwhelmed all else. "Assuming you live, of course."

Normally he'd have stopped and administered first aid, but was there even a point? The wounds were so numerous, his blood loss severe. He looked through the trees to the bald mountain ahead. It wasn't far. The ground already sloped heavily upward. If he continued, he could reach it in another ten minutes or so.

What other option was there? Spend another hour walking back to town hoping he did not collapse before reaching it? Already pain wrapped around his body like a cocoon, and it would only worsen over time.

In this forest of talking wolves and phantom eyes, Devin put his faith in the same cure as Jonathan. If it could cure the terrible disease ravaging Dunwerth, then perhaps it could cure him, too.

"Arothk," Devin gasped as he began his walk. The bite on his ankle added a fresh lance of pain up his leg, as if he didn't have enough agony to deal with. "You better be there, whatever you are, or I will be royally pissed."

He'd also likely be royally dead, but Devin tried to focus on the positive. Step after horrid step he crossed through the woods. No blue eyes watched him from afar, though he doubted he could see them if he tried. His head slowly grew dizzy. Time itself slipped from him, large portions in his mind becoming empty blackness focused on the steady motion of one foot after the other.

The forest ended. Devin didn't remember when he exited it, only came to a realization that he now walked steep, open spaces. There seemed no clear reason why, only that at an exact line halfway up the bald mountain the trees ended, the appearance giving it its name. Snow covered the rocky ground, reflecting the starlight back at him, almost blindingly white. A large number of boulders gathered near the mountain's sudden, sharp incline. Devin walked toward them, for where else was he to go? "Arothk!" he shouted. His voice echoed throughout the quiet night. "Arothk, are you here?"

Shouting stretched the shredded skin of his face. A strange thought hit Devin. It should hurt far worse than it did. Much worse. Just how delirious was he?

The wobbling of his legs gave him his answer. He collapsed to his knees. A glance at his side showed his coat bathed in blood. It'd be a fool's game guessing which of his wounds were responsible for which massive stain. Devin tried to stand but his body refused to listen.

"Not good," he said, his words coming out as a strained whisper. "Not good, Devin. Get up on your feet. Get up, damn it, get up or you'll die."

It seemed both his mind and body were just fine with that second option. His vision darkened. He braced his weight on his arms and heaved with each individual breath.

Should have turned back, he thought. *Should have . . . I should . . . Anwyn, take me into your arms . . .*

A rumbling noise pushed through his clouded mind and brought his gaze up to the mountain. Devin didn't understand, and he was too tired to try. The boulders were rising before him, snow rolling off stone arms and legs. They rose as his mind dropped low, and unconsciousness blessedly took him from the pain.

CHAPTER 3

The sounds of burning kindling welcomed the Soulkeeper back to consciousness. His eyes fluttered open. A small fire to his left cast flickering light across cave walls. Devin started to sit up and immediately regretted the decision. A dull ache awakened a path from his ankles to his forehead, as if every limb in his body had fallen asleep. Devin slowly breathed in and out as he waited for the numbing stings to subside. His mind felt more alert than any time since the wolf attack, so that was good. He scanned his surroundings as he waited. From what he could tell, he was at the dead end of a cave tunnel. Behind him it continued far beyond the light of the fire, while at his feet, it ended at a wide, rounded wall. So far it appeared he was alone.

"I live another day, Anwyn," Devin said aloud. "Perhaps you were watching out for me after all."

Once feeling had uncomfortably returned to his body, Devin sat up and welcomed the warmth of the fire washing over his face and chest. His coat lay to his side, and he was surprised by how little blood remained on it. Had . . . had his rescuer washed it? He shook his head, the surprise distracting him from more important matters. Devin lifted up his mangled shirt to examine the wounds on his chest.

Clear white lines ran across his tanned skin. Not weeping wounds. Scars. Devin traced his finger along them, awakening a hot, itching sensation. He released his shirt, swallowed his fear, and pressed his hand to the worst of the wounds upon his face. Rough scar tissue greeted his fingers. Whatever work had been done to him was beyond even the most skilled of surgeons. Somehow he was already healed without any apparent stitches or searing of the wounds. So either he'd been unconscious for months... or Arothk's healing powers were as good as Jonathan insisted.

Devin began every new day with a prayer to the Sisters, and he had no plans for stopping now. He muttered it aloud as he rose to his feet, pins and needles assaulting his waking limbs.

"Blessed be the morn, and the Sister who gave it," he said, and he let out a tired laugh. "Assuming it even is morning. You'll forgive me if I'm wrong, right, Alma?"

He leaned against the side of the cave to gather his strength and tapped his belt. Both his pistol and sword were gone. Devin looked down the tunnel leading away from the fire. He had no clue how deep into the mountain he was, nor if it was a straight shot to the surface. Even if he fashioned a torch, he wasn't guaranteed to find the exit without getting lost. That left waiting for his rescuer to return.

"So we wait," he said, looking to the fire. He furrowed his brow. He should be drowning in smoke, but instead the tunnel was clear. Devin scanned the top of the cave. Once he knew what he was looking for, he found it easily, a perfectly circular hole somehow cut or drilled into the stone. Whether it led to the surface or other parts of the cave, he could only guess.

"Well, someone's clever," he said.

"Not clever," rumbled a voice behind him. "Only old."

Devin spun. The voice came not from the tunnel but the curved dead end behind the fire...only now it wasn't a smooth wall but instead a cracking, shifting surface breaking free of the surrounding stone. Devin's hands clenched at his sides as he ordered himself to remain calm. He would not cower before the unknown, but instead meet it with his head held high.

A boulder broke from the wall, and then that boulder grew, chunks separating to become arms with three gigantic fingers. Legs emerged with a shattering of stone. A head slowly rolled from the center of the chest to the top of the newly outlined torso. Solid black eyes the size of Devin's fist peered down at him. The creature said nothing, only stared with what Devin guessed to be mild curiosity.

"Arothk," Devin said. "That's...that's you, isn't it?"

The creature dipped its head. A thin line cracked across its face, forming a mouth.

"Your tongue," it spoke. The voice perfectly matched the depth of the mountain they resided within. "Changed. Sloppy. Such shame. Without the Aeryal, you mangle the divine."

Arothk spoke with a strange accent, one Devin could not place. The s's and p's had a scraping sound to them, somehow produced without a visible tongue or lips.

"Aeryal?" Devin asked. "Divine? Forgive me, Arothk, but you speak of things I do not understand."

"It is A*ro*thk," it corrected, though for the life of him Devin could not decipher how the pronunciation varied from his own.

Its head tilted back, its arms sinking halfway into its body as they crossed over its chest. "Why have you come?"

"The village nearby," Devin said. Forming sentences suddenly became difficult. Magical creatures didn't exist. He knew this as fundamentally as he knew the sun would rise and fall with each passing day. They were merely stories, tales of a more whimsical and fantastical past. To witness stone come to life and speak tore at his mind with equal power as the teeth of the wolves tearing at his flesh. "They've fallen ill with a disease."

"Black marks upon flesh?"

"Yes," Devin said. "Like…like before."

"Then Viciss wakens," Arothk said. "Leave. Your village is not safe. Your time of humans ends. More will wake."

"More?" Devin asked. "More like you?"

Arothk shook its head.

"Not just me. Others. Not humans. The world before the sleep."

Each answer left Devin with a thousand more questions, but the ancient being appeared almost bored with him. It cracked its knees into itself to reduce its height and then turned to the apparent dead end it had crawled out of. Its hand flattened against the stone, melding into it. The wall shimmered with rainbow light, and then it parted like curtains opening before a stage, revealing that the tunnel led to no dead end but instead to an expansive cavern filled with stalactites and stalagmites reaching toward one another. A river ran deep through the heart, the faint light of the fire dancing across its surface. Mushrooms glowed a dozen effervescent colors beside its waters. The beauty of it struck Devin silent, and it was only after Arothk stepped into its recesses that he remembered to speak.

"Wait," he said. "The disease afflicting the villagers...you can cure it, can't you? Like you did years ago?"

Devin swore he saw sadness in those coal-like eyes.

"The cure is of my blood. I have little. Used much on you. Too much."

Guilt stung Devin in the chest. So there was a cure, but it'd been wasted on him? His inability to defend himself against the wolves doomed the men and women wasting away in Dunwerth?

"No, please," he said. "There must be some other way to save these people."

"No other way," Arothk rumbled, the first time it had raised its voice. It seemed the walls shook along with Devin's knees. "The Sisters' prison breaks. It holds us no longer. Black water rises, and it will not stop. Save your people? Then flee. Leave the sick."

Pieces of its chest cracked open, revealing a compartment containing his sword and gun.

"Your weapons of war," Arothk said, handing them over in its wide, flat hand. Devin tucked them into his belt, feeling the creature's judgment for merely owning them. He wanted to protest but he felt so small compared to Arothk. If only he could have more time to speak with it, to learn the knowledge it possessed. What did it mean, black water? The Sisters' prison? Viciss? The sleep?

"Please, don't go," Devin said. "I don't understand. What do I do? How do I help them? What do you mean, black water rises?"

Arothk placed its hand beside the cavern opening. The two dark eyes shimmered with a faint ghost-light.

"There was good among you," Arothk said. "Much good. But

Sisters placed you above all. Such shame. We might have found peace."

The stone closed in on itself, sealing Arothk and the majestic cavern away. The cave turned silent but for the crackling fire. Devin touched the wall as if needing confirmation he'd not just woken from a dream. The stone should have been cold, but instead it was warm beneath his fingers. Breathing. Almost alive.

"Sisters help me," Devin whispered. "What is happening?"

First talking wolves and now living stone foretelling doom. Deep inside him the foundations of his reality crumbled. The exhausted part of him wanted to kneel beside the fire, clutch his hands to his head, and pray until the conversation faded into distant memory. According to every holy book and scripture, there were humans, there were animals, and there were the Goddesses. There was simply no place for a being like Arothk, no neat little corner for his mind to slot it without potentially questioning every tenet of the Keeping Church.

Black water rises . . .

Devin slid his heavy coat over his shoulders, the fabric warm from lying beside the fire. He couldn't stay. Arothk's warnings were dire, and Devin had no reason to disbelieve them. The world was changing, the circumstances far beyond his understanding. To doubt the ancient creature risked dooming the entire village.

Devin blindly walked with his right hand brushing the cave wall. If Arothk could manipulate the stone, Devin had a hunch it'd be a straight path to the outside. It curved a few times, but his hunch proved correct when the first hint of starlight lit the distant hole that was the cave's exit. A cold wind fluttered against him, and he tightened his coat to protect against its chill.

The moon was low and the stars fading when he emerged.

The bald mountain loomed behind him, the dark forest before. After everything that had happened, Devin had but one silent prayer to the Sisters before he began his trek home.

Please, please, please no more wolves.

If there were wolves, they let Devin be as he made his way through the forest. Morning light soon scattered through the pines. With the reaping hour passed and the landscape lit by the sun, the feeling of watchful eyes vanished like the dew. He reached Dunwerth an hour later, beyond thankful for the quiet trip. Scattered glances welcomed him as he stumbled toward the mayor's home. He smiled and tipped his hat to the few men and women hurrying about, almost amused by how bruised and scarred he must look. Few offered greeting in return. Their eyes looked sleep-deprived, and their faces hollow. The specter of death was a heavy burden, and it had clearly weighed these people down for weeks.

"Good morning to you, Soulkeeper," a younger woman said as she passed him in the street. "Have you come for our reaping rituals?"

"I come to prevent them," Devin said, putting on a brave mask. "Do you doubt the power of Alma's grace?"

A sneer crossed the woman's pretty face.

"Alma did nothing while I lost my brother and his wife," she said. "Seems the only time any Sister notices us is at the reaping hour."

Devin politely bowed his head, refusing to argue. He needed to save his energy for a far more important discussion.

Jonathan sat in a rocking chair beside the door to his home, a wide hat pulled low over his face to block the morning sun. The man's snores greeted him.

"Wake up," Devin said, kicking the chair. The mayor startled to his feet with a huff. "There's work to do."

Jonathan followed him into the house. Hacking and coughing assaulted his ears from the entryway, and Devin tried to bury the guilt they elicited. His fault or not, it didn't matter now. Without Arothk's blood, he could only act on what he had power to change.

"Did you find him?" Jonathan asked once they were in his room and the door closed.

"I did," Devin said, tossing the grandfather's journal onto the side table with a thud.

"I knew it," Jonathan said, clapping his hands together. "I just knew it! What . . . what was it like, Soulkeeper?"

Devin tried to find the proper words to describe being in such a creature's presence.

"It was ancient stone," he said. "Like a mountain, thousands of years old, suddenly waking. Hearing its words was . . . humbling."

"And the cure?" Jonathan asked. The mayor's eyes sparkled with hope. "What of the cure?"

Devin inwardly winced, for this was the question he dreaded.

"I have none," he said. "Arothk's blood is the cure, and he would not give any to save the sick here in Dunwerth. He'd spent too much on me, Jonathan. I nearly died on my trip there."

The mayor's anger visibly spread across his entire face.

"Then . . . then it's even more your responsibility. You're a Soulkeeper! Why didn't you take that blood from him?"

Devin thought of his thin sword and tiny lead shot attempting to pierce the heavy stone that made up Arothk's being.

"There would be no taking," Devin said. "Either he gave it as a gift, or he did not. Even if I could harm him, I would not repay the kindness he showed me with murder."

Jonathan sat down on his bed, his hands rubbing over and over his bald forehead.

"Then what do we do?" he asked. His upper body was trembling. "How do we stop it from spreading?"

"I don't know," Devin said. "Truth be told, it doesn't matter. Dunwerth must be evacuated at once. Head south for Crynn. It might not be far enough, but it's a start."

"Evacuate?" Jonathan asked. "Wait, why?"

"Because Arothk insists doom is coming, and if we're to live we must flee the mountains."

"No," Jonathan said. "No, that can't be. This...this monster must be confused, or lying. Do you have any proof? What, pray tell, are we even fleeing from?"

Devin grabbed the mayor by the front of his shirt and lifted him off the bed. Urgency gave strength to his words. His anger added a dangerous edge.

"You asked me to trust you that Arothk was real, and I did," Devin said. "Now I'm asking you to trust me. Arothk said to flee if we wish to survive. Give the order. Evacuate the town, or stay here and watch everyone die."

CHAPTER 4

Devin was assisting the villagers in packing their belongings, focusing his efforts on the elderly, when Jonathan pulled him aside. They stood together beneath the welcome sun, not far off from where wagons were parked in the center of town.

"Soulkeeper, we've got ourselves a problem," he said.

"I can think of a dozen problems," Devin said. "But what is yours?"

"Well, here he comes now, actually."

A burly man with hair down to his shoulders and a beard twice that length trailed Jonathan down the path. His neck was splotched red with anger, and Devin had a feeling he'd already spent some time arguing with the mayor.

"Devin Eveson, this is Garruk," Jonathan said. "He has some disagreements with our plan."

"Damn right I do," Garruk said. He jammed a finger at Jonathan. "My ma is dying on the floor of your house and you want me to just leave her to suffer?"

"Those in my care can barely stand on their own," Jonathan insisted. "They won't survive the trip through the mountains."

"You don't know that," the burly man argued. "But I do know she'll die if she's left here to starve. That ain't a fate fit for no man or woman."

Devin hid his fury behind a stoic mask. There'd been no discussion the night before about leaving the sick in Dunwerth. The mayor had made this decision without consulting him, and it was a terrible one.

"We will bring the sick with us and pray for their survival," Devin interrupted. They both turned his way.

"I've already floated that idea," Jonathan said. "Four families have sworn to me they'll stay if we bring the sick with us, and I wager that number will grow by the time we roll our wagons out. We're fleeing the disease. It makes no sense to bring the disease with us."

Bringing the sick with them meant other healthy families might stay behind and suffer whatever dire fate Arothk had promised, yet demanding that all the sick remain in the village alone was cruel and inhumane. Only one option made sense, as much as he disliked the danger involved.

"Then I will stay behind with those who are sick," Devin said. "Your mother, and all others who are suffering from this plague, shall be under the protection and care of a Soulkeeper. Should they pass on, I will perform the reaping ritual for their souls. Will that suffice?"

"Cared for by a Soulkeeper?" Garruk said, scratching at his beard. "Yeah. Yeah I think that'll be fine. You'll stay true to your word, won't you?"

"We carry the fate of souls in our hands," he said. "If you trust us with so great a matter, then trust me in all else I promise. The sick shall be under my care, from life to the pyre. The world may end and my word will still remain true."

"Thank you," Garruk said. Now that the matter was settled he appeared almost nervous to be in Devin's presence. "Thank you kindly. You're a good man."

He turned and hurried away.

"Are you sure you're willing to do this?" Jonathan asked, watching him go. "You said yourself that staying here means death."

"My staying also means others will leave and live," Devin said. "Perhaps we might have discovered a better solution if you had told me of your plan to abandon the sick."

Jonathan looked away in shame.

"I hadn't thought of it, either, Soulkeeper. People started arguing about it this morning and they forced me to make a choice. You and I both know that those inflicted with this disease have no hope left for them."

"That doesn't mean they deserve to remain behind and die of starvation and thirst."

"They don't deserve to be sick at all," Jonathan said. "Forgive me for making what I thought was the best decision at the time."

Devin shook his head and sighed.

"You're right," he said. "None of this is just, and your decision was likely the correct one, all things considered. Just remember that survival is not everything. Animals survive. *We* help one another. Remember that as you lead these people east."

Many hours later, Devin paced through Jonathan's living room, the crackling fire his only source of light. He certainly didn't feel like a good man. Instead he felt tired and resentful of the enormous care required by the sick. He held a large bowl of soup, most of it uneaten. Of the nine people in the mayor's house, only two still had the strength to sit up and slurp from the spoon.

"I've not seen it progress like this before," Jonathan had told him before joining the last of the wagons trundling down the winding mountain road toward Crynn. "If the doom you predict comes, don't die for the lot. They're already dead."

Too many refused to eat, and those who slept seemed incapable of waking despite his nudges. Deciding enough was enough, Devin let the spoon sink beneath the bowl's surface and left for the kitchen.

"Don't die for them?" Devin said. He chuckled as he set the soup bowl on a table and picked up a wet cloth. "Sorry, Jonathan, but that's what I agreed to do when you summoned me here. Besides, after Arothk wasted his blood on me, it's only fair I stay back with those who should have been cured."

People had argued about leaving behind loved ones, but in the end self-preservation won out. Dunwerth was dying of plague. Though Devin and Jonathan did not specify the reason for evacuating, many reached the expected conclusion that anywhere was safer than their seemingly cursed town. Only one man had refused to leave, a husband wishing to die beside his wife. Jonathan came pleading for a solution, and Devin gave it to him in the form of some crushed herbs. A group held him and forced him to drink the herbs, which sent him into sleep that would last for many hours. By the time he woke, he'd be miles from town, and hopefully stay with the caravan instead of attempting to return.

"Would it have been better for him to die here?" Devin wondered as he wrung out the cloth to the sound of coughing.

"I don't know, Anwyn, but I hope you'll forgive me if I was wrong."

The night hours passed long and slow. Devin cleaned weeping sores as best he could. When it came time for the sick to urinate or defecate, Devin was there with fresh rags and changes of clothes. People loved listening to stories of Soulkeepers defending against bandits, hunting down murderers who plagued the streets of Londheim, and winning impossible competitions of skill with the pinpoint accuracy of their hammerlock pistols. Devin doubted many would huddle breathlessly around a campfire to hear him tell the story of wiping down of an old man's crotch and legs because he'd shat himself for the third time that night. People didn't want to know the real work of a Soulkeeper. They wanted tales of adventure.

By the time the reaping hour approached, Devin was ready to call it quits. He plopped down into the chair by the fire Arleen had occupied the night before. His heels pushed it back and forth in a steady, creaking motion. His hands were raw from constantly washing them, and he doubted he'd ever remove the smell of sickness embedded into the leather of his coat. Eyes closed, he listened to the coughing and hacking of the dying.

"I can only do so much," he whispered. "Help me out, Sisters. I'm drowning."

The chair rocked back and forth. *Creak, cough, creak, cough.* A morbid lullaby...

A ringing sound woke him from his light slumber. Devin lurched to his feet, his instincts sensing something amiss and forcing his sleeping limbs to move. He squinted, trying to adjust to the light, and only after a moment realized it wasn't daylight that blinded him, nor was it the glow from the now-dead fire.

Nine beams of soft blue light shone to the ceiling. They gave off a subtle chime, a noise more suitable to a cathedral than the stinking room. Devin's mouth dropped open in shock. The triangle-and-circle symbol of the Three Sisters burned across the sick men's and women's foreheads, carved by an unknown hand. The first hints of the rising souls swirled across the marks, casting a brilliant hue across the living room.

In all eight years of his official duty as a Soulkeeper, not once had Devin witnessed something akin to the spectacle before him. It wasn't just the sight of the souls rising in perfect unison without any need of his prayers or rituals. The reaping hour felt...strange. Powerful. What was once a brush of cold against the back of his neck was now an overwhelming flood of sensation. The walls of the world seemed weak and pliable, the stars holding the void at bay impossibly close.

His sleep-addled mind remembered proper protocol, and he quickly dropped to one knee and bowed his head.

"By Alma, we are born. By Lyra, we are guided. By Anwyn, we are returned. Beloved Sisters, take them home."

The ringing reached a crescendo. The nine souls vaulted into the air, bypassing the ceiling as if it weren't there. The blue beams rapidly shrank in size until they were a faint slice of light vanishing into the darkness. Silence followed in their wake, broken by the fire bursting back to life as if it had never died.

Devin slowly rose to his feet and wiped tears of both awe and exhaustion off his face. When the church had informed him of his mission, he'd expected a long, dull hike through the mountains to a sleepy village suffering a particularly vicious bout of the flu. Instead, he'd found himself in over his head, watching the world rapidly tumble off a cliff of sanity into an amalgamation he did not understand.

The smell of death, already suffocating, grew with each passing moment. Devin made for the door, deciding that any other home would provide a better night's sleep. He glanced at the corpses. They would need to be burned, but that could wait until morning. Devin entered the house beside Jonathan's, a small abode with a single bedroom. There were no sheets or blankets on the feather-stuffed mattress. That suited him fine. He kept all but his coat on, preferring to leave the bulky leather hanging on a hook by the door. A window was directly above the bed, and he pulled it open despite the chill. Fresh air felt wonderful after hours in Jonathan's cramped, sickly living room.

"Do we witness the end?" he asked the Sisters, fearing that the world itself would answer him before his Goddesses. "What Arothk said... is it true?"

Arothk's words echoed in his mind.

Your time of humans ends.

According to Anwyn's Mysteries, the world would end when the void-dragon crashed through the prison of stars and attempted to swallow the light of the First Soul, now disseminated throughout all of humanity. No part detailed living stone creatures or black water. Were the Mysteries incomplete, or did a brand-new threat emerge? Chilling thoughts, and they lent themselves to nightmares he was glad to forget when blessed daylight washed over his face through the open window.

The morning greeted Devin with the discovery that his horse had broken free from her stable and fled in the night.

"Not a great start to the day," he muttered as he surveyed the broken wood that had once been a stable door. Something must have spooked his horse, and badly. Given the spectacle he'd witnessed the night before, it wasn't much of a stretch to assume the two matters linked. He walked the outskirts of the town, but he saw no sign of her. Devin tried not to let it worry him too much, and he focused on the current task at hand.

Burning nine bodies would require a much larger than normal pyre, which meant Devin had to scout for an open area outside the town's limits. Dragging the bodies all the way into the forest would take far too long as well. He chose a gentle hill near the western end of town, the sides spotted with fifteen or so trees that would make for easy gathering of tinder and kindling for the enormous pyre.

As for the logs themselves, that was a simple but laborious task. Nearly every home had a large stack of firewood piled against a side of the house. Devin carried armfuls from the nearest home and steadily built a triangular outline to fill in with the logs. Once sufficiently full, he'd layer the kindling atop it, followed by the bodies and the tinder. It was heavy work, but Devin didn't mind. Everything else might be beyond his reasoning, but at least he could build a fire. Once the pyre was done he'd drag the bodies from the mayor's house and perform another familiar, comforting ritual.

Devin was halfway finished with the pyre when the ground began to shake. He dropped to his knees and relaxed his body, trying not to fight the suddenly angry earth. Snow cascaded down the peaks of distant mountains as multiple avalanches triggered. The noise built to a roar, a crescendo of snow and stone and cracking walls and snapping pines. Devin closed his eyes and focused on remaining calm. He was safe atop the hill. If he kept relaxed, no harm should come to him.

The earthquake ended. Devin slowly rose to his feet. His legs were unsteady, and he stared at the grass as if expecting it to betray him.

Another terrible omen, he thought. As if he needed any more of those after his horse fled. He gazed to the southeast. There ran a long path sloping through green hills for several miles before curling down the side of a mountain. The villagers were long out of sight, but he looked in their direction nonetheless and offered them a prayer. It'd be a cruel fate if they were caught in the path of one of those avalanches.

Something dark in the distance stole his attention. Devin squinted, trying to decipher what he saw. It looked like a shadow curling up the path around the mountain, but the sky was clear. What had been curiosity quickly turned to fear as the darkness approached at a blistering pace. It seemed made of shadow, yet the substance covering the landscape had a depth to it, and the way it flowed? Like a liquid, or . . .

"Black water rises," Devin whispered aloud.

The black water rushed up the path into the village. Though it appeared a flood, it made not the slightest sound with its passage. Devin watched, his feet locked in place. He felt imprisoned, as if in a dream from which he could not wake up. The black water crashed into the homes but did not wash the structures away. It moved nothing as it flowed through windows and around corners. Nothing stopped it, not even the hill Devin stood atop.

"Oh shit."

Devin sprinted for the closest tree. Its branches were thin but he'd have to trust them to hold his weight. The alternative was to be submerged beneath the black water, and every instinct in his body screamed to avoid that at all costs. Branches scraped at his face, needles poked at his eyes, but he climbed higher and higher. The black water was close, so close...

The water surged beneath him, quiet as a predator. Not even the air moved from its presence. Devin clutched the trunk and watched the liquid shadow pass. The sight was mesmerizing in its beauty. The water bore the color of midnight, yet the longer he stared the more that emerged from its depths. Faint stars swam just beneath the surface. Deep purples and blues shifted like cosmic smoke. Sunlight vanished into it. The physical world dissolved away beneath it.

All the while, silence.

Devin didn't know how long the water flowed. Time itself crawled to a stop in the presence of the water. His mind lost itself to the flow, the pine's branches and needles vanishing so it looked as if Devin hung in midair above an abyssal ocean of stars and void. The moment it receded, his mind broke free, and he gasped for breath. His muscles ached. His head throbbed. The unnatural quiet still sounded far too loud. The black water retreated down the hill, through the town, and vanished in the direction of Crynn. In its wake, it left complete and utter devastation.

What had been green grass was now a sickly gray. The pine needles beneath him had lost all color. The brown of the trunk was now black as tar. When Devin's foot touched a lower branch its needles fell, leaving the branch twisted and naked. Devin climbed down with reckless urgency. He didn't trust the tree to support his weight much longer. The trunk looked rotted and decayed.

When his feet hit the gray grass, the blades erupted into a shower of powdery smoke that stung his eyes and scraped his throat like a razor with every breath. Devin grabbed the side of his coat and pulled it over his face. It was meager comfort. Impulse said to flee to the dirt-worn streets of Dunwerth, but he fought it down. Had to remain calm. Had to keep track of where he was. If he ran blind and gagging he had as much chance of veering off track and dying as reaching the town's safety.

Devin waited out the cloud. Slowly the tears left his eyes, and though his throat was raw, cool air blessedly flowed across it. A long, terrifying field of gray separated him from apparent safety. Careful not to move his feet, Devin pulled his shirt over his nose and tied it there with a spare cloth he kept in one of his heavy coat's many pockets. Last, he removed his hat and pressed it flat against his mouth. He had no protection for his eyes, but hopefully he would be fine without.

Eyes closed, he took his first step. His foot brushed the grass, scattering a fresh cloud of ash into the air. Devin kept his breathing soft and steady. One foot after the other. Despite all his protection the powder coated his throat. But instead of gagging and gasping for air, he merely fought through an impulse to cough. The pain grew like an itch he couldn't scratch, but it was bearable. Soft breathing. Steady walking. His eyes watered but that was the extent of their suffering so long as he kept them clenched shut.

Devin counted steps, using them as a careful measurement as he closed the distance to the town. Between each one he paused, ensuring that his path remained straight. Even the slightest deviation might take him away from the town. After a minute he paused in place and counted to one hundred before opening his eyes.

It turned out there was no cloud to outwait. He stood at the far end of Dunwerth, the ground already beaten to dust by the foot traffic. Devin let out a sigh of relief as he lowered his shirt and untied the cloth.

"Thank the stars you warned us, Arothk," Devin said as he looked over what remained of the town. The walls of all the homes appeared to be in late stages of decay. A sickly black mold clung to them and stank of wet rot. When Devin pushed in the door of the nearest home it collapsed, the hinges breaking free with ease. Inside, the floor was a bubbling mass of mold. What had been a rocking chair was now a charred black collection vaguely resembling a human construction. The curtains had lost all their color and hung threadbare from their hooks.

Devin opened one of the cupboards and immediately regretted it. The owners had left behind a handful of apricots on a plate. Their yellow skin had turned sickly gray speckled with black spots. The brief smell that escaped before he slammed the cupboard shut was of sour milk.

"Sisters damn it all," he muttered, turning aside and retching. The smell refused to leave his nostrils. The floor creaked beneath his every step as he fled outside. He savored the fresh air, his arms crossed and his eyes closed as he tried to meditate. Every foul discovery heightened his anxiety, compounding a fear he refused to speak aloud.

Just how far did the black water flow?

A loud rattle of wood broke him from his thoughts. At first he thought it was the sound of a rotted home collapsing, but then he heard another noise, and then another. Movement coming from the mayor's house. A creeping horror slid down into his belly. The bodies of the nine he'd yet to burn...what had the black water done to them?

Devin loaded his pistol, drew his sword, and went to find out.

CHAPTER 5

Seven creatures wandered the street before the mayor's house. Creatures, for nothing about their jittery movements resembled their former humanity. The black water appeared to have sunk into their flesh, sapping away all color and leaving their skin an unnatural white. Their eyes were empty holes leaking gray pus. Their clothes had rotted away, leaving them naked as they fumbled blindly about. Long ropes of coagulated blood leaked from their nostrils.

"Goddesses above," Devin whispered, his mouth dropping open. These abominations defied every natural order of life. They were empty shells, their souls removed and taken to Anwyn in the heavens. They should be ash in a pyre, not walking, not moaning quietly as they stumbled about sniffing the air.

Their wet inhalations intensified. What had been aimless wandering shifted toward his vague direction. Could they smell him? Perhaps, Devin thought, but it didn't matter. He was a Soulkeeper, and he bore responsibility for those bodies.

Whatever their state, whatever the dangers they possessed, he would burn them on a pyre.

Devin carefully approached the closest walking corpse. They certainly could not see him, and their sense of smell didn't appear too precise. They drifted his way, their arms occasionally flailing at the air as if striking invisible opponents. Devin stopped halfway across the street and let the nearest come the rest of the way toward him. It snarled, granting Devin an unwelcome look into its mouth. Half its teeth were missing. The other half were cracked and chipped, forming uneven fangs. He saw no sign of its tongue, just a hollow crevice with a pool of dried blood collecting from its nose.

Devin planted his feet and swung. His sword chopped through the creature's neck with ease, the spine offering much less resistance than it should have. Black goop gurgled from the exposed neck cavity. The head went still immediately, but the same could not be said for the body. Its limbs trembled erratically, and its legs took two more steps before the body collapsed in on itself. Black liquid formed a puddle as the rotted flesh dripped off the creature's bones. There would be no burning what remained.

One down, he thought, the macabre display so terrible it did not feel real. *Eight to go.*

Two more closed in. Devin avoided a clumsy swipe by sliding to his left, then returned the favor with a thrust through the eye. Three steps to the side rotated his position so the impaled creature blocked the other's way. To Devin's relief, he discovered that puncturing the brain worked as effectively as removing the head. The body liquefied. Its pieces dripped off Devin's extended sword. The other dead creature moved toward him, both arms up and reaching. Devin dropped low, his feet spinning underneath him in an agile dance. The flailing arms hugged air.

Devin's blade slashed up and around, cutting a long gash across the walking corpse's throat.

A thick black substance oozed from the wound, but the creature remained otherwise unaffected.

Not good enough, he thought.

The corpse flung itself at him, and it was far too close to dodge. Devin slammed his body into it with his shoulder, hoping instead to fling it away. Its ribs cracked inward with the resistance of rotting fruit. The corpse staggered a step before immediately resuming its advance. Devin buried his blade into its face. Spasms shook its arms as they reached and clawed. A single swipe caught Devin across his neck, and he hissed in air at the sharp pain. He drove the sword deeper into the thing's skull, forcing the rapidly decaying body to its knees. His sword slid free, the blade caked in a disgusting liquid as the rest of the creature liquefied into a bubbling mass resembling tar and bones. Devin rubbed the back of his glove across the scratch as the corpse bubbled apart. It came back with a fresh smear of blood.

The remaining five corpses let loose a synchronized howl. They sniffed constantly, seemingly pulled by their noses as they abandoned their slow, steady shambling for a terrifying sprint. Devin fell back, fighting against full-blown panic. The blood. They smelled his blood. He lifted his pistol as he retreated and squeezed the trigger. The lead shot tore through the forehead of the closest, its fragile skull blasting apart like a smashed melon. Another lunged with its ragged teeth snapping. Devin gave it his sword to swallow, then viciously yanked to the right. The body toppled, blocking two others from reaching him but freeing up a third. Momentum carried Devin's left arm around, striking the onrushing creature with the heavy iron of his pistol. Its lower jaw cracked free from its skull and flew through the air until it collided with the wall of the mayor's home.

Any other foe would drop immediately, but still the corpse kept coming, now much too close to avoid. Devin cursed his combat instincts. Had to adjust. Only killing blows would have the slightest effect. Devin dropped to one knee and ducked his head. With the creature's upper body tilted heavily forward, and lacking any real sign of reflexes, it stumbled over Devin's prone form. He shoved himself to a stand, sending the corpse tumbling across his back. Devin stabbed it through each eye and then sprinted, hoping the injuries would be enough to break it apart. The final two gave chase, their loud, wet sniffles haunting him. Could he outrun them? Would they ever tire? Piss, he didn't know anything about these vile creatures, only that their presence filled his chest with horror.

A glance back showed them steadily falling behind. They couldn't see him, instead hunting him solely by smell. If he could use that to his advantage...

Devin cut right, lowering his shoulder to smash through the door of a small house. Inside was a rotted table, and Devin toppled it onto its side and stepped behind. The two walking corpses pushed single file through the door. The first creature rushed straight into the table and fell headfirst over it. Devin jammed his sword to the hilt in its skull, then retreated. The second one tripped over both table and corpse, the combined weight breaking the table in half. The thing flailed wildly on its stomach, the motions ending when Devin decapitated it with a single blow.

Devin left them where they lay. The street had fallen quiet again, but he refused to allow himself to relax. The mayor's house had contained nine corpses, but so far only seven had exited through the broken door and into the street. What of the other two? Devin reloaded his pistol with shaking hands. That was a question he could not let go unanswered. Begging his Goddesses for strength, he returned to the home and entered the main foyer. He heard a soft thumping to his right. Were they trapped in one of the rooms?

Devin crossed the soft wood floor and paused beside a bedroom door. No doubts now. The sounds definitely came from within. He carefully pulled the door open an inch, then used his foot to swing it open the rest of the way as he brought his pistol to bear.

Two corpses had lain in the same bed when the black water came. Their respective halves were woven together, a tangled mess of bone and muscle. The monstrous amalgamation tried to rise off the bed onto its three legs, but its two frail arms lacked the strength to lift it. Both heads smelled the blood on his neck and clacked their teeth together in a hungry frenzy.

Not even in his nightmares had Devin seen such a terrible sight. The shock of the day scraped his raw mind. He fell back on his training, repeating the words from muscle memory:

"By Alma, we are born," he said, leveling his pistol with the left hand. He pulled the trigger. The shot thundered in the tiny space. The left head went limp, black gunk oozing from the new hole in its forehead.

"By Lyra, we are guided."

He loaded the flamestone into the barrel, then fully cocked the hammer.

"By Anwyn, we are returned."

The lead shot slid into the barrel with a single pump of the ramrod. The right head snarled at him like a wild animal. He aimed straight for its forehead.

"Beloved Sisters, take them home."

The ringing in his ears from the two shots overwhelmed the sudden silence. He left the room, his path unknown to him. He moved as if in a dream. The world wasn't real anymore. All about him was a changed, dying, twisting chaos beyond all ability to understand. His past life felt stolen from him. His easy faith in the Three Sisters was now a desperate, violent struggle.

Devin found himself at the outskirts of town. The sun shone brightly from a blue sky atop the snow-capped peaks of Alma's Crown. All of it so peaceful. So beautiful. And then he looked below, saw long fields of gray grass and pine forests composed of black needles and rotting trunks. Cruel, hopeless questions assaulted his tired mind. Did any survive? Was only little Dunwerth affected, or had the black water washed away the entire world in an apocalyptic flood? Where was the blessing Lyra granted upon their lives? Where was the protection the Sisters represented against an already chaotic world?

Up there in the blue sky, Devin figured. *Not down here with us.*

At last he dropped to his knees, closed his eyes, and let the sorrow and despair break free in a torrent of tears streaming down his bruised, bleeding face.

Breaking apart made Devin feel that much more together once the tears stopped and the anguish dulled. Even through the collapse his mind had steadfastly worked, preparing a series of tasks. First was to gather whatever food he could for the trek ahead. Enduring the stench, he checked all the upper cabinets that went untouched by the black water's passage. Devin assembled a hodgepodge collection of bread loaf pieces and various jarred vegetables and fruits. The best discovery was a bowl of five crisp autumn apples set atop a shelf.

"Bless whoever you were for this gift," Devin murmured to the previous owner. Three of the apples made it to his pack. He devoured the other two. The bright green of their skin and tarty sweetness of their pulp were a welcome contrast to the bleak gray of the outside world. It'd have brought him to tears if there were any left in him to fall.

Water came next. Devin built a fire and set a few pots atop it. Once they were warmed he dumped snow he'd collected from the rooftops inside to melt. The black water didn't appear to have changed the snow on the ground, but he'd prefer not to test it until he absolutely must. Devin filled his large travel flask and then hooked it to his belt behind his waist. Food and water taken care of, that left one final detail: traveling through the dangerous new terrain.

Between all the abandoned clothes and beds Devin had his pick of materials for his new mask. He used his sword to cut and shape three thin bedsheets, then slid a thicker scrap of wool to form an interior layer. Sewing was hardly the forte of a Soulkeeper, but truth be told there was little difference between it and stitching a wound, something Devin had a tremendous amount of experience doing. He sealed the wool inside the four pieces so none would slip free. The longer, thinner sides allowed him to tie it into a painfully tight knot behind his head. The white cloth covered his face from just below his eyes all the way to underneath his chin, the cords of it digging deep into his skin.

Devin breathed in and out, testing the mask. Air passed through with only a bit of effort. He'd not want to do any sprinting with the mask on, but his normal hike should be fine. The only thing left was to protect his eyes. Much of the road from

Dunwerth to Crynn was worn dirt and rock, but there'd still be patches of unavoidable grass that might get into his eyes. His best idea was a thin piece of white cloth stretched wide, with thin holes he poked into it with his knife. He could barely see through it, but it was better than nothing, he figured, as he stuffed it into his pocket.

The sun was beginning its descent when Devin took his first step toward Crynn. It'd be dark soon, but he couldn't bear to stay the night in the remains of Dunwerth. Walking its streets was like walking among ghosts. A breeze blew over him, and he watched the black grass gently wave. No explosion of painful ash. It needed his touch to erupt. Devin couldn't shake the feeling that the natural world hated him now. He trudged along, wishing with every hill he climbed that he'd discover a world of green and blue on the other side.

No such discoveries awaited him those first few miles he crossed before setting up camp. It wasn't much, just a bedroll atop the dirt, his pack as his pillow. He built a fire using branches cut from nearby trees. Devin used his knife to slice up the rest of his fruit and ate slowly. The sweetness was divine compared to the stench he'd suffered through.

Devin hunched before his fire as the sun vanished behind the mountains. The welcome heat washed over his skin.

Do you really want to survive in this new world? he asked himself.

The insidious question refused to depart. There was no denying it, pretending around it, or silencing it with platitudes. If the entire world was like what he experienced today, was it worth all the blood and toil to endure? What life might he find besides endless suffering and rot? Right now his only plan was to travel to Crynn and desperately hope that his brother-in-law, Tomas, had survived the desolation. And if not? If the black water had washed as far as the city, and beyond? What of his sister, Adria? Did she survive in Londheim, or would Devin arrive only to find festering dead and corruption claiming the once-magnificent city?

Devin closed his eyes and whispered to his beloved Goddesses.

"Grace me with your presence this night," he prayed. "And please, don't forget about me. I'm here, Sisters, I'm alone, and I need you more than ever."

The Soulkeeper lay atop his bedroll, rested his head on his pack, and quickly succumbed to sleep.

CHAPTER 6

Devin's eyes fluttered open to see soft starlight. The world was dark, quiet, and cold. He lay still, certain something had woken him. His campfire smoldered to his right, mostly extinguished but for a few flickering embers. Devin thought to add more kindling, then paused. Something about the fire was...strange. It elongated, shifting in ways no fire should. The little lick of flame was no bigger than his hand, yet he saw it sprout arms, legs, and a head. Devin lay there and watched. If this little creature was a threat, he'd let it end him, for there was no hope for survival in a world where your own campfire became a sentient murderer. It turned left, then right, as if testing out its ability to move.

No, not move. *Dance.*

The little flame creature spun through the fire, its legs flowing over the wood like water. Tiny red footprints shimmered in its wake. As it turned, Devin saw two little imprints in its head, like black eyes. Every successive turn lessened the fear in Devin's heart. There was an undeniable joy to the creature's movements, and though it had no partner and no music, it danced nonetheless. Two arms reached upward as it twirled, the creature's essence melding together so it appeared to be a tornado of fire whirling atop a log.

So much for the Cradle being made for humans only, he thought, already feeling foolish for the admonition he'd given the mayor of Dunwerth. He watched this new creature dance about for several minutes, the tension in his muscles slowly easing away. Such a cheerful thing looked incapable of malice. Whereas the black water had mutated what already existed, turning wood to rot, grass to choking powder, and corpses to monsters, this creature appeared unique and untouched by any such corruption. Deciding to the void with being careful, Devin sat up in his bedroll and smiled.

"Hello there, little guy."

The creature's head sank into itself, then reemerged so it faced Devin. The tiny black orbs widened, and then, fast as a fleeing mouse, the flame dove into the heart of Devin's dormant fire. There was no evidence that the little creature had ever existed at all aside from the soft yellow glow that pulsed amid the embers. If Devin hadn't seen it in the first place, he might have never suspected a thing. He kept his movements and tone calm and gentle as he faced the campfire.

"Are you frightened?" he asked. "Please, do not fear me. There are too many frightening things in this world, and I would hate to be one of them."

A little bit of smoke puffed up from the fire. Devin rubbed his chin, thinking.

"Have you a name?" he asked. "Can you speak? Does a fire even know how to speak?"

A red and yellow head popped up from a little nest of ash. One eye squinted as it stared at him. It huffed, and a cloud of smoke rose in a ring from its forehead. Devin had a strong impression the action was one of annoyance. A smile stretched across his face.

"Forgive me," he said. "I am inexperienced in conversation with campfires."

Another huff.

"Not a campfire," Devin quickly corrected as more of it rose up from the logs. "A creature of flame, perhaps? I am sorry, but I do not know what to call you."

There was no other way to describe it. The creature's shoulders dropped low as if in a hearty sigh. It wagged one of its arms at him, then pointed beyond the fire. Devin lifted an eyebrow.

"I'm watching," he said, hoping that was what it wanted.

The creature nodded and then zipped out from the logs. It ran across the bare earth with legs moving so fast it seemed they were but one flowing entity dragging a thin red line. Up and down, back and forth, with the speed and grace of a humming-bird. Once finished it dove back into the fire. It'd been out for only twenty seconds or so, but by the time it reached the warm embers its size had shrunk by half. The lingering glow of its passage spelled out a single word.

FREKIN.

"Firekin?" Devin asked. That it knew human letters and words was intriguing enough, but he'd let Mindkeepers and the Wise debate those implications. Right now, Devin just wanted to make the little firekin comfortable. The way it huddled amid the ashes made it seem almost...cold. An idea struck him, and he shifted in his seat.

"Here, would you like this?" he asked, reaching into his pack. The firekin disappeared once again beneath the logs, then slowly poked its head up to carefully watch. Devin laughed. The act broke a stone vise clasped about his chest. This strange, intelligent being of fire had the skittish temperament of a bird. He did not feel like it belonged amid the corrupted landscape. But this new world was unfamiliar to him, and he did not yet understand its rules. The idea lit a candle of hope inside Devin where none had been before.

"Easy now, I'm not going to harm you," Devin said. He pulled out two long twigs from a pile he'd stashed in his pack. They easily snapped in half, and Devin offered the first to the firekin. It shifted a little in its perch, a visible shudder running through the flame as it watched. Devin waited, but it did not come for the twig. Fair enough. Just like befriending a fearful dog, his task was best done in steps.

"It's all right," he said. "I don't blame you for being scared. I'm scared, too."

He tossed the twig to the edge of the campfire. The firekin dashed out, its arms latching onto the twig and dragging it back underneath the blackened log. It settled atop the kindling, its legs disappeared beneath it, and its eyes shrank. A steady puff of smoke rose from the top of its head. The twig burned at an abnormally fast rate, becoming ash in mere moments. The firekin returned to its original size and hopped to the edge of the campfire, wiggling both its arms.

"Hungry for more?" he asked.

It puffed two little circles of smoke in answer. Devin's smile grew.

"All yours, buddy."

He tossed the remaining twigs into the fire. The firekin zipped to and fro, pulling the twigs into a tiny pile and then happily settling atop them. Devin let its joy become his own, and he wished for a thousand twigs to give this little creature.

"Have you a name?" he asked it. "Or is *firekin* your name?"

A little puff of white smoke drifted from the top of its head as it bobbed it up and down.

"Might I know it then?"

The creature hopped back off its twig pile and zipped along the grass to form another message before returning.

CRKSSLFF.

"I ... I don't think I can pronounce that," Devin said, laughing. "Might I give you a name more suitable for my tongue?"

The little firekin shrugged its shoulders, the human gesture enough to melt Devin's heart. He watched it as he thought for a proper name. The firekin softly swayed atop its kindling, puff after puff of smoke happily rising from its body. An idea for a name came to him, and its silliness felt like a perfect counter to the grave dourness of the previous day.

"Puff," Devin said. "No ... Puffy. Is Puffy suitable for you as a name?"

It nodded.

"Excellent," he said. "I know not where you came from, little firekin, but consider yourself welcome in my camp."

Devin couldn't be sure, but to his eyes the creature burned just a little bit brighter in response. He rested his head in his palm and watched it consume the twigs. The remainder of the logs shimmered as the firekin brushed off their ash and set them back alight. His campfire spread its heat, banishing the lick of cold that had settled upon Devin's skin. The little thing didn't seem to mind his watching, and Devin could only guess as to how much time passed before he finally could not keep his eyes open.

"I need to sleep," Devin said to the firekin. "Tomorrow will be another long day. There are strange creatures about, ones that aren't so friendly as you, and I must be strong enough to face them."

Puffy cocked its head to one side quizzically. It moved its arms in a circle.

"I don't understand," Devin said.

In response the firekin zipped out and ran a circle surrounding Devin's bedroll before returning to the campfire. It crossed its little arms, which melded into one another.

"You'll keep me safe?" he asked. Puffy nodded. Devin blinked away a few tears. "Thank you, little one. Thank you so much."

Devin lay down on his bedroll and turned so his head faced the flame. The firekin bobbed up and down while its little black eyes scanned the night. He smiled at it, wishing they could better communicate. Their bizarre midnight meeting was the first time he hadn't felt alone since the black water's rise. He watched it keeping guard until the weight of his eyelids was too heavy a burden.

Puffy was gone come morning. Nothing but ash remained of his campfire. Had it died or merely run off seeking more sustenance? Devin shook his head and refused to accept the former. The firekin lived. He would believe no other alternative.

"Blessed be the morn, and the Sister who gave it," Devin prayed as he prepared his breakfast. "And whoever sent me a little friend, thanks for that, too."

CHAPTER 7

Devin used the quiet solitude of his trek to ponder what exactly to make of his nocturnal visitor. Church doctrine rattled around in his skull, but nothing seemed applicable. The Sisters arrived upon the Cradle to find it floating barren amid the chaotic void. They blanketed the cold stone with grass and forests. They made the moon and sun and put them into an endless dance in honor of the eternal cycle they would soon create. They birthed the wolf and the deer, the raccoon and the grasshopper, spreading life throughout the Cradle. Then the Sisters reached through the void and took the light of the First Soul from the forever lands beyond. Within was the concepts of love, forgiveness, compassion, and selflessness. The Sisters gifted this soul to the humans, their most favorite of creations.

All of this was clearly detailed in the First Canon. What was *not* mentioned was any sort of living fire creatures, or giants made of stone. Had they existed before the Sisters arrived? It was an interesting thought, but that contradicted the idea of the Cradle originally being barren.

Devin held his breath and closed his eyes as he trudged through a thick patch of black grass that had grown across a smooth stretch of the road. Perhaps he was looking at it the wrong way. What if they weren't creations of the Goddesses, but instead their enemies? When the Three Sisters carried the First Soul back to the Cradle, the furious void took the form of a great dragon and tried to swallow its light. For a thousand years they battled until the void-dragon was defeated and fled far, far away to lick its wounds. The Sisters delivered the First Soul to the Sacred Mother, whose name had been lost to time, but her gift, the divine right of all her children to bear a soul upon birth, had elevated humanity to masters of the Cradle.

The blood of the void-dragon had fallen upon the Cradle during their battle, however, and it tainted the purity of the Goddesses' creation. While humans learned love and compassion, they also gained the capacity for hatred and cruelty. Devin wondered if perhaps these new creatures had been given form by the blood of the void-dragon, hence their strange and otherworldly forms. This meant Arothk and Puffy were physical manifestations of the void's insatiable hunger and hatred of light and heat, and therefore enemies of the Keeping Church.

"That's ridiculous," Devin said aloud, and he shook his head. The idea that something as playful as Puffy or as noble as Arothk could be tied to the void just didn't hold water. He refused to believe them enemies of the church. That answer was too easy, too cowardly, to be true. This left one final, and frightening, thought: Even the oldest and wisest of the church's teachings lacked all knowledge of these beings.

Goddesses above, what he'd give to have Adria there with him. His sister was far better versed in church doctrine and its long, convoluted history. Thinking of Adria punched his gut with worry. Was she fine, or did she suffer as he did through a bleak, corrupted world? Or worse, did she survive at all? Horrible thoughts to endure, but alone and lost in the wild, he had little else to occupy his mind.

Devin crested a small hill, and the sight below him stole away his dark thoughts. Below him, perfectly split in half by the winding road, was a giant clearing of healthy green grass sprinkled with melting trampled snow. Devin ran to its center, his pack sliding loose from his shoulder and onto the ground. He tore his mask from his face. Everywhere he looked he saw signs of life. Footprints in the snow. Blackened circles of campfires. Holes in the dirt where tired men and women nailed down their tents.

"The people of Dunwerth," Devin said, needing a human voice to pierce the quiet. "They live."

The story spread before him, as easy to read as a book. The gathered villagers of Dunwerth had camped in this little valley prior to traveling the Winding Steppes. The black water had come for them, corrupting all it touched…but then at the last moment it split, avoiding them like a river blocked by a tremendous stone. The people were spared. Why, he did not know.

Devin dropped to his knees and ran his hands through the grass. His eyes drank in the color. His fingers floated across the blades. He tore a chunk of earth free and breathed in the missing world. Devin lost himself to a fit of laughter, his hands crushing the grass and scattering dirt. He'd needed this, so badly he'd needed this, never knowing until the green spread before him amid a world of pale snow, black grass, and gray stone.

The Soulkeeper dropped onto his back and stared at the blue sky. For a brief moment he let himself believe that all was well, and that when he sat back up, the beautiful mountains of Alma's Crown would no longer bear the scars of the black water. The notion passed, as it must, but the joy fueled him in a way no food ever could.

"Did you save these people?" Devin wondered to the clouds. "Was it Lyra's hand that guided the waters aside? Or did you impose your will, Anwyn, for it was not yet their time?"

It didn't matter, not really. What mattered was that the villagers lived. Pulling himself up from the grass, he hoisted his pack over his shoulder and retied his mask across his face. If he hurried he might catch up to them before they reached the town of Crynn. Devin left the blessed circle of life and ventured onward to the worn path known as the Winding Steppes.

Dunwerth was surrounded by a beautiful series of valleys and hills nestled between the taller peaks of Alma's Crown. Leaving that relatively open section meant traveling a path through those peaks, of which there was only a single road, the Winding Steppes. It started off fairly flat and wide, like the dried basin of an enormous river, but as the day wore on the path narrowed, and to one side a canyon steadily grew steeper and steeper. The black grass vanished, a welcome relief, but it came with biting cold winds swirling down from the snow-capped peaks.

After several more hours Devin's road was little more than a slab of stone carved into the side of a mountain. To his right, always present in his weary mind, was a massive cliff. Devin had found it a little unnerving on his travel to Dunwerth. On his way out, after encountering the dangers the black water had seemingly awakened, the road was an anxiety-inducing torment.

The water might not have made it this far, he told himself as he pulled his coat tighter at the neck. The barren ground provided no evidence one way or the other toward its passage, so Devin allowed himself to hope. Every hour or so he encountered another sign of the villagers, usually in the form of a stiff corpse pushed against the steep cliff side. They were typically elderly, Devin noticed, lost to the cold and exhaustion of travel. A deep instinct demanded that he stay and escort the soul during the reaping hour. Each time he reminded himself of the blazing souls soaring heavenward the prior night. Perhaps this new world had no need for Soulkeepers and their rituals.

It wasn't until nightfall that he spotted a corpse bearing signs not of weather but of injury. Devin knelt beside the body and frowned. His gloved hand pulled away the young woman's stiff hair to reveal long red gashes across her neck and shoulder. A cloth was tied about her throat. It crinkled as he pulled it away, and he quickly let it go. Frozen blood had hardened the cloth. The woman's throat was torn open, with a bit of her exposed trachea hanging free.

No blade did this, he thought as he stood. His hand drifted to the hilt of his sword. *So what then?*

Devin debated his course of action. Whatever had killed this woman could still lurk nearby, assuming the villagers had not brought it down during the attack. Camping here was dangerous. On the other hand, the path was narrow, the moonlight often blocked by clouds, and his every muscle ached from exhaustion. Continuing on could easily result in him stumbling off the path to die at the bottom of the ravine.

Deciding he'd trust his sword and pistol over his tired eyes, Devin resigned to catching up with the survivors the following day. With so little wood in his pack, he grimaced away his discomfort and tore the clothes free of the dead woman's corpse to use as additional kindling. He used his own body to block the wind, and after a little bit of oil and a heavy striking of the flint, he set his campfire to blaze. Its meager heat was a welcome relief upon his numb face.

Once his limbs had thawed he debated what to do with the corpse. He had not the supplies nor the time to build a proper pyre. The best he could do was craft a burial mask with the snow, so he prayed that would be sufficient. He piled it high across her face and, after a moment's hesitation, piled more across the wounded neck and shoulder. No need to keep that grotesque sight visible. The reaping hour approached, its arrival more obvious to Devin's mind than any wind or sparkle of sunlight. It wasn't quite the same power as in the mayor's house, but it was close. Devin spoke the holy words, though he couldn't shake the feeling that they were no longer necessary in this new world.

"Blessed Sisters, take her home," he finished. The symbol of the three Goddesses flared blue in the snow, and then the soul parted from the body like a shot. It blazed into the heavens, a comet in reverse. Devin let out a soft sigh. At least he hadn't found a way to screw that up. That left one minor, wriggling detail. He had no pyre, yet the corpse was an empty shell needing to be burned or buried. Seeing no good solution, he gave up and shoved the naked body off the cliff to the ravine below.

"Sisters help me, I cannot wait to be among civilization again," he muttered. "I swear I've committed more blasphemies in the past two days than all the rest of my life."

Should he die before the dawn he'd plead his case to the Sisters for clemency. If he lived, well, then he'd have had a good night's sleep. Devin curled up as close to the fire as he dared, and he idly watched the flickering flames while wondering if his little firekin would make another appearance. He certainly hoped it would.

A long howl pierced his hazy mind, pulling him from sleep he was surprised to have entered. His eyes snapped open, a chill spiking from his heart to his throat. Wolves, this far up the mountains? That wasn't right. Could they have been chased here by the black water? Or had they been changed into an unholy abomination like the corpses and the grass?

That unwelcome thought pushed Devin to his feet. He drew his gun and loaded a shot down the barrel. His last encounter with wolves had left him near-dead, and only Arothk's intervention had spared him. Devin had a feeling no ancient stone creature would save him this time. Pistol ready, he freed his sword and scanned the pathway. He'd been too groggy on first hearing the howl. Which way had it come? Ahead or behind?

"Holy shit," Devin swore as he turned and slammed his back against the cliff. Another howl, except this time it came from seemingly everywhere. It made no sense. The bright moonlight allowed him to see far in either direction of the cliff-side road. No wolves. How could they be so close and yet not be seen?

A crackling of stone turned his head slowly to the cliff side itself. His eyes widened. His mouth went dry. Devin had pondered letting the firekin take his life if in the new world he had to fear his own campfire. That desire returned tenfold. An enormous leg of a spider slipped up and over the edge of his path and dug its claw into the hard stone. A second followed. Devin aimed his pistol between the two legs, waiting as if lost in a nightmare. A snarling wolf's head appeared next, drool trembling from its lips. Its eyes were closed. Its white teeth shone in the moonlight.

The rest of the wolf body followed, its four paws hanging limply from its body. No, it moved with the four ebony spider legs, each the length of a man, that sprouted from a bloody focal point in the center of its back.

The wolf's yellow eyes blinked open. Then two more, and then two more, until eight such eyes stared hungrily at him. The thing howled, and Devin saw the dripping fangs of a spider wiggling beneath its pink raised tongue.

Stay calm, Devin told himself, as if it could be that easy. His pistol sighted straight between the two largest eyes. Splattering its brains across the snow seemed the best plan. He stared down the spider-wolf, preparing to take his shot. So far it hadn't moved, only threatened from the edge of the cliff. His finger tightened on the trigger.

A new howl washed over him, and against his better judgment he spared a glance upward over his shoulder. A second spider-wolf descended from the sheer mountainside from high above. The first spider took advantage of his lack of focus and lunged. Devin's shot glanced off the side of its head, tearing off an ear and ripping open two of its eyes. The pain was enough to stop it in its tracks, but Devin didn't dare try to press the attack with his sword. Pistol holstered, the Soulkeeper tucked his head and sprinted down the narrow path.

"Fuck, fuck, fuck," Devin muttered as he fled. He could hear the creatures' snarls behind him, could feel the thudding of their feet upon the rock and snow. It wouldn't be long before they caught up completely.

Devin turned a sharp corner. The moonlight glittered strangely before him, his only warning before he slammed into what felt like a firm, heavy blanket. Thick strands of a spider's web held him securely in place above the stone path. Devin screamed as he struggled, succeeding only in entangling himself further. Strands clung to his individual fingers, his face, and his chest. His wrists and ankles moved as if in chains.

This time, panic was impossible to hold at bay. He kept expecting to feel the legs of the spiders wrap about him, spinning him around and around, wrapping him in webbing, preparing him for...

"Enough!" he screamed, using the cry to pull his mind free of its panic. The creatures weren't attacking. Not yet. He craned his neck to look over his shoulder, and strangely enough the two spider-wolves stood side by side on the path, which was too small for the both of them. Their long spider legs curled below the path and clung higher up the mountain to make room. They softly snarled, drool dripping from their mouths, but neither approached. Devin watched with detached horror. Were they playing with him? Waiting for him to pass out? Or did they possess unimaginable cruelty and wish to toy with him longer?

A feminine form shimmered into existence between the wolves. The light did not touch her. Only the glint of her long, clawlike fingers reflected the moon's embrace. Devin stared, convinced he was lost in a dream as she neared. One of those claws brushed across his neck. Warm blood trickled down his chest and throat, yet he felt no pain. Though this figure stood mere inches away, he saw only a deep black silhouette.

"What...what are you?" Devin asked, surprised by the slurring of his words. The world tilted off its axis, and his stomach churned unhappily. His mind fogged as if he'd drunk an entire bottle of rye whiskey.

"Hush now," a woman's voice spoke. So soft, so gentle and innocent. "Be not afraid."

"I'll try," he muttered. His eyelids drooped. "But I...I think it's too...too..."

His head hung low, his every muscle relaxed in the comforting grip of the web.

CHAPTER 8

Devin burst awake with a sudden clarity that baffled his previously drug-addled mind. He gasped in air, growing aware of a sharp pain in his neck. Everything around him was pitch-black, everything, that is, but for the long claw sunk an inch into his neck. Devin tensed, and he found his hands and legs thickly bound with webbing, holding him to what he believed was the wall of a cave.

The claw withdrew. A vague, lingering pain remained. Devin stared at the perfectly smooth black shape that was the woman's face. Well, she and her spider-wolf things hadn't killed him immediately. That had to mean something, right?

"Good morning," he said. "Or is it evening? One can never tell in places such as these."

The womanly form retreated. The silvery claws crossed over her heart, assuming she had one. He couldn't see a single feature of her body otherwise, not eyes or lips or clothing.

"Places such as these?" she asked. Her voice shivered through Devin's spine like tinkling crystal or the soft patter of rain upon leaves. Pleasant, almost achingly so, and he immediately wished for her to say more.

"Places like caves," Devin said. "Or monster dens."

"Is that what you think I am? A monster?"

"You're a shadow with claws. What else am I to make of you?"

One of those claws wagged before his nose.

"So ready to judge what you do not understand. How little humanity has changed. Would you trust me if I were clothed in silk, my lips painted cherry red and my hair laced with silver threads?"

"It'd help," Devin said. "Though I doubt it'd have mattered once your twisted little children chased me into your web."

"Those wolves are not my children." The silhouette paced before him. "Nor are they like the rest of my kind. I merely found them this morning, twisted and changed by Viciss's black water. I eased their pain and then guided them to food. They are innocent creatures of nature, and I would spare them from suffering."

The more she talked the more Devin noticed oddities with her speech patterns, particularly with her pronunciations. Occasionally she'd say something he did not immediately recognize, but could understand from context.

"Viciss?" Devin asked. "Who is Viciss?"

"He is the crawling mountain," she whispered with reverence. "The greatest of the five. He crafted me into who I am, and is worthy of praise."

"Crafted you?" Devin said, still struggling to understand. "Into what? Some twisted shadow of humanity?"

"I am neither human nor twisted," she said. No anger accompanied her rebuke, only wistfulness. "I am an artistic glory. A divine portrait. I am beautiful, little human. Viciss made me *beautiful*."

From within the void of her face he saw her eyes open. A sky of soft pastels swam inside her irises, steadily transitioning from pink to ocean blue. The dark silhouette of her body brightened like the rising sun, no longer absorbing light but instead exuding it from every surface. Devin's eyes widened, his heart halting for a long, agonizing moment. This woman...this woman did not lie. She was far from human, and she was so very, very beautiful.

Scales covered every inch of her body, but they were not hard and reptilian. They fluttered with her movements like soft petals of a flower. The center of her neck and chest were a vibrant white, with radiant waves of pink and then blood red spreading outward to her arms, back, and legs. Her stomach and abdomen were the only parts he saw that lacked scales, for instead they were formed of tough, green skin, like the stem of a flower. When she bowed Devin saw that her spine was outlined and protected with a similar stemlike covering that weaved its way up her spine to vanish beneath the crystalline rainbow that was her hair. Her fingers weaved amid her bow, and no longer did they shimmer like moon-kissed blades. Instead each long finger looked like a deep blue spinneret of a spider, all except for the middle fingers. They bore long, crooked stingers as black as obsidian. Those stingers were the only threatening image in her entire form.

"Your name," Devin breathed. "Tell me your name."

"I have not a name as you perceive them," the woman said. She stepped closer and tilted her neck toward him. "Human noses are unrefined, but please try."

Perfume washed over his face. It was a mixture of a dozen flowers, the morning mist upon a still lake, and a final lingering note of lavender. He breathed it in and tasted forgotten childhood memories of playing in the mud and wet grass after a rain. Devin's mind swam, and the moment the scent passed he ached for its return.

The woman stepped away. Her head dipped low and her arms crossed behind her. As if she were shy. As if she weren't an otherworldly beauty imprisoning Devin in webbed shackles.

"Never before existed a name so sweet," Devin said. "But my clumsy tongue cannot hope to replicate that. What might I call you instead?"

"When I walked your courts I was given many names. You may use Lavender, if you wish." Her pastel eyes shimmered. "A name for a name, human. Who are you?"

"Devin Eveson." He did his best to respectfully bow given his current predicament. "Soulkeeper of the Three Sisters and humble servant of the people."

"People?" Lavender asked. "Which people? The wealthy? The poor? Do you serve all people, or do you serve only the humans?"

"Forgive me, Lavender, but until two days ago I did not know there were other people besides humans."

She lovingly brushed her fingers across the side of his face. His skin tingled at the touch. It felt like being brushed by a patch of poison ivy.

"Your Sisters left you so ignorant and confused," she said. "But I am not here to teach you, Devin Eveson."

"Then what am I here for?" he asked, unable to help himself. "To be your dinner?"

"Dinner?" She smiled, revealing a row of perfectly smooth

teeth like water-worn marble, all flat but for two long and hooked incisors that did much to dispel the smile's comfort. "Do you fear I'll eat you, little human? Shall I turn your insides to jelly with my venom and drink of their nourishment to pass away the winter?"

"I'd prefer you not," Devin said, and he grinned along with her. "But I'd hate to be a rude guest."

Lavender laughed. A faint whiff of her name-scent trickled down Devin's throat.

"Fear not my web. You are a skittish animal, and I sought to prevent your harm, and mine, when you woke."

It was good hearing that she had no plans to turn him into porridge, but there still remained the awkward situation of him stuck to a wall.

"Then illuminate me," Devin told Lavender. "Why capture me like this if you mean me no harm?"

Lavender passed her hand from one side of his face to the other, her spinnerets weaving a thick sheen of webbing over his mouth. Her lips breathed cool air against his ear.

"I have slept for so long, human. I do not recognize this world, but you do. What you know, I must know. Where are your towns, your cities? How far has humanity spread in our absence?" Her long, powder-dry tongue drifted across his cheek. "You are beautiful, Soulkeeper, in a way that only humans are. I expect this to be most pleasant."

Something thin and sharp stabbed from Lavender's tongue into his ear. He tried to scream into the webbing but he felt his body relax instead. A haze settled over his mind, and it felt like he lost himself to daydreaming. He thought of his trip from Londheim, of visiting with his brother-in-law Tomas in the city of Crynn before continuing on through the Winding

Steppes to reach Dunwerth. He remembered the crisp chill in the air and the songs he'd sung as he walked the valleys of Alma's Crown.

Devin's mind seemed to grow bored with the images, and his thoughts wandered with it. He remembered holding his sister's hand as they knelt before two triangular pyres burning away to ashes the bodies of their parents. He remembered the cavalcade of orphanages afterward, and of his excitement at being brought into the church for training. It all flowed in his mind, one memory fluidly leading to another. There seemed little rhyme or reason. Sometimes he thought of his time in training to be a Soulkeeper, other times playing leatherball with childhood friends in the fields of Stomme.

One image in particular put a smile to his daydreaming face. It was of a blond Soulkeeper kneeling over a decapitated body on a long, empty stretch of road. A jagged two-handed axe freshly painted with gore lay beside her. She'd glanced over her shoulder and smiled at him, a bit of blood from her gray coat wiped across her nose, giving her a prominent jester's dot. It was Brittany, his wife, greeting him for the first time ever as she cleaned up the last of a group of bandits terrorizing a farming village in the southern vale.

The memory that followed clenched Devin's stomach tight. A ring of pines. A cold body atop an unlit pyre. Six years ago, it'd been, six long, painful years. Rage swelled inside his chest. He'd dealt with that sorrow once. He refused to suffer it again. His teeth clenched. His arms and legs tensed. This daydream, it wasn't a daydream, it was a prison, and by the Goddesses he wanted out. The webs shook and stretched at his pull, and suddenly a sharp pain stung his ear as Lavender gasped and pulled away from him, blood dripping from her tongue. The color drained from the petals of her skin, removing the last bit of light in that deep, dark cave. Only her pastel eyes shone, the slanted pupils widening with surprise.

"You relive moments of joy and yet reward me with anger," she said.

Devin's stomach cramped. He slumped in the webbed manacles, his every muscle exhausted. His lips parted, the webbing sealing them crackling like dry leaves.

"Joy?" he said. "You have a strange view of joy. I don't recall too fondly the loss of those I loved."

The woman let out a strange, hissing noise.

"Not a loss, but a soul's return to your Goddesses," she said. "Are Soulkeepers not tasked with the aiding and celebration of this? I know your kind once feared death. Have you now come to despise it?"

Devin lifted his head and stared straight into those mesmerizing eyes, trusting the strange woman to see his resolve despite the darkness.

"Lavender, as a respected Soulkeeper of the Three Sisters, I say this with utmost civility: Either kill me, or get the fuck out of my face."

Lavender recoiled as if struck. The pupils of her eyes slanted like a snake's. A flutter of petals sent waves of red and orange down the scales from her head to her toes, the color quickly replaced by utter blackness.

"Kings and lords once paid for my gift of relived memories," she said. "Women adorned themselves in lilacs and roses to mimic my beauty. I brought tears to the eyes of those whose lives I swam through. And yet you ... you disheveled, lonely servant of slumbering Goddesses would insult me so?"

"My Goddesses do not sleep," Devin said.

The walking shadow closed in, her glowing claws shaking before his face.

"Not anymore," she whispered. "But neither do we."

She left him there, the light of her claws vanishing so he hung in complete darkness. The sound of his breathing was the only reprieve from the silence. What he'd give for a torch, or the shining stars above. He loosely counted for about ten minutes before he started systematically working one individual bond after another, testing their strength. Wrist to ankle to wrist to ankle, figuring out which might give, which directions might have motion. He would not hang there awaiting death or worse. He didn't know how much time passed, for he had no marker. While awake, he strained and pulled. When his legs tired, he focused on his arms. When his shoulders ached with every breath, he loosely shook his weight from side to side, refusing to give the webbing even a moment's reprieve.

Hours, Devin was certain. So many hours passed. He gave his muscles a rare break and hung completely limp.

"Has my time come?" he whispered. "Take my soul into your hands, beloved Anwyn. Please don't leave me here to rot in a cave until the time of Eschaton."

A brief spark of illumination seared his right eye, and he turned his head away and closed his eyes. When he reopened them, he expected it to be gone, and it seemed it was . . . but there was light now. He saw the faintest gray of the cave's walls. Where did it come from? He twisted his neck as his eyes adjusted. No, not before him. Above?

A delirious smile stretched his face.

"Puffy?" The firekin had significantly shrunk in size since last they met. It no longer maintained a humanoid form, instead appearing like a tiny ball of fire no bigger than his little finger.

A singular little foot stretched from its lower half to pull it along the cave wall toward Devin's bound right wrist.

"*Shhhh,*" it said, its angry little eyes squinting at him.

At least, that was what he believed the creature said. It more came out like a long sizzle. Devin nodded to show he understood. Puffy continued its crawl along the wall until it reached the thick overlapping strands of webbing keeping his right arm locked down. The firekin looked to him, made the shushing sound a second time, and then touched his shackles.

Devin clenched his teeth and gagged down his scream as the webbing burst into flame. The heat seared across his wrist. Puffy leapt off almost immediately, drawing the fire with it. Devin's hand pulled free, and he winced at the swelling line of blisters and red skin. He slowly breathed out, his training taking over. This, he could handle.

Puffy scurried to the other hand, already appearing a little bit larger than before. It looked to Devin with its coal-black eyes, and he nodded for it to continue. Three more vicious spikes of pain later, he tumbled free to his knees. Puffy hopped down and stood before him. Tiny little arms spread from its body to haughtily push against nonexistent hips. One eye squinted.

"This wasn't my fault," Devin whispered. "I swear."

Puffy didn't look convinced. Devin decided there'd be better times to make his case. Now that he could see, it was easy to find his pack slumped against the nearby cavern wall. Devin's sword and pistol lay beside it. He retrieved both and, after a quick check, loaded his pistol. Having his weapons with him eased his tensions a tiny bit. At least now he might go down fighting should he be caught again. Once his pack was over his shoulder he turned to Puffy. The firekin shivered on the bare floor.

Devin held up one finger, then pulled the ramrod free from

his pistol. With his other hand he yanked the thick cloth mask he'd made in Dunwerth and tied it about the end. A crude torch, but it'd do for now. He offered it to Puffy, who happily hopped on and nestled in. The creature's size grew as it consumed the cloth.

"You can keep fire from spreading to my clothes, right?" he whispered. The firekin nodded. With no choice but to trust it, Devin slid the ramrod into one of the deeper pockets of his coat. Only the upper third poked out. Puffy shifted, somehow adjusting the weight of the barrel so it hung away from the coat's fabric. Devin readied his sword and pistol.

"Can you lead me out?" he asked.

Puffy rolled into a perfect sphere, shot out an arm, and pointed ahead.

"You're goddess-sent," Devin whispered, earning himself a little puff of smoke he could not interpret.

Devin cautiously traversed the winding cave tunnels, the firekin his light and guide. He passed in silence, his ears straining for the slightest noise and his eyes alert for a patch of darkness that didn't sit quite right. There were only a few places where the tunnel branched, and Puffy pointed out the correct direction for him to take. A soft wind blew against his skin, the temperature rapidly dropping with each footfall. Relief battled apprehension when he spotted the thick angular crack leading to the snow-kissed outside. Escape was close, so close, but he mustn't barge out recklessly. Devin leaned against the wall and listened for movement. Nothing but the wind. He glanced at Puffy, who shrugged its shoulders. Apparently the firekin detected no sign of Lavender, either.

Devin removed his pack and pushed it through the crack, then turned sideways to slide after it. The starlit mountain greeted him with a fresh gust of frozen air. Devin managed only a single step before he heard a soft cluck of a tongue.

"Soulkeeper."

Devin smoothly turned around. Lavender sat upon a lip of rock several feet above the cavern entrance. Snowflakes settled across her petal scales, adding a layer of white, like a cape, over the red and pink. Her hands clasped together and rested on the knees of her crossed legs. Now out of the cave he better saw the crystalline ropes that cascaded down like hair from her scalp. Starlight dazzled across them, a full rainbow of subdued colors, and with each movement of her neck they shimmered anew.

"Where're your pets?" he asked.

"Feeding," she said. She tilted her head at him. "You escaped."

Devin kept outwardly calm despite the hammering of his heart.

"Yeah," he said, glancing either way of the mountainside path. "It seems I did."

Lavender rose to her feet. Devin's pistol snapped up, aiming for the space between her pastel eyes.

"There's no need for bloodshed," he said. "Let me go and neither of us will see the other again."

"Perhaps *you* will never see *me*," she said. Webbing shot from her spinneret fingers, forming a bridge directly ahead of her feet so she might walk to the ground. "But I have drunk of your memories. You are a part of me now, another life that shall never dim within my mind, haunting me, my forever ghost."

"You make it sound disturbing when you put it that way." Lavender's feet touched the stone. He tensed his every muscle. The aim of his pistol did not waver. "Come closer and I will shoot."

"Then do it," Lavender said. She took another step, and another, until the barrel of his pistol pressed against the scales of her forehead. Devin fought against her mesmerizing stare but could not look away.

"What have I to lose?" she asked him. Blue tears trickled down her cheeks. "Centuries passed while we dragon-sired slept in a shadow tomb built by your Goddesses. My mind is a graveyard of humanity. I cultivated an entire world that no longer exists. I recognize only Londheim, but you've taken that city from us, taken it like you took all else. What comfort am I to receive? I sipped lives like your strongest wines, but its taste turns bitter after so many centuries. I do not want this new land. I do not wish to claw, scrape, and bleed to build what we once possessed. What might your bullet take from me that has not already been taken?"

"Then find a new purpose," Devin said. His finger twitched upon the trigger. "You said you walked among kings and queens? Do so again. Help us understand what is happening to our world."

Lavender's sharp teeth spread into the most bitter of smiles.

"Do you think I cannot smell the stink of terror leaking from your every pore?" she asked. "I shall find no acceptance, nor do I want it. Go. Run to whatever city you think still remains after Viciss's rage washed the world black. Leave me to my ghosts."

"And what of your wolves?"

Lavender stepped away from him, still showing no fear of his pistol.

"They shall hunt as they wish. Perhaps they will let you be. Perhaps you will murder them when they seek food." She glanced over her shoulder. Her tears were gone, replaced with sickening disgust. "Humanity has always been so good at murder."

She turned to black and slid inside the cave. A wall of webbing sealed the way behind her. Devin holstered his pistol and pulled the ramrod torch free from his coat pocket.

"You all right?" he asked the firekin. Puffy nodded, its flame settling tighter against the burning cloth. "Good. I hope you stay with me for a while longer. These mountains are cold and lonely, and right now, I'd rather not be either."

CHAPTER 9

As best as Puffy conveyed to him, Devin had been held prisoner in Lavender's cave for almost twenty-four hours. Catching up with the people of Dunwerth would be much harder, but he pushed himself to make up what ground that he could. By morning Devin descended the last of the Winding Steppes into the valley beyond. They'd traveled the entire night, too cautious to sleep anywhere where the two spider-wolves might still hunt. He'd hoped that upon reaching the valley he'd discover the black water's limits, but instead waving black grass greeted him. The only sign of life was the wide path carved through it signifying the villagers' progress.

"Still, we move on," Devin told Puffy. He'd stopped for a bit to secure the ramrod in his pack for safer travel, as well as wrapping another layer of cloth around the muzzle. It'd burned at a much, much slower rate than he'd expected, no doubt due to the firekin's masterful control. The cloth was food to it, and it rationed carefully.

After twenty miles Devin decided he could go no farther. He

settled down onto his back and let out a pained grunt. Puffy hopped free of the torch and zipped across the dirt to the edge of the blackened grass. Devin watched with a half-open eye. The firekin slowly curled into the grass, which ignited with an audible *whoosh*. Puffy settled into it, a small circle of flame forming about it. Devin couldn't see its expression, but he had a feeling it bore a look of happiness based on the steady puffs of smoke rising to the cloudy sky.

"Don't let me sleep for long," Devin said. "I just need a few hours, that's all."

When he awoke the sun was high overhead, for he'd slept all through the night. Devin struggled to his feet, and he cast a tired frown to where Puffy still calmly waited in its small circle of flame.

"I thought I asked you to wake me," he said.

The firekin burned a message into the dirt and then tilted its head sideways.

U SLEEP GOOD?

"Yes, but that's beside the point," Devin grumbled. He ate the last of his bread, downed half of his water, and then continued. Puffy traveled alongside him, flicking the edges of the black grass occasionally to fuel itself. Its preferred size seemed to be about the size of Devin's hand, and anytime it grew larger than that, it stayed on the bare dirt and hopped along until it shrank again. Devin chatted with it off and on, never receiving any answers but still enjoying its company. In many respects it reminded Devin of a child. When they stopped for a rest it peered into the contents of his pack, one time nearly setting the leather aflame. Other times it dashed to and fro ahead of him, as if impatient with Devin's steady pace. Despite its lack of facial features beyond those two solid black eyes, Devin found the firekin incredibly expressive. More amusing, he caught it mimicking his actions several times when it thought he wasn't looking.

"How long will you travel with me?" he asked the firekin when he stopped for a breather. "Have you any family or...how did Lavender put it? Perhaps friends that 'awakened' with you that you should find?"

Puffy slowly swayed in the center of a patch of black grass. Its eyes closed, rendering it near indistinguishable from a normal fire. Devin accepted the answer with grace.

"Your life is your own, little firekin," he said. "I only ask that I may call you friend."

A single eye popped open. Puffy's head extended up a bit so he might see its subtle nod.

"Thank you," he said. "Stay at my side as long as you wish, and should you ever leave, I will pray to the Sisters for your safety."

The fire flared a tiny bit. Anger, or happiness? He couldn't tell, and he did not have the courage to ask. Instead he drank the last of his water and resumed his trek, crossing the final miles to gaze over the field of grass between him and the walls of Crynn. The Dunwerth villagers' pathway veered wide of the town entirely, but why?

The walls are black, Devin thought as he lowered his spyglass. *But that's not enough to have chased them off. What then?*

The only visible building from his vantage point was the tall, blocky stone Tower of the Wise. If the world was kind, Devin's brother-in-law, Tomas, would be safe within its walls. Devin turned his focus to the open gate, but he couldn't see much. Something had to have chased away the villagers, but what?

There. A slumping form exited the doorway, its movements

painfully familiar. Just like the returned dead from Dunwerth. He focused the spyglass. No, not quite the same. It still had eyes, for starters. All its hair had fallen out, leaving its sickly pale flesh completely smooth and bald. Its mouth was completely covered over with a thick layer of what appeared to be dried blood, rendering it mute and unable to bite. The creature stumbled over the grass, and Devin noted how it did not erupt into black powder as it would with his own passage.

"Anwyn have mercy," he muttered. "The world *is* conspiring against me."

That the creature could safely move through the tall grass awakened a new worry. Devin scanned the field between him and Crynn. He'd been so focused on the town, and the path taken by the villagers, he'd not searched the field itself. Now that he knew what he looked for, he spotted them with ease. Slumped heads and shoulders rose inches above the swaying grass. They didn't move. They just waited. Hundreds filled the fields, his every turn finding more.

"No wonder the people avoided the town," Devin said as he put away his spyglass. He knelt so he might better address Puffy. "Listen, my brother-in-law lives in there, and no matter how bad it looks, I need to know if he's survived. We'll sprint our way to the town entrance, and I do not expect to be safe once we're inside. Given your nature, I confess I do not know if these creatures present you any danger, but I thought I should tell you my plan before we make the attempt."

Puffy elongated its form so it appeared taller, two little fists clenched against its hips as it nodded. Devin smiled.

"It's good to know at least one of us is brave."

Now there left the matter of his breathing. Devin used his

sword to cut a ring free from the bottom of his pant leg. Puffy watched, one eye lifted slightly higher than the other.

"I used my protective mask for your fuel," Devin explained. "I'm making do with what I have until we reach town and I can search for something better."

Puffy bounced up and down, its black eyes wide and shaking. A soft hiss emanated from it in quick, short bursts. Devin stared at it in bafflement. Was... was the firekin laughing at him?

"Have you a better solution?" he asked it. Puffy nodded. "Then be my guest."

Puffy dashed into the black grass without hesitation, immediately setting it on fire. This time it wasn't just licking the outskirts of a pathway or burning a circle for them to camp within. The firekin ran straight for Crynn, and in its wake spread an inferno. The grass erupted into flames in an unstoppable wave. Devin backed away from its heat with his arm raised to protect his face. It spread wider and wider, a triangular sea of fire and smoke. The legion of corrupted dead within howled and flailed their arms, but they were powerless against the fire's rage. The sky filled with ash. Devin feared nothing would stop it. He imagined that every inch of United Orismund seared with flame, fields and homes and forests stripped away, breaking nations down to a barren layer of earth matching what the Three Sisters found when they first set foot upon the Cradle.

Except it did stop. There seemed no reason for it, but the spreading wave hit a line several hundred yards to the east and west and halted before dwindling to nothing. The smoke drifted with the wind. After several minutes Devin could see a clear path leading directly to Crynn's gates. A tiny little flicker dashed toward him across the barren earth. Devin knelt and waited for

Puffy's triumphant return. Its coal eyes were wide and shaking, the flame of its body newly vibrant.

"I admit my defeat," Devin said, hoping his voice lacked any hint of the fear in his chest. "Your plan is indeed better."

Puffy gave an exaggerated bow and then hopped back along the path it had created as if it were no big feat. Devin tied the cut strip of gray cloth around his mouth and nose, this time to protect against the thick haze of smoke, and then followed with his sword drawn and his pistol loaded.

Devin's hope that the walls would protect the town quickly died. The all-too-familiar rot of black water washed the side of every home. Devin steadily walked the street toward the tower, his head on a swivel. To the best of his recollection, two thousand people lived in and around Crynn. No town of that size should be this unnaturally quiet. His black boots hitting the earth was the loudest sound in all of the town. His nervousness made him wish to talk to Puffy, but his hunter's instinct kept him silent. This place was dangerous.

A loud crash jerked his attention to the side. Clay shards of a toppled flowerpot rattled below a windowsill. The half-rotted curtain fluttered despite the lack of wind. Devin aimed his pistol for the home's door and waited. It cracked open. The former occupant stepped out.

"Sisters save us," Devin whispered. It wasn't dried blood that crusted over their mouths like he first thought when viewing the monsters through his spyglass. It was angry, sealed-over scar tissue.

The corrupted human took a step toward him, then another. Its blue eyes stared at him, analyzing with a disturbing intellect. Devin shook his head. Would it understand?

"Stay back," he whispered softly. "Or I will shoot."

His threat had the immediate opposite effect. The human

broke into a sprint on a direct collision course. Devin swore. He had no choice. The flamestone erupted within the barrel. His shot ripped a hole open between the eyes and a matching hole on its exit out the brain. The body dropped in a wet puddle of blood and gore.

In the quiet afternoon, that shot was an echoing thunder call.

"We need to hurry," he told the firekin as he quickly reloaded his pistol. Puffy crossed its arms, nodded, and then dashed to the nearby home. It crawled up the wall like a spider, leaving a tiny ashen trail in its wake. High ground was certainly desirable, but Devin doubted he could follow along rooftop to rooftop. Forget the wide gaps between homes. The buildings themselves couldn't even support their own weight, let alone his.

Devin spotted the first of the bald mute things watching him from a window at his left. It didn't attack. It didn't run. It just watched. Nerves clenched Devin's jaw tight. *Just move*, he told himself. Perhaps if he showed no signs of panic it'd let him be. And perhaps if he prayed hard enough, the Goddesses would descend from the heavens bringing him guards, horses, and a cheese-stuffed bread roll.

Once Devin was sufficiently far away, the creature exited the doorway and began following him step for step. Devin paused, and so did it. He carefully turned in place and lifted his pistol. Unlike the other monstrous creations he'd encountered since the black water, this one seemed to understand the threat of a pistol. It immediately dove to the side, cowering behind the corner of a home. Devin could have fired, but something about the scenario felt off. Staged, even.

Eyes peered at him from the window just above him. Waiting.

"Oh, fuck me sideways," Devin muttered. How many more might be watching? How many more were eager for him to waste his shot? Devin resumed walking, a plan formulating in his head. Perhaps it'd be best to stand his ground and force the creatures to attack? It could work, but the noise of battle might also summon more of them. These things weren't like the creatures in Dunwerth. These showed a sense of self-control, and perhaps a lingering intelligence from when they were alive. Now whether that was good or bad, well...

Devin decided *bad* when he found the road ahead blocked by three more of the corrupted humans. Their silence unnerved him further. They stood side by side, heads tilting back and forth, carefully watching him. A glance behind him showed two more lurking in the rubble of a collapsed home. Staring. Waiting.

Devin's careful walk turned to a jog. He turned early, and the second he did the ones ahead broke apart, leaping through doors or scattering up the street to most likely cut him off farther ahead. The coordination was terrifying. He so much preferred the mindless rotted things that had attacked him in Dunwerth. The second time he found his way blocked, waves of ice chilled Devin's blood. They were herding him. Three ahead, two chasing from behind. Fighting all five simultaneously while surrounded could be a fatal disadvantage. He followed the path they laid for him, and it led to what he feared: a thin dead-end road surrounded by tall homes on all sides. A sixth mute patiently waited atop the dead-end wall, and though its lips were buried beneath red scarred flesh, its cheeks tilted upward and its eyes twinkled with a distinctly human delight.

These corrupted humans made no noise, they bared no fangs, and they wielded no claws. Yet of all the things Devin had faced thus far, these frightened him the most, for their eyes still shone with human intelligence. Devin spun in place, trying to track each of the six mutes that had chased him into the dead end.

Two cut off his retreat, while three others lurked in windows and balconies.

"Come on, you bastards," Devin whispered. "Make a move."

The one atop the wall waited as perfectly still as a stone gargoyle. Pale eyes in a bald face hovered in the window on the upper floor to his left. Two more huddled mutes lurked at the edge of the balcony on his right, the walls of the building creaking from their weight. As for his two chasers, they crouched on their hands and knees, absurd hounds eager to charge their cornered prey. They breathed through their nostrils, the wheeze of their rising and falling chests their only sound.

Six corrupted humans, only one bullet in the barrel, and no time to reload for a second shot. His sword would have to handle the other five. Devin's eyes swept the perimeter once more. So be it. If the monsters were waiting for him to make the first move, then he'd use it to secure whatever advantage he could.

Devin's pistol spun, his upper body twisting to fire at the lone mute atop the wall. His shot blasted through its jaw and tumbled it off the other side. Before the smoke had even left his barrel Devin sprinted for the wall. He had to get his back to it. He had to prevent himself from being surrounded. The two on the street charged first, launching themselves with both hands and feet into a weaving, unsteady sprint.

Devin didn't slow as he neared the wall. The creatures were close, so close. He could hear their wheezing inhalations. He could smell the stink of the bloody flesh sealing over their mouths. He dropped his pistol and drew his sword with both hands. Devin ran straight to that wall and then up it two steps, twisting his body to face his chasers. His turn gave tremendous power to his sword, its wide arc cleaving the nearest monster in half at the chest.

When Devin landed, he shoved the blade forward, impaling the second creature as it leapt for him with long, reaching fingers. His killing blow pierced through the sealed flesh over the mouth, and blood gushed from the opening as the body dropped limp. Devin put his foot on the mute's forehead and kicked his sword free. Two more of the corrupted humans had already leapt from above, and he could not spare a second's delay.

Both landed mere feet from him, crumbling as they hit the ground in a tangle of twisting limbs. Like macabre contortionists they kicked and flailed as they got to their feet and charged. Devin had never faced a foe remotely like this, knew of no proper technique or defense against such wild, reckless assaults. He swung his sword as if chopping through a tangled section of weeds. A foot and arm went flying. Blood sprayed wildly. It didn't even slow their combined momentum.

They both managed to wrap hands around Devin's neck. Knees slammed his stomach and groin, elbows his face and chest. Blood from severed limbs dripped across his coat, thick and cold. The chaotic flurry of blows left Devin gasping for air that would not come. His eyes met those of one of the mutes, and he saw that it experienced immense pleasure at his suffering.

Fight through the pain! he inwardly screamed.

Devin swung his sword upward, breaking off their hands at the wrists. They separated cleanly... but their severed hands did not relent in their suffocating grip. Horror blanked his vision. Devin's sword hit the dirt and he immediately reversed its direction for another swing. He felt brief contact as his sword hit their bodies, but he could not see through the clouding of his vision. He could only rely on what he heard, that of breaking flesh and bone.

Devin staggered forward, the onslaught finally abating. He

yanked the hands from his neck, gasping as he flung one of them to the dirt. A gargle turned his head right. A mute rushed for him with its arms spread wide as if in need of an embrace. The left half of its face had been cleaved off by his blind swing, exposing bone and a naked eyeball weeping pus. Devin didn't quite dodge so much as drop to one knee and turn his shoulder. The corrupted thing grabbed air and then stumbled over Devin's body. It fell, and Devin severed its spine to put an end to it.

The final hand around his neck suddenly went slack, and Devin did not want to think about the magic somehow connecting it to its former body. He tore it off and flung it. Clean air slid down his retching throat, finally releasing the agonizing burn in his lungs. The relief was short-lived. The other wounded mute tackled him to the ground, its arms wrapping about his waist. Devin rolled with it, positioning his sword so the tip pressed against the corrupted human's chest. Their roll continued, the hilt struck ground, and the creature's own momentum impaled itself upon the blade.

Devin shoved the body off him and then pulled at his sword. No give. The blade was trapped within the rib cage. Devin's senses screamed warning. The corner of his eye spotted movement. Devin released the hilt in addled panic and rolled to the side. He'd killed only five. The sixth remained. The final mute dove off the balcony, scabbed hands reaching, nostrils flared, eyes wide and overwhelmed with fury. It would land atop him, and Devin had no defense but his bare fists.

A comet slammed into the mute in mid-descent, blasting it aside. Puffy clung to the bald mute, which thrashed on its back as the firekin grew in size, enveloping its body with steady, unstoppable flame. Pale flesh blackened. The firekin's body grew, and grew, consuming the creature, charring it to bone and fluttering ash. Its final breath was thin and raspy. Once the deed was done Puffy hopped off, shedding much of its size like a snake shedding its skin, except instead of old scales it left behind a great smear of liquid fire burning upon the street.

Devin swallowed down his unease, accepting another solemn reminder that not even his small, friendly companion was as innocent as Devin wanted to believe. Still, there was no denying the firekin had yet again saved his life.

"Thank you," he said, still weak and out of breath. "I'd be in sore shape without you, wouldn't I?"

Puffy hopped over to one of the buildings and used a finger that emerged from its side to quickly scrawl a message.

YUWELCOMFREND.

"Friends indeed," Devin said, and he weakly smiled despite the horror of the day.

It appeared the Goddesses had finally decided he deserved a break, for no more of the mute creatures lurked about as Devin resumed his travels to the tower where he hoped to find his friend. It took him only a few minutes to reorient himself, and he walked the last of the trip with Puffy hopping along the rooftops. Devin wasn't sure what he expected upon reaching the tower, but when he finally arrived, this certainly wasn't it. The Tower of the Wise was stone, not wood like the rest of the buildings in Crynn, and all along its base had collected an astounding mound of bone, ash, and rotting flesh.

"What in Anwyn's name happened here?" Devin wondered aloud.

The Soulkeeper checked some of the more intact bodies near the outer ring of the carnage. One creature lay on its back, its swollen tongue poking out a small hole in its scar-tissue mouth. Burn marks spread from its neck to its lower abdomen in a snaking, treelike pattern. Devin had seen such a pattern once before in the drawings of a textbook. It marked the unique burn scars of a lightning strike. Except lightning strikes were incredibly rare. Devin counted at least two dozen bodies bearing similar patterns.

That wasn't the only oddity he found in what appeared to have been a battlefield. Many of the corpses looked crushed as if by heavy rocks or bricks, yet no such objects lay anywhere in sight. Most bodies were torched with fire, many down to the bone. Devin could only guess if it was the cause of death or merely applied after.

Puffy looked equally upset by the sight. Devin asked if it would follow, but the firekin refused to step anywhere near the tower.

"I can't blame you," Devin muttered, turning his attention to the door. Its thick oak front was heavily damaged and splintered, as if cudgeled from the outside. Devin tested it with his shoulder. No give. He glanced about the many dead and decided if they couldn't force it open then neither could he. Still, there were other entrances.

Devin circled the tower, searching for the lowest window. The tower stretched four stories, and while there were no windows on the first floor, there were two on the second, one conveniently above a rather thick collection of ash and bone. Devin climbed the pile while doing his best to ignore the macabre sight. Once at the top he tested the bricks of the tower. They were smooth, but not perfectly so. He brushed his fingers along the wall, searching for handholds, and when he found one, he used it to propel himself as he jumped. His other hand caught the window's edge.

Once he'd pulled himself up, he spun about and waved to

Puffy. It dashed across the dirt, leaving a trail of lingering flame to spell its message.

IWATE.

Devin saluted with two fingers, turned on his heels, and hopped down from the sill into a dark, dusty archive of the tower. The light from the window was all he had to see. Multiple burnt-out candles hung from various chains. The archive was small, just a single bookshelf on each of its four square walls, but this wasn't the only one the tower contained. The Wise were the keepers of local lore, maps, and weather charts. Every city had one, and Tomas was Crynn's. Should you seek a cure to a snakebite, you came to a Wise and his little book of nineteen different poisonous species. Property dispute over where one's land ended and another's began? Seek a Wise. Basically the tower's entire structure was floor after floor of libraries and knick-knacks of questionable use.

Devin climbed the stairs from one floor to the next, a thick knot twisting in his throat. The walls of the tower were tall, and the corruption clearly hadn't reached the second floor. If Tommy had survived, the tower was where he'd be. One giant *if.* Devin couldn't shake his dread that up those stairs he'd find another of those awful blood-mutes…

The final floor was painfully tiny, with room for little more than a desk and a chaotic collection of books covering the floor. Two candles burned on either side of the desk. Devin stepped off the stairs, his breath catching in his throat. A blond-haired man lay slumped in his chair, his hands hanging limp by his sides, his open mouth drooling over the book he currently used as a pillow. He wore a disheveled bed robe and a long pair of soft leggings. A long, gratingly loud snore droned from his open mouth.

"Tommy?" Devin said, grabbing him by the shoulder.

Tomas yelped and jolted upward. His hand brushed Devin's. A tremendous sound of thunder shook the walls, and a force like a bolt of lightning flung Devin across the tiny room to tumble over a pile of weathered tomes. Tomas spun in his chair, a massive grin of relief spreading across his young face.

"Devin?" he asked. "Goodness gracious, it really is you! Oh, uh, sorry about that, a bit of a reflex I'm still working on. So, um, good news—I can cast spells now. Isn't that great?"

"Yeah," Devin said, half-buried in books. Static leapt off him in wild little sparks. "Just...fantastic."

CHAPTER 10

Their table was a tiny square slab of pine on the second floor braced by three painfully unsteady legs. Devin sat in one of the two chairs, his coat hanging over the back. A tall glass of wine and a half-eaten apple rested on a plate before him.

"I really am sorry about that," Tommy said. He paced behind his chair, unwilling or unable to take a seat for all his nervous energy. His friend was rambling, not that Devin minded. Hearing a familiar voice was like finding rain in a parched desert. "While most elemental conjurings require a fairly precise reproduction of what I like to call the verbal recipe, some of the simpler ones appear more like reflexes after the initial casting, requiring only mental reproduction of the necessary incantations."

"Let's take a pause here," Devin interrupted. "Before we get into . . . well, all that, I'd rather know how you're doing, Tommy. Surviving these past few days had to have been difficult."

Tommy's pacing halted for a split second. He drummed his fingers against his sides.

"Yes, it was very, uh. So. Every Wise has a collection some-where of older scrolls and texts that have been long since discredited—books on things like alchemy and palm readings." He wiped at his brow. "Anyway, these supposed instructions for spells are a petty amusement—at least they used to be. I think every member of the Wise tries at some point to see if they can utter the perfect words to conjure a fireball or change a clear day to rain. I considered it a childish wonder, that hope for some-thing magical, you know?"

As his friend spoke, Devin's worry steadily grew. Tommy's voice was trembling, and he'd purposefully dodged his question. Devin stood from the table and put a hand on his friend's shoul-der, interrupting his rambling. Tommy, so lost in his own mind, jumped at the touch.

"Tommy, it's all right," he said. "I'm here now. You're not alone."

Tommy froze. His jaw trembled. His hands shook.

"You're right, you know," Tommy said. "It's been difficult, real difficult. No, more than that. It's been fucking torture."

The tears finally broke free. Tommy flung his arms around Devin and clung to him like a raft amid a flood. His chest shud-dered with every breath. Devin quietly returned the embrace, his stomach sick with worry.

Devin had first met a young Tomas on the eve of his and Brittany's wedding a decade ago. Tommy, as he preferred to be called, had been a supremely chipper boy who looked the spit-ting image of his older sister. He had just been accepted into the training program of the Wise, a remarkable achievement for one barely turned fourteen. Three years later he was desig-nated the Wise of Crynn, granted to someone so young because no one else in the program wanted to travel all the way to the westernmost city in Unified Orismund. Tommy had known that was the case but didn't care.

"I get to read and study for a living," he'd joyously told Devin and Brittany as the three gathered in an outdoor market drinking oversized tankards of ale and wine. "Can you imagine a greater life than that?"

Devin wondered if that same innocent happiness would ever return, or if it'd be one more thing the black water corrupted and ruined.

After a minute Tommy pulled back, and this time he collapsed into his little rickety chair.

"Sorry about that," he said, wiping at his face.

"You have nothing to apologize for," Devin said as he took his seat opposite him. "I know this is hard to talk about. If it'll help, I can start with my story first. I've a tale to tell if you'd like to listen."

"You know I'm always up for a story," Tommy said, cheering up at the idea. "You've got a lot of new scars and bruises, so I bet it's a good one, too."

"Empathy, Tommy," Devin said. "Try to have some empathy, would you?"

Devin started with his arrival in Dunwerth, and he left nothing out of his recounting. Tommy quietly listened, his body relaxing for the first time since they met. His eyes lit up when Devin talked of Puffy, and his excitement was palpable upon hearing that the firekin had stayed with him through the journey.

"Might I meet it?" he asked.

"I guess I could introduce you two," Devin said, cracking a smile.

Last he came to his arrival in Crynn, and his discovery of the Dunwerth's villagers and their corruption.

"And that's my tale," Devin finished. "So much as it is."

"The Goddesses' presence in the world appears to be strengthening to counteract the evil of the black water," Tommy said, two fingers pinching his lower lip as he thought. "At least, that is my interpretation of these events. The reaping hour needed no ritual from you to take the souls of the dead in the mayor's home, and what other explanation do we have for the water's bypassing of Dunwerth's villagers?"

"It's a thought that's crossed my mind," Devin said. "But I'll leave that pondering to the Mindkeepers. I've told my story, so what of yours? How have you endured since this all began?"

Tommy shifted uncomfortably in his chair, but he seemed much more together than during his initial ramblings.

"The only warning we had were faint tremors indicative of a distant earthquake," he said. "Not uncommon given our proximity to Alma's Crown. I was logging it in my daily journal when the water arrived." He took in a long breath and let it out slowly. "It wasn't silent like you described in Dunwerth. I noticed its arrival from...from the screams."

Tommy looked around while wiping his sweating forehead.

"Goodness me, I forgot to get myself a drink."

Devin patiently waited as the young man hurried over to a cabinet, pulled out two small glasses, exchanged them for tankards thrice the size, and then filled them with wine.

"I think the Goddesses know how much I need this," he said as he returned to his seat. "Where was I? Oh. Right." He took a giant swig. "Once I heard something was amiss I went to the window and saw...I saw an ocean of shadow and stars stretching for miles and miles. I didn't know what it was, where it came

from, I just stood there by the window and watched. I think....
I think I was convinced the world was ending. What else could
it mean?"

Devin didn't have the heart to tell him that still might be the
case. Instead he took a sip of his own drink and gestured for
Tommy to continue.

"When it receded I saw people in the streets, and I thought
they'd survived," Tommy said. "Maybe it wasn't the end of the
world, I told myself. Sure, the houses looked a little worse, and
the grass outside the town seemed ready to die, but at least we'd
survived. At least we'd..."

Tears were building again. Devin quickly offered him a
respite.

"No," Tommy said, lifting a finger and waving it. "No, I can
do this. I was a coward then, but I'll relive it now. I hid, Devin.
I locked and barred the door, then hid under my bed with my
fingers in my ears like a child. The people who went underneath
that black water? They were changed. They were always *bleeding*, and they were angry. So angry."

He took another long drink and then gasped.

"Lyra's tits, that tastes good. Oh. Sorry for the language."

"Foul language is the least of my concerns right now," Devin
said. "When we return to civilization, and we're resting in a
nice warm bed in a crowded tavern, perhaps then I'll make you
offer a few prayers for Lyra's poor offended tits."

Tommy laughed, and the temporary relief loosened the bud-
ding tears in his eyes so they fell.

"Sometimes people screamed for help," he said. "Other times
I just heard them fighting. No one came to my tower. Not
at first. If...if they had, I don't know if I'd have let them in.
Not out of malice, just...none of this seemed real. It couldn't

be happening. These awful, terrible, nightmarish sounds were because I was losing my mind. I could handle that. The whole town wasn't dead or turned to monsters. That was ridiculous. That was insane, so surely I must be insane instead."

Tommy sighed bitterly at his tankard.

"Near the end of the second day I realized it was all real. I also made my first big mistake. I let one of those bloody things see me."

The young man sank into his chair and fell silent for a moment. Devin sipped his wine, the scene outside the tower falling into place. Once one of those creatures saw him, others must have started to gather. Noise would have drawn more, to create more noise, to draw even more...

"I think by then I *was* a little crazy," Tommy said, eyes snapping back into focus. "When those things first surrounded my tower I hid and begged whatever goddess might listen to spare me. Those things, some of them used to be my friends. These were the people I helped, who came to me for..." He stopped and shook his head as he collected himself. "The more I saw of them the more I knew that though they shared the same body they were nothing like the people I knew. I hated them for it, and as those things continued surrounding my tower I started taunting them. I've never been great with, uh, improper language, but by the Goddesses I did my best and then some. I flung old books. I laughed at the ones failing to climb the tower. I might have even, um..." His face flushed red. "Well, I have to urinate somewhere, you know."

"I guess that's true," Devin said. "None of those things are still alive, so how did that come about?"

"Well, it was during the whole 'book throwing' phase,"

Tommy said. "The world was ending, so do we *really* need Wise Dallert's treatise on proper cartographic principles? I kept the good ones, though. Even then, part of me was convinced I'd survive, I'd help rebuild, and there are some things we should know. So while curating what I'd throw and what I'd save, I came across... hold on, let me show you."

Tommy hopped up from his chair and hurried to the stairs. Devin rose as well and drifted over to one of the windows. It took only a moment's searching to find Puffy quietly burning a black spot atop a nearby roof. Devin waved at the firekin to show that he was alive and well. Two smoke rings rose in response.

"Here we are," Tommy said as he came back down, a small book in hand. It was fifty pages at most, and nothing seemed remarkable about it. The two retook their seats, the tome placed between them. Devin glanced at the burgundy cover. *Manipulation and Theory of Aethos Magic, a discussion by Salid Emberson the Wise.*

"Aethos?" Devin asked.

"Your guess is as good as mine," Tommy said as he flipped through the pages. "A lot of it is arguing against an opposing school of thought, and poorly done, I'd wager, given how Salid gives few examples of what that opposing school believed prior to posting his counterarguments. The writer goes into great lengths to argue the proper positioning of the little finger during incantations, at one point insisting that having it fully extended is like asking the Goddesses to turn you into a bullfrog. But he lists examples of 'Aethos spells' at various points in the book. I had good reason to believe they would now work, so I studied—"

"You had good reason?"

"Well, the black water solidly defied normal understanding,

so who was to say other previously derided ideas couldn't be useful? Oh, and did I forget to tell you? I had lightning sparking out of my fingers."

Devin blinked.

"That is something you failed to mention, yes."

"It was at its worst not long after the black water came." He squinted at his now empty tankard but decided against refilling it. "Though it's died down somewhat since. Sometimes if I snapped my fingers or drummed them too long on a surface, little sparks of electricity would zap from my fingertips. It was one of the reasons I was convinced I was insane. Once I decided I might actually *not* be insane, it was perfectly logical to assume that the sparks indicated a significant change, hence my decision to keep the book instead of throwing it in the face of another one of those creatures."

Tommy shifted uncomfortably in his chair.

"I read Salid's tome cover to cover and picked what appeared to be the simplest of incantations. Most involved some sort of elemental or energy manipulation, so I started small. Well. Relatively small." His face flushed a little. "All right, I admit it, I'd actually read that book before and attempted to cast its spells years ago while severely intoxicated. Is there something wrong with a nineteen-year-old wanting to throw a giant fireball in a cellar?"

Devin smiled at Tommy and did his best to reassure him. "The Fifth Canon assures us that with the greatest of faith we might walk lighter than our souls to the heavens. When I was fifteen I fasted all night in prayer and then, with my heart full of belief, I lifted my eyes to the clouds and stepped off a diver's cliff near Stomme. I flipped head over heels and splashed twenty feet down into the ocean. Trust me, Tommy, I know what it's like to fantasize of one's special uniqueness and fail spectacularly."

"You never told me that story before," Tommy laughed.

"You never told me of drunk Tommy rambling ancient spells in a cellar, either."

"True, true, you have a point, Mister Soulkeeper. Anyway, my earlier failures resulted in having studied rather thoroughly the proper pronunciation of Salid's words, so I read them aloud, and..."

The young man's smile spread ear to ear.

"Goddesses damn it all, Devin, I know the world's ending, but I summoned fire with my bare hands. Do you know how incredible that is?"

"I imagine it was...exhilarating," Devin said.

"Exhausting is a better way to describe it," Tommy said. "I shat bricks when that fireball leapt off my fingertips. Felt like I'd run a mile after it happened, too. I sat in the window and stared at the dozens of charred bodies and told myself, very slowly and very clearly, that even if I was insane I was going to have as much fun as possible amid my insanity. So while I waited for my pounding headache to fade I studied some other spells."

"Did they work?" Devin asked, curious. He'd heard a handful of tales over the years of supposed spells lost to time, ranging from petty (changing copper to gold) to absolutely ludicrous (pulling the moon from the sky, turning whole towns into fish).

"The vast majority, no," Tommy said. "I've not tried them all, and I have theories as to why certain ones work and others do not, but I'll not delve into that right now. I picked a few that seemed most likely to succeed and returned to the window. I only meant to cast two or three, especially after how physically demanding the fireball had been, but when I returned to the window something had...changed. The world felt electric. Hundreds of those creatures surrounded my tower by that point. I summoned a thunderstorm first, the angriest you can possibly imagine. Lightning shredded their numbers. Fire leapt from my fingers in torrents, then ice. It all *flowed*, Devin, like somewhere in me a dam had broken and nothing could stop the river. The essence, or the 'Aethos' as Salid might put it, permeated the air. It suffocated me, but every new spell was a cold, clean breath."

Brittany had often joked that her brother was too kind to swat a biting mosquito. Imagining Tommy wielding enough strength to tear apart armies and ascend to the realm of the Goddesses was impossible.

"I stopped sometime after midnight," Tommy said. "Though I don't remember choosing to stop. I think I just passed out on the floor. I've tried casting some of those spells since, but the moment has certainly faded. A single lightning bolt left me sleepy this morning. I can't fathom how in the world I managed that torrent."

"You didn't seem too exhausted from flinging me across the room," Devin said, and he lightly punched the young man in the shoulder.

"Careful now," Tommy said, and he winked. "You never know what might set this powerful wizard off."

Devin drained the last of his wine and thudded the tankard down with a chuckle. "Damn right, high and mighty Wise of Crynn. I'll do my best not to forget."

Tommy did his best to finish his own in one gulp. He

sputtered a little of it back into the tankard, then chucked the whole thing to the floor. It bounced with a nice, satisfying *clack*.

"So what now?" he asked.

"Now we prepare for the journey ahead. I'm not sure how safe this town is, but I have no desire to stay in it longer than necessary. How many days of food and water do you have stored in here?"

"Another week at least," Tommy said.

"Good." Devin rose from the table. "Pack it up. We're leaving."

It was late afternoon by the time they exited the tower. They'd taken everything dried and salted they could carry, as well as filled multiple water skins. Tommy had changed out of his bedroom attire and into the stuffy brown robes of a Wise. Nothing could contain Tommy's excitement at meeting the firekin, but there was one small problem: Puffy was nowhere to be seen.

"I wouldn't worry too much," Devin said. He adjusted the heavy pack on his back. "Puffy can be quite skittish at times, and I think it's shy when it comes to new people."

It seemed ridiculous saying so after watching the firekin burn one of the corrupted humans to ash and bone, but it was still the truth.

"So it's more like a cat than a human?"

"A little bit, but it's your hide if you want to say that to its face. I have no clue what might offend the sensibilities of living fire."

They walked the road to the town entrance. Devin kept a watchful eye out for any more of the corrupted humans. Between the charred field outside, Tommy's pile of corpses below his tower, and the few Devin had killed during his ambush, it appeared the last of the creatures were gone from Crynn. At no point did he spot Puffy following. By the time they reached the exit, Devin had begun wondering if the firekin decided to move on without him.

"Hey, Devin," Tommy asked as they made their way toward the path the Dunwerth villagers had carved eastward, giving Crynn a wide berth. "Is . . . is that it? Is that Puffy?"

Devin glanced behind him. A streak of fire danced its way across the charred ground from the city entrance. The two halted and waited for the firekin to catch up. Puffy arrived with a flourish of sparks, leaping up to pirouette onto the barren earth. It settled into itself, a single waving candlelight with two black eyes peering up at them.

"Puffy, this is my brother-in-law, Tommy," Devin said.

Tommy's smile was ear to ear, and he seemed unable to speak for a long moment.

"It's so *cute*."

One of Puffy's eyes slanted. It peered Devin's way with an unmistakable look of annoyance.

"I'll make sure he behaves," Devin said to the firekin. "Here. I got you something."

The Soulkeeper set his pack down and pulled out a wax-candle lantern he'd taken from Tommy's tower. He flipped it open, and Puffy happily hopped atop the wick. Pack over his right shoulder, lantern in his left hand, Devin gestured for Tommy to follow.

"Can I hold the lantern?" he asked.

Smoke bloomed out the top of the lantern in a rapid series of plumes.

"No."

They followed the trail of the villagers, Devin in silence, Tommy rambling semicoherently as the sun slowly set. The changes to the world had lit a fire to his imagination.

"Think of how many once-derided stories might now be true?" he wondered. "What if what we considered old wives' tales are faintly remembered pieces of history?"

"And I thought you were a man of science," Devin said, shaking his head. "Do you really think a blue goblin will steal away your old teeth if you put them under your pillow? Or that if you leave a small bowl of milk overnight on your doorstep you'll be blessed by a passing faery?"

"Milk and honey," Tommy clarified. "Just milk won't do it. Not sweet enough. And don't you give me that look, either. It might seem pedantic, but those tiny differences might be what separate fiction from reality in our strange new world. A lot of these old tales and fables will only contain partially complete information, for even the truest of stories will be warped over time from the retellings, but we work with what we know until something contradicts it. For example, did you ever read Hauncer's *Elemental Dance*?"

"Can't say I have."

"It's a retelling of an old Vibrant Isle tale, of how fire and water took human forms to battle over the fate of the island. In it, the fire creature is the villain. I presuppose that these elementals might in fact exist, and posit Puffy as proof. But what about the good and evil dichotomy? Does that fit? Were the fire elementals the villains?"

"I don't know," Devin said as he lifted his lantern. "Were you the villains, Puffy?"

Puffy narrowed its eyes and tilted its head like a disappointed parent admonishing a child. Devin laughed. It felt amazing to have company, even someone as talkative as Tommy. The world was that much more alive, that much more hopeful.

Grass rustled underneath Devin's foot. He froze. He'd not looked. He'd not even paid attention, only followed the path ahead. His tightening throat expected a burst of caustic powder. His eyes watered of their own. But it did not come. The grass was not black. There was no mistaking that dwindling yellow-green shade lit by the light of his lantern.

He looked up, and saw that starlight lit the valley ahead. A distant pond sparkled under the reflection of the heavens. Blue-tinted trees waved in the soft nighttime wind. For the first time in what felt like years, he heard chirps of the midnight songbirds. None of it bore the signs of corruption. As far as the eye could see, nature appeared untainted by the water's passage.

"The black water stopped," Devin whispered. Relief quivered through his entire body as the muscles in his chest and back loosened from tension he never knew he carried. "Goddesses almighty, the black water *stopped*."

Londheim. Nicus. Steeth. The church's capital in the Kept Lands, and Queen Woadthyn's throne in Oris. It all might still exist. Its people still woke with the morning, spoke with friends, bathed and loved and slept like all of humanity had before, and would continue to do so long after they were gone. The world had not ended. Hope was not all lost.

"I never..." Tommy said, and he frowned and shifted awkwardly. "I never really thought the black water would have gone forever. That seemed...not possible. Not *fair*, you know?"

Devin dropped to his knees. He brushed his hands across the grass, and he laughed with so great a release that tears swelled in his eyes. His friends, his family, they survived. The carnage unleashed upon the far west was still catastrophic, but it was understandable now. It was bearable. He could relinquish at least one of his burdens, for his sister was likely alive and well inside Londheim's walls.

"We're coming, Adria," Devin whispered softly. "We survived."

CHAPTER 11

Adria Eveson knelt beside the bedridden old woman in the tiny little room she called her home.

"This is the third time this week, Rosa," Adria said as she washed her hands in a small basin of fresh water. "You cannot expect such an ailment to improve overnight."

"You Mindkeepers are always so quick to call for patience," Rosa said. "When it's your knee crying out like a roasting goat, maybe then we'll see how patient you are between treatments. And don't frown at me, Adria. I can see it in your eyes."

A smooth porcelain mask, the right half deep black, the left shining white, covered the entirety of Adria's face but for two thin ovals for her eyes. She was indeed frowning behind it. For good or ill, Rosa had always been a sharp woman, and her mind had not aged along with the rest of her body.

Adria reached a hand into the folds of her ornate white-and-gray dress. Though it appeared to have no pockets, there were in fact dozens of them hidden within the overlapping fabric. Adria withdrew a slender bottle with a clear crystal stopper. The brown contents swirled, remixing the layer of white that had settled on the top. Adria had personally crushed the six roots and herbs within, work normally reserved for a novice, but none had been assigned to her church. Supposedly her little corner of Londheim was too dangerous for the younger, untrained students.

Adria withdrew one of Rosa's spoons from the basin and carefully poured her mixture into it.

"Piss on that tiny dose," Rosa said. "Can't you give me the whole bottle?"

Adria turned her mask to the woman.

"The whole bottle would kill you."

"That ain't as good a reason as you think it is, Mindkeeper."

Adria was glad for the mask. She'd hate for the spindly, darkhaired woman to see how frustrated and exhausted she was behind it.

"Take it," she said, handing over the spoon. "That's the last you'll receive for three days, Rosa, no matter how much you complain. Anwyn, not my medicine, will take you when it's time."

Rosa gulped the foul spoonful down. Adria opened the curtain to the lone window, spilling light across Rosa's bed. The elderly woman winced and turned from it.

"The sunlight will do you good," Adria said.

"Ain't nothing good out there," Rosa said. She sighed and closed her eyes. "And I got a full day's sun for fifty years working Quiet District's gardens. Didn't do me good then, won't do me good now."

Adria glanced out the window. Haggard men and women walked the street, most heading east to work the docks alongside the Septen River. A raven-haired mother carrying her child on her shoulders noticed Adria in the window and quickly averted her eyes.

"You're losing hope," Adria said, turning away. "Lyra's healing comes to those who believe and endure."

"Save that bollocks for the young, Mindkeeper. Come pray your prayers and be done with. I already got what mattered."

Adria had thought herself used to such sentiment. Perhaps not.

"I can leave now if you wish," she said stiffly.

Rosa let out another sigh.

"I'm sorry, girl. I've not slept well in weeks. Please, come pray your prayers. If I'm to walk again I'll need every little bit of help I can get."

Adria withdrew a small, well-worn leather book from one of her interior pockets. The book wasn't much larger than her hand, and like all other copies of Lyra's Devotions, it contained exactly seventy-nine pages, one for each prayer. Adria had memorized every page, but she'd learned that bringing it out during her visits to the sick and elderly added an air of ceremony to the process. She knelt beside the bed, the 36th Devotion open before her, and then slowly pulled away the blanket covering Rosa's right leg.

The knee was an uneven purple blotch, colored like someone had smashed an enormous grape underneath her skin. Adria was thankful her mask hid her grimace. No wonder Rosa had summoned her so quickly. It had grown significantly worse over the past two days. If the illness continued to spread at such a rate . . .

"Might you do something for me?" Adria asked. "Pray along with me this time, please. You must believe to be healed."

Rosa shifted uncomfortably, and her inability to meet her gaze did not go unnoticed.

"I'm sorry, Adria. I don't have it in me to lie. We both know this knee ain't getting any better."

Adria did know it, but she could not believe it, otherwise what hope was there? She gently placed both hands on the sick knee and closed her eyes. Rosa had been one of her first visits when Adria was assigned to the Low Dock church three years ago. Hearing her so defeated made Adria physically ill. Where was her fight? Where was her faith? Had the agony stripped her of both?

"Lyra of the beloved sun," Adria recited. "Hear my prayer. Your children weep for your touch, and so I come, and so I pray."

Most devotions began similarly, but this time Adria poured her heart into it. Perhaps she could compensate for Rosa's uncertainty. Perhaps she could show that it wasn't so hopeless. The disease didn't have to spread. Flesh could heal. Rot could recede.

"Sickness fouls the perfection you created," Adria continued. Her breath caught in her throat. Was it her imagination, or did the ground shake beneath her?

"Darkness mars the glory you shone upon us."

Another tremble. Her hands quivered as they held Rosa's knee. Something wasn't right. The hairs of her skin stood on end. The sound of the outer world faded in her ears.

"With bowed head and bended knee I ask for succor. With heavy heart and weary mind I ask for blessing."

The words came of their own accord. Adria felt like a helpless passenger trapped on a carriage that would not stop. Rosa let out a soft gasp but Adria dared not open her eyes. The end of the devotion neared. She knew the words, but something was changing in them. She could not control her tongue.

"This beloved soul requires healing, Lyra, my savior. Cleanse the sickness. Chase away the pain. Precious Lyra..."

Not ask. *Demand.*

"At my touch, heal this woman."

At last she opened her eyes and withdrew her hands. The purple was gone. The flesh was healed.

"Blessed be," Rosa said, staring with wide open mouth. Her gaze turned Adria's way, eyes alight with shock and wonder. Adria staggered to her feet, her back pressing against the wall. She pointed a shaking hand toward Rosa.

"No one must know of this," she said.

"But what you just did, it's..."

"I said no one!"

Adria's mask suffocated her. She ripped it off and stared at Rosa's knee as if it would suddenly change back. Reports of divine healing were thoroughly investigated by the Keeping Church. She'd known of several incidents since she moved to Londheim, and each and every one ended the same: with the Mindkeeper stripped of title and banished from the church in disgrace for their falsehoods. Adria clenched her hands into fists and finally met Rosa's worshipful eyes.

"I don't know what any of this means," she said. "Until I do, tell no one of what happened here."

Rosa slid off the bed, slowly shifting more and more of her weight onto the previously sick knee.

"This miracle should be shouted from the rooftops, but if you want me to keep silent, then silent I'll be." She shook her head. "What a fool I am. Praise Lyra, praise Alma, praise all Three Sisters, it looks like Anwyn's not ready for me yet!"

Rosa flung her arms around Adria and squeezed with far more strength than her withered frame should possess. Adria returned the hug, her body still locked in shock. She bit down on her tongue as hard as she dared. Nothing changed. Not dreaming, then, or if she did, it was a waking dream.

"I must go," Adria said. "I must...pray on this matter."

She replaced her mask and retied the leather knot in the back. A little bit of comfort returned to her at its cool touch. Behind that mask, she was the calm, collected Mindkeeper of Low Dock. Only her eyes might give away her fear and worry.

"Try not to wander about too much for the next few days," she instructed. "If you go bouncing through the market, people are going to ask questions you won't have answers for."

"Oh, I'll have the answers, Adria," Rosa said. She winked. "But I'll keep them to myself."

Adria exited the one-room home onto one of Low Dock's many winding stone roads. She was not fond of Londheim, but she'd learned to welcome the honest hardship of her little district. The dilapidated buildings around her were tall wood-and-stone structures with vaulted ceilings, seeming to almost curl overhead in an attempt to cocoon in the road from the sun, not that there was much need for it today. Shade from the overcast sky mixed with the deep gray of the stone to lend an almost blue atmosphere to Londheim. Adria hurried north, her eyes focused inward and her feet moving of their own accord.

A rare miracle, never to be replicated, Adria told herself. If her superior, the Deakon of Londheim, declared an inquisition into the matter she would deny any divine nature tied to the recovery. So long as she didn't seek to attract undue fame, the Keeping Church's leadership should accept her explanation.

Piss! My devotions!

Her mind was too scrambled after the incident. She'd left her book of devotions on Rosa's bed. She spun to return and immediately froze. Where...where was she? It wasn't possible. Adria knew every dark corner of Low Dock, for the men and women living there often could not go to the apothecary in the nearby

Tradeway District. Their professions were too seedy, the reason for their injuries often illegal. If you were stabbed in a robbery, whether you were the robber or the robbed, you came to her. If you couldn't make the trip, she came to you. Low Dock was her flawed, violent home, so why did it feel so foreign to her?

Adria studied the house to her left. The chipped 57 above the door meant Becca Langston lived there with her two sons. Why did it seem different? The stone bricks, Adria realized. Instead of clear, layered cracks in the sides they were perfectly smooth, as if the home were constructed of one single stone. Her insides shivered. Stone gargoyles with catlike faces smiled down at her from their rooftop perches. Those were usually confined to the mansions of Quiet District, for they'd fallen out of favor by the time much of Londheim was built.

"Sir," she said, stopping the first person she passed in the road. The older man turned and lifted an eyebrow.

"Might you need something, Mindkeeper?" he asked with the slow drawl most native to southern Londheim carried.

"Do you know Miss Langston?" she asked. "Her husband died three winters back?"

"I worked with her father," the man said. "Is something amiss?"

"I . . . I'm looking for her home. Is that it?"

Adria tensed. Would he notice? A man who'd lived in Londheim all his life would immediately recognize such a change . . . wouldn't he?

"Aye, that's her home," he said. His eyes lingered on the building. Adria could sense his steadily growing apprehension. "I must say, I don't remember it ever having them stone gargoyles before."

It wasn't just her, then. She couldn't decide if that should make her feel relieved or terrified.

"Thank you," she said. "May the Sisters watch over you."

She needed to think. That was all. A good moment to pray and meditate on what was transpiring. Adria hurried along, glancing at homes as she passed. Things looked so similar, with only the tiniest of changes to some. It was like coming home to find all her furniture rearranged. The changes weren't restricted to gargoyles, either. She noticed several homes with large open windows on second floors where there'd been only solid walls. For what reason could those exist in the cold climate of Londheim? Or was she jumping at shadows, only now noticing things that otherwise would have been easily ignored?

At least one clear identifying marker remained unchanged. The Sisters' Tower, located near the passageway through the stone wall marking the borders of districts, stood a clear sixty feet higher than any other structure in Low Dock. Despite its size, it contained only a single square room on the bottom floor, with no stairs, ladder, or opening leading higher. Many Mindkeepers theorized the tower was hollow throughout. Three marble statues overlooked the city at the top, one of each holy Sister triumphantly addressing Londheim with their hands raised in joy and wind blowing through their pristine robes.

Adria followed the road to the quiet corner containing the tower's entrance. Two soulless city guards stood guard before the door to prevent vandalism or unlawful entry. Adria was never comfortable around the soulless, doubly so after her baffling experience, and she did her best to address them with a clear, firm voice.

"I seek a moment of solitude to pray," she said.

Those born soulless had no desires, no wants, no imagination or creativity or sense of identity. They followed orders without hesitation or complaint unless those orders directly and obviously ended their lives. Because of this, they could be taught to have an owner whose orders must be followed above all others. With a bit of training they made perfect guards and laborers, and there were shops in the northeast filled with thousands of soulless workers. Their presence always unnerved Adria. The way they stared at her made her skin crawl.

"As you wish, Mindkeeper," they said in unison. No inflection in the slightest to their voices. They stepped aside, the one on the left gesturing for her to enter. Adria kept her head high and passed through them, suppressing a shiver.

For as long as recorded history could tell, the Sisters' Tower was a holy place of prayer for members of the Keeping Church. The room at its base was not much taller than her, and she could touch the ceiling with her fingers if she wished. Three enormous paintings covered the walls, one for each of the Goddesses. The first was of Alma, a woman in white with pale skin and golden hair, standing beside a creek at the break of dawn. She extended a dove toward the second painting, that of Lyra. Lyra cradled the dove in her arms, its white feathers a sharp contrast to her dark skin and even darker dress. Her long black hair spilled out across the grass at her feet. A stream flowed before her, its water sparkling in the high afternoon sun.

Last was the painting of Anwyn. The goddess reached out a gentle hand toward Lyra, seeking the dove. Her skin was so clear it was almost translucent. Unlike the other two, she stood naked for all to see. Her head was shaved and her face hidden behind a perfectly smooth porcelain mask. The sun set behind her, streaking the sky with red and orange rays. The masks of the Mindkeepers were homages to all three, Anwyn's porcelain painted half in Alma's white and the other half Lyra's black.

Adria bowed before the center painting of Lyra. As was

expected of a Mindkeeper, she felt closest affinity to the goddess of the day, the holy symbol of her sacred division. Alma created souls and delivered them to the world, and Anwyn accepted them into her embrace once life was at its end, but it was Lyra who watched over them during their stay in the imperfect world. Lyra offered guidance. Lyra shed her tears for their sorrows and extended her grace to any who sought a better life and a better self. It was that knowledge that Mindkeepers attempted to harness for themselves and then spread throughout the populace.

Adria placed her hands atop two circles in the intricately carved floor. Swirling lines connected each corner of the room, sometimes coming together to form elevated bumps of smooth stone. No records remained of the tower's construction, leaving scholars and bored nobles to make guesses as to their symbolism or purpose. For reasons she could not identify, Adria was certain that the proper place to pray was on her knees in the heart of the three paintings with her hands on the two center half spheres that rose from the stone.

"Praise be to the Goddesses of dawn and dusk, of life and death, and of the sacred days between."

The words steadied her heart. The tower was a holy place, a visible beacon throughout Londheim serving as a reminder of the ever-loving gazes of the Goddesses. No matter what happened, the Sisters would be there for her. They'd watch over her.

"Praise be to the creator of our souls, the nurturer of our souls, and the caretaker of our souls upon this life's ending. I pray to thee, Sisters. I ask that my words be heard. I ask that my heart be pure. Hear me, so I may hear you."

The stone circles warmed beneath her touch. The ground shook. There'd been minor quakes occurring for the past few days, and she initially thought it another. When the circles pulsed a pale blue underneath her fingers she thought otherwise.

"Guards?" she asked, spinning around as she hurried to her feet. The two soulless were gone. The floor was rising, taking her with it through the hollow tower. A deep, metallic grating noise, reminiscent of levers and chains and pulleys, came from the four walls. Adria put her hands behind her back and waited. This was clearly beyond her control. She would not panic and make the situation worse.

With a shudder, the platform came to a halt. Cold wind blew across her skin as Adria's insides shivered. Whatever hidden mechanics she'd activated had taken her all the way to the top. The three enormous statues of the Sisters surrounded her, but they were not as they seemed from below. Their form split at the hip, becoming a second version of the Goddesses facing inside the tower. Alma drooped low, her arms struggling to lift a single feather. Lyra covered her face with her hands, clearly weeping. Anwyn had removed her mask only to reveal a face equally smooth and featureless beneath.

Adria stood before the presence of the Goddesses, and while they showcased strength and exultation to the city, in private they wept and struggled with their burdens. Tears filled Adria's eyes and she did not wipe them away. This tower, this place, this spot...it was indeed holy, but not for the reasons they'd always surmised. She put a loving hand on Lyra's side and pressed forehead to forehead with the statue.

"You do weep for us," she whispered. "Please, whatever happens now, whatever miracle is passing over our world, know that I welcome it with open arms. I shall be ready to serve, even unto the end of days."

Adria pulled away from the statue and overlooked the city. She'd never seen Londheim from such a vantage point, and for the first time she fully grasped its sprawling size. Low Dock was such a meager part of it, and yet its trials often overwhelmed her. She could not imagine the strength of character the Deakon possessed to bear all of Londheim's burdens.

Alarm bells rang from the west. Adria turned, her gaze lifting to the roads beyond. A river of humanity approached, numbering in the thousands. They were not alone. Something was behind them, something she could barely see if she squinted her eyes. Something that should not be.

Far from Alma's Crown, in a sprawling field where should only be faded grass and gently sloping hills, came a cracked gray mountain.

CHAPTER 12

Descending the tower was as simple as returning her hands to the glowing blue spheres carved into the bottom of her platform. The two soulless guards gave way, either not knowing or not caring about what she had just experienced. Adria didn't give them a second glance. From the tower she had seen a throng of what appeared to be refugees approaching the city, and she would be there to help in any way she could.

Adria crossed through Tradeway, which was strangely quiet for midday. Cobblers, masons, carpenters, and barbers all gathered here, with seemingly every building in sight bearing a wooden sign of one guild or another. A few had customers, but most artisans stood at their doorways gossiping with their apprentices and neighbors. Adria hurried down the largest of the roads, a slowly curving half circle leading toward the western gate.

What had been strangely quiet became a madhouse within moments of leaving Tradeway onto the east-west through road.

The mayor's city guards lined the streets, barking at gawkers and onlookers to clear a path. The first of many travelers had already passed through the gate, herded toward some destination deeper into the city. Dozens walked before her, heads hung low, their faces ashen. They looked as if they fled a war zone, but what war could have struck them in the west? Bandit groups were small and disorganized, they were far from any coastal raiders, and even the Three-Year Secession decades ago had left the west relatively unscathed.

Another thought danced in her head, but she was too frightened to give it voice. It didn't matter that the city had changed overnight. It didn't matter that strange mechanics and pulsing lights had lifted her to the rooftop of a tower that had been dormant for centuries. Just because her hands bore healing magic did not mean the rest of the world had also changed...

Rows of guards marched beside the apparent refugees, their steel cuirasses and sallet helmets easily distinguishing them from the lightly clad villagers. They pushed and shoved away those who tried to speak with the newcomers, all while shouting for people to return to their homes. A trio passed by Adria, and one reached for her shoulder while telling her to disperse. He quickly stopped when he saw her mask.

"Forgive me, Mindkeeper," he said. "We're under orders to keep these people from speaking with the populace so they don't spread a panic."

"And I am no ordinary member of the populace," Adria said. "The mayor will not stop me from helping those in need."

"Don't misunderstand me," the guard said. "This order came directly from Royal Overseer Downing. If you disagree, take it up with him."

Adria quietly fumed. During what was known as the Three-Year Secession, South Orismund had attempted to secede from Unified Orismund, claiming that the Keeping Church had usurped too much power from the crown. Concessions by both the Queen and the church's ruling Ecclesiast had brought South Orismund back into the fold, but the result had been a drastic increase in autonomy for West and South Orismund. In addition to that was the election of the Royal Overseer every ten years by landowners to rule West Orismund in the Queen's stead. No one bore greater authority, not even Deakon Sevold, which meant there was no way for Adria to bypass the orders.

"Might I at least know where you take them?" she asked.

"Go ask your church," said another of the guards. "We have work to do."

The ground rumbled beneath their feet, as good a signal as any for them to continue on with their work. Adria took a step back and chewed on her lower lip, thankful for the mask to hide the unseemly habit. Several men gathered to her left, talking among themselves in the shade of a storefront's awning. They looked agitated.

"What's with the mountain?" one shouted to the passing crowd. "Where'd it come from?"

Guards reacted as if he'd set fire to a building. Two rushed him, one shoving the man's friends away, the other cracking him in the mouth with the butt of a spear. The man blurted out a garbled protest as he staggered away. The guard spun his spear, using a blunted hook at the base of the head to trip the man by the ankle.

"We said disperse, you cock-eating goat, so disperse before we take a few more teeth in tribute to Londheim."

He fled the moment his feet touched ground, his friends hurrying with him. Adria watched with her mouth open in shock.

"Such punishment for asking a question?" she demanded of the guard.

He gave his answer in the form of a rude, upward jab of two fingers. Adria shook her head and debated her next course of action. She could follow the trail of people to whatever destination they were being led to, or she could return to her church in Low Dock and await orders from either Deakon Sevold or, more likely, Vikar Thaddeus Prymm. But doing nothing would drive her crazy, so she slipped through the scattered onlookers in pursuit. She'd managed only a block before she froze. Traveling amid the refugees was a man in a long gray coat with a familiar folded tricorn hat.

"Devin!" she shouted, lifting her hand above her head. "Devin, over here!"

He looked up, eyes darting about the crowd. Adria waved higher, and the moment he saw her, a tired smile lit up his face. Her brother pushed through the crowd as she removed her Mindkeeper mask. He swept her into his arms with surprising desperation.

"It's so good to see you alive and well," he said. "I feared... no, forget what I feared. It doesn't matter. We're finally home."

The welcome surprises continued when her brother-in-law joined her and Devin, his shy smile making it seem like he was embarrassed to call attention to himself. An enormous pack hung from straps around both his shoulders. He carried a lantern in his left hand, which he carefully held aside to make room for her hug.

"Hey, Tommy," Adria said. "Things must be serious if Devin managed to drag you out from your tower."

"It's... it's been a curious trip," Tommy said, shrugging his shoulders. "I think I'll let Devin tell most of it. You won't believe us otherwise."

"Both of you, get back in line," a guard shouted as he approached the trio. "Dallying or exiting prior to interrogation is expressly forbidden."

Adria whirled on him, putting herself between them and the guard.

"You address the ordained Mindkeeper of Low Dock and one of the church's most respected Soulkeepers of West Orismund," she said. "Who are you to order us?"

"It's all right, sis," Devin said. "He's just doing his job."

The guard bounced his gaze between them, suddenly nervous.

"Those are the orders," he said, almost as an apology. "But Soulkeepers and Mindkeepers have their own orders, am I right?"

It sounded like he was pleading for an out, and Adria quickly gave it to him.

"You are correct," she said.

"Your friend, though," he said, pointing to Tommy. "He's neither Soulkeeper nor Mindkeeper. He goes with the rest of them, no exceptions."

"It's quite all right," Tommy said. He kissed Adria on the cheek. "It is wonderful to see you again. When things calm down I hope we can catch up together over a giant plate of biscuits."

Tommy left, accompanied by the nervous guard. Adria's insides churned with curiosity. What had happened outside Londheim? Why the refugees? And was it tied to the strangeness that had happened today?

"I've a lot of questions for you," Adria said.

"And I'll answer as best I can," Devin said. "But not here. To the western wall. We'll discuss more there."

Adria watched her brother stare at the distant mountain from atop the wall surrounding Londheim. It looked five to six miles away, and the sight of it put a pit of worry deep into Adria's stomach. Just as worrying were the new signs of battle etched upon her brother's face. Sweltering purple bruises covered his throat, new scars dotted his forehead, and a particularly brutal scar covered much of his left cheek. Whatever story Devin had to tell, she feared it would be nothing but hardship and suffering.

"Have things been, well, different here?" he asked, breaking the silence that had comfortably settled upon both of them during their walk to the wall. Such a vague question shouldn't have meant much, but Adria immediately sensed what her brother was alluding to. So it wasn't only Londheim...

"In many ways, yes," she said. "Why do you ask?"

Devin shook his head and finally turned her way.

"Because all the world has changed, Addy, and I'm not thinking it's for the better."

Adria looked over the wall to the throng pouring through the gates.

"I don't understand," she said. "If they don't want anyone to interact with these people, why aren't we setting up camps for them outside the city until we're better organized?"

"Because it's not safe outside," Devin said. "I'm not sure it's safe inside, either, but we must hope."

"Safe? Safe from what?"

Her brother drew in a long breath and then hesitated.

"This might take a while," he said.

Devin began with his arrival at Dunwerth, his encounter with the wolves, and then meeting the stone creature named Arothk. Every sane part of Adria told herself to doubt such outlandish nonsense. But perhaps it wasn't so strange after what she'd witnessed herself. Then came the black water. Adria shivered at the retelling, unable to imagine something so terrible. She wished to wrap her arms about her brother and comfort him, but he looked too lost in his own thoughts to even notice.

"I was worried it was the whole world," Devin said after a momentary pause. "With every flower, tree, and blade of grass dead, civilization would soon follow. Such a pathetic, ignoble end to humanity."

"Clearly it did not end," Adria said, careful to frame her comments as neutrally as possible. She wanted to believe her brother, and she also wanted to prove him undeniably wrong. "I see Tommy survived these events as well."

"He's got his own scars," Devin said. "I think he's the only survivor in all of Crynn. Can you imagine that, Adria? All that death around him. It's a miracle he stayed sane."

"You endured similar, and you're still sane."

Devin softly laughed, that sound precious to her ears.

"I'm not so certain. A lot of us have been asking ourselves that question. But I more meant...it's Tommy. You know how he is. After Brittany died it took him a month before he'd leave his home on his own. If it weren't for his books...." He shook his head. "I'd rather not think of it."

"What happened after you left Crynn?"

"We—"

Little quivers shook through the wall, traveling up their heels to the small of their backs. Devin faced the mountain, and she swore he looked ready to draw his pistol.

"Are you all right?" she asked him.

"No," he said. "I don't think I am. I'm exhausted, Addy. I've seen thousands die, and this whole world feels like one long nightmare I can't wake up from. I thought it'd be better when we arrived here, but it's not. The mountain is following us, Adria. It's *following us*."

"I . . . I don't understand how that's possible."

"*None* of this is possible," Devin said. He gestured wildly about him. "The whole world's turned upside down. The dead are walking, fire is alive, and Tommy can call down a strike of lightning with a few words and a wiggle of his fingers. If the sky opened up tonight and dumped a legion of locusts on our heads I wouldn't fucking *blink*."

The other guards on the wall were starting to stare. Adria grabbed her brother by the scruff of his shirt and yanked him closer.

"Get a hold of yourself," she said. "You're a Soulkeeper. Act like it."

Devin looked at her, really looked at her, and finally she saw a bit of his old self reemerge. His arms wrapped about her shoulders, and despite his larger size, he leaned his weight against her.

"I'm sorry," he whispered. "I've been strong for everyone else since this whole thing started. It feels good to finally break down a little."

"Until you tell me everything that's going on, I'd prefer you keep it at just a little." She grinned at him, just like she had when they were kids. "Or does my big brother need his little sister to hold his hand during story time?"

Devin wiped at his face as he shook his head and laughed.

"Coldhearted bitch."

"Unstable dick." She smiled. "Are we better now?"

"Such uncouth language for a Mindkeeper. And yeah, I think I am."

"Good. Now what in blazes did you mean by Tommy can call down lightning?"

Devin shrugged his shoulders and looked across the field to the mountain.

"I wasn't kidding when I said the world has turned crazy. I'll start with what I found when I arrived at his tower."

Every minute it seemed her brother's story grew that much more incredulous. She tried to imagine Tommy commanding the power Devin described but could not. It was like imagining a butterfly overcome with bloodlust. He kept silent on what Tommy had been through prior to his arrival, sticking only with what he had seen for himself.

"We caught up with the villagers from Dunwerth not long after we left," Devin finished. "After that, it was mostly a tedious march to cross the rest of the miles here to Londheim."

"And the mountain?"

The wall rumbled, as if the earth were aware of the question.

"We saw the distant peaks of it yesterday morning when we awoke," Devin said. "The ground's shaken ever since. As we've traveled east it's gotten nearer, not farther. It's been following us, Adria, and I can't explain how or why in the slightest."

Adria joined her brother in leaning over the parapets to watch the pale gray mountain. From base to peak it looked around one third of a mile high, and perhaps twice that in length. She could see individual peaks, sharp and angular. They appeared white along the tops, but something about the light and detail felt off. The color wasn't snow, more likely a discoloration of the rock.

The rumbling ground was growing more and more apparent. From the mountain, perhaps? But again, how, and why?

"We should get going," Devin said. "I'm sure the church needs every hand at its disposal."

Adria tucked her arm through his.

"Not yet," she said. "I expect we will both be busy for the next few weeks, so let us have our time together while we can."

Devin removed his folded hat and tucked it under his free arm. "Fair enough. But in return, you must tell a story of your own. I saw how you reacted to my questions. There's strangeness afoot in Londheim as well, isn't there?"

Adria bit her lip. Her other hand subconsciously drifted into her pocket to touch the smooth porcelain of her mask. Yes, there was indeed, and was it really any more fantastical than what her brother shared?

"I . . . I healed someone with my prayers this morning."

He lifted an eyebrow her way.

"Healed as in how?"

"Healed as in I put my hands on swollen, infected flesh, prayed, and then lifted my hands off perfectly healthy skin."

Devin whistled softly.

"No wonder you didn't immediately call me insane," he said. "Tommy theorized that the Goddesses' strength was returning to the Cradle. Perhaps he's correct."

"Or perhaps you're correct, and we're all going insane."

"That, too. I put it at a coin toss for either."

She withdrew her arm and they fell silent and watched the mountain. It was two miles away, maybe three at most, and there was no doubt at its approach. The first visible proof was when one of the larger hills collapsed in half, parting in a cloud of black earth to make way for the enormous bulk. They could finally see the base of it, and Adria stared for a good long time while her heart hammered inside her chest cavity.

"Devin..."

"I know," he whispered. "I see it, too."

The mountain did not move. It crawled. Six legs poked out on either side, the way a turtle's appeared from beneath its shell. Unlike a turtle, though, these bore massive claws the size of buildings, each leg bigger than the Sisters' Tower. It dragged its bulk straight through the dirt, carving a massive canyon in its wake. Each shudder forward sent shock waves. Most terrifying of all was its eyeless serpentine head. It hovered mere feet above the ground, every inch of it so dark it appeared made of onyx or obsidian. Though its mouth was closed, enormous streams of black water dripped down its chin and splashed across the churned earth.

"Goddesses help us all," Devin said. "It's not a mountain. It's...it's like the void-dragon walks the earth."

"'And the dragon shall throw down the stars so he might finally walk the Cradle,'" Adria recited. "'Then will the Sisters return alongside an army of great heroes shining with the light of their souls to slay the void. The Cradle shall be cleansed, its souls protected in Anwyn's hands, until Lyra builds the land anew, free of the dragon's corruption and perfect once more.'"

"The First Canon doesn't make that sound quite so terrible," Devin said. "But this isn't the time of Eschaton and the Cradle's destruction. I don't see any great heroes to do battle. Do you?"

Her brother often joked when he was nervous. As always, she hated it.

"I don't know what I see," she said, her short fingernails digging into the thick fabric of her dress. "I'm not sure I want to know."

Adria stepped closer to her brother, who wrapped a welcome arm around her shoulders. Together they watched the crawling mountain approach the edge of Londheim.

The guards stationed along the walls grew more frantic with each shuddering step of those twelve gargantuan legs. They ignored Devin and Adria, too focused on their own task. Younger men passed out crossbows and arrows from heavy packs on their backs. Older men with rank set up formations, focusing heavily upon the closed gates of the city. The idea that the crawling mountain would need to use such a gateway amused Adria. At least, it would have amused her, if everything weren't so dire.

By now they could hear the mountain's footsteps, not just feel it. The sound reminded Adria of when builders had demolished an old home in Low Dock for fear it would soon collapse. Those few seconds of breaking brick, erupting dust, and splintering wood were a pin fall compared to the thunderous scraping of the mountain's chest as it carved a canyon through the field.

"What might our weapons do against such a thing?" Devin wondered aloud. "You can't bring a mountain low with arrows. You can't crumble it with the strike of a sword. We're at its mercy."

"Quieter," Adria reprimanded. "You are to inspire hope in those around us, not drain it away."

Every guard looked frozen in fear. Word of the crawling mountain's approach spread among the citizens of Londheim down below. The rumble of their frightened cries joined the piercing of the earth. Smoke rose from the far eastern wall of the city. Riots, no doubt from people fleeing the city. Adria couldn't blame them. What else could you do against such inexorable creeping doom?

Half a mile west from Londheim, the living mountain halted. Its legs sank into the dirt and settled. The rumble ceased, and it seemed in the sudden silence that all the city held its collective breath. The rock of its face cracked along the top to reveal gigantic, piercing blue eyes. They looked upon the walls of Londheim. Judging it? Examining it?

A crack split from side to side of its face, then grew. The monster's mouth opened. Teeth like marble stalagmites and stalactites jutted from the obsidian surface. Black water poured out in waterfalls. Wind blew across Adria's skin as it took in one deep, long breath. And then the mountain roared.

The walls of Londheim shook. Devin stumbled to hold his grip on the parapet. Adria clutched her hands to her ears and pleaded to the Sisters. The head turned and from its gullet blasted a veritable river of black water to the north of the city. The sun glistened off the water's surface like oil. Stars shimmered in its waves. The river continued seemingly forever, covering every stretch of grass and tree visible from their wall. At last the flow ceased from its mouth, and the monster slowly turned its head toward the south.

"The black water you spoke of?" she asked amid cries of terror from both guards and citizens.

"That's it," Devin said. "This monster is responsible for all those deaths. Perhaps it *is* the void-dragon, Addy. It's taken enough lives to claim the title."

Adria watched, paralyzed by the implications of Devin's words. Here was the proof of all the strange stories her brother told, and the truth of her experiences that day. If this water existed, and mountains crawled, then all else was true. Tommy wielded storm and fire. The dead walked among the living. Ancient spider-women, sentient stone monsters, and living flame all graced their world. And for whatever reason, her prayer-clasped hands could heal.

Adria's heart seized in her chest. The dragon turned the gaze of its enormous blue eyes to Londheim. Black water bubbled from the corners of its mouth.

"Goddesses save us," Devin said breathlessly. "It can't happen here. Not like Dunwerth and Crynn. Please, Sisters, have mercy."

"Will the water climb the walls?" Adria asked.

"I don't know. And I don't think it matters."

The crawling mountain opened its throat once more. A deluge of shining black water roared toward the walls of Londheim. She thought of Devin's description of the rot that had overwhelmed Dunwerth. Buildings crumpling. All food turned foul. Those touched becoming twisted and vile. That horror took place in a small village with a couple hundred men and women at most. Two hundred thousand lived inside Londheim's walls, and there would be no chance to flee.

Devin extended his hand, and Adria took it so they might together watch the doom rolling forth. The river of black water silently flowed over the western road. Many on the wall screamed. Others dropped their weapons and ran. Devin locked her fingers with a vise grip, bruising her knuckles. Adria bit her tongue and stared straight ahead. She would not look away. She refused.

Two hundred yards from Londheim's city gates, the water violently forked to either side. Twin rivers rolled north and south, carving a perfectly straight line in the grass. Not a drop passed this sudden line of demarcation. The water continued until reaching either edge of the city and then dissipated. The fearful screams of the city dwindled to a murmuring chorus.

The mountain shuddered, its tremendous weight settling into the earth with a deep rumble. The blue eyes closed. All was still.

"What does it mean?" Adria asked after several minutes passed.

"It means we're still alive."

"But for how long?"

He offered her a grim smile.

"Until that thing awakens and decides otherwise."

CHAPTER 13

Three years ago a barrage of tornadoes and storms had devastated the southern half of West Orismund, tucked between the Oakblack Woods and the Triona River. Lack of homes, food, and money had driven hundreds to seek shelter in Londheim. The people had come in droves, whole communities banding together for safety on the road. The mayor had shuffled dozens into Adria's poor corner of the city, providing shoddy tents in alleys as their main form of shelter while the wealthy debated solutions to the problem. Adria forfeited hours of sleep each day making her rounds among the tent communities, fighting a losing battle against disease, starvation, and despair.

That hectic summer paled compared to the numbers streaming into her church in Low Dock begging for aid.

"Please, find a place to sit," she told a father holding two kids in his arms. She saw no sign of the mother. "I'll be with you when I can."

Adria honestly had no idea where they would find room.

An average sermon saw fifty to sixty people at most inside. By her last count, over one hundred refugees currently huddled in pews, against walls, or in any other available open space. Adria prayed to the Sisters that she and Sena were worthy of their trust. She tried to hurry down the aisle but a man on the edge of a pew reached out and grabbed the sleeve of her dress.

"Is Faithkeeper Sena here?" the frightened man asked. Adria narrowed her eyes. This man was a local, not a refugee like the others. Joshua, if she recalled correctly.

"She is, as am I," Adria said. "Is there something you need?"

His eyes vibrated like a deer aware of a hunter's presence.

"I, um, I just wish to talk to her. Only a moment, I promise."

Adria clenched her jaw behind her mask.

"If you seek comfort, seek it elsewhere for today. Right now the physical needs outweigh the spiritual."

Joshua looked appalled.

"I have attended *every* one of Faithkeeper Sena's sermons since she arrived. I deserve a chance to—"

"You *deserve* nothing," Adria snapped. "Have you a home with a roof over your head?"

"I...yes, I do, but..."

"These people don't. Return to yours while we worry about giving them theirs."

Joshua stormed out of the church, his neck as red as a rose bloom.

Could have handled that better, thought Adria.

Consoling the populace was not her forte. Mindkeepers were the quiet, studious members of the church, their faces hidden with masks and their time spent poring over books. Adria had memorized Lyra's Devotions and the Five Canons and could argue with the sharpest of minds why Vikar Seigmar's mournful writings bore greater wisdom than the uninspired rambling sermons of King Woadthyn the First. She wrote sermons, she studied history, and she traversed like a ghost through her part of the city learning its people, its difficulties, and its greatest needs. In her case, it had been an appalling lack of medical care for anyone in Low Dock, resulting in her spending countless hours researching herbal cures and basic procedures normally reserved for apothecaries. All this collected knowledge and skill was a vital asset to Sena, her assigned Faithkeeper.

Faithkeepers were in every way the opposite of Mindkeepers. Instead of dull garb and masks, they wore pristine white suits to stand out among a crowd. While Mindkeepers wrote the sermons for the ninth-day services, the Faithkeepers bellowed them out with thunder and zeal. Sena dined with donors, attended family gatherings to bless the feasts, and provided comforting shoulders to people during their daily tribulations. Faithkeepers were often the most well-known and beloved members of a neighborhood, and there were dozens of streets throughout Londheim named after them.

This was just fine with Adria. She did not desire recognition or praise. Adria was the mysterious woman behind the mask willing to dive her hands into the blood and shit to get things done. People might confess their dreams and heartaches to Faithkeepers, but they confessed their sins and flaws to the Mindkeepers. Adria firmly believed it was the latter that allowed real healing to begin.

The doors swung open, and two more women stepped inside. Blood stained their sleeves and trousers. They'd need attention, bandages, and yet another empty place to lay their bodies down. All things Adria was sorely lacking. The first creeping scratch of panic bored into her chest.

I can't handle this, Adria thought, turning in place in search of the church's Faithkeeper. *No one can.*

Finding Faithkeeper Sena was always a simple task. Her midnight skin was a stark contrast to the blinding white of her trousers, shirt, vest, and jacket. The woman looked no less exhausted than Adria. Puffy circles surrounded her bronze eyes. Sweat stains marked the collar and arms of her shirt. Her jacket and vest lay on the floor, two babes sleeping atop them. The Faithkeeper's triangle-and-rising-sun pendant of Alma, goddess of the dawn, hung from around her neck. Her head was shaved, a fact Adria was jealous of as she adjusted the sweaty mask covering her own face. It mattered not that it was a crisp fall evening; with so many people crammed into one building the heat radiated off every surface.

"Faithkeeper, might I have a moment?" Adria asked as she stopped at the end of a cramped pew.

Sena smiled and kissed the foreheads of the praying couple who knelt facing their little spot on one of many long pews. "Lyra bless you," she whispered softly as she put an arm around each man, careful not to interrupt their prayer. How the woman could still smile and act calm amid all the chaos was a mystery to Adria.

Sena walked sideways through the cramped pews, her expression nothing but pleasantness as she approached.

"What is it?" she asked.

Adria dropped her voice a little, wishing it weren't so loud inside the church. It was hard to hold a private conversation when the coughing, crying, praying, and arguing rumbled from every corner.

"This is beyond our capabilities," she said. "Go to the cathedral and beg for aid from Vikar Caria. I lack every herb imaginable,

I'm almost out of bandages, and some of these people don't even have proper clothes on their backs. Please, even a handful of novices would help tremendously."

"If the Vikar of the Dawn will send aid, then she will send aid," Sena said. "I'm not leaving where I'm needed to beg my superior to do her job."

"You know damn well Low Dock is the furthest thing from the Vikars' minds."

"And you know damn well that I don't agree," Sena said, her smile never wavering. In public Sena was all pleasantries and comfort, but in private she bore a willpower as sharp and stubborn as Adria's. Anyone who thought to intimidate the pleasant woman was quickly disabused of such a notion. "Vikar Thaddeus may treat Low Dock like it does not exist, but Caria has always been generous to me. She will remember, and she will send what aid she can. For now, our church has enough food and blankets to last the night. When morning comes, and I am certain our flock is cared for, *then* I shall go to my Vikar and ask."

Adria was glad her mask kept her glare hidden from the rest of the populace. The last thing they needed was the tired, hungry, and frightened scattered throughout the church to see their caretakers fighting.

"So be it," Adria said. "I shall assist with what limited resources are still available to us."

"You focus too much on resources we or the rest of the church possesses," Sena said. "There are others who may help, don't forget."

The idea slapped Adria with its obviousness.

"Will you be fine without me for an hour?" she asked.

Sena winked.

"This isn't my first season of strife," she said. "And it's not yours, either. Be swift."

Adria slipped out the church doors, put her back to the street, and tugged off her mask. She gasped as the cold air brushed her sweaty skin like a divine kiss. Too many people. Too many needs. Adria preferred her one-on-one sessions in people's homes. Combined with her mask, it was the perfect mixture of intimacy and distance. This veritable tide of humanity begging for aid? What could she do for all of them?

You could help them, you know, a fearless part of her whispered in the back of her mind. *Just pray. See if it happens again.*

The temptation squirmed inside her chest. There were many, many types of prayers within Lyra's Devotions. Some asked for rain. Some asked for food. She imagined kneeling in the center of the people, and bread appearing in her hands where none was before. They'd marvel and praise her name. They'd feel the goddess's love. They'd know it in their bellies.

Adria banished the prideful daydream as she slid her mask back over her face. No, even if she could work those miracles, she would perform those prayers in secret. The keepers of the holy scripts and shapers of the divine message were not meant to be praised and beloved by the populace. There was a reason she wore her mask, and it wasn't just to hide away her emotions. She almost ducked into an isolated alley and prayed for the bread anyway, just to see. Something, perhaps fear of failure, perhaps fear of success, kept her from doing so.

"It's time to help people," Adria whispered. "And you'll do it the old-fashioned way."

The people of Low Dock were some of the poorest, over-worked, and undersheltered of all of Londheim. Despite having little to give, they were also the most ready to help others of similar circumstances.

"Dearest child of Alma," Adria said as the first door of the first house opened to her. "Have you room beneath your roof to shelter a family in need?"

Adria returned with the setting of the sun. The chaos inside the church had settled down, helped in part by the eleven homes that had volunteered to shelter children and the elderly. Candles burned in evenly spaced candelabras hanging from the walls, casting long shadows so that even those crammed in the center of the pews could feel a sense of privacy. Adria heard soft weeping and the complaints of upset children as she walked the center aisle, but compared to earlier in the day the church was as quiet as a cave.

Faithkeeper Sena wasn't near her lectern or visible walking the pews. Retired for the night, Adria guessed. The far left end of the church had two doors side by side. Larger churches often separated the keepers' living quarters from the worship hall, but neither Adria or Sena had that luxury. Each door led to their respective office and bedroom. Adria gently knocked on the Faithkeeper's and waited. After a minute of no response she knocked again.

Gone, then, she decided. *Hopefully Vikar Caria will listen to Sena's requests and remember that even Low Dock deserves a fair share of aid.*

She returned to the lectern and sat with her back against it. Her head thudded against the wood. Every muscle in her body ached, and her voice was hoarse from addressing nonstop prayers, complaints, and requests. This would be the easiest day, she knew, and that made her dread the coming weeks all the more. Today the hearts of Londheim's people would be open to the plight of the refugees. They'd welcome and give and stand alongside strangers like brothers, but once the hard times came, the inevitable famine and overcrowding, the refugees would be outsiders once more.

Adria wanted nothing more than to go to bed, but it'd be negligent of her to do so while Faithkeeper Sena was still absent. Drawing in a deep breath of resolve, she rose to her feet and began a long, winding circle through the dark church. She said nothing to the families. If they requested aid, she would give it. Until then, she would let them be.

Halfway through her circle, the sight of a sleeping man curled up on the floor between the final two pews gave her pause. She squinted in the candlelight and leaned closer, and upon recognizing him, she gave his shoulders a shake.

"Oh, hey, Adria," Tommy said as he stirred. Sleepiness mixed with excitement, so that his smile looked incomparably goofy. It made her love him all the more. "I was wondering when you'd get back."

Adria held her finger to her lips.

Follow me, she mouthed.

Tommy more clattered to his feet than stood, a tattered blanket wrapped around his shoulders and chest. Adria led him out the door and to the side of the church. Her brother-in-law shivered and pulled his blanket tighter around him.

"It's so cold out here," he said.

"I find it's too warm in there," Adria said. She pulled off her mask so the chill air might blow across her sweaty face and neck. "How did the questioning go?"

"As I expected," Tommy said with a shrug. "A lot of vague questions and no patience for any detailed answers. I thought that, being one of the Wise, they'd be more interested in what

I had to say over the average Jack or Harry. Turns out that's not the case, though I don't think they believed I *was* a member of the Wise. It's the age, I know it. Society sneers at the young and beardless."

"Did you tell them about your new...abilities?"

Tommy shook his head, and he honestly looked upset.

"No. They didn't even ask. I was near the back of the line, and truth be told, they looked ready to be done with all of this by the time I had my turn. It wasn't a few minutes before they ordered me to keep my mouth shut and seek shelter in my designated district."

Relief swept through Adria's chest. Spells and rituals were considered blasphemous by the Keeping Church, the activities of heretical Ravencallers who (according to greatly exaggerated legends) dressed in black feather costumes and beak masks, killed innocents, and feasted upon the power of their soul come the reaping hour. Their name had been given because of their disposal of the dead, for instead of burning or burying, they strung up soulless corpses to be devoured by the ravens. Now that the crawling mountain had arrived at Londheim the church's opinion on magic might change, but for Tommy's sake, the less they were aware of him, the better.

"Try to keep all this spellcasting stuff to yourself for now, all right?" she asked. "Everyone's frightened and confused, and I'd hate for people to react poorly to your abilities."

Tommy frowned.

"You're asking a butterfly to close its wings and pretend it's a caterpillar. I'm not happy about this, but if you insist, I will try my best."

"Thank you." She lovingly put a hand on the side of his face and smiled. "Good thing you were assigned here, right?"

"No I wasn't. They tried to squirrel me away in some church on the north side of town. Like I'd put up with that. I came here once no one was paying me any attention."

Up north meant one of the wealthier churches, Riverside District maybe or even the old cathedral in Sisters' Way. Most would die to stay there instead of in her cramped, shoddy edifice down in Low Dock.

"There's no reason for you to stay here," she said. "Why aren't you at Devin's house? He has plenty of room for you."

"He never offered."

"I'm offering for him."

"What if he gets mad?"

Adria tilted her head and reminded herself to be patient. Tommy's mind did not work like other people's minds.

"Tommy," she said slowly, "You're homeless, and you're family. Devin will be mad if you *don't* stay at his house."

"If you insist," he said. Excitement immediately replaced his resistance. "I will get to see Puffy more often. I've been dying to ask it questions about who and what it is."

"See, there's always a bright side to things," she said, a sentiment she didn't quite share in her exhaustion but knowing that her brother-in-law needed to hear it. "Do you remember where he lives?"

"Seven-Five Sermon Lane. I'm bad at a lot of things, Adria, but dates and places aren't one of them."

"Head there now," she said. "I'll try to visit when things calm down."

"You better," Tommy said. He looked to the nighttime street. "Is it, um, is it safe to walk there now it's, you know, dark?"

Adria forgot that not everyone shared her comfortable

familiarity with Low Dock's winding streets and its downtrod-
den people.

"If you're nervous, go in the morning," she said. "Your little
spot between the pews will suffice for tonight."

"Good night, then," Tommy said. He opened up his blanket
enough to give her a hug. "And thanks for being here."

Adria gladly returned the hug. "I'm happy you're here, too,"
she said softly. "Londheim would be a sadder place without you."

Tommy blushed and wordlessly ducked inside the church.
Adria remained outside, slowly twirling her mask in her hands.
Her fingers traced the dividing line between the black and white
halves. Too often she did not feel like herself without that comforting distance separating her from those she conversed with.
Tommy was one of the few with whom she could. She needed
more people like that in her life, she decided. Now more than
ever. With so many dead, and many more suffering and soon to
join them, it'd be tempting to sink all the way behind the porcelain so none of the pain could reach her.

The rhythmic sound of metal hitting stone stirred her from
her thoughts. A lone man approached from down the street.
With every other step his cane clacked against the cobbles. The
cane alone would have identified him to Adria, but the tightly
fitted black vest and jacket signifying a Vikar of the church confirmed it.

"Vikar Thaddeus," she said, bowing low with her hands
clasped to her chest. "Is there something amiss?"

Thaddeus Prymm leaned on his cane and peered at her
through his spectacles. He was the oldest of the three Vikars in
Londheim, but in her opinion his mind was the sharpest. His
hat drooped to one side atop his thick gray hair. A silver sun at

the top right corner of a downward pointing triangle hung from two chains about his neck. The pendant was the symbol of Lyra, goddess of the day and patron of the Mindkeepers. Adria wore a similar pendant underneath her thick robes.

"Must there be something amiss for me to visit one of my churches?" the Vikar of the Day asked.

"In Low Dock?" Adria said. "Most often, yes."

"A stain upon my soul, then," he said. "How are you, Adria?"

"Do you wish the polite version or the real version?"

"Whichever is closer to the truth."

Adria laughed even as a few tears swelled up in her eyes.

"I feel like shit, Vikar. I've not had a day this long and tiring since seminary. Knowing that the days are about to get longer and harder only makes me that much more goddess-damned tired."

Thaddeus smiled at her.

"I see you share a bit of your brother's foul mouth," he said.

"I'm just the amateur," she said. "He's the expert at cursing up a storm to make the Goddesses blush."

Though Thaddeus was West Orismund's Vikar of the Day, and therefore responsible for all their Mindkeepers, Adria knew him on a fairly personal level. The nearest library of any worth was the Grand Archive nestled into the enormous construct that was the Londheim Cathedral of the Sacred Mother. Adria trekked there often to prepare Faithkeeper Sena's sermons. The Vikar was a devoted scholar himself, and over the past few years she'd developed a friendship with the elderly man during long discussions over tea in one of the archive's many reading rooms.

Thaddeus put a hand on her shoulder. The moonlight reflected off his silver eyes as he leaned in close.

"I know you feel it will get worse, but it will also get better, each in their own time," he said. "We demand the best of you, Adria, no more, and no less. Have you given that today?"

"I think so," she said with a sigh.

"Then worry not to the future. Focus on your little corner of Londheim and I will do my best to ensure that you have the supplies you need."

Adria's ears perked up.

"We will? When? And just in food, or also blankets and housing?"

"I can't say how Mayor Gaunt distributes the city storehouses, nor what Vikar Caria will assign of hers, but of my division's stores, we will be distributing what we can spare fairly throughout the churches. I hope to be done in a day or two with all of it, but you should expect an initial allotment come morning."

Better than nothing. Even if she might disagree with what might be a "fair" allotment, at least it meant she and Sena would be receiving something.

"So what brings you to Low Dock?" she asked. "A novice would have sufficed for such news."

"I've been making the rounds to all my Mindkeepers," he said, putting both hands onto his cane. "And I must confess, this was my last stop."

"It usually is for everyone here."

They both smiled, hers far more bitter than his.

"A novice cannot share the information I am here to share," he said. "I'm sure you have already received a great many questions about what is transpiring, questions you do not have answers for. Until we have studied this situation further, I'd like you to assure people that the final days of Eschaton have not come. The world is not ending. The sun will rise and fall like it always has.

Seek strength from the Goddesses in these trying times as we do our best to illuminate the darkness."

The church's stance went about as Adria expected. The answers wouldn't satisfy any of the people coming to her for clarity, but they'd at least attempt to tamp down the wilder fears and rumors.

"I understand," Adria said. "Thank you for coming to me personally. I will do my best to serve the people of Low Dock, and therefore serve the Goddesses and their divine glory."

Thaddeus tipped his hat to her.

"I expected nothing less from a bright child such as yourself," he said. "Now go to sleep, Mindkeeper. Consider that an order from your Vikar."

He turned to leave, but Adria was not quite satisfied.

"Wait, Vikar," she said. "What of the crawling mountain? Is it the void-dragon returned like some have said?"

Thaddeus's head sank a fraction of an inch lower.

"We must still study and learn," he said. "Things will never be the same, Mindkeeper, of that I am certain. Everything else is leaves of knowledge twirling in a thunderstorm. Perhaps in the coming days you can help me snatch a few from the wind. And Adria…"

He glanced her way.

"If that abomination truly is the void-dragon, there will be no peace for us in the coming months. I pray you are ready to do your part."

CHAPTER 14

Blistering light split the absolute darkness of Janus's prison. The cave floor rumbled beneath his feet. The dark water enveloping him rippled in chaotic waves. Janus flexed his muscular arms, pulling the chains clamped around his wrists to their limits. Only one person could be splitting open the cave wall: the dragon demigod who had first imprisoned him within.

"Hello, Viciss," Janus said. His soft voice cracked. It was the first time he'd spoken in...decades? Centuries? "Did you have a fine rest while the world moved on without you?"

The darkness formed a humanoid shape. A midnight sky drifted along its skin, eerily reminiscent to the black water submerging Janus up to the neck.

"It seems the centuries have not dulled your tongue," Viciss said. His voice was the smooth slither of a snake through rain-drenched grass.

"Things dull from overuse. My tongue remains plenty sharp."

Janus stood in the center of a deep pool, his arms chained

to the stone at the bottom. Black water fell behind him in a steady trickle from the cave ceiling. Listening to its bubbling had been his entire occupation since Viciss sealed him in those chains. Even during the Goddesses' enforced slumber it had overwhelmed his dreams. In its darkness stars and gaseous shapes flickered in and out of view, phantoms of other worlds to taunt him in his imprisonment.

"It is your mind that I require sharp," Viciss said. The dragon ducked underneath a long stalactite as he neared the edge of the pool. "How has it fared?"

Janus couldn't decide if it was an honest request or just another little insult to the dragon's least favorite creation. Even as his eyes adjusted he still could make out no features. Viciss, like Janus, was all things and nothing. Others would perceive the illusions. Janus saw the truth.

"My sanity remains, if that is what you wonder," he said. "I owe that to the Goddesses more than yourself. It is far better to sleep the centuries away than to endure them in complete darkness and solitude."

"You speak as if you are undeserving of your punishment."

Janus ignored it. If the dragon wanted to argue the rights and wrongs of his past, he'd rather return to the cave's cold silence.

"Speaking of centuries, pray tell me, dragon, how did the world fare in your absence?"

Viciss brushed another nearby stalactite. It shimmered into dust without a sound.

"The humans built and spread like ants but their inner hunger has only grown more ravenous. We are all but forgotten, and their lives are mere drudgery and exhaustion as they await their soul's escape. Damn the Goddesses for confining their reality so."

"That's the problem," Janus said. "There is no one to damn them."

"*We* are here to damn them," the dragon said. The tone of his voice could freeze rivers. "One by one we return to find humanity living without wonder. They are certain of their divine rule over all other things. It has glutted their pride. It has stunted their emotions. Never before has the need for the salvation we offer shone so clear."

"Salvation?" Janus asked. He shook his head in disbelief. "After all your children have suffered, after our banishment, after the death and bloodshed, you still care for the Goddesses' dull creation?"

"Humanity is not responsible for the failure of their creators."

"Then neither are you responsible for *your* failings. A convenient truth to spread, don't you agree? But that also means I'm not responsible for my failings, am I, Viciss? Strange how I'm still chained to the stone and swallowed by black water for using the gifts you gave me."

"Your pleasure in others' discomfort was no gift of mine," the dragon said.

"How else was I to perform the art you requested?" His ire grew, his voice gaining strength. "Remind the humans of their place, you told me. Show that we are not subservient to their Goddesses and laws, was that not the goal when you birthed me from within this mountain of flesh and steel? Did I not fulfill my task?"

"You were to remind humanity of their place," Viciss said. "Not wantonly slaughter every last man, woman, and child that crossed your path."

"You wanted me to paint, and so I painted," Janus seethed at the dragon. A million times he had imagined this conversation during his imprisonment. At last he had his chance, and he would not remain silent, not even to the demigod who gave him life. "You wanted humanity reminded of their wretchedness, and so I reminded them. You wanted the Goddesses insulted and mocked, and so I covered their ugly creations with my beauty. I did everything you wished, and for that you sealed me away within your own damn body. Why keep me alive if you despise me so?"

"Because the Goddesses demanded your death," Viciss snapped. "You were a hateful creation made in a moment of weakness, and that same weakness is why I kept you alive. Do not give yourself undeserved importance."

"Oh, but I am important," Janus said. He smiled, revealing his perfect rows of opal teeth. Each one contained its own unique pattern, but they all shared a swirling coloration of the entire visible spectrum. "I'm your pure embodiment. You loathe my existence for the reflection it reveals."

Based on the thunderous roar that shook the cavern walls and broke multiple stalactites, the dragon was beyond furious.

"I helped create the world, you wretch! You did nothing but destroy."

"Just as my maker intended."

Though the massive crawling mountain might be the dragon's body, the presence before Janus was its mind, and it frightened him far more than any stone claw ever could. The living, walking starscape extended a hand, fingers elongating into claws eager to tear apart the fabric of his existence, but at the last moment they pulled away.

"There is truth to your words, as much as I am loath to admit it. Your existence is my sin, but perhaps we might both atone. I come bearing a task."

"And what is that?" Janus asked.

Viciss lowered a hand to the black water rippling with universes beyond understanding and dipped a single finger beneath its surface. The shackle about Janus's left wrist snapped open, followed by the right.

"Travel southwest of here to the Oakblack Woods. There is a village of alabaster faeries not far into the forest, and they have in their possession an object I have hidden from the Goddesses. Bring it to me."

Janus lifted his arms above his head. Water dripped off his skin, the last of his prison rolling away. Tears of joy glinted in his emerald eyes. A hundred desires filled him, and he picked the first to come to his mind. The microscopic building blocks of matter bent to his will with a mere touch. The flesh of his hands stiffened, hardened, and shifted in color. With deep pleasure he looked upon his jade hands. Janus was an artist, his hands the brush, the world his canvas. Every creation a beauty, unlike the mottled carcass that was called humanity.

Janus clenched his hands into fists, crunching the stone back into flesh and bone.

"What is this object?" he asked.

"A starlight tear," Viciss said. "I will not say more. Secrecy is of the utmost importance, for I bring you into matters that led to the Goddesses banishing us into our imprisoning slumber."

Janus ran his hand over his bald head. Hair sprouted and fell down to his shoulders, the left half a vibrant green, the right as black as the night. He stepped naked from the pool and bowed low to the dragon.

"And once I return?" he asked.

"Then you may have your reward," Viciss said. "Free rein within Londheim to kill any and all keepers of the church."

Janus's smile spread ear to ear.

"With pleasure."

"Do not kill wantonly," Viciss warned. "Slay only the keepers. We seek freedom for the rest of the populace, not their annihilation."

Janus smirked.

"Speak for yourself, dragon."

Viciss's hand shot out in a blur. Long, shadowy fingers closed about his neck with the strength of a noose. Janus tried and failed to breathe as the dragon lifted his bare feet off the stone.

"I am done bickering," he said. Janus clutched at the darkness holding him aloft. "Disobey and I shall unmake your existence. You will feel the obliteration of each and every one of your individual cells. With Chyron's help I shall slow time's grasp about your mind so that each cell's death feels as long as a second. Do you know how many cells make up your physical shell, Janus? You will suffer for more than a billion years before the last of you is consumed."

Viciss leaned closer. His formless lips breathed warm smoke across Janus's face.

"But I, my dear creation—I will watch this torment unfold in mere minutes. Have I made myself clear?"

The dragon dropped him to his knees. Janus clutched his aching neck and shivered through wave after wave of horror.

"I understand," he said. "I understand, and I obey. Only the church's keepers."

"Good. I am not a merciless slave to rules, and I understand that casualties shall happen. Keep them minimized."

Viciss waved an arm. What had been a thin crack ruptured into an enormous doorway through the stone. Janus squinted against the surge of light. He was in the base of a mountain a mere hundred feet above the black grass. Half a mile in the distance, he saw the familiar walled city of Londheim.

"Do not tarry," Viciss said. "We have not lost our chance to save humanity, but it will only be through decisive action."

The shadow that was Viciss dissipated into thin air. Janus lingered a moment and then leapt from the side of the mountain. The grass swayed but held firm upon his landing. The warm sun bathed his naked skin, drying away the last remnants of the dragon's black water, the liquid embodiment of change. A long, deep sigh escaped his throat. To experience freedom again was overwhelming in its pleasure.

He brushed the black grass, sensing the corruption within. With a thought it returned to a healthy green for several feet in all directions. It seemed Viciss had been unable to contain his rage, not that Janus blamed him. His pale hands dug deep into the dark soil. The cool earth stuck to his skin, a welcome change from the isolation of Viciss's black water. His fingers curled and lifted. Dirt came with it, transforming into a pitch-black pair of breeches stretching down to his ankles. Janus dropped to his knees, his fingers plunging once more to the grass. When he stood he lifted up a long black coat, which settled comfortably over his naked arms and back.

Janus faced the slumbering mountain. Despite his rage, Viciss had stopped just shy of destroying the city. Such a pity. Londheim's collapse would have sent shock waves throughout the entire east, a good first step in reestablishing proper order in the Cradle. Sentimentalism. It could ruin even the mightiest of dragons. Disgust squirmed in his stomach as he gazed upon Londheim.

"So you've forgotten us?" he whispered to the huddled masses of humanity within. "You no longer fear the dark hunts? The call of the swamp ghosts, the spears of the lapinkin, or the howls of the living snow? You are kittens convinced you are lions. That era ends. The real hunters have emerged."

He scooped a chunk of earth into his hand and lifted it to his lips. His will channeled through the touch of his hands, shaping reality with his thoughts. Matter twisted, mutated. Dirt became blood. Stone became dense, ropy flesh and then a human heart. This new heart beat once and then died. Janus smashed it within his fist, his pulse quickening at the sudden surge of pleasure. Blood dripped across his bare chest.

"I'll come for you soon, dear humans," Janus whispered to the people of Londheim. But first, the dragon's task. He ran east, bypassing the city. A smile lit his face. It might be a few days before he returned to Londheim, but if he passed through a human village during his travel, he might still have a chance to work his art upon their bodies. After so many centuries of slumber, he had a thousand ideas to try...

CHAPTER 15

I'm not sure why we're doing research on religious matters," Tommy muttered as he plopped two dozen rolled parchments onto the table, kicking up a cloud of dust. He sneezed three times, each one angrier than the last. "Void-dragons? End times? This seems entirely a church matter."

"Because they know we'd be more likely to store writings considered to be heretical," said Malik Sumter. The older man sat on the other side of the table, a mountain of books on either side of him. They were inside the archive on the second floor of Londheim's Tower of the Wise, doing their best to locate any reference to the time of Eschaton or the existence of the void-dragon. Malik was the assigned Wise for the enormous city, and he'd gladly accepted Tommy's help when Tommy showed up one morning offering it. "The city's keepers are afraid, which means the people will be afraid. It is our job to help calm those fears in any way we can."

Tommy plopped into his own chair. It'd been three days since he'd arrived in Londheim, three very long days spent poring over books at Mayor Gaunt's behest for even the slightest clue as to what the living mountain might be, and why it'd crawled to Londheim's gate only to hunker down and settle into perfect stillness.

"I just don't see how wasting our time helps the people."

Malik closed the book in front of him and frowned over his oval spectacles. It was a frown to be jealous of. Malik's smooth skin was the color of candlelight, and somehow his frown put no wrinkle or dent in it. It was disapproval personified and placed onto a square jaw that Tommy had a hard time not admiring from the corner of his eye.

"Is something bothering you, Tomas?" Malik asked. "I can't help but notice quite a few of those scrolls have nothing to do with religious history."

Tommy rattled his teeth together. Of course the older Wise had noticed his uncharacteristic frustration. Nothing went unnoticed by those dreamy brown eyes.

Less schoolboying, more adulting, Tommy berated himself. Despite his sister's insistence, it was time to take a risk, otherwise he'd go insane.

"Malik, as you are my superior I feel compelled to inform you of something I have otherwise not mentioned since my arrival in Londheim."

The older Wise watched him with a perfect gambler's face. Tommy coughed and pulled on his collar. The archive was well ventilated, a tribute to the excellent builders and designers in Londheim's past, but suddenly it felt intolerably hot and stuffy. Perhaps he should stand next to a window for a minute or two before . . .

"What do you wish to share, Tomas?" Malik asked when Tommy did not continue.

"Tommy. It's—it's Tommy. That's what my friends call me. I'd like you to call me Tommy, too."

Malik's frown didn't budge in the slightest.

"Pray tell me that is not the reason for your distracted attention."

"Oh no," Tommy said. "No, no, that's not what is distracting me. It's more my ability to summon lightning and fire that's got me all tangled up."

It took a full three seconds before Malik responded. "Excuse me?"

Tommy sighed and rubbed his eyes.

"Look, I know that what I am about to tell you will sound insane, but I am asking you to suspend your disbelief for just a few moments while I explain what happened to me in Crynn."

"You told me you hid in your tower until the Soulkeeper, Devin, found and escorted you to Londheim," Malik said.

"And I did. But that's not quite . . . everything."

He didn't know where to begin, so he blurted out every detail he could think of in somewhat chronological order. The other Wise listened without saying a word. His frown tightened. Tommy revealed the casting of spells, the destruction he'd unleashed on the corrupted humans, his shock and subsequent delight, all of it. The only thing he kept to himself was Puffy's existence. It seemed a bit rude to step on Devin's toes in that department.

At last he finished. He slumped in his chair and sighed with relief.

"Whew. I feel so much better, Malik. Thanks for letting me get that off my chest. I've been debating for at least two days now, do I tell him, do I not tell him, and my sister was so worried . . ."

"Stop rambling," Malik said. He rose from his seat. "To the basement. Now."

"What? Why?"

"Tommy, I am faced with two distinct possibilities. One is that you are capable of wielding tremendous power using long-discredited arcane words and spells. The other is that you have completely lost your goddess-damned mind. The only reasonable action before we proceed in our research is to conclude which of the two is true."

"You know, when you put it *that* way it does sound quite reasonable."

They left the archive and descended the stairs to the basement. Normally it would be packed full of barrels and crates, but those stored foodstuffs had been quickly distributed over the past few days, mostly to Adria in Low Dock per Tommy's request. This left them a large, empty space with stone walls, a perfect area to showcase his newfound talents.

"You might perceive this as an insult," Malik said as he went from lantern to lantern upon the wall and lit them with a candle. "But I'm honestly hoping you're insane."

Tommy put a hand to his chest. "That's rather hurtful."

"Don't take it personally. If what you said is true, the entire scientific understanding of the world we Wise have built over the centuries is going to need a thorough deconstruction. Plus, the thought of you being able to incinerate me with a snap of your fingers is a little bit frightening."

"I'd never do such a thing."

Malik finished lighting the last lantern and blew out his candle.

"You said you flung Devin Eveson across the room without meaning to do so."

"I did, but accidents happen."

"That's also what I'm afraid of." Malik stepped beside Tommy and pointed to a bare wall. "Now do...whatever it is you do."

Tommy rolled up the sleeves of his robe, cracked his knuckles, and hopped his weight from foot to foot.

"All right." He clapped his hands together, then remembered. "Oh. One moment. I need my book."

Tommy ran up the stone steps to the first floor of the tower, ducked into his room, and grabbed Salid Emberson's Aethos book from his bedside table. He clutched it between sweating fingers as he rushed back down to the cool basement. An inner monologue of various spells cycled through his head. Should he stick with the easiest? The flashiest? Would lightning summoning even work in a basement? He was still lost in his own head when he hit the bottom of the stairs. Only by nearly bumping into a waiting Malik did he regain focus.

"What?" Tommy asked at Malik's perplexed expression. "I'm still new to this whole 'magic' thing. Can't expect me to have everything all figured out and ready."

"Just...get on with it."

Tommy stuck with the most basic of his spells, one he could conjure with only a single word spoken aloud if he recited the rest of the verbal recipe in his head. He didn't even need a quick reminder from the book he'd fetched. His hand casually flicked toward the wall.

"Aethos."

A thin zap of lightning streaked from his fingertips. It hit the stone and crawled in several directions before fizzling out.

"There. Do you believe me now?"

He looked over to Malik. His superior's mouth hung open, his eyes locked on the lightning's spot of impact. He'd dropped his candle to the floor. Tommy was a little surprised at how poorly Malik was taking it. To be honest, he'd grown quite used to having this power and it was hard to remember just how world-shattering the concept was when he first discovered the ability. Granted, he'd also been trapped in a tower by weird, mutilated living-dead things for a few days. Pretty much everything following the black water had left his brain a little scrambled and open to the weirder side of life.

"Tommy..." Malik said. He spoke as if startling awake from a dream.

"Yes?"

"Can you cast more?"

Tommy interlocked his fingers and stretched them until they popped.

"I can indeed. If you'd like, I can put on a damn show!"

Despite his bravado, Tommy quickly learned that his limits were far below what might be considered a "show." Three more spells took the wind out of him. The first was a blast of fire that scorched the stone and left far too much smoke inside their cramped quarters. The second was a small white orb that materialized within his palm. When he tossed it at the wall, it exploded into a swirling torrent of ice and snow. It took a bit to succeed in a third spell, for two new incantations conjured nothing but a sigh from Tommy's lips. At last he attempted a spell that would supposedly grant him a sword of lightning. Instead it created a temporary swirl of electricity around his fingers before fizzling away. After each spell Malik clapped his hands like a guest at an opera.

"Whew," Tommy said. He leaned against a thick wood beam. "I'm sorry, Malik, but I don't think I can do any more, not without a bit of rest. I feel like I sprinted from one side of Londheim to the other, and I'm starving like a coyote to boot."

"That is just fine, Tommy." Malik walked over to him and put a hand on his shoulder. "You and I, we're going to scavenge through every book in our archives for more viable spells."

Tommy hadn't felt so happy since he'd met Devin back in Crynn. The more people who knew about his abilities, the less strange it all seemed. The less lonely, too.

"I couldn't agree more," he said. "Shall we get started in the apocrypha section, or dig through the trunked material?"

"Not yet." Malik stared at their target wall. His square jaw rocked back and forth as if he were attempting to swallow something. His eyes barely blinked. "I want to see if I can cast these spells myself."

"But...are you sure? Maybe, maybe it's dangerous for those who first try? I might have been incredibly lucky, you know."

Tommy couldn't explain it but his mood immediately turned defensive. This was his talent. This was what made him special. If Malik could easily replicate what he'd done...

"I must know if this power is unique to the individual or accomplishable by anyone with the proper training and commands," Malik said.

"Does it matter?"

Malik crossed his arms and frowned down at him. It seemed his face became more square, if that were even possible.

"It does indeed. Imagine if the words to create your blast of fire became common knowledge throughout the city? What would life be like if even the roughest of sorts could wield such power? We have a responsibility to the safety of Londheim's people, and that means understanding the rules of our new world."

Tommy clucked his tongue.

"I guess you *could* do some bad things with these spells, but that feels like such a waste. Imagine everyone able to light their fires at night with a clap of their hands? What might we accomplish if we can summon and move stones with our minds, or conjure food and drink from thin air? It could be paradise!"

"I have studied history extensively, Tommy. Any force for good, if capable of evil, will inevitably be used for evil. It's just the nature of humanity."

Tommy frowned at him.

"Such a pessimistic viewpoint."

"It is a realistic viewpoint; now please, lend me the book."

Any more protests would be useless. Not only was Malik his superior, but his force of will was such that Tommy doubted he could say no to him for long. He flipped to the page detailing a simple zap of lightning and handed it over. Malik ran his fingers over the words.

"The pronunciations are based on the Orissian dialect," Tommy offered. "Particularly the original eastern."

"Tommy, this might shock you, but you were not the only one to study the old scrolls and spells when undergoing training," Malik said. He glanced up and winked. "I too spent a few days wagging my fingers and reciting lines when I thought no one was looking."

"I knew I wasn't alone!" Tommy said. "I was so certain the other Wise would mock me for it."

"Oh, they would. Consider it a time-honored tradition of the Wise. We make fools of ourselves, then enjoy calling others fools. Quiet now. I must concentrate."

Tommy anxiously watched Malik mouth the words to the spell. They were simple enough, just four in total and none longer than two syllables. Like all the others he'd successfully cast, the word *Aethos* featured prominently as the first or second word. It was the only constant so far that he'd noticed. After a terribly long time Malik shut the book, handed it back to Tommy, and clapped his hands.

"The spell will conjure after the last syllable, yes?" he asked.

"It should. Keep your hands outstretched and your fingers pointed, otherwise you might not know where it goes."

Malik did so, awkwardly shifting his hands this way and that as if deciding the proper pose. The sight provoked a laugh, which Tommy thankfully caught and strangled in his throat at the last second. The man was always so calm and collected. The idea that he could be nervous or uncertain had never even entered Tommy's mind. Once Malik settled on a position with his palms flat against each other and his fingers pointing to the wall, he blurted out the words of the spell.

"Aethos creare parvos fulgur!"

Nothing.

"Did I make an error?" Malik asked, his body still locked in place.

"Well, it sounded fine to me," Tommy said. "Perhaps slow down a little? You don't need to hurry the words. It's not a race."

Malik wiped his brow with the back of his hand and then resumed his stance.

"Aethos. Creare. Parvos fulgur!"

Not even the tiniest of sparks. Tommy could summon more lightning with his feet and a shaggy rug.

"Maybe you need the book?" Tommy offered hopefully.

Holding the book did not matter. Reading the words slower or faster did not matter. Malik spread his hands, he widened his palms, he sat, he stood, and he wiggled his fingers for dramatic effect. Nothing mattered.

"Are you *sure* I am saying the words correctly?" Malik asked after the ninth attempt.

"Aethos creare parvos fulgur." A casual flick of Tommy's wrist sent another thin bolt of lightning into the wall. "Earlier I only said *Aethos* because if I think the other three in my head, it will...still...what?"

Tommy could not interpret the look on Malik's face to save his life. Thankfully the bear hug that immediately followed settled that.

"You beautiful bastard," Malik said, shaking him in his grasp. "This is everything. Somehow, some way, you and possibly you alone have tapped into things we could only dream of. This is an opportunity seen once in a generation. We will journey into a brand-new field of study as true pioneers. Our names will echo on in history, Malik Sumter and Tomas Moore, the first scholars of the old magic!"

"That sounds wonderful, though I certainly don't *feel* like a once-in-a-generation pioneer. I mostly feel a little pooped."

"I've theories on that, theories we'll discuss in due time. For now, we collect books for our reading."

"Shouldn't we inform the other Wise of what we've discovered?" Tommy asked. "At least a cursory letter explaining the basics?"

"Oh, Goddesses, no," Malik said. "This is our discovery, and we shall reveal it when we are good and ready. Until then, we keep this tight to our chests, Tommy."

The Wise vibrated with the energy of a far younger man. The studious veneer he'd kept since Tommy's arrival had rapidly given way to excitement and curiosity. It was almost like meeting a brand-new person.

You aren't the only one affected by the black water, Tommy reminded himself. Yes, he'd seen his share of carnage and endured things he'd much rather forget. That didn't deny others the weight of sudden change and confusion at the arrival of the crawling mountain. Too many whispered that the world was at its end. Of course Malik would seem a little stiff and overly serious upon first meeting. No doubt this excited, eager-to-learn man was who he'd been before everything went strange.

"I guess we can keep quiet for now," Tommy said. "But I have one important condition that you must agree to before we begin this grand adventure."

"Name it."

"It goes Tomas and Malik, not Malik and Tomas. My name first. I'm the one throwing the lightning and fire, so it's only fair."

Malik's face might not crack at a frown, but his every feature widened upon his ear-to-ear smile.

"That, my friend, is a deal."

CHAPTER 16

What had once been pieces of a man were submerged half-way into the stone wall and then locked in place. He bore the garb of a Mindkeeper, though his mask was cracked in half and used to cover his crotch instead of his screaming face. Given the many broken bones and exposed tissue there should have been a fountain of blood staining the wall and street, but instead a frozen flow of gold painted large swathes of the surrounding area. As for the shape this poor man had been twisted into, there was no mistaking the downward-pointing triangle, with the Mindkeeper's severed head and golden blood-spray marking the bright daylight sun in the top right corner.

"I hope to fucking stars you know what this shit means," one of the many guards told Devin as they observed the macabre display. "Because we don't."

Devin certainly did not, but he would keep such thoughts to himself.

"We don't want anyone to panic," he said instead. "Block off both sides of the road until all . . . this . . . is taken care of."

The rattled guard nodded.

"Already on it."

Devin stared at the mutilated body, his mind racing. An order from Vikar Forrest had brought him here, and though it'd warned of a brutal sight, nothing could have prepared him for this. It wasn't just the body, either. Long, looping letters swam across the wall beneath the body. They appeared written with some kind of silver paint...no, that wasn't right. The wall itself had been turned *into* silver, but only where the beautiful script flowed.

Elegant calligraphy, and the ugliest of words.

The artist returns. Know his name.

Below that, in emeralds instead of silver or gold, was signed a lone name.

Janus.

City guards hacked at parts of the wall with shovels, but there would be no digging the dead Mindkeeper out. He was one with the stone. By Devin's estimate, they'd have to cut and scrape off what they could and brick the rest over, a permanent addition to Londheim's architecture. The thought gave him chills.

What kind of monster could have done this? he wondered. Nothing human, that was for certain. A creature awakened by the black water, perhaps? One with a severe hatred toward the Sisters and their Keepers. Devin grabbed one of the guards, a younger woman with a face so pale he wondered if she'd soon vomit.

"Interview everyone who lives on this street," he said. "Find out if anyone saw anything the slightest bit unusual, no matter how irrelevant they might think it is. Should you discover a clue toward who—or what—this Janus person is, contact Vikar Forrest immediately. Is that understood?"

The woman nodded. Wishing there were more he could do, Devin shook his head and walked away. His Vikar had requested he return when finished examining the scene, so best get that over with immediately.

All three Vikars worked and lived in the enormous Cathedral of the Sacred Mother located in the heart of Londheim. The cathedral was triangular, with towering stone walls believed to be over eight centuries old. Painted-glass windows showcased former Vikars preaching to crowds, slaying monsters, and healing the wounded. Something about the architecture stood apart from the rest of the city, built in a style no one alive remained to master. The walls jutted at strange, random intervals, creating little alcoves and sharp rises that ended in hollow towers. It looked less like it had been built and more like it had ripped itself up from the ground, majestic and proud.

Each of its walls was named for one of the three sacred divisions of the Keeping Church and their corresponding goddess: Alma for Faith, Lyra for Mind, and Anwyn for Soul. Devin climbed the steps to Anwyn's gate, passed through with a polite nod to the novices stationed on either side, and entered the Soulkeeper's Sanctuary. This section of the cathedral was dedicating to housing and training new Soulkeepers. The walls were decorated with scriptures from Anwyn's Mysteries carved into golden plaques, and the many paintings showcased their patron deity lovingly guiding the souls of the dead on from their bodies to the stars beyond.

The Vikar's office was separated from the many barracks by a long, carpeted hallway. At its end was a door laced with silver containing a triangle-shaped window in its center. Devin knocked twice and then entered without waiting for a reply.

"Rude as always, I see," Vikar Forrest Raynard said as he

looked up from his chair. As Vikar of the Dusk, he was in charge of all Soulkeepers in West Orismund. He looked like a tower of muscles given long blond hair and then wrapped in a painfully tight black uniform. A silver moon inscribed into the downward point of a triangle hung from a chain around his beefy neck, a larger, more ornate version of the one Devin also wore. The cold gray walls were nearly barren but for a single portrait of Forrest's wife and children hanging behind his head. Beside his desk leaned his only other decoration: the enormous axe he'd wielded during his time as one of the church's fiercest Soulkeepers.

There was no chair for his guests to sit, so Devin stood before the desk and crossed his arms over his chest.

"I surveyed the scene as you asked," he said.

The Vikar leaned back and crossed his arms. "And?"

"And that is some damn nightmare fodder. Do you have any idea what creature of the void did it?"

"No, I don't," Forrest said. "But it seemed the Mindkeeper's blood was turned to gold, did it not? In terms of clues, I have only one to go on, but it's not here in Londheim. Do you know who Gerag Ellington is?"

"By name only. He's a merchant of some sort, and a generous donor to the church."

"A lumber merchant, to be exact," Forrest said. "And he's a *very* generous donor, which means you need to walk on eggshells while interacting with him. Gerag owns a number of lumber camps along the northwest edge of the Oakblack Woods. It seems one of them, Oakenwall, suffered a similar…incident."

"In what ways?"

"The blood to gold in particular, though I don't have too many specifics. He reported it to me just yesterday, said he thought this was a matter best left to us than the Royal Overseer's soldiers.

Seems the camp was attacked by a lone individual, with only one man surviving. I haven't had a chance to send anyone to interview him for further details. Out of all my Soulkeepers, you're the one with the most experience with the black water and its changes. I feel it best you handle this matter."

Devin bowed respectfully.

"I will do all I can to prove your judgment correct."

"Good. Gerag's mansion is in Quiet District, house number two-seven. Interview the survivor to learn what you can. If you believe it's connected to Janus, travel to the camp to see the evidence for yourself. Whoever this wretch is, the sooner we put him or her down, the better."

"What about the living mountain?" Devin asked. "Shouldn't I be here if it attacks?"

"Oh please, so you can do what? Hit the side of it with your sword? Just do your job. We're at that thing's mercy, so there's no point in preparing for that possibility. No, we'll keep living our lives and doing what must be done. Right now, that means figuring out who the fuck put one of our Mindkeepers into a goddess-damned wall."

Devin moved for the door, eager to begin the investigation.

"Oh, and Devin?" the Vikar called as Devin's hand closed about the door handle.

"Yeah?"

"Remember. Eggshells. With Londheim sliding ass-first into chaos, we can't afford to lose a single copper penny."

Land was at a premium in Quiet District, and Devin had a feeling Gerag had come upon his wealth more recently than his neighbors. Though his plot was small, he'd built upon it a tightly cramped spire of a home, at least six stories tall by Devin's guess. That it was taller than every other home in Quiet District was surely no accident. It was such a ghastly sight, too. With no room to expand, the mansion twisted in on itself, still attempting to fit in gargoyles, windows, and balconies despite the confinement. The painted red wood had faded to an ugly rust color. Combine that with the brown shingles and the mansion looked like a picked scab atop the surface of Londheim.

"Wonderful," Devin muttered. "Truly the home of a pleasant, humble man."

A cast-iron fence surrounded the estate, the tops sharpened to an absurd point. Given how far apart they were, and how much higher the tips went above the final crossbeam, anyone who climbed the fence could easily slip over without harm. The appearance of danger was more important than the function. Another good indication that Devin was about to meet with an asshole.

Devin pushed on the front gate. Locked. He sighed and shoved his hands into his coat pockets as he waited. The sun was hidden behind a lazy stretch of clouds, meaning nothing combated the biting chill of autumn. Devin watched the windows, relieved when he finally saw one of the curtains rustle. A servant quickly rushed out the front door and crossed the five stone steps between the door and the gate.

"Forgive me for any delay, Soulkeeper," the elderly man said as he pulled a ring of keys from his pocket and began fumbling through them. "I assume you are Vikar Forrest's emissary?"

"Something like that."

"Good, good. Our master has been worried about the workers in Oakenwall. Very worried, indeed."

The iron gate rattled, then shuddered open a few feet. Devin slipped through and was surprised when the servant immediately locked the gate behind him.

"Is crime a serious concern here?" he asked.

"With the crawling mountain's arrival, Master has requested the front gate be locked at all times. He fears potential looters should things turn ill, and his home is precious to him."

"I see." Devin winced at the ugly mansion. "Very precious."

The inside was as hideous as expected. Gold covered everything within visible range of the door, even if it made no sense, such as the gold coat hangers and gilded door handles. Definitely new wealth, then, and Devin doubted it was solely through the lumber trade.

"Follow me, please," the servant said with a wide gesture of his hand. He led him down the hall and to the right, stopping before a wide oak door with a golden couple in repose above the doorway. "Master Ellington is waiting for you in his study. May your day be kind."

"And yours one of peace and prosperity," Devin said, tipping his hat. Swallowing down his unease, he turned the gilded doorknob and stepped inside.

The room was similarly overlavish, except in a different way. Instead of gold everywhere, every inch of the cramped room's walls was covered with finely detailed paintings, each one no doubt costing a pretty sum. A cursory glance showed scenes of markets and nature from all across the Cradle. The painters' styles themselves differed wildly, with only one or two landscapes appearing to have been done by the same artist. Devin had a feeling the plump man before him had bought them in bulk, not caring about style or taste but instead whether they were visibly expensive.

"Welcome to my humble abode," Gerag Ellington said, not rising from his red padded chair. "I hope Belford treated you respectfully."

"He was most pleasant," Devin said, guessing Belford to be the servant. "A professional servant often foretells a wise master."

A little buttering up of the chubby merchant. The smooth words exited his tongue almost on reflex. If he'd have thought about them for even a moment he'd have held them back. Gerag was an unpleasant man, though Devin couldn't quite place why. His skin was clean, his dark hair neatly trimmed and pulled back from his face. His face, Devin decided. He had a smugly punchable face. When he smiled, it resembled a cross between dog puke and a lizard.

"Yes, yes, sometimes I do feel proper servants are a lost art," Gerag said. "The soulless have ruined lazy owners, I say. Because they always follow orders, too many think that means soulless need not be carefully trained and observed during their first few years. Often that laziness extends to training of normal servants as well."

"An interesting thought," Devin said. It was anything but. Listening to people talk of training the soulless always made him uncomfortable. Like they were dogs and not humans.

"Perhaps, but that's not why you're here, no, no, you're not here to listen to me spout theories." Gerag gestured to the chair opposite him. "Please, do have a seat."

Devin sat down and shifted the chair back as much as he could. Like every other room in the mansion, it was a few feet too small to be comfortable.

"My Vikar informed me of an incident at one of your lumber camps," he said. "Though he only gave me a cursory explanation of what happened."

"That is because I can only offer a cursory explanation myself," Gerag said. "You'll soon see why." He clapped twice. Belford appeared at the door in an instant. "Bring Broder in here."

The servant quickly returned with a heavyset man wearing a new pair of trousers and a shirt that did not quite fit right. His hands were calloused, his face scarred, and his hair and beard as dark as his eyes. His every movement was quick and fidgety, like a mouse fearful of an unseen cat.

"Greetings, Broder, my name is Devin Eveson. I'm a Soulkeeper of the church."

Instead of speaking, the man offered his hand as if in greeting, quickly rotated it to either side, and then pointed to his ears. That explained Gerag's comment, then. Broder was deaf, and could not speak because of it.

A long-standing tradition of the Keeping Church was to care for many men and women deemed unfit to work or live on their own. They were known as Alma's Beloved, and they were taught skills of artistry and music with the finest teachers Orismund could offer. Over the centuries a hand lexicon had been coded and standardized for use in the church's cathedrals, and Devin had been taught that lexicon as part of his training as a Soulkeeper. He repeated his greeting, this time with a similar curling gesture of his wrist, followed by a quick spelling of his first name.

"Good, you two can communicate with one another," Gerag said. "It's been rough getting a story out of Broder since he returned from Oakenwall. He knows his letters, but not very well, and his ability to draw isn't much better."

"We can communicate, yes, but only in simple concepts," Devin said. Since Gerag had not yet offered, he pointed to one of the chairs so Broder might take a seat. The big man squeezed into the chair, and he looked decidedly uncomfortable. Devin noticed he held several small scraps of paper.

I look? he signed to Broder.

Broder reluctantly handed over the pages.

"Every week the finest, smoothest-cut boards arrive by wagon at Londheim's gates," Gerag said as Devin looked the pages over. "Yesterday they missed their first shipment in two years. Instead Broder arrived, alone. Those pictures are the best we could get out of him as to what happened. The one thing that is clear is my workers are not safe, if they're even alive at all."

That was putting it mildly. Broder's pictures were drawn with charcoal, and they showed multiple people in various states of disembowelment. One, though, appeared perfectly fine, yet Broder had circled the lower half of him multiple times. Devin pointed at it and lifted his eyebrow. Broder responded by signing letters one by one.

G. O. L. D.

Gold? The man's entire lower body was . . . gold?

After seeing the corpse embedded into the wall that morning, it shouldn't have seemed so preposterous to him, yet still it seemed to lack any sense or reason to it. Assuming this Janus person wielded the power to change people into gold, why use it on a person? And why only the lower half?

Broder perceived his confusion and pointed a meaty finger at the upper half of the man.

Black, he signed.

Devin had assumed that the upper half was colored that way because of the nature of drawing with charcoal.

Black? Devin signed back to show his lack of understanding. Broder thudded his hands on his knees as he thought.

Dead, he signed. *Insects. Time.*

Devin took another look at the drawing, piecing the words together. The lower half was gold, the upper half rotted flesh, perhaps filled with maggots or worms. The punishment wasn't rational, but symbolic. Devin tried to imagine what it'd be like to witness such a horrid fate inflicted on another and shuddered. No wonder Broder looked pale and constantly in fear of his own shadow.

All dead? he asked Broder. *No alive?*

Yes.

"Well?" Gerag asked.

"No survivors by the sound of it," Devin said.

"Then why'd he survive?"

A good question. His frown deepened, and he chewed on the side of his mouth as he thought for a way to phrase his next question.

Why you? he asked. *Why alive?*

Broder blushed slightly. He pointed to himself and then signed a word many people throughout the Cradle could imitate even without knowing any of the lexicon.

"He was defecating outside the camp," Devin explained to Gerag. He stared at the bizarre mutilations, and he imagined dozens of men all suffering such brutal fates, those that didn't have their bodies turned to rot and gold.

"Do you know who did this?" he asked.

Broder gestured to the last of the drawings. It was of a man with long hair, a heavy coat, and completely filled-in leggings. An arrow pointed to the left side of his head, along with a clumsily written word: *green.*

Green hair? Devin asked him.

Yes. Left. Right black.

So a man with green hair on half his head, black on the other, a long black coat, and black trousers. The description was definitely unique enough that it might be worth putting on a poster throughout the city. He made a note to speak with Vikar Forrest about it before any departure to Oakenwall.

Name? he asked, pointing to the drawing. He did not expect one, but to his surprise Broder signed the word for *tree*, followed by five letters.

J. A. N. U. S.

Devin handed back the drawings and thanked him. That was it, all he needed to know for this to be his top priority. Whoever had killed the Mindkeeper that morning had struck the lumber camp days beforehand. If there were other survivors, he had to find them and ensure their safety. The Janus monster clearly represented a supernatural threat, one whose nature they knew painfully little about.

Gerag noticed their conversation was over and summoned Belford to take the man back to his room. Devin stood and took him by the wrist.

I pray, and then gestured, *for you*.

Thank you, Broder signed. A little bit of life returned to his sunken eyes, and Devin wished nothing but the best for him. Once the man was gone he turned to the merchant.

"This is definitely a matter I shall investigate personally," he said. "I'll leave tomorrow at first light."

"Excellent. Before you go, I'd like to make one request, and that is for one of my soulless to accompany you."

"Is that so?" Devin's face twitched. "Might I ask why?"

Gerag clapped his hands instead of answering. The door to the study creaked open. Belford poked his head inside.

"Fetch Jacaranda for me, please."

"At once, Master."

Devin sat back down and fought for patience. Of course Gerag would make additional demands. Most of the time Soulkeepers were requested by entire villages, as in Dunwerth. The needs were significant, and the contract made with an understanding to that significance. Devin vowed his life to fulfill the stated need. Someone like Gerag? Requesting a Soulkeeper was no different than hiring an expensive mercenary. The Keeping Church would humor him so long as he kept his coffers open. It was the greatest reason why Devin preferred working in the wildlands to the far west instead of in Londheim.

"So Jacaranda is an interesting name," Devin said, deciding the silence was slightly more uncomfortable than discussion.

"It is indeed, but I chose it with care." Gerag rubbed his hands together eagerly. "Have you been to the Vibrant Isle, particularly the southern half of it?"

"Sadly, I have never been."

Gerag pointed to one of the paintings. A family gathered beneath a beautiful tree for a picnic. Its leaves were a purple so livid and pure it was surely an exaggeration.

"Jacaranda trees, native only to the Isle. They're a wonder to behold, my most favorite, truly . . . and so is my Jacaranda."

The door opened, and Jacaranda stepped inside. She was a smaller woman, pale of skin and similar in age to Devin. The hollow chain of interconnected circles tattooed across her throat marked her as one of the soulless. She wore a plain white shirt and a black pair of slacks buckled tightly at her slender waist. Her hair was fiery red and hung loose past her shoulders. True to her name, he saw her eyes were a deep violet. Devin started to rise from his seat and had to remind himself that such manners were unnecessary.

"I was requested," she said with the perfectly monotonous voice only soulless could create.

"Indeed, you were," Gerag said. "Jacaranda, this is Devin Eveson. You will be accompanying him on his mission to Oakenwall."

The woman turned her gaze to Devin. Their eyes met, and she stared for so long it made him uneasy.

"I see," she said.

Devin turned away from her.

"Mister Ellington, I understand the people of Oakenwall are important to you," he said. "But I do not have the time to keep an eye on one of your servants."

"Forgive me, Soulkeeper, but she's there to keep an eye on you," Gerag said. "I want Oakenwall investigated thoroughly, and there are matters to be dealt with that will not concern you when it comes to the leadership at the camp."

"The land is dangerous now, and..."

"And Jacaranda can take care of herself," Gerag interrupted. Anger flashed across his face, ugly and surprisingly fierce. It vanished as quickly as it came, replaced by an unnerving giddiness. "She is my personal guardian, so I assure you she is *very* well trained. I know the world is a dangerous place, but with my precious Jacaranda at your side, you will be that much safer."

"If you insist," Devin said, deciding not to bother protesting. Even if he put his foot down, a simple message to Vikar Forrest would likely overrule his decision.

"Excellent." The merchant slapped Devin on the shoulder. "I'll have her prepped overnight so she'll follow any and all orders you give her...within reason, of course. And don't go thinking to have some illicit fun with her, mind you. As I said, she is well trained. You won't like what happens if you try."

Devin was insulted that the pompous little toad thought he'd even consider it.

"We depart tomorrow morning from the southern gate. Make sure Jacaranda is dressed and outfitted for travel."

"I'll provide you both with fresh horses for the ride," Gerag said as they stood and shook hands. "With all the insanity about, I feel that the need for Soulkeepers is about to grow tremendously. Here's to hoping you and I have a long relationship ahead of us."

Devin would rather cut out his own eyelids.

"Peaceful days to you," he said, dipping his head.

"And prosperous nights and all that to you as well," Gerag said.

Devin spared one last look at Jacaranda. Her violet eyes followed him carefully. The expression on her face was passive, but he couldn't shake the feeling that it was a lie. The soulless was on edge, always watching, always ready.

"Tomorrow morning," he said to her as he passed.

"If Master wishes it."

CHAPTER 17

"Are you sure you'll be safe?" Tommy asked Devin as he prepared for his lengthy travel with Jacaranda. His brother-in-law sat at the table in his bed robe, a small bowl of cheese and nuts before him. Tommy had made himself quite comfortable at Devin's home. Several blankets lay strewn about the slender couch, intermixed with pillows and cast-off clothes needing a wash.

"Is anywhere safe?" Devin asked as he buckled his pistol and sword to his waist.

"Well, some places are theoretically safer than others," Tommy said, tearing a chunk of cheese free and tossing it into his mouth. "And outside Londheim seems particularly unsafe. At least here the grass isn't trying to choke us and the dead haven't risen up to kill us yet."

"Yet?"

"I can throw lightning my from my fingers, and a sentient being of flame is snoozing in our fireplace. Forgive me for keeping my mind open to possibilities."

Devin glanced to the fireplace while removing his hat from a hook on the wall. Normally the few logs would have burned to embers overnight, but Puffy had kept it carefully controlled so that one of them was untouched completely. The little firekin appeared to be flattened across the top of it, the black dots of its eyes closed into thin slits one could easily miss if not looking for them.

"Will you and Puffy be all right while I am gone?" he asked.

"Theoretically," Tommy said. When Devin glared he lifted his hands in apology. "Sorry, I forgot you are not a morning person. And yes, I've been getting along quite splendidly with the local Wise. Malik is a studious, focused man, though he is a tiny bit distracting."

"Distracting?"

"Well, he's, uh, Malik's a particularly…striking person to look upon."

Devin laughed lightheartedly at Tommy's blushing face and neck.

"Do I hear the first seeds of a crush blooming?"

Tommy harrumphed.

"He's also twenty years my senior, Devin. Please do not interject yourself into my romantic life. We have more important matters for us to focus on right now."

Devin squeezed his brother-in-law on the shoulder.

"As everyone is fond of saying lately, it seems the world is ending. Try not to be too picky or focused on work. We should enjoy what happiness there is for us in this life."

"Says the man trotting off to do some wealthy merchant's bidding," Tommy said. "Seems like you're the one who could use more happiness in his life."

Devin winked as he slung his fully stocked pack over his shoulder.

"My time with Brittany gave me enough happiness to last a lifetime. Take care, Tommy."

"You too, Devin."

Devin's house was located near the official center of Londheim, tucked away into a corner of the wall that bordered Church District. Normally it was a quiet walk, his few neighbors wealthy enough to afford sleeping in most days instead of waking with the sun. This time, however, he was surprised to see a trio gathering at the end of the street, the elderly Mr. and Mrs. Aggerson, and an odd cloth merchant who went only by his first name, Jomo.

"Good morning, Soulkeeper," Mr. Aggerson called with a wave.

"Did you plan on watching the crossroad oak as well?" asked his wife.

The two looked dressed for a ninth-day sermon, wearing plain but expensive gray clothes to protect against the chill. Devin shook his head, confused.

"Is there something amiss with the oak?" he asked.

"Oh, we hear it's changed with the arrival of the refugees," the missus said. "Ask Jomo, he's seen it."

"It truly is remarkable to witness," Jomo said, nodding. He was on the eccentric side, his clothes loose and blue and his mustache impressively long. Rumors put him as having been a wildly successful magician back east before he retired to Londheim. Given the dark-skinned man's overwhelming charisma, Devin found he believed it more than not.

Devin walked alongside them, still baffled. The crossroad

oak was an ancient tree at the cross section of the north-south and east-west throughways. No plaque or memorial marked its planting, but the roads were carefully cobbled around it, and had been for as long as anyone could remember. It was easily the most popular spot for weddings in Londheim, as well as proposals and celebrations.

"I do have a bit of time," Devin said. "So what would I witness if I accompanied you?"

"Oh you must accompany us, you must," Jomo said. "And I would not spoil the wondrous surprise, especially if you come with virgin eyes and ears. Step, step, all of you, lest we miss the sunrise!"

Over three hundred people gathered around the old oak tree by the time they arrived, the bodies forming a tightly sealed circle. Devin led the way, taking advantage of his status to politely request a bit of space for his group.

"Good, good, we're not late," Jomo said. He rubbed his gloved hands happily together. "I tell you, I have been awaiting for this ever since yesterday morn!"

The crossroad oak's size was extraordinary, its trunk at least fifteen feet wide. Thick, heavy branches curled and twisted in all directions, filling the air above it with wide green leaves. So far nothing about it seemed amiss, and Devin was familiar enough with each and every black branch. He'd raced his sister to the tree's apex numerous times while growing up, winning more often than he lost. It might seem cliché, but the crossroad oak was one of his favorite spots in Londheim to relax at the end of a long day.

"What exactly are we waiting for?" Devin asked after several minutes of awkward silence and shuffling.

"You'll know it when you see it," Jomo said.

"Sunrise, dear," Mrs. Aggerson clarified. "It happens at sunrise."

Just a few minutes, then. Devin stretched his arms and back to keep them loose for the coming travel, an eye on the tree at all times. The first rays of sunlight trickled over the walls of Londheim. Onlookers clapped and pressed closer to the oak. Devin frowned. Still nothing. The tree was as it always was. A soft rustle teased their ears. Branches gently swayed. The relaxing sound almost made him miss the blindingly obvious before him.

The leaves were flapping in a wind that was not there.

"Jomo..." Devin said.

"Hush now," the man said, his eyes never leaving the oak. "Just watch."

It started at the bottom, where the lower hanging branches offered their arms for eager children to climb. A soft light like fire shimmered through the leaves. What was a dark green in the late night was now a flourishing bloom of gold and red. The wave of color flowed upward, with each and every leaf folding itself in half before opening again.

No, not leaves. Wings connected to tiny brown circles like acorns detached from the tree's branches. Their light was so bright, the volume so tremendous as they flooded outward, that it made a mockery of the sunrise. A soft chorus accompanied their flight, like the rustle of leaves combined with the aria of a young girl. Each leaf sang it, and as they floated overhead Devin listened to the constantly shifting and changing song. The pitch deepened. The swirling vortex of wings condensed directly over the tree.

All is alive, and all is new, thought Devin. The vortex's eye blazed gold while pulses of orange and red flowed toward the increasingly widening outer circle. Devin heard words amid the song, strange and foreign, but they settled comfortably on his heart like a warm blanket. The sky above him burned like fire, and it was as wondrous and beautiful as anything Devin had ever imagined.

A single explosive crack marked the leaves' scattering. The song faded, and the leaf-creatures rapidly dispersed into distant red and yellow dots across the orange sky. They left behind a barren crossroad oak as if it were the dead of winter. Onlookers cheered and clapped. Devin shared in their joy. In the shadow of the crawling mountain, surrounded by the soiled grass of the black water, such vibrancy and life gave him hope.

"Do they come back?" Devin asked.

"Every nightfall," Jomo said. "I've been here for that as well, and it's not quite the same. They've dulled their colors, and they arrive over the course of an hour instead of one sudden flurry. Fascinating to witness, still, but it doesn't hold the magic of the sunrise."

"I wonder what they are?" Mrs. Aggerson asked. "I think they look like butterflies, don't you?"

"Indeed, butterflies, strange butterflies," Mr. Aggerson said. He took Jomo's hand and shook it. "I am so glad you told us. I much appreciated the show."

"Thank you all for the invite," Devin said, tipping his hat to the trio as he trudged south. "I cannot think of a better way to have started my morning. Enjoy the small crowds while they last. It won't be long until half of Londheim comes for a peek."

Devin arrived at the southern gate to find Jacaranda waiting for him with a thick pack of supplies strapped to her back. Her brown leather trousers and burgundy shirt looked like they'd

never been worn before today. Over this, she wore a long coat
that hung nearly down to her ankles. Her long, expensive daggers were buckled prominently at each hip.

"I see you are well armed," he said, smiling at the woman.

"I am adequately prepared for the journey," she said.

"I hope that includes food and blankets."

The soulless woman looked mildly confused.

"I said I am adequately prepared for the journey."

She spoke as if he were a toddler failing to comprehend a basic
idea. A little bit of Devin's cheer from witnessing the crossroad
oak leaked out with his sigh.

"Forget it. We've a long ride ahead of us, so let's get started.
Where are the horses stabled?"

Devin had worked with soulless before. At least ten dozen
occupied the lowest-tiered ranks of the city guard, the wealthy
often employed them as servants, and even the Keeping Church
accepted them as custodians. This was the first time, however,
that one had been explicitly assigned to him, and Devin disliked
every part of it. Traveling with Jacaranda had all the awkward
inconveniences of traveling with another but without any of the
benefits. One could not make small talk with a soulless.

"Is the sun bothering you?" Devin asked. The weather might
be cold but that didn't mean the rising sun couldn't sting the eyes
every time the road swung momentarily east.

"Squinting is unpleasant."

"I see that. Generally the sun is responsible." Jacaranda
remained silent, so Devin pressed on. Soulless did not act on

minor inconveniences. He'd once seen a soulless guard stand an entire shift in the rain because he didn't think to take two steps to the left to duck underneath a porch. "Did you pack a hat of some kind?"

"Master does not like how I look with hats."

"And your master isn't here right now, either."

Jacaranda gave him a blank look.

"I do not understand how that matters. Master said hats hide my hair and do not flatter my face; therefore I may not wear them."

Devin wished Gerag were on the road with them so he could slap the bulbous little toad across the head.

"Well, I think you'd look fine with a hat."

"Irrelevant."

Devin tried not to let it bother him. After all, Jacaranda was easily the most talkative soulless he'd ever met. Most would ignore comments sent their direction if they did not include immediate orders to follow. The two rode in silence for hours, skirting the limits of the destruction the crawling mountain had breathed southward upon its arrival at Londheim. Jacaranda watched him at all times. He tried playing a game of guessing what orders Gerag had given her, and the only one he was certain of was *Do not trust the Soulkeeper.*

The first day passed easily enough. Every other hour they'd see travelers fleeing to Londheim, and Devin often stopped and chatted with them while their horses rested. The people were frightened and confused, so Devin did his best to give them answers and hope in equal measure. When it came time to settle in for the night, Jacaranda aided in building the campfire but did not intend to sleep beside it.

"Master says I should not sleep close to fires," she explained as she dragged her bedroll far from the campfire. "He does not trust me to prevent burns."

"I hope you have an extra blanket, then," he said. "The nights are getting pretty cold."

"I am adequately prepared for the journey," she said.

"Yeah," Devin said. "You've told me."

So he slept alone beside the fire, enjoying its warmth on his skin as he relaxed after a long day of riding. Sleep came quickly, but sadly it lasted only a few hours before his eyes snapped open, followed by an immediate groan of annoyance. Ever since the black water's arrival he'd been unable to sleep through the reaping hour. Its presence was simply too powerful to ignore. Cold fingers brushed the edges of his spine. Electricity set the hairs on his arms and legs to rise. When the moment passed he'd be able to fall back asleep, but not any sooner. Deciding he might as well enjoy the silence, he looked up at the stars and drank in their beauty.

Grass rustled to his left. Devin's hand moved hidden beneath his blanket to his pistol. He'd loaded it before settling down for the night, just in case they encountered the odd bandit. He kept his eyes skyward, not revealing he'd noticed. No reason to panic yet. There was a good chance his midnight visitor was a curious animal, not a thief. Devin shifted his head ever so slightly until his pack was in sight.

No, not an animal. Human eyes stared at him. Devin counted to three and then lurched to a sit, his pistol swinging in his left hand to draw a bead on the interloper. Within a heartbeat Devin's finger was off the trigger.

"Hello there," Devin said. He tilted his pistol up and to the side. "Are you hungry?"

A pale-skinned boy knelt over Devin's pack, a half loaf of

bread wrapped in brown paper clutched tightly to his chest. Dirt layered his mussed hair. Blood stained part of his shirt. Every muscle in his body looked tensed for a sprint. The boy ignored Devin's question, his eyes focused solely on the pistol.

"Do you see this?" Devin asked. He showed the silver moon and triangle decorating the side of his pistol. "Do you know what this means? It means I'm a Soulkeeper, child. I won't hurt you."

"Another man said he wouldn't hurt me," the boy said. "He lied. He wanted me to . . . to touch him. I bet you do, too."

Devin's anger flared, and he kept it cool and hidden beneath his face. The last thing he wanted was this boy to think that anger was directed at him.

"I wish only to see you safe and well," Devin said. "Have you a family, or a home?"

"Black water took my family," the boy said. "Didn't take me. Won't let it. Won't let no one." His grip on the bread was so tight it crumpled between his fingers. "Thanks for the food."

"Wait," Devin said. The child put himself at great risk living so far from civilization, especially if he hoped to feed himself by robbing travelers. "Please, I only wish to help you. I'm a member of the Keeping Church. Come with me to Londheim, and I promise you'll receive shelter and food."

The boy took two steps back into the tall grass.

"You lie."

"I am nothing if my word is not true."

Fear and trauma were powerful poisons, and Devin had only his kind words to combat it. He remained patient, letting the child think through things on his own.

"You . . . do you promise?" the boy suddenly asked.

"I promise."

He looked down at the food, then back up at Devin. Debating.

A hand reached behind the boy, slender fingers locking against his forehead. The other hand drew a knife across the boy's throat, opening it up with a flourish of blood.

"No!" Devin screamed.

The boy collapsed onto his chest and convulsed. Jacaranda knelt behind him, calmly wiping the blood from her dagger. She spared Devin an emotionless glance before walking back toward the campfire, her dagger returned to its sheath. Devin's anger, already a boil, surged uncontrollably through his veins.

"Why?" he asked, leaping in her way. His fist tightened into a painful white-knuckle grip on the handle of his pistol. "Why would you do something so awful?"

Jacaranda tilted her head to one side. Mild confusion. No guilt or empathy. Devin doubted her pulse had even accelerated.

"Thieves are not to be tolerated."

"That wasn't a thief! It was a boy, just a starving boy."

"The boy held our supplies. You distracted him, I brought him down. Our supplies are safe."

As if it were that simple. As if the corpse bleeding out in the grass meant nothing. Devin lifted his pistol and sighted it between her eyes. Jacaranda stared back, unflinching. Her daggers were in hand, and he couldn't remember when she drew them. Speed. Stealth. Her training was good. Far too good.

"Soulless are not to kill," he said.

"I defended us. Did I err?"

"Yes, you fucking erred!"

He could kill her right there and be fully justified. One bullet and this soulless monstrosity would be gone, and to the void with whatever tantrum Gerag might throw about it. He imagined pulling the trigger. He imagined the satisfaction in seeing Jacaranda's body lying dead beside the boy she'd killed. Even if

Jacaranda was trained to kill, an act strictly forbidden, Devin would find no justice back in Londheim. Gerag had bought himself into the church's good graces. But his little puppet here? The one alone and vulnerable?

"What are your orders?" he asked her with a shaking voice.

"I am not to tell you."

"Are you to do what must be done to survive?"

"Yes."

"Then tell me your orders or I will put a bullet in your brain and use you as the kindling for the boy's funeral pyre."

"I am to defend myself," Jacaranda said. She twirled her daggers as she settled into a low stance.

"I'm sure you are. Tell me, soulless, which do you think is more likely to spare your life: trying to outrace my pistol, or telling me what your orders are?"

The woman froze as if calculating the odds.

"Very well." She stood up immediately. Her muscles slackened. Her daggers vanished into their sheaths. "I have many orders. Would you like me to detail them all?"

The change was unnerving to watch. Jacaranda didn't show the slightest concern for the pistol aimed at her forehead. It was like someone had flipped a switch, and now she was calm as could be. No grudge at being threatened. No hesitation at whether she had made the correct decision.

"Let's stick with the ones your master gave you explicitly for our trip," Devin said.

"Do accompany the Soulkeeper to Oakenwall," Jacaranda began. "He is helping Master. Do not allow sexual favors with him. He has not paid. Do not reveal your orders. He is not to know. Do not allow deviation on the trip to Oakenwall. There must be no delays. Do not leave Oakenwall until the status of its workers is determined. The people are valuable. Do ensure Nathan Evart's survival. Burn his home if he is missing or dead. Do not trust the Soulkeeper. Kill him if he abandons his duty to Master."

A spiteful part of Devin yearned to pull the trigger, put the soulless down like a rabid dog, but that was his anger and frustration talking.

She is a tool. A weapon. Blame the hand that wields her.

Devin holstered his pistol. Gerag deserved his anger, not Jacaranda. Perhaps it would not matter much, but when he returned to Londheim he'd lodge a complaint and see if he could start chipping away at the loathsome man's support in the church.

"A warning for you, Jacaranda. Don't even think of trying to kill me. It won't go well for you."

"I am highly trained," she said.

"So am I."

Devin debated what to do now. It was past the reaping hour, which meant either he could stay here for a full day and night to administer the reaping ritual, or he could have the boy buried and hope the recent changes in the world would allow it to escape without his intervention.

"Dig a grave and bury him in it," Devin said, deciding that as much as he disliked it, he couldn't afford to waste so much time. Other lives might be in the balance. "We don't have a shovel, so you'll need to use your hands. Break the earth with your daggers if you must."

"I require sleep," Jacaranda said.

"And you'll get it when the body is buried. That's an order. Consider it your penance."

All soulless would follow orders given to them unless strictly trained otherwise, such as those conscripted to be city guards.

Jacaranda searched for a particularly soft patch of earth and then dropped to her knees. Her daggers punctured the surface, breaking up the soil. Devin retrieved his pack, set it near the fire, and lay down to sleep. For the sake of his tired mind, he pretended not to notice the stain of blood along one side.

CHAPTER 18

Devin woke with the dawn. Jacaranda stood over a bare patch of dirt, steadily flattening it with her feet. Just now finishing, by the looks of it. Devin tried to ignore the first note of guilt that strummed his heart as he walked out to the field to piss.

"Is the grave complete?" he asked her when he returned.

"It is."

The woman was a sore sight. Large bags swelled beneath her eyes. Dirt covered nearly every part of her. When he looked to her hands he saw them sheeted with a drying cake of blood and dark earth. With his anger and shock subdued by the quiet morning, Devin's conscience reared its stubborn head.

Blame the hand that wields her, he recalled from the night before. Gerag might be responsible for Jacaranda's training, true, but it also meant Devin was responsible for every bleeding cut and scrape she bore from digging the grave.

"Come with me," Devin said.

She wordlessly followed him. He gestured for her to sit beside the dormant fire.

"Are you in pain?" he asked her.

"I am."

Devin ground his teeth together.

You damn asshole, Devin.

He set his pack beside him and retrieved a handful of supplies. Jacaranda watched him with disinterest. Devin dropped to his knees, uncapped his water pouch, and nodded.

"Give me your hands."

She offered them, and he slowly poured the cold water across her fingers and palm.

"Water is a necessary supply," she said.

"We'll cross two streams today. It'll be fine."

Devin gently brushed his hands over hers, testing for open wounds as well as removing the loose dirt. More water. Her fingertips were by far the worst. Those that weren't bleeding were covered with blisters.

"Anwyn forgive me," Devin whispered. Then, louder to Jacaranda, "I'm sorry. This was wrong."

The woman looked at him but did not say a word. He would receive no forgiveness from her. Soulless didn't understand the concept.

Devin wiped away the dried blood on her knuckles and confirmed that none needed stitches. He flipped her hands back over and washed away the dirt from her palms. When finished he withdrew the first of his bandages and looped several layers about her knuckles.

"Keep still," Devin said, holding the bandage tightly while withdrawing his sewing needle. "I don't want to hurt you more than I already have."

He sewed the bandages together, repeated the process on her other hand, and then washed her fingers a second time. Clear skin was starting to show, and he again reminded himself that he was an asshole. Most fingers bore cuts that'd heal well enough on their own if they didn't become infected, but the nails of her left little and ring fingers had both torn down to the skin. The ring finger was the worst, with half the nail still ripped back and bleeding.

"I need to remove the torn half of this nail," he said. "I expect this will cause some pain."

She said nothing. Devin withdrew a slender knife from his pack and pressed the blade at the tender intersection between nail and skin.

"On three," he said. "One. Two."

Three. Off came the nail with a quick swipe of the knife. Jacaranda hissed in a breath through clenched teeth. Devin quickly wrapped both fingers with bandages and began his work with the sewing needle as a scarlet dot stained the white cloth. A minute later he was done. He groaned along with his back and knees as he returned to a stand.

"I'll need to check them by midday," Devin told her. "Now lie down for a few hours. You look like you can barely stand."

"There must be no delays."

"A few hours won't matter."

"There must be no delays."

It was the first time he'd ever heard her raise her voice. Something akin to panic shone in her eyes. Was that a tear? No. Soulless didn't have emotions. This outburst made no sense.

"All right, all right," Devin said, not wanting to stress her further. "You can sleep while you ride. Is that acceptable?"

Jacaranda said nothing. Devin figured that as a yes. He offered her his hand, and she promptly ignored it as she stood. Regardless of the pain it caused her, she saddled her horse without help, mounted it, and was ready to ride before Devin even prepared his breakfast.

They rode their horses side by side at a calm pace, his eye always upon her. After a few hours she began to droop in her saddle. The road was too quiet, too steady. Devin reached out and took her reins. A little tug and the horses slowed. Jacaranda slumped further, her arms crossed in her lap and her chin to her chest. When they reached the first of the two streams they were meant to cross that day, he pulled the horses to a stop. Jacaranda might not like the thought of a delay, but Devin could see the effects of exhaustion on her, and he could not bear the guilt of her suffering further because of his mistake.

"Easy now," he whispered as he hopped down from his mount. He laid a blanket in the grass directly beside the stream, then unhooked Jacaranda from her saddle. For a brief moment he feared she'd wake up as he gently lowered her into his arms. Might she confuse it for forbidden sexual advances?

He has not paid.

The thought sickened him. Using soulless for concubines was strictly forbidden by both the church and the crown. Proving Gerag's guilt, however, would be a difficult manner, for no doubt Jacaranda was well trained against questions regarding her interactions with Master. Even investigating the matter would be difficult, given Gerag's generous donations to the church.

Thankfully Jacaranda remained asleep, and he set her down upon the blanket. Deciding his own back could use a break, he prepared a second blanket, nestled his pack underneath his head, and closed his eyes. He didn't sleep, nor did he expect to. Resting beneath the warm sun and listening to the soft gurgling of the stream was nice enough. These moments were why he relished his position as Soulkeeper, which had him always on the move somewhere throughout West Orismund. A common joke within the church went, "What is the difference between a Faithkeeper and a Soulkeeper?" The answer was twenty thousand miles.

When Jacaranda awoke two hours later, she bolted upright as if her life were in danger.

"Where are we?" she asked.

"At the first of the two crossings I told you of," he said. "We stopped to eat lunch."

"We mustn't delay."

"Lunch isn't a delay. It's lunch. The stream's right over there. Wash yourself up while I wait."

Instead of replying, Jacaranda began stripping off her jacket and shirt. Devin quickly put his back to her. Soulless did not show modesty unless ordered. Despite knowing she'd not care if he saw her nude, Devin still afforded her some privacy. Given her lack of self-awareness and her need to follow orders, observing her in such a way felt wrong.

"Come back when you're hungry," Devin called over his shoulder. He sat with the stream directly behind him. Chiding himself for acting like a twelve-year-old skulking around a public bath, he opened his pack and pulled out a thick wedge of cheese wrapped in wax paper. He broke off two chunks, rewrapped the cheese, and then retrieved a package of dry rye bread. He tore equal portions of it and set them all atop his pack. Last were two wooden cups he filled with the last of the water from his skins.

Jacaranda unceremoniously reached over his shoulder and grabbed one of the cheese portions. He glanced at her and froze. She stood completely naked, her pale body glistening from her dive in the stream. Her wet clothes were wrapped in a bundle underneath her arm, and she plopped them to the ground beside the fire to dry.

Devin turned back around and stared straight ahead, more annoyed than anything. Jacaranda retrieved her blanket by the stream, dropped it next to her clothes, and sat atop it while eating her cheese. Next came the water and bread, which she ate with the focus and determination of a woman on a mission. Once finished she curled the blanket about her and leaned closer to the small flame.

"We'll leave once your clothes are dry," Devin told her.

"Master insists no delays. My clothes will dry while we ride."

"You'll be cold."

"I do not understand why this matters."

Devin rubbed his eyelids.

"We ride when your clothes are dry. That's an order."

Jacaranda didn't acknowledge him. Instead she unfurled her blanket, lay atop it on her back, and stared at the sky. If not for the sound of her breathing, Devin could be convinced she were a carved and painted statue.

Once Jacaranda was dressed, Devin checked her bandages. Her worst two fingers were swollen, and he reapplied the wrapping to give them a bit more room to breathe. Devin wondered how much pain it'd caused her over the past few hours. Perhaps for the sake of his conscience it was best he not know.

They made camp at the second stream crossing, a good hour earlier than Jacaranda was pleased with. They'd reach Oakenwall early tomorrow, and after five minutes of arguing Devin convinced her that keeping their horses rested was better than riding hard and arriving at the logging camp in the middle of the night. The memory of their previous midnight visitor weighed heavily on his mind as he built another fire. So far they'd yet to see another soul since the boy. Probably for the best, Devin thought grimly. Jacaranda offered to keep watch but he quickly shot her down. The last thing he wanted was to wake up to another body.

The next morning came peaceful and calm. The sun shone brightly above them as they rode the wagon-rutted path into the empty confines of Oakenwall.

"Keep wary," Devin told Jacaranda as they slowly trotted between the log cabins. They were arranged in a clumsy square, with the lone road slicing through the middle toward the Oakblack Woods. Beyond them were horse and oxen pens, a half-dozen wagons in various status of loading and unloading, and a single open-faced barn.

"Do you see anyone?" Devin asked. The prolonged silence had begun to unnerve him.

"I see you."

"Besides me."

"No."

The two dismounted in the center of the cabin square. Devin's instincts screamed out a warning, but no sign justified it. The entire camp was dead silent. Not even the chirping of birds or barking of dogs broke the quiet. The loggers had fenced in a large portion of the nearby grasslands for their horses and oxen, though the animals themselves were missing. Devin guided both their horses inside and then locked the gate.

"To the forest," Devin said to Jacaranda, who had trailed him the whole while like a shadow.

By the line of trees leading into the Oakblack Woods the two found the macabre sight Broder had drawn. Bodies of men lay massacred across the grass, each one sporting a different, horrific mutilation. One man had his arms removed, turned to solid gold, and then repositioned so the metal hands strangled his own throat. Another seemed pinned to the ground by loops of grass, yet when Devin knelt closer, he saw they were actually shards of finely serrated metal colored and shaped like grass. They dug deep into his skin, opening veins and pooling dried blood beneath him.

Near the center of the carnage he found the scene of one of Broder's drawings, the lower half of the man solid gold, his legs braced as if caught midrun. It ceased at his waist, but where his upper half should be was instead a festering pool of rot. Bones lay scattered in all directions, lying within a black and gray mass that stank to the high heavens. Devin clenched his jaw and steeled his stomach. It seemed the entire upper body had separated from the lower gold half and collapsed to the grass.

Though Devin tried to keep his distance, Jacaranda investigated the gold legs like she would any other random object. Soulless knew no fear, nor did they care if something smelled foul.

"I have no explanation for any of this," she said after a moment.

"Join the club." Devin pointed ahead. "Come with me."

Near the forest Janus had created his most intricate work of art. Two men stood locked in place like statues. Their arms were raised high above their heads. Vines encircled their naked bodies . . . no, not encircled. Their flesh had *become* vines, and the blood that leaked through their torn skin bloomed into crimson flowers. Devin could still see bits of organs through gaps in the vines. The vines ceased at their necks, which remained solidly human, but that did not mean the horror stopped.

A thick round branch stretched from each of their mouths,

as if a tree had been planted inside their bellies and grown in an instant. Permanent expressions of horror were etched on their faces. Devin examined closer and immediately regretted it. The men's teeth had been pushed outward to make room for the branch. Perhaps it *had* grown from their stomachs, and Devin felt creeping panic in the back of his mind at the thought of this being done while the two men still lived. The branches interlocked with one another to form the outline of a doorway. Across the interlocked branches grew an impossible bloom of flowers. Spelled with roses amid the rest of the white carnations was a lone name: *Janus.*

"You are destroying evidence," Jacaranda said as Devin sliced and hacked at the flowers with his sword until the name was gone.

"That I am," he said. "And I don't care."

Every mutilated body, every sadistic display, only confirmed one fact for Devin: Whoever this Janus was, he loathed humanity to an insane degree. Sometimes he spelled words insulting a dead man with his own intestines. One man appeared perfectly fine until Devin cut open his chest to discover that his internal organs were solid stone. There was a glee to this murder, enough to frighten him to his core.

If there was something Janus sought to gain from this, Devin did not see it. Had he come to Oakenwall to kill before making his way to Londheim, or perhaps had Oakenwall merely been on his way? Most Soulkeepers were masters at tracking, and Devin considered himself a cut above the others in his sacred division. It didn't take long to identify the wide, flat feet of Janus passing through the doorway bearing his name and into the forest.

Beside those footprints was a trail of blood.

"Once Janus was done here he went into the forest," Devin

explained to Jacaranda after he'd called her over to him. "Most likely he was dragging a body, though dead or alive, I cannot guess. There's a lot of blood to know for certain."

"Then all of the loggers are dead," Jacaranda said. "We shall return to Londheim."

"No," Devin said. "Not yet. I need to know what Janus wanted inside those woods."

The soulless woman looked greatly displeased.

"The loggers are dead. Master says to return, so we must return. You propose a delay. There must be no delays."

Devin let out a loud sigh. Jacaranda was his responsibility, and he wasn't going to leave her alone. That, and as much as he didn't want to admit it, the horrific sights around him had set his nerves aflame, and he greatly preferred to have any sort of company with him as he searched.

"We don't know that the one he dragged with him is dead," he argued. "He could be alive."

"That is a lot of blood. He is dead."

"Do you know that for certain?"

Jacaranda stared at him for a long moment.

"No."

Devin loaded flamestone and shot into his pistol.

"Then in we go."

CHAPTER 19

The missing person continues to leave blood behind," Jacaranda said. She trailed two steps behind Devin as he led them onward. "He is certainly dead by now."

"We go until we find a body," Devin said. "That's the rules. I don't make them, just follow them."

He took perverse satisfaction in Jacaranda's confusion.

"Whose rules? Rules for what? I do not understand."

"Neither do I," he muttered. The forest was rapidly changing, and in ways that left him mystified. Thorn-covered vines sprouted along the trunks of the black oaks, encircling halfway up in a stranglehold. The brush of the forest, normally scattered and thin, tightened with weeds and bushes that looked entirely foreign, something that should not be possible in a region Devin knew like the back of his hand. The leather of Devin's coat was his only protection against the burs and thorns.

A thick wave of rot attacked his nose upon a soft hint of wind, and Devin fought back a gag. His first thought was that it was the dragged man they tracked, but the smell came from the right. He veered off anyway, needing to satisfy his curiosity. A short walk later he found the bloated corpse of a deer. It lay on its side with its belly opened as if by a sword. Red and purple vines emerged from the dirt surrounding it, their short, sharp thorns digging into the deer's skin on all sides of the gaping wound. Devin could not shake the feeling that those vines had been what ripped the deer open. Where there should have been blood and intestines instead was a massive growth of crimson flowers.

Jacaranda peered past Devin to the carcass and deliberated.

"It looks like flowers spilled out from its stomach and started to grow."

"Yeah," Devin said. "It does kind of look like that."

"Is that possible?"

Devin retreated back to the tracked path.

"I have no goddess-damned clue anymore."

The two of them walked deeper and deeper into the forest, and after an hour Devin felt his nerves begin to fray. Already the forest had become unknown to him, but now it was getting harder to see the sun through the thick canopy of leaves. Normally he trusted his innate sense of direction, and his ability to survive weeks in a forest if need be, but the weirdness of the vegetation robbed him of his confidence. Flowers appeared the wrong color, moss shimmered blue and yellow, and the cries of birds in the trees were of species he knew nothing about. At least the dragging body and its smear of blood was still easily tracked, but should they wander...

"Devin, do you hear that?"

He stopped, and in the absence of footfalls and crunching brush, he did hear the faintest sound.

Singing.

"It sounds like a woman," he said. "But a woman singing out here, in the middle of this forest…"

The hairs on his neck stood on end. The song lacked any words he could understand, just a long, continuous melody that could leave many of the professional singers in Londheim jealous. There was no doubt as to its source, either. It came from up ahead, the same direction that the tracks lead toward.

"Do you think it wise I ready my weapons?" Jacaranda asked. "I do not see any threats, but my knowledge of this forest is significantly limited."

Devin laughed, a dark grin spread across his face.

"Limited?" he said. "Yeah, that's one way to put it. I think it's wise, Jac. Very wise."

The soulless woman drew her daggers, Devin his sword, and together they followed the slightly trampled path spackled with blood toward the sound of a song. It wasn't far until he spotted a strange ring of trees, their trunks close enough together that they almost formed a wall. The trail led directly within them. Devin mustered up what courage he had and strode right in, to be greeted by the forest's singer in its center.

Its base was a rose pistil as wide as a tree trunk, its lovely red petals opened in full blossom. A seemingly numberless collection of vines sprouted from below, some snaking along the ground, others tunneling deep into the earth to reemerge elsewhere. A second row of petals opened up within the first, these a yellow deeper than the sun and speckled with soft red dots. Four stamens waved in an unfelt wind, their tips bladed and stained crimson. In the center of it all grew the creature's heart, a feminine shape with her arms crossed over her chest. She showed no facial features, just a lush of yellow-green vines, blooming flowers, and pulsing veins. A gaping hole opened where her stomach should be, and from within its depths came the lovely song.

It'd have been a beautiful image if not for the blood splashed across the vines and petals.

"Visitors to my forest?" asked a voice that lilted through the ongoing song. The tone quickly shifted when the featureless face turned their way. "Human visitors. *Trespassers*. Why have you come?"

Devin took in a deep breath and mentally ordered himself to remain calm. Yes, it was an enormous talking flower, but so far it was a *nonviolent* enormous talking flower. If they were lucky, it'd stay that way.

"A camp nearby was attacked by a man named Janus," he said. "Do you know of him?"

"I have met him once." The four stamens shivered. Devin could not help but notice the razor-sharp blades along their sides. "Viciss's avatar of change brought gifts. Do you bring gifts?"

The drag marks to the flower's base. The blood across its petals. It added up to a particularly unsavory image, one that Jacaranda put together just as quickly.

"The flower ate the body," she stated. "This is unusual."

"I am more than a flower. I am the songmother of the woods. I woo the deer. I calm the wolf. Every tree that grows, every plant that dies, I guide. I control. I make in my image."

Devin felt his knuckles ache from his tight grip upon the hilt of his sword. If the songmother turned violent, where did he even strike? He had one shot for his pistol, but would it do anything to the mix of vegetation within its heart? What exactly *were* the internal organs of a carnivorous flower?

"Forgive us, songmother," Devin said. "We bring no gifts,

but I assure you, we mean no disrespect by it. We were unaware of your presence."

The harsher chords within the song softened.

"Foolish. Ignorant. The deer contain more wisdom. The tick harbors greater purpose."

Try not to think too highly of us, Devin thought, wisely keeping that to himself. Instead, he gestured in the direction he thought Oakenwall was in and tried to bring the conversation back on track.

"The camp," he said. "Please, Janus murdered all of the men there, and I would know why."

"Why?" The songmother leaned closer. A scent of pollen and tulips washed over him. "Hundreds of years, we slept. Buried beneath the ground, like seeds. Locked in the sky, like water within clouds. We slept, so you might multiply like rodents. We are angry, and you ask why? Why?"

The petals shook with laughter.

"There is no place for you in my forest. I have no heart for you in my song. Be gone."

Not good enough. The songmother had called Janus the avatar of change, but what did that even mean? Why had he come to Oakenwall, and why slaughter the men? The songmother was his only lead, which meant he had to press the issue. He begged the Sisters for wisdom and stepped closer to the giant petals.

"Please, if you know of this Janus, tell us of him. Tell us why he came. Surely I do not ask for much?"

Vines crept across the trunks of the black oaks surrounding them. The impression of walls closing in was unmistakable.

"I ask you to leave, and you stay," said the songmother. The song deepened. "Always this way with humans. Soft flesh, no claws, blunt teeth, yet you believe yourself lord of beasts and sky. Make demands of your betters. Build homes upon land that was never yours."

"I believe we are being threatened," Jacaranda said as the feminine figure in the center rose to its full height.

"I believe you're right," Devin said as he raised his sword.

"You wish for answers?" the songmother shouted. "Janus came for the starlight tear. Does that knowledge grant you comfort? Does the name make up for the insult you inflict upon our kind?"

The bladed stamens whipped circles in the air.

"I am hungry," the songmother said. "And human blood has always tasted the sweetest."

Two of the stamens swung simultaneously from either side of Devin and Jacaranda. Devin slid to his knees and chopped overhead. The stamens retreated halfway, avoiding the cut. Jacaranda burst into motion beside him, weaving like a professional dancer through the thorned vines that covered the ground. Her daggers cut grooves into the thick red petals at the base of the songmother. They drew no blood, if the creature even had any to begin with. Its only reaction was one of annoyance.

"Do not mock me with your metal weapons," it said.

"What about a pistol?" Devin asked. He pulled the trigger, his shot perfectly aimed. The bullet hit the center of the feminine figure's forehead and exited the other side in a burst of water and petals. The songmother didn't even flinch. A cut across his arm from the stamen was his reward. Devin dodged, his sword deflecting a follow up hit.

Jacaranda took advantage of his distraction to cut three more grooves into the petals and then retreat. A stamen lashed for her legs, and she leapt over it with grace that left Devin stunned.

He considered himself a fine swordsman, but Jacaranda's reflexes looked as honed as a panther's.

"I do not know where to attack," Jacaranda said upon landing, so calmly and matter-of-factly that she might as well be telling Devin the weather.

"Forget attacking," he shouted as he dropped to his knees and slashed his sword above his head. The blade cut halfway through the stamen. Blue-tinted water spilled across his coat from the wound. "Just run!"

"Which direction?" Jacaranda asked. Though her voice strained with exertion, she showed no outward sign of fear or panic. For once, Devin envied her soulless condition.

"Away from the damn flower trying to eat us!"

She reacted immediately, retreating to the outer edge of trees and slashing against the vines that sealed them in. They weren't many, and they were thin enough that her daggers could cut through them in one blow. Devin followed after her, positioning himself to guard her against the stamens, his pistol holstered and his sword held high in both hands. The songmother leaned in closer, her song pulsing with rapid, almost guttural urgency.

"Where shall you run?" it asked. Thorns broke through the ground as vines emerged in all directions. "The forest is mine. The world is ours. We shall pick you from our bodies like a dog does to fleas... with its teeth."

All four stamens lunged simultaneously. Devin saw them coming and knew immediately he was doomed. His sword could not stop them all. He dug in his feet, then felt his balance immediately falter. The stamens pierced where he'd stood, but he was falling backward, Jacaranda's hand firmly gripping the neck of his coat. The two of them fell through the severed vines and out of the circle of trees surrounding the songmother.

"We are not safe," Jacaranda said as she helped him to his feet. Though the stamens could not reach beyond the circle, there were still hundreds of veins cracking through the dirt, and they approached the two of them like snakes.

"Then start running."

They ran without any sense of direction, easily outpacing the vines. All that mattered was putting distance between them and the songmother. Their sprint settled to a jog after a few minutes, for the vines were sparser. That jog became a walk only when there were no vines at all, and the sound of the flower's song had faded into the quiet rustle of the forest.

"It would be wise to avoid further contact with that creature," Jacaranda said when they paused to catch their breath.

"Couldn't agree with you more."

"What do we do now?"

"Now?" Devin shrugged. "I'd say we're out of leads, which means it's time to exit this awful forest." He glanced at the sky, thought a moment, and then pointed. "That way should be the direction out."

They walked in silence. Devin's certainty lessened with each passing minute. The forest was so strange that he recognized no familiar sights, and even reliable markers, such as where the moss grew upon the sides of trees, seemed off. Devin wasn't sure he would call himself lost, but as the minutes dragged on, he feared that they were taking a more parallel path to the forest's edge than he'd have liked.

"Do you hear that?" he asked Jacaranda near the end of an hour.

"I hear many different things."

"I mean the crying."

Jacaranda stared at him blankly. Devin frowned and asked

her to remain still while he listened. He couldn't quite place the direction, but it sounded like the crying of a young child. Had there been children at the lumber camp? He didn't know, but if there were, perhaps one had survived?

Devin slowly approached his best approximation of the source. The closer he walked, the more certain he was of the crying. Under any other circumstances he would have called out to the child, but now? The rules of the world were cracked and shifting. Void's sake, a giant singing flower just tried to eat him and Jacaranda. The tears could be of a child...or they could be a trap. He drew his pistol just in case.

Devin held a finger to his lips when Jacaranda started to follow. He turned back and continued, now certain as to the source of the noise, that of a tree not far in the distance. The more he neared, the more certain he was of it being a young girl crying.

"It's all right," he said as he stepped around the deep black oak. "I'm..."

A tiny woman no taller than the length of his hand sat atop a white lily, her weight bending the stem sideways. Her skin was darker than any other Devin had laid eyes upon. It almost didn't look like skin, but instead as if she'd been carved from smooth, malleable onyx. Her short hair was equally black, if perhaps a shade lighter. Four wings resembling those of a dragonfly sprouted from just below the shoulders, the higher two larger than the bottom. Her dress was a dark green and appeared woven from the leaves of the forest.

"Oh!" the faery said as she pulled her hands away from her face. Little tears fell to her lap, each one shimmering like a tiny fleck of diamond. Her wings buzzed, and faster than his eyes could perceive she was in the air.

"Please-don't-shoot-don't-shoot-I-promise-I'm-nice."

"Is it a threat?" Jacaranda asked from the other side of the tree. Devin couldn't imagine so, but he'd been plenty surprised since the black water's arrival. He recognized words in that verbal explosion, but she spoke at such a mesmerizing clip he could only guess. Her eyes focused on his pistol as she hovered, and Devin realized he still held it at the ready.

"I'm Devin Eveson, Soulkeeper of the Three Sisters," he said as he carefully lowered his pistol. He didn't want to antagonize the creature if she was friendly. "It's nice to meet you...?"

The faery crossed her arms over her chest and sniffled one last time. She dared take her eyes away from his pistol to meet his, and when she next spoke her words were slower and clearer, even if still delivered at a rapid clip.

"I'm Tesmarie Nagovisi," she said. "I said please don't shoot, I promise I am friendly."

A tiny pin of guilt stabbed Devin in the heart. Here he was, towering over the tiny woman with pistol drawn, and he was worried about *her* threatening *him*?

"Forgive me, Tesmarie," Devin said. "I do not mean to frighten. I raised my pistol in self-defense."

Her wings fluttered to life and sang a pleasantly low hum as she lifted up to his eye level.

"You're forgiven. Maybe. I need to know if you're-friendly-first-so-we'll-see."

She sounded like a wagon barreling downhill to higher and higher speeds. Jacaranda stepped around the tree, and she showed not the slightest surprise or reaction to witnessing the existence of a faery.

"Will she be of use to us?" the soulless woman asked. "Or will she be a distraction?"

"I'm not sure," Devin said. "A lumber camp was nearby here,

Tesmarie, and its people were attacked. I'm trying to find the man responsible. A...creature of the woods, it called itself a songmother, claimed Janus came here in search of a 'starlight tear,' whatever that might be. Have you heard of one?"

"Starlight tear?" Tesmarie said. "No, well, maybe, I shouldn't, I've been...preoccupied, that's it, busy-doing-things-um-I'd-rather-not-talk-about-it."

Her speech increased with her apparent nervousness until she spoke at such a rapid pace he could only guess at her words.

"Pardon me, little one," he interrupted. "My slow ears struggle to follow your voice."

"Oh, sorry," she said. Tesmarie's hands weaved before her. The air thickened about the faery, then shimmered into a pink and purple bubble enveloping her. When it popped, she flicked her bangs away from her face and frowned. "You humans experience the world much too fast. You miss out on so many wonders that way."

Whatever she'd done, her movements were now slower and her speech clearly understandable.

"Thank you," Devin said. "It is an honor to meet with...forgive me, I do not even know what you are."

"I'm an onyx faery," Tesmarie said. She tilted her head. "Has it really been that long? Do you know nothing of the fae?"

"Until last week I thought the fae were stories we told our children."

Jacaranda stepped between them before Tesmarie might respond.

"Do you know of what Devin seeks or do you not?"

Tesmarie frowned at the rude interruption.

"Well, yes, I believe I do."

"Then take us there."

Tesmarie side-eyed the woman.

"I don't take orders, especially from those whose names I don't even know."

"My name is Jacaranda. Now show us the way."

"Or you'll do what?"

Devin grabbed Jacaranda's wrist before she could draw her dagger. Tesmarie zipped a dozen feet higher into the air. A twirl of her wrist created a slender sword within her grasp, from hilt to blade glowing as if formed of moonlight.

"Should have known, should have known, should have *known*. Humans hate fae. Call us thieves and pranksters and bad omens..."

"No, please," Devin said. He glared at Jacaranda. "You are not to harm Tesmarie under any circumstances, is that clear?"

Jacaranda's arm immediately relaxed.

"There must be no delays," she said. "If Tesmarie does not help, she is a delay."

"Thank you for explaining it so succinctly," Devin said dryly. He looked up to Tesmarie. "Forgive her, please. Soulless are not the best when it comes to meeting new people, but I promise we mean you no harm."

"Soulless?" Tesmarie said. Curiosity snuck into her voice. "How is that possible? Have the Sisters abandoned you?"

The question stung deeper than the faery could have known.

"No," he said. "But sometimes I wonder if we have abandoned the Sisters."

Tesmarie opened her hand. The moonlight blade vanished into mist.

"This starlight tear, you're not planning to take it, are you?" she asked.

"I seek to know who and what this Janus is. If he wanted the starlight tear, I only wish to know its purpose."

"Then I shall lead you to it, but only if you promise that…" She stopped to glare at Jacaranda. "That…soulless…behaves."

"You heard her, Jacaranda," Devin said. "Stay on your best behavior."

"I do not behave. I do not misbehave. I follow orders."

"And if I order you to behave?" he asked. Jacaranda stared at him and said nothing. "Good enough for me. Please, Tesmarie, if you'd be so kind, lead the way."

The faery looped two circles in the air.

"All right then, follow me!"

She dashed into the woods like a shot. In less than a few seconds she was out of sight, gone so fast neither Devin nor Jacaranda could even begin to follow. A second later Tesmarie returned.

"Sorry, sorry, silly me," she said. "I forgot that for how fast your time moves, you walk so slow."

"We walk only as fast as our two legs may take us," Devin said. "Some of us do not bear the luxury of wings."

Tesmarie pirouetted three full revolutions in the air, dropping several feet before springing back up to eye level.

"They are pretty neat, aren't they?" she said. For the first time since he met her she smiled, and it warmed Devin's heart.

The faery fluttered ahead, this time at a far more sensible pace. Devin was glad to have her, for without her he'd be lost in this weird forest. Worse, he'd have returned to Londheim without learning anything about whatever Janus had come to the Oakblack Woods for. Devin used his thick coat to protect against the scraggly weeds and briar patches they pushed through, and he stomped down a few of the weaker ones to allow Jacaranda easier access after him. Tesmarie, meanwhile, casually fluttered up and around every obstruction, seemingly clueless as to their difficulty in following her.

"Several times now you speak of us moving fast," Devin asked as he navigated yet another briar patch. "Yet to my eyes you are the fast one."

Tesmarie hovered at the other side of the patch, and she frowned and scrunched her nose as she thought.

"It's not that *you* move fast," she said. "Your *time* does. Mine is much slower, which to your eyes makes me seem like I move much faster than I do."

Devin rubbed at his eyes.

"That doesn't...I don't think I follow, little one."

The faery crossed her arms as she hovered up and down in thought.

"How about this...imagine two rivers. One is a rapid current. The other is a slow, steady trickle. Put a leaf atop the water of each, and it will move with the speed of the current. In the rapid current, the leaf will vanish quickly. In the slow, you will follow it with ease. Does this make sense so far?"

"It does."

"Now imagine that the two rivers are in fact the same river. Time moves fast for you, like the rapids. Time moves slow for me, like the steady trickle. Pretend my words and actions are like the leaves, easy for me to follow, but fast for you in your rapid pace."

Devin tried, he really did, but this felt more like something Tommy would love to argue about over a campfire. As far as Devin understood it, time was time, equal and fair to all who lived upon the Cradle. He decided to let the matter drop and instead focus on not getting scratched to pieces by the briar patch. Dozens of yellow flowers hung from long vines at the end of the patch, and Devin dipped his head beneath and thankfully emerged with only a single scrape across the back of his hand. He shook his coat to loosen a few broken, clinging branches.

"This is far from my first time within the Oakblack Woods," he said. "Yet I recognize none of these plants."

"None of them?" Tesmarie asked from up ahead. "How strange. So even some plant life vanished with us."

Devin glanced over his shoulder to check on Jacaranda. The woman walked with rigid spine through the patch, not even bothering to push aside the branches scraping across her legs and thighs. Devin winced, fearing how many cuts he'd need to attend to once this business was over. Sending a soulless with no sense of self-preservation into a dark, cluttered forest seemed like a cruel punishment in hindsight. Just one more wonderfully wise fuckup he'd made on this entire trip.

"Be careful," he said. Unsure if Jacaranda would understand or know how to obey the simple command, he decided to elaborate. "Do not get pricked by thorns if you can avoid it."

Jacaranda turned her attention to her legs and arms, carefully obeying his command. With her attention downward, she walked straight into the yellow flowers hanging from the vines. Powder exploded out of their bell cups, and it shimmered black in the forest air. Panic spiked through Devin's veins as Jacaranda gagged, her face immediately swelling.

"Jac!" Devin screamed.

He held his breath as he rushed to her side and yanked her free from the patch. She tumbled to the ground, her lips a frightening shade of blue.

"Oh no, no, no no no-no-no-no," Tesmarie said. She zipped

to Jacaranda's side. "Why didn't you duck? Those are poisonbells, those are bad, bad-bad-bad. Devin, lift her up, do it, do-it-do-it-do-it!"

Devin slipped one arm underneath her shoulders and the other below her knees. Where were they to go? Whatever poison-bells were, the speed with which their pollen took effect was beyond any toxin he'd witnessed in his years as a Soulkeeper.

"Need time, more time, more time," the faery said. She clenched a fist, summoning her moonlight blade into existence. Devin met her gaze and saw steeled determination worthy of a being ten times her size. "Don't move. I need to carve a rune upon your forehead."

"What for?" he asked.

"For her!" Tesmarie cried. "No time, stay-still, stay-still!"

She landed atop his nose, her wings softly fluttering to keep her balance. Her blade cut shallow grooves into his skin. Devin clenched his jaw against the stinging pain and kept his carefully trained muscles still. Tesmarie knew what she was doing. She had to, for otherwise Jacaranda would die. The blade carved a circle first and then sliced and cut seemingly at random within that circle. No blood dripped down his face. Did the blade burn and not cut? He dared not ask, lest he disturb her concentration.

Tesmarie finished cutting whatever symbol she wanted, released her fist to disperse the blade, and then clapped her hands together.

"Chyron enthal tryga!"

Her palms slammed into the center of his forehead. It felt like a house dropped atop him. Devin gasped as his mind performed cartwheels. The sounds of the forest slowed. His body became molasses. A deep part of him shrieked against the wrongness of everything, and he feared it would break his mind completely, leaving him a drooling fool to starve and die in the middle of the Oakblack Woods.

Devin closed his eyes in an attempt to regain his bearings. His eyelids obeyed, but it seemed ten minutes passed before they fully shut. His chest moved to inhale. The cool air flowed like honey down his nostrils to his lungs. Half an hour passed between the first beat of his heart and the second. Words calmly slid into his ears, each one an interminably long drone with a mountain of time between them.

"Too....

far ...

too ...

far ...

come…

back…

Devin

come…

back…
to me, Devin!"

Devin's mind slammed into his body and restarted at normal speed and pace. He gasped in a breath of air and opened his eyes. Things were returning to normal, at least somewhat normal. Tesmarie hovered before him, relief mixed with urgency on her dark features.

"Oh, thank the dragons you're here," she said. "Quick, quick, follow me."

Devin lurched to his feet. Waves of disorientation assaulted him. It took a moment to recover, and once he had, he spared a glance at Jacaranda. Her face was fully swollen, the tip of her tongue pressed out between her blue-tinted lips. She wasn't breathing. Wait, no…she was, only slowly. Very slowly. Devin looked around, realizing for the first time just how much had changed. A yellow leaf fell from one of the trees, its descent a slow, graceful weave back and forth. It fell less than a foot over the course of several seconds. Tesmarie's wings were no longer an imperceptible blur but a beautiful rainbow of colors reflecting off the clear chitin.

"What have you done?" he asked. His voice sounded strange to him, deeper, flowing like water yet echoing repeatedly in his ears.

"Slowed your time," she said. "Like me. Like the trickling river. Now stop dallying and run!"

Devin shifted Jacaranda's weight in his arms and then followed Tesmarie as she flew through the trees. The air felt sticky against his skin. The grass crunched beneath his footfalls, and it remained pressed low after his passing. A soft wind blew through the trees, creating a steady, comforting roar above his head.

"Where are we going?" he shouted.

"Not far."

The vegetation thickened as the ground sloped downward. Devin used his shoulder to brush aside a low-hanging branch. When it slipped off it did not spring back immediately. Instead the leaves shifted like a dance, tilting away from him as the branch slowly straightened.

More brush beat at his arms and legs. Thorns cut holes in his trousers, and he had no choice but to endure. The ground's uphill slope intensified, more branches formed a wall in front of him, and then at last Devin broke through.

A pond sparkled before him. Dragonflies hovered over it, their slow hum mixing with the croaking of a hidden frog. Tesmarie pointed to a flat spot beside the pond.

"Put her there, but do not let go!"

Devin set her down, careful to keep a hold of Jacaranda's hand. He had no idea what magic surrounded him, nor why he must keep contact with Jacaranda, but he wasn't willing to risk putting the woman's life in further danger. Tesmarie hovered several feet out, frowning at the water as she drummed her fingers against her chin.

"Two minutes should do it," she said. "I hope."

Devin watched mesmerized as the faery extended her right leg and then twisted about. Her foot carved across the water. The ripples spread at a snail's march. Tesmarie danced and danced, drawing a strange, circular rune atop the water's surface. She was a wonder amid this frozen canvas.

Is this the world she lives in? Devin wondered. She'd grumbled that humans passed through time too quickly. Seeing everything so calm and slow, he now understood her analogy with the rivers. Mundane movements gained a sense of fluidity. The twisting of leaves was a gentle ballet. Flying insects moved in careful circles he'd not noticed before. Even the ripples of water took on a hypnotic quality.

"Drink!" Tesmarie called to him. Devin startled, his concentration broken. "Have her drink!"

The runes on the water glowed with a sudden pulse of purple light. Devin reached his cupped hand into its center and lifted it. The liquid ran down each side of his palm like tiny waterfalls, leaving drops in a stalled rain as he brought his hand to Jacaranda's lips. He used his other hand to carefully pry open her mouth and pin her tongue to her jaw. The opening was small, and so much water had already spilled free of his palm. Devin prayed it would be enough. He lowered his wrist and twisted it, sending a crawling stream past her blue lips and across her swollen tongue.

A soft pink sheen flashed across Jacaranda's pale features. Devin opened his mouth to question it but his words died on his tongue. The color had started to return to Jacaranda's lips. Her chest heaved up and down as she violently struggled for breath. The swelling dwindled. Her face calmed. Last came a single cough expelling a cloud of black powder from her lungs, which Tesmarie turned her back to and blew away with her wings.

"What magic is this?" Devin wondered aloud.

"Not now," Tesmarie said. "This won't feel good, but if you stay like this any longer you might not ever leave."

"What do you..."

The faery snapped her fingers. A thunderous explosion of sound assaulted his ears. Jolts streaked up and down his spine like a wave crashing over him. Devin let out a confused gasp and then it was over. The world returned to its normal speed and time its normal flow. Jacaranda looked up at him, perfectly healthy and perfectly calm as ever.

"I do not remember how I came here," she said.

Devin fought off a wave of nausea as he stood. His skin tingled, and it felt like his insides were rioting in protest of the sudden departure of magic.

"I'm not sure you'd believe me if I told you."

He offered her his hand. She ignored it and flipped up to her feet on her own. Wet soil from the pond clung to her back and rear. She showed no sign of caring.

"We must continue," she said. "There must be no more delays."

Devin laughed despite the growing pain throughout his every muscle.

"Indeed," he said. He turned to Tesmarie. The little faery looked relieved as she wiped sweat from her brow. "Thank you so much. You healed her."

"Yes and no," Tesmarie said. "She's better but I didn't cure her. Instead I made her like she was then and not now."

"'Then' as in before she breathed in the poisonbell's fumes?"

"Correct! About two minutes ago, to be exact."

Talking wolves. Corrupted black water. Time-controlling faeries. More and more it seemed the world was a waking dream, but there was nothing dreamlike about the intense ache in Devin's limbs.

"I feel like I sprinted a dozen miles," he said. "Is this... normal?"

"Your body is not meant to live in the world I live in," Tesmarie said. "I promise I would not have done it if I thought we had enough time. Poisonbells are aggressively lethal. Everyone knows not to touch them."

Devin brushed his forehead, and the symbol she'd cut there to enact her spell. "So will this leave a scar?"

The faery peered up at him.

"Probably. I didn't cut deep, but your skin is as sensitive as a flower petal. In case you're worried, the runic design is intricate and beautiful. Consider it a decoration."

"What do you think, Jac?" Devin asked. "How's it look?"

She spared a glance his way.

"It looks like you were wounded."

"Can't argue with that."

Jacaranda climbed up the wet slope away from the pond.

"No delays," she shouted over her shoulder.

"Always on point, that one." Devin dipped his head in respect to Tesmarie. "Would you lead us again, little one? It's clear we are in over our heads."

"Of course I will," Tesmarie said. A chipper smile lit up her face. "Always happy to help a friend, yes?"

"Yes," Devin said. He smiled back. "Friend indeed. Oh, and if you would, could you point out other obvious things that might kill us as we travel?"

Tesmarie winked at him before flying ahead of Jacaranda.

"You two are just so helpless, you know that? Well, you're under Tesmarie's care now. Trust me, and I'll lead the way!"

CHAPTER 20

Are any of these poisonous?" Devin asked as they walked through a flowerbed full of knee-high buttercups, only instead of a normal yellow their petals pulsed between red and purple as if a heart beat within their stems. Concentrating on all these strange new plants was proving increasingly difficult.

"Not those flowers," the faery said over her shoulder. "Though I'd still suggest not eating a winecup."

"Winecup?" Devin asked. "I assume named so because of their color?"

"Color? Oh no, no." She laughed. "Eat one of those and you will get completely sloshed in the bucket. I hear they're popular at human parties. Well, they were. I suppose not anymore."

"The songmother referred to a great sleep," Devin said, stepping over a long, thorned vine as thick as his arm. He tried tracing it back to the root but he never saw where they began. "And you've mentioned a similar sleep. What is it you mean by that?"

"I mean what I say, that we slept," Tesmarie said. "Hundreds of years, it seems."

"But where did you sleep? How did we not find you? And does that mean you existed upon the Cradle centuries ago, among our kind?"

"So many questions," the faery said, and she playfully zipped a circle around Devin's head. "Questions, questions, questions, but I'll answer as best I can. I say the Sisters banished us to a sleep because it's the closest thing that makes any sense. One day we were part of your world, and then the next we...weren't. We didn't die. We weren't undone. I was aware of time passing, but just...vaguely. Like the world was continuing in another room while I stayed in my bed and watched between naps."

Devin tried to imagine what that was like. Hundreds of years in slumber, with only a tiny sliver of understanding as to what happened around you. He remembered his conversation with Lavender, and her bemoaning the passing of time, and the deaths of all humans she'd known. How strange to think there was an age when these creatures had existed alongside them, however far in the past it might be.

"We were aware of your kind during your slumber," Devin said. "But only as stories and fables. Perhaps we knew those stories were true, once, but as time passed our belief in them faltered."

"Well, you believe in us now, right?"

She accentuated the question with a quick twirl inches away from his nose. Devin laughed despite the exhaustion and horrors of the day.

"Yes, little one," he said. "I'd be insane to deny it otherwise."

"How long until we arrive?" Jacaranda asked from behind them. "Master wished me to return quickly, and we already know the loggers' fates. This starlight tear is for your curiosity only."

"I came to discover why Janus attacked your camp," Devin said. "As far as I'm concerned, we're still learning why."

"It's fine, let the soulless one be cranky," Tesmarie said. "We're almost there anyway."

There was a village of faeries, according to Tesmarie. She'd insisted that the starlight tear was kept in a shrine, and that if they asked nicely they could view it.

"Are you sure we'll be welcomed?" Devin asked. He gritted his teeth as an oak branch scratched the side of his face. "A lot of magical creatures I've met don't seem very happy to meet me in return."

"Oh, I'm sure it'll be fine," Tesmarie said. "At least, I think, maybe, we'll-find-out-just-how-happy-because-we're-here!"

Tesmarie stopped before what looked like any other tree in the dark forest. He saw no homes or signs of life across its many branches. Devin knew the faeries were diminutive in stature, but it still seemed improbable that they housed an entire village inside the trunk.

"Are you sure?" Devin asked.

"Am I sure?" Tesmarie laughed. "You ask silly questions sometimes."

She flew to the center of the trunk and pressed her hands together atop a prominent knot. At once the bark split open like a curtain, forming a passageway inside. Devin's mind reeled. What he witnessed, the open space, sunlight, homes, none of it should fit in that impossible space.

"Follow me," the faery said cheerfully as she flew inside.

"Well, you heard the woman," Devin said to Jacaranda. "Best we not keep her waiting."

Devin passed between the bark, which formed an entryway a

dozen feet long. He didn't need to duck, which surprised him. Devin stepped out into a circular clearing that was hundreds of feet wide. Wooden walls stretched high above him, seemingly touching the blue circle of sky. Built upon either side of a dividing line of grass were stick and mud homes with leaves interlocked together to form their roofs. They piled onto one another, dozens and dozens, so that they filled all the space across the walls. Their similarity to doll houses sold at the Londheim markets was unmistakable.

"Hello?" Tesmarie called as she zipped through the air. "Is anybody...home?"

A soft gasp escaped her throat. Devin halted in the center of the village, dread swelling inside his chest. There was a reason no one had come to greet them. Lying beside his foot was a small faery similar in size to Tesmarie, only whereas Tesmarie's skin was a deep black this one was white like marble. The faery lay on her back with her neck tilted at an awkward angle. Scarlet blood stained her skin and leaf-sewn dress.

Devin turned and found two more lying beside one another on a rooftop. One was missing her arm. Another was missing his head entirely.

"What...what happened...what happened to everyone?" Tesmarie asked. She zipped from home to home, calling out names. "Jeshua? Seyna? Cassia? Poeme? Please...someone... anyone?"

Jacaranda joined Devin's side. He noticed that her daggers were in hand, and she gently turned them within her grasp.

"The village was attacked," she said.

"You soulless have a knack for stating the obvious."

"It is because I am confused as to by whom, or what."

Devin walked the dividing line through the village center.

He saw more bodies tucked into little corners, all slain with severed limbs or long cuts that opened up their insides. Now that he had time to study the structures, he saw that many buildings had their rooftops caved in or their walls punctured in half. Whatever was responsible for the assault had been viciously thorough. It didn't take long before Tesmarie abandoned her search for survivors and floated to the ground in the village's center. Tears rolled down her cheeks and plinked like diamonds upon the smoothed bark. Devin went to her, and he knelt down so she might hear his softened voice.

"I am sorry, little one."

"It's awful," she said. "I was here just yesterday and everyone was alive. They were alive, and happy, and beautiful-and-wonderful, and now, and now, and now-they're-dead-oh-dragons-help-me-I-don't-want-this-I-don't-want-to-be-alone."

She bawled into her hands. Devin sat on his knees and quietly waited. He wished to comfort her, to offer her some sort of embrace, but given their difference in size he had not the slightest clue as to what would be appropriate. So he waited, keeping an eye out for whatever monster had slaughtered the faeries. There was something that confused him, but he did not want to broach it just yet. After a minute her tears slowed. Her breathing calmed, and it looked like she'd regained some measure of control over herself.

"Sorry," she said, as if she had anything to apologize about.

"Tears are most appropriate for a sight such as this," Devin told her. "Do you think you can talk now?" She nodded. "Please, I hope I do not offend, but I must ask. These faeries, they do not look as you do."

Tesmarie sniffled.

"I'm an onyx fae, and my friends here, they were alabaster fae.

They took me in after…after I left my other home. They were so kind, Devin. They wouldn't hurt a bug or worm, not even the icky kinds. Who would do this?"

"It could be the Janus person whom we have followed," Jacaranda offered. Devin shook his head. Something about that felt off. Whoever this Janus was, he'd shown great pleasure in killing and mutating humans, whereas he'd brought a gift to the fellow human-hating songmother. Nothing about this felt like Janus's style, not the target, not the apparent method of killing. He couldn't discount it, though. Perhaps the fae had not turned the starlight tear over to him, and he'd punished them in return?

"Tes, you said the starlight tear was kept in a shrine. Might you show me where?"

"I guess," she said. Her wings fluttered to life. "This way."

The shrine was at the far end of the divide, nestled up against and into the wood barrier. Its construction was noticeably more detailed and ornate than the surrounding homes, and little colored stones hung from string tied to its rafters. Tesmarie pointed inside, but because Devin towered over the building, he could see nothing.

"In there," she said. "I was told it was sacred, a shard of an actual star that fell to the Cradle. It should be—"

Tesmarie's scream was Devin's only warning. The roof blasted open, and from within the building shot a blur of shadow the size of a cat. Devin dropped to one knee and brought up his sword. The shadow struck the steel, and despite its small size, Devin felt the impact of a tremendous weight jar his elbow backward and twist his shoulder. As quickly as it'd attacked it leapt away, slamming into the wooden barrier a dozen feet off the ground.

"What is that thing?" Jacaranda asked.

"No clue," Devin said. He raised his pistol. "But it needs to die."

There was no substance to the creature's body, not even a fluid one like smoke. It was an absence of light, a void where space should be. Its back legs and tail were feline, but its front paws were more akin to human hands. Its six fingers dug into the wood with ease despite having no claws. The creature bore no head, no neck, no visible eyes or ears. How it sensed them, Devin could only guess, but it clearly could tell their location. The moment he raised his pistol it dodged aside. He tracked it to another curve of the wall, not pulling the trigger until it momentarily halted.

The flamestone's eruption thundered in the clearing. The bullet hit the monster square in the chest...and then bounced off with a high-pitched *plink*. The monster tensed, its body turning directly toward Devin.

"Well," said Devin. "Shit."

He dove aside as the creature lunged through the air. Its hands and legs scraped grooves into the ground upon landing, halting its momentum so it might leap again. Jacaranda took advantage of its distracted focus and lashed into its hindquarters with her daggers. They left shallow cuts, and if they drew blood, Devin saw no sign of it. He brought his sword up, his legs tensed to defend. If it turned on Jacaranda he'd flank it. If it went for him, he'd hold it back and pray his sword was enough to deflect its bizarre body.

The monster did neither. After a quick swipe to force Jacaranda back, it stood on its hind legs, vibrated like disturbed water, and then split itself in half. From the lower half a feline form sprouted to match its hind legs, coupled with a catlike face and paws. Its eyes were ghostly shadows. The other half shriveled slightly, its mass traveling downward to become a childlike abdomen and legs. From the top half sprouted a small head with the features of a newborn babe. It blinked its ghost-light eyes and smiled at Devin.

"Three bodies, one soul." It spoke with a deep resonance, the words coming from both cat and child. *"Disappointing."*

The cat dashed toward Jacaranda, the child toward Devin. He swung his sword, embedding the blade an inch into its side. The blow only nudged it slightly off course, and nothing halted its momentum. The blade sliced along its side as it continued onward, leaving a small trail of shadow blood. Its fist slammed Devin's knee, and he screamed, fearing the kneecap shattered. How could it possess such power?

Devin rotated, his other knee connecting with the monster's face. It felt like kneeing a stone wall. The thing slid back a step, the space enough for Devin to bring his sword down across its neck. He pushed every scrap of his strength into it, for he knew the longer the fight went on, the more likely he would suffer another blow to something far more vital than his knees. The blade cleaved down into its body, halting just above its waist. The monster squirmed and struggled, somehow still alive.

Horror fought against Devin's concentration. He wanted it away from him. He wanted it dead. Twisting the blade, he flung the thing across the clearing. The monster child rolled across the ground, its body plowing through several of the faery homes. When it came to a stop it pushed itself up to its knees. Its separated halves lashed toward one another with long, black syrupy strands. Two faery corpses lay near it, and it grabbed one in its little six-fingered hand and raised it to its mouth. Rows upon rows of shimmering cobra teeth grew from its gums. A single bite ripped the faery in half, and it chewed with obvious satisfaction.

"So you can heal," Devin said as he limped across the distance. "Good to know."

It swallowed down the other half and then snarled at Devin like a wild animal. In return he shoved his sword straight into its open mouth and down its throat. It bit the blade, its cobra teeth shattering. Devin shoved it down harder, telling himself to ignore its form. It wasn't a child. It wasn't a helpless babe. Just a monster needing to be killed. He pushed until the tip of his sword pierced out from the small of its back. When he ripped his sword free multiple pieces fell to the ground. Long, shudder-inducing strands still connected them like veins or ligaments.

Devin gave them no chance. He hacked at the strands, at the chunks of the void, hacked and cut and stomped on every little piece until it seemed a puddle of darkness had splashed across the grass. Soft wisps of white smoke rose from its surface, and to his relief he saw the darkness evaporating away like water in high summer heat.

A cry behind him spun him about. The other half! He readied his sword to aid Tesmarie and Jacaranda, but he need not have worried. Tesmarie swirled around the creature as a black-and-blue blur, her moonlight sword shredding line after line into its skin. Jacaranda merely played the distraction, stabbing at its sides whenever Tesmarie fled away. The thing's strength was clearly waning, while Tesmarie's sword seemingly pulsed longer and brighter with her growing fury.

"You killed them!" she shrieked as her moonlight blade ripped a massive gash across its feline nose. "You-killed-them-you-killed-them-youkilledthemyouawfulhorriblemonster!"

She moved so fast Devin could not track the faery's movements. It just seemed like an aura of blue-white light surrounded the horrid creature, and then it collapsed in a shower of void shadow. Tesmarie hovered above it, panting with exhaustion. Diamond tears fell like stardust from her eyes. Her hands went limp. The blade vanished. Her wings barely kept her afloat.

"Is it dead?" she asked, her voice strangely slow and detached.

Devin sprinted so he might catch her as she fell. He cradled her little form in his palms. She looked so broken, both physically and mentally, that it pained Devin's chest.

"Why does she lie there?" Jacaranda asked. "I see no injury."

"Not all injuries are inflicted upon the flesh," Devin said. He raised Tesmarie higher and shifted his fingers so she leaned upward against them. Her eyes fluttered open. A soft smile spread across her onyx face.

"Oh, did I fall?" she asked as she wiped the tears from her face. Devin realized they were actually dry like dust upon his skin, perhaps truly made of diamond as they seemed. "Silly me."

She rose to her feet but instead of flying away she hovered the short distance to Devin's shoulder and sat upon it.

"You don't mind, do you?" she asked.

"Of course not."

Devin turned to Jacaranda. The soulless woman had just finished cleaning her daggers and slid them back into their sheaths.

"Are you injured?" he asked her.

"My fingers are bruised, my hands contain multiple cuts, the nail is half missing from where you removed it..."

Devin winced at the recounting of what he'd forced her to endure while digging the dead child's grave.

"Wounds needing to be tended to immediately," he interrupted.

Jacaranda shook her head.

"I endured no significant injuries during the fight."

With the apparent threat taken care of, that left the shrine where the monster had emerged from within. Devin walked over to inspect it. With the shrine's destruction upon the monster's arrival, Devin had no trouble kneeling down and examining where the starlight tear had been housed. He brushed aside a few broken pieces of torn wall and then recoiled.

A wriggling line split the air in the heart of the shrine. It was as long as his forefinger, as thin as an eyelash, and seemingly composed of pure shadow. The way it moved, it was as if it bore no substance. It was a rip in the world itself, a scratch on a painting or a crack in a sculpture.

"Have you seen anything like this before?" he asked Tesmarie. The faery shook her head.

"What do you think it is?" she asked.

"The stars are our protection from the void's eternal desire to swallow the light of our souls," Devin said. "I may be wildly off the mark, but that seems like a tiny little sliver into the void itself. I'd wager the monster we killed came from within."

"What made it appear, then?"

"Maybe removing the tear from the shrine?" He started to shrug, then halted, worried he might unbalance the faery on his shoulder. "I don't know, and I sure as shit don't like that Janus is now in possession of it. If it has any connection to the void, then its power shouldn't be in the hands of a lunatic with a passion for slaughtering humans."

It seemed there was little else to learn. He wished he could banish that strange line, for what if more monsters escaped through? A horrible thought, but at least out here in the woods it was far from civilization.

"Tesmarie, I would not leave the bodies of your kin in such an ignoble state," he told the faery. "Have your kind a funeral ritual we might perform?"

"We bury them," she said. "Granting our life back to the earth and stone from which we came."

"Then burial it is."

He had no shovel, not even a spade. Thankfully the ground was soft beneath the grass that divided the village, and it tore easily when he stabbed it with one of his spare daggers. Tesmarie fluttered away to give him space while Jacaranda watched.

"This will take..." she started, but Devin immediately interrupted her.

"It will be done," he said. "No questioning it."

Jacaranda's face twitched ever so slightly.

"Very well," she said. "Shall I assist you to speed up the process?"

He thought of her digging into the earth with her hands and shuddered.

"No," he said. "You've dug enough graves. Leave this to me."

It took about an hour, but at last he dug what he believed to be a large enough grave. Next came a thorough search of the homes, with Tesmarie helping to point out any bodies he might miss. One by one he laid the little faeries in a row. They looked like stiff, beautiful dolls, and it pained Devin to think of what this village had been like before the monster of the void had torn them asunder. It must have been a wonderful place, full of life and buzzing dragonfly wings. Such a pity he saw only its quiet, hollowed ruin.

When the last were laid to rest, Devin poured the dirt back over the bodies, burying the alabaster forms beneath a layer of dark soil.

"I would pray to the Sisters that they show mercy and bring their souls to the heavens," Devin said awkwardly. "But I do not know what gods or goddesses creatures such as you pray to, nor if you have souls to take."

"The dragons made us," Tesmarie said. She'd perched back on his shoulder, and she'd spent the past ten minutes sniffling as she watched the familiar faces added to the pile. "And the dragons will take us. You...you can pray if you want, though. It'd make me feel better."

Devin lowered his head and whispered a simple prayer to Anwyn. Perhaps it was improper, asking a human goddess for a magical creature's aid, but in his heart it felt right.

"Be with all of us here, Anwyn, both the living and the beloved deceased," he prayed. "We are all in need. Grant succor and comfort to us living, and your love and mercy to the dead. To those in this grave we say good-bye, but only for a time, for we shall meet once again."

Tesmarie dusted his collar with diamonds, but when he glanced her way she was wiping her eyes and smiling.

"You're pretty good with your words," she said. "For a human, anyway."

"I try my best, little one. I hate to ask another favor of you, but might you lead us out from the forest? So much of the woods has changed that I fear my tracking skills may not be reliable."

Tesmarie meekly nodded.

"I will," she said. "But only on one condition."

"What is that?"

"You let me stay on your shoulder. My wings could use the rest."

"A fair deal," Devin said, and he weakly smiled despite the horrors of the day. "Consider yourself always welcome at my side."

CHAPTER 21

I never thought I'd be so happy to see the sky," Devin said as their trio emerged from the woods to the edge of Oakenwall.

"It's especially beautiful at sunset," Tesmarie added. She fluttered off his shoulder. "Though I doubt you humans can see all of its colors."

Devin couldn't imagine what other colors might be hidden within the yellow, orange, and red streaks painting the sky, but he didn't doubt her, either. Ever since the arrival of the black water it seemed each day offered a new reminder of their ignorance to the world.

"So what will you do now?" Devin asked the faery. "I must return with Jacaranda to Londheim and report what we found. You are welcome to come with us, if you feel it will be safe."

"Safe?" she asked. "Why would Londheim be unsafe?"

Devin suddenly found himself awkwardly trying to answer.

"Because humans are frightful, superstitious people," he said. "And I do not know how they will react to seeing one such as you."

Tesmarie fluttered her wings and bit down on her lower lip. Her eyes bounced between him and the forest. She'd been subdued ever since leaving her village, her chipper tone replaced with a solemn, dignified pain.

"I...no, I'll be fine on my own. Just fine. You stay safe without me, you understand? No more running into dangerous forests, breathing in poisonbells, and almost being a songmother's dinner. Bye-bye Devin. Bye-bye, soulless one."

Tesmarie hovered backward toward the trees. There was no hiding her hesitation. Devin waved good-bye and then started for the empty logger camp. Jacaranda, who had stood silently during the entire exchange, suddenly spoke up.

"Her usefulness outweighed her distraction. It is better if she remained with us."

"Can't argue with you there," Devin said. "But it's not our choice."

The first thing Devin did was check on their two horses. They were still inside the fence, and he retrieved a bucket from the nearby workshops, filled it with water from the trough, and ensured that both drank their fill. When that was done he returned to Jacaranda, who had not moved from her spot in the middle of the camp.

"We're staying here until morning," Devin said as he began the process of building a fire. "Consider it an order not to argue or object. We both could use a long night's rest."

Jacaranda wordlessly accepted the order and began calmly examining the cabins one after another. Devin was vaguely aware of her as he lit and then carefully kindled his fire. Right now he wanted nothing more than a freshly cooked meal, and the squirrel he'd shot on their way out of the forest would do nicely. Jacaranda returned to the fire carrying a long stick wrapped in a discarded shirt. She lit it like a torch and then left without explanation. Devin assumed she was lighting the fireplace in her chosen cabin. He kept the spit turning, his mouth drooling at the smell.

Several minutes later Jacaranda emerged from a cabin and sat down beside him.

"Find one you liked?" he asked. Sure, soulless were terrible at conversation, but he'd decided that wouldn't stop him from trying. Better to pretend Jacaranda was a normal human than going on as if she were a thoughtless doll.

"The cabins are equally hospitable."

"If they are all equally hospitable, how do you pick which one to sleep in?"

"I have not picked."

Devin frowned at her. "Then why..."

He looked to the cabin she'd entered and immediately swore. Smoke billowed from its windows. Devin lurched to his feet despite knowing it was already too late. Flames licked the curtains and seared the walls. What in the Goddesses' names could he do about it? Put it out? With what? He looked to Jacaranda, confused, and then remembered the orders she'd revealed to him.

Do ensure Nathan Evart's survival. Burn his home if he is missing or dead.

"Who was Nathan Evart?" he asked.

Jacaranda sat beside the cook fire and stared at the roasting squirrel.

"I do not know."

"How did you know that cabin was his?"

"Master told me what to look for."

"What did he tell you to look for?"

"I am not to say."

Of course not. Devin hadn't the strength to force the answer out of her. She'd cracked earlier and revealed her current orders, but pressuring her harder to betray Gerag might lead her to fighting back. That, and he was just plain exhausted. It had been one very, very long day.

"Forget it." He pulled the spit free from the fire and set it aside to cool. "Let's just eat."

They finished their meal in silence. They drank from their water skins, then refilled them from a giant trough that collected rainwater. Twice Devin heard the buzzing of insect wings and looked about earnestly. A dragonfly the first time, a large beetle the second. His disappointment contended with his relief. The people of Londheim were still acclimating to the presence of the crawling mountain. How might they react to an onyx faery zipping to and fro?

The sun completed its descent by the time Devin decided to pack it in. He called Jacaranda over and re-dressed the bandages on her fingers. The swelling had reduced somewhat, and so far he saw no signs of infection. Couldn't hope for much more than that.

"Since you burned that one down, I figure you can bunk in one of the others," he told Jacaranda as he finished wrapping the last of her fingers.

"The weather is not a danger," she said. "I will sleep outside."

"A bed will be more comfortable."

"My comfort is irrelevant so long as I do not injure myself."

Devin sighed. It might not be safe sleeping under starlight beside the forest. What other bizarre creatures might lurk within? If plants could talk and manipulate, what of the insects? He shuddered at the thought. If a wasp started speaking to him, he'd put a bullet through its body. His mind could only handle so much change. The last thing he needed were the bastards of the insect kingdom explaining why they were about to sting him to death.

"Do as you wish," he decided. "I'll be in that cabin over there in case you need me."

"I will not," she said.

"You never know."

The cabin Devin chose was the smallest of the lot, containing a single bed, a crudely built dresser, and a locked chest underneath the bed. No doubt the key was lost somewhere among Janus's many victims. Devin surrendered its contents to the mysteries of the universe and climbed atop the straw mattress. He collapsed onto his back and let out a long groan. Damn did it feel good to lie down. Devin used his bedroll as a pillow, closed his eyes, and whispered his nightly prayer to the Sisters.

The reaping hour arrived. Devin's eyes snapped open. He'd hoped that his exhaustion would allow him to finally sleep through it. No such luck. As always he felt the shiver in the air. The world grew unnaturally quiet. Grumbling against the cosmic injustice, he flung off the thick blankets and made for the door. The cabin was well insulated, and the blankets combined with the fire he'd built left him coated with a thin layer of sweat. A brief walk in the cool night air sounded divine while he waited for the moment to pass.

It took him a full second to understand what he saw, for it made no sense. Piercing the clear night sky was a thin white line. It was close, so close, and almost like ...

Devin sprinted barefoot to the center of the camp, his fears confirmed by a beam of light rising from Jacaranda's head. Her eyes were closed, her body stiff. The symbol of the three Sisters shone translucent blue across her forehead.

"No, no, no," Devin said. What happened? How had she died? He fell to one knee, repeating the words of the reaping ritual.

"By Alma, we are born. By Lyra, we are guided. By Anwyn, we—"

A soul shot through the pale beam, but it did not travel up to the heavens. It traveled downward, piercing through the glowing symbol on her forehead and vanishing with a tremendous crack. Air blasted outward, knocking Devin off his feet. He watched from his rear as the beam vanished. The reaping hour came to its end, and to mark its passage, Jacaranda sat up in her bedroll and shrieked at the top of her lungs. There were no words to it. No form. Just long, meaningless, overwhelming shock and horror.

"Jacaranda?" he asked. Her scream buried his words. Her eyes were open. Her fingers clawed the flesh of her face. Devin grabbed her blanket and tackled her into a makeshift cocoon. His strong arms pinned her hands at her sides, preventing her from damaging herself further. Jacaranda screamed, and screamed, each one a little bit weaker as her voice cracked and she gasped for breath.

And then suddenly there were words within the mindless howling.

"Let me go," she shrieked at the top of her lungs. "Let—me—go!"

Devin released the bundle of blankets and limbs. Jacaranda

thrashed away from him, tripped over her own feet, chose to crawl. Once on the other side of the fire she spun about and scooted farther until she could rest on her hands and knees. She looked like a wild animal frightened for its life. Devin slowly held his hand out to her. He kept his words gentle in hopes of preventing further alarm, but that soothing calm in his voice did not match the panic in his heart. This was unprecedented. A child of the Goddesses lacking the soul Alma was to deliver upon birth, a tattooed and claimed soulless, was now awake. Aware. Alive.

"It's all right," he said. "I wasn't trying to hurt you. I just wanted to restrain you before you hurt yourself."

"Don't touch me," she said. Her fingers clasped the hilts of her daggers. "Don't come near me."

"I'll stay right here," he said. His pulse pounded like two drums on either side of his neck, but he clenched his teeth as a way to focus. Panic would harm them both. Had to stay collected, puzzle this out.

Jacaranda stared at him, her gaze never leaving his. The silence grew heavy. After a time she started to look bewildered. Her hands shook. Her head twitched as her eyes widened with alarm. Color started to drain from her face and neck. Devin watched, frightened and unsure, until he realized what was happening.

"Breathe, Jacaranda," he said. *"Breathe."*

She sucked in a single ragged gasp, and that intake of air shuddered through her like a jolt of lightning. It seeped back out through her lips slowly, and was then followed by another deep inhale. Each inhalation looked like it absorbed her entire faculties, her shoulders pulling back and her chest thrusting out. The color returned to her lips, and her body's shakes lessened. Devin sat down and patiently waited it out, for it did not take long before her breathing came naturally.

"Th-th," she said. He tried not to react. It was like watching a child grow leaps and bounds in mere seconds. "Thank you."

"You're welcome," he said, as if he'd actually done anything. He smiled at her to hide his own panic. "Are you...are you all right?"

"I—I don't—what?" she said. "What do you mean? Physically? Mentally? No, Devin, I'm not—I'm not—damn it, this is, this is..." She was starting to cry. "I don't...do I sit? Stand? My words, who chooses them? I'm fine. Not fine. Lies. I can lie. I can lie?"

"Stay calm," Devin said. He'd encountered many people having undergone a recent trauma, and he relied on that experience to help Jacaranda through. "Focus on one thing at a time. Breathe in, then breathe out. Place your hands where you'd like them to be. Breathe in, breathe out. Sit how you feel comfortable. Breathe in, breathe out. Close your eyes, or leave them open, whichever you want. In, then out."

He watched her do as he said with frightening intensity. What could she possibly be feeling? To regain a soul after a lifetime without, did that make her a stranger to her own body? Her own *life*? Jacaranda's tears swiftly vanished as she followed his commands. When at last she was calm, she looked at Devin and asked a simple question with a million possible answers.

"What am I?"

Devin swallowed hard.

"I don't know."

Her lower lip trembled.

"That's not...I don't want to hear that. Please. Tell me an

answer. I . . . I don't think I care if it's true. Inside me, I feel it, this . . . this need."

"All right," Devin said. "I will explain as best I can for how I understand it. Maybe that will help you. Alma did not deliver your soul to you when you were born. Instead it was given to you mere moments ago, and it seems to have . . . awakened you in ways I cannot hope to understand. You lived your previous existence through basic survival instincts and a strict need to follow orders. Right now, you're making decisions for yourself. I'm sure it's overwhelming, to say the least."

Jacaranda shifted more to a sitting position, the fire still between them. Time passed, tense and quiet. Was she analyzing his guess? Debating her future? He couldn't imagine the chaos within her mind. There wasn't a way to know without asking, but it felt like patience was vital if he wished to help the woman through this ordeal.

"Might we talk?" he asked after a several minutes.

"I cannot stop you from talking," she said.

"It's not *my* voice I wish to hear."

Her eyes flicked his way, and he could not read the emotions they held. After a moment's hesitation, she nodded.

"Go ahead."

Devin decided to go with the most pressing question on his mind.

"What do you remember?"

"All of it," Jacaranda said. Her eyes stared into the fire and refused to budge. "My memories are my own. I remember the sounds, the sensations, even the reasons I made decisions. They happened to me, only I feel as if I wasn't . . . there for it. I don't know how to explain so you'll understand. It's like I stepped into a stranger's life, only it isn't a stranger. It's me. Every bit of it."

"So it's like a dream?"

She frowned and looked confused.

"I don't know, Devin. Perhaps? I have never dreamed so I cannot compare."

There was another strange idea he figured the Wise would be interested in. Were dreams connected to souls? If so, did that lend greater importance to their meanings? Devin tapped his fingers together as his thoughts raced.

"How do you feel when you look back on, well, your life before tonight?" he asked. Jacaranda seemed to be steadily growing more sure of herself, and he hoped to keep her talking. Each answer grew more thoughtful, and the muscles in her arms and legs slowly relaxed.

"I walked through my life perfectly numb. Dulled. I never felt emotions. I never chose an action, I merely...acted. If someone insulted me it meant nothing. If they touched me, kissed me, I never responded with anger or guilt or pleasure..."

She was staring at her fingers. The bandages he'd wrapped them in.

"No matter how much it hurt," she whispered. "I did what I was told."

Devin's guilt gnawed at him with renewed vigor. His petulant anger had meant her suffering.

"I'm sorry," he said. "For keeping you awake that night, for making you dig until you bled. It was wrong of me. One day I pray you will forgive me."

"You're not the only one who needs forgiveness." She turned her hands before her as if studying them for the first time. "I killed a child. I took his life, and I felt nothing. He wasn't the first. Am I a murderer, Devin?"

"No," he said. He stood on instinct, his anger pushing him

to his feet. Jacaranda slid back two steps and pulled one of her daggers halfway out of its sheath. "No, you're not a murderer. You never chose to take a life. The blame isn't yours, Jacaranda, and neither should you bear the guilt. Others gave you orders. Others trained you to be what you are. Let them bear the responsibility."

Jacaranda stared at him, and he met her gaze without flinching. Everything within her was a swirling vortex of emotions. Her gaze hardened, and her rage was so naked and unrestrained it frightened him. She leapt to her feet and grabbed her pack from the ground beside her.

"You're right," she seethed. "Another *was* responsible."

And with that she trudged on the path northward.

"Wait, what are you doing?"

"I'm going to Londheim," Jacaranda said. She spun on him. "I'm going to find Gerag, and I'm going to shove a dagger so far down his throat he shits steel."

"You're far more evocative with your language now," he said. She glared death and fury his direction. "Sorry, sorry. I make bad jokes when nervous or confused, and right now, I'm both."

"I don't care about your confusion. I know what I want to do, and so I'm going to do it. Gerag treated me like I was his doll. His precious little doll. He deserves what I shall give him."

"I'm sure he does," Devin said. "But this isn't worth your life."

"My skills are more than enough to handle the likes of him."

"That's not what I mean. Gerag isn't some lowly dockworker. The church will investigate. I'll be brought in for interrogation and forced to lie to keep you safe, a task I might fail. Soulless who commit murder are *executed*, Jacaranda. You just regained your life. Don't throw it away."

"Then I shall explain," she said. "I'll prove I'm no longer

soulless. I'll tell them of all he did to…to…" She looked away, her entire face and neck matching the color of her hair. "I'll be doing Londheim a favor. How could anyone execute me once they know I've awakened?"

"Because you're terrifying!" He didn't mean to shout. He was afraid she would leave. "Do you know how many soulless are within Londheim alone? How many are servants for the wealthy? Over one hundred are city guards. Even the church has their soulless custodians. The idea of them waking, feeling, behaving human, it…it's too much. And if you're the first, they might decide you're an oddity best eliminated and never spoken of again."

"But I'm not soulless," she said. Her face was a heartbreaking mixture of fury and despair. "Doesn't that matter?"

"It does to me," Devin said. "But I am not the rest of the world."

Tears trickled down to her chin. Her feet rooted in place. Her gaze bounced between the northern horizon and Devin's campfire. Bandaged fingers traced across the chain tattoo upon her neck.

"Will the world truly be so hostile to me?" she asked. "To what I am?"

"I don't know," Devin said. "But it'd be a cruel fate for you to awaken now only to spend the last of your days in a cell or fleeing bondsmen."

Jacaranda wiped away her tears.

"Cruel," she said. "As if nothing else in my life has been cruel?"

He winced as if she'd thrust a needle into his heart.

"I know. I mean, I don't know. I know nothing of this, what

it means, and how you feel. I'm overwhelmed, and surely you are, too. Please, at least sleep on this. That's all I ask."

Jacaranda crossed her arms and looked away. Devin held his breath as he waited. He would not force her to stay. For good or ill, Jacaranda's life was now her own.

"I'll decide come morning," she said. "Good night, Devin."

And with that she marched to one of the nearby cabins and shut the door behind her. In the sudden silence Devin lifted his eyes to the heavens and raised his palms.

"What the fuck, Sisters?" he asked. "Just... what the *fuck*?"

If Jacaranda were the only one to awaken, her life would forever be in danger. If all other soulless awakened, violence and chaos would follow. No transition from slavery to free people would happen without blood. It'd be for the best, he knew that, but the situation had surely arisen because of the Sisters' failure to deliver the souls in the first place. Why the delay? Why the sudden return? What did either mean to his faith in the Sisters' divine nature? Questions without definitive answers, and he'd only drive himself crazy chasing solutions in his mind.

He returned to his cabin, but sleep was slow in returning. When he awoke the next morning, he did so with a pounding headache and a tightly clenched stomach. Devin dressed and relieved himself, groggily wondering what in Anwyn's name he would do about the situation. A tiny part of him hoped it had been a strange, vivid dream. That part of him was a coward, though. Easier to hope it had never happened than deal with the difficult consequences.

He saw no sign of Jacaranda, so he lit a fire to cook their breakfast. The flames helped chase away the last of the morning's chill. Devin kept his eyes on the door to the cabin Jacaranda had slept in. Had she already left for Londheim? He wouldn't blame her for abandoning him, especially after his stunt with the child's burial. Hopefully she stayed out of trouble if she did. Even if she hid her tattoo, she posed a memorable figure. If one of Gerag's servants or acquaintances saw Jacaranda on the street and identified her...

The cabin door opened. Devin sat up straighter, his heart racing with sudden nervousness he could not explain.

Jacaranda emerged looking like a completely different person. Her fiery red hair was carefully cut at a length close to the chin. She must have raided spare clothes from all of the cabins while he slept, for every piece appeared different. She wore a red oversized shirt, untucked and hanging past her belt. For her trousers, gone were the soft brown cloth, replaced with a pair of sturdy blue breeches that stretched all the way to her ankles. What he guessed to be the remains of a white shirt was ripped and torn into a makeshift scarf wrapped tightly about her neck, obscuring her chain tattoo.

The brown of the coat, the burgundy shirt, the blue breeches, the white scarf, all slightly off and clashing. It reminded him of when a toddler learned to dress oneself. His absolute favorite part of her new ensemble was the tall, wide-brimmed hat settled atop her head. A smile blossomed on his face the moment he saw it.

"I was right," he said. "You do look good in hats."

Jacaranda looked momentarily taken aback.

"Are you mocking me?" she asked. She removed the hat and held it before her. "Do I look foolish? It's big for me, I know, but I saw it and loved it and..."

Devin slowly moved as if to avoid startling a frightened animal. His hands closed around the brim of the hat and gently pulled it from Jacaranda's fingers. He set the hat atop her head and turned it so its silver buckle was centered above her face.

"If you love it, then wear it," he said. "You're dressing for yourself now, not anyone else."

Jacaranda smiled at him. Her violet eyes shone, and he saw her truly happy for the first time in perhaps her entire life.

"So I will," she said. It seemed she caught herself. Her arms crossed over her chest and she backed a few safe feet away. "I spent the night thinking. For now it seems reasonable for me to trust your advice. You were...kind to me. After I buried the child, you apologized. No one has ever apologized to me, no matter how terrible their actions. You even looked away when I..." She blushed a little. "Stood naked before you."

Devin awkwardly coughed.

"Yeah, that was, um, a thing."

"Don't think you're fully forgiven," she said. "The blisters on my fingers hurt way too much for that."

"Sounds fair." He glanced northward, imagining Londheim in the far distance. "Are you still angry with Gerag?"

"I am," she said. "More than you could possibly understand. What keeps me calm is the freedom I now possess. To dress myself this morning. To look over clothing and decide if *I* wished to wear it. Imagine wearing a blindfold your whole life, and then one day someone rips it off. Nothing can compare. I have spent my whole life dying of thirst, and now I drink of limitless water."

"Try not to get drunk on it," Devin said.

"You cannot get drunk off water."

Devin laughed.

"I see we still need to work on our analogies and metaphors."

She blushed, embarrassed. He tried to playfully smack her

shoulder to show he meant no offense and immediately regretted it when she took a step back. It wasn't a matter of trust, either. He recognized that instinctual reaction, that twitchy fear of another's touch.

He hasn't paid.

"Your hair's a big change, too," he said, pretending not to have noticed her shy away. While she processed her trauma, he'd give her a cautious amount of space. "Why did you cut it?"

"Because Master hates..." She caught herself. Visible revulsion shuddered through her. "Because I wanted to, and so I did."

Nice. Two dumb, awkward things in a row. He was really on a roll this morning.

"Well, I've cooked us up some grub," Devin said. He gestured to the cook fire. "Eat up, and then we can get on our way."

She walked to the fire and stopped just shy of it. Her gaze lingered on the bowl of porridge mixed with honey he'd prepared for her. She bit her lower lip in thought.

"Something wrong?" he asked.

"I was deciding if I wanted to eat it," she said.

"And?"

Jacaranda shot him a wink as she plopped to her rear, grabbed the bowl, and began wolfing it down.

"I've decided I do."

CHAPTER 22

Is that the last of them?" Faithkeeper Sena asked as Adria shut the door behind her.

"In a sense," Adria said. She pulled off her mask and wiped sweat from her brow. Her long dark hair stuck to her forehead, and she used her fingers to pry it away. "A few more sought potions I simply do not have. They didn't sound content with only prayers, either. They're loitering outside the entrance. I don't have the energy to force them away."

"Then I'll do so for you when we're done here," Sena said. She leaned back in her chair. The two were inside the Faithkeeper's private room, drinking in the quiet and solitude after another hectic day in the church. "I have something to ask, though. A silly thing, really, but it's been digging at me all day."

Adria twirled the mask between her fingers and looked away. Had the older woman sensed something amiss? Or would she reprimand her for not putting her whole heart into serving the people?

"Your prayers," Sena said. Adria's heart immediately spiked with panic. "You're reciting them wrong."

Adria tugged at the collar to her dress, wishing she could have something less cumbersome and hot to wear, such as Sena's expertly tailored suit.

"Am I?" she asked. "I'm sorry. The exhaustion must be catching up with me. I'm not surprised I fumbled a word here or there."

"You're not fumbling," Sena said. She leaned back in her chair and clicked her long fingernails together. A hint of worry snuck into her voice. "I've listened closely now. Every single prayer, no matter which you offer, you have changed a word or dropped a verse. You've been my Mindkeeper for too long, Adria. I know you can recite each and every one of Lyra's Devotions from memory. Void's sake, you could probably list their possible variants from old Orissian translation. You're erring, and on purpose, but for the life of me I cannot decipher why."

Adria finally met the other woman's gaze. She wasn't a good enough liar, and Sena was far too experienced at reading others, for her to deny the truth. Her best bet was to rely on the Faithkeeper's trust in her.

"I am erring," she said. "But it is for my own reasons, and I swear to you, they are important. I...I don't feel comfortable explaining why, nor safe to do so. Not yet."

Sena frowned at her.

"Does your faith waver during these trials?"

"No," Adria said, more forcefully than she meant. "No, please, my faith has never been stronger. This world is different now, and I'm doing what I know to adjust. Will you allow me my little secret?"

The Faithkeeper's eyes narrowed.

"This was merely a matter of curiosity," she said. "But now you have me worried. Has something happened, Adria? Are you in danger?"

Loud knocking on the door interrupted the conversation before she might answer. Faithkeeper Sena rose from her seat, smoothed out her trousers, and then opened the door with a practiced stern expression on her face.

"Yes?" she asked, as if it would take a goddess waiting outside to justify her coming to the door.

Adria couldn't see outside but she recognized the voice that spoke.

"Forgive me, Faithkeeper. I know it's late but I must speak with Adria. It's important."

"What is the matter, Rosa?" she asked as she stepped around Sena at the door. The older woman backed away. Her hands twirled nervously together. Adria noted that she stood perfectly balanced on both her legs. If the knee she'd prayed over had regressed, she showed no sign of it.

"It's my friend," Rosa said. "Please, we need your help. She won't stop bleeding."

Rosa led them back to the pews. Only half were filled with sleeping men and women, a fact Adria was proud of. They'd spent hours setting up tents and residences for all of them, slowly giving the refugees a sense of home beyond the church. Most appeared asleep, or trying. By the door sat a younger woman with her back propped up against a wall.

"That's her," Rosa said. "That's Laura."

Adria crossed the room, Faithkeeper Sena trailing a few steps behind her. Her cranky mood quickly shifted to worry as she neared Laura. Sweat caked her hair to her face and neck. The woman's normally dark skin was visibly shades lighter. Tints of blue washed over her lips. She held a bloodied rag between her legs, her pale green dress stained with blood around the crotch.

"Hello, Laura," Adria said with cheerfulness she did not feel. "What's the matter?"

"The bleeding," Laura said. She sounded drowsy and eager for sleep. "Won't...stop bleeding."

"Were you cut?" she asked. Laura weakly shook her head. "Is this your flow?" Another negative shake. Adria gently lifted the woman's dress and took the bloodied rag away from her. Performing such an exam there in the entrance hall of their church was hardly ideal, but Adria feared to move the woman. The walk to the church looked to have drained what remained of her strength.

Sena arrived holding two candles; one she put beside the young woman, the other she held aloft. Adria examined as best she could, coming to a third question she feared to ask.

"Are you with child, Laura?"

Confusion put a bit of life into her drowsy words.

"What? No...I...I mean I could be, my last flow was three months ago, but..."

Adria gently pressed on the woman's abdomen. The muscles immediately seized, providing her with her answer. She replaced the rag, gently brushed her forehead with a clean hand, and then stood. The other two women gathered closer.

"I fear she's lost a child and it's taking her with it," Adria whispered. "There's nothing we can do but keep her comfortable and wait. If the body can pass it soon, she'll have a chance."

"Bullshit," Rosa seethed. "Heal her, Adria. You know you can. This is far more important than my damn knee."

Again panic snarled Adria's stomach. She'd not recited a single prayer perfectly since healing Rosa's knee. The potential consequences for wielding such a power were far too much for her to grasp. The people might revere her as a saint or bury her as a monster.

"Rosa," Adria hissed. "You promised."

"Promised what?" Sena asked. She held her candle like a sword, her free hand crossed over her chest. "Speak quickly, Mindkeeper. This woman is dying."

"Adria can heal her," Rosa said, turning her attention to the Faithkeeper. "She did it with my knee, and she can do it with Laura. All she has to do is pray, that's it, just fucking pray."

"Don't tell tales," Adria said. The lie passed poorly off her tongue.

"What, are you scared?" Rosa asked. She jabbed a finger toward her. "Fine. Be scared. Let her die."

"You can't put this on me," Adria said. She felt like a cornered animal. "I didn't cause this. I'm not Lyra. Her life wasn't born into my hands."

"Her life is in your hands *now*, Mindkeeper, so save her or let her die. Either way, it's on you."

Sena's eyes bored a hole into Adria's skull.

"I pass no judgment," she said. "Not without understanding. But if you know a way to keep this young woman alive, I expect you to do so."

Adria didn't want this responsibility. She didn't want this gift. The world was frightening enough. Why must people live and die by her faith? Must her prayers to the Goddesses bear fruit in such a physical, immediate way? Let others wield miracles. She just wanted to make her little corner in Londheim a better place.

In the end, her desire to help others won out. Selfishness could not withstand her guilt, nor her sense of duty. Adria pulled her mask over her face and knelt before Laura. The mask's comforting separation solidified her decision. So be it. Doubting it now would only prolong the woman's suffering.

"Listen to me, Laura," she told the dying woman. "Hear the words I say and repeat them as best you can, all right? Can you do that for me?"

"I'll try," the woman more mouthed than said.

Adria fell to one knee and crossed her hands over Laura's abdomen. She closed her eyes and said good-bye to her old life. Once Sena saw her, things would never go back to the way they were.

"Lyra of the beloved sun, hear my prayer. Your children weep for your touch, and so I come, and so I pray."

The words flowed so easily off her tongue. Her doubt eased away. She'd run from herself since the crawling mountain's arrival. No more.

"Sickness fouls the perfection you created. Darkness mars the glory you shone upon us. With bowed head and bended knee I ask for succor. With heavy heart and weary mind I ask for blessing. This beloved soul requires healing, Lyra, my savior. Cleanse the sickness. Chase away the pain. Precious Lyra, at my touch, *heal this woman.*"

Laura let out of a soft gasp of air and then slumped. Adria pulled back.

"Is she...?" Rosa asked. Adria shushed her. She watched the young woman through the eyes of her mask. Color steadily returned to her face and lips. Her breathing deepened into that of a heavy slumber. When Adria removed the heavily stained rag, no more blood flowed.

"Let her sleep," Adria said. "As for you, go, and tell no one of what you saw."

Tears ran down Rosa's cheeks.

"You're a miracle, Adria. Thank you, thank you, thank you." She flung her arms around her neck. "Goddesses above, thank you for sending her to us."

Rosa placed a kiss atop Laura's forehead and then exited. Adria stood in the darkness, her mind receding deeper and deeper behind the white and black of her porcelain mask. She waited for Faithkeeper Sena to address the miracle, her heart steeled against whatever she might say. So far, the woman revealed no emotion beyond intense concentration.

"My room," she said. "Now."

The two returned to Sena's room, the older woman leaning against the door with arms crossed as Adria sat atop the bed. Adria felt weirdly guilty, like she'd been caught doing something inappropriate by her schoolteacher all the way back in seminary.

"How long?" Sena asked.

"Since the crawling mountain arrived."

"And how many times?"

"Just the one time with Rosa's knee," Adria said. "I haven't tested it since."

Sena locked their gazes. Adria couldn't look away if she wished; the other woman's forceful personality was too strong. Even the mask was meager comfort.

"Is this why you've been erring with your prayers, to prevent these miracles from occurring?"

Adria nodded. Silence fell between them. She didn't know what to say, and Sena looked lost in her own mind as she struggled to understand. One thing worried her above all else, and she finally gave it voice.

"Will you tell others?"

The Faithkeeper ran her hands across her temples to the back of her shaved head, as if pulling away phantom strands of hair from her face.

"I don't know. You saved a life tonight, Adria. How many others might you save if we make your gifts public?"

"And how many investigations will the Keeping Church launch?" Adria asked. "How many will shift their faith from the Goddesses and onto my own self? What of the other Faithkeepers and Mindkeepers? How many will doubt their faith and compare it to my own? My prayer came true the moment the mountain crawled to the gates of our city. What if... what if this power I have is not of the Goddesses?"

"Is that what bothers you the most?"

No, ashamed as she was to admit it, something else bothered her worse. Sena was her friend, and a fellow servant of the Sisters. If she could tell anyone, it had to be her.

"I'm not a fool," she said. "If my prayers heal at a touch, then I bear a gift of tremendous importance. If they truly are blessings from the Goddesses..." She closed her eyes and imagined the separation between the world and her true self deepening behind her mask. "The greater the gift, the greater the task. Whatever fate they set before me, I am terrified of it. I'll stumble. I'll fall. Anointed prophets and healers don't live long lives, Sena. They die abandoned and alone, as martyrs and madmen. How do I embrace such a fate?"

Adria let the quiet tears fall behind her mask. She'd bottled up this fear from the moment her hands lifted off Rosa's knee and she saw clean, healthy skin. Night after night she'd prayed that other members of the church showcase the same talents. Anything to make her less special. Anything to reduce the burden awaiting her.

Sena put a hand on her shoulder, then pulled her in for an embrace. Adria closed her eyes and accepted it, but her hands stayed at her sides. She felt too numb to return Sena's gesture.

"I will think on what I have seen and heard," Sena said when she withdrew. "As for you, stay at your brother's house for tonight. Get away from Low Dock and its people and its refugees. Focus on yourself. A well that runs dry is of no use to anyone."

"If you insist," Adria said.

"This world is not ending," Sena said. "It's enduring birthing pains, but a new one will emerge. You'll help guide us to our first steps, Adria, I promise you."

Adria smiled behind her mask.

"I wish I had that same confidence."

Adria exited the church, and the moment the doors closed behind her she breathed out a long sigh.

"A penny for a poor woman, keeper?" A voice spoke from the dark, startling her from her thoughts. A woman lay beside the bottom steps, her dirty hair long and gray. "Or maybe a silver penny if you're feeling generous?" she added.

"I have nothing to give," Adria said. "Come inside if you need shelter and food."

The woman smiled, revealing multiple missing teeth.

"Too loud. Too crowded. Here suits me just fine, miss keeper. I'll buy what I need."

Adria pulled several copper pennies from one of her pockets and placed them inside the woman's eager palm. She knew she should discourage begging at the church steps, but to the void with it. The woman likely needed alcohol or herbs to sleep the night away, and given the amount of misery in the world since the black water's arrival, she had no desire to judge.

"Stay warm," Adria said before hurrying down Low Dock's familiar streets. Candlelight shone in the occasional window. Lanterns hung from sparsely placed poles, rare enough that she mostly walked by starlight, and she drank it in with greed. There was a reason she'd become a Mindkeeper and not a Faithkeeper. Some people fed on companionship, conversation, and noise. She was drained by it. Fantasies of her future blinked in and out of her mind. In some she was revered as a holy prophetess, men and women eagerly awaiting hours for her touch. In others she knelt atop a platform awaiting the executioner's axe while crowds called her a heretic and a Ravencaller.

Adria passed a cramped shed built in the space between two homes. A drunk man stumbled from the door. He laughed when he noticed Adria watching from the corner of her eye.

"Pleasant nights t'ya," he said.

"The night may be pleasant, but if you don't sleep soon, your morning will not be," Adria said.

"Spare me the advice. I already got my fun, didn't I, girl?" The man tipped his hat before he disappeared down the street.

Adria glanced to the night woman standing in the shed's doorway, her body thinly covered by the blanket she held. Their eyes met. The woman slowly nodded, and she flashed a handful of silver before tucking it away. She was safe. No intervention necessary. Adria slowed her walk so the drunk man gradually faded farther down the street. She heard the loud *thunk* of the shed door closing behind her. Adria hoped that was the woman's last for the night. Too often such girls came to her in the mornings with bruises and cuts needing to be cleaned and bandaged. The violence of the buyers seemed to know no bounds.

A strange hooting pulled her attention to the rooftops. An owl, in Londheim? She couldn't quite place the direction, but she heard it again and again. Seeing the rooftops rankled her nerves. Gargoyles leered down at her from their perches. No matter how many times she told herself it was ridiculous, she could not shake the feeling that they watched her with their stone eyes.

The hooting abruptly turned into a screech, followed by silence. Adria froze in place. It had come from an alleyway to the right. Inaction was seductively easy. The reptilian selfishness of her mind urged her to let it be. Adria forced her legs to move. Someone needed her help. She sprinted down the road and then slid to a halt before the alley. A scream stuck in her throat and refused to release. Her hands shook at her sides. Her eyes spread wider than the holes carved into her mask.

A massive wall of white feathers huddled over the shredded carcass of the drunk man from earlier. Clawed feet dug into his body and stomach, pinning him to the ground. The creature's head curled over its shoulder and rotated ninety degrees to stare at her. Bleeding flesh hung from its coal-black beak. Wide yellow eyes blinked at her from beneath the perfect snow-white circle that was its face. Deciding she was no threat, it turned back to its meal. The beak scooped up a large part of the rib cage and ripped it free. Bones snapped and crunched with terrifying ease.

"That's not an owl," Adria whispered aloud, as if convincing herself. "It can't be an owl. Owls aren't that big. Owls don't hunt humans."

Her words stole back its attention. Adria's heart hammered in her chest. The creature swallowed down the rest of the bones and then spread its wings to reveal speckles of black feathers interspersed among the white.

"But I do," said the owl. "Shall I hunt you?"

The massive creature's claws clacked upon the stone as it took a step toward her. Each one looked the size of her forearm. Its beak was bigger than her head. Those enormous eyes imprisoned her. Was this what happened to mice when they spotted a snake? Her arms stretched out defensively before her as a desperate prayer of devotion tumbled out her lips.

"Blessed Sisters, I seek your protection. Bind the darkness so it may not touch my flesh. Show mercy so I may stand in the light."

It was the shortest of Lyra's Devotions, a prayer she'd whispered a thousand times when she first walked the dark streets of Low Dock and feared every set of watching eyes. The owl lowered its head upon hearing those words. *Clack, clack, clack,* the claws bringing it closer. Those eyes, she could not look away from those eyes! Every part of her mind screamed to run, but the thought would not travel to her legs. She could only stand there, arms up, lips stammering out prayers behind her mask.

"No Sisters," the owl said. Its wings spread wide, a single flap lifting it several feet into the air. "Just us."

Tears ran down her face. Her hands quivered like shaken rabbits.

"Blessed Sisters, I seek your protection. Bind the darkness so it may not touch my flesh. Show mercy so I may stand in the light."

Another flap and the owl surged toward her, its legs extending, its claws opening wide to grab her. Adria knew her death had come. Her final words were a most earnest plea against the terror of those claws and the pain they'd inflict while ripping her frail body apart.

"Show mercy."

An enveloping circle of brilliant gold light flared across the stone, lighting up the night as bright as day. The owl let out a single high-pitched cry as it slammed to a halt in midair. Its body shattered and twisted. Its beak cracked in half, its claws ripped, feathers and gore splashed outward. The warm fluid splashed across Adria's monochrome dress. Blood slid down her mask, dripping from the eye holes to her cheekbones. The circle around her faded away. The carcass instantly dropped into a disgusting crumple of feathers and bones. One eye was hidden behind a wing; the other remained locked open and staring at a wall. Their hypnotic spell broke. Her mind regained control of her body, and she used that freedom to drop to her knees and scream.

Adria tore her mask free from her face so she could retch. Her vomit joined the gore upon the earth. Cold sweat poured from her forehead and neck. Her heart felt ready to burst. She wiped at her mask, frantically cleaning off the blood with a scrap of her dress as if her life depended upon it. Once satisfied, she flung it back over her face and closed her eyes. She fell away from herself and into the carefully controlled persona of a Mindkeeper. Goddesses help her, she wanted to flee her body and go to a world where she hadn't just eviscerated a creature that shouldn't exist with the mere words of a prayer.

Seventy-nine devotions, she thought as she lurched to her feet and exited the alley. No doubt remained within her: All seventy-nine would be at her disposal. This went beyond healing. This went beyond everything. She'd already feared wielding the power of miracles to heal and bless. Now she bore the power of death. Adria leaned against a ramshackle home and crossed her arms over her body. The city guards needed to be informed and Londheim's people warned in case more owls hunted elsewhere. All things she'd do, in time. But not now.

"Please Alma, please Lyra, please Anwyn, pass this cup to another," she pleaded. The stench of blood filled her nostrils. She closed her eyes and imagined her mask as a wall between all the world. Only she and the Sisters remained. Silent. Alone, together. "I cannot do this. I can't. Please, Goddesses, I can't, I can't, I can't..."

CHAPTER 23

Jacaranda and Devin stopped just in sight of Londheim's gates so their horses might rest. The day was pleasant enough, the sun bright and warm on their skin as they sat upon the grass. Jacaranda hoped it'd be a foretelling of how the remainder of the day would go.

"You'll need to enter the city before I do, and on foot," Devin told her as they munched on the last of their rations. "Gerag will suspect something amiss if I return with a red-haired woman who somehow isn't his former soulless."

"I could disguise myself," she said. "Maybe hide my hair entirely?"

"There's no reason to risk it," he said. "Hiding your face or hair will draw more attention, not less."

Jacaranda shrugged. Until she got her feet underneath her, she'd rely on the Soulkeeper's judgment.

"What shall I do once I'm in the city?" she asked.

Devin crunched a nut between his teeth.

"Good question. I'd say make your way to my home and slip inside when you think no one is watching. If I give you directions, do you think you can manage?"

Jacaranda shot him an indignant look. Since she'd awakened he'd shown an annoying tendency to treat her like a child.

"My training included hours of poring over maps of Londheim, and my skills at stealth are better than yours. Yes, I think I can manage."

"Sorry," he said, lifting his hands in surrender. "No offense intended. It's just your first time inside the city as a free person. I don't know how that will affect you. The amount of people might be a bit overwhelming."

Jacaranda ate her own handful of nuts and washed them down with a drink. Better to eat than say something mean when Devin was just trying to help. Besides, as much as she didn't want to admit it, she *was* nervous about entering the city alone. At least, she assumed the fluttery butterflies in her stomach and the vise tightening around her lungs and throat was nervousness.

"I guess you're right," she said. "I'll humor you for now. If I'm to enter the gates alone, where shall I say I come from? And what name shall I give?"

Devin thought for a moment, a familiar look crossing his face. It was as if he receded into himself, the outer world vanishing so he might decide.

"Answer that you're from Ostenbrook," he said. "It's a small village far to the north. You're frightened by what's happening and came to Londheim for safety."

Not a bad idea. The reason also helped explain any nervousness or fear she might show at being discovered.

"And my name?"

He shrugged.

"It doesn't matter so long as you're consistent."

It was beyond weird to ponder something so unique as naming herself, even if it were just to fool some guards at the gates.

"How about...Anthea?" she said, figuring she'd stick with the flower theme.

"That'll work," Devin said. "Don't slip up, though, or it might lead to more questions."

"Then I won't slip up," she said. "But I cannot predict everything. What do I do if the guards discover my tattoo?"

The chain tattoo underneath itched with soft heat. She hated remembering its presence, hated everything it represented.

"If you try to enter the city and then flee upon discovery, Gerag will hear of the red-haired soulless who fled the gates," Devin said. His tone had stiffened. His eyes locked on hers with deadly seriousness. "If you don't run, the guards will bring you to the Mindkeepers for interrogation. At best they'll return you to Gerag. At worst..."

He drifted off.

"What are you saying?" she asked.

"I'm saying being discovered isn't an option. Once you approach the gates there is no backup plan. If that distresses you, then we can look into other, safer courses of action. We might find a smaller village to the east that hasn't been too adversely affected by this whole 'end of the world' thing. You could hide out there, just another refugee fleeing the black water."

Jacaranda shook her head. She would not flee from a threat. Londheim was where she needed to be. It was where her vengeance would be had.

"No," she told the Soulkeeper. "Gerag's reckoning is coming, and it will be at my hands. I'll make it through the gates unnoticed, I promise."

"Have you ever made a promise before?"

Jacaranda frowned, taken aback.

"No," she said. "I guess I haven't."

"Then don't start making them now unless you're certain to keep them." He dug into his pocket and pulled out a small iron key. "My home is at Seven-Five Sermon Lane. It's in a quiet neighborhood, so I suspect you won't have any trouble entering my house unnoticed. Don't expect me until late. I need to report the events at Oakenwall to my Vikar, which will be a long tale on its own. I'll also meet with Gerag and settle the official request for aid."

"What will you tell him?" she asked. The thought of seeing him again filled her with a mixture of anger and disgust.

"I'll tell him the truth, in my own way," Devin said. "The soulless woman who accompanied me from Londheim disappeared in Oakenwall, did she not?"

Jacaranda tipped her hat to him, and she smiled at his "truth."

"That she did," she said. "Good luck, Soulkeeper. May we both succeed with our lies."

Jacaranda traveled ahead while Devin waited with the horses. A strange sensation slowly settled over her as the distance grew between them, strange enough that she focused upon it. Alone . . . she was alone. She'd been alone before while soulless, of course, but now she was keenly aware of it. She stopped in place. There was no one to make her continue. There was no one to make her stay. If she so desired, she could return to Devin and refuse to enter Londheim. She could vanish and never see the Soulkeeper again. By the void, she could strip naked and run for the hills.

The more she dwelled on the matter, the heavier her feet became. No, there were far more options than that. She could twirl and sing. She could dig a grave with her hands. She could slit her wrists and bleed out, wasting the gift given to her. Whatever her mind could conceive, she could enact. Even the simplest act of breathing was a decision to be made. Faster, shallower, held for thirty seconds, blasted out in wheezy gusts. She'd been so focused on the larger decisions, things Gerag would give orders over, she'd overlooked the nature of the life she now lived. *Everything* was a decision. How wonderful, this overwhelming paralysis.

Jacaranda took a step toward Londheim, and did so because she wanted to find Devin's home. She breathed in and out with steady breaths, for she wished to remain alive. No, more than that. She found living suddenly wildly invigorating. The next minute she ran, pushing her legs to their limits. After that she ripped up some grass and inhaled its scent. To think she'd found joy in picking out her clothes and yet overlooked the complete control she had over every single *second* of her existence.

Her elation had mostly settled down by the time she neared Londheim's gated entrance. That unwelcome sensation of nervousness replaced it. She found herself repeating her new name and home over and over in her mind. Anthea from Ostenbrook. She was afraid of the changing world. Once inside, go to Seven-Five Sermon Lane. Anthea from Ostenbrook. Changing world. Seven-Five Sermon Lane.

The soldiers at the entrance had separated traffic into two lanes, with those entering the city forming a line on the left half. A bespectacled man with an enormous book and a stick of charcoal interviewed them before entry. Jacaranda tightened her scarf and took her place at the back of the line. Her insides squirmed, and with a mixture of fascination and horror she realized her breathing had become rapid and shallow. Jacaranda forced herself to breathe regularly. Perhaps not everything was reliant on her decisions. The beat of her heart, for example, or the tingling in her fingers as her line steadily moved forward. So strange to control one's body but also have it behave autonomously.

When it was her turn she stepped up to the two bored soldiers and the man with the book.

"Name?" the older of the two soldiers asked.

"Anthea."

The man with the book started scribbling, and after a pause, he glared at her. Jacaranda froze. What did he want? Was something wrong with her name? The soldiers looked annoyed with her, too.

"Full name, woman," the soldier added. "None of us have all day."

Piss. She hadn't thought of that.

"Anthea Flowers," she said, going with the first thing to pop in her head.

Anthea Flowers? Do you know how absurd that sounds?

She put a hand on her scarf, the chain tattoo beneath burning her skin. Upon realizing what she was doing she quickly dropped it back to her side.

"Anthea...Flowers," the man with the book said. The tone in his voice revealed his disbelief. "Search her bag."

She handed her pack over, which the younger soldier opened carelessly. There wasn't much left inside, just a change of clothes, tools to sharpen her daggers, and a bit of food. Nothing inside to directly link her to Gerag.

But of course, she forgot about the pack itself.

"This is nice leather," said the older soldier. "Very nice."

"Where are you from, Anthea?" the book man asked.

"Ostenbrook," she said.

He squinted at her.

"And where did a woman such as yourself obtain such a nice pack? Did you steal it?"

Think, think, think. Her current clothes were a mishmash of what she'd found at the logger's camp. They wouldn't believe her wealthy enough to buy such a well-made pack. She could claim she was a servant to one of the noble houses. She'd memorized their various names and symbols while under Gerag's control, but there was always the tiny chance the soldiers would look into that connection, especially after she'd made a fool of herself multiple times.

"It's not stealing if you take it from the dead," Jacaranda said. "Some well-to-do man and his family thought it'd be safe up north."

"I take it that it's not?" asked the soldier.

"Why do you think I came south?"

The soldier searching her pack shrugged and handed it back over.

"She's got nothing," he said.

The book man clucked his tongue at her.

"You should be thankful Mayor Gaunt is a man of compassion," he said. "I'd turn you away if it were up to me."

Then good thing it's not up to you, you smug bastard.

Jacaranda bit her tongue. The temptation to voice the statement aloud was much stronger than she'd anticipated. The guard tossed the pack back to her. She slung it over her shoulder and tried to hurry away.

"Wait," the book man said. "Have you anywhere to stay?"

Goddesses above, she was a terrible liar. She spun and decided to go with the truth.

"I, yes, a friend," she said, begging they would not inquire further. He rolled his eyes, marked something in his book, and then dismissed her as if she were an annoying insect. The motion humiliated her, but she was free, and she quickly vanished into the crowded streets of the city.

Londheim felt overstuffed ever since the crawling mountain arrived. What had once been clearly defined sections of prosperity and poverty were heavily blurred. In such a chaotic state it was easy to blend in with the refugees and simply wander. It took her twenty minutes, but at last she arrived at Sermon Lane. It was a quiet neighborhood, just like Devin had described, formed from a single road that curled around into a broken circle before coming to a dead end. The homes started in the sixes, so it didn't take long to find home seven-five. Satisfied that no one watched her from nearby windows, Jacaranda calmly approached as if she'd always lived there. She slid in the key, turned it, and stepped inside.

A younger man slouched sideways in a comfy chair beside the fireplace. He wore a loose pair of white drawers and a robe hanging open from his scrawny shoulders. In one hand he held a tattered book opened to a page near the middle. In the other danced three luminescent orbs slowly changing from red to blue to yellow. The young man was so entranced he did not notice her entrance until she cleared her throat.

"He . . . hello?" Jacaranda said.

The three orbs instantaneously vanished. The man flailed as if struck, dropped the book, and with the grace of a two-legged pig toppled headfirst off the side of the chair. His feet were the only part of him she could still see, the ankles resting atop the chair's arm.

Something deep inside Jacaranda erupted uncontrollably. Tears swelled in her eyes. Laughter, she realized, an act she'd witnessed a thousand times before. Nothing could stop it. She clutched a fist to her mouth but it did no good. When the man's head poked up from behind the chair, his neck as red as an apple, her laughter only worsened.

"I'm sorry," she said. "Please, I . . . I . . . I'm so sorry."

Jacaranda could barely control herself. This laughter, it felt so good, so freeing. The only reason she wished it to stop was so she could catch her breath.

"It's, um, quite fine," the man said. He glanced down at his mostly naked self and flailed at the robe until his clumsy fumbling resulted in something resembling a knot. "Devin didn't tell me we'd be having a guest over."

"He didn't know he'd have one until our way back to Londheim," she said. "It is nice to meet you . . . ?"

"Tomas Moore," he said after a pause. "But most people call me Tommy."

"Greetings, Tommy," she said. She tipped her head in respect while touching the center of her chest. "My name is Jacaranda. Devin has offered me a place to stay until things become more . . . clear."

"Yeah, that sounds like Devin all right," Tommy said. He scratched at his head and looked around the small, cluttered home. "Sleeping arrangements will definitely be tricky, though. I guess you can have the couch. A few pillows should do me fine on the floor."

"You don't want to share the couch with me?"

His entire body froze like a deer sensing the presence of a wolf. Giggles escaped Jacaranda's throat. Heavens help her, this was a problem. She already felt light-headed. Any more laughing and she might pass out. Tommy realized she was teasing him and narrowed his face into a cockeyed glare.

"How do you know Devin again?"

"I accompanied him to Oakenwall," she said, deciding that if Tommy lived with Devin, he must be worth some measure of trust. "What of you?"

"He's my brother-in-law."

"I see. How kind of him." Jacaranda knelt down and retrieved the book Tommy had dropped. "So what is it you were reading when I interrupted?"

The man looked ready to yank the book from her grasp, but every time his hands moved forward he pulled them back to his sides.

"Please, please, be careful, that book is *very* old and *very* important."

She skimmed the pages, most of it appearing to be nonsense. It wasn't nonsense, though, she knew that. Those three orbs shimmering in his hand were no worldly creation. Jacaranda offered him the book, waiting until he put his hand upon it to speak.

"Is this how you summoned those orbs?"

His fingers locked onto the leather cover.

"I, uh, have no idea what you're talking about. No idea. What orbs? Where did you see them? I was just sitting here reading, that's all. Been a rough week so I decided a cozy day beside Puffy would do me well."

And Jacaranda thought she was a terrible liar. Tommy had her beat by miles.

"Puffy?" she asked.

"Did I say puffy? I meant, um, stuffy fire. Yes. Nice and warm and stuffy. Silly you, imagining things I certainly didn't say or do."

What in the world was he blabbering about?

"Sitting by a fire does sound good, though," Jacaranda said. She removed her hat but kept her coat on, using the long leather as a sort of blanket to sit upon. Her scarf slipped a little as she sat. She quickly adjusted it and hoped Tommy had not noticed.

"So can I get you anything?" Tommy asked. "We're not exactly stocked with delicacies, but I could get you some water or raspberry wine."

"Water will be fine, thank you."

Tommy ducked into the next room, looking grateful to escape. Jacaranda pulled her coat tighter around her and stared into the crackling fire. She felt herself coming down from her high, a not entirely unwelcome sensation. Her awkward host returned with a large wooden cup nearly full to the brim with water. To her surprise, four chunks of ice floated in the center. She sipped the cool water as Tommy slumped back into his chair, his own tall cup of wine gently swirling in his hand.

"I'm glad you're here," she said. "It is much better to talk with someone than sit in silence awaiting Devin's return."

"I do try to be friendly," Tommy said. He smiled at her. "And my sis always did say I was the life of a gathering."

She took a larger sip. Her ice clacked against the wooden side of the cup.

"The ice is a nice touch," she said. "How did you get it?"

He winked at her slyly.

"That is my little secret."

"Just like those three orbs?"

He coughed on the wine he'd started to drink.

"I'm sorry, Jacaranda, but I doubt you'd believe me even if I did try to explain."

"Try me." Tommy shifted in his seat. She sensed he wanted to tell her, but something was holding him back. Shame? Fear? A vow of some sort? "How about this," she said. "A secret for a secret. Does that sound fair?"

His brow furrowed.

"I doubt you have a secret anywhere close to as significant as mine."

In answer she tucked her fingers into her scarf and gently pulled it down to reveal the chain tattoos across her throat. Exposing it left her feeling far more naked than if she'd stripped off her coat and shirt. Tommy's eyes widened upon realizing the mark's significance.

"That mark, that means you're, but you don't act like..." Tommy stopped to scratch at his head. "You're a soulless who no longer appears to be, well, soulless. That's a first, and not just for me, I mean, a first for the entire Cradle. Damn. You seem to be taking this change rather, uh, well."

"I am trying my best," she said, quickly lifting the scarf and feeling immediately better upon doing so. "But there is my secret. Care to share yours?"

He took in a long deep breath and braced himself as if expecting to be punched.

"I can cast magical spells."

Jacaranda had assumed as much just by those floating, shimmering orbs.

"Is that it?" she asked.

Tommy looked dumbfounded by her nonchalant response.

"You're not surprised?" he asked.

"Devin and I were nearly killed by a singing, man-eating plant. The only reason we lived was through the help of an onyx-skinned faery capable of manipulating time. Upon leaving the forest, my soul plunged from the sky into my body, awakening me. The existence of magic is not the biggest surprise of my week."

"Oh. Wow." Tommy gulped down the rest of his wine and

then grinned at her. "But now that you've teased me with that tale you'll need to tell the whole thing. More water?"

Jacaranda stared at Tommy's nearly empty cup. She'd never imbibed alcohol before, only witnessed its effects on others. There never appeared a reason for its use, given its detrimental effect on sense, reason, and dexterity. Now, though, she thought of herself overcome with laughter and wondered.

"I think I would like to try that wine after all," she said.

"Now that's the spirit! No, uh, pun intended."

He took her cup, left the room, and quickly returned with it half full of a dark crimson liquid.

"Have you ever had wine before?" he asked.

Jacaranda accepted the cup and took a tiny sip. Initially she tasted sweetness, and as she let it swirl across her tongue a strong tartness crept in. She swallowed, grimacing a little at a sudden hit of bitterness.

"No," she said. She took another gulp, enjoying the warmth this time as it traveled down her throat. The scent of raspberries lingered in her nose. "Not once."

"Then let's be smart and keep you at one cup," he said, eyeing her warily. "It can be a bit dangerous to drink wine so... eagerly."

Jacaranda drained the last of it, set her cup down, and then belched. The act was a perfectly normal bodily function, but strangely this time she felt embarrassed. Color flushed in her cheeks. This feeling, it was like a desire, and keenly focused on what someone else thought of her. Would Tommy disapprove of the belch? Was that why a tiny bit of heat built in her cheeks and neck? That was ridiculous, but she apologized for it anyway.

"Sorry," she said, surprised that it actually made her feel a tiny bit better.

Tommy grinned at her and shook his head, thankfully saying nothing. Jacaranda finally removed her coat, and she relaxed upon it with a satisfied groan. It felt so good to lie down and stretch her back after the hours on the road. She gazed into the fire as an airy tingle settled over her mind. The result of the wine, she assumed.

"Before you begin your story, I guess I should be honest," Tommy said. He gestured to the fire. "Though I'd say the final decision's up to you, Puffy. I think it's safe to trust her, but I also have a history of being completely and utterly wrong about people."

Jacaranda wondered, not for the first time, if Tommy might be missing a few pieces in the head. Who was he talking to? She followed his gesture and stared at the fire. The strangely flowing fire. The fire that formed a head and lifted up and blinked at her with two coal-like eyes.

Perhaps she was not as accustomed to the absurdity of the world as she believed.

"Hello?" she told the fire.

The head plopped back down and vanished. A long, curling strand of flame replaced it, the top spreading out to form five individual fingers. And then it waved.

The hand vanished, and the tiny little head reemerged, the black eyes peering at her expectantly. Jacaranda's chest warmed, and her mouth dropped open of its own volition. She reckoned her face looked similar to when she'd witnessed others playing with kittens they found in an alley or cooing over slobbery newborn babies.

"I *love* it. And its name is Puffy?"

A circle of smoke puffed up in response.

"I'm teaching it ways to easily communicate," Tommy explained. "A circle is yes, an X is no. Isn't that right, buddy?"

A fist emerged from the fire. Two of its fingers suddenly shot straight up in a recognizably rude gesture.

"It, uh, learned that one on its own."

Jacaranda laughed, finding it easier and easier to do with the aid of the wine.

"I am so happy to have met you," she said. "The both of you."

Tommy smiled at her, and he lurched to his feet as if reaching a sudden conclusion.

"Oh, piss on being smart," he said, grabbing Jacaranda's cup along with his own. "It's time for a refill."

CHAPTER 24

Walking the afternoon streets of Londheim felt undeniably strange to Devin. People were tense, more so than when he'd left. He passed boarded-up windows and broken statues, statues he didn't remember being there in the first place. Twice he found himself lost at a dead end, and no matter how certain his brain insisted he'd made no wrong turns, he could not deny the crowded walls and cramped homes blocking off his passage.

"This isn't the city you remember, Devin," he muttered to himself. This wasn't like with the black water. Things weren't rotted or breaking down. No, it felt like there was just *more* to the city. More buildings, more walls, more homes where there used to be gaps or little corners of grass. It felt like pieces of Londheim had also been hidden beneath a stone, and now he saw what had always been.

When he reached the Ellington mansion he was mildly surprised to see an armed guard standing beside the front door. The guard, a bald, copper-skinned man with a dark patch of hair below his lip, calmly approached. His sword swung loosely from the scabbard belted to his waist. More surprising was the long rifle hanging across his back by a leather strap. Firearms were not cheap, nor the flamestones required to operate them.

"What do you want?" the guard asked. All business, no charm. Devin pulled the moon-and-triangle necklace from underneath his shirt and showed it to him.

"I am Soulkeeper Devin Eveson, come to speak with your employer."

"Anyone can fake a charm."

Devin suppressed an impulse to roll his eyes and instead drew his pistol.

"And this?" he asked, the symbol of the Sisters flashing in the sun.

The guard stared at it a moment and then suddenly relaxed. He unlocked the gate and flung it open.

"Come in. I will inform Master Ellington that you are here."

He used the same key to unlock the front door, then gestured for Devin to follow. They passed through the garish rooms, the guard leading him to the same cramped parlor where he'd first met Gerag four days prior.

"You will wait here until he arrives," the guard said. He stood by the door, crossed his arms over his chest, and stared ahead as if Devin were no longer there. Devin took a seat in an overly padded chair and examined the guard. Something about his outfit seemed vaguely familiar. He wore long white trousers and a loose white shirt with a plunging neckline and short sleeves to showcase the girth of his arms. Most peculiar were his vibrant red shoes, almost like a calling mark . . .

"You're a member of the Faultless Eye," Devin said, making

the connection. For the first time the man seemed interested by his arrival. He dipped his head in respect and offered a faint smile.

"You are correct, Soulkeeper," he said. The Faultless Eye was a highly esteemed mercenary band known for their skill with firearms. Devin had never met one before, but he'd grown up listening to stories of their incredible deeds. One of his favorites had been of a pistol duel between a Soulkeeper and an Eye, the outcome of which always seemed to change depending on the storyteller. Sometimes the Soulkeeper won, sometimes the Eye, but most often their bullets connected in midair, with both accepting it as a sign from Anwyn their deaths were not yet nigh.

"Might I have your name?" Devin asked.

The man sized him up with his faint brown eyes.

"Tye the White," he said. Faultless Eyes forfeited their last names upon entering the group, with their new title recognizing their shooting accuracy when in combat. If he remembered correctly, white meant an accuracy somewhere in the high eighties. Green was the lowest at seventy-five percent. Any lower and you were removed from the mercenaries in disgrace. Their leader Anloch claimed the title "the Red" for having never once missed in battle.

"It's nice to meet you, Tye," Devin said. "I didn't know the Eyes made their way this far west."

"We go where the gold and silver demands," the man said.

"And I take it demand is high here in Londheim?"

Tye grinned at him. There was something unwholesome about that smile, and it turned Devin's stomach.

"The demand is high everywhere, Soulkeeper. Many believe

the world is dying, and they will pay a great price to stave off their perceived doom."

Devin drummed his fingers across the arm of his chair.

"Do you believe the world is dying?"

"Perhaps it is, perhaps it isn't," Tye said. "When the pyre consumes my flesh, is that not the end of all things so far as my own soul is considered? What does it matter then if the world continues or not?"

"So all that really matters is the coin?"

"And the things it buys, yes."

"If the world ends, your coin means nothing. Perhaps you should care a little bit, just in case?"

Tye spread his hands in a gesture of concession.

"That, or perhaps I should ensure that I die at the same time the world does."

The door opened and Gerag Ellington walked in with a huff. Devin noticed that his black hair wasn't carefully slicked back like before, and his shirt was only half-tucked into his trousers.

"Devin, Devin, good to have you back," Gerag said, sounding slightly out of breath. He glanced to Tye. "There's been an accident downstairs. Go clean it up for me."

"Of course."

Devin fought to keep his face passive as Tye left. An accident? Of what kind? Gerag plopped down in a chair near the fireplace and wiped his brow.

"Downstairs?" Devin asked casually, hoping maybe to pry a morsel of information.

"You saw what land I have to work with," Gerag said while waving his hand dismissively. "I built down as well as up. It's only prudent. But we're not here to discuss construction. What did you discover at Oakenwall?"

"Mr. Ellington, I must regretfully say that Broder was correct. None of your men survived Janus's attack."

Gerag brushed it off like a bad business transaction.

"Did you, uh, did you find anything interesting or of note inside the camp?"

An image of Nathan Evart's cabin burning to the ground flashed through Devin's mind.

"No," he said. "The camp was quite empty."

Gerag wiped at his unkempt hair, and he looked much relieved.

"Well then, I guess that's tragic but expected. Everyone's suffering lately, are they not? Say...where is Jacaranda? Why is she not with you?"

Devin hesitated. This was it. An unsuitable answer might leave him wondering. He hated lying, and did not consider himself good at it. There was, however, a way to dance around the edges, keeping unwanted information back. That skill he'd developed for years as a Soulkeeper. You didn't tell a dying person they were dying. You told them they needed to focus on resting and getting better. When you found the body of a missing child, you didn't tell the parents to what extent the child suffered. You speak of the heavens, and the everlasting nature of her soul.

"Jacaranda touched a plant I have not encountered before," he said. "Its pollen was poisonous, tremendously so. There was nothing I could do to help her."

Of course Tesmarie could help her, but no need to tell Gerag about that. The merchant slumped in his chair. His face reddened, conflicted between anger and sadness.

"So she's dead?"

"I'm sorry, Gerag. Your soulless ceased to be in Oakenwall."

Slightly strange wording, but he could not bring himself to completely lie. If only he could hide behind the mask his sister wore. Perhaps then he might more easily focus on the good the lie would bring.

Gerag's calm face crumbled with a sudden surge of rage. He bared his teeth like an animal. His eyes glistened with uncontrolled emotion. When he lurched to his feet he paced the floor as if unable to contain his energy.

"No. No no no. She was under your care, Soulkeeper. This is your fault. Yours, you hear me? This . . . this travesty is a debt you will never repay."

"I never requested her to accompany me," Devin said. There was no hiding his anger, nor his bitterness. "But don't worry. I'm sure you can buy another soulless at the sanctioned auctions in Nelme."

"Jacaranda was not replaceable!" Gerag shouted. "I don't want some other soulless I have to train from scratch. I want my damn girl back, you hear me?"

Dozens of his workers dead, the entire camp destroyed, and yet all he cared about was Jacaranda? His stomach twisted. His girl? What exactly was Jacaranda's role in this house? Her role with Gerag? Perhaps it was best he did not know. Knowing might result in him acting, and gutting the largest benefactor to the church would have him charged with murder no matter how he explained it.

"I'm sorry," Devin said. "But I cannot help you."

A frightening change swept over Gerag. The anger vanished beneath a calm, smiling façade. His hands ceased shaking, and he stood and met Devin's eyes with a firm gaze. Back in control. Back in charge.

"So be it," he said. "Rest assured the church will know of my displeasure in regard to your conduct. When I send a message, I send it loud and clear, and I send it with gold. The church will receive no pay for your services, nor will they receive my generous monthly donation until I feel I have been adequately compensated."

Devin's hot rage suddenly turned cold. He glared at the disheveled man, a look he normally reserved for rapists and murderers.

"Thousands of refugees are barely surviving on the graces of the Keeping Church," he said softly. "You would have them risk starvation because of your displeasure?"

"I'm sorry, Soulkeeper," Gerag said, gesturing to the door. "But I cannot help you."

Tye waited for him at the front entrance, his arms crossed over his chest, his back leaning against one of the two doors. Devin noticed that his rifle rested beside him. The mercenary did not move out of the way as Devin approached.

"I hope your meeting went well," Tye said.

"It did not."

Tye smirked. He didn't seem to really care. What he did seem to care about was impeding Devin's departure. When Devin reached for the other door, Tye slid to the center to block.

"Your pistol," he said. "Are you as good with it as people claim?"

Devin was in no mood to banter.

"Sometimes better, sometimes worse," he said. "It depends on the teller. Is there something you want, Tye?"

"We should have a contest sometime. A friendly one, of course, with no wager but our pride. I'd like to see what you are capable of."

"I don't play games."

Tye stepped aside, and his smirk took on a hard edge.

"A game doesn't stay a game if the stakes are high enough," he said. "Have a pleasant night. Never come back here again."

Devin shoved the door open and flashed a rude gesture with his fingers above his head as he walked away.

"Gladly."

The day dragged on forever, with Devin waiting over two hours before managing to interrupt his Vikar's busy schedule for a discussion about what he'd learned of Janus...which sadly wasn't much. The only conclusive thing they reached was that Janus wanted what Tesmarie had called a "starlight tear," and that he was considered Viciss's avatar of change. Anything beyond that was pure conjecture. Even worse, Forrest informed him that a Faithkeeper had been slain during his absence. It sickened Devin knowing he could offer little help in locating the demented bastard, and come the end of the day he wished for nothing more than to collapse into his chair by the fireplace. When he opened the door to his home he saw that fate would not be so kind.

"Tommy?" he asked. His robed brother-in-law stood in the center of the room, back to him, with his arms lifted up above his head. Jacaranda sat on the floor near the fire, laughing in fits. "What in Anwyn's name is going on?"

Tommy spun. His entire body locked in place like a frightened deer upon seeing Devin. The turn exposed what he'd been doing, but it only added more questions. A shape hovered in the air between him and Jacaranda. It shimmered and glistened a rainbow of changing colors, an otherworldly look for a very worldly creation: a limp penis with long, dangling balls.

Tommy's senses finally caught up with him, and he banished the image with an erratic flourish of his arms.

"I, uh, I—I—I learned how to make illusions," he said, as if that explained everything.

Devin shut the door behind him on instinct.

"So you made...that?"

"I challenged him," Jacaranda said. "I said, make the one thing you'd never have the guts to make." She stopped to giggle. "And so he did. You won, Tommy!"

She took a long gulp from a cup beside her. The red wine he saw within went a long way to explaining the situation.

"It seems so," Devin said, wishing he were just hallucinating it all instead. "And how did this happen?"

"Oh, I accomplished that by imagining an image and then saying the spell's words. It's simple stuff, really."

"That's not what I...forget it." He didn't need to know what resulted in this little absurdity. The alcohol was likely enough reason. Devin removed his coat and hung it by the door. Both resumed laughing, he presumed at his discomfort. A connection clicked in Devin's mind, and it was so ridiculous he couldn't help but turn to his friend and close the distance between them.

"You can conjure up any image so long as you imagine it?" he asked Tommy.

"Pretty much, yes."

"So...whose nether regions did you imagine?"

The deathly embarrassed look Tommy gave him was answer

enough. Jacaranda broke with laughter. Devin put a hand on horrified Tommy's shoulder and leaned in.

"I send Jacaranda here for safety, and upon meeting her, you get her drunk and then magically show her your penis?"

Jacaranda clutched her arms to her abdomen as she rolled, laughing so hard she looked like she might die. Tommy blubbered an incoherent defense that died out in seconds. He spared a glance at Jacaranda, and then gestured for Devin to follow him to the other side of the room, acting like he needed to share an important secret. Once sure Jacaranda would not overhear him he lowered his voice to a whisper.

"She's very pretty," he said.

"I'm aware of that, yes," Devin said.

"She's also weirdly dressed."

"Don't be rude, Tommy."

"I'm just saying, she's going to stand out in a crowd."

That much might be true, but all three Goddesses would walk the world before he admitted as much to his tipsy friend.

"Let's make a deal," he said. "How about we let Jacaranda worry about how she dresses, and you worry about whether you're casting spells for ridiculously improper purposes?"

Tommy gave him an off-kilter salute.

"Your wish is my command," he said.

"Good, now go get dressed. You're still in your robe from this morning."

He looked down.

"Oh, I am, aren't I?" Instead of leaving he squinted at Devin's forehead. "Hey, did you get a new tattoo or something?"

Devin touched the runic spirals Tesmarie had carved into his skin. Explaining would be a long story, one he wasn't yet ready to get into.

"Tommy. Dressed. Now."

"Right!"

And with that he trudged into Devin's room, where a second dresser contained Tommy's new clothes that they'd bought after his arrival at Londheim. The door shut. Devin removed his pistol and sword, hung them from several large hooks near the front door, and then sat with Jacaranda by the fire. She eyed him mischievously.

"I see you've made yourself at home," he said. "Did everything go well at the gates?"

"Mostly," she said. Now that her laughing fits had ceased, she appeared a bit more together. "No one saw my mark, if that's what you're worried about."

That was all they could hope for. Devin nodded, feeling suddenly awkward and unsure. He hadn't thought too far ahead when it came to Jacaranda's immediate future. He couldn't keep her cooped up forever, but every single trip outside would put her at risk. If only there were a way to remove the damn tattoo on her throat.

"Have you tasted wine before?" he asked, deciding to switch the topic to something more lighthearted. He'd had enough serious discussions for the day. Jacaranda tilted her cup and stared into the tiny puddle of liquid at the bottom.

"No one gives alcohol to soulless," she said. Bitterness crept into her voice. "No point to it."

"I'm sorry," he said. He wasn't sure for what, but it felt appropriate to say. Her stare never left her cup. She was agitated about something. Devin kept quiet, letting her decide whether to broach the subject.

"How did your talk go?" she asked. Her eyes lifted momentarily. "You know. With him."

"Worse than I'd prefer, but he didn't seem to doubt me when I told him you were deceased, so at least there's that."

That didn't seem to make her feel any better.

"He'll replace me. He won't want to, but he'll replace me. He always needs...he needs..."

She clenched her jaw tightly shut. Her emotions had been high when he entered his home, and they easily transitioned into sadness with the aid of the wine. Tears trickled down her face, and she wiped them away. Devin wished to hold her hand, or put his arm around her shoulders. He wisely did neither.

"Jacaranda, I want you to know something," he said. "I will never pressure you to tell me all he's done. If you'd like to talk, I will listen. If you'd like advice, I will offer it. All I ask is that you give me some time before you take any act against him. Can you do that?"

She nodded. Her knees pulled up to her chest, and she rested her head atop them.

"I don't want to think about him right now," she said softly. "I was happy. He ruins that."

"Fair enough," he said. "How about instead we start settling you in? While you're here, my home is your home."

"A home of my own," she said. Her original mischievous look returned, a welcome sight. "That sounds wonderful."

Tommy readily offered his couch to Jacaranda, insisting pillows and blankets would be enough for him on the floor. Devin gladly removed his boots from his aching feet and finally sat down in his chair. Tommy hustled about, already declaring where a new dresser and closet would go, and how they could divide the room for Jacaranda to have more privacy.

"You need somewhere to put your things, after all," Tommy said.

"My things," Jacaranda said. She spoke as if the words were dancing on her tongue.

Devin scratched the stubble growing on the side of his face and pondered. Jacaranda had only the clothes on her back and the daggers strapped to her legs and waist. At bare minimum she needed a few more outfits than the ragtag assortment she'd collected from the dead loggers.

"We'll go to the market tomorrow and pick you out an assortment of clothes," he told Jacaranda.

"I think . . . I think I'd like that," she said.

Everyone settled down, preparations ready. Puffy flickered and flared his body out, increasing the warmth of the fire. They chatted merrily, and Devin's stress slowly drifted away. After half an hour the door opened, drawing their attention. Adria stepped inside and removed her mask. The smile that had been forming on her face immediately retreated into caution when she noticed Jacaranda's presence.

"You have a guest," she said.

Devin lurched to his feet and crossed the small room to embrace her warmly.

"Thanks for coming, sis," he said.

"Who's the woman?" she whispered.

Devin wasn't sure the best way to explain everything. He barely knew where to begin.

"Jacaranda, I'd like you to meet my sister, Adria," he said, figuring that was a good start. Jacaranda shyly waved.

"Pleased to meet you," Adria said. "Might I ask how you met my brother?"

"We traveled to Oakenwall together."

Adria frowned as she pulled off her gloves and put them into hidden pockets. He could sense her unspoken question, and so did Jacaranda. Without any other explanation, Jacaranda took her scarf and slowly unwrapped it from around her neck. The dark chains shook from her nervous swallow.

"You're Gerag's soulless," Adria said, now even more confused.

"Was," Jacaranda snapped. "He doesn't own me. He never did."

Such a reaction was impossible for a soulless. Adria's mouth dropped open, and she struggled to find words.

"This...this can't be, Devin. The implications of a widespread awakening is...it's unfathomable. Are you certain this isn't an act Gerag taught her?"

Jacaranda looked ready to strike.

"I'm awake," she said. "I'm *here*, and you want to dismiss my existence as an act?"

Devin slid closer to Jacaranda and positioned his arm and shoulder between her and his sister.

"I was there," he told Adria. "I saw the soul enter her body during the reaping hour."

Adria gave him a tired, bewildered smile.

"And I thought I was the one with surprising news," she said. "I...Devin. What is that?"

The Soulkeeper couldn't help but laugh when he turned his shoulders. There in the window, looking almost ashamed with her arms crossed behind her back, hovered Tesmarie.

"That's a friend," Devin said. He opened the door, and the faery quickly darted inside. She kept beside his shoulder, quiet and nervous. Adria gaped in shock, but Tommy's reaction was far more welcoming.

"Is...is that a faery? Goddesses above, you're so pretty. Are those diamond eyes of yours real?"

"Of course they're real, they're my eyes," Tesmarie said, giving Tommy a strange look.

"Don't mind him," Devin said. "I'm surprised to find you here in Londheim. I didn't think you would follow."

"Well, I wasn't going to, but then...I don't..." She looked away. "I don't have anywhere else to go, and you did offer, after all, and-I'm-sorry-and-this-is-embarrassing-but-but..."

She abruptly fell silent. Devin thought of how he'd first found her, crying alone behind a tree, and he knew he would not leave her to dwell alone in sorrow. Whatever the reason she chose to come with him, he'd accept silently until Tesmarie broached the issue herself. His offer had been genuine, but first, he had one last thing to check.

"Do firekin get along with faeries?" he asked the fireplace. A ring of smoke puffed up in answer. "Then there's no decision at all. Tesmarie, consider yourself welcome in my home."

Tommy looked pleased as could be, but Adria froze in place as if seeing a ghost. Devin had to stifle a laugh. He'd forgotten that his sister hadn't been around various magical creatures as much as he had. As the faery zipped to the fire to introduce herself, Adria slid closer and lowered her voice.

"I assume you have a story to tell?" she asked stiffly.

"That I do," Devin said. "But not quite yet."

Devin ducked into his kitchen, found the nearly empty bottle of raspberry wine Tommy and Jacaranda had shared, and then carried it out with him to his chair. He plopped down with a satisfied sigh and looked around at the bizarre assortment of people and creatures he'd collected over the past few days.

"To new friends," he toasted, only somewhat sarcastically. "May we not be at each other's throats by the end of the week."

Devin threw his head back, closed his eyes, and drained the last of the wine.

"All right," he said, putting the bottle down. "Now where in Anwyn's blessed name do I even start?"

INTERLUDE

The Aeryal lifted one by one from the ground, forming an enormous circle encompassing the sleeping city of Londheim. Their heads bore two opposing faces. One looked upon the city while the other gazed to the wilderness. Their perfect stone bodies moved in unison, as did their thoughts. Their arms rose skyward in careful reverence. Unspoken messages flowed between them like a peaceful river. They stood on four muscled legs, each one facing a different cardinal direction. Stable. Noble. Unchanging like the thousands of words carved upon every inch of their bare arms and chest.

They were the keepers of the divine, the tongue of the Goddesses, and every single word was spread among the hundred.

"Protect the divine," they spoke in unison. "Preserve the divine."

One swayed to the left before returning straight. There was nothing special about that particular Aeryal, only that it was the first. The next in line did the same, followed by the next, and the next. That motion traveled the circle until it reached the original first, who then swayed to the right. Magic swelled within their carved words, and with each tilt of their bodies it flared. Back and forth. Back and forth.

The Aeryal closed their four eyes. Low rumbles escaped the throat of their rear faces, so deep only a few rare animals could truly hear them. The faces watching Londheim opened their mouths, and spoke their mantra with ever growing power.

"The divine is eternal. Let there be no barriers. Let there be no walls. All as one, one shared among all."

The speed of their swaying rapidly increased until none remained still. The infinitesimally small words carved upon their bodies shimmered. Crafted by Gloam and blessed by the Goddesses, the Aeryal wielded tremendous power, but with that power came a singular focus, incorruptible and ever-lasting. Together they began to speak, each one's words unique. One word per second. One hundred Aeryal. Six thousand each minute. For half an hour they swayed beneath the stars and bathed Londheim with their words.

At last their mantra came to an end. Their four legs sank into the earth. The twin faces closed their eyes, their minds already searching for their next destination. With their recent awakening they had found the world to be a massive, seeping wound. Words shared meanings. Local accents, once a tiny flourish of style, had grown like cancer so men and women could hardly understand one another. Foreign tongues bred mistrust and fear. These were deep cuts to the divine, irreparable if centuries more were allowed to pass.

The Aeryal would bandage the wound. They would clean up this mess of blood and verbs.

When the humans woke the next morning they would notice nothing different. The words inside their minds had been tweaked and bent with the skill of expert thieves. Their mangled divine was now pure. Their speech was perfect truth, as had always been, as would ever be. Memories would mold to fit the new accents. Those who once could not understand one another now would, and they would not remember a time when they could not. Only a select few might feel that something was amiss, the poets and writers who dedicated their lives to understanding hidden linguistic flows. They'd feel it like an old pair of shoes suddenly not fitting quite right. Some would adjust. Some would be driven insane.

A meager price to the Aeryal. Protect the divine. Preserve the divine. They knew nothing else.

The sun rose, and the Aeryal vanished beneath the grass. Miles and miles to the west, Soulkeeper Devin Eveson led his refugees toward the city of Londheim, the crawling mountain not far behind.

CHAPTER 25

Faithkeeper Sena stood in the doorway of the Creshan mansion, as she had for the past two minutes, trying to say good-bye.

"I really must be going," Sena said. "The hour is already late."

"Yes, yes, of course," Mr. Creshan said. He shook her hand once more, a pleased smile on his mustached face. "It is good to know our money goes to a fine cause."

"That is what's important," Mrs. Creshan said, hovering beside her husband in a dress a little too tight and far too expensive. "With so many suffering we are thrilled to help the church serve the people."

"Please, let us know if there is anything else we can do to help," Mr. Creshan added.

Of course there was plenty, but Sena knew they weren't interested. Their large home could foster a dozen people with ease, but the two times she'd carefully floated the idea it'd been soundly ignored. Money they could hand over; they had plenty of that to spare. Inconveniencing themselves? A whole different matter entirely.

"I will keep you in my thoughts," she said instead. "Pleasant nights to the both of you."

Sena stepped out the door, their good-byes trailing behind her. She breathed out a long, exasperated sigh through her nose. She'd hoped to be back at the church before dark, but the Creshans had insisted she stay for dinner. Sena cursed her weakness. Since the refugees arrived, skipping meals had become a regular habit for her. The idea of a full-course meal had won over her beleaguered stomach. Dinner led to dessert, and dessert led to a friendly drink of wine. She'd have skipped out far sooner, but the Creshans were long-standing friends of the church. Insulting them was not an option.

The sun hid behind the walls of the city, the sky a red smear fading into black. Sena dug her hands into her pockets and walked at a brisk pace. Quiet District was a good mile and a half from Low Dock. She glanced nervously at the sky. Rumors of the great owl Adria killed had spread like wildfire, and the city guard found bloody pools all throughout Londheim suggesting there were more than the one. Even more concerning for Sena were the three different keepers of the church found dead and mutilated over the past week, all by the hand of the monster known as Janus. He was targeting them and leaving grotesque messages behind, and no one had a clue as to why. Goddesses above, given the states of the corpses, no one even knew *how*.

Sena whispered a prayer to the Sisters and hurried on. The temperature plunged with the receding sun, and she shivered beneath her jacket.

"Evening, Faithkeeper."

Sena held back her startled cry with well-trained poise. The streets were uncharacteristically empty lately, but not everyone could afford to hide in their homes. A lamplighter stood at the corner of an intersection beneath a tall black iron lantern. She wore brown trousers and a thick wool sweater, the unofficial uniform for the lamplighter guild. In her left hand she guided a long pole with a lit flame to the lantern's wick, lighting it without even looking.

"Good evening, lamplighter," Sena said.

"Sorry if I scared you," the woman said. She pulled the pole back, rotated it around, and used a hard metal hook to close the lantern. "People say the night ain't safe for soulful and soulless alike. You take care now."

"Frightened people say many things," she said. "Do you not fear the rumors?"

"Of giant owls and tunneling goblins?" The lamplighter laughed. "Mayhap I am, but people need light, and I need my wages." She tapped a dagger tucked into her belt. "I'll be fine. Save your prayers for more important women than I."

Sena bid her good-bye and continued down the street, her arms crossed over her chest. The clack of her boots upon the stone were like little alarms in the quiet night. It stunned her how quickly the city had changed. Men and women should have been traveling to taverns to eat and drink the night away. Gamblers should have been standing at the occasional alleyway, trying their luck with the card slingers. Even the night women were out of sight, and Sena wondered if their clients would start arriving sooner and sooner in the day so they might return home before dark.

The Faithkeeper passed a gloomy tavern, the six patrons inside looking like they huddled in anticipation of a storm. She debated joining them. In there she could rent a room, pay for a meal, and wait out the night. Only the many refugees under her care kept her walking. They'd be worried at her absence, and rightfully so. Her responsibility was to her church, her own fear be damned.

Two blocks later she encountered a man in the middle of the street approaching from the opposite direction. Her stomach twisted immediately upon seeing him. A long, loose coat hung from his shoulders, the bottom almost scraping the street. His trousers were as black as his long hair, at least, the right half. The other half was the deep color of jade. He walked with his arms spread wide, as if he were greeting an old friend. His pale chest was bare. His face bore a madman's smile.

"Faithkeeper!" the man called. "How wonderful it is to meet you this evening."

Though he wielded no weapon, she knew he was dangerous. Her every instinct screamed to run.

"And you are?" she asked. Her rational mind tried to dismiss the fear. He'd done nothing, only greeted her. Surely she was being impulsive. The night and its people had never frightened her before.

"I have many names, though I fear most are now forgotten," he said. "Please, call me Janus."

The name burned through her like a hot iron. A sudden wave of fear locked her every muscle rigid.

"Stay away," she said.

"You don't command me, little Faithkeeper," he said. "None of your kind ever has."

He was close. Too close. She took another step back, feeling her paralysis finally breaking. Janus seemed to notice, too, and his wide grin shrank.

"Don't run," he said. His voice had softened. His green eyes imprisoned hers. "If you run, I shall chase. Those who die in my wake shall be your fault, not mine."

Sena squeezed her eyes shut, and the spell finally broke. She turned to flee, but Janus was faster. He dropped to one knee and slammed his hands atop the street. Stone roiled underneath his touch. A cracking line shot straight from him to her, and her mind struggled to understand. What had been firm cobbles beneath her feet was now thick mud. She sank into it, the mud coming up above her shins. Janus stood and approached with a casual smile.

"Remain still and you will not suffer," he said. "I won't even draw a single drop of blood."

Sena lunged onto her stomach and dug her fingers into the cobbles. Her nails cracked and bled, but she pulled herself free of the mud and staggered into a run. She glanced over her shoulder to see Janus laughing.

"Well. I tried, Viciss. I really did."

She sprinted as fast as she could, with no real destination. She just had to get away. Each time she glanced over her shoulder, she saw Janus following. His body moved as if he were casually jogging, yet he easily kept pace.

Up ahead she saw a familiar sight. The tavern. The people inside, they could protect her. Sena veered toward it and collided at nearly full speed against the door. Its lock rattled in protest. She beat it with her fists and then shifted to the window. She could see the men and women inside. They stared at her in shock.

"Open the door!" she screamed.

The man nearest the door leapt out of his chair and came

running. Sena stepped back, and she spotted Janus from the corner of her eye. He was close, so close. She slammed a hand on the door, panic overwhelming her every action.

"Hurry!"

Janus reached the corner of the building and stopped. His hand pressed against the wood, then seemed to sink into it as if it were water. Nothing rational explained what she saw next. Green veins spread in all directions from his touch, the wood itself changing and becoming something else. They slashed through the boards and rippled through the windows, converting even parts of the glass. It took less than a second for them to encompass the entire tavern, and with the door so close she could easily make out what those green veins were.

Grass. He had turned portions of the building into grass.

The tavern groaned and fractured from all sides. The structure's supports were split. Its walls were segmented. Sena fled the collapsing building. She could only hope the men and women survived inside that cloud of debris. Her lips rambled random prayers. Her head ached from adrenaline and fear. The cacophony of breaking wood and shattering glass sang a mocking chorus in her ears.

Sena ran. Janus followed.

"Miss? Miss, are you all right? Is he bothering you?"

Sena spun, exhaustion slowing her limbs. She'd passed the lamplighter on her route, and she was jogging toward her with a worried expression on her face. She sought to help, but this wasn't some perverted thug or desperate cutpurse. Janus reeked of the void.

"Run," she shouted at her. "Just run, please!"

The lamplighter turned to Janus, and she could tell by the drawing of her dagger she had no such intention.

"You best walk away, young man," she said. "The keeper seems mighty upset."

"He'll kill you," Sena pleaded. The lamplighter didn't turn her way. She was too busy staring down Janus.

"Is that so?" Janus asked. His gait didn't slow in the slightest. The lamplighter pointed her dagger angrily.

"You take one step closer and I'm going to carve my name into your skinny white chest."

Janus paused. The way he looked at the woman gave Sena shivers. As if deciding whether to murder her were a casual thing. He took one long, single step, halting mere inches beyond the weapon's reach. His mad smile spread.

"Try."

The lamplighter lunged with her dagger. Janus reacted with unnatural speed, stepping in closer and latching onto the lamplighter's wrist. He smiled as the lamplighter struggled to break free.

"I'm going to give you a gift for your bravery," Janus said. "I will make you a beauty all of Londheim shall remember."

The lamplighter's body stiffened, and her mouth opened in silent shock. The dagger dropped from her hand. Gold spread outward from Janus's touch. Not covering skin and hair, no, not that. Changing it. Becoming it.

"But do you know what humankind does to beauty?" the strange man asked. "They will rip and tear it apart. Greed destroys decency, respect, and everything good the Sisters tried shoving into your weak little shells. They will remember you, but they will still break you to pieces."

Janus forced the lamplighter to her knees. The gold swarmed over her, her movements turning rigid. Sena watched in horror as Janus rapidly shifted and changed the positions of the lamplighter's arms and legs with his free hand. He twisted fingers, bent an elbow, and turned wrists so they rose up in supplication. He pulled back the head, extended the jaw, and adjusted strands of hair. Janus molded her like a potter with a mound of clay. In that moment, Sena did not exist. There was only the artist and his craft.

A lifetime of horror passed in a handful of heartbeats. Janus stepped back and observed the solid gold statue of the lamplighter on her knees, a permanent expression of terror on her face as she cried to the stars.

"Did I not keep my word?" Janus asked, turning his attention to Sena. "Is she not beautiful?"

"You're a monster," Sena said. Only her fear kept her tears in check.

"We're *all* monsters to you. If we don't fall to our knees and proclaim your superiority you view us with horror and disgust." Janus smirked. "You hate us for committing the sin of being different. Well, Faithkeeper, I've some bad news for you. I don't *care* what you think of me. Your disgust is as meaningful to me as the rage of an ant dying beneath my heel. Perhaps less, for the ant has done nothing to earn my ire. But you? Your kind?"

The fingers of his right hand curled. His fingernails extended while everything from his wrist down smoothed into polished steel. His left hand changed similarly, but instead of shining metal his skin and flesh hardened into bark. Thorns encircled two of the fingers. Crimson flowers blossomed from his knuckles.

"I'll give you a choice," he said. "The natural touch of the wild, or the heartless steel of humanity. Which shall it be?"

"Neither," she said. "I'll never be your art."

Janus tilted his head to the side. Not upset, just mildly confused.

"You ran. People died. Why run again? Do you want a grand escort of souls to accompany you to the heavens?"

Sena fled. She had endured a thousand trials throughout her life, and she'd defeated each and every one with raw determination. She wouldn't give up, not when she had breath in her lungs.

Janus, it seemed, had had enough. The ground splintered to her right and then curled around ahead of her. Thin metal rods burst upward, trapping her behind a chin-high fence. Spikes adorned their tops, each one curling slightly and colored to resemble a flower bud almost ready to bloom. When she flung her weight against the bars they did not even budge.

There was only one direction she could go, and Sena ran while knowing in her gut there would be no escape. Janus was guiding her. Trapping her. The small gap between the two buildings she entered ended at the back of a third. Nowhere to flee. Nowhere to escape. Sena tried anyway, spinning in search of a window she could enter or perhaps a way to scale to the rooftop. She found none.

Janus stepped into the entry. His long coat fluttered. His jade hair glowed in the moonlight.

"I must thank you for the sport," he said. "It's been centuries since I walked among your kind. How I missed it terribly."

Sena put her back to the wall. Her knees weakened, then buckled. Her hands clasped in prayer. The 17th Devotion was her favorite for its simplicity. She'd whispered it to herself as a child after the death of her parents. She'd repeated it as a mantra after her foster father came into her room to touch her when he was drunk. It'd been a long, long time since she poured her heart into those words, but she did now, for the next time she spoke them she might be in the presence of the Goddesses.

"I am blind, but Lyra gives me sight. I see darkness, but Lyra gives me light. The light I see dwells in me, and it is blinding. I am blind, but Lyra gives me sight."

Sena watched Janus approach, an easy smile on his face and a relaxed swing to his hips. She wiped away her tears. She would not give him the pleasure. She continued the devotion, an endless loop sweeping away the last of her horror. Her insides hollowed. Her fear of death crumbled to acceptance. Janus leered down at her. His right hand had returned to flesh, but the gnarled, twisted bark of his left had only grown.

"The light I see dwells in me," she whispered as he pulled back for the lethal swing. "And it is blinding."

A brilliant sun erupted from Sena's chest. All its power, all its wrath, shone into Janus's face. He let out a pained cry and violently lurched his body away from the light.

"Fuck!" he shouted. He flung his arm to his eyes and staggered sideways.

The sun vanished mere moments after. The dark returned to the alley. Sena didn't think. She didn't question it. She jumped to her feet and ran right past Janus. He swung wildly for her, missing entirely. Once back in the street she sprinted for the Creshan mansion. She dared not look behind her. She dared not see if Janus chased.

"Is something the matter?" Mr. Creshan asked when he opened the door to his mansion after her fifth time slamming her fists against it.

"Please, can I stay the night here?" she asked.

"Of course. You're always welcome."

The wealthy man had servants bring her a change of clothes and direct her to the guest bedroom. He didn't ask what had happened, and for that, she was thankful.

Once settled into her room, Sena took the small chair before the vanity, moved it beside the window, and sat. Her forehead rested against the cold pane. From her second-story room she could see the entire front lawn and much of the street.

I understand now, Adria, she thought. *This power. This fear. It's like holding fire.*

Sena watched for any sign of Janus, watched for hours as the night crawled on, watched until her eyes closed and she did not have the strength to open them again.

CHAPTER 26

I'm not sure you're ready for this," Devin told her as the store owner set the bowl down between them. Jacaranda's eyes widened.

"You couldn't be more wrong," she said. She grabbed a slice of her apple bread and swirled it through the thick sweet cream that overflowed the bowl. Once it was fully enveloped she stuffed it all into her mouth. The taste hit her immediately. Her insides quivered. Her upper body turned to jelly.

"Goddesses above," she said through her mouthful. "How do you not eat this every day?"

Devin laughed as he dipped his own piece of bread into the cream.

"Because that would be expensive," he said. "Besides, treats stop being treats if you eat them too often."

The two sat opposite each other at a table inside the confectionery's store. Devin had offered to accompany Jacaranda throughout the city and she'd jumped at the chance. There were dozens of things she wished to try, and it helped having Devin's guidance, as well as his coin. So far they'd watched the crossroad oak flourish alive with color and song, toured the courtyard of cherries located within his church's grand cathedral grounds, and diced away a few dozen copper pennies at a streetside den that Devin refused to say whether or not it was legal.

"That sounds like a lie you tell children," she said, licking cream off her fingers. She ripped another piece of bread off and slammed it through the cream as if attempting murder. It wasn't like she was used to poor food. Her meals at Gerag's estate had been well prepared and varied, for she usually ate what Master—

Shit, shit, no, what Gerag ate, not Master. She winced at the simple mistake. It was still too easy to slip back into her older mind-set.

"I'm surprised you've never had anything like this before," Devin said. "Given how Gerag's a fat slob, I'd assume this was a daily offering."

"It makes no sense giving desserts to soulless," she said. "Besides, eating sweets like this might have ruined my... figure."

Devin performed admirably at keeping his sudden anger concealed behind a pleasant smile.

"Fuck him," he said. "Your figure is just fine."

"I'm glad you approve of my figure."

His neck started to turn a faint shade of red. Jacaranda was both pleased and alarmed at how much joy it gave her to see that reaction. She winked at him and then resumed eating. The ratio of bread to cream on each bite shifted further and further toward the cream side until she gave up and began lifting the cream directly from the bowl with her fingers.

"Careful now," Devin said. "You're going to make yourself sick."

"How so?" Jacaranda asked. "I'm still hungry, and each bite tastes as fantastic as the first. Are you saying both my mind and stomach are fools?"

"Yes," Devin said. "I am."

In response she sucked cream off her finger hard enough to make it pop when she pulled it free.

"Then I guess I will just have to get sick."

Once the bowl was licked clean (quite literally, for Jacaranda was determined not to waste a single scrap of it) Devin leaned back in his chair and crossed his hands over his lap.

"So where to now?" he asked. "Is there a place you've always wished to go but couldn't?"

"Not particularly," Jacaranda said. "I never...wanted things. I never experienced boredom or curiosity. I obeyed orders, and if I had no orders, I just quietly existed until I did."

"Would you like me to offer suggestions?"

"Sure," she said. "So long as it remains my choice."

"Well, assuming they haven't been canceled, there will be some horse races at the Sinegard farmstead in about an hour. It's about a mile east of the city, so we could easily make it in time. There's also the gunsmith tourneys. One should be taking place all day not too far from here."

"A shooting contest?" Jacaranda asked. "Would you participate?"

Devin laughed.

"We're forbidden," he said. "Gamblers always bet on Soulkeepers, and the tourney organizers hate that we're too honest to bribe."

That killed what little interest Jacaranda had.

"What else?"

"If you'd prefer something less respectable, Low Dock has a knuckle-box ring; winner stays champion until they finally go down. It gets real heated once the workday ends."

"Everything you recommend is competitive. Have you nothing beautiful or playful to recommend?"

"By all means," Devin said. "Feel free to chip in for ideas. Perhaps if we swing through the market we might find a mummer or some singing troupes. It's anybody's guess if they'll be any good, though."

Jacaranda ran memories through her mind, trying to isolate things and places that would have meant nothing to her soulless self, or even better, things that would have completely baffled her.

"A garden," she suddenly blurted. "There's one off Sable street, just shy of where it connects to Hemwick Lane. Do you know of it?"

"I do."

"I'd like to go there," she said.

"Are you sure?" Devin asked. "It's in Quiet District."

Which meant it was in the same district as Gerag's mansion. There was a chance they might stumble upon one another, ending her hopes of a normal life inside Londheim.

"I'm not letting Gerag dictate what I can and cannot do," she said. "I did enough of that when I was his soulless."

The two exited the store and out into the bright sunlight. Jacaranda pulled her hat lower over her head to hide her vibrant hair and then secured the scarf about her neck. She hated having to constantly check, but one slipup might be all it took for someone to notice. A Soulkeeper escorting a disguised soulless could cause rumors, rumors they could not afford.

Upon Devin's insistence they took a detour on the way to Quiet District.

"You said you wanted to see something beautiful," was all that he'd tell her as way of explanation. He took her down a quiet street full of stores advertising the more splendid wares someone living in the nearby Quiet District might prefer: jewels, necklaces, fine chairs and desks, glassware, and the like. Devin stopped them before one in particular. Jacaranda punched his arm upon seeing the name of the store. *Multav's Mirrors*.

"You think you're clever, don't you?" she said.

"I have my moments."

While Londheim might not be famous for its mirrors (that was Nicus by the sea, with its abundant access to sand) there were still a few craftsmen who had learned the style and brought it west. A burly man stood beside the store's door, his hairy arms crossed over his chest. He glanced over the two as they approached, and he nodded upon seeing that Devin was a Soulkeeper.

"Welcome," the man said, and he opened the door for them.

The store was long and slender, its walls painted white. Seven mirrors hung upon the wall, their craftsmanship clearly of the highest quality. The largest was nearly three feet tall and shaped into an oval. Silver leaf decorated its sides, shaped and curled to look like vines. The top of the oval bore diamonds arranged like the petals of a flower. Not even Gerag could afford a mirror of such fine quality. Jacaranda twirled before it, mesmerized by her reflection. She'd seen herself only rarely in pools of water, but now she scanned her face with a clinical examination: the paleness of her skin, the fire of her red hair poking out from underneath her hat, the allure of her violet eyes.

Jacaranda knew she was beautiful, for she had been told it

often as a soulless, but it had been a simple fact processed and remembered in case she was asked. It'd borne no meaning, no understanding. Now she saw it, and it made her vaguely uncomfortable. She compared herself to the many women they'd passed walking the streets, and she realized she stood out among them, from the perfect angle of her cheeks to the slender point of her nose to the statuesque curvature of her chin. Of course, why wouldn't she be of startling beauty? She was Gerag's perfect little flower, after all. His most prized possession.

"Obviously I can't afford anything like that," Devin said after giving her a lengthy time to look. "The little hand ones on the counter were more of what I was thinking."

Jacaranda glanced at the twelve or so tiny mirrors laid into bone and ivory handles.

"No," she said. "I think I'm fine without. May we please go?"

"Of course." Devin politely nodded to the shopkeeper who'd patiently waited off to the side in case they had questions. "Are you all right?" he asked once they were back out on the street.

"Just my stomach," she said, not entirely a lie.

"I warned you."

"And I say it was still worth it." She did her best to relax. His planned gift of a small mirror was touching. It wasn't Devin's fault her mind was so messed up. "Now to the garden, or have you any other distractions?"

The enormous garden was completely walled in with ivy-covered stone. The only entrance was through a gate that bore the name of the original wealthy founder and was guarded by an older man with a straggly beard more appropriate to a youth just exiting puberty.

"Miss Valber left the gardens for the whole city to enjoy, but a donation would be most appreciated," the man said. "In these troubled times, the arts often go unappreciated by those who need it most."

Devin slipped a few silver pennies into the man's offered hand. The old man tipped his hat to them and quickly pocketed the coin.

"Enjoy the garden, lovebirds," he said. "Do try to behave."

Jacaranda grabbed Devin's hand before he could offer a correction, and she pulled him toward the ornate gates.

"We will," she promised.

"Presumptuous of him," Devin muttered as they walked a path created by thousands of smooth, colorful stones. Much as he might complain, she noticed he had not released her hand.

"Are you saying we're not two heart-struck lovebirds madly dashing into a quiet garden for a wild and tempestuous affair?"

His neck flushed, and he squinted one eye in a glare she found all the more precious.

"I see you've discovered the joy of teasing," he said, reluctantly pulling his hand from hers. "You'd have been a nightmare as a child."

"Why can't I be a nightmare now?"

He did not answer, only laughed and gestured for her to follow. The path led through dozens of bushes, most of them various colors of roses from the brightest white to reds that made her own hair look pale by comparison. Upon Devin's insistence she leaned next to one of them and slowly inhaled their scent.

"It's smells...lovely," she said. "I don't understand. How does a scent evoke such emotion?"

"You should ask a poet, not a Soulkeeper," Devin said. "We tend to be terrible at flowery language."

"Was that a pun?"

"Was it funny?"

"No. Leave the puns to Tommy, please. You're no good at them."

This time she took the lead as Devin trailed.

"I thought it was a little funny," he grumbled quietly to himself.

Flowers were not the only decoration within the garden. As they wound closer to its heart they passed more and more statues carved out of smooth white limestone. Jacaranda studied them, fascinated. They were all of people, most of them children in the nude. The way they were posed implied motion despite their stillness, and she could not believe how much emotion she could read into their little faces. Mouths open with laughter, eyes bright and dazzling, their arms flung out to the side as they ran, tumbled, and climbed.

"How does one learn to carve so intricately?" she asked. She touched the head of a babe suckling from her smiling mother's bosom. They'd entered a series of tall hedges, and the statues had shifted from children to adults engaged in mundane, daily routines. "These feel like thoughts made real."

"I couldn't tell you the individual steps," Devin said. "But I do know it is a skill like all other skills. Miss Valber could carve these statues because she carved hundreds of others like them, just not as beautiful and flawless. Time and practice. Hardly the sexy answer most want to hear, but it's the truth."

"Speaking of sexy," Jacaranda said as they turned a corner through particularly tall hedges to discover a statue of a man carrying an enormous boulder upon his back and shoulders. His erect penis was prominently displayed, not helped by the statue being placed on a pedestal so it was at eye level. That the penis was swollen and round for the first half of the length, and thin like a reed for the second half leading to the tip, was not lost on either of them. A lone word, *burden*, was carved across the pedestal.

"This one is definitely...interesting," Devin said.

"Indeed," Jacaranda said. She adopted a flat, careful tone. "So what emotion do you think she wished to convey with this piece?"

Devin tilted his head to one side.

"Erections can come at even the most inopportune times?"

Jacaranda felt laughter threatening to escape, and she clenched her jaw as tightly as she could to hold them back.

"Maybe we should bring Tommy here," she offered. "He could use the inspiration."

"You mean he could add another penis to his repertoire?"

Giggles escape through her teeth. She couldn't contain herself any longer.

"Had Miss Valber even *seen* an erect penis?" she asked. "Dear Goddesses, it looks more like a chicken drumstick."

Devin tilted his head the opposite direction.

"Maybe that was the intention," he said. "Just trading one cock for another."

That did it. She was done. Jacaranda laughed and waved her hand in front of her as if warding away the bulbous monstrosity.

"Please, let's go," she said as she recovered. "I don't want to look at that thing anymore."

"Careful turning more corners," Devin said. "You might poke your eye out."

Goddesses help her, that set her off all over again. They passed more statues and flower arrangements, but she barely noticed them. When she exited the garden she felt refreshed and alive. There was so much to the world that had been denied to her, not through Gerag's orders, but by the very nature of being soulless. Witnessing the careful thought and dedication of the sculptors felt like waking up a limb that had been asleep for two decades, only without the pins and needles.

"Where to next?" Devin asked.

"You still think we might find a mummer or two at one of the markets?"

"I do."

"Let's go, then," she said. "Far too much of my life was spent without laughter. I've catching up to do."

They did indeed find some mummers, a trio surrounded by a crowd who alternated between singing songs and performing with puppets from behind a thick curtain strung between two trade stalls. They kept their songs bawdy and their performances silly and crude. The city craved something lighthearted to forget the dread of the changing world, and she did not blame them. Jacaranda laughed and sang along with the crowd.

Once that was finished Devin bought them little pies stuffed with vegetables, and they ate as they walked eastward to the river. At one of the piers they found an unoccupied bench and sat so they might rest their tired legs. Jacaranda felt like they'd traversed half the city, though she knew that was nonsense. Londheim was enormous, and she had seen only a tiny fraction of it. Instead of intimidating her, it only filled her with determination to see that much more, to experience everything the winding streets and crowded buildings could offer.

Jacaranda shifted slightly so she sat close enough to Devin to lean her body against him. Together they watched boats lazily drift across the water. The touch of Devin's body against hers, even if just shoulder to shoulder and elbow to elbow, caused her heart to race. Was it nervousness, fright, or revulsion? She didn't know. An insane desire to kiss him flashed through her mind. How might he respond? Would his lips be soft, his touch tender? Or would they be rough, aggressive, just like...like...

The desire died instantly. Jacaranda clenched her jaw and fought down the revulsion. No, damn it, not now. Not when she was happy. As if in rebellion to her own mind she looped an arm around Devin's and embraced it.

"Thank you," she said. "Today has easily been the best day of my life."

"You've not had too many for comparison," Devin said. "But I'll happily take the default win."

She pulled away. Her heart hammered inside her chest hard enough that she wondered if Devin had felt it. Goddesses above, was this the sort of thing people dealt with daily? No wonder men and women rambled out poetry for hours and wrote countless stories about love and courtship. It was so confusing and exhausting, how else might one figure out what the fuck was going on?

"It'll be dark soon," she said after several more minutes of watching the river. "Should we head home?"

Devin stood, and she stood with him, assuming that was a yes. Instead he paused a moment, inwardly debating something.

"You probably should," he said. "If you'll forgive me, I won't accompany you. There's something I need to do first."

"And what is that?"

"I'd rather not say. Even we Soulkeepers need some privacy on occasion."

Jacaranda was surprised by the response. He...he wouldn't tell her? Why wouldn't he tell her? Was he hiding something? Did it involve her? The deluge of wonder and curiosity was thoroughly new and unexpected, and it took her a moment to collect herself.

"Oh, all right," she said, and smiled as if not bothered in the slightest. "Stay safe."

"You too."

He hesitated a moment, as if still deciding something, then bowed low. The grand sweep of his arm and the removal of his hat made it seem like he bowed before a queen.

"Farewell, milady."

"You're such a fool," she said, but she offered him her hand anyway. He kissed it gently upon the knuckles. The warmth of his lips upon her skin sent a pleasant tingle up her arm and down her spine.

"What can I say, you bring out the fool in me."

Devin replaced his hat atop his head and casually strolled away. Jacaranda watched him go, her feet rooted in place. She couldn't believe how strongly the desire to follow pulled at her chest. She didn't just want to know where Devin went, or why he preferred to go alone, she *needed* to know, almost as badly as she needed air in her lungs. She bit her lip. Her inward debate lasted but a moment before she followed after Devin at a sufficiently safe distance. She had extensive training at stealth and trailing another unseen. What harm could there be in satisfying a little curiosity? Besides, if she did her job right, Devin need not ever know.

Devin stopped at the entrance to a large, gated patch of land. Well-cut grass formed a wide barrier between the fence and the rest of the city, for no one wished to live or work so close to a graveyard. A nondescript iron fence surrounded the triangular lot. A shack was built just beside the front gate, a lone torch hanging from its corner to illuminate the entrance.

"Why are we here?" Jacaranda whispered as she watched from afar. Devin knocked on the gate, waited a moment, and then warmly greeted an elderly man who stepped out from the shack. They talked for a bit, too distant for her to make out the words. Eventually the old man returned to his shack and Devin wandered deeper inside the graveyard.

Jacaranda circled the fence, an eye on Devin the entire time. He seemed to have an exact destination in mind, for he did not wander or tarry. She vaulted the fence once he was far enough in, then followed. There was nothing to hide behind, so Jacaranda had to rely on the darkness and Devin's blind spots to remain hidden. She slowly approached, coming as close as she dared. Devin was before her, kneeling at one of seemingly hundreds of unmarked graves. The ground was flat, the grass cut low, so she hunkered down and slowed her breathing to a crawl so she might listen in.

Devin carefully set three candles to form a triangle about the patch of ground. He used a knife from his belt to carve connecting lines in the dirt between them. All the while he remained completely silent. Jacaranda feared her breathing might be detectable in such a quiet, somber place.

"By your will, not mine," Devin whispered in prayer. Jacaranda knelt lower to the grass. A pang of something tightened inside her chest. Guilt? Awkwardness? Something about peering in on such a private moment felt wrong to her, but in a way she couldn't hope to express. If not for her fear of alerting Devin to her presence, she'd have left then and there.

"By your power, not mine. By your grace, not mine. Please, Sisters. Let this be the final reaping hour for her. Overlook her no more. Take her soul into your hands. Alma, Lyra, Anwyn... please, take her home."

The reaping hour came. Jacaranda knew by the thin beams of blue light that shone in the distant dark, souls shooting to the sky throughout Londheim. Devin prayed louder, pleading, begging. Whatever he desired, it was surely not granted, for the heartbreak was evident in each and every tired word he prayed. She blinked and discovered that tears had swelled in her eyes. Why did she feel this sorrow? It wasn't hers. Whatever Devin suffered, it was unknown to her, but it hurt her heart all the same. An impulse to go to him flooded her, and she took a single step before realizing she'd done so.

One step, that was all, but the soft crunch of grass was enough to turn Devin's head. Jacaranda froze. She felt like a rabbit before a wolf. He said nothing, and she had nothing to offer in return. His shoulders shook as he took a long breath in and then let it out.

"Go home, Jacaranda," he said. His voice trembled.

"I only wished to..."

"Go. Home."

She retreated out of the graveyard and over its iron fence, all the while a burning heat lighting up her neck and face. By the time she arrived at Devin's home she'd mostly recovered.

Tesmarie snoozed upon a padded shelf, and Jacaranda made sure not to wake her as she retreated to her room and locked the door. She was still awake when she heard Devin come home. Jacaranda sat atop her bed with her legs crossed underneath her and her head resting in her fists. She stared at the door of her room, wondering if he'd knock. Wondering if her stupid mistake would forever tarnish all the joy they'd experienced throughout the day.

No knock. Just quiet. Jacaranda did her best to sleep, but it came in random, uneven fits. They said nothing of it the following morning. Jacaranda doubted they ever would.

CHAPTER 27

Adria led the early-morning prayer with the handful of volunteers inside her church, but her mind was elsewhere as she asked the Sisters for mercy and guidance throughout the day.

I'm not asking for certainty, Devin had told her that morning. *All I'm asking is for legal precedents involving soulless. We need to know what future Jacaranda might have.*

There were no precedents, though. That was the entire point. When the first soulless appeared decades ago they'd been small in number and cared for by the church. Faithkeepers prayed over them constantly, and Mindkeepers searched through old tomes for answers. None came, and nothing changed. The soulless lived and died, and that was that. As the number of soulless grew, so too did the burden of feeding and housing them. The textile mills in the north had been the first to sue for the right to employ soulless, and many industries quickly did likewise. Every legal decision was based on the accepted premise by both church and state: The soulless were human but not truly *human.* They were akin to expensive livestock, with strict regulations to prevent abuse and cruelty.

Her prayer ended. The mostly female group scattered. Some would cook meals to share with those still bunking inside the church. Others would gather donated bread from bakers to bring to the families housing refugees. Two elderly sisters collected the previous day's clothes and washed them in tubs behind the church. Keeping everyone fed and clean was a tremendous task, and Adria knew she couldn't have done it all alone, not even with Faithkeeper Sena's help.

Normally Sena was in charge of the morning prayers, but she'd not returned since the previous day. Her absence bothered Adria greatly. Given her encounter with the enormous owl, and the Soulkeepers' search for whoever was murdering keepers, Adria feared the worst had befallen Low Dock's Faithkeeper.

"Would you like us to fetch more water from the well?" one of the refugees asked her as she walked the center aisle, pulling her free of her thoughts.

"If you could, please," she told him. The man nudged his husband beside him, who lay on the pew with a pillow over his face.

"Wake up," he said. "Time to earn our keep."

The other man grunted and made a rude gesture with his hand.

"You volunteered us, didn't you, you asshole?"

"Such fitting language for a church," Adria said. The man lifted the pillow, saw her watching him from behind her mask, and paled.

"Shit. Uh. Sorry. Sorry. Sisters forgive me."

The two men hurried for the door. Adria paid them no mind. Currently she was daydreaming of a few minutes of peace and solitude in her room before she began her own errands. When she heard the two men stop at the door and call out a greeting, she realized her solitude would have to wait.

"Good morning, Faithkeeper," they said in unison.

Adria spun to see a disheveled Sena offering them both a polite nod. Dried mud covered the bottom of her normally crisp white trousers. Her fingers were bandaged. Adria kept her body still and relaxed, not wanting to give away her worry to the rest in the church.

"Welcome back," Adria said, as if Sena had been gone for a few minutes on a morning stroll.

Sena walked right past her on the way to her room.

"We must talk," said the older woman, and Adria followed.

Sena sat atop her bed, flung her jacket off beside her, and then stared into nowhere. Adria patiently waited. Whatever trauma she'd endured, she'd tell it at her own pace.

"I was...attacked," Sena said after a long while. "He looked human, but he wasn't. And my prayers, they...they..."

Adria sat down beside her and gently put her hand over Sena's.

"Take your time," she said. "I'm here to listen. All else can wait."

Sena described her night, starting with leaving the Creshan mansion. Adria kept silent, but her mind reeled at the thought of a man able to change flesh to gold at a mere touch of his hand. When the Faithkeeper told of the brilliant sun summoned by her devotion, Adria wanted to weep. She wasn't alone. She wasn't the only one with this power.

"And now I'm here," Sena said as she finished. "What do we do, Adria? This is far beyond my expertise."

"The devotion," Adria asked. "Do you think if you recited it you might re-create the blinding light?"

"I don't know," Sena said. "What are you thinking?"

"I'm thinking it's time we speak with a Vikar. There's too much we don't know that our superiors might be able to illuminate."

"And if they do not believe?" Sena asked. "Or worse, believe we've sold our soul to the void and become Ravencallers?"

Such a thought should have been ridiculous, but Adria remembered how frightened she'd been the first time she healed another. These gifts shook the foundations of the mind. Who could predict how a man or woman reacted to that?

"We'll reveal ourselves to Vikar Thaddeus," she said. "He's a friend. He knows I'd never give in to such blasphemy."

"I shall trust your judgment," Sena said. "Let us not delay. If we leave now, we can catch Thaddeus at the Cathedral of the Sacred Mother just after his morning prayers."

Adria and Sena sat beside one another on an ornate hickory couch with padded white cushions. Seven candles flickered in the chandelier above. In the northern tip of the cathedral, within the heart of the Deakon's Garden, was a mansion known as the Old Vikarage. The three Vikars of Londheim, plus the Deakon himself, all shared the extravagant abode, affording them ample opportunities to discuss with one another the overwhelming work required to oversee the Keeping Church's presence in West Orismund. The two keepers sat in one of many little rooms with bookshelves, chairs, and couches meant for sipping tea and quiet reflection.

"It's not too late," Sena said softly. "We can still walk away."

Adria shook her head. No, enough was enough. This feeling of secrecy and paranoia had to be dealt with or she'd lose her mind. It was time her Vikar knew of the power they, and potentially hundreds of others, wielded with their prayers. After they'd insisted on the importance of their coming and demanded a private audience with Thaddeus, a novice had finally relented and brought them to the Old Vikarage. There they sat, two cups of untouched tea cooling before them, as they waited.

"Have faith," Adria said. "The Sisters have given us these gifts for a reason, and it was not to suffer or die at the hands of our own church."

"Perhaps you should read more into the history of our church."

Adria winced.

"A forgotten time. The heretical purges died with the beliefs of hundreds of void-dragons walking among us."

"And a mountain has crawled to the gates of our city," Sena said. "Who knows what old beliefs will come roaring back with it?"

The door to their room opened before Adria could respond. The two quickly rose to their feet and bowed in reverence to the Vikar of the Day. Thaddeus arrived with a small escort of four. Three were young novices, and he quickly bid them to disperse. The fourth was a man dressed in matching brown trousers and shirt. His eyes were a milky white, and he walked while holding Thaddeus's sleeve. Adria fought to remain calm as she greeted her Vikar. Sena stood beside her, her head bowed in respect to another sacred division's Vikar.

"I must admit you have piqued my curiosity," Thaddeus said. He gestured to the blind man. "I've brought Titus with me as you asked. Now what is it you wish to show me, and how does this pertain to the madman killing our keepers?"

"Not yet," Adria said, taking the lead since it was her Vikar they addressed, and her idea to meet with him in the first place.

"Hello, Titus, it's been a few years since I last saw you. Have you gotten any better at the lute?"

"My playing has much improved since I last performed at your church," Titus said, and he smiled. "My singing voice, I must sadly say, is still the same croaking frog it's always been."

Titus was one of Alma's Beloved, whose organization Adria considered one of the finest the church had ever adopted. It traced all the way back to the first Ecclesiast, Cassandra Anklare, who established the Beloved as a rebuke to those calling for a merciful culling during a brutal four years of famine.

"If you'd follow me, please," Adria said, and she gently took his hand into hers. "I want you to lie down on this couch."

"If the lovely lady insists."

Vikar Thaddeus watched them intently, no doubt puzzled by what they were planning. Adria led Titus to the couch, and he settled down atop it as if for a nap. Adria and Sena exchanged a glance. They'd been unsure who should try first, but with Sena having been the one to encounter Janus, it felt better to let her start. If she succeeded, her testimony on what the murderer could do would carry that much greater authority.

"Titus, I am Faithkeeper Sena," her friend said as she knelt at his side. "I doubt you remember me, for you were just a boy, but I was there when we brought you in to the cathedral."

"Of course I remember you," Titus said. "What might I do for you, Faithkeeper?"

"Lie still, and repeat everything I say," Sena said. "Can you do that?"

"Sounds simple enough. Sure."

Adria shifted nervously from foot to foot. This was something neither had done before, particularly Sena. The woman held Adria's copy of Lyra's Devotions, and she flipped it to the page containing the 22nd Devotion. Sena had cautioned against trying a new prayer, but Adria had held fast.

"Pain may fluctuate. Fevers come and go. We need something no one can doubt, proof that would remain strong even before a court of law."

Titus had been a member of Alma's Beloved for nearly two decades. He'd interacted with hundreds of people within the church at all levels of status. No one could claim this a con or deception, not if this worked.

Sena closed her eyes, placed her hands across Titus's closed eyes, and began reciting an opening line Adria knew all too well.

"Lyra of the beloved sun, hear my prayer."

The words flowed easily off her tongue. The last of the prayer ended and Sena withdrew her hand. Adria held her breath. Would he be cured? Had his sight been restored?

"Is that it?" Titus asked. His eyelids crept open. They were the same milky white.

"It appears so," Thaddeus said, and he shot Adria a look.

"Do not be discouraged," she said, putting a hand on Sena's shoulders. "The Sisters' gifts may vary."

It was her turn. She knelt and closed her eyes, her hands gently folded over Titus's face.

Focus, she told herself. *Stop worrying for yourself. Think of the gift you are about to bestow.* If this worked, she'd be giving sight to a man blind since birth. His entire life would be changed for the better. Shame on her for thinking about how this might make her appear a fool. *Sisters have mercy, does my selfishness know no bounds?*

Adria reached into her pocket and pulled out her mask. When she slid it over her face her fears eased away. Mindkeepers were both purity and sin, perfection and imperfection coexisting in a

dance set into motion since the blood of the void-dragon corrupted the First Soul. True Mindkeepers did not crumble under
emotion. They gave no pause to the smallest blessing or the
greatest sin. They did not elevate self above the world, for how
else could they lend their aid to the suffering? The world craved
the touch of the holy, and she would give it regardless of the cost.

"Lyra of the beloved sun, hear my prayer. I kneel with heavy
heart, and before a man pure of soul but impure of flesh. Shower
your mercy upon us, I beg."

A tremendous power trembled within Adria's breast, stronger and much more sudden than before. The gifts of the Sisters passed through her hands. Its song parted from her tongue.
Thaddeus gasped behind her. Did he, too, sense it?

"Let no suffering last eternal. Let no earthly form deny star-
born perfection. That which was broken be made anew."

Adria lifted her hands, curled them before her heart, and
waited. Titus stirred, his head tilting as her prayer gave way to
silence. His eyes opened, clear and green as fresh cut grass.

"Is that...that..."

His mouth dropped open in shock. He looked around like an
awestruck child and struggled to speak.

"Thaddeus?" he said. "It's...it's you, isn't it?"

The Vikar had tears in his eyes.

"That it is," he said.

Titus openly wept. He flung his arms around Adria's shoulders and showered kisses upon her neck.

"Thank you," he whispered again and again. "Thank you so
much."

Adria endured the outpouring with quiet dignity. This was
how it was always meant to be. No matter the joy, no matter the
sorrow, she'd be the pillar they could cling to amid a storm.

"I—I need to go for a walk," Titus said. "I need to see the market, the cathedrals, the river. Shit, the tree, I need to see that damn crossroad oak people won't shut up about."

"In time," Thaddeus said. "But first I ask you to show me a courtesy after all the kindness our church has shown you."

"And what is that?"

The Vikar reached into his pocket and pulled out a small brown purse. The interior rattled of silver.

"Find an inn and pay for three nights," he said. "Come morning, purchase a change of clothes at the market. Tell no one of what has happened here, nor that you were a member of Alma's Beloved. At the end of those three days, return to the church. I shall be waiting for you."

Titus looked like a child who'd been gifted the world. He spun between the three of them, showering all with thanks and praise. When he left, Thaddeus shut the door to their room, locked it, and sat in a chair facing the both of them. The gentleness in his smile was long gone. Adria had seen him in this mood rarely when they studied in the archive, but she remembered it well. His sharp mind craved information like a mongrel craved fresh meat. Nothing would sate him.

"It is time you both explained yourselves," he said, pulling his spectacles from his face. "Are you the only one capable of doing this, or can Sena do so as well?"

"I can," Sena said. "But I have tried only a few, and the prayers that work for me are not always what work for Adria."

Her Vikar nodded, absorbing the information.

"So are we the first?" Adria asked. "No one else has shown the same powers we possess?"

The Vikar's face darkened.

"Only one," he said. "But his is a tale opposite yours. Do not worry for him. Tell me your story, each of you. When did this first start? Was it the same time for the both of you, or different?"

"I first healed someone the day the crawling mountain arrived," Adria said.

"And you?"

Sena braced herself.

"I did so out of desperation. If not for the Goddesses, I'd have died at Janus's hands."

"Janus?" the Vikar asked. "The Janus responsible for murdering our keepers in the dead of night?"

"I believe so."

Thaddeus pulled his chair closer, and he pressed his thumb and forefingers together as he concentrated.

"Tell me everything," he said. "And I mean everything."

CHAPTER 28

Tucked into a corner of the market district was an unmarked building with thick wood blinds covering its windows. Malik skipped the front entrance and led Tommy to the side alley where another large door awaited. He knocked three times and then stepped back.

"You sure this is a tavern?" Tommy asked. "It looks more like a shuttered home."

"They try to keep it hidden," Malik explained. "Helps keep the beggars away."

"Seems a bit stuffy-minded. How do they attract customers?"

"Through recommendations, of course. Trust me, Tommy, once you try their rosemary braised lamb shanks you'll be wanting to tell the whole world."

The door opened and out stepped a clean-shaven servant in a finely tailored suit.

"This way, please," he said.

Though the building had seemed to be two stories from the outside, inside was a single expansive room with a vaulted ceiling. Dozens of candles hung from chandeliers, casting a soft glow upon the hard oak tables. Shoulder-high barriers criss-crossed between the tables to form isolated sections. Tommy felt woefully out of place as the servant led them past tables of dining lords, traders, and high-ranking members of the Keeping Church. He even saw two Soulkeepers merrily chatting over thin, wide bowls of a pale-green both that smelled of minty perfection. Tommy made a mental note to ask if Devin was aware of this place.

"I am, um, not sure I brought enough coin with me," Tommy said as he sat. Malik waved off his concerns.

"Calm yourself. Neither of us will be paying. I keep a tab in the name of the Wise Organization. Londheim's budget will easily cover a few meals."

Well, that was a relief. Tommy tapped his hands on his legs, telling himself that no one was paying him any attention. By the Goddesses, though, he wished he had taken a bath before coming, or at least combed through the disheveled wild animal that was his hair. When Tommy had nearly fainted at his research table, Malik pressed him on his eating habits. Upon finding out it'd been nearly twelve hours since his last proper meal, Malik forced him to come along, leaving him no chance to clean himself up. Thankfully the tables to either side of them were empty, meaning no one should catch whiff of sweat and musty books. To their left, though, a trio of women whispered as if the survival of the kingdom were at stake. They sipped soup from fine crystal bowls with incredible calm, steady movements. Tommy could see why. Their outfits alone likely cost more than Devin's house. Shit, just the *spoon* looked more expensive than his entire life's earnings.

One of them glanced his way. Tommy turned his attention to his own table with his heart hammering. He felt like a burglar being spotted climbing a fence.

A different man returned to their table, his long black hair carefully tied in a loose ponytail. Tommy tried not to stare. It was as if the restaurant had gone out of its way to hire the most beautiful men in all of Londheim. Tommy ran a hand through his own hair in a failing attempt to unflatten the left side he'd slept on.

"Greetings, esteemed gentlemen, my name is Tynek," the servant said. He clasped his hands before his fitted vest. "Your choices are either the honeyed duck with cherries or carved rosemary lamb."

"Duck for me, lamb for my friend," Malik said, ordering for them. "And a strawberry red from Nelme for each of us."

"Very good."

Tynek bowed low and whisked away. Within seconds he was back with two crystalline glasses filled with a sparkling crimson liquid.

"Enjoy your meal," Tynek said.

"So," Malik said when the man had left. "We have some time. Let me hear what you mean by 'schools' of magic. I believe you said something to that effect right before you almost fainted."

Tommy took a gulp of his wine, set the glass down, and immediately found himself distracted.

"Holy shit, that's sweet."

Malik grinned at him.

"That wine is likely older than the both of us. Enjoy."

"Am I allowed more than one glass?"

"You are."

"Then damn right I'm going to enjoy."

He drained the rest, thudded the glass down, and let out a satisfied grunt.

"So, schools. I'm not sure if that's the proper way to describe the distinction. *Disciplines* could also work, or *classes*. What I'm getting at is that all the spells I've managed to successfully cast share unique words in common. Not only that, but these individual words appear to have their own distinct concept or power associated with them."

"Interesting," Malik said. "How many are there?"

"As of what I can figure there are five: Aethos, Viciss, Gloam, Nihil, and Chyron. There might be more, but I've yet to discover them."

The older Wise slowly rubbed his forefinger over the top of his glass as he thought.

"I've seen you cast many Aethos spells. I wager it has something to do with fire and frost?"

"In a sense," Tommy said. "Involving elemental energies is a better way to say it. Fire, frost, explosions, lightning; all the fun stuff, really. Viciss is something like change, or mutation. If it involves turning one thing to another, it always appears to be a Viciss spell. Chyron is the one I'm most certain of, and that's time, either speeding it up, slowing it down, or potentially becoming 'unstuck,' whatever the bloody madness that means."

"You've not given it a try?"

"Goddesses, no," Tommy said. "I don't want to see the future, the past, or anything in between. I can barely handle the present as it hits me."

Malik laughed. His brown eyes sparkled in the dim light.

"Fair enough, Tommy, fair enough. All of these do sound familiar to me except for Gloam. Is it a recent discovery?"

Tommy drummed his fingers atop the table, thinking. He

caught one of the pretty ladies glaring at him from the corner of his eye and quickly stopped.

"I think I tried the first...yesterday? Two days ago? I need to get on a regular sleep schedule again, I really do, all these days and nights are just merging together into one long book study. Chronicling the history of our discoveries is going to be a massive headache, I can already tell. Maybe we should keep a journal of some sort for posterity's sake or..."

Malik reached across the table and settled his fingers atop Tommy's wrist. Tommy's attention immediately snapped into an eagle's focus on that light pressure. There was nothing to it, just a polite, patient way to interrupt his rambling, but that did not stop the shivers rolling up his arm and down to his stomach.

"Tommy," Malik said. "Focus, please."

"Sorry," Tommy coughed. He reached for his drink, remembered he'd emptied it, and then cocked an eyebrow in surprise. With the stealth of a phantom the servant had scooped away his empty glass and returned it completely full. He drank another half of it, thankful for the delay. The cool wine burned upon reaching his stomach.

Hoo-boy. Watch the liquor, Tommy, or you'll be dancing atop this table before long.

"What was I saying?" Tommy asked as he set his glass down. He didn't wait for an answer. "Right, Gloam. It took me a few hours to really nail down my hypothesis, but my belief is that this school of magic involves understanding and manipulating thought, perception, and emotion. So far it's been the most difficult for me to cast, but with how often I've come across that key word, I'm convinced of its importance."

"I assume that's why you've not demonstrated to me one of its spells?"

"Correct," he said.

Malik leaned back into his chair. Though his eyes were upon him, Tommy knew the man's thoughts were far elsewhere. He had a way of sinking into his own mind, his features freezing calmly in place to hide the intense concentration. In those times he looked less like a living human and more of a doll. An attractive doll, mind you, but still a doll.

"And what of the last one?" Malik asked, snapping back into motion as if nothing had happened in the past five seconds. "Nihil, was it?"

"That's the only one I can't quite pin down," Tommy said. "I've managed just two of its spells, and neither shared any obvious theme. I'd normally posit that *Nihil* was a lesser part of the casting, but these two spells also lacked any of the other four words, nor did they share any other verbal component."

The servant might have been a phantom with the wine, but Tommy noticed his approach with their food from halfway across the room. He leaned back in his chair to give Tynek space to set the two steaming plates. His mouth began to water at the sight. His lamb chop was practically swimming in a dark sauce that smelled of rosemary and heaven.

"Please enjoy," Tynek said, bowing low.

Tommy sliced off a piece. The meat melted in his mouth. The sauce rolled across his tongue like a food-borne massage. Tommy's hunger less awakened and more exploded into spontaneous existence. He devoured his meal, and when finished he took another sip of his wine, slumped back in his chair, and sighed long and loud.

"Damn."

Malik grinned at him. His duck was half-finished on his plate before him.

"Do you understand now what I explained earlier?" he said. "Recommendations are all they need. Try not to tell too many people about this place. I enjoy the short waits for a table."

Tommy simmered in his posteuphoria haze as Malik sliced away at the duck with his fork and knife. His movements were precise as a surgeon's, Tommy noticed. Very confident. Very strong. He fantasized what it'd be like if those hands grasped not hardened silver but something much softer, much warmer, and then moved with those same disciplined movements...

"...yet to try?" Malik finished.

Tommy snapped out of the daydream. His mouth dropped open an inch as he fought to control his panic.

"What was that?" he asked.

"Back at the tower," Malik clarified. He wiped his hands on a folded cloth and then dabbed a bit of fat from his chin. "You said I had not yet tried all schools of magic. Do you think there is reason I should?"

"Well, of course," Tommy said, glad to be back on a topic he understood. "We have far too little information to work with to make any real assumptions. Why can I cast spells and you can't? Not a damn clue. Perhaps these individual schools are separate for a reason. Perhaps some people can master one or two but not others? What if you are incompatible with Viciss or Chyron but gifted with Gloam? The best way is to experiment."

"What Gloam spells do you have?"

"Hold on, I'll show you."

Tommy reached for his pocket and then stopped. His hands were still coated with grease. He quickly wiped them on his cloth napkin and then pulled out a long, rolled piece of paper.

"I should have at least one Gloam spell on here somewhere," he muttered as he scanned the list.

"Tommy, what is that?"

He glanced up. "Spells I've successfully cast. Why?"

"You carry them around with you?"

"Of course I don't carry them around with me. The various tomes and books are still safe in the archive. These are just copies." Tommy couldn't read Malik's frozen expression. Perhaps it was best he didn't. "Anyway, this one, riiiight...here."

Tommy flipped the scroll about and pointed to the list. Malik scanned over it, his frown deepening. It wasn't unhappiness, Tommy had learned. The harder he concentrated, the more his face shifted that way.

"What exactly does this spell do?" he asked.

"I'm not certain," Tommy said. "When I tried it I heard whispers of voices and ideas from all directions. The source scroll was heavily damaged by fire. I could not make out much more than the required words."

"And so you'd have me try this uncertain spell in the middle of a crowded restaurant?"

"It's not that crowded."

"Tommy, the *crowded* part is not the...very well. I need not worry. I'll fail this one just like I have failed all the others."

"You will if you go in with that attitude."

Malik glared vicious death. Tommy lifted his hands in surrender and then leaned back in his chair. His mentor memorized and rememorized the three seemingly simple words. He tried each one separately, tasting them like he did the wine. At last he pushed the scroll away, breathed out long and loud, and then brought his gaze to Tommy.

"Gloam legere tavrum," he said. It seemed the air around him rippled. Again he tried, this time slower. *"Gloam legere tavrum."*

Tommy shook his head. It felt like something was knocking on his temples. Soft, hesitant, and thoroughly alien.

"Malik," Tommy said. "Wait, I'm not...so...sure..."

His mentor ignored the warnings. His eyes were clouding over. He spoke a third time, and with every syllable a funnel of air whirled between them. A lance of lightning shot from Malik's forehead to his. Could no one else see this? Could no one else hear the sudden tempest roar?

Tommy? The voice spoke within his mind. It was no doubt Malik's, only it bypassed his ears and shot straight to his brain. A recent memory bubbled upward of its own accord. *Is this...you?*

Tommy tried to focus but struggled impotently. His thoughts were scattering like cockroaches before a sudden light. Heavy sleep lined his eyes despite his confusion and panic. Memories lurched into his consciousness with no apparent reason or connection. Him and Brittany using flowers and their mother's powders to play dress-up on a sleepy afternoon. Tedious study sessions back in Steeth. Vomiting so hard he thought he'd die after eating part of a frog on a dare. A dream from last night. The first time he masturbated when he was ten and had been horrified by the sudden stain across his trousers. These memories surfaced, popped, and vanished into a blackness blanketing his mind.

Malik, please, he begged.

It's...it's all right, Tommy. I'm gaining control.

Sure enough, the scattershot memories slowed. His mind felt less like an avalanche and more a steady trickle. Malik was a composer inside his head, summoning memories instead of music with the waves of his hand. At first he'd flailed and spun every which way, but now they were smoothing over. Tommy hovered in a giant black void. His memories shimmered into existence, and he saw them as his eyes saw them, and he remembered his thoughts as they'd been in that moment. Somehow, he knew Malik hovered next to him, seeing and reliving exactly the same.

I'll pull us back, Malik's voice echoed. *I'll take us here to the present, and then I'll leave.*

The memories rolled forward at a steady pace, calm and controlled to the point of pleasantness to reexperience them again. Reading through his many books while Malik worked next to him. Malik suggesting they eat a meal. Their walk to the restaurant. Tommy's exuberance upon tasting the food. The tastes washed over him again, and they had a startling clarity. The deep hunger was gone, and he could identify each flavor with clinical preciseness. He felt sad when the memory moved on. Now the taste of wine. Him observing an empty plate. Looking up.

Him staring at Malik's hands as his mentor ate. The fantasies he'd imagined swirled like secondary clouds to the periphery of the memory.

"Oh fuck," Tommy said. The words escaped his lips, and his grasp on reality hardened. He was sitting in a chair. They were in a restaurant. He was mortified. Fear and humiliation slammed away the mental connection, the lightning tether dissipated, and suddenly they were quiet and together, facing each other with their real bodies and addressing each other with their physical voices.

"Fuck, fuck, fuck," Tommy said. He couldn't even look at Malik. His eyes drilled holes into his empty plate. "I'm sorry, Malik, I'm so sorry. That was inappropriate of me, I know, very inappropriate. I'm beyond embarrassed. My mind shouldn't be that undisciplined. I cannot begin to guess your sexual preferences, and even if they *did* tilt a certain way that doesn't mean you'd be interested in *me*, but oh fuck me, fuck, fuck, I ruined everything, didn't I?"

Malik's hand once more settled atop his wrist, but this was not the same polite interruption. His fingers curled into his. The pressure increased, not much, just enough to keep skin against skin. Tommy looked up, hope battling despair. Malik did not appear upset or angry. If anything he looked amused.

"Do not be embarrassed, or ashamed," Malik said. "The fault is mine in traipsing through your mind when neither of us fully understood the consequences. And as for your...fantasies..."

The heat in Tommy's neck traveled all the way up to his ears. He must look like a ripened tomato ready to fall off the vine.

"I will not say your feelings go unappreciated, but you should understand that I am many years your senior. I am in a position of authority over you, and that complicates things greatly. You mentor under my apprenticeship, and you work alongside me in the study of something wondrous and new. Do you understand why that makes any physical and emotional connections complicated?"

Tommy could hardly believe what he was hearing. It was the pardon of a queen while dangling from the hangman's noose. It was the sound of water rushing through a desert. It was the sound of the *slightest chance* something more might happen, and by the Goddesses and all the magic in the world, he was ready to cling to that like a man adrift.

"I understand perfectly," Tommy said. "So I forgive you, you forgive me, and then we both move on like this never happened?"

"Not quite like it never happened," Malik said. His mischievous grin lit a fire in both Tommy's heart and groin. "I've touched a school of magic! Hurry, let us return to the tower. I want to read every single Gloam spell you've found, and when that's done, I want to search for more!"

CHAPTER 29

It wouldn't be dark for another half hour but already the city appeared empty. Devin passed homes with lit candles hidden behind heavy curtains. Londheim was like a ship battened down for a storm, only the storm was giant owls and a mysterious psychopath murdering keepers. A novice had come bearing a letter demanding his immediate arrival at the Cathedral of the Sacred Mother. At the foot of Anwyn's Gate leading into the cathedral grounds he discovered more than fifteen other Soulkeepers gathered in waiting. It seemed he was not the only one to receive a summons.

"Hello, Devin," Lyssa said as Devin joined her in the back of the group. "I thought for sure you'd be scouring the wildlands instead of sulking here in Londheim."

"And I would if I had a choice," Devin replied. "I'd rather brave the black water than risk another errant shot from your pistols."

The freckled woman grinned at him, and Devin grinned right back. Soulkeepers often traveled alone, sometimes going months between trips to speak with their Vikar. Devin only recognized a handful of those gathered at the steps, but Lyssa had trained and graduated alongside him twelve years ago. Her auburn hair was pulled up in a bun, adding age to an otherwise youthful face. She wore a tricorn hat similar to his, only slightly smaller and sporting five raven feathers tucked into its band.

"Do you still have the scar?" she asked.

"It seems highly inappropriate to show my ass on the steps of the cathedral."

Lyssa punched his shoulder with strength far greater than a woman of such diminutive size should possess. More Soulkeepers trickled over, increasing their numbers to twenty. Deciding it enough, Forrest clapped his hands to gather their attention.

"I'm going to keep this short," he shouted. "Some bastard named Janus has been hunting our own, and the city guard don't have the manpower to find him or the skill to bring him in if they do." He lifted up a large sheet of paper with a man drawn upon the front. It was one of the wanted posters that had been nailed throughout the city for the past several days. "He's a strange-looking sort, half his hair green instead of black, wears a long leather coat and no shirt. This might sound unbelievable, but we have corroborating accounts confirming he can change anything he touches into anything else."

"That's putting it gently," Lyssa shouted. "I saw one of the Faithkeepers he killed. Janus turned him into a goddess-damned statue before breaking off his head."

Murmurs spread through the twenty Soulkeepers. Devin had not heard of that one, but he'd seen the Mindkeeper melded into the wall with his blood turned to gold, not to mention the horribly disfigured men at Oakenwall.

"Enough," Forrest said, his deep voice easily carrying author-ity to silence them. "Janus has always struck after dark, so until he's found, expect to be sleeping during the day and patrolling at night. Be warned that as of late our city's gone to shit. We've got confirmed deaths by giant fucking owls, for starters, so keep an eye on the sky. The church has also been told of fox people, living gargoyles, and shapeshifting dogs. They're all rumors, but at this point, I wouldn't rule anything out. Better to be jumping at our own shadows than dead to some new nightmare creature. Split up in pairs and choose your districts. If you can't agree, I'll start making the decisions for you. Good luck, and may Anwyn watch over you."

Lyssa nudged Devin with her elbow.

"Care to be my date for the night?"

"I'd be honored."

Devin strolled through the group of gray-coated Soulkeepers to Forrest. Overall the mood was darkly jovial. There was an energy to confronting the unknown, and a palpable sense of finally *doing* something instead of idling in the shadow of the crawling mountain.

"Got a district for me?" the giant man asked Devin when he saw him.

"Is Low Dock still available?"

"Sure is. Keeping an eye on your sister?"

"What can I say, I'm a good brother." Devin crooked a thumb over his shoulder. "Lyssa will be with me, too."

"Have fun," Forrest said as he jotted it down into a small notebook. "Try not to die."

Lyssa and Devin walked side by side through the quiet streets of Low Dock. The moon shone bright and clear in the sky above, removing any need for the street lanterns. Devin held his armed pistol with its aim loosely pointed toward the sky. Lyssa's custom brace of pistols were equally armed and ready, except she kept them in her holsters, the two softly swaying with the swing of her hips. Few could match her speed when it came to drawing a weapon, be it her pistols or the slender short swords strapped to her thighs.

"I wasn't there when the black water came," Lyssa said after Devin finished telling her of when it flowed through the town of Dunwerth. "I missed it by only a few miles. My first experience with it was stumbling upon a tremendous black field split by the road traveling north from Pathok."

"Did you disturb the grass?" Devin asked.

"Disturb it? I knelt down where the corruption started and stuck my face close enough to smell it. Gave myself a fucking eyeful when I brushed a patch with my hand. I'd rather pour salt on my eyes than go through that again. I truly thought I'd be blind for the rest of my life."

Devin knew he shouldn't laugh but did so anyway.

"If it makes you feel any better, I was convinced the entire world had turned into that choking grass. At the first patch of green I found, I dropped to my knees and bawled like a child."

Lyssa chuckled.

"I do feel a little better," she said. "So has Forrest sent you on any pointless errands?"

"Wouldn't call it pointless, but he sent me to a lumber camp to see if Janus had struck there before coming to Londheim."

"And had he?"

Devin winced at the remembrance.

"Yeah. He had. What about you?"

"Forrest sent me to Roros to see if the black water had reached that far."

This wasn't too surprising. The hills near the town of Roros bore the distinction of being the only place in all the Cradle where flamestone was mined. Because of this it was heavily guarded and its mines strictly regulated by the Queen.

"I imagine if the world ended, Roros would be one of the few places to survive," he said.

"Pretty much," she said. "The guards there had it boarded up tighter than an ant's asshole. Other than that, the trip there was pleasant enough. It's the priority that irked me. The world may be ending, but by the Goddesses, we'll still have the tools needed to kill ourselves."

The two traveled the district, several hours passing quiet and uneventful. Devin was thankful. Lyssa, not so much.

"If anything interesting is happening in Londheim, it's not here in Low Dock," she grumbled. "We should be in bed."

"Does it matter if we sleep during the night or sleep during the day, so long as we sleep?" Devin asked, trying to remain upbeat about their assignment.

"I was thinking in the *same* bed, so yes, a little."

Devin blushed. The two had slept together multiple times since their training, stopping only after Devin met Brittany while traveling to Stomme. No, that wasn't quite true. There'd been one more time, three weeks after his wife's death. His mind and heart had been in a dark pit of loneliness and isolation, and he'd desperately clung to Lyssa's burning light of humanity. He was deeply grateful, but that moment of intimacy had been their last. Unfairly or not, Lyssa was now linked to Brittany's death in his memories.

"You'd find me a poor partner," Devin said. "Out of practice and more awkward than romantic. I must refuse for the sake of my pride."

Lyssa rolled her eyes in an exaggerated manner.

"Please tell me you haven't become one of those Estranged Isle exiles who thinks Anwyn desires us to die as virgins."

"It's a little late for that."

"They also insist that oaths of celibacy will return your virginity. Apparently it's never too late to decide that the awesomeness of fucking is more than our meager souls deserve."

Devin's laugh was a pleasant thunderclap across the sleepy district.

"I've missed you, Lyssa," he said. "Much more than I realized, and likely more than you missed me."

She looked down from the sky and winked at him.

"Don't sell yourself short," she said. "It's nice chatting with someone not so easily upset or offended. Seems most town mayors or village elders believe their pure daughters are besieged by monsters or impregnated by Ravencaller magic when they turn up 'in a family way.'" She laughed. "I wish you'd been there with me, Devin. This haggard old woman was insisting to me that her granddaughter was possessed by a lustful ghost." Her voice rose a pitch and she added a scratch to it. "*'I saw her when she thought we was sleeping,'* she tells me. *'She was moaning and moving like a man was atop her, I swear, but she was all alone in that bed.'*"

Devin had encountered similar situations, particularly in the farthest reaches of West Orismund, where visits from doctors, teachers, and the Wise were a rare occurrence. He tried to be tactful when addressing such concerns. He had a feeling Lyssa did not.

"What'd you tell her?" he asked out of morbid curiosity.

"I told her the obvious. I said she'd caught her granddaughter masturbating and to give her some privacy next time. Old bat threw a fit and asked if such impropriety should be punished. Punished? I told her to be goddess-damned grateful. Fingers can't impregnate her granddaughter, but a neighbor boy's cock sure can."

Devin laughed despite himself. Layers of mental armor slipped off his mind. The public persona of Soulkeepers was of skilled, armed protectors of life and manipulators of souls. Their arrival in a town often signified a dire need of some sort: a spreading disease, mass burials, or bandits thought to be beyond the reach of the Royal Overseer's soldiers. People saw them as invincible, but Devin knew better. He remembered Soulkeepers-in-training getting homesick in their early days as a novice, remembered their broken bones and bleeding noses during training, foul jokes over meals, smuggled bottles of rum and beer, and awkward, uncomfortable sexual escapades between young men and women in cramped wooden bunks. They were human, and it felt good to be one with someone who understood that.

"When daylight comes, would you like to find a tavern somewhere and toast to old times?" he asked her.

"Sure," Lyssa said. "I assume you also haven't given up alcohol?"

"Are you kidding?" he asked. "No sex *or* alcohol? I might as well—"

A shadow crossed over the moon. Devin shoved Lyssa aside and brought his pistol up to bear. A deafening screech assaulted his ears and threatened to disrupt his aim. Wings and feathers and reaching claws whooshed through the spot where Lyssa had stood. Devin pulled the trigger, immediately sensing he was already too late. His shot splintered harmlessly into the side of a building. The enormous owl flapped its wings with enough force to blow the hat off Devin's head and rapidly ascended back into the night sky.

Lyssa rolled to her feet. Her pistols appeared in her hands as if she'd merely willed them out of their holsters. Two more rolling cracks of thunder echoed through the street from her flame-stones' eruption. If either shot hit, the owl showed no sign of it. Together the two Soulkeepers watched the bird of prey fade into the distance.

"Holy shit," Lyssa said. Her pistols remained aimed at the fleeting shadow despite being empty. "Holy shit, Devin. Holy shit."

"Did you believe the owls imaginary?" he asked her.

"It's not that," she said. "I nearly died. Just like that, I'd be owl food. Holy shit."

A somber reminder that an empty street did not mean safety. One moment they were laughing and discussing their journeys as Soulkeepers, the next, diving for their lives. Holy shit, indeed.

"We need to keep moving," he said. He put a hand on her shoulder. "Better us than someone else."

Lyssa pulled herself free of his touch.

"I know my job," she said. "And forget splitting our attention. We both keep our eyes on the sky."

They reloaded their weapons and continued their patrol of Low Dock. All hint of their jovial banter was buried beneath steady gazes and careful examination of their surroundings. The owl's attack had unnerved him greatly, so when Devin heard sudden pounding against wood from around the corner he had to stifle a jump. The two Soulkeepers exchanged glances, and Lyssa gestured for Devin to take point. He drew his sword as she readied both her pistols. After a silent count to three he rushed the corner, and upon discovering a scrawny man beating against the locked door of a bakery, he brought his pistol to bear. Disappointment quickly replaced his adrenaline. No half-green, half-black hair, just sweat-stained brown locks atop a young dockworker.

"Hey there," Devin said as he lowered his pistol. "What is the matter, friend?"

The man ignored him. His fists struck the door with a steady rhythm. A simple glance through the window showed the small bakery closed and empty. What was he hoping to accomplish?

"I said hello, friend," Devin called again, this time with far more edge to his voice.

The man spun about and shoved his back against the door. He looked haggard and bruised. The bottoms of his brown trousers were stained from the waters of the Septen River. His eyes locked onto the drawn pistol.

"What?" he asked. He sounded perturbed, as if the two Soulkeepers were annoying interlopers. Hardly the respect they deserved.

"The place is closed," Lyssa said. "Why the fuss?"

"I'm hungry," he said as if that explained everything. He scratched at his neck. His skin looked pale and unhealthy, as if he hadn't seen the sun in years.

"Hungry or not, there's no food to be had here," Lyssa said. "Go home. Find yourself a big breakfast come morning."

"Can't sleep," he said. "I've given up trying."

The dark circles underneath his eyes certainly lent evidence to that, but overall he looked wired and edgy, not tired. Something about his movements seemed off, though Devin could not quite decide why. Like he moved in spurts. Certainly not drunk, but then what?

"Do you know where the local church is?" Devin asked. The man nodded. "Good. My sister is a Mindkeeper there. Go to her and ask for a nocturnal medicine. She'll give you something that will knock you right out."

The man nodded twice, three times, four, five.

"Maybe," he said. "Maybe, maybe."

And then he ran full tilt up the street. Devin watched him go with a deep pit in his stomach.

"Did any new powders or mushrooms arrive recently in Londheim?" he asked.

"Not that I know of," Lyssa said. "Just the standard weeds from the south. They don't wind you up, though. Quite the opposite."

The strange man ducked around a corner and out of his sight. Devin decided to ask Adria if she'd encountered similar behavior. If something new had hit Londheim, especially in its overcrowded state, it could be …

Movement drew his eye. On the rooftop, not far from where the man turned. Shadows crawled. He caught the faint outline of wings.

"He's in danger," Devin said. "Follow him, hurry!"

They sprinted over the cobbles. A terrible cry added an extra burst of speed to their steps. That wasn't a man in pain. That was a man dying. Devin drew his sword and pistol as he turned the corner, anticipating the worst and still not prepared to view it.

Two monsters huddled over the man's corpse. They looked made of stone, with crooked backs and clawed three-toed feet.

Long, reptilian wings sprouted from their shoulders. Though their arms and legs resembled those of a human, their faces were akin to a panther's, with narrow eyes, a broad flat nose, and long, pearly-white canines. They were unmistakably gargoyles, only instead of decorative objects meant to shunt water away from rooftops, these breathed and snarled and ripped meat off the dead man's ribs and into their stone mouths. They heard the Soulkeepers' approach and turned. Their eyes shone a sky blue with little white veins crackling throughout.

Lyssa's extended pistols remained as still as the statues the gargoyles were supposed to be. She showed no outward panic or fear. Life-or-death training had taken hold. No doubt she analyzed the gargoyles with the same clinical mind-set as Devin. The gargoyles opened their bloodstained mouths and growled in unison. It sounded like angered mountain lions, only strangely higher-pitched.

"Their skin may be real stone," Devin said. "Aim for the eyes, or the throat if you can't."

Her aim shifted to the left gargoyle. Devin trained his pistol to the right. The four of them remained still, each pair tensely watching the other. Waiting for movement. Seeking weakness. The left gargoyle spread its wings and growled again, the pitch even higher. Lyssa fired before the sound could even leave the monster's throat. Blue blood erupted from its mouth in a spray. As the force of the bullet rocked its head backward she fired again, this time into the skin directly beneath the jaw.

Lyssa's shot forced Devin to take his own. The bullet ricocheted off the other gargoyle's skull. The monster flapped its wings in a frantic, graceless rhythm compared to the calm beats of the giant owls. Its skinny legs aided its ascent with a jump carrying it up to the nearby rooftop.

"Check it," Lyssa said, her calm voice out of place after the detonation of three flamestones. The shot gargoyle wasn't moving, but that was evidence of nothing. Devin holstered his pistol and rushed toward the body, his sword pulled back for a thrust with both hands.

The second gargoyle dove headfirst off the rooftop. Its teeth opened wide, eagerly extending those four long canines. Devin had no time to think. Training took over. His body was primed for a thrust, so he shifted his aim skyward and tensed his legs and elbows. The gargoyle's momentum carried it into contact, driving the sword down its throat tip first. Devin had a brief second to feel the cold, wet insides of the gargoyle's mouth before the weight of the body made contact.

The two slammed into one another in a chaotic tumble of arms, legs, and wings. Devin's head hit the ground first. The sudden crack flooded his vision with giant black splotches. His sword ripped out of his hands. Something sharp raked his chest. Claws? Teeth? He didn't know. He rolled onto his stomach as the weight slid off. His hand shot to his waist where he kept a hunting knife. Had to arm himself. Had to fight.

Fingers closed around his elbow. His panic nearly caused him to slash Lyssa's hand off at the wrist.

"Nice kill," she said. "Keeps us at an even one and one."

His vision was returning, however slowly. He settled his eyes on the stiff gargoyle lying beside him. His sword remained embedded up to the hilt in its throat. Grimaces and groans accompanied his push to stand.

"Should we get you to an apothecary?" Lyssa asked.

Devin put a foot on the gargoyle's head and yanked his sword free after a few tugs.

"Nothing's broken," he said. "I'll be fine."

He stood over the gargoyle. It'd been surprisingly difficult to pull out his sword. Despite dying mere seconds ago its entire body appeared locked in rigor mortis. Even stranger, he saw no sign of blood anywhere. He knew these things could bleed. He'd seen the spurt from the one Lyssa gunned down.

"Bizarre, isn't it?" Lyssa asked. She joined him in staring at the dead creature. "It makes you wonder, are all of the gargoyle statues alive? Were they alive all these centuries, or only when the magical creatures emerged?"

Good questions, and all of which Devin had no answers for.

"We'll need to call for some guards to clean up the mess," he said.

"Lucky them."

It wasn't much, just a low scrape of stone against stone, or claw against cobble. Devin dropped to one knee and spun. The first gargoyle they'd "killed" was very much alive, and it lunged at him with open mouth and reaching claws. Its aim was too high, and Devin ducked even lower as he swept his sword in an upward arc. The creature landed between the two of them with a howl. Blue blood flowed from the cut across its chest, joining that which dripped from the earlier bullet wounds.

Instead of charging again it flapped its wings and soared into the air. The gargoyle circled like a hunting falcon, the two Soulkeepers its wounded prey.

"Buy me time to reload," Lyssa said.

"I don't know if I can fight it off," Devin said. It took much of his strength to remain on his feet.

"Then just look scary," she snapped. "I only need a few seconds."

Devin had witnessed Lyssa reloading her weapons countless times during their training, and she'd gotten only faster with age. Her fingers curled the pistols downward, her thumbs pulling back the hammers and then smoothly dipping into two pouches belted on either side of her waist. Out rolled a flamestone into each chamber. Her hands twisted again, rotating the pistols so they faced upward. Another smooth motion rolled two lead shots wrapped in cloth out of two higher belt pouches and into the barrel. Last she twirled them downward, sliding the barrels over two short rods of metal poking upward from her custom belt. When she lifted her loaded pistols to the sky, a mere five seconds had passed from start to finish.

Not once did her eyes leave the circling gargoyle.

"Come on, you son of a bitch," Lyssa breathed. "Make the dive. You know you want to."

Perhaps the gargoyle knew they were prepared. Perhaps it didn't care. Two loops lowered its height significantly, and the third sent it spiraling into an uneven dive toward the Soulkeepers. Devin stood his ground and trusted his friend. Lyssa's pistols moved in tiny little shifts, tracking the dive, anticipating its movements.

Fire burst from the barrels. Two loud cracks announced the bullets finding their marks. The gargoyle plummeted off course and smashed into the side of a building. Devin's eyes widened, and he had but a half second to dive aside before the gargoyle's body ricocheted off and slammed through the street at a dizzying roll. Lyssa instinctively held an arm up before her, and then the two collided into a rolling tangle of limbs.

"Lyssa!" Devin screamed. He pushed to his feet and ran to where she lay upon the cold stone. One of the gargoyle's wings rested atop her like a blanket. Her eyes fluttered, and then she let out a pained groan.

"Never lucky, am I?" she said.

Devin sighed with relief. "Are you all right?"

"More or less," she said, gingerly rising to her feet. She clutched her right arm to her abdomen and hissed in sharply. "I'm thinking less. Motherfucker broke my arm."

Devin turned his attention to the dead gargoyle. At least it looked dead, but he was taking no chances this time. He watched the flow of blood cease from its wounds, something familiar about the sight. He used his sword to open up a new cut on a flank of skin relatively free of bloodstains. When Lyssa asked what he was doing he merely held up a finger and asked for patience.

After a minute or so he saw the first blue drops of blood coalescing along the wound.

"I was right," he said. "I *have* seen this before."

"Seen what?" Lyssa asked. "Something turn to stone?"

"It's not turning to stone," Devin said. "It's slowing its own time."

He lifted his sword with all his might and brought it slamming down upon the gargoyle's neck. The blow severed its head, and the instant the spine broke, the body thrashed wildly. Blood spurted from the gargoyle's many wounds. Whatever magic had frozen its time was spent. Devin moved to the other and with two quick whacks severed its head as well. Blue blood flowed across the cobbles.

The two Soulkeepers quietly surveyed the mangled remains of the two creatures and their unfortunate victim. It seemed neither wanted to break the silence. Devin certainly didn't. His mind was too busy reeling from the implications of this discovery. How many gargoyles were perched upon the corners of Londheim's taller buildings, particularly in the older districts such as Church and Quiet?

"Summon the city guard," Lyssa said softly. "No civilian should see this."

"Agreed. Go get your arm looked at by an apothecary. I'll spread orders to break and shatter all gargoyles from their perches. A few may be real, or maybe all, but it's the only safe course to take."

"We'll need to get permission from the mayor, or perhaps even Royal Overseer Downing."

Devin looked to the shredded corpse of a man he'd talked to mere minutes before. To the gaping hole in his chest where the gargoyles had torn open his rib cage and devoured his intestines.

"Then we get it," Devin said. "Come daylight, every last one of those gargoyles is coming down."

CHAPTER 30

Jacaranda waited until the stars were out before emerging from her bedroom fully dressed and armed. She peeked at the couch and saw Tommy snoring atop it. Good. She slipped to the door, then paused as the one person still present and awake let out a little cough to draw her attention.

"Where are you going?" Tesmarie asked. She fluttered up from her new makeshift bed. It was on a shelf with two rolled-up strips of cloth plus a small collection of loose cotton. It looked like the fanciest bed for the world's tiniest cat.

"I'm going out," Jacaranda said, keeping her voice soft to prevent waking Tommy.

"But-but-but Devin says it's dangerous at night. Plus you have your, you know…" She twirled her finger before her neck. "Your mark."

Jacaranda subconsciously tightened the white scarf covering her tattooed chains.

"I have my own matters to attend," she said. "I ask that you not speak of this to Devin."

Tesmarie flew back to her bed and sat on its edge with a sad huff.

"What if he asks? I'm not good at lying, Jacaranda. I'm, well, actually kind of terrible at it."

"Promise me," she insisted. "If Devin knows, he will want to help, but this is something I must do on my own."

"All right, I promise," the faery said, looking miserable. The fire popped. Jacaranda glanced at it in time to see strange ripples across the top of the flame. Tesmarie heard and promptly translated. "Oh, and Puffy says he won't tell anyone, either."

Jacaranda had planned to sneak out unnoticed, but now she was unsure. If Devin came home before her, the slightest interrogation would crack Tesmarie like an egg. Nervousness bubbled in her chest. How might he react? Would he be angry with her?

A surge of anger blasted the thought away. What did it matter how he reacted? She was not his soulless. Jacaranda lowered her hat over her face and pulled her long coat tighter about her neck and shoulders.

"Don't worry about me, either of you," she said, stepping out the door. "I am no stranger to the night."

Jacaranda had been many things for Gerag Ellington, and one of them was his loyal assassin. Nine times she'd climbed through windows into bedrooms and private studies to eliminate a rival in business or, more often, someone who had slighted Gerag and his new wealth. Countless other nights she'd protected his illegal shipments as they were slipped through the streets under the noses of the city guard. Going out alone was second nature to her, a skill as well trained upon her soulless self as eating and bathing.

Jacaranda hurried down the quiet street, then turned south.

Each road she passed was easily named in her mind. Part of her training had been two straight days of staring at maps of Londheim and committing every detail to memory. Her instructor had not told her she could sleep or take sitting breaks while doing so. The crippling pain in her legs and back was so horrible by the second day that Gerag had brought in a masseuse and ordered her to take a full week of bedrest. The instructor had suffered dearly for that oversight. She'd even been the one ordered to cut the tendons from his heels.

No amount of training or stealth seemed necessary for tonight, though. *Empty* did not begin to describe how the streets felt. People were in hiding. Windows were boarded over, less than a quarter of the streetlamps were lit, and the few patrols of guards she spotted were enormous groups detectable from blocks away and therefore easily avoidable. Jacaranda cut through enclosed alleys whenever possible, but sometimes it couldn't be avoided. At one major crossroad she paused and scanned each of the four directions, seeing no one. She started to cross and hesitated upon realizing she'd forgotten a vital fifth direction: up. She looked to the black sky, the stars, the moon...

And the shadow of an owl that passed over the moon.

Jacaranda picked a direction and sprinted. Her hands clutched the hilts of her daggers with white knuckles. The nearest cover was a shelter of the kind that had sprung up all throughout Londheim since the refugees arrived: long slabs of wood and cloth wedged into open crevices to create a shanty. Jacaranda fled toward it with one eye on the sky. She saw nothing but stars. That was meager comfort. The stealthy predator would likely take her before she knew it approached.

Jacaranda slid to a stop just within the shanty and breathed a sigh of relief. To her surprise, she was not alone in that dilapidated space. Two adults and a child huddled at the far end. Their bodies were covered with thick ash-gray coats and matching gloves. Wide, flat hats rested atop the heads of the two adults, while the small child wore a headscarf. They looked at her with pale yellow eyes, a peculiar family trait. A wave of nausea interrupted Jacaranda's attempt to address them. Their faces. She couldn't identify their faces. It was like a haze in her brain. Male? Female? Black? White? Nothing was coming through.

"Is something wrong?" the one on the left asked in a masculine voice. He lifted his hand toward her. For one brief moment she swore she saw red fur and palms like the paws of a canine. Light like stardust passed over her vision, and suddenly it cleared. The couple weren't strange, faceless beings. No, they were a tired man and woman with smears of dirt splotches on their faces and rags stuffed into the interior of their coats for warmth. A little girl huddled before them, her arms crossed and her cheeks red from the cold.

"S-sorry," Jacaranda said. She sheathed her daggers. "I'm sorry if I disturbed you."

"It's no bother," the man said. He smiled wide. Though his face was dirty his teeth were immaculate. "We're just taking a respite from the weather."

"Papa," the little girl said, tugging on his coat. "Look, look, she's *different*."

Jacaranda followed her pointing finger to her exposed throat. Her scarf. It'd slipped during her run. She spun sideways while tugging the fabric up below her chin. Her every muscle tensed. Hate it as she might, she would kill to protect her freedom.

"I don't know what she's talking about," Jacaranda said.

The husband and wife exchanged glances.

"No, I think we do," the husband said. "Her eyes have always been the sharpest. Do you fear us, Jacaranda?"

Jacaranda positioned her palms atop her daggers. She'd never given them her name. Something was deeply amiss. Whoever this man (was he a man?) might be, he showed no fear of her undrawn weapons. He stepped closer, and closer, his eyes locked onto hers. The pupils took on a feline slant.

"You are not alone," he said, his deep voice an edge above a whisper. "This fearful world will make room for the old even if blood must be shed. Should you ever feel ready to use those daggers of yours in the purpose of good, seek us out."

"Seek who out?" she asked. Those pale eyes paralyzed her.

"We are the Forgotten Children. Whisper our name, and you will find us."

Back to a tired, poor, dirty man and his family. His wife smiled at Jacaranda so sweetly.

"You'll kill to protect your freedom?" she asked. Her hands wrapped lovingly about her daughter. "So will I."

Her teeth were suddenly far too white and far too sharp. Jacaranda felt violated. Could they read her thoughts? Did they do so even now? Just what *were* these three? She took a step back, and then another. The threat of the great owls above seemed meager to the trio down here below.

"Merry hunting," the father said. The three rushed past her to the street and then off into the night. They ran fast, faster than a human was capable of. Jacaranda clenched her teeth and pretended not to notice. Damn all the oddities and bizarre things that threatened to swallow up Londheim. She just wanted her vengeance.

Jacaranda kept a roof or awning above her head the rest of the way, and like a thief in the night she slipped into Quiet District. Only here did she really have to worry about guards patrolling the streets, for even in potential end times the wealthy kept a firm hold upon their valuables. Despite the earlier scare, Jacaranda knew there was only one safe way to approach, so to the tops of the towering spires she climbed. She jumped roof to roof, sliding through twisting bell towers, crocket-coated spires, and interlocked balconies with railings adorned with stone triangles. She climbed one last spire, circled around its top, and looked upon the ugly, overly stretched mansion of Gerag Ellington.

Nothing could have prepared her for the visceral reaction she felt upon seeing it. Every daydream of returning had been painted red with rage and the satisfying spilling of blood. Gerag suffering. Gerag pleading for his life. A singular focus had fueled her, protected her, but now daydreams broke before reality. Locked-away memories lurched wildly through her consciousness, and no discipline could shove them back.

In that mansion she'd knelt nightly at the side of a bed stinking of sweat and expensive tobacco. Gerag loomed before her like a creature more appropriate to the dark entangling forest of the Oakblack Woods than a civilized city. Sometimes he forced himself into her mouth. Sometimes he merely finished upon her face and chest. Never in her. In his own words, she was too valuable an asset to risk dying to an unwanted pregnancy.

The memories assaulted her like stirred hornets. She couldn't keep them away. The taste. The smell. The sensation of semen on her tongue. She'd never cared. She'd never resisted. He'd lanced pins through her nipples, dripped hot wax across her labia, and ordered her to perform her best imitations of pleasurable noises.

Sensations rolled over her along with the memories, and it was as if she relived each and every one for the first time.

Jacaranda closed her eyes and bit down on her tongue. She had to regain control. The brutal memories faded first, for those she could easily process. Gerag was a beast. He was vile. Of course he would inflict pain and call it pleasure. More stubborn were the memories where he wasn't cruel. Memories when he was in his kinder moods. Being soulless did not remove physical sensations. It only meant she didn't care. Now she *did* care, and in far too many moments she remembered her pleasure in having Gerag inside her, the enjoyable way her body had tightened about him, how it increased her natural breathing rhythms and flushed her neck with heat. She remembered the heightened sensitivity of her skin as he kissed her every inch.

Guilt wrapped each memory in spiked chains. How could she murder him if she felt such things? How dare a single memory of him not overwhelm her with disgust? Was she confused? She'd spent her entire life absent from her body. Could she really be angry at how it was used? The guilt weakened her protective walls. More memories burst through. Deeper fears.

What would happen if he captured her? Could...could she go back to what she'd been? Could she live with a real chain about her neck instead of one made of tattoos? For a brief moment she envisioned herself under Gerag's power and it weakened her knees. She slumped, tears rolling down her cheeks. She'd never experienced anything like these emotions. Jacaranda failed to understand any of them. Horror at the thought of his hand on her skin. Terror at losing control of her life. Guilt for her past actions, no matter how ardently she protested that they were not of her own making. Rage at herself for being so helpless before her doubts and fears.

All because of that mansion. That fucking mansion, and its fucking owner. She'd thought to scout it out, but now she wondered if it'd be best to burn it all to the ground, rendering it impossible to return to the mansion's hidden rooms, its underground trade, and its cruel master with his sadistic perversions. His every whim, she unable to resist. For some that might dampen the joy. For Gerag, it only excited him further.

Oh shit.

Jacaranda turned to the side and vomited air and stomach acid.

"What is wrong with me?" she whispered. She stared at her shaking hands as if they betrayed her. "It's just a building. It's just a place."

Jacaranda heard the gunshot a fraction of a second before bits of wood splintered free from the shingles and pelted her legs. She immediately turned and slid down the side of the spire opposite Gerag's mansion. The smooth stone bruised the ridges of her spine until her feet caught the next spire and wedged her in place. Damn it, she'd been here too long. Her high perch might go unnoticed by nighttime travelers (assuming there were any in Londheim anymore), but a dedicated guard would observe more than just the road. She could only count herself lucky that the opening shot had missed.

Another gunshot, and she flinched involuntarily. The lead clacked upon the opposite side of the spire. It might be her imagination but she swore the sound was perfectly lined up with the position of her head.

Have to move. Have to get out.

The need for patience pushed back against her panic. If she waited for the next shot she could flee before the shooter reloaded. She pressed her knees closer to her chest and dropped even tighter into the V-shaped wedge between the spires, making herself as small a target as possible. Come the third shot, she'd roll free and sprint away from the mansion. Patience. Patience.

That third shot never came. Her nerves steadily frayed. Was the shooter summoning more guards? Gerag had heavily relied on Jacaranda to keep himself safe. With her dead he'd likely overcompensate until he crafted a replacement. There might be more than just the two guards he usually kept inside the mansion protecting his secret basement.

"I hope you're not waiting for me to waste a shot," a man's voice called from somewhere atop Gerag's mansion roof. "I have the entire night to kill. Can you say the same?"

Jacaranda bit down a curse. No, she couldn't. She envisioned the layered rooftops of the stretched mansion and used the man's voice to guess where he hid. All of the vantage points would provide easy shots against her if she fled to either side of the spire.

"Come now, don't be shy. Surely you know I'd have killed you with my first shot if I wished. Let us talk a bit to alleviate the long, tedious night."

Responding meant confirming her sex. Even that was more than she wished to reveal. If this shooter also noticed the color of her hair underneath her hat, or perhaps the color of her eyes... what would it take for Gerag to question Devin's story about her untimely death?

"No? Still plan on hiding? Well, I guess that leaves me no choice."

No choice? What did he mean by that?

The answer came in the soft thud atop one of the lower portions of the mansion rooftop. It seemed this mysterious shooter had come to her. Jacaranda readied her daggers. She'd be easier to hit at such a short distance, but at least she could attack back. Better to risk death fighting than fleeing from an unseen bullet.

Jacaranda waited until she heard the first footstep and then rolled to the left. She slid down the side of the spire to the lower portion that smoothed out onto a flat ridge with tiny iron spikes. In that brief second she took in her foe, analyzing him with cold intellect more akin to her soulless self. He was a muscular man dressed in white. To her surprise, his rifle was slung across his back instead of readied to shoot. A sword hung lazily from a loose grip in his right hand. Weirdly, his buckled shoes were a bold red.

Does he truly just want to talk? she wondered as her feet touched the rooftop. Perhaps he did. Perhaps not. Her mind was set. One way to prevent Gerag from hearing her description was to kill the man who'd spotted her. She sprang off her toes, a bladed missile aimed straight for the man's chest. Based on the smile on his face, he was far from displeased by the prospect. Her daggers lunged forward like the fangs of a biting cobra. The man swirled his sword, parrying both safely to the side, and like that, the battle began.

Jacaranda had never faced someone who fought in such a fluid, elusive way. He didn't challenge her speed by attacking faster than she might parry. He didn't challenge her strength with powerful chops that dared her to block. His grasp on his sword never tightened beyond that lazy, comfortable grip. She'd slice and lunge with ever-increasing aggression and he'd casually bat aside the thrusts he could not dodge. When she tried to surprise him with a sweep of her leg, he hopped over it like a child playing a game of jump rope.

With no apparent reason or timing he suddenly swung onto the offensive, his curved sword looping into circles and figure eights. It drove her mad. Her training was based on the concept of a dance, with each of her actions forcing a reaction from her foe and vice versa. Him? He moved through a series of maneuvers with little regard to her own actions, confident he knew what her reactions would inevitably be. Half the time he didn't need to parry or block her swings because of her poor aim. Other times he deftly sidestepped and ducked, sometimes before she herself had made the decision to attack. With the small space in which they fought, it should have been hard for him to remain so maneuverable, but he used every inch as if he'd spent his entire life there.

"This is one way to pass a night," the man said as his sword ricocheted left to right, batting away her trio of thrusts. "Please, tell a man your name. It feels wrong to be so intimate with a complete stranger."

Jacaranda couldn't shake the maddening feeling that he wasn't trying to harm or kill her. There was something almost playful about his occasional jabs. She couldn't decide if he was the better sword fighter, or if his style was so different from her training that she was making poor decisions all throughout the confrontation. She pulled away from another strange, slanted weave of his sword and backed to the edge of the rooftop. Sweat dripped down her face and neck as she sucked air into her lungs. Instead of denying her rest, the man crossed his arms, his blade carefully tucked into his armpit. Beads of sweat trickled across his copper skin.

"How rude of me," he said. "Asking for names without giving my own. I am Tye the White, third rank of the Faultless Eye. With whom do I have the pleasure?"

"Anthea," she lied. "Are you Gerag's new hire?"

"Are you familiar with his old hires?"

Damn it. Stop giving away information.

Jacaranda pulled her hat lower, guarding her face from the moonlight. It took all her willpower to keep from checking the position of her scarf.

"I'm paid to know things," she said. She'd encountered several hired killers in her life, working both for and against Gerag. Perhaps she could fool Tye into thinking she was one of them. It wouldn't be unusual for rival businessmen to strike during the chaos. Hard times were coming, and all of them would be jockeying to be the ones who survived, if not thrived.

"And what do you know of my master's mansion?" Tye asked.

"It is poorly guarded by a single man more eager to play than to protect."

"How harsh," the man said with a laugh. "If you weren't alone I'd have sent my first shot straight through your forehead. I only play games when I know I will win."

The insults and the ego merged into a red feral rage in her mind. What she'd give to grab him by that patch of hair beneath his lip and rip off his entire lower jaw. She leapt into a new frenzy, all her skill and training pushed to its limits. Who the fuck cared if he didn't wish to dance with her. She'd make him. Jacaranda ensured that her every strike would embed somewhere fatal. As counterintuitive to her training as it was, she forced herself to ignore his every action. He would respond to *her*. If she took a cut to her arm, she'd live. If he didn't parry or dodge her stab for his heart, he'd die. A trade she'd happily make.

Jacaranda thrust once, twice, kicked him in the stomach, and cross-slashed while falling back a step to avoid a desperate counter. Their blades connected. She hooked her right dagger inward and then twisted, pushing Tye's sword farther outward. Her left hand shot through the opening, her dagger aimed at his eye. He dodged backward, but not without injury. It wasn't much, just the tip of her dagger lancing a portion of his lower lip, but it felt like a significant victory. Between the two of them, she'd drawn first blood.

Tye weaved away, adding separation between them. Jacaranda allowed it, a part of her also enjoying the brutal exchange. When she was soulless she didn't care about the battle except as a means to accomplish what Gerag asked of her. For the first time she felt pride in her abilities, and satisfaction at proving herself equal to or better than her foe.

Tye wiped the back of his hand over his mouth and glared at the large splash of blood staining his glove. Jacaranda thrilled at seeing his pristinely white outfit tarnished.

"That's enough," he said. "You've become a poor guest. It's time you leave."

"No good-bye kiss?" she asked, unable to help herself.

Tye grinned. Blood rolled down his chin from his split lip.

"I don't kiss my whores."

He looped his sword in a long, wide circle and then dashed forward with nightmarish speed. There was no playfulness to his probing thrusts, no amusement to his relentless assault. He predicted her parries and forced her to exert additional strength to shove aside a killing blow. The distance between them vanished, and while that should have favored her smaller daggers, he elbowed and kicked with each twist and turn of his sword. Jacaranda's mind screamed for her to take the offensive, but she couldn't spare the second to even breathe. Tye was in complete control of this fight, and that meant her defeat was inevitable.

Jacaranda shifted left to avoid a punch that never came, realized his sword was twisting around for a slash at her side, and tried to block with both daggers crossed. Instead his fist struck her across the face, followed by the solid sword hilt cracking down atop her skull. Flickering lights danced across her vision. She flung her daggers up above her in anticipation of a killing chop. As always, she predicted wrong. Tye retreated two steps while twisting his body. His hands moved with practiced smoothness as they sheathed his sword and swung his rifle off his back, over his shoulder, and into his waiting right hand. He held it out from his body like a pistol, his finger on the trigger, the long barrel pressed against Jacaranda's forehead.

"To your knees," he commanded. "And drop your daggers."

Jacaranda wanted to retort. She wanted to respond in some way to salvage her pride. The cold metal on her skin denied her the ability. Tye's glare was death. The slightest misstep would scatter her brains across the mansion rooftop. She slowly lowered herself. She released the hilts of her daggers, and they clattered atop the stone.

"Tell whoever hired you that you're abandoning the job," Tye said. "If I see you again, I'll put a bullet through your heart before you even know I'm near. Is that understood?"

She glared to hide her growing fear. His finger tightened on the trigger.

"Is that understood?"

"Yes," Jacaranda whispered softly.

He slung his rifle back over his shoulder.

"Good. Now get the fuck out of here."

And with that he leapt off the rooftop edge. Jacaranda looked to her daggers, a raw impulse clamoring for her to grab them and assault while Tye's back was turned. What stopped her was the sight of his right hand holding the hilt of his sword, and the bare inch of steel showing between hilt and sheath. He was ready for it. Perhaps even hoping for it.

Jacaranda waited until he was out of sight, counted to thirty, and then fled the other direction. No matter how hard she ran, no matter how much she gasped for breath, no matter the path she took or the sweat that ran down her neck and chest, she could not outrun the reawakened horror at kneeling before another man, looking up at him helplessly, and telling him yes.

CHAPTER 31

A worried Tesmarie perked up at the sound of the door unlocking. She fluttered from her bed and increased the speed of her personal time flow to match the pace of humans. As much as it annoyed her, she knew it helped the fast-time humans understand her. Jacaranda slid through the door and shut it with quiet, stiff movements.

"Hi-hi-hi, Jac!" Tesmarie said, as loud and excited as one could do so while still whispering. "How'd your night go?"

Jacaranda looked her way with glass eyes and a statue for a face.

"Poorly."

The human trudged into the kitchen and returned with a browning apple. She sliced off chunks with her dagger and popped them into her mouth. Never one to give up easily, Tesmarie fluttered closer. Jacaranda looked so miserable. Surely there was something she could do to cheer her up, right?

"I'm sure whatever it is you'll do better next time," Tesmarie said. "Every new sun is a new life to succeed and flourish."

Jacaranda ignored her. She sliced off a chunk from the brown side, bit into it, and immediately spat it back out. Her brow furrowed in confusion.

"What?" Tesmarie asked. "Have you never eaten a bad apple?"

"No, I have, it's . . . I've never cared that something tasted foul before." She looked mortally wounded. Tears had begun to fall from her bloodshot eyes. "It's awful."

She cracked a window and tossed out the half-eaten apple. Tesmarie tried to be sympathetic but was confused and unsure.

"Jacaranda . . . are you all right?" Tesmarie asked.

"I'm going to bed," the woman said, brushing past Tesmarie. The faery had to zip out of the way to prevent being bowled over. "Tell Devin not to wake me."

The door thudded shut. Tommy's snoring ceased for a moment, then resumed. Tesmarie returned to her bed and folded up her wings as she nibbled on her nails. The last remnants of the night crawled on by. An hour later Devin came home. He looked no happier than Jacaranda, but unlike her, he bore multiple bandaged wounds. His hands removed his coat and unbuckled his weapons with an absentminded steadiness that showed that Devin's thoughts were deep in his own head.

"Goodness, Devin, are you hurt?" Tesmarie asked.

Devin's gaze broke. He weakly smiled at her and offered her his wrist at chin level. Tesmarie landed atop it and fluttered her wings happily.

"I'll be feeling these bruises for a while," Devin said. "But they'll heal in time."

"Time is the best healer," Tesmarie said, bobbing her head up and down. "Did you get into a fight? Was it something scary? I could help you, you know, if you'd only ask!"

"I'll keep that in mind," he said as he walked to his room. "Say, Tesmarie, do you know anything about gargoyles?"

"Gargoyles? Of course I do. Are you saying you *don't*?"

"Is that surprising?" Devin asked. "There's plenty I know nothing about."

"Yes, but there's gargoyles all over Londheim. I even chatted with a few on my way here. So you humans don't even remember *them*?"

"We knew them only as statues," Devin said. He sat on his bed and used his free hand to pull his boots off one by one. "Two of them killed a man tonight, and they tried to kill me as well."

"What?" Tesmarie said. "Why would they do that? Gargoyles are so friendly!"

"Friendly." The Soulkeeper's grim laugh gave her chills. "They did it so they could eat him, Tes."

Her confusion only grew.

"Gargoyles eat mice, rats, and birds. Why do you think they were so popular in Londheim? And they most definitely do *not* eat humans!"

"I saw it with my own eyes," Devin said. "I'm sorry, but the world's changed from what you remember. It certainly has for us." He gestured toward the door. "My night was long," he said, asking without asking.

"Of course." She spread her wings and floated to the door. "You...you sleep tight, Mister Devin. I'll make sure things stay nice and quiet for you."

She sulked her way to the main room's couch. Devin quickly shut the door behind her. The fire crackled softly, drawing her attention. Firekin had no means to speak, so they communicated with subtle movements of the flame around them. She doubted humans could see it, what with their bodies in such hurries, but she could easily detect the rise and fall of flickering letters.

Tesmarie sad?

"Maybe a little," she said. "Devin and Jacaranda also seem sad. Do you think I caught it from them?"

Puffy dipped in and out of the fire.

Tesmarie lonely.

Memories of her village flourishing in the heart of the Oakblack Woods stung her mind with the ferocity of wasps. The smiles of her friends. The love of her family. The welcoming hum of a hundred wings zipping through the air.

"I'm not lonely," she snapped. "I'm bored. That's it. Faeries aren't meant to be cooped up in colorless rooms with scraps of sun coming in through pieces of glass. I'm going out."

Tesmarie zipped for the door. Several loud pops from the fire turned her back to Puffy. The firekin's beady black eyes swelled with worry.

Human city. Not safe.

Tesmarie shook her head. No. Humans were easily frightened and confused, she knew that, but they weren't evil. Londheim might not be the city it once was, but she fully believed it could be her home. She just had to give it time, and time was something she was most excellent friends with.

"I'll be fine," she said, offering the firekin her biggest, widest smile. "I'll see if I can find you some sandalwood chips to snack on. Does that sound good?"

Puffy sank into the heart of the fireplace. There was no sign of his beady eyes.

"I'll take that as a...yes," Tesmarie said, holding firm to her desire for an enjoyable day. She flew high above the houses as she scouted for a good place to spend some hours. She'd be a blur to any who looked up and noticed her passage. No reason to worry. She saw plenty of quiet streets and tucked-away neighborhoods, but she was looking for something *interesting*. Apparently that would be a hard task in Londheim. No doubt they did most of their fun things indoors. Humans had always been weird like that.

Surveying the city from up high allowed Tesmarie to better assess its grand scope. She drifted toward cramped districts with rooftops that seemed to intersect with each other at odd angles. Arches linked buildings with no apparent purpose. Walls merged from one building to the next, combined with an apparent love of needless additional balustrades and buttresses across the ancient spires. A great commotion filled the street around one spire in particular, and she adjusted her path toward it.

A crowd of two dozen gathered loosely around a squad of armed men near the entrance. They all held part of a thick length of rope. She traced it upward to a gargoyle perched near the top of the tower, the rope bound around its neck. The soldiers pulled and released with a steady rhythm. The crowd's cheers urged them on.

"What...what are you doing?" she asked. It was obvious what it *appeared* they were doing, but that couldn't be right. They wouldn't be that cowardly, that cruel.

At first glance it seemed the gargoyle's feet and claws were part of the stone it huddled upon, but she knew that not to be the case. The creature possessed amazing strength and was trying to keep itself on its perch, but it could not match the combined might of the men below. It broke from the stone, tearing chunks of the outcropping with it in its claws. The gargoyle plummeted and broke upon the cobbles. Its blood painted a blue splatter in the heart of the crowd.

Panic seized her. Tesmarie zipped over to the other gargoyle and put her hands upon its flat nose. Gargoyles spent daylight with their bodies practically frozen in time, a gift that allowed them to live for hundreds of years. They could not individually manipulate its flow like Tesmarie, though she'd heard they could freeze up if in danger or significantly harmed. She touched the bubble about the creature and whispered words invoking the power of Chyron. The bubble shimmered momentarily into view and then popped. Warmth flowed into its feline nose. The gargoyle's eyes groggily opened.

"Fly!" she shouted. "Please, fly and hide before you must sleep again!"

"Why?" it asked.

"Humans…humans hate you now," she said, too ashamed and uncertain to repeat the reason Devin had given her. "You have to go. Warn the others if you can."

The creature rubbed the side of its face against her. Tesmarie hugged its stony ear.

"I shall do as asked," it said. "You are a true friend."

Its reptilian wings spread wide. A small hop sent it floating off the building's edge. Tesmarie heard screaming from the crowd below.

"A good day," she whimpered. "It's going to be…a good…day."

She flew without caring where. Her eyes soaked up her surroundings in a dull haze, for her mind was locked far away in a horrible cave echoing again and again with the sound of the gargoyle's body striking ground. Puffy had warned her, hadn't he? Human cities were unsafe...but that wasn't how she remembered the world. Her mother had told her stories of Londheim, the city of peace, where humans and dragon-sired lived in harmony. Had her mother lied? Or had too much changed over the centuries they'd slept?

Tesmarie lowered herself onto the top of a stake holding up the thick fabric roof of a stall in the heart of Londheim's southern market district. She curled her legs to her chest, rested her head on her knees, and sniffled. Tears slid down her face and fell atop the brown fabric. They hardened into little diamonds that sparkled in the morning light.

"It's not all bad," Tesmarie told herself even as she cried. "There's...there's Devin. He's nice. Jacaranda hasn't tried to kill you. Puffy's a little lazy but always good for a laugh. The food is good, and Tommy brings you strawberries...I don't need to go home. Who misses home? Not me. Not this faery."

You're not welcome here, Tesmarie Nagovisi.

She shook her head and cried away the horrible memory of her banishment. The tiny pool of diamonds grew. After a few more sobs she folded up her wings and lay on her back. The sunlight bathed her. She closed her eyes and pretended she was on a wide oak leaf drinking in the morning rays. It didn't matter that she cried. It didn't matter that homesickness ate a hole the size of a mountain in her stomach.

"Mommy?"

Tesmarie opened her eyes. The stall she lay upon was butted up against a multiple-story home. A human child peered at her from the sill of an open window. His skin was dark like hers (at least, as close as human skin could approximate her own), and his eyes were big brown walnuts rimmed with white. She sat up and spun to face him, baffled that this little youngster could think she was his mother.

"Mommy!"

The boy thrust his finger at her, and she realized he wasn't calling her his mommy, but summoning his own. Tesmarie curled her legs back to her chest and lowered her eyes. She didn't want to fly away. She liked this spot. More importantly, if she left she'd have to decide on a new place to go, and right then her paralyzed heart was incapable of making such a decision.

The boy's mother arrived at the window. Her annoyed expression rapidly changed to caution when she noticed Tesmarie's presence.

"Go play with your sister, Mason."

"But, Mommy..."

"Go. Now."

The boy retreated from the window. The woman crossed her arms over her chest and warily eyed Tesmarie. Her hair was tightly braided into several dozen strands and then those strands themselves tied together with a white bow that matched her pretty blouse. She put her elbows on the windowsill and leaned out. No words, just that hardened, weary gaze.

Tesmarie wiped her nose with the back of her hand, blinked away her tears, and then put on the best smile she could manage.

"Hello," she said. "My name's Tesmarie! What's yours?"

The woman looked surprised to hear her talk.

"Nora," she said. Nothing else. She looked cautious and hesitant. Did she fear for her child? Dragons help her, what stories did these humans believe about faeries after all these centuries? Did she think she'd come to take her boy away? Steal his eyes and mix them into potions?

"Should...should I go?" Tesmarie asked as the tense silence stretched on.

A silent argument waged within Nora's head. The moment it ended, her body visibly relaxed.

"My husband runs the stall you're on top of," she said. "Don't scare away any customers and you can stay."

Tesmarie smiled.

"Thank-you-thank-you-thank-you!"

Nora nodded. She still seemed uncertain, but Tesmarie was determined to prove her good intentions.

"Try to behave," Nora said. "I've work to do."

With that she vanished back into the home. Tesmarie picked up her crystalline tears and carefully sprinkled them over her hair, letting her momentary sorrow lend beauty to her presence. Time to gather herself. She didn't mind crying, but crying was not supposed to be on the list of goals for the day.

Tesmarie sat at the edge of the fabric, her feet dangling off the side, and watched the people of the market go about their day. Surrounded by noise, life, and light, her heart slowly awakened. It didn't take long for people to notice her presence, but most seemed curious or amused. One man offered a slice of peach to her, and she eagerly accepted it. Another man came later with a buttered piece of bread. After such boring food at Devin's, the market was a paradise of wonders. A trio of girls visited later who wished to give her flowers. Tesmarie tore two red petals free and weaved them together into a little circlet. She curtseyed for the girls, who curtseyed back with tremendous gales of laughter.

Hours passed with pleasant speed. She ate, waved at shoppers, and, if a large enough crowd gathered, twirled and danced through the air to their delight. It was enough to tire out even the most excitable of faeries. Eventually Tesmarie curled up just shy of the edge and slept.

She awoke past midday, with much of the traffic dwindled down. Tesmarie rubbed her blurry eyes and then noticed Nora watching her from the window.

"You put on quite a show," the woman said.

"Uh-huh," Tesmarie said. She yawned loudly and stretched her arms. "Do you mind if I come back tomorrow?"

Nora smiled for the first time.

"Consider yourself welcome here," she said.

Tesmarie set her wings a-buzzing. Before the woman could react she planted a soft kiss on her cheek.

"Bye-bye-bye," Tesmarie said, zipping back to Devin's home, her heart a million times lighter than when she left.

CHAPTER 32

Adria lay on her bed and massaged away one of her now-common headaches. It was just past midday, and this was her first moment of peace since morning. She'd asked Sena to allow her an hour of rest before waking her. Of her requested hour, she spent maybe ten minutes of it lying on her bed before a firm knock stirred her from the hazy place between wakefulness and sleep.

"I pray this is an emergency?" she called from her bed.

"Not an emergency," came the muffled reply on the other side of the door. "But I do come with a summons from Vikar Thaddeus."

Void-dragon have mercy, Adria thought.

"One moment."

She hoisted herself up from the mattress and smoothed out her dress and hair. Last came her mask. Did the church's Oathkeepers stand to either side of the door, ready to arrest her for heresy and unholy spellcasting? If so, she'd at least go out dignified.

Her fingers closed about the handle. She felt weirdly resigned to her fate no matter what choice the three Vikars, and likely Deakon Sevold above them, reached. Shouldn't she be worried? Then again, what could she fear? The Sisters themselves answered her prayers. Death lost much of its fear against that comfortable confirmation. She thrust open the door and stepped out.

No Oathkeepers waited with their shining silver armor, black-masked faces, and immensely sharp scythes. Just a young novice looking mildly impatient.

"The summons, please," she said.

"None to hand over," the acne-faced teenager replied. "I mean, none to hand over, Mindkeeper. Vikar Thaddeus requests you meet him at the Sisters' Remembrance."

That was odd. Not at the Old Vikarage, in Thaddeus's private study, or even at the Grand Archive? The Sisters' Remembrance was a short walk from Lyra's Door along the western side of the wall surrounding the Londheim Cathedral. Its purpose was as a glorified resting hall for the ashes of former Vikars, Deakons, and wealthy patrons of the church. Adria hadn't visited it since her training days as a novice, when she'd been forced on several "educational" tours through the portraits, statues, and expensive belongings of long-dead men and women. Funeral pyres were good enough for the laymen, but apparently Deakons deserved golden urns spotted with gemstones and laced with silver.

"I will leave immediately," Adria said. "You may go, novice."

The boy (because that was all he really was, a young boy being assaulted by the changes leading into adulthood) quickly bowed and hurried off. Adria remembered scurrying around with hundreds of vague orders and requests during her own time as novice. She almost missed not having a shred of responsibility beyond following basic orders.

Adria returned to the main hall. Sena lingered at the lectern with three women wearing laughably large hats that were supposedly in style all the way east in the capital city of Oris. If that was the style there, then Adria loved her cramped, twisting city that much more.

"Faithkeeper, if I might have a word?" she said.

Sena quickly apologized to the women and followed after Adria, who slipped away to one of the walls and crossed her arms. She was careful to keep her limbs still to hide her growing nervousness.

"Yes, Mindkeeper?" Sena asked once she had joined her. Adria noted the hint of annoyance in her tone. She'd interrupted a discussion with potential donors to the Low Dock church, and Low Dock did not have many donors in the first place.

"Vikar Thaddeus has summoned me," she said. She need not explain why. Sena's face immediately molded into a controlled mask, as smooth and emotionless as the porcelain sticking to Adria's skin.

"Only you?" Sena asked softly.

"It seems so. Perhaps he..."

Adria paused. Another young novice hurried in through the door of the church, a sealed scroll in her hand. She spotted Adria, rushed over, and offered up the scroll.

"From Vikar Caria, Faithkeeper," the novice said.

Adria took the scroll, dismissed the girl, and quickly unrolled it. Her eyes flitted over the text in less time than a heartbeat.

"It's a summons to the Faithkeepers' Sanctuary," Sena said. "I'm to speak with Vikar Caria."

"They've come to a decision," Adria said. Sena nodded in agreement. The two shared a look. It was possible they both walked into a clandestine arrest, and if so, this was likely the last time they would speak with one another. Adria started to stammer something meaningful, but words did not come easy. Sena abandoned them entirely and embraced Adria with their foreheads touching.

"I pray Alma keeps you in her mercy," Sena said. "No matter our path, stay strong. The Sisters blessed us for a reason."

"And if that reason is to die a martyr?"

Sena pulled back, and she smiled despite their worry.

"You Mindkeepers," she said. "Always ready to believe the worst in people."

Adria hurried out of the small church before she might lose her nerve. The old woman who had taken up a permanent residence at the bottom of the steps called after her as she rushed past.

"Something serious, keeper?" she shouted, then cackled as if it were the best joke ever told.

Adria ignored her and carried on. The walk to the Londheim Cathedral was one she'd taken a thousand times. She knew each stone by heart, or at least, there was a time she did. Houses seemed bigger or smaller than they once were, full of alcoves and deep shadows that were not there a mere month prior. Many windows were boarded over, and those that weren't were covered with heavy drapes. Why? Did the people fear that the hunting owls would crash through open windows?

A tired family passed her by, and while normally she'd never give them a second thought, something about them felt... unusual. She glanced over her shoulder but could see only their ash-gray coats and wide hats. Something had been strange about their faces, but she could not voice exactly what.

Adria grew more unnerved, and it seemed all of Londheim conspired to frighten her further. Her walk took her past a boarded-up home with an elderly woman sitting with her back against the shuttered door.

"Good afternoon, Mindkeeper," the woman said. She smiled, revealing a clean set of white teeth. "May your day be bright."

False teeth, Adria told herself as she continued on. Just like the hair on the little girl hopping ahead of her, which fell all the way to her shins. Surely it couldn't be real. Her parents dashed from where they huddled in an alley and grabbed the child when they saw her coming.

"Don't play in the road," they scolded as Adria passed. She felt their eyes on her mask. "It's not safe."

Not safe? What did they fear now? Her? And if so . . . why?

But her mind did not want to grapple with that. Nor did it want to acknowledge how these apparent refugees shared similarly long hair and blood-red eyes. A family trait from the southern coast, she told herself. That was all. Her eyes flicked to empty spots where gargoyles had perched mere days before. Where had they gone? Had they been destroyed, or did they hide elsewhere, waiting for night to come so they might feed?

Adria did her best to push her unease out of her mind upon reaching Church District. She bypassed the grand steps leading up to Alma's Greeting, curled around the southwest corner, and followed the northerly road. The Scholars' Abode passed by on her left. It had been added two centuries after the cathedral's major renovation, not too surprising given the scholars' late addition to the sacred division of the Mind. The building lacked a lot of the cathedral's interlocking architecture. Instead it contained rows and rows of doors, each one leading to a private bedroom and study for the assigned scholar. There were stories of scholars not leaving for years, having their food delivered and their bedpans changed by novices. Needless to say, scholars were often viewed as reclusive, scrambled-brained versions of Mindkeepers.

The Sisters' Remembrance came next, and it looked downright gaudy compared to the Scholars' Abode. It was twice the height of the abode, and the front entrance was flanked by giant pillars that were intricately carved with a wavy semblance of fire. Four stained-glass windows triple the size of a man were built on each of the four sides. A large statue of Anwyn stood on a raised dais in the center of the rooftop, one arm covering her breasts, the other reaching to the left with an open palm, forever waiting to receive the dove from Lyra's care. Her head bowed low, and coupled with the slight hunch of her shoulders, it gave Adria the impression that the goddess struggled under a terrible unseen burden.

Vikar Thaddeus stood beside the front entrance, his hands resting comfortably atop his cane. His face was solemn. No novices accompanied him, nor any members of the sacred divisions. Adria climbed the three steps to the door and bowed low in respect to her Vikar.

"You summoned me?" she said.

"Indeed I did," Thaddeus said. "I'm sure you've surmised the reason."

"The reason, yes," she said. "But not the place. Why are we at the Remembrance?"

Thaddeus removed his spectacles and cleaned them with a bit of cloth folded into a pocket of his pristine vest.

"What do you know of this particular building?" he asked her. "Of its history?"

She started to answer and then stopped herself. What *did* she know of the building? She'd paid little attention to the tours during her training, and once she'd attained her rank of Mind-keeper, she'd used her access to the Grand Archive to study far more interesting matters.

"Not much," she said. "For centuries it has housed the ashes of those our society deems important. As for its construction... I guess I have always assumed it was built around the same time the cathedral underwent its first major renovation."

Thaddeus smiled at her.

"You're mostly correct," he said. "Mostly."

He extended his arm toward her, and she gently slid closer so he might use her shoulder instead of the cane. They did not enter the Remembrance as Adria had expected. Instead he led her down the steps and around the building's corner. As they walked he spoke.

"The building was constructed not long after the major renovation, but you err in thinking it has always served as a tomb for dead Vikars' ashes. In those earliest days of the faith, our church had a much different purpose for this stone memorial."

On the northern side was a single set of stairs dug into the earth to reach a simple wooden door. It looked out of place against the rest of the building's opulence. Adria had seen it before but assumed it was used by novices so they could work and clean without being noticed at the front. Thaddeus pointed at it with his cane, confirming their destination. They carefully took the steps one at a time.

"Is it locked?" Adria asked as she reached for the door.

"Not this one," Thaddeus said. "But this is merely the first door of many."

She pushed the door open. Her heart shuddered at the sight beyond. She'd expected a cramped hallway into some tucked-away corner of the Remembrance. Instead she revealed a dark stone tunnel carved into the earth.

"What is this?" she asked.

Thaddeus reached around the corner of the door and retrieved an unlit lantern. He pulled a small but ornate tinderbox from his pocket and handed it and the lantern over to Adria.

"The first major renovation to the Cathedral of the Sacred Mother was about eight centuries ago," he said, calmly watching her light the lantern. "Around that same time the Keeping Church underwent the first of several major schisms."

"You mean the heretical purge," Adria said. It seemed like clockwork every half century a radical thinker would desire to worship one of the Sisters as greater than the other two. Little scripture supported these theories, for even the oldest scraps of paper discussed the intimate link between the three Sisters and their role in creating, transporting, and cherishing the soul.

"Indeed I do," Thaddeus said as he accepted the lantern back from her. "But where nowadays we view church schisms as arguments of the power and roles of the Sisters, back then things we take for granted as bedrock tenants were still being established. There were people who wished to worship beings separate from the Sisters entirely. They gave names to creatures and things and lifted them up as equals to the divine three. And for them, I must admit to the shame of our church, our forefathers built the sunless cages."

Adria's eyes widened behind her mask.

"Here?" she asked. "Below the Remembrance is a church-sanctioned prison?"

"Of sorts," Thaddeus said. He watched her closely, and even her mask was not enough to protect her from those silver eyes. "Are you afraid, Mindkeeper?"

Of course she was. The church would have imprisoned and hidden away only a specific type of prisoner...one she might well qualify as.

"How many heretics have starved away in the sunless cages below the Remembrance?" she asked.

"Two hundred seventy-three," the Vikar said. "And I have studied each and every one of their supposed sins in preparations for today. I am not here to trap you, Adria. I am here to illuminate you. More is at stake in Londheim than you know."

He gestured into the darkness with his lantern.

"I have never doubted your faith, or your resolve," he told her. "Do not make me question it now."

Pride swallowed down her fear. Together they walked the stone tunnel's steadily downward slope. After fifty steps the tunnel turned sharply to the right and ended at another door. A window with two thick bars was built into its center, and a helmed man peered through it.

"Greetings, Vikar," the burly man said.

Thaddeus smiled politely. The door opened with a loud creak of rusted metal. Inside was another tunnel, this one lit with four equally spaced lanterns hanging from the wall. Despite them the air did not reek of smoke, which meant there was some manor of ventilation dug into the stone. Thaddeus released his hold of Adria's shoulder and led the way with loud, echoing cracks of his cane upon the smooth stone floor.

"To the best of my research this prison has not been used since the late 1200s," Thaddeus said. "The church even discussed sealing off the entrance at one point, but the cost kept it from happening. Easier, and cheaper, to ignore it entirely. And so for two hundred years we've forgotten this little stain upon our history. I myself had been down here only once in the past twenty years, but then..." He shrugged. "But then the world changed."

They passed cell after cell, the iron bars rusted and twisted. Doors hung on broken hinges. The insides, however, were immaculately swept and cleaned, as if with enough dusting one could hide the purpose of these dark cages. Adria wondered how many souls lingered on after death instead of ascending in the reaping hour. She had never been one to believe tales of ghosts and hauntings, but if there were such places, this would be one of them. The air stuck to her skin, pulling her downward, threatening her with a burden centuries older than herself.

Thaddeus's voice quieted, as if he, too, felt the omnipresent weight.

"Before you came to me, we had been aware of only one other man capable of drawing power from the old scriptures and lessons. That's who I'd like you to meet, Adria. I want you to see the danger in what you represent."

A lone man sat resting against the back wall in the next cell. Adria was stunned that he still wore the black-and-white robes of a Mindkeeper. Equally stunning was the leather strap buckled around his head, completely covering his mouth. A small lock dangled from its center. His hands were chained together, as were his feet. Holes in his outfit revealed fresh cuts and bruises. His brown hair was long and dirty, his skin tanned, and his face broad like many of the southern coasters. His pale gold eyes observed them calmly, as if he awaited them in a private study instead of a forgotten prison.

"Who is he?" she whispered.

"Mindkeeper Tamerlane Swift."

She recognized that name. Tamerlane was a member of the

leadership council, a passing face she'd seen a handful of times during her education prior to her assignment in Low Dock.

"Why is he imprisoned?" Adria asked. Her heart feared the answer. "Does healing the sick deserve such cruelty?"

Thaddeus leaned heavily on his cane. He stared at the man as he would a dangerous animal.

"Lyra's Devotions were culled together from many sources," the Vikar said. "Some were considered falsely attributed to the Goddesses, or not worthy of belonging in a collection of praises. Perhaps you are aware of them?"

"There are thousands of scrolls filled with apocryphal material," Adria said, mesmerized by the man. "They are not my area of study. The apocrypha tend to be the domain of the scholars."

"Then let me illuminate you," Thaddeus said. "While some apocryphal writings are disregarded because of their poor quality or questionable sources, others strongly contradict established tenets of faith. Writings full of anger and retribution, by an author who would elevate the power of the soul over the Goddesses themselves. Do you know of what I speak?"

"The Book of Ravens," Adria said.

"That's right. Have you read it?"

"I have not."

"I have," the Vikar said, and he glared at the imprisoned man. "It does not contain blessings like Lyra's Devotions. No, it carries curses."

Adria's throat constricted as she pieced it all together.

"Is that why his mouth is covered?" she asked. "To prevent him from cursing the guards?"

Thaddeus solemnly nodded.

"His voice is his weapon, and it is far harder to take that away than a sword or a pistol."

Adria took another step closer to the prisoner. Her fingers touched the iron bars. She had never met a true Ravencaller before. They were largely figments of ancient times, their teachings relegated to bored teenagers seeking to add excitement to their tedious life. No one took them seriously, yet here was a respected Mindkeeper who had betrayed his faith to follow writings long since condemned as heretical. Why would he do so? What had spurred him down such a dark path?

"Why not cut his tongue out completely?" she asked.

"Because we hoped with enough convincing he might undo his curse."

"What was the curse?"

"Come," he said. "I will show you."

Thaddeus led them to the last cell in the long tunnel. Lanterns illuminated the square cage. The door had been completely removed from its hinges. Dozens of pillows covered the cold ground, and in one corner she saw an ornate table recently brought down from the surface. Two Mindkeepers stood just within the entrance, and they bowed respectfully at the Vikar's presence. And there, in the center of those pillows, lay the cursed man.

His skin was thin and stretched, its texture and yellowish color reminding her of uncured leather. Scabs covered his bald pate like a pox. He was naked from the waist up, granting Adria an unwelcome sight: the twisted, unnatural spiral of his ribs as they jutted against their fleshy restraints. The man gasped in his breaths with a low, droning moan. His teeth were gone, leaving behind only black gums. Of his face, only his eyes remained the same, while his nose, lips, and chin all twisted and stretched as if someone had turned his skin to mud and given it a good stir.

"Sisters have mercy," Adria whispered. Her hands curled into fists at her sides. Her teeth clenched as she fought down a surge of revulsion. Each of the man's fingers looked like they had been broken and then allowed to heal at the wrong angle. Who would do this to someone? Even the lowest of humanity deserved a clean death over this atrocity.

"It never becomes easier," Thaddeus said, and then to the attending Mindkeepers, "Please, give us a moment."

The two bowed and then left. Thaddeus replaced their watch. A long-necked bottle of water rested in the center of the table and the Vikar took it in his left hand. His right gingerly propped the cursed man's mouth open so he might slowly, carefully trickle in drop after drop. Adria kept out of the cell. It felt like her feet had turned to stone and sunk into the ground.

"I pray I do not sound cruel," she said. "But killing him would be a mercy."

"Indeed it would," Thaddeus said. He did not look at her, too focused on ensuring that the steady drops did not increase. Much more and it seemed the wheezing man might drown. His tone, however, conveyed his disappointment in her. "So think, Mindkeeper. Why does he yet live?"

Adria forced herself to look beyond the figure's physical mutilation. She saw his leggings and recognized them as made from silk. Extremely expensive, and only importable from textile mills east of Nicus. A wealthy man, then. Was he a major donor to the church, and that was why they kept him alive? No. That didn't feel right. Her eyes flicked to the table. Various personal effects cluttered its top. One was a book she recognized, a gold-trimmed, numbered edition of Lyra's Devotions from the initial printing by King Woadthyn the First. Its wealth was startling in the dank, ancient stone. She was aware of only one copy in all of Londheim, but why would the ...

And then it hit her. She didn't even want to guess. It was too horrible to voice.

"Thaddeus," she asked breathlessly. "Whom did Tamerlane curse?"

It took a long while before the Vikar responded. The delay only added power to his answer.

"Deakon Sevold," he said.

Deakon Sevold. The Keeping Church's appointed spiritual master for West Orismund. Only the Ecclesiast and Queen Woadthyn had greater authority upon the Cradle.

"Why did you bring him here?" she asked. "He ... he should be attended by the best Mindkeepers. Scholars should be studying his condition. He needs sunlight, and fresh water ..."

Her voice trailed off. Of course Thaddeus knew these things. Her Vikar knelt beside the Deakon and lovingly brushed his malformed head.

"We brought him down here hoping we could convince Tamerlane to cure him. It didn't work. Tamerlane insisted he could not undo the damage no matter how intensive the ... persuasion we used. After a week we decided down here was the only place we could be absolutely certain to keep the Deakon's condition a secret."

It made sense, of course. In such tumultuous times, knowledge of the Deakon's condition would only spread panic and fear. The citizens needed to believe that its leadership was in control. She had a feeling that if they could not cure him, they'd eventually announce he'd passed away in his sleep. Even that was better than his current condition.

"We Vikars have assumed control over his duties," Thaddeus continued, as if he could read her train of thought. "We've managed to use the chaos of the living mountain's arrival as a cover for our constant refusals against meeting with the Deakon. It's not a permanent solution, however. That's why you're here."

Of course that was why. She'd showcased an ability to heal with the Sisters' power, and who in the church's opinion was in greater need of it than the Deakon of West Orismund?

"I do not know if I will be able to help," she said.

"Right now, the only thing we *know* is that helping the Deakon is beyond our capabilities," Thaddeus said. "Our *human* capabilities. But you have shown a power that belongs to the Goddesses themselves. What other hope do we have?"

Fair enough. Even if this poor, cursed man weren't her Deakon, she'd sweat and toil to help him. That was who she was. More importantly, that was who she was supposed to be if she was to walk the path of wisdom bestowed by the Goddesses.

Adria took the Deakon's malformed hand. His skin felt like it looked, dry and tough. A long, shuddering whistle marked Sevold taking in a larger than usual breath. Did he retain his senses? Was the man's sharp mind still functioning within the broken shell of a body? Such a terrifying thought. She had to help him. She had to set him free. The question was, how?

Her mind bounced through the seventy-nine devotions. This was no disease or birth defect. No prayer explicitly dealt with curses. They dealt with real matters, as she'd always thought until recently. Real, as in hunger, pain, and loneliness. Which were appropriate for a man cursed by Ravencaller magic?

In the end she decided to use the same prayer she used to heal illness and mend broken bones. This was a corruption of the body. If her faith was strong, the Sisters could work through her, and nothing was insurmountable to their touch.

"Lyra of the beloved sun, hear my prayer," she said softly. Her head lowered, so close to his bony chest she could hear the Deakon's heartbeat. "Your children weep for your touch, and so I come, and so I pray. Sickness fouls the perfection you created. Darkness mars the glory you shone upon us."

The calm, steady rhythm of the words at first soothed her chest, but then something struck at her peace of mind. A discordant note. An angry rhythm. As the Sisters' power swelled within her, so too did a fiery heat focusing at her touch.

"With bowed head and bended knee I ask for succor."

The heat grew. The anger grew with it. She opened her eyes without realizing why. Crackling red and black lightning greeted her. It sparked from random parts of his skin, arcing across the leathery body as if it were densely packed thunderclouds. Her training kept her going through the shock.

"With heavy heart and weary mind I ask for blessing. This beloved soul requires healing, Lyra, my savior."

At Lyra's name immense agony crippled her hands. She shuddered as if stabbed in the spine. That rage...that rage! She could feel it twisting the flesh into its current form. It burrowed deep into every bone. That discordant note pulsed harder. This rage had but simple, basic urges: twist, break, turn, change.

Adria's tongue was already swollen. Thin tears fell behind her mask. To her ears, the prison cell was silent. To her mind, it was a constant, thunderous roar threatening to drown out her pitiful words.

"Cleanse the sickness. Chase away the pain. Precious Lyra... precious Lyra..."

The sinister lightning swirled about her hands, stinging her, begging to be let in. To twist and change her as well. Adria wrenched her hands away. The thunder became a whisper. The red-and-black lightning became mere spots over her eyes that gradually faded. Sevold went limp in his pillows. Perhaps he let out a sorrowful cry at her failure. Perhaps she only projected.

"I'm sorry," she said. "This curse, this power... it's completely foreign to me. I don't understand it, and because of that, I don't know how to fight it."

Thaddeus slowly nodded.

"Thank you for trying, Mindkeeper," he said. There was no hiding the disappointment in his voice. "Perhaps in time you may save our Deakon from his fate."

She did not share his optimism. Goddesses above, what lent such power to that rage? How did it dismiss her so easily? Her fingers shook from the remembrance. For one split second she'd felt it starting to take root in her bones. Just one second, but the joints had already begun swelling and her fingers curled outward to the surrounding muscle's displeasure.

"I pray that I do," she said. It was about as noncommittal as she could manage. She stood on weak knees. Vertigo immediately assaulted her. She grabbed at the bars and held still until it passed. The Vikar said nothing as he patiently waited.

"Was this all you required of me?" she asked once her strength returned and she was fully in control of her faculties. Her fingers still ached, but that she could manage. Thaddeus pointed the bottom of his cane toward Sevold's body. He'd fallen asleep by the looks of it, or at the least, his eyes were now closed when they'd been open before.

"The era we walk has become one of power and change," he said. "Our members die at the hands of a man named Janus, for reasons we cannot fathom. Creatures stalk the night, and even our best Soulkeepers struggle to survive. A mountain has crawled to our doorstep, and our scholars wonder if it is the void-dragon itself come to end the time of humanity."

He cupped her chin in one hand and lifted her face. The other hand carefully removed the mask so he might look upon her true self.

"You carry a gift that may save our people," he said. "And I pray you and Sena are but the first. The world has become a dark place, and I would give my life for the Keeping Church to be the brightest guiding light. Our previous understandings of heresy and magic are void. I have witnessed your blessing, and I have witnessed Tamerlane's curse. It does not take a Vikar to understand which walks the righteous path."

Thaddeus offered her his arm, and she took it. Together they walked past the Mindkeepers waiting at a respectful distance, followed by Tamerlane's cell. It might be a trick of the light, or her mind playing tricks, but she swore she saw him smile behind his muzzle.

"I've talked with the other Vikars," Thaddeus said. "We shall judge you by your actions. If you bring healing and relief to a frightened, dying populace, then you walk in the Sisters' light and we will do all we can to support you. If your path results in hatred, curses, and death?" He nodded toward Tamerlane's prison. "Then you shall find yourself in a cell beside his."

Adria slid her mask over her face. She needed it to breathe easier. She needed it to hide the overwhelming emotions threatening to break her down to a sobbing mess on the prison floor.

"Thank you," she said, meager words to convey the relief in

knowing that the Keeping Church would embrace her awakened gift. "I shall only be a light. I shall only a blessing. On this I swear my soul."

Thaddeus smiled at her, but that smile did not touch his silver eyes.

"Much is expected of those to whom much is given," he said. "Never let me regret this, Adria. If you put the people's faith in the Goddesses at risk I shall personally turn the key locking you into a forgotten cell. On that, I swear *my* soul."

CHAPTER 33

Janus slowly brushed his fingers across the dry pool of blood. Not red, like a human's. No, this was a deep blue color that seemed to glow beneath the light of the moon. There was no corpse, but Janus had witnessed the slaughter firsthand. It'd taken all his self-control not to shred through the riotous crowd.

"Do not kill wantonly," Janus muttered, echoing the command given to him by his dragon creator. "If only the humans followed such rules."

Janus rose to his full height and gazed upon the building the gargoyles had perched upon before they were ripped from the rooftop and smashed to pieces. It was a small but pristine church, its wealth grotesquely displayed with an overabundance of gold inlaid upon door frames, windowsills, and triangular painted windows. A tall iron fence surrounded the church, no doubt to protect it from thieves during the night.

He smirked. A church so wealthy it sought to protect itself from those its wealth was meant to serve. So very...human.

"No more fences," he said as he placed both hands upon the

bars. His magic coursed through the iron, shifting its structure at the most infinitesimal level. Iron turned to water. It splashed upon the cobbles and gathered into puddles, but Janus was not done. He dipped his finger back into the gargoyle blood and swirled it so it mixed with the water. Another simple thought and the blood lifted off the stone entirely.

"Let us weep when the war is over," he whispered. "Let the stain of blood mark only our victories and not our defeats."

The words of a brilliant avenria, the raven folk whom Raven-callers unknowingly imitated with their extravagant feather costumes and long, ornate beak masks. He had yet to encounter an avenria since returning to Londheim, but he figured it was only a matter of time. They would not sit idly by while the fate of the awakened world was decided.

Janus kicked the doors of the church open and strode into the candlelit center aisle. Eight people lay about, most sleeping in the pews but for a plump-looking woman in a white suit conversing with a man by the pulpit.

"You stay," he said, pointing at the Faithkeeper. "All others, leave."

Some panicked and fled immediately, the word *Janus* on their tongues. Others looked ready to defend their Faithkeeper. Janus rolled his eyes at them. The reason he was forced to attack at night was to minimize extra casualties. He'd hoped the church would be empty, but it wasn't, and now here was another temptation for him to cast off Viciss's orders and have fun slaughtering the whole lot of them.

"On the count of three, I will execute every last person inside this building," Janus said. To highlight the point, he lifted his right arm. His forearm twisted, the bone itself rotating three full revolutions and elongating into the form of a corkscrew as the skin turned to steel. A man beside him thought this the best time to attack, his bare fists striking Janus across the neck and shoulder. The blows were as effective as wind upon a stone.

"One," Janus said, whirling upon the man and slamming the sharpened tip of his arm directly into the man's gut.

"Two." His arm slowly rotated with audible snapping of the bones at his elbow. The blade burrowed while pulling the man's bleeding, convulsing body closer.

"Three." They fled, every last one of them. Janus watched them leave with a twisted pit in his stomach. Viciss demanded that he kill carefully, with minimal loss to those not serving the church. Yet when the dragon awoke, he unleashed black water across the west, killing untold thousands in his rage. The dragon demanded what he himself could not deliver. The unfairness of it gnawed at him relentlessly.

"No no no, not you," Janus said as if reprimanding a child. He flung the corpse across the room. It slammed into the church doors with a wet smack, pinning them shut so the fleeing Faithkeeper could not escape. The chubby woman spun about and clung her fists to her chest. Panic widened her eyes as she screamed.

"Let me go," she said. "We've done you no harm, none!"

"You are part of a great machine known as the Keeping Church," Janus said as he crossed the room. "You wear its robes, take coin in its name, and wallow in its privileges. The Keeping Church has done me great harm, woman, as have your Three Sisters. You're a part, even if your hands are clean. You're a piece, a cog, a bolt, a screw, and when it comes to the church's sins, *you partook.*"

Janus's hand closed about her neck, and he flung her violently to the ground. She let out a pained cry. His heel dug into her spine. Words escaped between her blubbers.

"Blessed Sisters, hear my prayer. May Anwyn look down upon me with kindness. May her heart be moved by my suffering."

"That's enough out of you," Janus said. The last thing he needed was another damn spell from a desperate keeper causing him harm. He yanked the woman by her strawberry-blond hair so she looked his way. His free hand jammed into her mouth. She tried to bite him but he'd anticipated the instinctual reaction and already shifted the outer layer of his skin to steel. Her teeth cracked. He touched her slippery tongue and let his magic flow into her, changing her. The tongue turned to lead.

"Better," he said as she moaned indecipherably.

He dragged her through the pews to her pulpit. The amount of gold carvings across it turned his stomach. There were even a few rubies and sapphires inlaid into portions to give the appearance of flowers. More hypocrisy from those who claimed to "serve." Why the common folk didn't string all the keepers from the rooftops by their toes baffled him.

"You could have avoided this," he said as he kicked the pulpit aside. He shoved her back against the wall and pinned her there with a hand upon her throat. "Did you not read the messages I left for your kind upon the walls of the city? Have you not heard of my killings, or did you merely not understand my demands? All of you keepers, you're to cease your teachings, your lectures, and your misbegotten prayers. Death awaits you otherwise."

She was trying to answer him, so he stuck his fingers back into her mouth and returned her tongue to its normal form. The Faithkeeper retched twice before finding her voice.

"You'll never stop us from serving," she said. "We…we're the Sisters' chosen. We'll give our lives if we must."

Janus glared at her.

"Is that so?" he asked. "Or perhaps my message is still not clear enough. I need to be bolder. I need to be *louder*."

He grabbed her wrist with his left hand and pressed it to the wall above her head. He imagined the change, then let his magic flow out through him, rearranging matter to make it happen. The skin of her hand and wrist attached to the wall as if it were part of her own body. He did the same to her other hand, then stepped back to give himself space to work. A low, guttural moan escaped from the deepest part of her.

"Stay still," he said. "I'd hate to make a mistake."

Janus's fingers took the shape of knives, and they easily parted the flesh of her abdomen. He punched through the fat and muscle before tearing her open as easily as unfolding a piece of paper. The squirmy intestinal workings of a human body spilled upon the floor, and he kicked a stubborn rope of it off his foot. She screamed, but not for long. He almost kept her alive to prolong her suffering but let her die instead. He'd spoken truthfully, after all, and her struggling might cause him to err.

First, the boring busy work. He scooped out organs like pulp from a pumpkin he planned to carve. Lungs, liver, heart, intestines, all of it into a wet, stinking pile. Once she was completely hollowed out behind the rib cage he cut a center incision directly up to the breastbone, then flayed her like a fish so that her ribs were clearly exposed. Only from her neck up remained together.

Janus paused to think, then pressed his fingers to her face. The woman's skin hardened into a single sheen of gold. As for the pile of organs and blood at his feet, he touched it as well, but only to drain it of color.

That's the easy part done, he thought. *Now for the tricky part.*

Blood was tremendously important to humans, and they

likened it to life itself. Only the soul was revered more highly. He could use that. The greater the shock, the greater the likelihood they would remember and commit his message to memory. Janus grabbed a large chunk of the woman's fat and pressed it to the ribs. The chunk changed to his will, becoming a massive array of thin, pink veins. It wouldn't be her actual veins, but to any human who came to observe, it'd certainly look like a natural part of her body. The tangle slithered into various parts of her exposed form, latching onto bones, ribs, and pieces of flesh. Once tethered, the other ends shot to the ceiling, becoming a massive web as they merged stone to vein.

Janus guided each and every strand, and it took all of his concentration. With how thin, and how many, it'd be easy for the web to lose any semblance of order. Worse, the veins might tear, especially when applying weight. He couldn't have that. Not until his art was discovered, and the rumors could spread like a disease throughout Londheim.

Once every single vein was finished he passed his fingers over the dead woman's wrists, freeing her from the wall. She swung forward a foot before coming to rest. Janus watched closely to ensure that the many bands could support her weight.

"Excellent," he said, but his tone did not match the word. Already he felt drained, his exhilaration becoming subdued disappointment. This wasn't enough. Would it ever be enough? He retreated down the center aisle to view his artwork from afar. Disgusting filth escaped the interior of a gilded body. Its veins burst to the ceiling, supporting her while also conveying a singular message. The several hundred veins crisscrossed each other to connect to nearly every corner of the ceiling. There seemed to be no apparent order to the entanglement, but if one stood in the center of the aisle the various gaps and overlaps came together to form one single word.

ABANDONED.

Janus exited the church to a dark, empty street. City guards were likely on their way, so he shifted his entire body, molding skin, clothes, and hair into his preferred disguise. He hobbled down the street, a burning hole in his stomach refusing to let him feel proud of his accomplishment.

"They're not learning," he raged to the night. "They're not *listening.*"

The pleasure in crafting the art did not last. It never did. He would have to paint or sculpt again, each message louder than the one previous, until they finally understood. Their Goddesses had abandoned them. Their faith would not save them. Only as equals to the dragon-sired might they survive, and things were so far from equal.

"I've tried your way, Viciss," he said, shaking his head. "But now we do it mine."

One way or another, the people of Londheim would receive his message, even if he must craft it with their own bones and blood.

CHAPTER 34

Jacaranda flitted through the crowded morning market, Tommy at her side and a tired and grumpy Devin trailing behind her. She'd noticed that the past few days of night patrols often left the Soulkeeper in such a state.

"I could be sleeping right now," he said as they paused before a stall selling racks and racks of beaded necklaces and bracelets. "I *should* be sleeping right now."

"Have you no sense of excitement?" she asked as she eyed the collection. The stall's merchant kept back so they might browse, but his jittery arms and wide eyes made him look like a wolf about to pounce.

"Devin has no sense in a lot of things," Tommy said, lifting a dangling bracelet for a closer look.

"It's beautiful," Jacaranda said. The bracelet was an alternating string of black and violet beads, each one smoothly polished. "Who's it for?"

"Me, of course. Who else?"

She batted her eyelashes at him, deciding it might be fun to hone a particular skill set she had painfully little practice with.

"Why, I thought it might be a gift for me. After all, wouldn't those black and violet beads match my eyes so much better?"

Tommy blustered for a moment and then turned to Devin for help.

"Solve this without me," he said. "I'm not foolish enough to get involved."

"Fine," Tommy said, handing it over to Jacaranda. "It does match your eyes better anyway."

Jacaranda slid the beads around her wrist and lifted it to catch the sunlight. She'd already convinced Devin to buy her a new wide-brimmed hat made of fine dark leather, and as for Tommy, he'd purchased the long dark gloves she wore from one of the first stalls they visited. Since she had no money of her own, she'd quickly discovered how easily a few well-timed smiles or pouts could loosen the drawstrings of their purses.

"Beautiful," she said. "Thank you so much, Tommy."

"Sure thing," he said as he paid the smiling merchant. "Where to next? Should we find some exotic delicacies? Maybe see what new styles are in fashion?"

Trade boats had arrived upon the Septen River carrying goods from Stomme to the east. Hundreds of men and women pulsed through the market district to browse the new wares and learn what life was like closer to Unified Orismund's capital. It was a welcome reprieve to a city that had been living each day in the shadow of the living mountain, always tense and fearful of what might happen if it waked.

"Everywhere," Jacaranda said, filled with energy from the excitement. "I want to see everywhere and go to every shop and stall."

"She's going to eat us alive," Tommy said, not seeming to care she was right there to overhear. "Thank the stars Malik is letting me move into the Wise tower for free."

"I didn't know your relationship had reached such a state."

"You're in a relationship?" Jacaranda asked, momentarily halting. "That's wonderful. Is he as kind as you? And why have you not introduced me?"

"I, no, it's..." Tommy flushed red with embarrassment. "It's not like that at all. Quite the opposite really, Malik made that awkwardly and painfully clear. It's just, there's some spare rooms in the Wise tower, and your house is a bit full to the brim with guests."

Jacaranda was unsure of how to react, so she merely smiled in sympathy. Devin, on the other hand, loudly smacked Tommy across the back.

"I'm sorry, Tommy. I really am. I could tell you were rather infatuated with him."

"Was I that obvious?"

"For good or ill, you always wear your heart on your sleeve."

"It seems far more often for ill than good," Tommy said. "I wish I could hide my adoration as well as you do."

Devin stiffened with embarrassment.

"And what does that mean?" he asked.

Tommy only winked. Jacaranda felt a warm buzz fill her chest, and she pretended not to have noticed the exchange as she hurried ahead. Her mood buoyed further when she noticed a curious gathering near a street stall selling a collection of hats. Most were children laughing and pointing, and they certainly weren't fascinated with finely tailored headwear. Her gaze followed their pointing to the awning that gave the stall shade...and to the onyx faery dangling upside-down off the side of it by her toes.

Jacaranda nudged Devin with her elbow so he also noticed, and together they approached the stall.

"So this is where you're running off to during the day," he said after crossing the distance.

"Hi, Devin! Hi, Jac!" Tesmarie shouted to them. Her wings buzzed to keep her perpendicular to the ground, and she swished her arms and laughed as the children did likewise. She looked so happy as she bathed in the sun. Certainly the little pile of food beside her helped in that regard. "Come to play, or buy some hats?"

"Neither," Jacaranda said. "We just wished to greet a friend."

Devin flipped a silver penny to the merchant family underneath the stall.

"For dealing with the little one," he said as explanation. The two waved to Tesmarie and then continued on with their browsing.

Guards were a common enough occurrence as they made their way from the southern end of the market district to the north. Jacaranda kept a careful eye on each one they passed. She wore a white scarf across her neck to hide her mark, but that cover did not remove her paranoia. Devin and Tommy stopped at a stall selling heavy coats, so she continued onward, perfectly content to browse alone.

"Rabid soulless? That a jest?"

The phrase stole Jacaranda's attention to a trio of well-dressed men gathered around a balloon of a man outfitted in Orismund's finest silks. The four sat on stools facing a table loaded with sliced rolls and a single bowl of melted cheese they took turns slathering over their bread.

"No other real way to describe it," the merchant said. "They're going violent, and it's spreading like a goddess-damned epidemic. It's particularly bad in the north. Heard they're putting soulless down by the dozens in the new workshops. If you got yourself some spare gold crowns, invest in textiles. That shit's about to get rare."

"Invest?" one of the local men with him snorted. "We're barely skirting off famine, a damn mountain might crush the whole city for reasons only the Goddesses know, and you think we should be investing?"

Mr. Pompous Balloon wagged a finger in his direction.

"Always think long-term with your coin," he said. "Famines come and go. Sure, people need food, but they'll always need clothes, too. There's no reason to let them get one part cheap just because another's getting too rare and expensive. Same goes for property. You should be hovering over estate auctions like a hawk. Starving folk rarely get their wills in order."

It took all of Jacaranda's self-control to keep her daggers sheathed. Her good mood broke beneath waves of rage. She wasn't alone. Other soulless were waking, but unlike her, they did not have a kind Soulkeeper to help with the transition. No, they had cruel men and women willing to murder them like rabid animals.

"Are you all right?" Devin asked, startling her.

"I...yes, I'm fine. Really." He clearly didn't believe her but she shook him off. "I'd like to be alone for a little while, all right?"

"Sure thing, Jacaranda," he said. His pleasant tone did not match the worry in his eyes. He pulled a few copper and silver pennies from his pocket and handed them over. "That should be enough to keep you entertained for the rest of the day. Stay safe, you hear?"

"I will," she promised.

She left the market and traveled east. The long walk calmed her rage but did little to remove her guilt. There were better things she should be using her time for, things more than decorating herself with little trinkets and gloves. Was this how life was when not soulless? Endless easy distractions so that difficult tasks kept sliding further and further into the future?

Stop it, she mentally yelled at herself as she arrived at the docks along the far east edge of Londheim. *You enjoy your time with Devin and Tommy. Don't feel guilty for that. It's your life. Live it as you wish.*

Jacaranda sat on a bench overlooking the many docking boats. Rich smells brushed over her with each gentle gust of wind. The earthy aroma of the dark riverbank soil. The sharp scent of pine tar on the docks and hulls. The steady flow of the water reminded Jacaranda of when she'd bathed in the river on the road to Oakenwall. Devin had kept his eyes to himself, but the thought of him watching her set her heart to flutter in a strange but not unpleasant way. Fascinating, the way sounds and scents tied together with various memories to elicit emotions. Sometimes, like with the river, she welcomed the sudden excitement. Other times, such as whenever her mind shot to her years under Gerag's control, she loathed it with a passion.

"Something the matter, miss?"

Jacaranda startled out of her thoughts, yet another unaccustomed sensation. Soulless did not daydream.

"Excuse me?" she asked the burly man, a fishmonger based on the bloodstained apron and thick bucket of stinking unpleasantness in his left hand. That apron was the only thing covering his bare, hairy chest, and given how the sky looked ready to snow, she had to commend his fortitude.

"Sorry, didn't mean to startle you. No sap here is good enough to have a pretty lass like you for a wife, so I thought something might be amiss."

"Perhaps I am full of surprises?" Jacaranda asked. She brushed her hand across her bangs, flattered. She'd been complimented before while soulless. The flowery words had been meaningless then, objective opinions on skin, hair, and bone structure unwelcomely offered as facts. Yet now a smile bloomed on her face. No wonder a few charming words could disarm even the most guarded of hearts. Something about his earnest compliment made her feel happy, and perhaps slightly embarrassed for reasons she couldn't hope to understand.

"Hah, perhaps you are," he said. He dumped his bucket of fish heads, spines, and unwanted guts into the river. "Serves me for making assumptions. Good day to you."

"And you, too, fishmonger."

The man sauntered off, and Jacaranda turned her attention back to the river. The shipments from Stomme had arrived in a grand fleet, with boats anchoring at every dock and many more waiting their turn farther out. These boats announced their names in a myriad of ways, with chiseled letters on their bows, colorful flags fluttering from their masts, or symbols in the hands of figureheads carved into the prow. There was one in particular she searched for, and it didn't matter that it took an hour of waiting before she found it.

The smaller boat docked several rows to her left, too far for her to read the name on its bow. The flag, a sickle wrapped in white cloth over a green field, was enough to confirm it the *Hawkins*, the trade ship of the Petyrn family, who mostly dealt with dried corn and beets grown on their sprawling family estate. Mostly. Jacaranda pulled her hat lower on her head and turned away.

The crew of the *Hawkins* might appear to be unloading its cargo, but Jacaranda knew better. Only the cheaper, bulk-rate goods would reach the markets and stores today. The real value of its haul would be transported come nightfall, and Jacaranda would be there to greet it.

Under normal circumstances the docks should have been alive with sailors gambling, singing, and flirting with the night women come to ply their trade. It seemed they'd been told of Londheim's dangers, for the docks were empty but for the unlucky few stuck on guard duty. The bars and taverns nearby were crammed full to the brim, and based on the noise coming from the boats, those who couldn't find room were bunking inside.

For Jacaranda, this was just fine. She passed unseen alongside the river, the *Hawkins* her unerring destination. A single guard stood bored beside the ramp. Any more would attract attention for such a small ship. A lantern hung from a hook on the prow, casting its yellow light across the dock. Jacaranda observed its gentle sway as the boat rose and fell atop the water, memorizing the dance of the shadows it cast.

It didn't matter that the guard was bored and spending more time paying attention to cleaning his fingernails. Even if alert, she'd have still buried her dagger into the back of his head without him noticing her approach. She carefully guided the body down so it wouldn't make a noise hitting the wood, then bent him over at the waist so he was hidden behind a stack of crates.

Jacaranda raced up the ramp and to the door of the captain's quarters. She knocked twice with the hilt of her dagger. Stealth wouldn't be necessary here. After all, it was perfectly normal for her to accompany these nighttime transactions.

"What is it, Troy?" the captain, a short, stocky man named Malin, shouted from within.

"I am not Troy," Jacaranda said, her voice perfectly even. "I am Jacaranda."

That was enough to get the captain up and to the door. She heard him grumbling from the other side, speaking to someone with him.

"The bitch's got some damn good timing, don't she?"

Malin flung open the door. He wore only a loose, untied pair of breeches. His long brown hair was unkempt and his skin layered with sweat. An amused younger man lay in the cabin's lone bed, his nakedness hidden by a blanket. The light of two candles on the desk flickered in the sudden intake of air.

"What do you want?" Malin asked. "Shipment's not to . . ."

Jacaranda slammed her fist into the lump of his throat. He staggered into the cabin, retching violently. She slid through the opening and pulled the naked man from the bed. Her heel ended on his throat, pinning him. His hands flailed ineffectually at her ankle and shin.

"Are you a member of the crew?" she asked. She relented enough pressure so he could answer.

"Not crew . . . bed warmer."

"Which brothel?"

He gasped in a breath of air.

"The Gentle Rose."

"Then get out and pretend you were never here."

The young man was more than happy to oblige. The moment she pulled back her leg he fled out the door, the thin sheet his only covering. Jacaranda turned back to Malin and reacted only with mild annoyance to his attempt to stab her with a dagger he'd somehow obtained. A slight shift to the left caused it to miss wide of her neck. She struck the interior of his armpit to pop the bone out of joint, then dipped low to swipe with her dagger. The blade cut cleanly through his heel, severing the tendon and dropping Malin with a howl. For good measure she stabbed through the other heel as well. It paid to be thorough.

"That should keep you still," she said. Right now she wasn't interested in Malin but the cargo manifest atop his small desk. She slid into his chair and flipped it open. To anyone else it'd appear to be a full account of the vegetables brought in from the Petyrn estate. To Jacaranda, who'd been trained to handle much of the illegal trade, it was a simple translation of extra words, symbols, and seemingly random numbers that dotted the page. By her reading Gerag had gotten greedy, no doubt spurred on by the long delay in shipments from the east.

"So why does Gerag want me dead?" Malin asked as she read. "He even tell you? Six years of loyal deliveries and this is the shitty thanks I get?"

He still believed she was a loyal soulless in service of her master. A desire, no, a *need* to disabuse him of this notion overcame her.

"I'm not doing this for that asshole," she said. "I'm doing this for me."

Malin had nothing in response to that. Her reaction simply did not make sense. At best, he'd assume her to be putting on a show Gerag had instructed her to perform. That was fine. He'd soon understand how far off he was. She slammed the manifest shut and stood from the chair.

"If I hear you scream I'm coming back to kill you," she said.

"Fuck you," he said without much conviction.

Jacaranda stepped around his prone body, avoiding the pool of blood as best she could. Malin's dagger lay a few feet outside his grasp. She kicked it into a corner. If he felt like crawling for it during her absence, then good on him. She hesitated a moment after shutting the cabin door, curious if he'd be brave enough to holler for help. He was not. Jacaranda opened the hatch and dropped into the *Hawkins*'s cargo hold. It wasn't very expansive, and she had to duck as she walked to one corner. Multiple crates were stacked up there, two of them clearly broken. She pushed those aside and drew her dagger as she leaned over a third.

You can handle this, she told herself.

It took two minutes but at last she wedged the crate open with her dagger. The top creaked as she shoved it aside. Prepared as she was, seeing inside still jolted her spine. Three soulless sat curled up in the crate, barely visible in the starlight coming through the open hatch. Two were young women, the third a short-haired boy. Not a one was older than sixteen. They looked up at her with blank stares. Awaiting orders.

"Get out," she said.

They obliged. Jacaranda saw their muscles twitch and strain from the movements. They wouldn't have been sealed in there for the entire trip, only before arriving in port, but that still put them stacked in like bricks for twelve hours at the minimum. The three stood side by side with their heads bowed toward their chests to avoiding hitting the top of the hold. Jacaranda's nerves burned with growing anxiety. She had to remain focused. Had to keep herself poised.

"Wait here," she said. Even ordering them around tweaked with her mind.

Jacaranda climbed out of the hold. Something was wrong. Someone was missing.

"You haven't bled out, have you?" Jacaranda asked upon opening his cabin door.

"Still breathing, no thanks to you, cunt," Malin said. He'd balled up a sheet from his bed and wrapped them about his heels. The dagger remained in the corner. Stupid man. He still thought he had a chance to survive this.

"Where is the fourth?" she asked.

"The what?"

Jacaranda grabbed the manifest off the desk and tossed the heavy book onto his stomach.

"The manifest says four but I only count three. The notes don't say she's dead, so where is she?"

The idea that this was some perverse game of Gerag's finally abandoned Malin. He stared at her with a fresh wave of bewilderment.

"What the fuck is going on? Why does a goddess-damned soulless care about my cargo?"

Jacaranda kicked him as hard as she could in the testicles. He howled as his entire body convulsed. She gave him a handful of seconds to recover and then knelt atop him, each knee pinning a shoulder. With one hand she held his head back by his hair. The other pressed the blade of a dagger against his throat.

"Don't you ever call them cargo again, you understand?" He wearily nodded his head. "Good. Now answer the damn question."

"One of the, uh, women started acting strange," Malin said. "It was like nothing we'd seen before. Had to keep her tied up and drugged for the last two days of sailing, otherwise she'd have flung herself into the river. I told Gerag I wanted her off my boat immediately, and if he didn't come get her I'd..." He seemed to think better of his intended language. "I'd solve the problem myself."

Jacaranda's vision darkened all along the edges. What colors she saw in the candlelight shifted solely to red.

"A soulless acting strangely," she said quietly. "Crazy, even. Did she fight, Captain? Did she curse and yell and try to take her own life?"

"Now-now-now, she wasn't no real girl," the captain said. His eyes widened with realization. "This ain't a slave ship. You of all people should know that. She was just like any other soulless when we loaded her. Something went wrong in her head on the way over, that's all."

Something went wrong in her head.

"Where is she?" Jacaranda asked. It took all her concentration to keep her physical body still. Her mind was burning with rage like an uncontrolled wildfire.

"I told you. Gerag came and got her. Seemed quite happy about it, really, once he had a chance to chat with her a bit. Said she'd be going to auction immediately."

"Happy." Angry tears stung her eyes. "Of course he'd be happy."

She cut his throat before he even knew she'd decided to kill him. A fresh wave of blood spilled across the cabin floor. Jacaranda stared at the flow and tried to find pleasure in the kill. How many young men and women had he ferried down the Septen to become Gerag's little playthings? Her own implicitness ruined it. Her choices or not, she'd been the one who came under cover of darkness to lead the soulless to their destinations. Damn her memories. Part of her wished she'd remembered nothing of what happened prior to her awakening.

Jacaranda returned to the dark cargo hold. The three soulless stood in the exact same spots. There was something strange in the way they watched her...or perhaps that was just projection. No. There was nothing behind those eyes. No curiosity. No desire for freedom. For once Jacaranda understood why so many remarked upon the unsettling presence of a soulless.

"Who are you waiting for?" she asked them.

The older girl, a pale-skinned redhead, answered for them.

"We are not to say."

As expected. The soulless were trained at the Petyrn estate before being shipped west, and part of that involved insulating both Gerag and the Petyrn family from potential blame if the soulless were caught and interrogated. They'd only follow the most basic commands unless you knew the code words. Since this was the first ship to arrive since the black water came, there was thankfully no chance that Gerag could have changed them.

"Your blood, my soil," she recited. "Your flesh, my garden. Your life, my rose blooms."

The words squirmed like worms on her tongue. Ownership, everything implied ownership, control, master over slave. How could she let this continue? She wanted to help them. She wanted to spare them the indignity and suffering of being sold into Gerag's underground market. But what orders could she give? *Be free?* They wouldn't understand that. She was still grappling with that concept herself. Perhaps she could give a series of instructions detailing feeding and clothing oneself, but no matter where she sent them the chains on their necks would identify them. People would ask questions. Someone would claim them eventually.

The helplessness of it tore at Jacaranda's insides. Gerag's entourage would be here soon to claim them. Enslave them. Sell them to sick men and women with plentiful coin and unconventional desires. Jacaranda wrapped her arms around the young boy and cried, letting her tears fall upon his head. The boy did not hug back. It had not been commanded of him.

"I'm sorry," Jacaranda whispered. "This is the best I know to do."

A dark part deep inside her insisted she slay all three. Her hand touched the hilt of a dagger. Better death than mindless enslavement. Better that the shell of a body return to the soil. But was that what she'd have preferred? Jacaranda had come over on one such boat. Gerag had been especially taken by her, and her eyes. Would she have preferred that a stranger slice open her throat all those years ago, denying her the chance to awaken now? Extinguish the possibility that she might find joy and happiness and peace?

Jacaranda let go of her dagger. Among all these imperfect solutions, she would go with the best she knew of.

"Do you know what a member of the city guard looks like?" she asked them.

"We do," they answered in unison.

"Leave this boat. Walk the roads of the city. Do not repeat the same path if you can help it. Once you find a guard, tell him or her you three are lost and need to be brought to the Cathedral of the Sacred Mother. If the guard does not do so, keep searching for another who will. Am I understood?"

"Understood." Again in unison.

"Then go."

Jacaranda lingered in the cargo hold as the three climbed up and out. If they arrived at the cathedral they'd be brought in and questioned, but of course they'd reveal nothing. Gerag would not dare try to claim them. It'd bring far too much attention his way, and require explanations he would not have. Most likely the three would be kept as servants for the church. They'd spend a life sewing, cleaning, and cooking, but far better that than being some bloated bastard's fuck toy.

. . . started acting strange . . .

An awakened soulless held prisoner, tortured, and sold. She wouldn't need to be trained like the others. Her reactions of fear, of pain and disgust, would be real. It'd be everything Gerag's buyers wanted.

Jacaranda's hands clutched the hilts of her daggers as she fought off wave after wave of horror and revulsion.

"Never," she hissed. "Not while I breathe, Gerag. You couldn't keep me, and no matter how many I have to kill, you won't keep her."

CHAPTER 35

Whenever night fell over Londheim a change swept through the cramped stone buildings. Shadows sank deeper. The wind sang louder. Tents and lean-tos dotted the slightest openings, dark and covered as if they were recently erected tombs. Worsening matters was a heavy fog that rolled off the Septen River, gradually thickening as the night wore on until neither Devin nor Tommy could see beyond a few dozen feet ahead of them. The hanging lanterns illuminated slender circles beneath them and little else.

"I'm starting to rethink my involvement in this," Tommy muttered.

"Remember, this was your idea, not mine," Devin said. After their trip to the market, and an admittedly immature grumbling about his frustration with his nightly patrols, Tommy had offered to accompany him.

"I might get to use my magic again," he'd said excitedly. "I mean, actually on something, and not a basement wall."

"Always focusing on the positive," Devin had laughed, but it didn't seem so funny now. If anything happened to his brother-in-law, he'd never forgive himself. Perhaps he should have been sterner and refused.

"I swear, it feels like I don't recognize this city anymore," he said as a particularly thick wave of fog rolled over the street.

"I have a theory on that," Tommy said.

"Do you now?"

"I do! It seems, based on my talks with Puffy and Tesmarie, that we once coexisted alongside these magical creatures until they were...put to sleep? Banished? Removed from the face of the Cradle? Something like that. My thinking is Londheim was changed with it to erase all evidence of their existence, or maybe we were just made blind to those things. Now that everything's woken back up, so to speak, I think Londheim changed back to how it was."

"Meaning what?"

Tommy shrugged.

"Meaning that maybe we're seeing where some of these weirder creatures used to live, and not humans?"

"A nice theory," Devin said, and he pointed ahead. "Does it explain that?"

A strange object blocked the middle of the street. It was shaped like an ovoid, as tall as his chin, and it awaited like an offered gift. The outer surface appeared made of some sort of mudlike substance. Countless thin strands of...something... ran through it, like straw or twigs, only its texture was undetectable given the dark brown coating. It almost looked like the earth had shoved up an egg from below its surface. No smell emanated from the outside, but he wondered if that'd be the case if he cracked it open.

"I have no idea what that is," Tommy said.

"Try a guess. That's what you're here for."

"I mean, it seems a little bit like an egg, and it's got a crack here, and here. I think we should discover what's inside."

Devin grimaced at the thought.

"I'm not sure I *want* to know what's inside."

"I'm not too curious, either, Devin, but if something hatches out of it and starts eating people I'm going to feel a tiny bit responsible."

Impeccable logic. This only soured Devin's mood further.

"Fine," he said, slowly approaching the ovoid with his sword drawn. "But you better be ready to roast whatever comes out with your magic. If I'm some newborn monster's first meal, my soul will haunt you for eternity."

"There's an interesting thought. Can a Soulkeeper build you a funeral pyre if you're nothing but bones and stomach acid? Where do you think the soul will emerge from? Your skull? Or from the blob that was your brain matter?"

Devin grinded his teeth together.

"Not. Helping."

He shoved his sword a few inches into its side. It was softer than he expected, and it easily parted for his sharpened blade. Devin pulled it free, his mind racing. The giant thing before him seemed vaguely familiar, which made no sense at all. Was it the texture? The shape? He used his teeth to remove the glove from his free hand and then pressed his fingers to the side. Cool to the touch, and surprisingly dry. With his sword as a wedge, he pulled at a chunk. The tearing sound triggered another memory, and with sudden, horrible clarity he knew exactly what this ovoid was.

"Of course," Devin said. His stomach churned. "Of course it is."

He sheathed his sword, donned his glove, and used both arms to rip and tear at the crack. One last violent shove opened it completely. A few loose bones spilled to the street. Dozens more remained embedded in jumbled facsimiles of a human skeleton. He saw a piece of a metal from a breastplate, a large brown flap of trousers, and a perfectly preserved straw hat. His stomach doing knots, he stepped aside so Tommy could see.

An owl pellet. The largest owl pellet in the whole fucking world.

"It's a..." Tommy started, and then he also made the connection. His face paled significantly. Devin wondered if he'd vomit. He felt like doing the same.

"Humans playing in waste," a booming voice spoke from above. "How appropriate."

Shock and horror wanted to lock Devin's limbs in place, but that reaction meant death. He slid to one knee and spun, drawing his pistol faster than he might blink and aiming it at the enormous owl lurking from the rooftop. Tommy lacked any such honed reactions, and he stood slack-jawed where he stood, his hands hanging limply at his sides.

"Is something the matter?" the owl asked. It turned its enormous white head. Its yellow eyes hovered in the fog. "Are you frightened?"

Not a hint of worry or fear in that deep, pleased voice.

"Yeah," Tommy said, answering for the both of them. "I think I'm scared shitless."

Devin couldn't wrap his mind around the creature's size. Its beak was as big as his chest. Its claws punctured the stone architecture like it was paper. Adria had described her encounter with the owl to him, and this creature easily dwarfed the other.

"We don't want to fight," Devin said, praying that maybe he could defuse the situation. "We're only protecting our people. That's all."

"I wish no battle, either," the owl said. Its head bobbed lower. "We hunt. We eat. Does not everything?"

"This isn't the same," Devin said, though he painfully wished he had a better argument than that. "You're murdering innocent people."

The owl rotated its head in a half circle and stared sideways at him.

"How many creatures do you hunt, human? Are they innocent? Life or death. Predator and prey. All the same."

"I beg to disagree," Tommy said. He immediately wilted beneath the owl's gaze. "I mean, if that's all right with you. We're not rabbits, though. We're people. You can't just hunt us!"

Stone cracked underneath the owl's clenching claws.

"Why not?" it asked. Its head twirled back to its proper position. "I am bigger. I am faster. I am stronger."

"We are blessed with souls by the Three Sisters," Devin said. He inched his hand closer to his sword hilt. "Through them we are granted dominion over the soulless of the wilds, from the smallest insect to the largest bear. We are to care for life, just as that life is granted to us for our survival. What say you, nameless owl? Have you a soul within that proud chest?"

The owl spread its wings to the fullest of its span and let out a shriek capable of shattering glass. Devin braced himself as if enduring a mighty wind. Whether courage or cowardice kept his pistol silent, he did not know.

"Nameless, you call me," it said, "for you know not my name. Soulless, you claim, though you know not the magic in which we dwell. You call me proud, yet why should I not be? I am Arondel the Beautiful, Queen of the Winged and cherished knight of the Dragons. You humans have not changed. Foolish. Dull. You will find greater purpose in my stomach than in serving your precious Sisters."

"Devin," Tommy whispered, sounding an inch away from

panic. The owl's feet clutched the rooftop edge so hard that chunks of stone were cracking free and falling. Devin shook his head, trying to convince his friend not to do anything rash.

"You know it not, but I called for truce," the queen owl continued. "I wished to know of your people. I wished to see what you became while free of us, as your Goddesses always wished. I have seen. I have learned. I am *unimpressed*."

"Stay back!" Tommy shouted. *"Creare parvos fulgur!"*

"No, wait!" Devin cried, but he was already too late. The ball of flame shot from Tommy's fingers toward the enormous owl. Its wings folded before it like a shield, protecting the rest of the body from the ensuing blast. Smoke rose to the sky, and within its cloud emerged the perfectly still form of the owl. The wings' feathers should have easily withered against such tremendous heat. Instead not a single one bore sign of ash or char. They unfolded, and Devin had but a fraction of a second to fire before the owl dove from the side of the building.

The flamestone roared, a pale comparison to the thunderous shriek that accompanied the owl's dive. His shot missed wide, as Devin had badly underestimated the creature's speed. An enormous beak closed about Tommy's waist before he finished the first syllable of another spell. A simple turn of the head lifted his friend off the cobbles, and another turn flung him right back down with a painful crack. A single clawed foot slammed down atop him, pinning him, crushing him.

"Londheim was ours before it was ever yours," the owl said. The calmness to its voice only heightened its deadliness. "We shall not leave. If neither do you, then let us hunt one another. We shall see whose tongue tastes blood first."

Its wings cast a tremendous curtain across the street. Wind blasted across him from the mighty beats of those wings. The claws relented. A terrible shriek split the night as the owl tore into the sky and flew east. Devin watched until he was certain it would not circle about and then hurried to Tommy's side. His friend had pushed himself up to a sitting position, and though he looked bruised and shaken up, Devin could find no serious injuries.

"Devin?"

"Yeah, Tommy?"

"I have regrets."

Devin stared at the fleeting darkness that was the queen owl.

"Go on home," he said. "I'm not sure there's much we can do out here anyway."

Relief flashed across Tommy's face, immediately followed by guilt.

"Are you sure you'll be all right without me?" he asked. "What if you run into Janus?"

Devin offered Tommy a hand, then gestured to the fog bathing the street once he was on his feet.

"We might pass one another and never notice. Do you know the way back to the Wise tower?"

"Know it? Yes. Want to walk it alone? Um. Not really."

Devin slammed his pistol back into its holster.

"Come on," he said. "I'll make sure neither of us becomes owl food on our way."

Devin's exhaustion bordered on crippling by the time he reached his house, and it wasn't the physical kind. He inserted his key and turned it only to discover the door already unlocked. That wasn't right. He'd locked it upon leaving...

He crept the door open while keeping one hand on his sword in case someone had been foolish enough to break into his house. No burglar awaited him, just Jacaranda sitting on the couch facing a low-burning fire. Devin closed the door and removed his sword and gun belt. The sound of metal and leather was unbearably loud in the heavy silence.

"Trouble sleeping?" Devin asked. Jacaranda hadn't even budged at his arrival.

"Something like that."

The hurt in her voice was as easily detectable as the fireplace in the dark. A chill had crept into the air, so Devin tossed another log into the fire from a tall stack beside it. A grateful Puffy emerged to wave in thanks before returning to the embers. Devin settled into the chair by the fire, guessing that Jacaranda would prefer a bit of space. Her outfit reminded him of when she'd first joined him on the road to Oakenwall. She'd removed her scarf, and she held it in her hands, softly rubbing it with her thumbs.

Devin said nothing as he rocked in his chair. If she wished to talk, then she'd talk. Until then, he'd relax while watching the fire burn.

"How do you do it?"

He glanced her way. Her cheeks were wet with tears. Something had clearly happened that night, but what, he could only guess.

"Do what?" he asked.

"Go on," she said. "Trying. Breathing. Living. When everything looks like shit and your heart doesn't want to do anything but hurt." She sniffled. "I can't even sleep. That doesn't make sense. How can I be too tired to sleep? Am I that badly broken?"

Still not revealing why she was upset. Did it involve the chains on her neck? Her memories of servitude? He didn't know, so he answered as best he could.

"Everyone reaches low points in their lives," he said. "It's like you've fallen into a pit, and it's cold, dark, and lonely. Sure, you could climb out, but you've a sense of how much strength it will take to make that climb. Sometimes it's so much easier to lie down, close your eyes, and tell yourself, 'Tomorrow, I'll make that climb tomorrow.'"

"That's one way to describe this...paralysis," Jacaranda said. "Have you fallen into such a pit before?"

"I have."

"When?"

Devin's tired mind slipped back into the past. Like many things in his life, it all came down to one single, awful moment.

"After my wife's death. I didn't handle it very well. At all, really. I insisted to anyone who'd listen to me that I was done as a Soulkeeper. I blamed myself. I blamed those who attended her in her final hours. I blamed the Goddesses for their cruelty. Brittany was also a Soulkeeper, and a far better one than I, yet all our work was rewarded with her death and my suffering?"

Devin had mostly made peace with her passage over the years, but reliving the memory scratched and dug at the deep scar. He shook his head and forced his mind out of the old rut lest it stay there.

"By the end of the week I'd stopped eating and all but imprisoned myself in my own home. I couldn't make myself care. Every piece of my life linked to memories of Brittany, her laugh, her smile, her flaws and jokes, all of it. My grief felt inescapable. I've been trained on what to say to others who lost loved ones. I know the prayers of comfort to offer when I light a funeral pyre. None of that helped. I didn't want the Goddesses' consolation. I wanted to scream and rip down the stars and demand they face my rage. I wanted them to feel *my* pain. Such hubris, but grief warps the mind, and it does not play fair."

Devin fell silent. He needed a moment to let the ancient feelings disseminate back into the cobwebbed corners of his mind. Embarrassment kept him from admitting that he had stood atop his roof and screamed at the stars, daring the Sisters to prove they were paying attention.

"How did you pull yourself out?" Jacaranda asked.

"Adria saved me," he said. "As she often does. Every morning she came in, sat down at the table, and asked me how I was doing. Was I eating? Was I sleeping? If I was hungry, she brought me bread and honey. If I needed to talk, she listened. I...I shouted some awful stuff at her, Jacaranda. I didn't want to feel better, but she dragged me out of that pit kicking and screaming."

There was one morning in particular that had finally snapped him out of his downward spiral. He remembered the hurt on his sister's face, the barely concealed exhaustion and desperation.

"I didn't realize the toll it was taking on her," he continued. "This one morning I asked her why she bothered. Why was she so insistent I pull myself out? She said because Tommy was even worse, and she didn't think she could reach him. That was when I finally saw how tired she was. In what spare time she had after her Mindkeeper duties she was splitting her attention between Tommy and me, trying to hold us together, and here I was, wallowing in my grief. I hadn't even seen Tommy once since Brittany died."

Devin rubbed his hand across his eyes and face. There were no tears there, but they were close, like a distant thunderstorm.

"So that afternoon I grabbed two bottles of cherrysilver wine, walked to his home, and announced we were going to drain those bottles dry while we reminisced on how awesome Brittany was." He couldn't help but laugh. "Not exactly the advice a Soulkeeper should be giving others, but hey, sometimes you must use what works."

He rocked back and forth in the chair, remembering that night. It'd been the first time he'd accepted Brittany's death as a part of his life instead of some cosmic disruption ending all semblance of order. He'd allowed himself to smile at her memories and joke with Tommy about how crazy she could get while fighting with her giant, custom-built axe. So easy to tell others to cherish your memories together instead of dwelling on the loss. So hard to do once lost in the tempest of grief.

Jacaranda shifted atop the couch and clasped her hands, her face locked in deep thought. Devin couldn't begin to imagine what it was like to process these emotions for the first time. Brittany's death had wrecked him, and he'd had a lifetime of experiencing love, happiness, anger, and loss. But what did Jacaranda struggle with? What personal monster clawed at her insides?

"So the way to endure the pain and hurt," Jacaranda said, as if she'd solved a mathematical problem. "It's through others?"

"Most often, yes," Devin said. "This world is much too hard and cruel to endure alone. From the first day the Sisters gave us life, we were meant to love and support one another. Sadly that basic tenet of our existence is also the hardest to keep."

Jacaranda nodded slightly. He noticed her violet eyes constantly flicking in his direction. She shifted her weight again. Was... was she nervous?

"Jac, is something—"

"Will you—" she interrupted, then blushed. He gestured for her to continue. "Will you sit beside me?"

Devin smiled. "Of course."

He moved from his chair to the couch, leaving a small space between them. Jacaranda quickly erased that space and rested her head atop his shoulder and her body against his arm.

"I want to thank you," she said.

"For what?"

"For being...good. If I'd awakened earlier, or a few days later, it wouldn't have been you who helped me. It wouldn't have been someone kind. And it makes me realize just how lucky I was for you to...to find me."

Devin swallowed down a blob of guilt bubbling up his throat.

"I'm not so good, Jacaranda. Have you forgotten the grave I made you dig? The lack of sleep and your cut fingers?"

She closed her eyes and turned her face further downward.

"I remember a lifetime of people treating me differently for being soulless. What they said. What they did. Compared to all that...it's easy to forgive you, Devin. It's so easy, because without you, if...if I'm without you, I'm alone, and I don't want to be alone. I'm a damn freak with a curse on my neck and I cannot go through this alone anymore. I can't. I just can't."

By the Goddesses, she was so strong. Even as she confessed her brokenness he saw the incredible strength holding herself together.

"I will always be here for you if you need me," he said. "Take a single step my way and I shall run all the rest. Put your trust in me and I will move the entire world to prove I'm worthy of that trust. Truth be told, it's the least I could do."

She did not answer with words, but by the visible relaxation of her body against his. Silence settled back over the dark room, but the tension had been punctured and drained. Devin listened to the crackling of the fire and Jacaranda's slow, steady breathing.

"I think I can sleep now," she said softly. "Is this all right?"

"Of course it is."

Jacaranda stretched her legs out across the couch and slid lower so that her head leaned against Devin's thigh. He rested his hand upon her shoulder, and she squeezed his fingers once to let him know her appreciation. It was not long before her breathing turned shallow. Devin watched her sleep, troubled by the blood he saw on her boots and the faint spray of it staining her shirt.

Time rolled along, the night approaching its end. Devin shifted so his lower back was more comfortable, and he shivered a bit. He had no blanket, and he had not the heart to risk waking Jacaranda getting one. The fire was lower than it should be, given... hold on. Puffy's two little coal eyes were watching him quietly, as if waiting for him to notice. Devin raised an eyebrow in its direction, and Puffy stepped its whole body free of the fire to stand at the edge of the fireplace. It waved through the air, slowly spelling out letter after letter.

SAD?

Devin smiled at the firekin's concern.

"We all need to be sad sometimes," he whispered softly. "But I think she'll be fine."

Puffy thought a moment before spelling again.

SLEEP?

"I hope to. It's been a long night."

Puffy thrust its hands onto its hips with clear purpose and nodded. It dove back into the fire and swirled around the edges. The light of it steadily dimmed, yet at the same time, the heat coming off it dramatically increased. Warm waves washed over

Devin's skin, and he relaxed his muscles and sank into the couch. The heat, combined with the increased darkness, pulled his eyelids closed.

"Thanks, little one," he said. The siren call of sleep beckoned, and he was happy to accept. "Better than any blanket."

The fire flared once in appreciation and then settled into a nice, steady rhythm of cracks and pops. The warmth and noise easily soothed away the bittersweet memories of Brittany's carefree smile hidden behind a mask of snow atop an unlit pyre.

CHAPTER 36

Tesmarie shifted and rolled restlessly atop the rough fabric above the hatmaker's stall. It wasn't the sudden drop in temperature that bothered her, for her onyx skin gave little care for the cold. It was the lack of sunlight. Dreary clouds sealed away the sun, and given the angry chill in the wind, she wouldn't be surprised if it started to snow later.

"Where did everybody go?" she grumbled. Only yesterday the market had teemed with life. Now the number of bodies cluttering the rows had dropped significantly, and they lacked the same level of joy and mirth. One brief respite, and everyone was back to fearing rumors and eyeing the living mountain as if it might strike at any moment. Tesmarie dangled her head over the side and looked at the upside-down Nora currently running the stall. The woman had wrapped a heavy quilt around her shoulders and covered her braids with a thick but pretty scarf.

"Today's a quiet day," Tesmarie said.

"People spent more than they had yesterday," Nora responded.

"Today they're tightening purses and realizing that just because some boats arrived, things aren't returning to how they were."

"So today will be dreary and boring?"

A hint of smile tugged at Nora's chapped lips.

"If it will make you feel better, Faithkeeper Nolan is giving his ninth-day sermon at the mummer's stage not far from here."

"Ninth-day sermon?"

"Informal prayers every three days, a full gathering of prayers and lecture on the ninth. Something to do with the church and their obsession with triangles. There's usually a hundred or so gathered there, so when it's over they'll spill out across the market. I'm sure you'll get your daily allotment of fruit and cheese then."

Tesmarie rocked her head, enjoying the way her upside-down hair swished from side to side.

"I don't come here just for the food, you know."

"You could have fooled me."

Tesmarie pulled herself up. Well then. What was a faery to do? It sounded like she'd have to wait for the ninth-day sermon to end, however long that would be. She yawned and stretched her arms. Perhaps a nap would do well to pass the time. She'd not slept well last night, especially after listening to Devin and Jacaranda's intimate conversation. The two had sounded so tired and broken. Tesmarie had spent the whole time pretending to sleep while hoping they'd finally kiss and hug and be happy.

"Why does this world have to be so hard?" she wondered. She tucked her hands behind her head, folded up her wings, and lay on her back. "Someone messed up, that's it. It certainly wasn't meant to be this way. I wonder who?"

Was it the dragons? The Sisters? Or maybe something else entirely? After all, it hadn't been the demigods and goddesses who had banished Tesmarie from her village, nor had they slain the alabaster fae of her new home...

"No, no, no-no-no," she said. "No more crying. I am done crying."

She crossed her arms and huffed again. Sniffled. Maybe wiped a single diamond tear away. The blanket of clouds lazily rolled along the sky, and she watched them with steadily growing boredom. Boredom was good. Boredom rarely led to her crying. Her eyes slipped closed more often than open. The sounds of the market lulled her frantic mind. Yes, a nap would suit her just fine.

Something thick and heavy fell across her. Tesmarie cried out in shock and confusion. She turned, looped, and jostled into a frantic cartwheel. Her wings twisted, one bending at an awkward enough angle that she shrieked. The ground approached, but it was weird, hazy, and then her descent halted suddenly with a painful smack to her forehead. Not ground. Glass. The floor was covered with it. Her weight shifted, and suddenly she was sliding to the side. Another glass wall stopped her. She only barely folded her wings in time to avoid a second painful bend. Her head struck the glass, spilling stars across her vision.

"What...what's happening?" she asked. Her voice came out drunken and distorted. Tesmarie shook her head and forced herself to react. Something was wrong. Her life was in danger. She spread her wings and flew her approximation of straight up... only now there was a giant piece of cork blocking the way. She hit it shoulder first and failed to make the slightest indent. Tesmarie fluttered back to the glass floor, horror steadily dawning on her. She knew where she was, what she was in. What else could it be?

A corked glass jar.

"Got you," a pleased, muffled voice spoke from above. Tesmarie held on to the side of the jar for balance as her captor lifted the jar. She saw the smiling face of an older woman with wrinkled skin and six strings of beads and stones hanging around her neck.

"Let me go!" Tesmarie shouted at her. Her fists banged futilely against the glass.

"Let go?" she asked. "Oh no. Not likely."

Tesmarie spun, trying to see through the thick distortion of the jar. Nora, why wasn't Nora doing anything? There she was, only she was talking with a customer. Her captor had waited until she was preoccupied, the fiend! The ugly woman quickly put her chest between the two and hustled away. Tesmarie clenched her fist and summoned her moonlight blade. Oh, she'd make the bitch pay once she...

The moment the light sparked from her fingers the woman jostled the jar violently from side to side. Tesmarie screamed as her body slammed into the unforgiving glass. She couldn't orient herself in time before the next jostle, and with each blow her strength waned. Her heart hammered within her chest as panic set in, but she knew how dangerous that was, too. There were no holes in the jar, nor in the thick cork sealing her inside. Already she felt light-headed, made worse by the pain emanating from her bruised and battered body.

"No escaping," her captor chided, as if she were a naughty child. "I'd hate to hurt you."

Too late for that.

Tesmarie leaned on the glass and struck it repeatedly with her fists. Even if she couldn't escape on her own, she didn't have to. The wrinkled woman carried her past dozens of people throughout the market, and Tesmarie shouted to them at the top of her lungs.

"Help! She's kidnapped me! Stop her, stop her, stop her!"

Finally a man looked her way. She stood up a little straighter, and at his confused look, she shouted it again. "I need out!"

The man shot a look to her captor, and he frowned with distaste.

And then he turned around.

And then he kept walking.

"Where are you going?" Tesmarie asked. She slammed her fists against the glass, not caring that blood started to flow from her knuckles. "Help, help, I need help!"

Her frustration grew at how no one looked her way. Could they not hear her? Maybe the glass muffled her voice more than she realized?

There, a woman carrying a bushel of apples! Tesmarie waved her arms and hopped up and down. The woman asked something of her captor, words too quiet and distorted by the jar for her to make out.

"Just taking her where she belongs," her captor replied.

And... and that was apparently enough. The woman barely shot her a second glance. Several more men spared her a worried look before resuming whatever they were doing. The only one who seemed to really care was a young boy being dragged through the market by his mother.

"Mom, it's the faery!" he shouted while pointing with his free hand. Tesmarie dared hope, but then the mother tugged his arm so hard he grimaced with pain. "But, Mooommm!"

Maybe it was the lack of air, but suddenly Tesmarie found she couldn't much stand anymore. She slipped to her rear in the center of her bottle. These... these people. Hadn't she danced and sung for them? Had they not given her presents and laughed? Yet now she received only subdued, embarrassed glances. Couldn't they see her trapped in that bottle? Who could look at this predicament and think it was all right? Tears fell from her eyes to ping and clatter off the glass. Her captor paused to look around, spotted an empty alcove, and rushed inside.

"Oh my," she said. "Oh my, oh my, are those what I think they are?"

Tesmarie grabbed at her spent tears and clutched them to her breast.

"No," she said weakly. How dare her captor look upon her suffering and desire more from her? These tears were hers. Her sorrow was *hers*, damn it.

The terrible woman clutched the bottle to her chest and looked about, as if suddenly worried someone would steal her precious treasure. She sprinted, the movements jostling Tesmarie against the sides of the glass. The little diamonds spilled from Tesmarie's hands. Her captor did not stop until she found a deep alcove behind a permanent stall and the back of a store of some sort. Finally alone, the woman lifted the jar to her face and leaned in so close her bulbous nose flattened against its side. Her breath fogged the glass.

"Oh my, oh my, they *are* diamonds," she said. "You are just a wonder, aren't you? And I thought your wings would be the real draw. Can you cry more, my dear? Cry more, and I'll poke a hole in the cork, just for you."

She'd rather suffocate. Everything hurt, even her heart. If her captor was upset, she didn't show it. A shrug of her shoulders, and she started back toward... wherever she was headed. Home? A shop? A new, better prison? Tesmarie thought of being caged like a pet and broke down further. Her tears slipped over her hands, unable to be stopped. Little diamonds. Her diamonds.

"Pardon me, but I do not believe that belongs to you."

Tesmarie blinked through her tears. A man had stopped her

captor at the entrance of their little alcove. She could barely make out his long dark coat. Her captor stood to her full height and sneered.

"And who are you to say so, young man?"

In response the man shot out his hand and grabbed her captor by the throat. The woman gargled out an unintelligible protest.

"Who must I be to call you a monster?" this strange man asked. "A king? A prince? Must I have wealth to know that you imprison a living being inside that jar? Tell me, so I may become him. What is the minimum power required to protest your heinous acts?"

Her captor wheezed and flailed at the iron grip about her neck.

"Beauty in a glass jar," the man continued. "That's what I see you holding. I'd make you the same, but there is no beauty in you to behold. Just ugliness and want."

He gently took the jar from her captor and, using only one hand, popped the cork free. Tesmarie gasped in a wonderful breath of fresh air. Her wings weakly fluttered until she could lift herself out. She felt lost in a dream. This wasn't happening. None of this was.

"I hope you are well, my dear," the stranger said, and he flashed her a smile. He wore no shirt despite the cold, and his hair was split between shades of green and shades of black.

"Who...who are you?" she asked him, certain she'd seen him somewhere.

"My name is Janus," he told her, and an image of a wanted poster immediately flashed into her mind. "I've come to save you."

Magical power flowed from Janus's hand and into the woman's body, as visible to her eyes as a rainbow, and just as shimmery.

The skin on her captor's body began to turn translucent. It wasn't disappearing, though, for she could see the texture changing as well. Hardening into glass, Tesmarie realized with detached horror. Glass spread to her teeth and nails, and then sank into her muscles and bones. Even her clothes turned crystalline clear. The pulpy insides, however, did no such thing. Blood pulsed through visible veins. Intestines twisted and slithered inside the grotesque mess that was a human's innards. The woman's eyes locked in place despite the wiggling of the connected cords. Faint tears slid down her glass cheeks.

Two men had heard the argument begin and approached the secluded alley. Upon seeing Janus's "artwork" they immediately screamed and fled. Tesmarie shared in their horror. Only her confusion and pain kept her from vomiting. Somehow, through some cruel magic, the woman was still alive.

"It took me years to understand this," Janus said as he stepped back to observe his handiwork. "Not all art must be pleasant to the eye to be beautiful. There is an undeniable pull to the truth, however wicked."

Tesmarie floated away from the horrific creation. She tried telling herself she'd been a bad human ready to kill her, or worse, but she could not shake her revulsion.

"Is she ... is she in pain?" she asked.

"Oh, most certainly," Janus said. He smiled at the glass-and-guts construct. "I left her nerves intact. They're the little yellowish spiderwebs connected to her spine and brain."

Tesmarie didn't know what nerves were but she understood pain. The way her captor's eyes shook, the way the visible heart hammered at a hundred miles an hour ... she was screaming. Somehow she heard that phantom howl despite the woman's mouth being sealed into a tight-lipped frown. Air whistled in and out of her nostrils, producing her only sound, that of a constant, desperate wheeze.

Janus might have saved her from her captor, but witnessing that grotesque artwork had her fearing him more than any fate in a glass jar.

"Please," she said, unable to look at it any longer. "Please, kill it. It's too awful."

"Humanity itself is awful. Would you have me kill them, too, Tesmarie?"

Tesmarie fluttered a few feet into the air.

"How do you know my name?" she asked.

Janus flashed her a smile of rainbow opal teeth.

"I have seen you during your displays in the market," he said. "Come now, stay with me a while. I would have us talk."

Talk was the furthest thing from Tesmarie's mind. This man was dangerous, and no doubt whom Devin and his fellows scoured the night searching for. She clutched her hands into fists, torn between fleeing and using her moonlight blade to slice apart the glass-and-gore construction. It made no sense, but she felt weirdly responsible for her captor's suffering. If only she'd paid attention, if only she'd not slept so low to the ground, none of this would have happened.

"I-th-th-thank-you-for-the-help," Tesmarie blurted. She rotated in air and tried to shoot for the sky, but Janus was somehow faster. Terrible pain shot through her back and spine as his fingers closed about her wings. A scream escaped her lips. If she struggled harder, she might rip them right out from their sockets.

"I'm sorry, little faery," Janus said. "But consider this a much-needed lesson."

Numbness crept throughout her wings. A sudden weight dragged at her shoulders, and she gasped at the new pain. Janus calmly put her atop his shoulder once the numbness had completely enveloped her, and to her horror, she saw that her wings were no longer thin, translucent chitin. Their rainbow of color was replaced with a dull gray. Stone. He'd turned her wings to stone.

"Please, don't," Tesmarie whimpered. "I won't tell anyone, I swear, please, let me go."

Her wings rested against his shoulder, and his support was the only reason they did not tear the skin off her back. She might not be inside a jar, but she felt just as confined, and just as powerless.

Janus returned to the bustle of the market, carrying Tesmarie with him. Nearly everyone stared, discreetly or otherwise. Slowly people began to recognize him from the wanted posters, which led to a wildfire of panic. Most quietly fled, as if making even the slightest noise might earn his unwanted attention. Shops slammed their doors shut. Men and women in stalls ducked behind them, and Tesmarie heard several praying as they passed.

"Think back to when you were inside that jar," Janus said, seemingly oblivious to those fleeing all around. "I want you to remember the way the humans looked at you amid your imprisonment. I want you to remember how not a single man or woman lifted a hand to help you."

"They were just confused," Tesmarie said. Did she believe that? She didn't know, but deep down in her core she wanted to deny every single word this man said. "These people, they, um, most don't know what I am. They couldn't hear me. They'd have helped if they understood, I know it."

Janus gave her the most patronizing of smiles.

"Your naïve innocence is heartwarming, Tesmarie, but it proves the need for my lesson."

"And what is that?" she asked. "That humans are awful, terrible things who hate me? Well, you're wrong. I-I-I played with them, and sang, and danced with them, and they brought me fruit and laughed, and-and-they gave me other gifts, too. Can you explain that?"

"You're a lovely novelty, Tesmarie. You're tiny and cute, and because of that, they do not see you as a threat. That's why they're happy to embrace you, but it's not as equals. You never will be equal in their eyes. If these humans had their way, they'd adopt you like an exotic pet. Yes, they'll love you. Yes, they'll give you food and padded pillows to sleep on. They'll laugh as you perform your tricks and smile as they listen to your songs, but the moment you try to escape the caged life they've given you?"

He snapped his fingers, making her jump. Where her wings connected with flesh exploded with pain.

"Down comes the lid to your cage. You're free only so long as you stay on your leash, which is no freedom at all."

He resumed his walk, and as the roads gradually widened Tesmarie discovered their destination. A large crowd gathered up ahead around a small stage with a curtained backdrop. The man addressing the crowd wore a finely tailored suit so white it bordered on obnoxious. Faithkeeper Nolan, Tesmarie assumed. Janus had brought them to the humans' ninth-day sermon.

"Janus, what are you going to do?"

He gently lifted her from his shoulder and set her down atop a windowsill overlooking the square. His opal teeth flashed amid his wide smile.

"I live in no cage," he said. "And so I work to take my city back from those who stole it."

His right arm became a blade of steel so long and sharp it

mocked the talents of human smiths. His left thinned and extended, bone liquefying, skin becoming hardened bark with serrated glass leaves. He gave the people no warning. Only a handful turned when the first man died, his entire body cleaved in half by that impossibly sharp sword arm. Then the long, branchlike whip lashed across a half dozen, and the people realized they were under attack. By then it was already too late.

Tesmarie sobbed as she watched Janus tear through the crowd like a savage predator of blood and gore. Not even bone slowed the cut of his steel arm. In gruesome juxtaposition to those perfectly clean amputations were the glass-shard leaves ripping flesh and muscle in wild, uneven directions. People fled in all directions, some dragging wounded with them to escape Janus's fury. The monster paid them no mind, for he carved a swathe directly to the mummer's platform, where Faithkeeper Nolan cowered on his hands and knees. The whip looped around him, covering him from neck to ankle. The leaves dug into him, sinking deeper and deeper, but not tearing. Not yet.

"Amid all this you merely knelt in prayer?" Janus asked him. The screams of those in flight formed a chorus of mockery. "Did you think your prayers would stop the bloodshed?"

"Sisters have mercy," the Faithkeeper cried out.

"They're not the ones holding your life in their hands," Janus said. "I am."

The branch arm tightened, and now those leaves ripped and tore, now they showered blood and spilled intestines, and Tesmarie was screaming, screaming out of horror and desperation as they ripped and tore, ripped and tore.

"Stop it!" she shrieked. Her moonlight blade appeared unbidden in her hand, but what might she do with it? Cut off her own wings so she might flee? Her sword trembled. She almost did it. In that moment, forfeiting her flight to live grounded and slow almost seemed better than witnessing another second of the slaughter.

The chaos finally summoned a trio of soldiers armed with spears. Their leader halted at the edge of the massacre, stunned by the sight. The other two were soulless like Jacaranda had been, and they patiently waited for additional orders.

"Run away," Tesmarie screamed at them. "You can't help!"

Her warning only startled the leader from his stupor. He pointed his sword at Janus.

"Kill him," he said.

The two soulless soldiers rushed into the clearing with eerily synchronized timing and steps. Janus brought his gaze their way and frowned in disgust. He shook a few ropes of stubborn intestines off his sword arm.

"You'd use these unfortunate shells as your slaves?" he asked. "Has your race no limit to its depravity?"

The two soldiers pulled their spears back for thrusts as they charged. Janus casually strolled to meet them, showing no worry for their weapons. The soldiers thrust in unison, and Janus weaved between them as if he'd known the exact attack they'd make before it began. In a single looping slash he decapitated both of them. Their bodies crumpled to the ground with a wet clatter of armor and blood.

"Soulless deserve peace. They deserve pity. Not you, though, slavemaster." The third soldier shuddered considerably. "You deserve a far worse fate."

Janus's arms retreated back to their normal pale flesh. His legs bound across the clearing with staggering strength. The soldier didn't have time to move or react. Tesmarie doubted that it'd have mattered if he did. Janus slapped the spear out of the man's hand, clearly dislocating several fingers in the process. His smile spread ear to ear. His fingers jabbed against the soldier's chest.

"I'll give your worthless mass a purpose," he said as the man's body went rigid. "After all, a painter must have his paint."

Janus's fingers suddenly sank several inches into his rib cage. A deep red color washed over every part of his body, even his clothes. His legs buckled. His features began to goop and lose focus. Like a wax figure melting, Tesmarie first thought, but that wasn't quite right. Beads of sweat rolled off his skin in sudden waves. His helmet melded into his hair. The color deepened, washing over everything, every last detail...

Oh dragons and goddesses, he was becoming blood, all of him, blood, the bones and muscle and tissue liquefying into a crimson waterfall that splashed across the clearing and sank into the cracks of the cobbles and the floorboards of the stage. His head was the last to change. Did he feel it happening? Did it hurt? The violation of it? The horror? Tesmarie frantically sped up her time. She couldn't watch. She couldn't bear to witness each drop splashing down and the ripples growing and the stink of fresh blood clogging her nose with her every breath.

An eerie silence replaced the horror. Tesmarie reluctantly slowed her time, for Janus stood before her, waiting, watching. The two of them were all alone in the clearing, alone with the bodies and the blood.

"Please, let me leave," Tesmarie pleaded. "I don't want to be here. I don't want to see this."

"Does this shock you?" Janus asked. "Does the killing leave you numb? You must crush these instincts, Tesmarie. What you have witnessed is the inevitable confrontation approaching all of us dragon-sired now that we have reawakened to a world that forgot us. Even those who love you will grow to fear you by the end."

"You're wrong," she said. "It doesn't have to be this way. It doesn't!"

Janus knelt so they might see eye to eye.

"I am not as old as some of Viciss's other creations, but I saw much in my time before the dragon imprisoned me," he said. "I saw hundreds of our kin slaughtered for the most petty of reasons. Human minds are weak, broken things created with the same false dichotomy that the Goddesses clung to since they set foot upon the Cradle: all things in pairs, one or the opposite. Alive or dead, male or female, day or night, good or evil. The most powerful of all? Us or them."

Tesmarie felt her insides trembling. There was power to his words, and worse, it felt like he spoke the truth. This truth brought no comfort, for it was a bladed weapon that sliced her sides and bled out her hope, joy, and peace.

"We are *different*, Tesmarie. To a human mind, you will never be *us*, only *them*. I have seen the horrors humanity is willing to inflict on those who are separate, who are different, even among their own kind. We are that much more distant. We are that much more endangered."

Janus stood to his full height, and it seemed a change swept over him. His intensity lessened, and the muscles in his frame visibly relaxed. His smile became almost jovial.

"You may leave soon, little faery," he said. "I must admit, my selfishness keeps you here. An artist's pride, if you will, for I would not have my art go unappreciated."

"Art?" she asked. "How could anyone call this art?"

Janus sadly shook his head. He didn't look at her as he talked, his attention on the ground as he paced the area.

"The act of creation does not always mirror the final result," he said. "Sometimes suffering and brutality must precede a wellspring of beauty."

Janus knelt amid the bodies and dipped a single finger into the pool of blood that covered everything. His eyes closed. His body gently swayed. The air itself began to shimmer with a steadily growing power. Magic swirled through the market, drawing in the power of the dragons and then flowing out through Janus's touch. The blood shimmered, its dark, dirty red growing in vibrancy. Janus stood, and his hands pulsed that same lively color.

Crystals spiked into the air at his sudden sway to the right. The outer layer of these formations was perfectly clear, while the interior contained thin tendrils of the blood they grew from. Janus drifted back to the left, his hands weaving like those of a dancer. The crystals cracked, tilted, and sharpened under his control. The frozen blood slowly shifted into shapes deep within frighteningly sharp pentagonal cones. Mesmerized, Tesmarie watched them form. Birds in flight. Schools of fish. Deer, crows, foxes; animals of sky, earth, and water all painted into miniature replications and locked inside their crystalline prisons.

Janus swayed faster and faster. Sweat dripped from his brow. Bone, flesh, and tissue ripped and melted away into a giant disgusting pile atop the wooden stage. Only the blood would be molded. Though the spray was chaotic, the formations were controlled, even beautiful. The larger pieces began to connect, the sharp points of one seemingly melting into the sides of another. What had been a simple clearing before a mummer's platform turned to a wondrous cavern. Light shone through the crystal, casting red shadows in the shapes of the animals frozen inside.

Still Janus was not satisfied. He slammed his fists into one side of the cavern that had swallowed them up. The side cracked and then swelled outward like an inhaling lung. A lash of his arm, and cones of blood shattered. Their shards layered the bare ground, shimmered, and then spread out to form a perfectly smooth walkway. Last he turned his attention to the stage. He calmly walked to the pile of bones, skin, and tissue so he might rest his hands atop it.

The mass rumbled and swirled as if captured within a tornado. It started with the bones. They clacked and grew atop one another, becoming the skeletons of human statues. Cracked, dry muscle layered atop them, followed by skin as smooth and immovable as marble. These statuesque humans gazed in frozen wonder about the new blood cavern Janus created, yet still the monstrous being was not satisfied. He gave the naked statues picks and axes, shovels and wheelbarrows, every possible tool humanity might use to plunder the wondrous crystal formations and their animals safely kept within.

Tesmarie clutched her arms to her sides and held back her horrified gasp. Each and every tool was crafted of the bones and flesh of their fellow humans. Linked ribs became the wheels of the wheelbarrows, skulls and femurs its trays. Arms and legs fused together to become handles of shovels. Curled fingers and toes linked into the teeth of rakes. Hair of all colors threaded through the cracks to give them strength. Dried skin layered over the rough edges to smooth them over.

At last Janus was satisfied. He lifted his arms and smiled as he took in the sight of his art and basked in its otherworldly beauty.

"What I have crafted in moments they could never create in years," he said. His opal smile tilted her way. "Remember the awesome power we once wielded, little faery. Remember humanity's jealous fear of it, and remember the steady erosion of our gifts in the name of coexistence. I assure you their primal cortexes have not forgotten."

Janus touched her wings. Their weight vanished, stone becoming chitin, gray becoming a gossamer rainbow.

"Live for your beauty," he told her. "Don't die for their hatred."

He touched the smooth floor and it opened for him, creating a set of stairs leading down into a deep chasm. It slammed shut upon his descent, swallowing him. Tesmarie hovered in his absence, the quiet interrupted only by her soft, miserable crying. She wiped away some of her tears.

"No," she told his lingering presence. "No, no, no, no. You're wrong. I know you're wrong! They...they..."

But what point was there in arguing to emptiness? She flew toward the cavern's ceiling. Her small frame easily fit through a triangular opening near the ceiling's center. She flew higher, leaving the red crystalline structure behind. Dozens of humans gathered around its edges, many of them brandishing armor and weapons. What would they do with the building? Tear it down? Could they, given how strong the crystal appeared?

Tesmarie took a straight line between the market and Devin's home, her wings buzzing as fast as they allowed. A squirming paralysis clutched her mind, the horror of everything ricocheting about inside her skull. The city could not pass below her fast enough. Devin had left a window cracked open for her, and she zipped right on through. He sat in the rocking chair beside the fire, and she slammed into him without warning, her knees on his stomach, her face buried into his chest. Her arms clutched the soft fabric of his shirt as if wrapping him in an embrace.

She didn't know what she expected, but when his hand ever-so-gently settled atop her back like a blanket, she melted down into a fresh wave of sobs. It was only a ghostly pressure, but it was her first returned embrace since waking up in this new and changed world. Tesmarie dusted Devin's shirt with diamonds, letting out all her pain, all her confusion and betrayal. Janus was wrong. She had to believe that, or this comfort and sympathy she felt from Devin were lies. She wanted no part of a world as cruel as that. Let her naïveté kill her if it must.

At last she felt she could cry no more, and she wiped away the tiny glittering pile.

"What is wrong?" Devin asked her once it was clear she was composed enough to speak. "Tell me so I may help."

"His art," she whispered. She felt the phantom weight of stone wings on her back and nearly broke once more. "Janus made me watch him craft his art."

CHAPTER 37

Adria looked up from her prayers as the door to the church burst open. A young novice rushed down the aisle to the pew where Adria knelt. Sweat covered the boy's face and neck, and splotches of both were colored red.

"It's an emergency, Mindkeeper," the novice said after a rapid half bow. "Your skills are needed at the southern market district."

Your skills?

Adria immediately assumed the boy meant her hidden healing powers but caught herself before responding. There was no reason yet to believe that.

"What happened?" she asked.

"Janus attacked the crowd at Faithkeeper Nolan's sermon," the novice said. "It's...it's bad. We need all skilled healers to come."

Not my prayers, then, but my talent with a needle.

Faithkeeper Sena's ninth-day sermon had concluded an hour ago, and she'd left for a midday meal with some wealthy attendees who'd visited from Quiet District. Adria didn't like leaving the church unattended, but if it was an emergency…

"Please lead the way," she told the boy. "I shall follow."

The two hurried out of the church and down the steps. For once the old woman was not there to harass her for copper. Good. Maybe she'd finally taken up a spot in a shelter instead of constantly begging. Adria tried to pry information out of the novice during their walk, but he had little to offer.

"I'm sorry, Mindkeeper," the boy said. "I only know what I saw before Faithkeeper Maria sent me away. There was, there was…" Adria belatedly realized the boy was struggling not to cry. "There was a lot of blood, and a lot of hurt people."

Adria put a hand on the boy's shoulder and walked alongside him.

"Stay strong and lead," she said. "Save your tears for in private. If it is as bad as you say, the friends and family of the wounded will look to us for strength, even down to the smallest novice. We must give it to them."

The boy sniffled and stood up a little straighter.

"I understand."

They resumed their hurried jog. Adria could tell they were nearing their destination, not by passing through one of the many archways leading into the merchant district but by the crying and screams of pain. She steeled herself for a horrific scene, and even then she had to stifle a gasp behind her porcelain mask.

A crystalline structure as wide as the road and taller than most nearby buildings blocked the way through the market. Adria saw an entrance but refused to peer further inside. She wasn't sure her mind could handle whatever might be within right now. A large swathe of space before it had been cleared out for the wounded. Injured men and women lay in haphazard rows, some on blankets and pillows, most just on the bare ground. Several apothecaries moved from person to person, dressing wounds and applying stitches while a handful of Mindkeepers and Faithkeepers held towels and cloths against gaping wounds to stanch the blood flow. A few even held torches for cauterizing wounds.

City guards formed a loose barricade to keep away gawkers, and they quickly moved aside to allow Adria and her novice to enter. Together they walked the rows, listening to the cries and wails. There appeared two distinct types of injuries: those with cleanly severed limbs, and those who were horribly scarred and mangled as if attacked by wild animals.

"Who is in charge?" she asked. She wished she felt as calm as her words sounded.

"Maria," her novice said, and he pointed to a tall Faithkeeper with the deep tan and curly hair of a Vibrant Islander. Her white suit was stained from head to toe in blood. Adria thanked the novice and joined Maria's side. The Faithkeeper held a torch in her right hand while her left pinned down a weeping man whose arm had been cleanly sliced off at the elbow. A second man knelt on the other side and helped hold him still.

"The more you move, the more I burn unnecessarily," Maria said.

Adria tapped her on the shoulder to gain her attention.

"Adria of Low Dock," she said in introduction. "What happened here?"

"Janus happened," Maria answered. "Did you bring your stitching needles and thread?"

Adria withdrew her little metal tin containing both from a hidden pocket. Maria saw it and nodded.

"Good. Find someone bleeding and make it stop."

She turned back to the man beneath her and, without

warning, thrust the torch against the weeping circle of flesh and exposed bone. Adria stepped away, and she noticed that the novice had clutched his fists to his mouth.

"I...I can't," the novice said before dashing toward the line of guards.

Adria watched him go, and she didn't blame the young man in the slightest. She slowly turned in place, the sounds and sights of the horror seeping into her body. Two children nearby shared matching sliced stomachs, their intestines poking through the perfectly smooth gashes. A woman without a leg shrieked as presumably her husband clutched a blood-soaked towel against the severed limb. The nearest Mindkeeper sowed stitch after stitch into the face of a passed-out woman whose face looked like it had been chewed to pieces. Row after row of bleeding, suffering, dying.

The little tin shook in her hands. What good would it do? What help would it be against such brutality?

Adria stuffed the tin back into her pocket and hurried to the woman with the severed leg.

"Move the towel," she commanded.

The husband glared at her with mistrust.

"Where's your torch?" he asked.

"I don't need one. Move the towel or I shall order a guard to make you."

He relented. The towel peeled back, revealing bone and meat where the cut had cleaved directly above the knee. Blood poured from still-open veins. That the woman was alive bordered on a miracle. Adria put her hands directly against the bone. Warm blood trickled across her fingers. The words of the 36th Devotion floated across the surface of her mind. This was it. There was no turning back.

"Lyra of the beloved sun, hear my prayer," she whispered.

The words flowed off her tongue with ease. She closed her eyes. Somehow seeing the healing happen felt like a betrayal to the miracle. Warmth grew beneath her touch. The flow of blood ceased. The touch of bone softened. Her prayer neared its completion, and she spoke the final words with great weight and reverence.

"Precious Lyra, heal this woman."

She opened her eyes to see pink skin underneath her fingers. Even the blood had dried and flaked away, leaving a smooth stump where the leg had been severed. The woman had ceased screaming and instead quietly sobbed, as did her husband.

"What did..." he asked, struggling for words. "How...Sisters above, thank you, thank you."

Adria pushed herself to her feet. One down. Dozens more to go. The husband grabbed her wrist before she moved on.

"Your name?" he breathed.

"Adria," she answered without thinking.

"The Goddesses bless you, Adria. They bless you. They bless you!"

Next were the two children. They writhed beside one another, not yet attended because, cruel as it sounded, they would not likely survive any traditional treatments. Adria knelt between them, and she softly stroked each of their foreheads.

"Lie still if you can," she told them. "This won't take long."

She pushed the thin rope of intestines back into the girl's stomach, then laid her hand over the wound. Eyes closed, she prayed the 36th Devotion. When she opened them, only a single white scar marked where the cut had once been. Then came the boy's turn, and though he squirmed and screamed when she put his intestines in, his motions ceased the moment her prayer began.

"Precious Lyra, heal this child."

Another long scar. Another life saved. Others were starting to notice now. An eerie silence seemed to have fallen over the onlookers at the line of guards. Adria moved to an elderly man whose entire left half was ripped and torn as if he'd rolled through a hundred shards of glass.

"The children," the man said. "I saw...are you a miracle worker?"

"Hush now," Adria said. "Let me pray."

From Adria's experience it would have taken over sixty stitches to close that many wounds. Her prayer needed none. The old man sat up once she was done. His hands shook.

"Surely you are the Sacred Mother reborn," he said, reaching for her mask to remove it.

"Keep such blasphemy to yourself," Adria said. She yanked the mask back over her face and fought against a rising panic attack. "Go home."

The old man went to the crowd, but he did not go home. Instead he began shouting to the others.

"Who is she? Who is the Mindkeeper with the dark hair and the touch of the Goddesses?"

"Adria! Adria, lady of miracles!"

The name spread like wildfire through the crowd. Adria shuddered at the sound. She wanted none of this praise, and it sickened her stomach hearing such a lofty title like "lady of miracles." It seemed she wasn't the only one worried, either. Faithkeeper Maria pulled her close so her low voice might be heard over the growing din.

"What in Anwyn's name is going on?" she asked. "How are you healing them?"

"I'm only praying," Adria said. "The Sisters do the rest."

"I've prayed over them as well, but my stitching is closing the wounds, not the Sisters." Maria looked to the rows of dead and dying. "I guess it doesn't matter. Keep going. Others still need you."

And so Adria moved to the next, and the next, prayers on her tongue and healing flowing from her hands. Deep exhaustion settled over her body, steadily worsening with each wounded man and woman she healed. The words of the 36th Devotion grew tired on her tongue. The syllables began to lose meaning. The prayer, the request, it shaped this power she wielded, and when she knelt beside a man bleeding profusely from a cleanly severed leg, she pushed her fingers into the wound and simplified the prayer tremendously.

"Precious Lyra, at my touch, heal this man."

Faint light poured forth from her hands, sealing off the muscle and bone with a thin, pale layer of scar tissue. Adria gasped as vertigo lashed her mind. With each prayer she was starting to feel...something within the bodies of those she healed. A lurking power that responded to her prayer and then latched onto her soul, drawing strength out of her and into itself. This deep ache was far beyond anything she'd felt in her life. It was like a thousand nights spent awake without sleep coming together into one singular moment of exhaustion.

"Lyra be praised," the previously wounded man said. He didn't sound too worshipful, but no doubt he was still in shock. He lay on his back with his eyes closed, sleep rapidly overtaking him. "Lyra...be praised."

Adria nearly toppled over when she tried to stand. Faithkeeper Maria grabbed her by the elbow and guided her to her feet.

"Stay strong," she said. "There are only five left. Will it help if I bring them to you instead?"

Adria nodded.

"Yes. I would be grateful."

She slipped back down to her knees and focused on keeping her breathing calm and meditative. The first arrived, carried in a blanket like a stretcher. Adria set her hands over the person's chest. She didn't look to see the wound, nor the look of hope and pain on his face. Her mind was struggling just to focus on her prayer. She couldn't risk empathy.

"Precious Lyra, at my touch, heal this man."

One by one they came wounded, and one by one they were carried away healed. Some sang praises to the Sisters. More sang praises to the Mindkeeper who healed them. When the last of those injured by Janus's attack was lifted away she dared hope that would be the end, but more were starting to gather at the ring of guards. The crowd was swelling, and the first of many cried out for Adria's attention.

"My leg," shouted one. "It's broken and healing wrong."

"My mother's dying," shouted another. "Please, if you could just…"

"The water lung's taken hold of my father…"

More voices. More in need. There weren't enough guards to shove them away, and several of the Mindkeepers and Faith-keepers had to join them in holding the line. Adria could feel the desperation in the air. How many lives might she save with just one more prayer? How much suffering could she unburden the people from?

One cry in particular pierced through her haze.

"Adria? Faithkeeper Adria? Your brother swore! He swore you would help!"

She looked up at an older man with a shaved head and a black beard holding a young girl. He pushed against the arms of a guard attempting to keep him at bay. The limp gaze of the girl gave Adria an ill feeling.

"Bring him," she said. Maria heard, and when she asked who, Adria pointed to the older man. "Him. With the girl."

The man hurried over, and the moment he found an empty spot of ground he set the girl down. Adria noticed how rigid the girl's body was, how still her chest.

"She...she tripped," the old man said. "People were running and screaming. I tried to get to her, I tried, Adria, I tried, but no one listened. Arleen, she..."

The rest broke into sobs. Adria knelt closer for examination. Dark bruises covered much of the girl's body from being trampled by the crowd. She put her fingers against Arleen's temple. No pulse. What a cruel fate. Others with shattered bones and ripped flesh she could save, but a young girl who hadn't even been there when Janus attacked, with only bruises to show how much internal damage she'd suffered, was beyond her.

"I'm sorry," Adria said. "She's gone."

"No," the older man said. Then, louder, "No, she can't, she can't be! Pray over her, please."

"But..."

"Try!" he shouted. Tears streamed down his face. "We lived through so much, Adria. The Goddesses cannot be so cruel."

There were many different prayers within Lyra's Devotions, but none dealt with returning the dead to life. Adria wanted to argue that, but what argument could stand up to the overwhelming power of grief? She turned her gaze to the young girl. So beautiful. So full of promise, all stolen by the monster Janus and his unexplained hatred toward servants of the Keeping Church.

Is it possible? she silently asked the Sisters. *Can even the dead return if the soul remains within?*

Adria crossed her hands over the girl's chest and closed her eyes.

"Lyra of the beloved sun, hear my prayer," she whispered. "Your children weep for your touch, and so I come, and so I pray."

No change. She continued the prayer, waiting for that sudden connection with the body and the faint drawing of power. It never happened. The prayer left her lips, her plea carried up to the heavens, but Arleen's heart remained still as a stone. Adria pulled away from the body and now faced an act equally dreadful—breaking the hope in the older man's eyes.

"I'm sorry," she said. "I can only heal. I cannot bring back the dead."

He let out a wail that surely could not have been human. It was too wrenching, too broken. Adria swallowed down her sorrow and forced words to emerge off her tongue. "Talk with Faithkeeper Maria when things have calmed down. She will put you in touch with a Pyrehand to handle the reaping ritual."

The man lifted Arleen's body and walked away looking lost and dazed. Adria rested on her haunches, the sound of her breath weak and shallow in her own ears.

"That's it," Faithkeeper Maria shouted to the city guards. "Get them out of here, all of them."

"No," Adria said. Her voice was hoarse. When did that happen? "Let them come."

Maria listened, organizing the sick and wounded into manageable lines. She didn't care how they decided who would be first, or how they kept the crowd orderly. Adria merely sat there and waited until a sickly-looking woman knelt before her with bowed head. Her skin was strikingly pale.

"The consumption," the woman said. Adria took her hands and shushed away any further explanation.

"Precious Lyra," she said. "At my touch, heal this woman."

The color returned to her cheeks. Life returned to her face. She flung her arms around Adria, weeping tears against her black-and-white porcelain mask. Adria kept perfectly still, simply waiting for the display to be over. She was too exhausted, too numb. Another came, and another, bearing broken bones, feverish bodies, and wet, bloody coughs. Prayer after prayer, she gave of herself to them.

"Precious Lyra..."

"Precious Lyra..."

Precious Lyra.

Precious.

Precious.

Hands grabbed Adria's shoulders, catching her from a fall she'd not known she'd started.

"I've got you," Devin said. "It's time for you to come home. Your body cannot withstand more."

To others it might have seemed like nothing, but to Adria it meant the world. She grasped her brother's hand and pressed it to the forehead of her mask.

"Thank you," she whispered. The world spun around her. "I don't think I can walk."

"Then lean against me."

Word of Adria's healing must have spread like wildfire throughout Londheim. How many sick and injured would come seeking relief?

"What of the crowds?" Adria asked.

"I shall handle the crowds," Thaddeus said, his deep voice

piercing the din. Adria hadn't realized her Vikar had arrived... but then again, she was hardly aware of the location of her own hands and feet, let alone others. "You deserve your privacy and rest, Mindkeeper."

More and more guards had filtered into the area over the past half hour, and by the looks of it a rather large entourage of both soldiers and physicians had accompanied her Vikar. With their spears and shields they pushed back the crowd, indifferent to their cries of intermixed frustration and need. Adria leaned on Sena and did her best to watch. There were at least six Mindkeepers in the area now, and at Thaddeus's insistence they gathered around Adria.

"You'll each have an escort of soldiers," Thaddeus said. "Return to your churches. The physicians can handle those that Adria healed."

"A miracle," one of the Mindkeepers said.

"The Sisters bless you, Adria," said another.

Adria smiled at them to show her appreciation, then remembered she still wore her mask. Well, hopefully they'd understand.

"It is indeed a miracle," Thaddeus said, and he glanced at Adria. "And may the glory and praise be sung to the Sisters amid the stars for what they have done this day. Now return to your church. Answer no questions on your way there. Leave the people wondering which of you is Adria so they know not whom to follow."

The guards shouted for the people to disperse. Shields slammed against bodies that, for whatever their reason, refused to move.

"Adria!" cried the crowd. They shouted it in protest of their dispersal. They cried it out in worship. They spoke it with fear and reverence in equal measure. "Adria! Adria!"

"Just ignore them," Devin said as he shielded her. "You've done everything you could."

Adria clung to her brother's comforting frame. Her head tilted as she settled her jaw on his shoulder. Her tired eyes drifted to the rooftops.

A man knelt on one knee at the edge of a distant shop. His clothes were long and dark. Half his hair was a bright green, the other a deep black. There was no doubt that he was watching her. Smiling at her. He could be but one person. One terrible, cruel, wretched being. If Adria had any strength left in her she'd have shrieked the name and sent the soldiers after him, but instead she had but a single whisper before her legs gave out beneath her and the dizziness inside her skull blanked out all thought.

"Janus?"

CHAPTER 38

An interesting choice for a meeting place, Janus thought as he stood before the Hive-Tree in the center of Londheim. The sun had already set, so the tree's many leaves had returned from their day of feeding upon the nectar of flowers to share with the greedy heart at the center of its enormous trunk. Janus had watched the morning eruption of leaves and color twice since Viciss granted him his freedom. Both times he'd been resentful of the many gawking humans, of their childish pointing and dull gasps of surprise and confusion. Such beauty was better than they deserved. There had once been an entire forest of Hive-Trees before humanity had come westward with its axes and torches. Now only one remained, a curious amusement for the race that had wiped out its kin.

"I suppose I should not blame them," Janus told the Hive-Tree. He lovingly brushed the tree's black bark. His mind could sense the minute vibrations of the beating heart, and he closed his eyes to absorb the welcome presence. "Humans are little more than locusts. Eat, breed, and destroy is all they know how to do."

"You are wrong, Janus, as you often are."

He turned and fell to one knee with bowed head.

"You bless me with your presence, dragon."

The featureless shadow that was Viciss approached the Hive-Tree with his arms crossed behind his back. Janus wondered what form humans would perceive him as. Human, perhaps? Or would he be a shadow to them as well, a void given form, a sentient mass of heavenly bodies and distant stars? The similarity to his black water was inescapable, and sometimes Janus wondered if the demigod's presence went out with it when he breathed across the land.

Whatever the form, though, it hardly mattered. The streets of Londheim were dead at night. Already the dragon-sired had begun reclaiming the city back into their rightful hands.

"Your contempt toward humanity is undeserved," Viciss said.

"Perhaps," Janus said. "But it does make the killing easier."

Viciss ignored the comment, his attention instead focused on the last Hive-Tree in all the Cradle. He put a hand upon the tree, his swirling black digits sinking into the bark as if it were liquid.

"My poor, lonely child," he whispered to the tree. "Stay strong amid your isolation. Perhaps one day I will spare you from this city and make your race anew. For now, take my blessing, and let your beauty be magnified tenfold."

Veins of gold spread from his touch throughout the bark. The deep green leaves fluttered as if preparing to take off. Their edges spread wider, fuller. Healthier, Janus knew. The trunk's color steadily brightened from its deep black to a vibrant copper. Viciss withdrew his hand. The branches swayed as if in a heavy wind, and then all simultaneously lowered in the Hive-Tree's best approximation of a bow.

Janus's heart panged at the display. There was a time when the five dragons walked the Cradle without fear. There was a time they created merely for the beauty of creation. It might take blood and fire, but Janus swore to use his power to make that time return.

"I witnessed your spectacle at the marketplace this morning," Viciss said, breaking the silence.

Janus's instincts cried warning. He kept his voice passive and pretended not to notice.

"A bit messier than I'd prefer," he said. That, too, was a partial lie. If he had his way the entire city would be drowning in blood. "But the many Faithkeepers and Mindkeepers throughout the city have been far too confident in their duties. I wasn't inspiring the necessary fear. Now I am."

"And the human civilians?"

"Collateral damage."

Viciss himself never moved, but his rage slammed Janus to the street. An unseen weight pressed his neck to the cobbles, and another closed around his throat, denying him breath. The demigod knelt before him and softly lifted his chin with a single finger. Viciss bore no eyes or mouth, but Janus could sense the seething anger toward him.

"I said no wanton killing."

The tension eased about his throat so he might answer.

"I had...reason," Janus gasped. "Killed Faithkeeper...as asked. The rest were...part of...the art."

The pressure on his throat and neck relinquished.

"I know your obsessions drive you, Janus. Consider this your lone warning. Another moment of self-indulgence like that and I will unmake you to your core."

"Forgive my arrogance," Janus said. "Is your displeasure why you have summoned me?"

"No," the dragon said. He rested against the Hive-Tree as if it were the curved body of a sleeping lover. "I have need of your wisdom, should you have gained any during your excursion through Londheim."

"Ask it, and I shall answer," Janus said. Now was not the time for disrespect.

"The Sisters appear weak and uninterested in this world. Our imprisonment taxed their strength, but I wonder if the centuries of watching humanity falter sapped their resolve. No matter the reason, they have not made a move against us and we must act accordingly. Preparations near completion, but one aspect still requires consideration."

"And what is that?"

"I require a member of the Keeping Church. They may be from any sacred division, and of any rank, so long as they are beloved by the people. Humanity's faith in the crumbling establishment must be broken if they are to evolve, and I need a replacement."

"And what will the fate be of this lucky chosen? I presume it involves that starlight tear I fetched from the faery village."

Viciss pressed his forehead to the Hive-Tree's bark and then withdrew.

"Not yet, Janus. We are close, so very close, but this is a secret that cost us our freedom all those centuries ago. Bring me my chosen. The future we dragons desire shall soon come to pass."

The demigod vanished without a shimmer of color or vibration of movement through the air. Only the Hive-Tree's somber drooping of its branches signified Viciss's departure. Janus felt a sting of sorrow that he could not share the simple creature's adoration of the demigod who granted him life.

As for the newly given task, he didn't need to give it much thought. Throngs of worshippers had already chosen for him.

"A keeper beloved to the people?" he wondered aloud as he began the process of changing his face and body. "I believe I know just the woman."

CHAPTER 39

"How's she doing?" Jacaranda asked as Devin shut the door to his room.

"She's still asleep," Devin said. "These prayers must take a lot out of her. It's like she's suddenly come down with a fever."

"I'm sure she'll pull through," Jacaranda said. She sat on the couch, an empty cup in hand. She should have put it away, but she needed something to keep her hands occupied. It seemed when her anxiety and worry heightened, her fingers gained minds of their own. "If she has any of your stubbornness, she'll be up and about in no time."

Devin laughed as he settled into the chair by the fire. Night was approaching, and no doubt he was relaxing before going out on patrol. Hopefully Jacaranda could dissuade him of that notion. She didn't know how loyal he'd be to the Soulkeeper organization, nor the troubles that might befall him if he didn't keep his post.

"Hey, Puffy?" she asked. The little firekin's eyes emerged from the heart of the flames. "Might we have a moment alone?"

Puffy bobbed its eyes up and down twice. Its form expanded while flattening, becoming more like a blanket or kite. After a few seconds it whisked up the chimney. The fire on the logs dwindled in the creature's absence.

"Is something the matter?" Devin asked. He tilted his head slightly, and though his voice remained light, almost carefree, she could tell he was carefully guarding his emotions.

"Devin...I need to ask you a favor."

"Whatever it is, ask, and I will do my best."

Jacaranda struggled for the right words. Requesting his aid would require voicing traumas of the past she desperately wanted to forget. It felt humiliating to expose what had been done to her, like an admission of being a lesser human. This wasn't her fault, she told herself. *Stop feeling shame for what was done by evil men.*

"Devin, my role in Gerag's estate was...complicated," she said. Her shoulders pulled inward, and she found herself sinking into the cushions of the couch as if she could shrink herself down to nothing.

"Gerag...used...you, didn't he?" Devin said. "It's all right. You don't have to tell me, Jac, not if it's too difficult."

Jacaranda suppressed a shudder through her spine.

"No, I mean, he did," she said. "But there's more to it. I wasn't just his—his plaything." How to explain? How to admit the role her soulless self had served? "I was their manager. Their caretaker."

"Their?" Devin asked.

Jacaranda took in a deep breath and slowly let it out.

"The other soulless. Gerag smuggled them in from East Orismund. They were taught to please. To fake pleasure. And then they were sold."

Devin's jaw hardened. His hands clenched into fists.

"He sold soulless as sex slaves to the wealthy," Devin said. "That isn't just illegal. It carries a penalty of death."

Jacaranda knew that, of course. That was why she'd escorted the soulless to Gerag's mansion. It wasn't just to keep Gerag's hands clean. It was so she could execute anyone who spotted them, or worst-case scenario, the soulless themselves lest they be interrogated and potentially implicate Gerag.

"Do you remember the cabin I burned back in Oakenwall?" she asked.

"I do."

"Sometimes the soulless would be so young as to attract suspicion. Those were dropped off the boats a few miles out from Londheim and taken to Oakenwall instead. A man there named Nathan Evart would take care of them until buyers arrived for their...their merchandise. That way it was the buyer's responsibility to smuggle them into Londheim, not Gerag's. Nathan kept notes of these 'shipments.' I was to burn the building to hide the evidence."

Devin was trying, she could tell he really was, but his anger bubbled over beyond his control.

"That motherfucker. I'll hang him by his toes from the city gates. I don't care how much he donates to the church; evidence of an underground sex trade will be the end of him."

"I hope you get your chance," she said. "I'm going to his mansion tonight, and I'd like you to come with me."

For the first time Devin looked taken aback.

"What? There's no reason for you to risk your life like that. If you share the logistics with me I can present evidence to my Vikar. The church will authorize a raid on his home for further proof. I understand you want your vengeance, but with a little patience we—"

"No, it has to be tonight," Jacaranda interrupted. "I infiltrated one of their boats and interrogated the captain. There's to be an auction. A special auction." This time it was Jacaranda who struggled to keep her emotions under control. "One of his soulless women awakened, Devin. She awakened, just like me, and he's *still going to sell her.*"

Devin flinched as if stabbed with a knife. Every trace of an argument vanished in an instant. He rose from his chair and approached the door. Something about the way he moved frightened her. It was like a shadow passed over him, erasing any kindness, worry, or compassion. All that remained was a fierce determination.

"Get your daggers," he said. "We've a job to do."

It was an order she was glad to follow. They moved under cover of darkness, two thieves slipping through the fog on the way to Quiet District. Jacaranda had changed into the same dark clothing she always wore during her midnight excursions, and she covered the lower half of her face with a red cloth. Between her hat and her mask, only her eyes were visible. Devin hid his face likewise, though his coat alone might still identify him.

"You realize if you are seen it may prevent you from ever living a normal life within Londheim," Devin said when they stopped just inside the district gate.

"It doesn't matter," she said. "This is the right thing to do, isn't it? Something good? Something worth dying for?"

"Yes," he said. "I think it is."

Jacaranda took the lead, and she kept close to the fences and the nearby mansions to reduce the chance of being seen. At last they reached the sprawling rectangular mansion next door, and the two peered around the side corner at the fenced-off entrance. Six armed men loitered about, casually chatting with one another.

"That's a lot more guards than usual," Devin said after they retreated.

"A high-profile auction," Jacaranda said. "No one is taking chances."

"Then how do we get inside?"

"Tell me, Soulkeeper, how often do smugglers use the front door?"

He grinned mischievously.

"What would I do without you?"

"Live a much more boring life, I'd wager," she said.

"Not a worthwhile trade. Lead on, Jac."

Given Gerag's paranoia, he naturally did not wish for constant parades of young men and women to be noticed entering through the front door of his home. This paranoia extended to the entire premises of his estate, but that had left him with a bit of a predicament. The cost of land in Quiet District was at a premium, and he'd been lucky to nab his cramped little plot. Most of the construction on his mansion had been completed by the time Jacaranda fell into Gerag's control, but she remembered how proud he'd been to showcase his brilliant plan.

"How could anyone possibly link the soulless to my home in Quiet District," he'd bragged to his servant Belford while Jacaranda stood idly nearby, awaiting orders. "When the entrance isn't even *in* Quiet District?"

Like most districts, a brick wall separated Quiet District from the others, but its wall was much thicker and taller. Supposedly it was to ensure protection for their valuables, but Jacaranda thought it was only so they could feel the tiniest bit more special than those who lived with less. This larger wall required much more maintenance, for which the members gladly paid. This meant it was common for work crews privately hired by its wealthy to paint, plaster, or relayer bricks. Over the two years it'd taken Gerag to build his mansion, the sight of workers all around the area was common—so common, in fact, that no one paid attention when his men started removing portions of the wall so they might access the ground beneath.

Jacaranda led Devin back through the entrance of Quiet District and then skirted along the dividing wall. They were in another residential area, but with Low Dock's greater proximity, its homes were much less extravagant. Jacaranda found the particular home with ease, for she'd passed in and out of it hundreds of times over the past decade. It was a squat building with stone walls and thick wooden shutters. Two dozen bird statues perched from the gutters, a strange touch left over from the previous owners before Gerag purchased it.

"Is it locked?" Devin whispered.

"Always," she whispered back. "But that won't be a problem."

Lock picking had been one of the easier skills she'd picked up as a soulless. It required concentration, patience, and a keen understanding of basic mechanics. The first two came easily as a soulless, and the third was a matter of study and practice. She withdrew her torsion wrench and hook pick from their little slots in her custom dagger belt. It took less than a minute for her to properly position the pins. Once it was unlocked she put away her pins but did not open the door. She waited for Devin to ready his sword and then gently turned the knob and pushed inward.

The interior was quiet and empty. The two quickly slipped inside and shut the door behind them. Another wave of disgust and disorientation struck Jacaranda as she looked upon the dusty furniture and vacant shelves. This shell of a home was tied to a thousand memories, and so few of them were good. She'd led dead-eyed men and women through here to their sexual enslavement, sometimes even children; damn that fat fucker Gerag.

"Where's the entrance?" Devin whispered.

Jacaranda took him to the back bedroom. The house was purposefully kept clean but sparse, with only the occasional room rented out during slow months to disguise the building's actual purpose in Gerag's various reports to the tax men. This meant there was nothing unusual about the large bed and ripped mattress, at least until one pushed it aside and lifted up the loose floorboards beneath to reveal a sloping set of stairs leading to a long dark tunnel.

"You're kidding me," Devin said. "He built an entire tunnel?"

"So far as I know, Gerag runs the entire market for illicit soulless in all of West Orismund," Jacaranda said. "People will pay a lot of gold crowns for a well-trained soulless that is completely unknown to the church and state. Building this tunnel was merely a cost of doing business."

"What do people want them for?" Devin asked. "Is it just for... you know?"

"Gerag never asked questions, and neither did I."

Because she hadn't cared. She'd watched life after life pass through this tunnel, kept in pens, and then taken back out in the hands of their buyers. Over the years she'd picked up hints, though. Most were used for sex, but not always. Some buyers wanted to make sure Gerag trained the soulless to adequately react to pain, or to show fear. Some buyers specifically requested that their soulless not be trained at all to keep the price down.

Those, Jacaranda suspected, were tortured and killed for their new owner's pleasure. Whatever the appetites, Gerag was there to provide.

Jacaranda realized her hands ached. She'd been holding the hilts of her daggers much too tight and forced her body to relax.

"What should I expect once inside?" Devin asked. He adjusted the mask covering his face and checked his pistol to ensure that the loaded shot inside had not slipped loose in the barrel.

"A locked door with a peephole, at least one guard, and then the pens we—they—keep the soulless in until purchase."

She started to descend but Devin grabbed her by the shoulder.

"Wait," he said. She turned, frustrated that he would delay when they were so close. What if the auction had already begun? Generally the important sales were done right after the reaping hour, which gave them half an hour at most, but Gerag easily could have started early if he thought all the big buyers had arrived.

"Remember, we're here to rescue the awakened woman," Devin said. "Not to find and kill Gerag."

"Nothing will stop me from killing the bastard if I see him," she warned.

"And I don't plan on stopping you," he said. "But things are about to get hectic. If it comes down to the prisoner's escape and your vengeance, I only ask that you make the right choice."

Jacaranda hopped into the tunnel and gestured for him to follow.

"Stop worrying about my making the right decisions," she said. "Worry about us making it out of here alive."

The tunnel was pitch-black from end to end, so they traveled with one hand in front of them and another hugging the wall.

It didn't take long to cross, for the tunnel only needed to dip underneath the wall dividing the districts and then up into the hidden basement Gerag had built beneath his mansion grounds. At the end was a slanted outline of a door, the light coming in through the cracks shockingly bright in the deep dark. Jacaranda paused a dozen feet away and held her hand behind her until Devin walked into it and halted. She touched his shoulder to help her orient herself to his body and then leaned in close.

"Give me your pistol," she whispered into his ear.

"Do you know how to use it?"

Jacaranda scoffed at him.

"Any fool can use a pistol at this range. Just pull the trigger and watch them die."

Devin took her hand in his and then slid the pistol into her palm. She gripped it, surprised by the weight. The pistol was much heavier than it looked.

"Stay here," she whispered.

Many buyers entered Gerag's mansion through the front under pretense of parties or business, but some of the more frequent clientele didn't like to be seen constantly exiting with soulless servants. Those were entrusted with a key to the outside house and the location of the secret tunnel. Jacaranda hoped that given the high-profile nature of tonight's auction, it wouldn't be unusual for one of those coming to enter through the tunnel. She crossed the rest of the distance to the bright outline of the door, pressed her body against the tunnel's wall, and used the coded knock.

Twice. Pause. Twice more. Pause. Once.

A square of painfully bright light shone into the tunnel as a tiny window slid open in the middle of the door.

"You're arriving late," a familiar voice said. It was Belford, Gerag's most trusted servant. The recognition almost froze Jacaranda in place. Gerag fancied himself master of all things sexual with his soulless in training, but Belford...Belford taught the more intricate details. He had been the one to teach Jacaranda how to dress, how to eat, how to bathe and braid her hair to make herself beautiful to Gerag's guests. If she possessed any semblance of a father, it was him.

"I know," she said. She placed the pistol into the window and pulled the trigger.

The shot seemed to echo forever inside that claustrophobic tunnel. Jacaranda flinched each time, her breath caught in her throat. Logically, she knew she should bear equal hatred toward the old man as she did Gerag, but it just wasn't there. She felt no sharp pleasure in delivering revenge, only a sad ache as a piece of her estranged past died in a bloody heap on a cold cellar floor, his brains splattered out the back of his skull.

"We won't have much time," Devin said, pulling her out of her morbid reverie. Damn it, she fell into these states far too easily. Had to keep focused. Had to fight the wellspring of emotions that were as new to her as the day she was born. "Can you pick the lock?"

"There's no lock to pick," she said. "Just a deadbolt."

Jacaranda's hand was more than slender enough to slide through the opened window and pull aside the bolt. The door shuddered, she withdrew her hand, and then together they stepped over Belford's corpse and entered Gerag's soulless prison.

From floor to wall to ceiling, the rectangular room was thick, ancient stone. At the end of the room was an open doorway leading to a stairwell. Six cells divided the space, three to each side of the slender walkway. Metal bars formed their perimeters with steel-enforced wooden doors as the only entrances. Within were a bed, a waste bucket, and a small table with cups of water.

"Why keep them like prisoners?" Devin asked. "No soulless would ever attempt to run away."

"You forget what they were trained for," she said. "A soulless will not resist an order unless its life is clearly in danger. Sometimes...sometimes that instinct needed to be broken entirely to satisfy a buyer's demands. The cruel ones who wished for the soulless to cower, beg, and refuse. It takes time to eliminate that reflex, Devin. Time, and a lot of cruelty."

All but one of the six cells were empty. Jacaranda approached as if walking through a dream. The smell of the room threatened to steal her mind away to a thousand memories she never wanted to relive again. Each cell contained dozens of phantom girls and boys, good little puppets dutifully obeying their masters no matter the cruelty or degradation. It flooded her stomach with bile. It pricked her eyes with stubborn tears. The only saving grace, the only fact she could cling to that kept away the despair, was knowing that none of them had been aware of it. Only the most basic sensations of pain and pleasure registered, and they carried no preference to either. Consent was an irrelevant concept. Shame was as distant as the stars.

But someone in that last cell did care. She was aware of her surroundings, and she most certainly did not desire a lifetime of slavery and degradation. Jacaranda unlocked the cell's door and flung it open. The woman inside winced and covered her face with her arms. She wore a beautiful golden gown, and yellow ribbons were tied into the curls of her short blond hair. Her skin had been scrubbed clean in preparation for the auction, and even in that cell Jacaranda could smell a hint of perfume wafting off her body, a strong scent of flowers and incense.

All the pretty dresses and all the perfume in the world could not hide the multitude of bruises that covered her arms, neck, and face. Captain Malin had mentioned how strangely his "cargo" behaved, how they'd needed to drug her lest she throw herself overboard. Jacaranda didn't want to imagine the violence the sailors had unleashed on her to keep her subdued. Imagining it might overwhelm her mind with anger beyond her control.

Jacaranda had a million things she wished to tell the frightened young woman cowering at the far end of the cell. How she understood the trauma she'd been through. How she'd awakened herself, and had experienced the mind-breaking phenomenon of having been there for her entire life, but yet not. Instead she leaned on that door and quietly said, "Hey. Please, don't be afraid."

"They always say that," the woman said. She kept her arms over her face. "Don't be afraid. It's always a lie. You're lying, too, aren't you."

Jacaranda shot a glance at Devin, who was examining the other cells with a look of distaste.

"I'm not lying," she said. "And I can prove it."

"How?" the woman asked. Finally she peered over her arms. In answer, Jacaranda pulled down her scarf to expose the chain tattoos across her throat.

"Because I'm just like you," she said. "I was Gerag's, and then I awoke. I've come to free you, too, if you'll trust me."

Goddesses above, there was so much hurt in that woman's eyes. No Soulkeeper had welcomed the girl when her soul plunged into her body like an unwanted invader, only violence and imprisonment. Jacaranda saw a spark, a faint, fearful spark of hope deep in those beautiful blue eyes.

"So you know," the woman said. "You know what it's like."

"I do," Jacaranda said, and she offered her hand. "And I'm here to help."

The woman pushed herself to her feet and absently brushed away dirt on her dress. It seemed now that she believed freedom might be a real possibility, her actions started to gain life, and a sense of urgency finally entered her voice to match the situation.

"Who are you?" she asked.

"Jacaranda."

"Marigold."

The fat fuck loves his flowers, doesn't he? Jacaranda thought.

The sound of a door opening traveled down the stairwell. Footsteps echoed from above, followed by the growing light of a torch. Jacaranda put her back to Marigold and drew her daggers. Devin heard and readied his pistol.

"The crowd's ready for the girl, Belford," Tye the White said as he rounded the steps. The moment he saw Devin and Jacaranda he froze. A smile creased his lips.

"Oh, how delightful."

Devin fired, but he misjudged the mercenary's reaction. He didn't flee up the stairs for help. Instead he rolled deeper into the underground prison. His legs were pumping the moment his feet touched the floor. Jacaranda pushed Marigold into one of the cells as Devin prepared to intercept.

"Stay inside," she told her. "Just until he's dead."

Outnumbering Tye two-to-one should have given them a significant advantage, but the slender gap between the cells wasn't wide enough to allow them to fight side by side. Their only hope was to get on opposite sides of the mercenary and trap him, but he was far too ruthless to allow them such an opportunity. Devin took the initial brunt of his attack, his larger blade clumsy and awkward in the confined spaces. Tye's curved sword was far better suited to the environment, and he weaved side to side, almost daring Jacaranda to slip past.

Jacaranda watched the battle with her every muscle locked tight. If only she could find an opening. If only the space between the cells wasn't so damn tight. Devin and Tye traded blows, testing the other's speed and strength. It was beautiful to behold, even amid such dire circumstances and surroundings. Both men were among the best in the world at what they did, and they feinted and pivoted in ways that less-skilled observers would not even notice. Tye never let the intensity increase no matter how hard Devin tried, for the moment he closed in, Tye's superior mobility would prove too dangerous. Their swords weaved, danced, and retreated, but Devin would not relent. He might not have had Tye's mobility, but he did have the greater strength, and he needed only a single opportunity to take advantage.

Devin finally caught Tye flatfooted, and he swung with a strong chop the mercenary had no choice but to block. Their swords crossed, and the Soulkeeper flung his weight against Tye's to close the distance between them. His heel looped around Tye's, they turned, and at last Devin managed to position himself on the opposite side of the mercenary. Jacaranda twirled her daggers, eager to have a go at the infuriating man.

"Oh dear," Tye said. "You have me trapped at last. What shall I do?"

Even now he mocked them. He wasn't afraid they could utilize the advantage. He wouldn't let them. A cornered rabid animal could not match this unrelenting rage. Tye's fighting style, which had been maddeningly fluid, became as blunt and brutal as a spiked hammer. Punches, elbows, and kicks accompanied his powerful downward slashes. He bounced between the two of them without any obvious tactic and reason; it was as if he were merely bored with one and turned his attention to another.

Instead of pressing their advantage, they each were on their heels, defending with desperation to match his insanity. The hilt of his sword split her lip open. One of his punches blacked out her eye. Every time she tried to counter he was gone, this tornado in white now enveloping Devin. How did someone learn to fight like this? What kind of training must he have undergone to develop instincts so finely honed? Jacaranda had but one hope, and that was that Tye exhausted himself with such a display. Surely he could not go on for long. The hottest of fires always burned out the quickest, after all.

Time, however, was not on their side. Heavy footfalls were their only warning that someone else had finally noticed the commotion from the underground cells.

"What's going on down—oh shit."

A man in padded leather armor exited the stairwell looking shocked and confused. He drew his slender sword, and suddenly it was Devin and Jacaranda trapped with an enemy on either side. Devin broke to face the new threat. Jacaranda couldn't decide if she should be flattered or horrified that he thought her capable of handling Tye on her own.

"Get her out!" Devin shouted as he blocked a heavy chop of the guard's sword.

Jacaranda was trying, but Tye had long surmised their goal. Protecting Marigold had forced her to remain within the hallway, allowing him to slide past her and position himself directly before the open tunnel door. At least this kept him in one location, and she tried to use that to her advantage as she launched into another series of attacks. Her daggers clanged and twisted off steel as his sword batted and twisted with expertise born of a thousand hours of practice.

Tye's vicious pace receded back to the earlier, calm control he'd shown at the start of the battle. He wasn't the intruder here. Reinforcements would come eventually. His every parry and thrust seemed designed to antagonize her and drive her to desperation. Worst of all were his words, which he wielded as any other weapon.

"Abandon the job, I told you," he said. He kicked the side of her knee, and it took both her daggers to block the nearly lethal chop for her neck. "I guess it never was a job, was it, soulless?"

Jacaranda fought on through her panic. She'd not lifted her scarf or mask back up after exposing herself to Marigold.

"I only follow orders," Jacaranda said, figuring it still worth the attempt to fool him. She barely missed a thrust at his chest, his deft weave of his body allowing him an easy swing at her exposed side. It might have even been a killing blow if not for how lazily he swung it. He wasn't done with her, she realized. He wanted more out of her. He wanted to taunt her with his knowledge.

"Such beautiful eyes you have," Tye said. He snickered at her glare. "I believe Gerag had a soulless of his own with violet eyes. Oh, how he lamented her mysterious disappearance when he first hired me to be her replacement."

Jacaranda forced strength into her limbs. She hacked and slashed at the damn mercenary with every shred of her skill, but it was like trying to attack her own shadow. No matter her predictions, no matter her speed, it just seemed like he was never where she expected.

"Her complete replacement," Tye added. His foot collided with her stomach, and she gasped in pain. She'd barely even registered the movement of his leg, he'd snap-kicked her so quickly. "Not just in keeping him protected, mind you, but also in training the new recruits. You know about that, don't you, Jacaranda?"

She did know about that. She knew about the clinical sex sessions, sometimes three or four soulless given orders of how to please Gerag as he lay on his bed and critiqued their performance. In all her years, Gerag had never shared a soulless prior to sale. Perhaps he'd been more upset about her departure than she anticipated. Perhaps he thought that it'd be necessary to keep the mercenary loyal. It didn't matter. She wasn't going back. Tye would die. They'd all die.

Desperation pushed her to act, but not in the way Tye expected. She turned and dashed for the opposing wall, kicked off it, and turned into a sudden, full-on sprint despite the cramped conditions. She leaned forward, her daggers pulled back for a dual thrust. Tye fell back accordingly, his sword low and ready to parry. But Jacaranda wasn't trying for a lethal stab, and Tye realized far too late to react. She leapt feet first without slowing her momentum. Her heels collided with his ribs. His sword tried to curl in from its parry but only smacked ineffectually against her hip with the flat edge. They both collapsed, her atop Belford's corpse, him rolling through the door to the tunnel. She didn't dare wait to see how badly he was hurt. Jacaranda staggered to her feet, grabbed the door, and slammed it shut. Her shaking fingers swiped at the lock until it turned.

The door shook as Tye slammed into it from the other side,

but it held firm. The mercenary peered at her through the still-open window. Their gazes met. He didn't say anything, not a word, only grinned at her with the amused look of a hunting wolf momentarily separated from its prey. *The chase is not over yet*, said that smile.

And then he dashed into the tunnel and vanished amid the dark. Jacaranda slammed the little wooden window shut all the same.

"Our time's up," Devin said. She turned to see him pulling his sword out of the chest of the guard who'd come down the stairs. "We need to get out, and we need to get out five minutes ago."

Jacaranda returned to the cell Marigold hid within and offered her hand.

"Come," she said. "We have no choice but to run."

She led Marigold to the stairwell and paused beside Devin. The Soulkeeper had just finished reloading his pistol and cocked the hammer all the way back.

"What are we looking at for upstairs?" he asked.

"We'll come up in Gerag's bedroom," she said. "You'll turn right at the hallway, go to the end, and then left. That'll get us to the front door. Auctions are held on the fifth floor. If we're lucky, their guards will be with them or eating a buffet on the fourth. That means a straight shot to the front door."

"And the six guards waiting outside."

"Do you want to risk the tunnel with Tye potentially waiting outside?"

Tye's rifle had been slung across his back that entire fight. Both of them could imagine what would happen if he drew it on them while they were trapped in the dark confines of that tunnel.

"So be it, we fight and kill the six," Devin said. "At least surprise will be on our side."

Jacaranda squeezed Marigold's hand.

"Are you ready?" she asked. The woman nodded. "All right. Let's do this."

Devin led the way, Jacaranda following as they emerged in Gerag's gaudy bedroom. The door leading into the mansion was disguised as an enormous wardrobe that had been bolted to the wall. The bedsheets were an ugly orange, the bedposts and nightstand layered with gold. Even in private he seemed determined to showcase his wealth, if only to reassure himself.

They burst through the bedroom door. A confused servant startled at their arrival and dropped the tray he was holding. Devin kicked him to the wall to move him out of the way. Jacaranda slit his throat as they passed. *No one is innocent here*, she told herself. *No one sees you leaving*. The following hallway was empty, and when they turned, only a single guard stood watch at the door. He barely had time to realize they were there before Devin's sword rammed through his gut and out his back.

Devin paused at the front door and met Jacaranda's gaze. He readied sword and pistol and then mouthed a countdown while she watched.

Three. Two. One.

He barreled through the door with his shoulder and then curled left, Jacaranda shadowing him and turning right. Devin stabbed the nearest guard through a crease in his armor, impaling him from side to lung. Jacaranda's dagger punched into the ear of a man leaning beside the door while smoking from a long pipe. The rest cried out in surprise, and they frantically reached for their weapons. Devin's pistol roared in the empty district, a clean shot through the skull. Jacaranda crisscrossed her blade over the next man's throat, showering blood across the walkway. She didn't see Devin kill his third, only heard his sudden, pained cry. Her third yanked his sword free of its scabbard and swung at her, but he was young, and he was afraid. She sidestepped it with ease, then ended his life with a stab right through his jugular. Just like that, the six were dead, with only one of them having had a chance to lift a weapon to defend himself.

All the while, her hand never let go of Marigold's.

The three sprinted down the street, Marigold huddled protectively between the two of them. They fled without secrecy or hiding this time, needing only speed and distance to reach safety. The sound of gunfire would attract the rest of the various lords' and merchants' retinues. They'd likely give chase. Too much was at risk for their masters to allow an intruder to escape, not to mention the potential fallout of Gerag's entire operation being exposed. The three of them didn't slow until they passed through the archway of Quiet District. It was only then that Jacaranda let herself believe they'd finally escaped.

"We did it," she said as they settled into a jog. "We actually did it."

Gerag's tower was but a distant spire when they heard the shot. It didn't register to Jacaranda, not at first, and by the time she realized it, it was already too late. Marigold's body jolted, and her legs stumbled. Jacaranda held her aloft, her eyes locked open and her mouth dropped. *No. No no no no no.*

"Get down," Devin said, grabbing both of them and pulling them off the road and into a cramped alley between two homes. The three collapsed to the ground, safely out of sight of Gerag's distant home. Jacaranda stared at Marigold, her shaking hands flailing uselessly at her sides. Her entire mind was paralyzed. Blood seeped through Marigold's clothing from the bullet wound that had opened up her chest.

"This, this isn't fair," she said. "Devin, please, do something."

Marigold gasped in slow, wet breaths. She didn't try to sit up. She barely had the strength to look at them. Devin examined the wound but only for a heartbeat.

"Jac, I'm sorry," he said.

"No," she screamed. She took Marigold's hand and clutched it with all her strength. "Marigold, please, look at me. Look at me. You can survive this. You...you...you're strong, you'll hold on."

Words were tumbling out of her mouth. She couldn't focus. Her rage and despair swirled together into the anathema of thought. This wasn't how it was supposed to be. They'd rescued her. They'd saved her. Marigold was supposed to experience the world like Jacaranda had, make her own choices, and decide her own fate. To bleed out now, in cold, barren streets, was too cruel. She clutched Marigold's face in her hands, and she kissed her forehead as she wept.

"No, don't," Jacaranda said. "Please don't. Don't die."

Perhaps it was the blood loss. Perhaps it was the shock. Whatever the reason, Marigold lacked the rage Jacaranda felt. There was no fury at the world's sick betrayal. No, her voice instead carried hopeless resignation wrapped in sorrow, and for some reason that made her final words so much worse.

"Can't die," Marigold said. "I never lived."

Jacaranda cried over the still body. She wept into hands stained with blood. Distant shouts echoed through the fog, prompting Devin to gently wrap his arm around her shoulders.

"We have to go," he said. "They're still in chase."

She sniffled and released Marigold's hands.

"Will her soul ascend?" she asked quietly.

"Normally I'd say if the Sisters are kind, yes," he whispered. "But if the Sisters were kind Marigold would still be alive, so I don't know. I only pray it does."

That wasn't good enough, but at least it was honest. Devin offered her his hand, and she took it and ran. They fled through the fog-covered streets, two thieves in the night with nothing to show for their efforts but spilled blood and a corpse cooling beneath the light of the moon.

CHAPTER 40

After two hours of praying over the sick and injured, Adria fled to the Grand Archive in desperate need of rest. These prayers, they took something out of her, draining a reservoir she didn't yet understand. Much as it had during her time in seminary, drowning herself in a book revitalized her mental faculties. Though the archive was lined with enormous windows, she'd found a darker corner to settle down in and relax. Given the book she read, it only seemed appropriate.

Keepers write of the Sisters' perfection, and of how that perfection is mirrored in the human form; so began the opening chapter of the Book of Ravens. *Yet the human form is far from perfect. It deteriorates. It sickens. It malforms. It dies. The church knows this, and so it casts the blame for these imperfections upon the void-dragon's blood spilling across the First Soul. The truth is far simpler. Humanity is imperfect because the Sisters are imperfect. Understand this, and you will understand how the world came to be.*

Adria rubbed her temples. The Grand Archive had a single copy of the Book of Ravens, and to even read it one had to have ascended to the rank of keeper. This one was exceptionally old, and she had to squint to read the tiny, faded text. She was on her third rereading of that opening chapter, and not from awe at its carelessly crafted argument. The unknown author wrote with fiery passion, true, but much could be rebutted by simple theological arguments or quotes of scripture. No, what fascinated her was the page on the opposite side, provided as evidence as the chapter continued on.

Malformation, it was simply titled. The words of the curse that had been used on Deakon Sevold. It was a prayer similar to Lyra's seventy-nine devotions, but instead of requesting the Goddesses' love and warmth, it invoked wrath and destruction.

Anwyn of the Moon, hear me! This flesh before me hides its rot. This smile belies its sickness. These bones deny the weakness within. Anwyn, hear me, Anwyn! Tear. Break. Sunder. Show me truth.

"Am I disturbing you?"

The inquiry was polite and soft-spoken, but it still caused Adria to jump. Realizing the identity of the inquirer only jostled her further out from her concentration.

"You are always welcome, Thaddeus," she told her Vikar. "I only ask that you forgive me if I'm a poor conversation partner. These past few days have been...tiring."

Tiring didn't begin to describe how she felt sometimes. Though Thaddeus was an elderly man with the gray hair and a walking cane, he seemed the more lively one as he settled into a chair beside her.

"I am not surprised," he said. "Word of your deeds has already spread beyond Londheim, did you know that? Just this morning a couple came to the cathedral requesting directions to your church. They traveled all night from Kelyk Township in hopes of being first in line for healing."

"How wonderful," Adria said. "Soon we'll have people traveling all the way from the Kept Lands to be disappointed that I cannot pray over each and every request."

Thaddeus chuckled and clicked the bottom of his cane on the floor in amusement.

"I see that this work takes much out of you. Perhaps it is a blessing my prayers cannot harness the Sisters' power the way yours do. The novices would have to carry me home on a cart."

"Can you set up such an arrangement for myself?"

"If you request it." He put a hand on her shoulder and gently squeezed. "Though I doubt you will have visitors all the way from the eastern coast, Adria. I hope you do not resent losing your shining uniqueness, but even in Londheim you are no longer the only keeper capable of healing."

Adria did her best to keep her face passive. "Is that so?"

"It is indeed." Thaddeus eyed her carefully. "Faithkeeper Tommen Jorr discovered this quite accidentally in the middle of a sermon yesterday morning. He confided this to Vikar Caria, and she gave him the same instructions as I gave you: to serve the Sisters faithfully, and lead none astray."

Adria relaxed into her padded chair. First her, then Sena, the imprisoned Tamerlane, and now Tommen. To have so many discovering this power in Londheim surely meant others all across the Cradle were equally gifted by the Sisters.

"Then we witness an awakening of sorts," Adria said. "Perhaps in time all keepers will possess the same power?"

"It'd certainly ease your burden, wouldn't it?" Thaddeus said. "Not that I blame you for hoping so. I know a taste of the responsibility you have endured, given my position as Vikar. I wouldn't wish it upon anyone who didn't desire it."

"It's not a matter of desire," she said, trying to articulate her thoughts. Memories of that morning after the attack on the market threatened to break her resolve. Goddesses, what she'd give for a good few hours of sleep right now. "I...want to help people. I want to heal them. That's *all* I desire. I don't want crowds whispering my name in reverence. I've had a taste of fame and it is not for me."

"Is that why you hide more and more behind the mask?"

Adria touched the black-and-white porcelain covering her face as if on instinct. She'd forgotten she even wore it. The masks were not required to be worn once inside cathedral grounds, especially in areas like the archives where no civilians would be present.

"I'm not hiding," she said. The moment the words left her lips, she realized how defensive they sounded, and how reactionary. Were they even true? Thaddeus's raised eyebrow showed he certainly didn't believe so.

"All right, perhaps I am," she said. "I'm used to being the quiet servant who deals in whispers and sins, not as a healer whose name is spoken in reverence by the crowds. The only thing I want crowded around me are bookshelves. It's good that Tommen is a Faithkeeper. He will be better suited to the attention."

"We all have our talents," Thaddeus said. He pushed his spectacles higher up the bridge of his nose. "But sometimes we must learn skills that do not come easily. You have a brilliant mind and a heart of unending compassion. Londheim would be a better place if it heard more of your words, and not just those you compose for Sena's sermons."

Another gentle correction. She'd given everything of herself to heal the people with her prayers, yet Thaddeus expected more of her. He always expected more. Even when he'd assigned her to the Low Dock church she'd felt his disappointment in her settling for such a quiet, unimportant district.

"Can we talk of different matters?" she asked. "I'd love to focus my mind on anything other than myself right now."

"Such as the curse inflicted upon our Deakon?"

Adria glanced at the book she held. Irrational panic seized her chest. The Book of Ravens was expressly forbidden throughout all of Orismund, and possession of it could lead to expulsion from the Keeping Church, or worse. Of course she had both permission to read it and an explanation for doing so, but that did not prevent her pulse from pounding within her veins.

"If I can heal broken bones and torn limbs through the power of the Goddesses, then removing a blasphemous curse should also be within my capabilities," she said. "The Deakon, he...he clearly suffers. I can help him, I know it, so I thought if I read the words, saw how it was summoned, then maybe I'd figure out a way."

"And has reading it helped you?"

Adria chose her words carefully.

"I am as fascinated as I am horrified by what I find written here," she said. "While much is wrong, much is correct, only framed in a terribly slanted way by what I can only call the author's angry bias. These curses themselves, though...the author claims the power is from the Goddesses."

"Clearly false," Thaddeus said. "Such vile powers cannot have come from the Sisters, only the void."

"How do we know?" Adria dared ask. "Our free will also comes from the Goddesses, and it can be used for both good and evil. I wonder if the tremendous power of the Sisters can be used in the same manner. And if it *does* come from them, then that means surely the power to break the curse *also* comes from them."

"You insinuate that the Sisters would allow faith in them to be wielded for malice and harm."

"Is history not full of such examples?"

Thaddeus bit back his initial retort so he might dwell further on a response. When he did speak, it was careful and deliberate.

"The Book of Ravens, from its first word to its last, seeks to remold the Sisters into petty, flawed deities unworthy of love and devotion. I do not deny there is power in those words, for I have seen the horror it has unleashed upon our Deakon. What I vehemently refuse to entertain is any argument that denies the love and compassion I have felt, and the holy experiences of a lifetime spent in prayer and service to others. We have both felt the power in a prayerful gathering. We have both felt the faint touch of Lyra on our hearts, and we have seen the shimmering light of souls rising to the heavens to be cared for in Anwyn's arms. The Book of Ravens sees only deception and hate. Never forget that."

Adria bowed her head, humbled.

"I will not," she said. A tired smile cracked her lips. "But this was hardly the relaxing banter I was hoping for when I suggested we speak of something else."

Thaddeus softly laughed.

"Forgive this old man. You are precious to me, and I fear anything happening to you from my own inaction. Yes, let us talk on other things. In fact..." He showed her the book he carried, an untitled collection of scrolls rebound inside a leather frame. "This, and not the news about Faithkeeper Tommen, is why I sought you out. I believe I have made a discovery you will find most fascinating."

"And what is that?"

Thaddeus's silver eyes gleamed behind his spectacles.

"The name of the mountain that crawled to our doorstep."

Now that was interesting. She gestured for him to continue, for he obviously had something to show her in the book he held.

"I've been speaking with multiple scholars about the void-dragon as of late," Thaddeus explained as he opened the book and began carefully turning the pages. "Before the Ninth Council of Oris settled the matter, there was a lot of debate over the concept of the void-dragon. Have you studied the Ninth Council's various issued rulings?"

"Not recently," Adria said. She bit her lower lip and thought. The Ninth Council had been convened in Oris in 1150 U.O., some three hundred years ago, mostly with the intent to clarify the separation of powers between the Keeping Church and the Royal Crown. She'd studied it during her years in seminary but only remembered a vague mention of the void-dragon.

"I don't blame you for not remembering," Thaddeus said. "It likely seemed obvious to you as a novice, but that council's twelfth ruling declared that there were no lesser dragons, no servant creatures, no little whelps the size of your thumb to whisper sinful ideas into your ear, that sort of thing. There was the void, and the dragon that resides within. Nothing else."

Adria nodded, her memory finally jostled loose. The Second Council of Nicus had used that precedent some two centuries later in its dogma-shaking ruling that the void-dragon was not an actual living, sentient creature but instead the personification of the many concepts of the void itself. An entire industry had built up around protecting one's soul from the void-dragon, be it costly prayers, tear-soaked trinkets, or whatever else charlatans and greedy members of the church could devise to separate the faithful from their coin. This ruling had burned that industry to the ground, and in Adria's mind, good riddance.

"So what does that original ruling have to do with the crawling mountain?" she asked.

"All councils allow dissenting voices to their rulings. It helps avoid embarrassment should a ruling be later changed or revoked entirely. Oris's Ninth Council had a dissenting opinion to the twelfth ruling, and it referenced a certain collection of scrolls for its insistence that there was more than one dragon in the void." He lifted the leather binding off his lap. "This collection."

The Vikar handed over the book to Adria's eagerly awaiting hands. She saw that he'd opened to a scroll that was actually a short letter that had been retranscribed. While Thaddeus talked she read.

"The letter was written by a Soulkeeper when humanity's reach was yet to spread much farther west than Londheim. Wealthy investors were attempting to settle villages for trappers and miners all across Alma's Crown, but they had significant difficulty in finding people willing to move. Read the reason why."

The letter opened with the Soulkeeper grumbling about performing duties for wealthy backers of the church (it was good to know some things never changed, Adria thought dryly). After that the Soulkeeper's ire turned to the many villagers who worked the fields surrounding Londheim who refused to move west as instructed.

> These dunderhead yokels won't pack their belongings for Dunwerth and Pathok. Aggressive prodding proves insufficient, for unless escorted all the way through the mountains they turn 'round and take up residence with relatives in the valley. I've tried reasoning with them, but they will

not be persuaded. The superstitious lot insist it a curse to live in Viciss's shadow, so you have two choices, Vikar. Either dig the dragon out of Alma's Crown, or send me more soldiers. At this point, I'll take whichever one returns me to Londheim the faster.

S. K. Rodwick Baurns

"That letter dates back to 643 U.O.," Thaddeus said when Adria lowered the book. "Viciss, a dragon buried all the way out in Alma's Crown. The same area with the earliest appearance of the black water. Just this morning I spoke with the only surviving family from Pathok, and do you know what, Adria? They reported seeing the crawling mountain mere hours after the black water's arrival, approaching their village from even farther to the west."

So ridiculous and yet at the same time so completely plausible. Sometimes the most absurd possibility was the correct one.

"You think the people were right," Adria said carefully. "That Viciss, an actual dragon, was buried in Alma's Crown."

"I have more evidence supporting than against," Thaddeus said. "And what else would you call the crawling mountain? I believe Viciss is its name, and that somehow our ancestors hundreds of years ago knew far more about it than we do."

"So Viciss is the void-dragon?" Adria wondered. She rubbed her forehead as she tried to work through the possibilities, as well as the many scriptures and prophecies foretelling the damage the end-times monster would unleash. "Wouldn't that mean the world is coming to an end?"

"Perhaps," Thaddeus said. "Though I'd say our understanding of what this dragon is has been slowly warped over the centuries, starting with the assumption that it didn't exist. By the time the Second Council of Nicus stripped the void-dragon of all names, the scholars recorded over two hundred monikers in use. Most names had sprung up over the past few decades hand-in-hand with the list of cures, protections, and charms to protect against them, but what of earlier? What if the prevalence of multiple names means the blatantly obvious...that there are more than one?"

Adria could sense his subdued excitement.

"You have other names you believe are true," she said.

"I do. I scoured all of our oldest letters and documents, particularly those not written by church officials, but they are few and far between. I've developed a growing suspicion that the heretical purge of 659 U.O. was not just for removing insulting dogma about the Sisters but also references to these dragons. Still, I discovered two other names of similar age that emerged unscathed. One was a dragon named Gloam, whom the writer, a Londheim chemist, blamed for his experiments in metallurgy failing. The other was 'Chyron beneath the waves,' whom a fisher in Wardhus gave as an explanation for what happened to his missing partner after a storm."

Wardhus was the trading town at the far end of the Septen River where it emptied out into the Gulf of Ianor. That they might invent their own dragon, this one in the ocean, wasn't too farfetched, but at the same time if Thaddeus's ideas were correct...

"Have we received any message from Wardhus?" she asked. Thaddeus shook his head.

"The Triona River is too strong for most boats. We'll need someone there to make the trek on foot to Watne, which might take weeks." He grinned at her. "Are you envisioning a mountain crawling from the ocean floor to carve across the sand, perhaps on its way to Nicus?"

"That's exactly what I'm pondering," Adria said. "It's human nature to think we're the center of everything, but what if our situation in Londheim isn't unique? The black water that came from the west stopped at Londheim...but what of South Orismund? East Orismund? What if this...Gloam...appears and threatens our Ecclesiast in Trivika?"

Thaddeus slumped in his chair, his excitement suddenly tempered with frustration.

"We're blind out here in the west," he said. "The boats from Stomme gave us some information, but nothing beyond the East Orismund border. Steeth could be demolished and the Kept Lands sunk into the ocean for all we'd know. What I'd give to be in Trivika right now, and have access to their ancient archives. Have they any other names from the distant past? If there are multiple void-dragons, and they walk the Cradle...what are the theological ramifications? Where did they come from? What is their goal? Are the stories correct, and do they seek to banish the stars and swallow the light of the First Soul?"

Adria stood from a chair and clasped his hands in hers.

"Do not wear down your heart asking questions you cannot possibly have answers for," she said. "It's only been a few weeks. Give it time. Londheim still stands, and I bet the other great cities do as well."

He smiled up at her.

"Let us both pray you are correct." The old man leaned on his cane and rose to his feet. "Oh, and before I forget, I have officially relieved you of your duty in Low Dock church. The work your prayers perform is much more important than researching and writing a few sermons and applying ointments to old men's bones. I've also prepared you a room in the Soft Voice, just in case you cannot find peace and quiet in your old room at the church."

"Thank you, Vikar," Adria said, uncertain of how to feel. The Soft Voice was a bell tower dedicated to the Mindkeepers in the Cathedral of the Sacred Mother, reserved for teachers, their students, and those who served directly under the Vikar himself. "Has Sena been informed of these planned changes?"

"She has."

Adria bowed in appreciation.

"I will think this over," she said. She didn't want to abandon Sena, and she had every intention of remaining in Low Dock to help those in need, but it was nice knowing she had a place to flee to when the work overwhelmed her and the prayers drained her strength down to nothing.

Thaddeus said his good-byes and retreated from her private corner, leaving Adria standing before her chair feeling adrift and uncertain. Restlessness itched at her limbs despite her exhaustion. Her Vikar's new discoveries had awakened her curiosity, and it drove her mad that there appeared no way for her to research into it further without exhaustive scouring through old documents and letters. If only so much of the earliest history of Unified Orismund had not been lost to the ages. What she'd give for five minutes with a historian of the time, or...

"Goddesses above, I'm an idiot," she muttered. She *did* know someone who'd lived at the time, even if she'd not interacted with her much. Adria rushed out of the archive and to the streets, not bothering to retrieve gloves or a scarf for her trip despite the deep chill in the air.

By the time she arrived at Devin's house, the first light flakes of snow had begun to fall. She knocked impatiently at the door and was surprised when Tommy, not Devin, answered.

"Oh, hey," Tommy said. "Come on in. Devin's still asleep, if that's who you're here for. So's Jacaranda. Not together, of course, I didn't mean to, you know. Imply stuff."

Adria shut the door behind her and, after a moment's hesitation, removed the mask and pocketed it. She was among friends and family. If she couldn't be herself here, then the mask might as well be a permanent tattoo.

"I thought you'd moved into the Wise tower?" Adria asked, gently shifting the focus of the conversation so he'd stop blushing.

"Yeah, well…" Tommy plopped down into the chair beside the fireplace and kicked his heels to get it rocking. "Malik and I, we had some issues regarding our research and I, uh, did not handle it well. I decided to come over here for a few hours while I cooled down."

"Would you like to talk about it?" she asked. "I can even put my mask on if it helps."

Tommy shook his head and laughed.

"Nah. It's fine, Addy, I promise. We're dealing with some pretty powerful and ancient stuff, so we're bound to disagree on its uses and interpretations. I just needed a relaxing environment and some good wine to put myself back together. Thankfully I've got plenty of both here!" He reached down to a metal goblet on the floor beside the chair, then glared at its lack of contents. "Well, plenty of the first, anyway. Be right back."

He hopped up and sauntered into the kitchen. Cabinet doors smacked open and closed, and she heard the rattle of silverware.

"So if you're not here for me or Devin," he shouted from the other room, "then who are you here for?"

Adria turned her attention to the pillowed shelf on the other side of the room, and the eavesdropping faery lying on her stomach in its center.

"Tesmarie," she called out. "Might you come here a moment?"

The faery's wings buzzed to life, and she hovered upward with an expression akin to a child caught with their hand down their trousers.

"I wasn't listening, I promise," she said. "All right, I was listening a little, not on purpose, though! You two talk…really…loud."

Her voice drifted off. Adria smiled at her to show she wasn't upset.

"Please, I have questions, and I think you may have the answers."

"Oooh, is that it?" The faery zipped to the couch in the blink of an eye and delicately sat atop Adria's knees. "I'd be happy to help! I thought helping was what I'd be doing more of here, honestly, since your brother seemed like he needed lots of it when we first met. Have you heard him talk about what he goes through at night? Giant owls trying to eat him and then there's the gargoyles, which I still can't believe but I don't see your brother as the lying sort, and they're trying to eat him, too. Not to mention that horrible monster, Janus…"

"Tesmarie?"

She cocked her head to one side.

"Yes?"

"Might I ask my question?"

Her wings fluttered a bit.

"Of course! Didn't I say I'd be happy to help?"

Something loud and metallic banged from inside the kitchen.

"Goddesses above, this cork is tighter than Lyra's…" Tommy

paused, and Adria could clearly envision the young man's panicked realization that she was in the adjacent room. "Lyra's, uh, nothing, nothing's tighter than this cork." Then, lower, mumbling as if she somehow wouldn't hear, "Gonna burn this wart-licking cork to ash with a fireball if it don't come loose, 'reckless use of magic' be damned."

Adria stifled a laugh. How in all the Cradle did her brother stay sane with friends like these?

"I was wondering if you could tell me about the void-dragons?" Adria asked Tesmarie.

"Void-dragons?" Tesmarie crinkled her adorably tiny nose. "I don't know any 'void'-dragons, just the five Dragons of Creation."

Excitement spiked in Adria's chest.

"The Dragons of Creation?" she prodded.

"Oh, you surely must be joking," Tesmarie said. "You don't even know *them*? Chyron, Viciss, Gloam...any of these names ringing a bell?"

"Hey, I know those!" Tommy shouted from the kitchen. A loud *pop* interrupted him, followed by the sound of liquid splashing across the floor. "Oh, come on, now it goes?"

Tommy returned to the living room holding the open wine bottle and with a massive red stain across his shirt and bed robe.

"What are we talking about?" he asked. "Sorry, I was preoccupied for a bit, but it sounds like you've finally taken some interest in the schools of magic?"

Adria felt as if a multitude of tumblers in one giant lock were finally sliding into place inside her head.

"One at a time," she said, holding a finger up at Tommy. "Tesmarie, you were saying?"

"The Dragons of Creation! Chyron, Viciss, Gloam, Aethos,

and Nihil. They're the ones who made, well…" Tesmarie shrugged her shoulders. "People like me. The dragon-sired. Chyron crafted us onyx faeries, for example. As for Puffy, I think it was Aethos, right?"

One smoke circle fluttered up from the fire, its symbol for *yes*. Adria had forgotten the firekin was even there, but it too offered corroboration. So if Thaddeus was correct…

"What of the crawling mountain at our city gates?" Adria asked. "Is it the dragon Viciss?"

Tesmarie tucked her arms behind her back and hesitated.

"Well… I've never actually *seen* the others before. Chyron's the only one I've met, and he was super sweet. Didn't look much like a dragon, though, but a faery like me, perhaps a few inches taller. The mountain could be Viciss, I guess, but it could also be one of the others. Has anyone tried asking?"

A few brazen men had shouted to the mountain not long after it arrived. They'd received no response, not even a trickle of black water. For the most part the rest of Londheim had tried to move on with their lives while quietly praying that the mountain remained dormant. Adria told the faery so, earning herself a confused shrug.

"I'm sorry I couldn't be more helpful," she said.

"You've been beyond helpful," Tommy said, and it looked like he was as excited as Adria. "This not only confirms my schools theory but offers an explanation for their existence! Oh, Malik is going to be *so* jealous of my discovery."

Adria stood and took the bottle from Tommy so she could down a large swig.

"Not yet," she said when Tommy reached to take it back. "First you explain what you mean by schools of magic."

"Fine. Of the spells Malik and I have managed to re-create,

they've all belonged to one of five categories, or as some of the older books call them, schools of magic. Aethos is destructive elements, lightning and fire, for example. Chyron clearly represents time. Gloam is something akin to thoughts and reason. Viciss involves transition and change. Of the five, the strangest is Nihil. That school eludes Malik and me, though our best guess is a sort of controlled chaos or discord. If these schools also represent dragons, then Nihil would be the one I want to meet the least."

Adria filed the information away in her mind. She bit down on her lip, more tumblers clicking.

"Tesmarie, Devin said you could slow and speed up time," she said. "And Chyron, the Dragon of Time, is your creator?"

The faery bobbed her head up and down.

"He sure is, and he gifted us with his blessings. That's how I do . . . well, what I do."

"So the dragons represent concepts," Adria theorized. "Your spells draw power from it, and their creations share gifts in a similar vein, such as Tesmarie's innate time manipulation granted to her by Chyron, the Dragon of Time."

Tommy finally snatched the bottle from her hand.

"If you were to put a dagger to my neck and force an answer, I'd say you have the gist of it," he said. "I'm personally a fan of this theory. It makes my spellcasting seem all the more badass. I'm not just casting spells, I'm harnessing the *power of the dragons*!"

He shook a shaking fist to the heavens for emphasis.

"Boom your voice all you want," Tesmarie said. "You still look like a drunken jester who just rolled out of bed."

Tommy hoisted the bottle.

"I'm not drunk yet," he said. "But I'm barreling headfirst toward that happy destination. Care to join me, Tes? I'm sure I could spare you a few drops."

Adria pulled her mask out from her pocket and slid it back over her face.

"You two enjoy yourselves," she said. "I must speak with my Vikar. This illuminates so much."

She waved to the both of them and then hurried out the door.

"Hey, Puffy," she heard Tommy call out from the other side. "Does burning alcohol do anything for you like drinking it does to us?"

Prudence dictated that she chastise Tommy for thinking an intoxicated embodiment of fire was a good idea. Adria was too excited to bother. She had confirmation of not only the void-dragon's existence but a number of names, magical concepts attached, and even a more formal title as the Dragons of Creation. No doubt the emergence of magical creatures was tied to Viciss's reemergence, and with all this they could focus their investigation on the various lore books and apocrypha.

She was so lost in her thoughts that she barely noticed the elderly woman limping after her.

"Keeper?" she asked. "Keeper Adria?"

She turned, then choked down a groan. Goddesses help her, it was the old woman who lurked at the bottom of her church's stairs.

"Yes?" she asked. Dread sank into her chest at the thought of her requesting prayers instead of coppers. Was this what her life would become? Accosted by strangers for healing of every scrape and ache?

"Just one moment," the old woman said. She hobbled as fast as her limp allowed. "Please, I need only a moment, and then I'll never bug you for coppers again."

"If you need a blessing of the Sisters, I must apologize, but wait until tomorrow. Today has left me exhausted."

"Oh, no, no," she said. She smiled. Her teeth were whole instead of missing, and they shone a myriad of colors. "The last thing I want from you is a blessing."

She lunged with speed far beyond what her meager frame should have allowed. One hand closed across Adria's mouth, muffling her scream. The other latched about her throat, choking the air from her lungs. Adria pulled at her wrists, but she was so strong they moved not an inch. The woman, suddenly not so old, and not so feminine, lifted her off the ground. Adria's feet kicked. Her hands flailed. She tried to pray one of her protection devotions, but not a sound escaped her crushed throat.

"No prayers," her attacker said. Gray hair deepened, half turning black, the other half green. The crackly old voice was replaced with one deep and masculine. "Just sleep."

Adria looked to either side, hoping someone might intervene. The street was empty but for a middle-aged couple frozen in conversation. Frozen most literally, she realized. Their bodies had been turned to colorful ice. Dark spots blotted out her vision. Fire burned inside her lungs. The last words she heard before losing consciousness were a frustrated lament.

"Consider yourself blessed Viciss wants you alive."

CHAPTER 41

Snow blew inside with the cold wind when Devin pulled the door open to his home.

"Is something the matter?" he asked, surprised to find two full-fledged Mindkeepers shivering on his front step. He'd expected novices.

"Pardon the intrusion at such a late hour, Soulkeeper," said the older of the two. "But by chance is your sister here?"

"No, she's not," Devin said. "What brings you here?"

"A matter of some urgency," said the other, an eager woman half his age. "A person of great importance to the church is in need of her prayers, but we cannot find her at the Soft Voice, nor at her room in Low Dock."

The first twinges of worry tugged at Devin's chest. Not for the person of great importance; he knew that was code for a wealthy donor. It wasn't like his sister to just disappear. He glanced over his shoulder at Tommy, who was reclining in the chair beside Puffy's fire. His brother-in-law was nursing a rather brutal headache with a tiny shard of ice pressed against his forehead.

"Do you know where Adria might be?" he asked.

"She left just as we were getting started," Tommy said, *we* meaning him and the completely unconscious faery snoring atop his shoulder. "She said she had to meet with her Vikar."

The older Mindkeeper overheard and shook his head.

"Vikar Thaddeus has not seen Adria since she left the Grand Archive this morning. Is there perhaps somewhere she'd have stopped along the way? Time is of the essence, and I cannot stress how important it is we..."

"You're right," Devin interrupted. "Time is of the essence, so please inform whoever it is you're begging for that they need to wait while I look for her. Assuming she's fine, maybe she will visit them with her healing prayers...or maybe they'll wait in line like everyone else. Understood?"

Neither Mindkeeper looked pleased, but there wasn't much they could do about it.

"I suppose," said the older Mindkeeper. "If you need any assistance, please do not hesitate to contact us. Oh, and when you do find Adria, please tell her to come immediately to—"

Devin slammed the door in their faces and turned to Tommy.

"Adria vanished on her way to speak with her Vikar," Devin said. He removed his heavy coat from its peg and slid it over his shoulders. "That's not like her. We need to go look."

Tommy pushed himself up from the chair, which sent Tesmarie sliding off to a graceless landing on her rump. She startled awake and streaked back into the air with a buzzing of her wings. Tommy appeared not to notice her plight in the slightest.

"I'll join you," he offered. "But where do we start looking? Surely she's fine, right? Maybe holed up in some nook of the Grand Archive and fell asleep..."

"Look for who?" Tesmarie asked as she rubbed the sleep from her eyes.

Devin buckled his sword belt about his waist, then holstered his pistol.

"My sister," he said. "She vanished somewhere between here and Church District. We have to make sure she's all right."

"Oh. Oh! I can help with that."

"You can?" he asked.

"Sure I can!" she said. She buzzed over to the door and hovered in front of his face. "If I concentrate really hard, I can, um...how to put this...I can see times other than the 'now' time, as if they're happening all around me. Once I do, I'll follow her past self to wherever it is she's at now."

"Are you sure it'll work?" Devin asked. He couldn't shake a nagging worry that something was deeply wrong. The knowledge that there was a madman named Janus hunting down members of the Keeping Church only worsened his anxious nerves.

"It's how I followed you to Londheim and figured out where you lived," Tesmarie said. "So long as I'm not looking too far into the past it should be easy."

"Then I graciously accept your help," Devin said. He glanced to Tommy. "The weather's cold. I've spare shirts and sweaters in my closet. Get dressed in something warmer."

Devin went to Jacaranda's door and gently knocked while his brother-in-law added some layers against the biting wind.

"Come in," she said softly from the other side.

Devin pushed the door open and entered Jacaranda's candlelit room. She lay on her bed reading a book that she'd convinced Tommy to buy for her at the market. Ever since Marigold's death she'd remained quietly inside her room, and Devin had done his best to give her the time alone she needed. Jacaranda looked up when he entered, her fingers marking her place on the page. Her expression revealed nothing.

"Adria's missing," he said. "We're going to look for her."

He wasn't sure if Jacaranda would join them after their terrible night, and it wasn't like she had any real connection with his sister. She surprised him by shutting her book and reaching for her daggers from where they lay atop her bedside table.

"I'll be just a moment," she said.

The four gathered at the front of Devin's home. Fog settled over the street, obscuring the thin layer of snow building atop the cobbles.

"Be real quiet while I do this," Tesmarie instructed. She hovered in place with her back to the door and her eyes closed. "Oh, and I might sound a little funny when I talk. Time about me is about to get real loosey-goosey."

Devin kicked his legs and crossed his arms to keep warm. It seemed late autumn's bite had come on strong, ushered in by the light snowfall. Tesmarie didn't seem too bothered by the cold, for she wore the same dress she always wore, which left much of her arms and legs exposed. He couldn't help but be a little envious.

The faery whispered words he could barely hear. Her hands lifted, her fingers curling into different contorted shapes. Pink light shimmered around her body, then receded into her dark skin. Only her eyes seemed to maintain a bit of that gleam when she opened them. A smile lit her worried face.

"There she is," she said. Her words slurred, spoken as if her entire body moved through molasses. "Follow me."

She more drifted than flew forward, yet gravity's pull seemed just as incapable of touching her as when her wings fluttered at a thousand miles an hour. Devin pulled his hat lower over his face to keep the snow from his eyes and then followed, the rest falling into line. This was the street leading to his home, yet with the fog, snow, and cold it seemed alien to him. He felt certain that eyes watched him, as certain as when he walked through the forest outside Dunwerth.

It wasn't long before Tesmarie came to a sudden halt. Her hands crossed over her mouth, and she cried out as if in pain. The noise only confirmed the dread that had been growing in Devin's gut since hearing of Adria's disappearance.

"What is it, Tes?" he asked.

Tesmarie didn't answer immediately. She shook her head side to side, muttering the word *no* repeatedly. Devin put his fingers a few inches away from her face and snapped them twice in rapid succession. It seemed to work, for she turned his way and spoke with a calm seriousness he'd never heard in her voice before.

"He took her," she said. "Janus. He took her."

Images of the Mindkeeper half-melded into the southern market wall flashed unbidden through his mind.

"Is she still alive?" he asked.

The faery weakly nodded.

"I think so."

There was that, at least. Devin loaded his pistol with flamestone and lead shot. If that monster had his sister, then there was no way tonight was ending without a battle. He gestured to Tesmarie, who, after a shudder, resumed her gazing into the past.

"He's carrying her," Tesmarie said as she led them down one road and to another. Her voice resumed its slow, plodding sensation. "Talking to her, but I don't think she's awake to listen."

"Saying what?"

"It doesn't work like that. I only see, not hear."

Devin knew the faery capable of far greater speed of flight and wished he could somehow urge her on faster. Each passing second felt interminably long. His fingers twitched against the grip of his pistol. The cold wind seeped through every crack in his coat and stole away the warmth from his skin. For the first time in his life he hated Londheim: its crowded architecture, its cobbled roads, its constant stink of fish and water.

"She'll be fine," Tommy said as they walked. "I mean, it's Adria. She's the best, and she has her prayers now. Remember how she exploded one of those owls? I bet we'll stumble upon a giant mess of Janus goo and bones any second now."

"Tommy," Devin said. "I appreciate you trying, but please... no jokes, all right?"

He blushed a little and nodded.

"Sure. Sorry."

Though they traveled in a relatively straight direction, Devin couldn't decipher their destination. Where was that bastard taking his sister? A bloody chaos of horrifying ideas bounced inside his mind, and it took all his training to silence them so he might focus on the task at hand. If Janus wanted to kill his sister, he'd have done so immediately, not carry her unconscious body through the city.

Unless he wants to make an example of her.

The night passed slow and painful. Tesmarie had to stop often to recast her spell, and each time it took longer for her to, as she put it, "locate the proper time." She fluttered at an even slower rate, until eventually Devin placed her on his shoulder and had her point in the direction to walk. They passed through two districts, and still they had no clue as to the final destination.

Late into the second hour Tesmarie abruptly stopped them in front of a dilapidated building in the adjacent district to Tradeway. Not a thing about it appeared unusual, especially now that so many buildings in Londheim had boarded up their windows or covered them with thick curtains. Tesmarie, however, was certain of its importance. She floated to the door and halted as if confused by its presence.

"In there," she said, pointing. "He took her in there."

Devin cast a glance at Jacaranda. She drew her daggers and nodded in silent understanding. The two took up positions on either side of the door. He tested the door handle, unsurprised to find it locked.

"Know any spells to open a door?" Devin whispered to Tommy. His brother-in-law scrunched his face as he concentrated.

"Not without alerting half the neighborhood," he whispered back.

"I'll get it," Tesmarie said. She shivered as a pink aura flickered and then vanished from her skin. Her eyes returned to their normal diamond color. She zipped through a slender gap in the boards covering one of the windows, and a moment later, the lock clicked. Devin pulled the door open a crack, and Tesmarie quickly flew back out.

"Is it empty inside?" Jacaranda asked.

"I think so," Tesmarie said. "But...but never mind. You'll see."

Devin led the way inside, Jacaranda at his heels. At first the building appeared like any other home in Londheim. The entry opened directly into a living room containing a fireplace and chimney. A hallway beside led further into the house, which, given the home's small size, he expected to be little more than a bedroom and a pantry.

"Where did he take her?" Devin asked softly. The two doors at the end of the hallway were both boarded over, and it appeared there was no other place to go.

"You mean you don't see?" Tesmarie asked.

"See what?"

The faery didn't answer. Instead she flew to the fireplace and gently landed.

"It must be protected," she said. The other three gathered around her to watch. It seemed Tesmarie was studying a bare patch of wall just beside the fireplace, her hands crossed behind her back and her lips pursed. "But protections like this don't like it when you mess with them real bad, like...this!"

She put her hand against the wall—which then sank into it half an inch as if it were made of liquid. Her wings fluttered, and she shot upward and then to the right, tracing a rectangular shape, once, twice, three times...

The wall wasn't a wall. It was a narrow entryway receding inward toward a gray stone door with no visible handle or lock. Devin rubbed at his eyes, feeling the beginnings of a headache. Just looking at the door burdened him. He stepped closer and put his hand atop the stone. Light emerged from little cuts and divots, forming a shape resembling an hourglass. When he pushed, it offered no give.

"How did Janus get inside?" he asked.

Tesmarie cast her spell a second time, returning the pink aura to her eyes.

"He put his hand upon the door," she said, her voice so slow it bordered on comical. "The hourglass glowed, and then it opened for him. I can't see more." She snapped out of her spell and pouted her lower lip. "I'm sorry. I wish I could be more helpful."

"You've been more than helpful," Devin assured her. He turned to his brother-in-law. "This feels like your area of expertise now. Can you make sense of that symbol?"

"It doesn't look like there's much to decipher," Tommy said. "It's an hourglass. If Janus gained entry by saying a password of some sort we could maybe discover a connection between it and the symbol, but by merely touching it? We have nothing to go on."

Tommy brushed the door with his fingers. The hourglass symbol shone back to life, then faded when he withdrew. Still no give.

"Perhaps there is a hidden trigger, and your fingers must apply pressure at certain locations?" Jacaranda offered.

"A decent idea," Devin said. "Tes, can you show me where Janus put his fingers?"

Pink shimmered over Tesmarie's eyes, and she stared at the door for several long moments before banishing the spell.

"All right, I think I have it memorized. Um, Devin, use your right hand. Put your thumb there"—she pointed—"and your forefinger there, index there…"

He did exactly as instructed, but even when all five fingers perfectly matched where Janus had touched the door, it remained locked. Devin swore and pulled his hand away. There must be something they were missing, but what?

"Is there any spell of yours that might open the door?" he asked.

"I could try," Tommy said. He scratched at his chin and stared.

"It looks like it's pretty thick stone, though. I'm not sure fire will do anything. Maybe if I concentrated a lot of lightning at it, but there's the possibility it's been protected in some way."

"Protected how?"

Tommy shrugged.

"Void if I know. I'm still a beginner at this sort of thing, remember?"

"Let's take a step back and think before we start trying to break down the door," Jacaranda said. "What is the purpose of this lock in the first place?"

"To keep people out," Tommy said as if it were obvious.

"No," she said. "Not just people. *Humans*."

All three turned to Tesmarie, who hovered in the air with her arms crossed behind her.

"Um, I guess I can see," she said softly. The faery fluttered to the door and gently put her hand atop it. The hourglass symbol flared with light and then vanished completely, as did the door, revealing a long dark tunnel. Devin sighed with relief. They weren't stuck. He still had a chance to save his sister.

"Can you still see Janus's path?" he asked.

Tesmarie cast her spell but then quickly banished it.

"He took her through that door, I'm sure," she said. "But beyond that is, well, it's lots of magic, and I mean lots." She clutched her elbows and held her arms to her chest. "A-scary-amount lots."

Even Devin, with his normal human senses, could detect the power emanating from the tunnel in waves. What lurked inside? For what purpose did that monster bring his sister here? Whatever the reason, he'd lead the way to find out.

"Can you give us light?" Devin asked.

Tommy snapped his fingers and muttered, *"Aethos creare lumna."*

A perfect orb of daylight shimmered into existence above his hand. It appeared the tunnel didn't travel far before reaching a second open doorway. Devin stepped inside, the stale air wrapping around him. He couldn't shake the feeling that something hummed in the deep nearby, its vibration rattling his teeth. There appeared no reason for it, but he found the air somehow harder to breathe. Dread increased with his every step. He half expected an ambush at the doorway, but none came. Lest his fear overwhelm him, he stepped straight through the door and into the room beyond.

The room was a perfectly spherical dome whose walls were lit with small, twinkling lights. No, not lights. Stars, as if the walls were windows to a distant night sky. Their soft glow illuminated a perfectly smooth floor made up of an enormous gray stone slate. In the center, shimmering with unearthly power, was a triangular well cut from stone. Alma's rising sun circled the sides of the bottom third, Lyra's full sun the middle, and Anwyn's moon the top. Thin rivulets of light swam from the stars toward the center of the dome's ceiling and collected into long, thin strands that fell like a drop of rain into the well. The drops looked composed of water, except it shone a pale white in the darkness and flickered like fire. Devin knew immediately what it reminded him of: a burning white soul rising up to the heavens.

"What is this place?" Tommy wondered. His eyes sparkled like a young boy's on his birthday. "It's so...so...wonderful."

Devin approached the triangular well. A faint blue aura shimmered about the stone sides, the exact same color as the beams that guided souls to the heavens above. He looked inside the well, and though it resembled a rippling pool of water, he knew that was a lie. Whatever swirled within bore no physical shape whatsoever; his mind only gave it a liquid form as it struggled to ascertain something not of this world. In the very center of the well, hovering just above the surface of the "water," was a smooth spherical orb made of clear diamond. White light rippled about it, bursting brighter every time a drop of whatever star-substance fell from the ceiling to touch its surface. A thin line, no thicker than a strand of spider silk, stretched from the bottom of the diamond orb to flow into the shimmering, raging white fire that filled the rest of the well. This wasn't the light that made up a soul, not quite. The color wasn't as vivid, the white not as pure.

"What do you think it is?" Jacaranda asked. She looked greatly unnerved by whatever swirled in the center of those three triangles.

"I haven't the faintest idea," Devin said. He stepped away from the well. Though its blue-and-white color conveyed feelings of cold and calmness, in reality he was painfully hot standing in its presence. Beads of sweat had already formed across his forehead.

"The room is empty, and I see no doors other than the one we entered," he told Tesmarie. "Can you tell where they went?"

The faery shook her head.

"I told you, my magic won't work in here. It's like asking me to find a spark while staring at the sun."

Devin swore. There had to be something hidden in that giant room. He joined Tommy at a portion of the long, spherical wall to see if he had any ideas.

"I thought I had a pretty good grasp of magic," his friend said.

"Malik and I had defined the schools, interpreted the words, and seen its supposed limits." He shook his head and gestured around the room. "This is beyond anything I've ever conceived. That well in the center is collecting something, and while I can only guess, my gut says it somehow involves stars and the cycle of souls. Someone put a lot of work, and a *lot* of magic, into creating this room. The question is... why?"

Devin put his back to the wall and took in the surroundings. Something about the place felt familiar; if only he could piece it together. The stars, the well, the bare stone...

Suddenly it clicked.

"When the Sisters arrived upon the Cradle there was only stone and water floating in the void. The Sisters created the stars to hold back the darkness, and upon seeing the Cradle's emptiness, they despaired."

"You're quoting scripture?" Tommy asked.

"The First Canon," Devin said. "It's from the story of our creation, and how the Sisters delivered the light of the First Soul to the Sacred Mother." He gestured about the room. "Does it not match?"

"I guess, but why make a replica?"

"If I knew that, we wouldn't be stuck here."

"Hey, I recognize this!" Tesmarie shouted. They both turned. Tesmarie hovered above the well and pointed to the diamond orb in the center.

"Get back, Tes," Devin said, fearful of how close she hovered to the shimmering essence. "We still don't know what that—"

Her tiny hands brushed the orb. A sound like thunder clapped through the room. The floor shook. Stars rippled as if space itself were a disturbed lake of water. Devin readied his weapons, convinced they'd sprung a trap. Tesmarie zipped over to his shoulder, looking ashamed and worried.

"There," Jacaranda said, her own daggers at the ready. "The wall."

A line split the stars, then rotated, creating a circular hole of pure darkness in the center of the wall. Tendrils of shadow drifted like smoke through the opening, but they did not rise to the star-ceiling but instead sank to the stone as if burdened with a heavy weight. Devin aimed his pistol at its center, already doubting that his meager stone bullet would do anything to what emerged. That tear, that opening, it was a much larger version of the black scar that had marked the temple in the massacred alabaster faery village. Just like then, a monster emerged from the void to enter their world.

Fingers pierced through the hole. The darkness clung to it like oil. Arms followed. A perfectly bald head emerged, tilted to the ground so they could not see its face. The breach among the stars shrank as the monster passed through, closing behind it. The blasphemous thing rose to its full height, an imposing eight feet tall with arms so long its six-fingered hands rested upon the floor.

Tesmarie whimpered, and Devin swore out of revulsion. Where there should have been a face was instead a great swirling vortex of darkness, a sinking pit without a shred of light that rotated and churned for an eternal distance. Devin could stick his hand, his arm, his entire body into that devouring maw. It bore no eyes, no nose, no hair or fingernails, just a hungry mouth that could feast upon the entire world and not reach its fill. Devin looked upon a moving embodiment of the void: furious emptiness given form and substance.

And then it spoke. Its voice was a whisper of the reaping hour.

"Trespasser."

Devin fired at the center of its head. He watched in horror as the bullet froze in midair just before contact. A soft white light enveloped its surface. The bullet drifted into the vortex, starting along an outer edge before rotating inward, growing smaller and smaller with each revolution but never entirely vanishing on its path toward that infinitely distant center.

"Anwyn be merciful," Devin whispered.

The monster took two lumbering steps and then flung its arms forward, its hands reaching greedily for them. Jacaranda deftly stepped aside, her daggers a blur as they scraped its skin. Devin was forced to drop into a roll as the six-fingered hand swooshed the air just above his head. He came up swinging, his sword hammering at the nearest joint twice in rapid succession. He'd have cut through any normal bone and flesh, but the oily darkness appeared as strong as steel. Tesmarie had far better luck. Her moonlight blade slashed through the darkness like a heated knife through butter. Inky liquid shadow erupted from the cuts, splashed the ground, and immediately evaporated into pale smoke.

Tommy used the distraction to ready one of his spells. His hands slammed together. Words of power leapt off his tongue.

"Glaeis astam!"

Ice gathered above his head, assimilating into the form of a long, thin spear. Tommy pantomimed a throwing motion. The spear shot toward the monster as if thrown with the strength of a giant, its aim directly for the monster's face. With such size and force, the spear should have ripped the monster's head off its body. Instead the ice shimmered and broke into shards, each one swirling into the shadow vortex to be consumed.

"Aim for the body, not the head," Devin shouted. Goddesses damn it all, was Tommy not paying attention when he fired his bullet?

"Um, yeah, I see," Tommy said. He wiped sweat from his forehead and began another spell as Tesmarie swooped in for another pass. Her moonlight blade ripped a gash open across its chest, oily shadow spurting out like blood. Some landed across her wings, and she shrieked as if burned. Her wings ceased fluttering. Devin dove to catch her, and thankfully Tommy covered him with a sudden plume of fire erupting from his fingertips. The flames licked across its body, and deep patches of the darkness bubbled and hissed into black smoke.

The monster of the void released what Devin guessed to be its version of a scream. Wind sucked into its face, shrill and howling. Devin whispered a prayer to the Sisters to combat his growing horror. This monster, this blasphemous existence, simply should not be. It did not belong in their world. It should not walk the land they walked.

Tesmarie didn't appear to be physically injured from the splash of darkness that had struck her, but she clearly was not well. Devin fled to one of the walls and gently set her down, all the while the monster sucked in air and flailed at the flames on its body with its six-fingered hands.

"Are you all right, Tes?"

"I'm c-c-cold," she said. Her body shivered as she clutched her arms to her chest. "I d-d-d-don't like it."

"Stay here," he told her. "We'll win without you, I promise."

With Tesmarie recovering, that left Devin and Jacaranda to occupy the monster's attention. Devin readied his sword in both hands and rushed to attack. The monster had subdued the flames, and though it lacked any expression given the vortex that was its face, there was no doubt it was infuriated. Its hands punched and twisted with heightened urgency. Devin dodged the first two, but a third punch connected with his shoulder, and he gasped at the impact. It felt like being struck with a sledgehammer. He dropped to the ground and rolled. It was a wonder his collarbone wasn't shattered.

Jacaranda launched into an assault to buy Devin time. Her daggers punched tiny little holes into the skin, the deepest she could manage given its toughness. Any other foe would have died under the barrage. This monster, however, acted as if she were as threatening as a bumblebee. It swatted at her, its arms coming in at strange angles given its double set of elbows. Jacaranda danced through the jumble of limbs, but even with her skill it was only a matter of time before a blow connected.

An elbow struck her forehead, dazing her. One of its hands latched onto Jacaranda's arm and yanked her to a halt. The other looped around her like a rope, one elbow bending at her neck, the other at her throat. It lifted her off the ground with ease, her struggles like the protestations of a mouse in the grip of a hawk. It didn't crush her, though it certainly had the strength to do so. Instead it brought Jacaranda closer and closer to that swirling vortex of a face. Eager for her. Hungry for her.

Devin stabbed and thrust into the monster's abdomen, and a wordless scream poured from its throat. Nothing, his attacks did nothing, he was slicing stone with a feather, he was cutting a tree with a spoon. Jacaranda would die, and he would be helpless to save her.

"Aethos creare fulgur!"

Another plume of fire exploded off Tommy's fingertips, this one more tightly focused than the last. It bathed the monster's elbow, causing the inky darkness to shrivel and bleed. The fire roared hotter, Tommy screaming as his strength poured into the spell. The arm severed and dropped to the stone. Jacaranda twisted and struggled at the lone hand holding her, but she could still not break herself free. Devin took a running start and leapt, his sword swinging high above his head.

For once his sword cut into the monster's flesh. It wasn't much, just an inch, but it was enough to splash a small amount of shadow blood across Devin's body and make the thing release Jacaranda from its six fingers. Jacaranda hit the ground and rolled. Devin retreated as well, shocked by the intense cold seeping through his coat from where the blood landed. It evaporated in an instant, but he trembled at the thought of it striking his bare skin.

"Doesn't like fire," Tommy rambled nervously. "So fire good, face bad, body shots...Devin, I think I know what to do!"

"Good," Devin shouted. "Then do it!"

"All right, but hold it still. I need time."

Devin would have loved to hear how Tommy thought they could do just that. He sidestepped another lunging grab, then cried out as the second set of elbows bent at a sharp angle and slammed into his gut. He stabbed at it with his sword in retaliation. The metal slid off it, his only reward a tiny trickle of leaking shadow. Jacaranda fared no better with her daggers. He'd seen her fighting style, and he knew she fought to bleed out her opponents with lethal cuts to various arteries. There was no such hope here. Her cuts meant nothing. At best they annoyed the monster, which swung its twisting, weirdly bent arms at them in constant frustration.

All the while Tommy spoke as if in a trance.

"Aethos creare," he said. *"Aethos creare, Aethos creare."*

A spark of light ignited between his closely cusped hands. His mantra continued, and he widened the gap with each repetition. The fire swelled between his palms, growing with every inch he pulled his hands apart. Devin and Jacaranda attacked with ever-growing ferocity, refusing to allow the creature a chance to stop Tommy's spell. Devin found it easier and easier to fight alongside her, his familiarity of her speed and skill having grown considerably since their first battle against the songmother way back in the Oakblack Woods. He attacked when she retreated; he held firm when she needed an opening. Despite its incredible strength, they gave the monster no openings, no easy movement. They might sting it like mosquitoes, but by the Goddesses, they were a swarm.

"Aethos taban secus fulgur!" Tommy screamed, and then, immediately after, *"Duck!"*

Devin and Jacaranda dove to either side of the monster. The orb of fire was as large as Devin's chest, and it passed mere inches from his elbow before slamming directly into the shadow creature. Devin thought the ball of fire would explode, as most of Tommy's spells tended to do, but not this one. The fire slowed tremendously upon making contact with its oily skin, and then it *burned*. That hovering inferno drew the rest of the creature into it with a hunger to match the monster's gaping maw.

The rest of its chest slipped inside the inferno, then its waist and elbows. They melted as if within the center of a blacksmith's forge. The creature's long arms flailed about, reaching for something that wasn't there. In sank the arms. Up went the legs, drawn into the fire as if gravity meant nothing to that blistering yellow orb. The fire swirled into an infinite vortex, surrounded it, enveloping the chaos, the two mutually annihilating the other so that the orb shrank into nothing and then vanished. Not a single puff of smoke remained of either it or the creature, leaving the room suddenly quiet and dark.

"Holy fuck," Tommy said. His curse echoed in the silence. "It worked."

Jacaranda sheathed her daggers and helped Devin up to his feet.

"What was that...thing?" she asked.

"I don't know," Devin said. He grimaced from the pain in his shoulder. Goddesses above, that was going to be a lovely bruise. "The First Canon mentions only one creature held at bay by stars that hates fire and light."

"Wait. Wait." Tommy pointed at the vacant spot of air where the monster had vanished. "Are you telling me that scary thing was the fucking *void-dragon*?"

"A tiny part of it, maybe?" Devin said. "The stars are supposed to imprison it, but I guess when Tesmarie disturbed the well, it somehow weakened them."

"Unbelievable," Tommy said, not listening. "I slew the void-dragon. I'm a damn hero."

Devin slapped him on the chest.

"Good luck convincing anyone of that."

Tesmarie sat looking glum by one of the walls, and Devin knelt down before her to talk closer to her level.

"Are you all right, little one?" he asked her.

"I think so," she said. "I'm just a little cold, but being cold is fine, right? Humans are cold all the time."

"That we are, especially in the mountains."

She gave her wings a test. They appeared to buzz just fine, at least to his eyes.

"I'm sorry if you need more time to recover," he told her,

"but that's time I don't know if Adria has. Can you tell me more about what you recognized?"

"I think I can," she said. The faery flew back to the well, this time far more careful not to touch any part of it. She pointed to the perfectly spherical diamond. "Do you remember the starlight tear I tried to show you from the alabaster village? That's it, right there."

Devin stared at the orb. So that was what Janus had fetched from the forest? The starlight tear was involved in this strange room and its triangular well, but what was the true purpose? For what reason would he need an object that seemed to imperil the very stars that protected the Cradle from the ever-encroaching void?

"I'd say for now we let it be," he said. "The last thing we need is another one of those...monsters coming through."

"Couldn't agree more," Jacaranda said. "But this doesn't answer where Janus took Adria."

Devin shook his head.

"There must be a door or passageway somewhere in here. All of us, if we look together, I'm sure we'll find it."

And so they searched every inch of the room, the well, and the wall of stars. Devin's confidence withered with each passing hour. They searched for hidden runes. They scoured the floor for any variation in its smoothness. Tesmarie flew among the stars, tracing lines with her fingers in case another door required her touch. If it existed, it did not react.

"Damn it," Devin screamed as he kicked the wall. "Goddesses damn the whole fucking mess of it!"

He didn't know what to do. He didn't know where to go. Adria was here, right here, and somehow she was gone. Helpless didn't begin to describe how he felt. Instead of answers, he only had dozens more questions to add to his gut-wrenching terror as to what Janus might do to his sister. His frustration was bubbling beyond what he could control, and he felt as impotent before it as he was in this strange room.

Jacaranda put a hand on his shoulder and pulled him away from the stars.

"We've been here all night," she said. "Maybe when we come back fresh we'll have a better idea of how to find her."

Devin glanced at Tommy, who merely shrugged his shoulders.

"My brain is fried," his brother-in-law said. "I'm not saying we give up, but I don't think another two hundred laps around this room will lead us anywhere. Besides, maybe there's options we haven't considered."

"Like what?" he asked.

"Like maybe there is no secret door, and Adria never left."

Devin clenched his hands into fists and fought back an urge to vomit.

"Are you saying she was fed to that…thing…we killed?"

"I'm saying we have to accept it as a possibility."

"I don't have to accept a goddess-damned thing," Devin seethed. "She's not dead, you hear me? She's not dead, she's not gone, and she sure as fuck wasn't eaten by that void-creature we killed. Is that clear, Tommy?"

His brother-in-law took a cautious step back.

"Sure," he said. "Whatever you say, Devin."

They were all looking at him now, frightened or upset by his uncharacteristic outburst. Shame calmed the frustration twisting apart Devin's insides.

"I'm sorry," he said. He rubbed at his eyes and addressed the others. His bones felt made of glass. His emotions were a raw scrape of throbbing pain at the back of his skull. "All of you, I'm sorry. You've helped so much, and I couldn't do this alone."

"You needn't ask," Tesmarie said. She tried to smile despite her own clear exhaustion. "And we'll get your sister back, I know it! Tommy just needs some time to think and puzzle it out."

"Sure," Tommy said, with only a fraction of the faery's confidence.

They left through the door of the chamber. Upon their exit the stone smoothed out, the hourglass symbol flared with light, and then the illusionary wall shimmered back into view. Devin watched the change happen and wondered if he'd ever know his sister's fate. And if he did... would he want to?

"I need some solitude," he told the others once they exited the vacant house. "I'll meet you back home."

"Are you sure that's wise?" Jacaranda asked.

"It has nothing to do with what's wise," he said. "Good night, for what's left of it, anyway."

Alone he walked the streets of Londheim, but in his mind he was far from solitary. A never-ending maw hovered over his vision, swirling with horror and nightmares. He thought of his sister, captive and helpless, confronted by such a monster.

Sisters, please, he prayed within the tormented echo of his mind. *Please, of all the fates, don't let that have been hers. Don't do this. Not to her. Not to me.*

Devin's heavy footsteps echoed long and loud upon the stone, but he did not fear the swoop of an owl or a lurking monster in the fog. Morning wasn't far, and truth be told, a dark part of him would have welcomed the chance to release his confusion and exhaustion through his sword in a shower of blood and gore.

CHAPTER 42

Devin stopped at the gates to the cemetery and rapped them twice with his knuckles.

"Are you napping again, Willem?" he called when no one came.

The door to the accompanying shack opened, and out came a man Devin did not recognize. He was far younger than Pyrehand Willem, who had managed the graveyard for the last two decades. Based on the uneven stubble across his chin and the youthful skin, Devin guessed the Pyrehand had obtained his rank within the last year.

"It's Jeffrey," the young man said. He pulled his leather coat tighter across his body and shivered. "And I'm sorry for the wait, Soulkeeper. This close to morning is the hardest time to keep the eyes open."

"Where is Pyrehand Willem?" Devin asked, ignoring the excuse.

The new Pyrehand shoved his hands into his pockets and

hunched his shoulders, as if trying to capture every shred of heat released by his body.

"Disappeared," he said. "Might have fled east, or maybe an owl got him. It's hard to tell anymore these days."

A pang of loss rippled through Devin's breast. Willem had been one of his few connectors to the past, a tenable link to his late wife, Brittany. He'd been a good man, and a good friend, during the hard months after. Losing him curdled his already sour mood.

"May the Sisters watch over him," Devin said. "I seek a moment of privacy. Consider yourself relieved of your post for its final hour. Eat, sleep, do whatever you wish, but I ask that I not be disturbed."

Jeffrey shifted his weight from foot to foot in uncertainty. Cities like Londheim were far too large, and the numbers of Soulkeepers far too low, to deal with the number of reaping rituals necessary every given day. To handle that toll, the church had created the Pyrehands, men and women trained solely in Anwyn's Mysteries. They did not travel, or fight, but instead were assigned a district and its accompanying pyre and graveyard. They were inferior in rank to a Soulkeeper but still prided themselves in their abilities. Relinquishing their duties to a Soulkeeper was generally seen as an insult.

"You just want some privacy, yeah?" he asked. "I'll be here in my home, but I won't leave until the dawn. Will that suffice?"

Devin fought back a sigh. The young were always the most ardent sticklers for rules and protocol. Old Willem would have been thrilled with an early end to his post. Once the reaping hour passed, the Pyrehands were little more than glorified babysitters to the dead.

"It'll do," Devin muttered. Jeffrey unlocked the gates, and Devin leaned his weight upon them to open them wider.

"Pleasant nights," Jeffrey said before returning to the relative warmth of his tiny home.

The thin layer of snow crunched beneath Devin's boots. He passed through the rows with easy remembrance. After a soul departed the body, the remains were burned upon the pyre and the ashes scattered into nearby fields and forests. If the soul remained, though, then it faced the ignoble fate of burial. For the longest time a burial was seen as a rejection by Anwyn, indicating some hidden sin or blasphemy. Some ninety years ago the Keeping Church officially denounced this belief, but many traditions remained, the most prominent being the law against naming or numbering gravestones.

Every row was identical to the last. Small triangles made of three stones marked the location of the graves, each triangle carefully swept free of snow by the graveyard's Pyrehand. Without names or records there'd be no shaming of the dead for the failure of the soul to separate from the body. No seeing a name on a tombstone and wondering what they had done in life to deserve their transitory state.

Devin walked to the seventh marker in the ninth row. Markings might have been illegal, but that had not stopped him from carving a nearly imperceptible groove into each of the three stones that rested above his wife's grave. He knelt in the snow and leaned closer, confirming his location. The silence of the dead settled over him. So many times he'd come here when his heart was troubled. Devin feared this might be the last.

He bowed his head and pressed a gloved hand into the snow to rest palm first atop the cold ground. Eyes closed, he let his attuned mind wander. A graveyard was a powerful place. Beneath him dozens of souls awaited Anwyn's summons to the starry sky. If he held his breath and cleared his mind he sometimes believed he could touch their presence. Their ethereal power would wash over him like the warm, comforting light of a campfire. In rare moments he convinced himself he felt a connection to Brittany's trapped, restless soul. Other times he swore he imagined it, for surely on some quiet night over the years the goddess Anwyn had called his beloved home. That confusion, of not knowing where her soul lay, was the worst.

Jacaranda's footfalls were expertly placed and quiet, and only the unnatural silence allowed Devin to hear her approach. He kept his stance low and his head bowed. Talking was the furthest thing from his mind.

"I asked for solitude," Devin said.

Jacaranda crossed her legs underneath her and sat opposite him in the snow. She'd pulled her hood off her head, and her red hair was dusted with snow. Her violet eyes sparkled in the moonlight.

"Don't you remember?" she said. "I'm not compelled to follow orders anymore."

Devin put his hand atop the triangle between them. The part of him that was decent and good reminded himself that Jacaranda had suffered just as much as he had, if not more. The petty and wounded part of him wanted to lash out and refuse any comfort and companionship.

"Why did you follow me?" he asked.

"I...I don't know the right way to say this," she began. "I'm sure it won't mean much, not with your sister still missing, but... but I want to try, all right? I want you to know I appreciate your coming with me to Gerag's mansion. Maybe it won't help, but I hope it does."

Devin looked away. He didn't want her to see his bitter smile.

"I promised to help you with your revenge that first night you awakened," he said. "How could I not go? I'd shoved aside your cares to focus on my own for weeks. Don't thank me for coming. Curse me for waiting so long."

"I did not come to curse you. How could I?"

"Are you sure? The rest of the world's been happy to shit on me; it only seems fair you join in."

Her hand settled on his shoulder. He looked up, expecting hatred or pity on her beautiful face. Instead he saw worry.

"Devin," she said softly. "Are you back in the pit?"

Cold tears struggled at the edges of his eyes.

"I don't know," he whispered. "I feel so worthless. That void-monster would have killed us all if not for Tommy's magic. When you were in its grip, I was so certain you'd...I feel so helpless, Jac. My gun and swords are meaningless in this new world we've awoken into. All my training, all my preparation and sacrifice, and I can't protect anyone I care for."

Jacaranda brushed her other bare hand across the side of his face, tracing warmth upon his chilled skin. She did not cower from his naked emotion. Those violet eyes met his with nothing but compassion.

"Is that what breaks you?" she asked. "You fear you cannot protect us?"

"I know I can't," he said. "I couldn't save the miners in Oakenwall. I couldn't save Marigold from Gerag's possession. Tonight it was my own sister who needed me, and I failed like I've always failed. I've failed you, Adria, Brittany..."

His guilt crushed him into silence. His hands clawed the earth and snow. His jaw trembled with his every breath. Shivers shook through his upper back and shoulders, and he felt himself a beast struggling to escape a cage.

"Brittany's death," she said. "You blame yourself, don't you? How did she die, Devin? Please, tell me. I need to know why you think it was your fault."

"My fault?" At last his tears began to fall, more stubborn than the cold itself. "No, it wasn't her *death* that was my fault, Jacaranda. She passed away from pains in her chest. I wasn't even there when it happened. I arrived a few minutes before the reaping ritual."

Jacaranda looked to the triangle of stones between them. Her sharp mind made the connection. Still no pity as he expected. She said nothing, only waited for him to continue. Her gaze was a weight upon his already tired shoulders. He wanted to explain his grief to her. He wanted to break himself down into pieces so she might see the true wreckage of his existence.

"If only I'd prayed harder," he said. "If I'd more cleanly drawn the symbol of the Sisters upon the earth. I even saw it, Jacaranda, I did, I saw the brief shimmer of the luminescent memories and emotions that were her soul break free of her forehead...and then I reached out for it."

Devin lifted his palm and stared into its center. He remembered the orb of light steadily rising within the blue shaft stretching up to the stars themselves. To touch a soul would burn your flesh to the bone, but for one brief moment he thought he could reconnect to his lover. He would touch, not fire, but the eternal personification of his love. It was a fool's delusion.

"I pulled my hand away for only for a split second," he said. "But it was enough to damn her. The soul retreated back into her body. I prayed, I begged, I cursed the Sisters and covered the ground with their symbol...it changed nothing. The reaping hour passed, and her soul remained."

Devin forced himself to a stand. He couldn't bear the close proximity to the grave anymore. Jacaranda stood with him, and she brushed loose snow from her knees.

"When I found you here that night," she said. "You were performing another reaping ritual for her soul, weren't you?"

Devin softly nodded, and he felt almost embarrassed to admit it true.

"The whole world changed. My sister heals with a touch. Tommy commands fire and lightning. I thought that perhaps things had changed for me as well. Perhaps I could finally do what I failed to do years ago, and send Brittany's soul through the void to Anwyn's waiting arms. I didn't, of course. I failed like always."

Jacaranda took his hands in hers, and he was touched by the simple gesture.

"Why does this bother you so?" she asked. "Brittany's soul is in the Goddesses' hands, is that not what you believe? Even if it takes until the end of all days for the Sisters to call her soul onward, she'll still make the voyage."

"Because..." Devin felt heat growing in his neck. Could he be so vulnerable as to admit it? He couldn't look at Jacaranda. He couldn't speak the words if he saw her violet eyes watching him intently. "Because I thought, if she moved on, then maybe I could move on, too. That maybe I was finally ready for another to occupy that same place within me that she once did."

Jacaranda's silence lingered heavily, each second a prolonged torment. Fog rolled alongside them. Scratches of daylight peeked over the distant walls.

"Do you love me, Devin?" she asked softly.

"I don't know," he whispered back. "What I do know is that I am blessed to be in your presence, and that your smile is a warm fire across my heart. I know that whatever time I spend with you is never enough. Is this love? Perhaps not yet, but it's close, and I'd give anything to make it closer."

Jacaranda moved beside him. Devin didn't know what her response would be, and he both feared it and anticipated it in equal measure. Her left arm slid about his waist underneath his coat. Her right took his hand and guided it over and around her shoulder, tucking her body against his in a gentle embrace. She pressed the side of her face against his shoulder and slowly, softly, exhaled.

"Do I love you?" she whispered. For whom she asked, he did not know.

She stood on her tiptoes and gently kissed his lips. Electricity sparked throughout his entire body. There was a trembling hesitancy to her kiss that made it feel all the more special, like catching in your palm the first snowflake of winter. When she pulled away, they each inhaled shallow breaths.

"I don't know if I can," she whispered. "The thought of anyone touching me floods me with panic, but—but not you. Not in the same way. Give me time, Devin. I don't think I love you yet, but maybe one day."

For Devin, that was more than enough. He cherished her embrace. The times since the black water had been lonely and isolating. He'd been wrong to think his troubles unique. Everyone carried different burdens, true, but they carried burdens nonetheless. All the world was changing, and if they were to survive, they'd need to cling to one another. They needed to trust one another. Tommy, Adria, even little Tesmarie and Puffy, they were his lifeblood now.

Devin leaned his head against Jacaranda's and wished he could give her a shred of the comfort her presence offered him. Time slipped away, and Devin did not regret a single second of it. The way she shifted showed that something bothered her, and he patiently waited for her to give it voice.

"I'm scared of Gerag," she said, finally breaking the silence. "He knows I'm alive now, and that you were involved. He might send Tye after us, or reveal my escape to the church."

Devin had given some thought to the problem, but not as much as he should, given Adria's disappearance. He let the situation slide through his mind, the pieces of it breaking down into options and decisions.

"Once Adria is safe, you and I will hunt down and kill Gerag Ellington, no matter the consequences afterward," he said. "He's a man undeserving of a burial, but you ... you deserve the world."

Jacaranda playfully snickered at him.

"Is this how a Soulkeeper flirts?" she asked.

"This is how a man who has not flirted or courted in six years does, perhaps," he said, laughing.

She kissed his cheek, her lips just as electric as the first time, and then leaned her head atop his shoulder. Together they watched the sun crest over the walls of Londheim. Lancing golden rays pierced the surrounding fog, and for the first time that night Devin realized the two of them were not alone.

"Devin?" Jacaranda said, stiffening against him, her shoulders twisting so his grasp about her broke. She pulled her arm away from his waist, her hand naturally falling to her dagger.

"I see them, too," he said softly. "Stay calm. They can do no harm."

Men, women, and children drifted through the fog. They walked with their heads to the sky, searching for something they could not find. Their skin was pale as the moon, their clothes muted as if covered by a fine layer of dust. Their outfits varied wildly in styles, like locked moments of time drifting about with ethereal quietness. An elderly man approached them directly, though he showed no sign of seeing them.

"Tasha?" he mumbled to himself. "Where are you, Tasha? Grandpa promised you kisses when he returned home."

Devin took Jacaranda's hand in his and clutched it tightly. The ghostly man passed through them, his gait never slowing. His passing was a layer of ice sweeping through Devin's body from one side to the other. He let out a soft gasp. Little could compare to that strange touch. The presence was frost, yet fire seemed to burn from every inch of his skin.

Did the Sisters grant them this vision? Or was this another part of the changing world? He watched these wandering souls and gave his heart to them. In the time of Eschaton it was said that even these would be carried home in Anwyn's arms as the earthly realm was swallowed into nothing and made anew, a perfect place free of the void-dragon's corruption. Then they would know peace. For now they looked skyward, as if they knew that was where they belonged. Each one whispered and muttered to themselves the names of loved ones and forgotten places, lost in their own world of memories.

Devin searched these wanderers without admitting to himself the reason. He didn't want to give it voice or form, as if that alone might deny it happening. The bodies were steadily fading into the fog as the sun rose higher. Their numbers thinned, one by one, until in the far corner of the graveyard he saw his most precious ghost.

"Brittany?" Devin said. He dared not believe it. There she was, dressed in her finest coat and gray Soulkeeper garb. Her tricorn hat tilted to one side atop her head, just as she always preferred it. Jacaranda slipped her hand from his. Confused emotions whirled through him at a rapid pace. Six years after her death, he could see her. Talk to her. He walked without realizing it, closing the distance between them. She lingered in the fog, eyes to the brightening sky.

"Brittany," Devin said, louder. "Brittany, it's me!"

She paused. His heart lit like a bonfire. Her eyes, her perfect blue eyes, turned his way. At first they showed only confusion, but then a tiny spark of recognition twisted her head. Her brow furrowed. Her mouth opened slightly. Every move she made was an instant link to a thousand memories, each little habit equally beloved.

"Devin?"

He'd carried a wish to hear her speak his name since the reaping ritual. The snow crunched beneath his boots as he ran. His arms reached out as if diving to save her from falling off a cliff. All else faded to black in his vision, just her, shining like a pale candle.

Brittany vanished into the fog before he ever touched her. He collapsed to his knees. His chest heaved. The sun rose higher, its warmth a mockery. The Soulkeeper stared into nothing, his entire mind numb. He didn't want to move. He didn't want to speak. He didn't want to do anything.

Jacaranda's hand gently settled atop his shoulder.

"She saw you. She remembered you. I hope that gift was enough."

His tears fell upon the snow. The weight of the night broke him. His arms slumped. Long-closed wounds bled afresh, and he wondered how long until the hurt would cease. He wiped at his face, painfully aware of Jacaranda's presence.

"Fuck me, I'm a mess."

Jacaranda laughed. It was so pure. So genuine. She knelt beside him, took his chin into her hands, and gently turned his gaze her way.

"It's time to go home," she said. "Don't make me carry you."

Her smile lit his darkness. Joy among misery. Compassion among sorrow. She was everything a Soulkeeper could wish to be, and it made him cherish her that much more.

"I don't need to be carried," he said. A broken laugh sent more tears rolling down his face. "But if you'd like, I'd love for you to walk at my side."

CHAPTER 43

Darkness greeted Adria's eyes when she opened them. Her stomach hitched, and for a moment she feared she'd vomit. Where was she? What was going on? She tried to move but nausea pinned her body firmly in place. A sound thumped in her ears. A heartbeat. Was it hers? If only she could sit up...no, she was already standing. Her feet shifted side to side. Not imprisoned, then; only her hands were locked in place.

"It wakes," a voice spoke from the darkness. Adria's breath caught in her throat. She knew that voice. Her most recent memories crashed into her, and it took years of trained discipline to remain calm when she responded.

"It does."

A soft blue light wafted upward like electric mist from her feet, though its presence upon her carried a weight like water. In its steadily spreading glow she caught the grim smile of Janus hovering mere feet before her.

"You do not cower, plead, or threaten," he said. "There might be hope for you yet."

"Flattered," Adria said. She tugged again with her arms. She could see her robes and most of her body in the glow, and that included two metal poles sticking up from the smooth ground. The poles ended with two circles, each one a manacle about her wrists. A bizarre construction of metal surrounded her on either side, taller than her and containing dark rivets and juts that she had no names for.

"Indeed, you absolutely should feel flattered," he said. "Your brother and his friends search for you even now despite the danger. Their meddling summoned forth a sliver of the void. A shame they killed it. I can't think of a more fitting fate for a Soulkeeper."

"They'll find me," she said. "And when they do—"

"Spare me," Janus said, cutting her off. "We have more important matters to discuss."

The madman paced before her, his hands clutched behind his back like a debating professor. Adria watched him, noting his jittery movements, and how his cheek twitched like someone kept pricking him with a needle.

"Viciss finally told me the reason for your captivity," he said. He looked torn between laughter and rage. "The reason for everything, really, the chambers, the secrets, our own centuries of imprisonment. Such a cosmic joke. A world-shattering blessing will soon be placed into your hands. Frail human hands of a human woman. Are you worthy, Adria? Can *any* human be worthy?"

Adria ran the seventy-nine prayers of Lyra's Devotions through her mind. Which of them might help her here? None of them begged for harm, only aid, succor, and strength. Perhaps the circle that had protected her from the owl, but that had lasted only a moment.

"You ask a question I cannot answer," she said. "Worthy of what? What blessing could you offer that I would not refuse in a heartbeat?"

"My blessing?" He laughed. "Your mind thinks so small, Adria. The dragons themselves offer this blessing. Only a fool would refuse."

Perhaps if she could disorient Janus she might escape the manacles around her wrists, not that she'd have any idea where to go afterward. Darkness stretched in all directions, deep and ominous. Sena had encountered this monster before, and lived. What prayer had she used...?

"Perhaps I am merely a fool," she said, trying to stall.

"I think not," he said. "If you were, I'd have turned your body to lilies and scattered it across the river, a much kinder fate than the ash the Goddesses would leave you as."

He wasn't paying attention to her, not really. Janus was absorbed into his own thoughts, debating something she was not privy to. That was fine with her. She started quiet, hoping her whisper would go unnoticed.

"I am blind, but Lyra gives me sight."

Janus's palm slammed across her mouth, silencing her.

"Oh no you don't," he said. His forehead pressed against hers, and his jade eyes twinkled in the ethereal glow. "I would have us talk, but if you insist on misbehaving I will send you back into unconsciousness, and this time I'll make sure the journey is far more painful and unpleasant than the last."

Adria felt a sensation like fire burn across her lips. When Janus removed his hand she tried to open her lips, but something was wrong. The skin stretched, but it would not open. Her mind rebelled against the reason, but the more she struggled the more certain she was of the bizarre horror he had inflicted upon her. Her lips no longer existed. Her mouth was but one smooth covering of skin.

"Much better," Janus said. "I have things to say, and you have things to hear, so let's prevent you from doing something you will regret."

Adria nodded, for what else might she do? Janus resumed his pacing. His jade eyes watched her carefully, analyzing the slightest twitch or emotion she revealed.

"Your precious holy texts are correct when they say the Sisters arrived upon a barren plane of rock and decided to create life upon it. What they neglect to mention is the *first* world they built. From the beginning, they created with a flawed mentality: Their creations were either perfect or imperfect, and they could not stand the latter. They created a painted world, beautiful but pointless. Its inhabitants were no more alive and wondrous than an elaborately carved rock."

Janus paced before her, the speed of his steps steadily increasing along with his story.

"The Sisters deliberated upon their failures, singling out various aspects of existence they simply did not understand. They flooded these aspects with a piece of their own essence to give them form, substance, and power. Their lone act of brilliance, the creation of the dragons. Chyron, master of time both beginning and ending. Gloam, king of thought and reason. Viciss, lord of cyclical change. Aethos, the purest of them all, the embodiment of energy in all its forms. And last, Nihil, seed of all discord and conflict.

"The dragons set about correcting the mistakes of the Sisters. Chyron declared that all beings have their end, whether it be days or centuries, to lend urgency to their lives. Nihil's gift swept through the land, and no longer would beings thrive solely through symbiotic exchange, but through conflict. Let animal and plant devour one another, destroying the weak and elevating the strong. Gloam looked upon the Sisters' sentient creations and gifted them with doubt, fear, and uncertainty. They would not walk certain of the Sisters' presence, their minds locked in rigid, preapproved patterns, but instead would question everything so that invention and creativity could flourish. Viciss shaped the seasons and the tides so that there was always a sensation of change and renewal. Aethos lent his aid to the others, shaping the world with eruptions of lava, shifts in tectonics, and great downpours of rain so that the land could support a great variety of life instead of coddling a few, singular creations.

"The greatest of these new beings shared in the dragons' gifts and contained the same innate mastery over elements, time, and thought. They were homages to the creator, sharers of the responsibility to breed a world full of life and awe. These were the dragon-sired, most beloved of all, and for thousands of years we walked the Cradle in a true paradise."

Janus turned her way, and she trembled beneath his seething hatred and disgust.

"And then the Sisters created *you*. The supposed culmination of every lesson the dragons had imparted. Even then their pride interfered. This human race would bear no link to the dragons, and would share none of their innate gifts. You'd be theirs, only theirs, their precious little children. They tried to downplay the aspects they did not understand. They denied you claws or scales so you would be vulnerable, and therefore cooperate instead of compete. They gave you short lives so you would rebel against the pull of time. Sermons and rituals would tame your doubts, and the Keeping Church would ensure that all questions were answered with unyielding faith. You would either master the elements like fire, or hide from them like the storm."

Janus shook his head. There was no hiding his disgust.

"The Sisters should have seen what would come next. Your frail, confused species would only crumble beneath the superiority of the dragon-sired. Instead of burying you beneath the sea, the Sisters reached through the void and clutched a piece of the same infinite power that gave them existence. The First Soul. Their indisputable proof of their preference of humans above all other creations."

Adria struggled against the sealed-over flesh of her lips. As dire as her situation was, she was fascinated with the monstrous man's knowledge. Here was a being that had walked the land alongside dragons, who spoke of the Goddesses with intimate knowledge. Perhaps he would kill her, perhaps he would give whatever "blessing" he spoke of, but either way she would attempt to garner what knowledge she could. Janus saw her attempting to speak, and after a momentary hesitation, he passed his fingers across her face. She felt the seal break. Cool air breathed across her teeth and tongue.

"What of the void-dragon?" she asked. "Is it true? Did it attempt to swallow the light of the First Soul?"

"I don't know," Janus said. He smirked. "I wasn't there. But I do know that your tales of the void-dragon's blood being the reason for your flaws and sins is utter nonsense. Like all their creations, your flaws were of the Sisters' own making."

Thin cracks of light were beginning to grow upon the ceiling, and Adria realized they were faint only because they were so far away. A brief vertigo passed over her as she suddenly understood that she stood in the center of a domed opening thousands of feet high. Nine little streams of light pulsed like veins toward her from all directions before connecting to the machinery flanking her sides. Where in Anwyn's name was she?

"Why tell me this?" she asked. "Why do you care what I know, or what I believe?"

"The gift you are to receive would crush the weak. This power would sow chaos in the selfish hands of a coward." Janus was not mocking her. He wasn't angry. His eyes shook with intensity. His words carried such earnestness it bordered on desperation. "For once, just once, humanity might become worthy. They might become *free* of imprisonment to the Sisters, no longer chained to their life-and-death cycle of souls. You could lead them there, but it involves a heart and mind willing to go beyond rote dogma and slavish loyalty."

He shook his head and clenched his teeth. Adria could hardly believe how panicked he suddenly looked, how unsure.

"Viciss requested a champion, and so I have chosen you. I cannot have chosen wrong. I cannot! You have heard my words, Mindkeeper. The Sisters are imperfect. They have failed, again and again, and they have failed you most of all. This gift, this burden, could you bear it? Is your heart willing? Did I make the right choice, Adria? Tell me, did I?"

Adria licked her dry lips. He pleaded for an answer. He hung on her every word. For once since waking up, she held a scrap of power over him, and she would not waste it.

"Anwyn of the Moon, hear me," she said. She felt the power reverberate within her head the moment the first syllable left her tongue. Janus stiffened instantly, as if a great chain had wrapped about his form. "This flesh before me hides its rot. This smile belies its sickness. These bones deny the weakness within. Anwyn, hear me, Anwyn!"

Janus's skin bubbled as if it floated atop a pot of boiling oil.

"Tear."

Flesh ripped and separated seemingly at random to expose muscle.

"Break."

He screamed as his arms and legs twisted at irregular angles. His fingers bent backward. His ribs collapsed inward.

"Sunder."

A force like a charging bull smashed Janus to the ground, grinding and twisting his mangled form so that nothing remained as it should. The last words exited Adria's tongue with a sudden calmness, a finality to the power she had already wrought.

"Show me truth."

Janus lay on the smooth ground in a frighteningly similar replica of the state to which Mindkeeper Tamerlane had cursed Deakon Sevold. Adria tugged on her manacles, trying to see if she had any room to move. Not much at all, but there was some give. With enough time, and perhaps with a bit of blood and torn skin, she might finally...

Janus laughed, and laughed. His malformed body twisted and shaped like clay. In mere seconds he had undone the damage. Eyes crazed with rage stared into hers, and he flashed her his opal teeth.

"Did you think my body as unmalleable as a human's?" he asked. "That the distortion of change into corruption might affect one who is the embodiment of Viciss's will? You would *curse* me, Mindkeeper? *Me?*"

Janus closed the distance between them. At any moment she feared he'd kill her with his rapidly mutating hands of blade and bone. His lips hovered beside her ear. His words were a seductive whisper, and they trembled from his barely controlled intensity.

"You whispered the words of a Ravencaller. You invoked

forbidden power. Here, in this chamber of demigods, you tossed aside the Sisters' demands so you might survive." He leaned closer. His warm breath blew across her neck. "I chose perfectly."

His hands were on her wrists before she knew what was happening. Janus broke the constraints, bent down, and grabbed the two sides of whatever construction she stood within. With a screech of metal, he slammed them shut over her, locking her inside. While the sides were solid, a large portion of the substance before her was translucent, and through it she saw Janus staring at her. Smiling at her. She pounded at the sides, but he said not a word before he walked away into the darkness.

At her feet, the blue liquid swirled higher and higher.

CHAPTER 44

Devin had not expected to sleep when he lay down on his bed to rest his sore muscles, but his exhaustion had different ideas. He stirred hours later with his head pounding and his throat cracked and dry as a desert. However much he slept, his body desired more, but it'd have to wait. Daylight slipped through the cracks of his drawn shutters, and in their thin rays he dressed for another excursion to the strange chamber underneath the city.

When he exited he was surprised to find Tommy, Jacaranda, and Tesmarie all waiting for him in his living room.

"There you are!" Tommy said, and he hopped up from his seat. Of all of them, only he seemed to be awake and energetic. "It's a long story, maybe not that long, I guess, but nonetheless with Tesmarie's help and a timeshroom I believe I cracked the code to the underground chamber's power conduit."

Devin rubbed at his eyes and tried to focus through the cobwebs of his mind.

"Say that again, but make sense this time," he said.

"Oh, um, all right," Tommy said. "How's this: I spent all night at the strange chamber and I think I know where Adria is."

That got his attention. Devin glared at the group, his frustration mounting.

"What? Why didn't you wake me?"

Jacaranda lifted her hands defensively.

"Don't ask me," she said. "I woke up ten minutes ago. This is the first I'm hearing of it myself."

"Fine. Please, forgive my rudeness, Tommy. How did you discover where Adria is?"

"Tesmarie gave me a mushroom that made me not need to sleep a wink," Tommy explained. "Something about time manipulation and hypersleep. That's why I called it a time-shroom, earlier. A little joke, you . . . right, not in a joking mood, sorry. Anyway, it looks like whatever the well in the center is, it started to activate. There's a thin line of light leaking from it to a wall, and I surmised that if it was conducting the substance of the well toward some specific direction, then surely a tunnel was also there following it."

"So you found a tunnel?" Devin asked.

"Yes. It took a few hours, but I finally found a panel on the wall where a star was not a star, but a button that activated . . . honestly I don't know what it activated, but it caused a door to appear."

Devin felt his excitement and dread growing in equal measure. They might still save Adria from Janus, or they might discover whatever terrible fate had befallen her.

"Are all of you ready to go?" he asked.

They nodded in affirmative. Even Puffy hopped out of the fire and stomped its feet atop the brick of the fireplace.

"You too?" he asked.

Puffy bobbed its head up and down. Devin could not describe how touched he felt. A few weeks ago he'd not even known most of them, but here they were ready to give their lives to help him save his sister.

"Thank you," he said. "All of you, thank you for being here when I needed you. I pray I can ever repay your kindness."

"We're not doing this to get paid," Tesmarie said, and she swirled around Devin's head and harrumphed. "Stop being a silly human and grab your sword and pistol."

Devin donned his coat and hat, then began the process of buckling his sword belt and holster to his waist.

"What about the church?" Tommy asked as they watched. "A few more Soulkeepers wouldn't hurt."

Devin glanced at Jacaranda's exposed tattoo on her throat, then the onyx faery and firekin. The Keeping Church knew about none of these three, nor that they lived with him in his home. The same went for Tommy's magic, and Devin could only guess as to what the church would think of that.

"The Keeping Church may not approve of my friendship with any of you," he said. "Worse, they may view you as threats to Londheim. If I must choose between all the Soulkeepers of Londheim and you four, I'm taking you four. Now let's go save Adria."

The five traveled through Londheim, a most bizarre assortment for a rescue team. Devin carried a torch in his left hand, Puffy safely disguised within its flame. Tesmarie huddled inside one of his deep pockets, explaining only that she felt uncomfortable going out in public since Janus attacked the market. Devin remembered the address well enough that he needed only the occasional reminder from Tesmarie as to where to turn. When they reached the dilapidated home, it was strange to look upon it in the sunlight. Nothing about it appeared special or unique, but he could still feel that intangible sense of power rolling outward in all directions. Even the men and women passing by on the street gave the home a wide berth, as if they, too, could somehow sense the chamber of stars and monsters hidden underneath.

Once inside, Tesmarie swirled away the illusionary wall like so many grains of sand and then put her hand atop the center until it opened. Devin drew his pistol and placed the cold barrel against his forehead. His eyes closed, and those around him fell silent as he whispered his prayer.

"Lyra, guide our steps this day as you do all days. Protect the life Alma gave us, and should we fall, deliver us swiftly into Anwyn's embrace."

He lowered his pistol, and the heavy silence broke with Tommy's sudden, awkward exclamation.

"Oh! I almost forgot!" He dug into his pocket and came out holding what appeared to be a flamestone, except instead of red it was colored a strange swirl of yellow and orange. "I made this while waiting for you and Jacaranda to wake up."

"What is it?" Devin asked as he accepted the gift.

"Well, when we fought that horrifying void-monster thing, your pistol wasn't exactly...how do I say this nicely...doing anything of significance."

"That's one way to put it," Devin muttered.

"Well, since we might encounter another one of those things, and fire was effective in destroying them, I made you that. It's a flamestone, but with a time-delayed spell enchanted into it that will trigger upon any significant burst of energy."

Devin rolled the flamestone between his thumb and forefinger.

"Try again, Tommy."

His brother-in-law scratched at his chin.

"Put it in your pistol and pull the trigger. You'll shoot one of my fire spells, so aim carefully."

"Interesting," Devin said. "Are you sure it will work?"

"Uhh... mostly sure?"

Devin put the flamestone in a separate pouch from the rest.

"Emergencies only, then," he said, and he winked at his friend.

They returned to the chamber of stars. Immediately Devin sensed a change in the air. The stars pulsed with new life. The well itself appeared to overflow with the blue-white essence that dripped into it from the domed ceiling. Just as Tommy described, a small line of it poured over the edge, the light a little wider than his finger. It raced toward the star wall and then vanished.

Tesmarie flew among the stars for a moment while muttering to herself. Tommy joined her, and after tracing a few formations they found the specific one they'd mentioned. Tommy pushed it with his thumb. Instantaneously an opening appeared where the stream of star essence reached the wall, exposing a long tunnel lit only by that thin glowing line in its center.

"How far does it go?" Devin wondered.

"Half a mile at least," Tommy said. "We didn't go far before we decided it best to turn around and bring everyone."

"A wise decision," Devin said. He took point, Jacaranda and Tommy not far behind. They didn't speak, and even Tesmarie fell silent after a few minutes as she hovered around their shoulders. Everyone's nerves were tightening, their minds preparing for battle. Puffy shuddered atop his torch after a minute. Devin had not even considered that the firekin might be afraid, but those little black eyes were spread as wide as they could go.

"Do you not like it here?" he asked as they walked.

Puffy enlarged its head slightly so it could shake in the negative.

Time and distance lost any semblance of meaning as they walked the long dark tunnel. It never turned, though many times it dipped lower, taking them deeper and deeper into the earth. No fire burned on Devin's torch but what composed Puffy's body, diminishing their light but preventing the release of any smoke. A distant hum greeted them, steadily growing louder with each step they took. The vibrations were deep and thick enough that he felt it in his bones. After another lengthy slope downward they saw an end to the tunnel and a massive room beyond.

"Be ready for anything," Devin whispered. Power pulsed through the tunnel, much stronger than before, and at last he recognized the sensation. It was the same heightened intensity he felt during the reaping hour. Pistol leading, he exited the tunnel and stepped into a room from another world.

The center chamber was a dome like the first, only a hundred times as grand. No otherworldly stars graced the ceiling. An uneven mixture of flesh and metal hung above their heads, the support rafters switching between iron and bone seemingly at random. White veins pulsed with stardust instead of blood, and it was their light that granted them sight. The ground was smooth but soft, and with a pale pink color to it. Devin feared to stab it with his sword lest blood spurt forth and his mind break trying to understand. Nine different beams of light converged from various tunnels into an enormous steel heart at its center. Multiple pipes connected to the top and bottom like veins and arteries, but it was not blood that pumped through them but instead that blue-white star essence from the peripheral chambers. The walls of this heart were clear like glass, the interior swirling with a bluish liquid that flowed like smoke.

Inside that heart Adria beat against the sides and screamed.

"Sisters be merciful," Devin said. "Get her out of there!"

He ran across the soft ground, the others at his heels. Panic coursed through his veins. That blue smokelike liquid covered her head, and by all rights she should have drowned, yet Adria clearly was awake and drew breath. He was now close enough to hear her, and she shouted at him from inside.

"Run!" she begged. "Run, now, while you can!"

"Not a chance," Devin shouted back. He circled the heart but he saw no door, no opening, nothing. Out, out, he had to get her out! He touched the glass, trying to decide whether it'd be safe to shatter it with Adria so close to it inside. His insides squirmed. Large parts of that heart might be steel, but there was no denying what his senses told him. Not glass, no, that he could understand. Instead it felt like flesh; this barrier was some sort of clear membrane sealing his sister inside. Devin struck it with his sword, but the sharp edge did nothing, not even scratch it.

Slow, steady applause turned him from the heart to the green-and-black specter of Janus emerging from one of the other tunnels.

"You've proven more resourceful than I anticipated," Janus said, casting a disapproving glare at Tesmarie. "Though perhaps I should not give you humans credit when the aid of dragon-sired allowed what progress you made."

Devin positioned himself between Adria and Janus, finally able to put a face to the monster that had been attacking his fellow keepers of the church.

"Release her and I'll let you live to stand trial," he said.

"A trial? By a court of your fellow ignorant sacks of meat and blood?" Janus shook his head. "I shall not be judged by those who cannot begin to understand the importance of our actions. Put away your weapons and sing praises to the heavens, all of you. You shall witness humanity's potential salvation. There is no reason to resist. Your sister is not in danger; quite the opposite. We shall make her as a goddess. Your people will revere her as you do your Sacred Mother, but unlike her, your sister's name shall be remembered, and echo on throughout the coming centuries."

Devin wanted no part of that, and he doubted his sister did, either. He cast his torch to the ground and readied his weapons. Jacaranda twirled her daggers, and Puffy reluctantly hopped off the torch and glared with his beady black eyes. Devin could not interpret the strange man's look. Was he disgusted by them, or was it merely pity?

"Let her go," Devin said. "I won't ask you again."

"Indeed, you won't," Janus said. "I gave you a chance, which should be enough for Viciss to find me faultless in what I do next. Let statues of gold and silver bear witness to the coming miracle. We have no need of a living audience."

Janus's right hand elongated into a sharpened blade. He smiled, eager for battle. In return, Devin shot him in the face with his pistol. It should have been lethal, but his lead bullet was a weapon for a different world, not this land of magic and power. Janus's face and neck molded from flesh to steel the instant his finger pulled the trigger. The bullet ricocheted off his cheek, leaving not a dent.

"Come now," he said. "I offer swordplay and you betray me with a cowardly shot? I thought Soulkeepers were to be the most honorable of humans."

"You kidnapped my sister," Devin said as he readied his sword. "Forgive me for thinking you'd prefer anything resembling a fair fight."

"Keep him surrounded," Jacaranda said softly as she stepped up beside him. "Our only hope is the magic of the others."

"Understood," Devin said, as much as he hated the feeling of uselessness.

The two rushed the madman. Janus tilted his head to one side, as if amused by their teamwork. His other arm twisted into a second blade, just as brilliantly sharp as the first. The next thirty seconds passed in a blur. Devin cut and slashed wholly on the offensive. Janus made no attempts to counter or seize initiative. He merely parried and blocked, feeling out their speed, each individual arm moving as if they were of separate minds. Twice Devin thought he could shatter those thin sword arms with the weight and power of his sword. Neither time did those powerful downward chops even dent the fine edge of the blade.

Jacaranda feinted a dual thrust, sidestepped, and then slashed for his shoulder. Janus rotated his upper body underneath, twisted so his hip slammed into Devin's hip, and came out of the turn slashing. Devin barely blocked in time, otherwise his head would have gone rolling across the floor. Jacaranda pressed again, thinking herself at an advantage with Janus's back to her. It was a lie. Janus pulled his hair off his head as if it were a wig, and three more eyes sprouted from his smooth, bald skull.

Jacaranda was so taken aback that she faltered in her footsteps, sapping her thrust of power. Janus trapped her extended arm between his elbow and his side.

"Your design limits you," Janus said. "I share no such weakness."

Devin swung his heavy sword in a chop at the opposite angle. Janus blocked it, twisted his sword arm so the sword slid along the bladed edge, and then kicked Devin in the chest. Jacaranda jammed the dagger of her free arm at Janus's spine. It pierced the jacket but not the set of silver scales that emerged from underneath the tearing skin. Janus released her arm, spun to face her, and slashed with both arms. She moved to block, but suddenly the swords were not swords but whips. The leather cords easily bypassed her meager block. Tongs lashed her skin, and she screamed at the pain.

"Glaeis astam," Tommy shouted. An ice spear formed above his head and shot straight for Janus's chest. Janus's whips reverted back to pink flesh, and he caught the spear on its travel. It melted into water in an instant, the spear doing little harm besides wetting his jacket.

"Was hoping for better than that," Tommy said. He started to cast another spell but Janus was ready for him now. Devin and Jacaranda converged from either side, attempting to be a distraction. It didn't matter. Janus was faster. He was the one fully in charge of the battle. Before Tommy could even finish another syllable Janus had crossed the distance between them.

"You steal power that is not yours to wield," Janus said as he rammed a fist into Tommy's gut. His other hand clutched Tommy's face, his fingers digging into skin. Little streaks of yellow lightning arched across where they touched, but Janus seemed not to notice the same power that had flung Devin across the room back in Crynn's tower. "Your words are treacherous leeches. Choke on them."

Tommy's entire body shuddered. His eyes widened, and suddenly he began to gag.

"You-you-you-let-him-go!" Tesmarie screamed, her moonlight blade a constant swirl of light carving rings across Janus's arm from wrist to elbow. His jacket exploded into fragments.

Pale blood trickled from the wounds that quickly resealed. It was enough to cause Janus to release poor Tommy, who collapsed to his knees and violently hacked and coughed. Blood trickled down his lips. He hitched, his face turned blue, and then he vomited. Black lumps squirmed amid the mess.

Leeches. Tommy was vomiting leeches.

"Learn your place, fae," Janus said. He caught Tesmarie by the ankles, struck her against his wrist to daze her, and then flung her across the room. She hit the soft ground and rolled, her pathetic whimper enough to spur Devin back to his feet.

"Get away from him," he said. "You're nothing but a monster."

"A monster?" Janus asked. He laughed at the insult. His fingers passed over his opal teeth, sharpening them into jagged points that would look more at home within the mouth of a lion. "Must you insult what you do not understand, human, or should I act the part to spare you the trouble?"

Jacaranda sprinted toward Tommy's choking form, but Janus spun her way and wagged a clawed finger.

"His fate is sealed," Janus said. "Worry for your own."

He leapt at them, his bare chest now a wall of muscled fur. His hands bore claws thicker than a bear's. Devin slashed and cut with his sword, his cuts barely drawing blood. Janus countered with a painful slash across Devin's arm. Blood poured down the interior of his jacket. That'd definitely need stitches, assuming he lived long enough to treat his wounds. Devin scored a cut on Janus's arm, earning him a brief reprieve, and Jacaranda dove in to take advantage.

It seemed Janus was merely toying with them. What Jacaranda thought was an opening was merely a trap. His knee found her stomach, his meaty fists her chest. She staggered back, her breath momentarily sapped from her lungs. Devin swung another high chop at Janus's neck, knowing he had to distract the madman lest he slaughter Jacaranda where she stood.

"Persistent, aren't you?" Janus asked as he caught Devin's sword arm at the wrist. His other hand latched onto Devin by the scruff of his shirt. Devin's free hand grabbed him in kind and he tried to yank himself free, but it felt like wrestling with a mountain. He kicked and kneed to no avail. This frightening relic of a forgotten past did not care in the slightest. The fabric of Devin's shirt stiffened. Changing. Becoming fur.

"Monsters," Janus said. His own face elongated like a wolf's. "Shall I make you what you believe I am, Soulkeeper?"

Puffy leapt atop Janus's back, scurried to his neck, and then flared with heat. Flesh burned but a moment before Janus twisted and reached for the firekin. His hand turned to ice, his burning shoulder immutable stone. Puffy struggled to keep a hold, but its size visibly dwindled in proximity to the ice. Blue fingers closed about its shrinking body.

"I always heard you firekin were the most reckless of Aethos's children," Janus said. "Why risk death to protect these meager beasts?"

Janus had released Devin's sword hand to swipe at Puffy. Was that how little he feared the steel blade? Perhaps so, but Devin would not waste the chance. He pulled his sword back and thrust, not for any vitals, but that blue hand. Devin might not be able to pierce steel, but he sure as the stars above could crack some ice.

His sword pierced through one of Janus's fingers and split his thumb in half. Puffy wiggled free as Janus cried out in pain. He flailed his arm, the ice turning to bark just before making contact with Devin's face. The impact sent Devin rolling across the ground, blood spilling from his scraped cheek. Goddesses above, Janus hit with the strength of a dozen men. He dragged himself up to his knees and sucked in a ragged breath. This fight couldn't last much longer. He had to end it now. He slipped his fingers into a pouch on his belt and palmed the special flame-stone Tommy had given him.

This better work, he thought as he slid the vibrant ball into the chamber and fully cocked the hammer.

"More bullets?" Janus asked as he approached. His face and neck shimmered as they hardened back into steel. His missing fingers regrew from the base of his hand. "I thought you'd learned."

"Forgive a stubborn human," Devin said. "I thought I'd try something new."

The hammer dropped, its sharp spike splitting the flamestone in half. It erupted inside the barrel as normal, but this time its kick was like a mule's against his arm and shoulder. A tiny shimmering red orb shot from the barrel and crossed the distance between him and Janus in the blink of an eye. The moment it touched his black coat it erupted into a tremendous plume of fire, charring the entire upper half of Janus's body as if he had bathed in oil. An explosive force immediately followed, ripping off pieces of flesh and flinging Janus several feet through the air. The vicious man hobbled to his feet upon landing and fled toward one of the side tunnels, his shoulder and neck still aflame.

Jacaranda rushed to Tommy's side and pried open his mouth now that Janus no longer stood guard over him. She dipped her fingers into his throat, grimaced, and then yanked out three more leeches. Tommy immediately sucked in air, and the color returned to his face.

"Are you all right?" she asked.

"Sure," Tommy said, his voice weak and flimsy. "Just a little traumatized, but otherwise I'm good."

Devin staggered to his feet. Half of him thought to chase after Janus. The other half wanted to return to his sister. In the end, Janus made the decision for him. Once within a side tunnel Janus grabbed a side of the wall and pulled a layer of stone off as if it were as malleable as a cloth curtain. He stretched it from one side of the tunnel to the other, and then it solidified into a barrier of pure steel, safely locking him on the other side.

"Forget him," Jacaranda said. She pulled on Devin's arm. "We have to get your sister out of there."

They ran back to the flesh-and-metal heart. Smoky water had enveloped the entire inner chamber, yet somehow Adria continued to draw breath.

"How do we open it?" he asked her.

"I don't know," she shouted. "Janus was the one who closed it around me."

"A spell," Devin said, whirling on Tommy. "Surely you can use a spell?"

"But...but...but nothing's safe," Tommy insisted. "What should I do? Melt her inside that tube thing while trying to burn her out? Lightning will conduct, and any blunt object could easily crush her if strong enough to break the outer membrane."

Devin felt his rage growing with his helplessness.

"Um, maybe I can try this?" Tesmarie said. She ran a loop around the heart, her moonlight sword carving into the metal. It only showered the area with sparks and barely left a dent. Swords did nothing. Magic put Adria more at risk than not. No door. No opening. What in Anwyn's name were they to do to get her out?

Whatever process Janus had begun reached critical mass. The floor shook with a tremendous beat, and then again a few seconds later. Then again. And again. A true heartbeat. Veins throughout the dome pulsed with electricity. The beams pulsing through the nine tunnels expanded with a tremendous roar of power, each one as large as a man's arm. Lightning streaked through the air above, erupting without any visible source or destination.

Adria pressed her forehead to the membrane so he might hear her better.

"Leave me," she said. "You have to go. It's too dangerous."

Devin would not move. It did not matter that his hair lifted toward the ceiling. It did not matter he tasted copper on his tongue and smelled a powerful stench of ozone and blood.

"I'm not abandoning you," he swore.

"Listen to me," she shouted. "Devin, *listen*."

Thin strands of electricity sparked off the metal of his sword and pistol. He paid them no mind. Adria's gaze was as powerful as the storm above.

"Do not die here with me, do you understand? Do not die here. *Go. Run*."

"Come on, Devin," Tommy said, pulling on his arm. "Do as she says."

The others had already fled, and his brother-in-law did not even wait to see if he followed when he released his coat and joined them. Devin put his forehead to the translucent flesh and spoke above the din.

"I love you, Adria," he told her. "You'll live through this, you hear me? You'll live."

Adria smiled at him despite her fear.

"Run, you damn fool."

Devin fled to the tunnel they'd entered from. The others waited for him there, and once he exited the chamber he turned to watch the culmination of all that had been put in motion. The interior chamber steadily brightened, the blue replaced with sparkling white light. It swelled with power. It pulsed with magic. The cavernous dome trembled, and all at once a beam of light ripped from the ground to the ceiling. The steel heart ruptured into pieces. Adria lifted to the air, the swirling beam of starlight tearing through her physical body. That beam splashed across the massive dome and swirled into a tremendous vortex of light. Higher and higher she rose, her head flung back, her arms out at either side, a long, singular scream pouring out of her throat.

Beat, beat, beat. It came not just from the floor, but from the chamber's domed ceiling. Its walls. Air sucked in with the beams from the other tunnels. Devin had never before felt so small and worthless. He was a parasite inside a massive heart. He was an ignorant savage watching the cosmic substance of eternity. The noise and light and wind reached a crescendo, and the beam holding his sister aloft flared so bright he had to turn and look away lest he go blind.

The light faded. The heartbeat ceased. The chamber plummeted back into darkness, then lit once more with the light of stars pulsing through shrinking veins in the ceiling. Adria slowly floated back to the ground, and she lay atop the broken steel and bloody membrane that had been her cage like a butterfly returning to its cocoon. All was still, and the silence was as deafening as the tempest that preceded it.

Devin raced to her side and flung his arms around her. Little shocks of electricity leapt from her body to his, but he didn't care. The pain meant nothing. What meant everything was the slow and steady inhalations of his sister's chest.

"She lived," Devin whispered. Tears of relief fell from his eyes. The others joined them, and they quietly shared in his happiness.

"What did it do?" Jacaranda asked.

"This chamber, the tunnel...surely they were constructed with a goal in mind," Tommy said. "As to what...I can't even guess."

"It doesn't matter," Devin said, and he kissed his sister's forehead. Theories could wait. Fear for the future did not matter to him in the present. No matter what had happened, it was a far cry from the terror his imagination had unleashed upon his mind over the past day. "Adria's alive. All else can come later. For now, we take her home."

CHAPTER 45

Devin heard a soft rustle behind him, and he knew it was a courtesy. If Jacaranda desired so, he'd have never heard her climb to the roof of his house.

"Come to join me?" he asked. The woman crossed the snow-covered rooftop to sit beside him.

"If you wanted solitude, I figure your room is more convenient than a rooftop," she said.

Devin laughed halfheartedly. His mind felt raw. Too many emotions. Too much confusion. If he slept for the next twenty-four hours he doubted it'd be enough to fully recover.

"You'll only mock me if I tell you why," he said.

"Give me some credit, Devin. I'm a better person than that."

He sighed. *Fine.*

"Remember when I said I didn't take it well when Brittany died? Well, in the midst of that depression I climbed to the roof and screamed at the Sisters at the top of my lungs. The addled logic was that by being higher up, I was closer to the stars, so maybe there'd be a fractionally better chance they'd hear…"

Jacaranda smiled, and Devin jabbed a finger toward her.

"See? I told you that you'd mock me."

"I'm not mocking," she said. "I'm only smiling."

"Smiling counts."

She threw up her hands.

"If smiling is mockery, then I mock you daily."

"Good thing I'm used to it."

Jacaranda elbowed him in his side. The motion drew her closer to him, and he noticed she scooted herself so that their thighs and shoulders touched.

"Anyway," Devin said. "Ever since that night I've come up here when I need to be alone. It might be only symbolic, but I *do* feel closer to the Sisters, and the troubles below me feel the tiniest bit farther away."

Jacaranda's head settled against his breast. Her right hand slowly traced along his neck and chest with her fingertips, as if tentatively exploring the touch of his coat, his shirt, and his skin.

"Would you like me to leave so you may be alone, then?"

"Not in the slightest."

Some time passed as they huddled together against the cold. Devin stared at the sharp, angular rooftops, but his mind was always on Jacaranda's presence beside him. Her warmth against his chest was a ray of sunlight during the spring thaw. Devin tried to remember his life before the black water washed over Dunwerth. It was simpler, certainly, but in hindsight he didn't know how he endured those months, no, those *years* of traveling the roads alone. No one to confide his troubles in. No one to be strong when he was weak.

After Adria, Tommy, and even Lyssa had pulled him from his grief over Brittany's loss, he thought he'd made peace knowing he'd never love another in the same way. Now he wondered at how many relationships he'd starved himself of in the name of that supposed "peace." Jacaranda was hardly the first to show him interest over the past few years, but she was the first with whom he'd dared wonder at the possibility of a future.

"Are you worried for your sister?" she asked him. Devin pulled his thoughts back to the here and now. Indeed he did, and those nagging questions as to what happened to his sister had brought him to the rooftops. Adria slept in his bed, and had for several hours. Though she showed no sign of physical injury, he couldn't shake the fear that *something* had to have been done to her. He just didn't know what. Tommy had left for the Wise tower promising to research into it, but Devin doubted his brother-in-law would find an answer in his old musty tomes.

"I am a little worried," he said. "But she's tough as nails. She'll pull through, I'm sure of it."

Jacaranda drummed her fingers against his ribs.

"I don't know how you do it, Devin. I never worried before, but now I'm worried for her, and for you, and even for myself. Does anything ever stop the worry? It's so . . . tiring. I'm not sure I've experienced a more bothersome emotion."

"That's one way to describe it," Devin said. "These doubts don't go away, not really, but you find ways to overcome them. The Sisters are that strength for me. What we do, from the smallest of daily actions to the once-in-a-lifetime decisions, it shapes us, defines us. We choose who we are, and who we want to be. The Sisters granted us a soul to forever remember those choices, and to fill those eternal memories with compassion, love, and joy. We are light from the stars brought to earth, and so I do my best to shine in the time I am given."

Jacaranda squirmed uncomfortably.

"What of me?" she asked. "I was given no soul for the longest of time. Did...did my choices not matter? Do *I* even matter? Maybe something was always wrong with me, or they judged me and found me wanting, and that's why they never sent my..."

Devin knew there were a thousand better ways to handle this but he was tired, he was hurting, and he couldn't stand listening to Jacaranda belittle herself so. He leaned in close and pressed his lips to hers, silencing her with a kiss. At first she remained still from shock, but when Devin moved to pull away she thrust herself at him, locking him in place with her sudden desperation. Devin closed his eyes and let it last, and last, until they gradually separated amid trembling breaths and melting bodies.

"Nothing is wrong with you," he said. "You're as wonderful and beautiful and close to perfect as this imperfect world allows."

Jacaranda returned his arm around her shoulder and held his hand in hers.

"That's not true, but it feels good to hear, so you may say it again."

"What, that you're beautiful?"

She winked at him.

"Oh, I know I'm beautiful. I meant the rest."

Devin moved to kiss her a second time, but she flicked him on the nose as if he were a misbehaving puppy.

"Control yourself," she said. "We're both ready to pass out from exhaustion. Let's save the rest of our kisses for somewhere warm and private."

"I'll hold you to that."

Jacaranda snuggled closer against him.

"I look forward to it."

They stayed together for what felt like hours, though he knew it was perhaps twenty minutes or so. Clouds drifted along the gray sky. Thin smoke lines floated up from a hundred chimneys. The road they lived on was peaceful, which made the clomps of hoofbeats from the occasional carriage and the laughter of scrambling children sound that much more distinct in the quiet. A soft ping, like a landing pebble, sounded not far to his right. Jacaranda shuddered slightly in his arms. Devin glanced in the noise's direction, saw nothing, and turned back to find Jacaranda staring at him with a puzzled look on her face. A circle of blood spread across her red shirt just shy of her left breast.

"Devin?" she asked. The name slurred on her tongue as she collapsed. Devin was too stunned to do anything but catch her. Warm blood flowed across his hands and into his lap. The eyes of some other person (certainly not *his* eyes, this wasn't happening, this was happening to someone else) stared at a hole in the back of Jacaranda's coat.

"Jac," he said. It was hard to speak with every muscle in his body locked in place. "Jac, no, no, don't..."

But she wouldn't look at him. He forced those shaking hands to lift her up (stranger's hands, not his) and though her eyes were open they weren't seeing anything, not a thing, not a goddess-damned thing. She couldn't speak. She couldn't breathe, wouldn't breathe...

A man's laughter struck his mind like thunder. Devin tore his gaze to the nearby rooftop, and the man casually strolling across the slanted shingles. His long, unbuttoned coat flapped in the cold wind. Smoke wafted from the barrel of the rifle slung over his shoulder. His pristine white trousers and shirt matched the color of the thin snow. His smile matched the lifelessness of the fog.

"I warned her," Tye the White said. "I said I'd put a bullet through her heart before she knew I was near. And to think you of all people were working with her, Soulkeeper." He laughed again. "You deserve one another. Shall I have your Pyrehand combine your ashes into one sad little pile for all eternity?"

The mercenary hopped over the slender gap to the adjacent rooftop. A calm haze washed over Devin, burying his shock and horror deep down into a pit to be suffered later. Cold rage breathed life into his limbs. He gently lowered Jacaranda's body, hesitating only slightly to ensure that it did not slide upon the shingles. Once that was done he rose to his full height, donned his tricorn hat, and pulled it low over his face. His hand drifted to the handle of his pistol.

"Yes, let us play a game," Tye said. "Do you think you can draw faster than I reach you with my sword?"

Devin pulled the hammer back and tilted the pistol to show that it was empty. Then he dropped the weapon to the roof and held his sword in a two-handed grip.

"I won't kill you from afar," Devin said. "When you die I want your blood on my hands."

Tye drew his sword and lazily sauntered to the edge of the rooftop.

"Overconfidence suits you," he said. "But you're out of your depth here, Soulkeeper. I'll be impressed if you manage to stain my clothes with *your* blood, let alone draw a drop of mine."

"Then let's find out."

Tye jumped the slender gap. His coat fluttered in the wind.

The moment his red shoes touched the stone, Devin initiated the battle with a reaching slash with fully extended arms. Tye easily parried it aside and then slid closer. He feinted a counter-thrust, but Devin didn't buy it for a second. He had a feeling for how Tye battled, and a sneaking suspicion that Tye relied on no one surviving their first encounter with him. These early parts of the fight would be spent on the defensive, the goal to tire out his foe.

Devin refused to play along. He kept his dodges to a minimum. His sword hardly moved more than a few inches to bat aside the occasional thrust. The combatants paced one another, analyzing weaknesses, sensing openings. Devin swept his long sword in waist-high arcs from side to side. There'd be no parrying those, only dodging away or hard blocking. Blocking wasn't what Tye preferred, and the dodge expended energy he was trying to save. Still Devin did not stop. Back and forth. Keeping him dancing. Daring him to take the offensive.

"Amusing, really," Tye said as he turned sideways, Devin's sudden thrust tearing a hole in his red coat. He was trying to act relaxed, unbothered, but Devin heard the heavy breaths slipped in between every other word. "This isn't even the first rooftop battle I've had this week."

Devin increased his intensity the slightest amount. To an unskilled watcher, their fight would look lethargic, almost bored. Their bodies kept loose, their attacks only single slashes and thrusts with no follow-ups. Tye wanted him to attack in the midst of his rage. He wanted him to burn out like wildfire. The fool. He could never understand his smoldering, seething anger.

"Are you hoping I'll make an error?" Devin asked. He steadily advanced, deciding he'd observed enough to have a feel for Tye's preferred reactions to his various attacks. His sword never stopped moving, one slash immediately followed by another. It was time to be as relentless as the tide. Tye parried some, dodged others, always ensuring that he continued in a loose circle to prevent being pinned against the rooftop's edge.

"Do you think I'll tire?" he continued.

Another increase in the speed of his steps. Tye was fully retreating now, for Devin had solved the puzzle that was Tye's fighting techniques. Redirecting the energy of Devin's attacks didn't help if Devin was relying on those redirections to keep his sword in motion for another strike. More and more the mercenary was forced to block, and each contest only conveyed what Devin already knew: He was the stronger fighter.

Once their fight took them back to the rooftop center Tye attempted to steal the initiative. He parried, adjusted his feet, and then slammed his shoulder toward Devin's exposed chest. Devin accepted the surprise hit. Good. He wanted Tye searching for openings. Parry and riposte. Thrust and counterthrust. This was the dance he'd trained years for, all the way back to when he was a child sweating under the hot summer sun in the training yard within the Cathedral of the Sacred Mother.

Tye tried following with an upward-curling slash. Devin trapped it low, stepped inward while shoving the steel in a reverse arc, and suddenly he had Tye fully exposed before him. All his strength poured into a downward punch against his neck, the blow easily disorienting the mercenary. He tried to retreat, but not before Devin swung his sword around for another blow. The sword's edge cut across Tye's forehead, opening up a shallow wound that bled profusely given its location. The mercenary smacked away the follow-up thrust and then retreated a step to gain his bearings. He wiped at his forehead, trying to keep the blood out of his eyes.

"That's a lot more than one drop," Devin said. His voice sounded strangely hollow. He wished he could feel enjoyment in the mockery. He wished he could take satisfaction in seeing the man suffer. He didn't. Everything was locked away in a vault of cold horror, and it would stay so until Tye bled out at his feet.

Tye twirled his sword before him, deftly switching its hilt from hand to hand.

"At least Soulkeepers are somewhat worthy of their bloated reputation," he said. "Let me show you how I earned mine."

Tye kicked off the shingles into a ferocious leap. His sword slammed against Devin's block, and the moment he landed he slashed again, and again, hammering away with all his strength. The distance between them shrank, and suddenly it wasn't just the sword attacking him but fists and elbows and knees. Devin had experienced this barrage already, unlike the surprise it'd been when infiltrating the Ellington estate with Jacaranda. The memory of her fueled his defenses with a surge of rage that broke free of his emotional cage. Tye relied on the shock of switching from a passive, energy-redirecting combat style to overwhelming savagery. That shock almost always meant his foes went on a panicked defensive, but not this time.

Not this goddess-damned time.

Devin met Tye's fury with fury. He howled like the wolves of Alma's Crown. He kicked and head-butted as if he were weaponless. Their swords slammed into each other and groaned with constant contact. Tye unleashed a flurry of punches into Devin's gut, and Devin responded with an elbow to the throat. When the mercenary gasped for air he followed it up with the hilt of his sword to the face, knocking out two teeth. Tye swept his leg, but even falling didn't stop Devin's attack. He swung while dropping sideways, a shallow cut across Tye's arm that was mostly deflected by his thick coat, and then they both rolled across the shingles.

Devin's feet found purchase and he dove back into the offensive. He forced two rapid parries with lethal slashes toward the throat, then snap-kicked Tye in the crotch. Sheer will kept the mercenary going. Devin's legs pumped, and their swords collided. They glared through the gap of their blades, each shoving their weight against the other.

Their swords separated, Tye roundhoused Devin across the cheek, Devin kicked in two of Tye's lower ribs, and then they staggered apart. Tye crouched down as if preparing for a lunge, so Devin retreated further, wanting enough space to react in time.

Except Tye wasn't preparing an attack. The rifle slipped from his shoulder. His speed rivaled Lyssa's as he slipped a flamestone out from a belt pouch and into the chamber. Devin knew he had to prevent the man from finishing, but his momentum had him traveling away from Tye, not toward him. He had a half second to react and so he went with the first idea to come to mind. His own pistol was nearby, and he dropped to a skid and scooped it up with his free hand. Loading it faster than Tye with his head start wasn't feasible, but that wasn't the plan.

The pistol sailed end over end through the air. The flat of its hilt smacked Tye directly in the forehead, further tearing the cut already there. The lead shot slipped from Tye's fingertips, and though he reached for another Devin was already moving. He leapt feet first at Tye's chest. The mercenary shifted his rifle to block, and they collided in a tangle of elbows, knees, and fists.

Tye retreated closer to the rooftop's edge, desperate for some separation. Instead of following, Devin swept up the rifle in his left hand and slammed the hammer back with his sword hilt. He stood with the rifle out as if it were his pistol. Tye glared at him from his defensive stance. Blood trickled down from the cut on his forehead. His sword wavered in his grip, which he no longer held in his easy, comfortable way but instead with white knuckles.

"It isn't loaded, you damn fool," Tye said.

Devin's finger tightened on the trigger.

"I know."

The hammer dropped, its spike piercing the flamestone and detonating its power. There might not have been a lead shot to fire but the energy still burst out of the barrel in a flash of smoke. Tye screamed as both light and powder stung his eyes. Devin dropped the rifle, braced himself, and hesitated for a half second. Tye anticipated an attack and dove blindly—and the moment Devin saw the direction, he lunged with the full power of his legs. His arms shoved the blade forward, the tip piercing between ribs to rip into the mercenary's chest.

Tye gasped. He tried to breathe in, hitched, and then coughed blood. Devin rammed his sword all the way up to the hilt. True to his word, Tye's blood poured across his hands. Devin twisted the hilt. He wanted it to hurt. He wanted the bastard to suffer and scream and writhe on his sword for years to make up for the sorrow festering in his heart. Let that sharpened blade of steel tear apart muscle and bone in retribution for a world so heartlessly cruel. Alma, Lyra, Anwyn: Devin felt betrayed by them all.

Devin grabbed Tye by the jaw and propped him upright. The

dying man's eyes were still open. His lungs sucked in weak, wet inhalations of air. Good. Maybe he'd still hear. Maybe he'd still understand.

"This world is not the end," Devin seethed. "And I hope the Sisters burn you in the next one."

Devin ripped out the sword with a tremendous spray of blood. He kicked Tye in the chest as he collapsed, booting him off the rooftop to crumple upon the street below. It still wasn't enough. It'd never be enough. Already his tears were starting to gather. His rage had nothing left to burn. His bloodlust was sated. All that remained was his sorrow escaping its temporary imprisonment, and oh how it consumed him like a river finally bursting free from a dam.

Devin's sword clattered atop the shingles. His shoulders sagged. He turned to Jacaranda's body, his cruel mind taking in every detail and permanently burning it to memory. The confused expression on her pale face. The few errant strands of red hair fluttering across her nose. The drying blood surrounding the hole in her chest.

"Why?" Devin asked the silence. Years ago, at that same spot, he'd raged at the Sisters for taking Brittany away. Now he wanted to do the same but he felt too damn old and weary. His insides were hollowed out. Even crying was beyond his body's current capabilities. His feet moved of their own accord. His hands wrapped about her shoulders and held her close. The absence of any reaction stood out beyond even the stink of death. No acceptance of the embrace. No subtle shifting of muscles or hints of breath. Just a shell he clung to his body, embracing it with naked emotion he'd never allowed to show. He pressed his forehead to hers and looked upon a face both beautiful and lifeless.

"Please, Sisters," Devin said. No heart for the rage. He had only pitiful sorrow. "Don't do this. Don't hate me so. I can't...I can't do this again..."

A single flicker of hope pierced through his darkening mind. Devin lifted her body with strength born of desperation. There was still a chance, however thin and fleeting.

"Adria," he whispered.

CHAPTER 46

Adria woke to a violent rocking motion shooting through her. She lurched to a sit as every part of her body flared with painful awareness. Concepts filtered into her tired mind. She was in a bed. It was dark from heavy blankets covering the window. Devin was beside her, his hand still on her shoulder from shaking her awake. He was crying.

"Devin?" she asked. There was something different about him, a light within his eyes dimming with each passing moment. The sight of it frightened her, and she pretended not to see.

"I know you're exhausted," Devin said. "But please, you're the only one who can help me."

Help? Help with what? The last thing she remembered was being encased within a gigantic heart of steel and skin, and a blue ethereal liquid filling the entire chamber. All else had become a blur.

"Devin, what happened?" she asked, still struggling to find her bearings.

"Jacaranda. She's been shot."

Adria had meant since she'd been submerged within the blue liquid, but now she understood her brother's sudden urgency. The terrible sorrow on his face added to her growing clarity.

"Take me to her."

He offered her his arm and she accepted it gladly. Her body felt strangely foreign to her, and she needed his firm presence to keep herself balanced as she set her bare feet upon the floor. Devin guided her to the living room. She did her best not to stare as she walked. That light in his eyes, leaking from his lips, shimmering within his skull...it was almost blinding.

Jacaranda's body lay on the couch. A trail of blood led from the door to the center cushion, and a pool of it grew underneath her, sticky and dark. Adria knew the moment she laid eyes upon her that Jacaranda's life was spent.

"Devin, I'm sorry," she said. "She's already dead."

Devin refused to listen. He was stammering and punctuating his every word with weird tics and hand motions.

"Your prayers," he insisted. "Your miracles, they...they can help her. Try, Adria, please. I'm begging you."

Her resistance withered under his red-eyed pleading. She'd suspected Jacaranda had become important to her brother, but now she saw just how much. Adria separated from Devin and walked on wobbly legs to the couch. She knelt and put a hand on the open wound in Jacaranda's chest. Her eyes closed.

"Lyra of the beloved sun," she whispered. "Hear my prayer."

The rest of the 36th Devotion came to her, but she did not voice it. The words echoed in her heart, and she saw with her eyes the power they wielded. The devotion sent reverberations across a supernatural world bound together by physical constraints. It wouldn't be enough, though, she knew that. Jacaranda's soul had already begun the extraction process upon her body's death. Curing the flesh, even if she could, would not save her from the reaping hour.

But perhaps there was another way...

"The man who shot her," she asked. "Is that his body outside?"

Devin glanced at the half-open door to the home, baffled. He'd not told her of the man's presence. She hoped the urgency of the situation would keep him from asking how she knew.

"It is," Devin said. "Why?"

"Bring him to me."

Her brother looked reluctant to leave Jacaranda's side, and only her deadly serious glare finally hurried him out the door. He returned moments later with the dead man slung over his shoulder. Copious amounts of blood stained his coat and trousers.

"Where do you want him?" he asked.

"On the floor."

Devin set him down near the door. Panic licked the edges of every action her brother took. Adria knew he was struggling to keep himself together. His desperate hope that she might heal Jacaranda was the only thing keeping him from breaking apart completely.

Adria knelt beside the mercenary's body and put her hand on his smooth forehead. Her skin burned as if she touched fire. Her nervousness intensified her twisting stomach and pounding heart. She closed her eyes, and even then she was not granted complete darkness. Stars blazed across her vision.

"Devin, I know what Janus did to me," she said.

Her brother seemed to sense the gathering power. His voice dropped to a low, cautious volume.

"What is it?" he asked. "What did he do?"

In answer, Adria curled her fingers, raised her arm, and pulled the soul free of the dead man's forehead. Its light lit the room, now in a physical sense beyond the mystical. Adria stared deep into its center, and it felt like falling. This man (Tye, she knew instantly) lay bare before her, all his memories and emotions wrapping about her like a warm sweater. She could feel the polished wood and cold steel of his rifle as he sighted for one of a hundred kills. She could feel the sting of sweat in her eyes, feel the burn in her muscles from his days of training, experience his selfish elation whenever he took a woman to bed.

That soul, that singular universe of thoughts, sensations, ideas, and emotions, was now hers to command. The spiritual collection burned with power. Adria pointed to Jacaranda with her free hand. The words of the prayers...they mattered, but only as guidance. They focused the wild storm of energy. They gave substance to desire. Adria knew this with absolute certainty, like a great mystery had been pulled from her mind, a thick curtain of ignorance given way to bare truth.

"Precious Lyra," she said. "Heal this woman."

Devin would not see it, but she did with sight granted by the strange machinery hidden beneath Londheim. Thin tendrils of Tye's soul streaked out like cast-off ropes. They mended flesh with a touch. They reset the pierced organs and replaced the lost blood. Tye's soul faded the tiniest sliver as it expended its power. Pieces of memories jumbled or blurred. Adria gritted her teeth, frightened by how easy this all was. She walked to Jacaranda's body, carrying Tye's soul with her. The flesh was mending, but there was still one key act remaining. Jacaranda's soul looked like a jittery firefly trapped within a jar. She gripped it with her other hand, soothing it, calming it. Power flowed from Tye's soul into her, and she redirected it into Jacaranda's.

Little tendrils so thin they looked like spiderwebs spread throughout Jacaranda's body, giving it life and light. They took hold, anchoring her soul, making the connections to permanently absorb the emotions and memories that the mind would forget with time. It was like witnessing a flower blooming in spring, and it conveyed the same immense satisfaction. This anchoring was what had been missing when she prayed over poor Arleen in the marketplace, but back then she'd been blind to the process. Now she saw. Now she commanded. A single, unseen jolt swirled through Jacaranda's physical form. She gasped in a deep breath of air as she lurched to a sit. Devin clutched her immediately, holding her against his chest as he sobbed with relief.

"Thank you, Sisters," he said as his tears bathed Jacaranda's neck. "Thank you, thank you."

For her part, Jacaranda looked only tired and confused. She slumped in Devin's arms, accepting his embrace as she closed her eyes and relaxed. Adria turned her attention to the soul hovering just above her palm. She fell back into its center. Tye's memories folded, shifted, and reopened to her slightest whim.

Show me your kills, she thought.

One by one they flashed over her eyes, her mind living them as if they were her own memories, her own actions, even her own emotions at the time she pulled the trigger. Adria watched men, women, and children fall dead from perfectly aimed shots to their chests and foreheads. She watched skulls cave in. She watched sprays of blood cover walls, streets, and grass. Tye's satisfaction swelled in her belly. His enjoyment at the kill put bile in her throat. This man. This monster. He viewed life like such a cheap, inconsequential thing. She saw Jacaranda fall. She felt Tye's elation at fulfilling his promise. She felt his smug amusement at witnessing Devin's suffering.

Adria pulled free. She stared at the soul in front of her, this embodiment of existence, this white fire. An intense rage threatened to overwhelm her judgment. What good was this man? For what reason should he entertain an audience before the Sisters? Her fingers shook. She wanted to smash the soul to pieces. She wanted to rip into its core and send those hateful memories and emotions scattering to the void. Let her, not Anwyn, play the role of the reaper.

The rage passed. She was too exhausted to maintain it for long.

"Be gone," she whispered to it. "Find your judgment at the hands of the Sisters."

No shimmering blue light. No need for runes and rituals or waiting for the reaping hour. A simple flick of her wrist and the soul shot through the ceiling to the heavens, to become part of whatever mysteries lay at the end of their earthly days.

With the soul's departure her mind steadily cooled like a sword pulled from a furnace and thrust into water. A thundering wave of fear replaced it. This power, this startling vision of the spiritual world—for what purpose was it given? She noticed Devin watching her. She could not read his physical expression, but that no longer limited her. The light of his soul swam over him, and she needed only to brush it with her mind to see the fear and confusion swirling through her brother with equal intensity.

"Not yet," she said, sensing his many questions. There was one last thing she must do. Adria put her hand to her chest. The almost imperceptible soul-threads throughout her body latched to her hand, and it took only the tiniest shred of strength, like a drop of water drawn from a lake, to send light rolling off her fingertips in waves. Tye's body burst into white flames, burning so hot even his bones turned to ash. Adria watched this empty shell void of light be consumed, and given the horrid sins of its soul, she could not imagine a more appropriate fate. No pyre. No burial. Just ash.

"Adria?" She turned. Devin stared at her with calm, controlled horror. She noticed that Puffy had poked its head up from the fireplace, those beady black eyes vibrating with worry. Tesmarie also stirred from her little pillowed perch, and she held her blanket to her chin as she stared. All of them, so terrified for her, for what she'd become. She didn't blame them.

"What did Janus do to you?" her older brother asked.

The answer seemed so simple compared to the implications.

"The reaping hour and its rituals," Adria said. "I have become them. I am the prayers. I am the burial mask."

She clenched her fist, her sheer will scattering the gray pile of ash that had been Tye the White.

"I am the pyre."

EPILOGUE

Janus stood before the mouth of the crawling mountain as it split open with the roar of an earthquake. From afar the change would be imperceptible, the gap a mere ten feet or so, but from so close Janus could see the vast cavernous darkness within. Starlight reflected off clear quartz teeth the size of buildings. Black water rolled between the teeth and fell to the grass like an encroaching fog.

Minutes later a star-filled shadow exited between the teeth and floated to the ground.

"They've begun stealing your power again," Janus grumbled to the demigod.

"It is no theft when the power is granted freely," Viciss said. "We are embodiments, not jailers."

"Perhaps you should reconsider your roles, then. A Soulkeeper somehow harnessed Aethos's power into his pistol. Nearly took my damn head off."

Viciss glanced behind him. The titanic jaws closed with another earth-shaking rumble.

"We've returned for mere weeks and already humanity shows its ingenuity. Our imprisonment led to their stagnation. The Sisters' decisions are not the best for even their own children, as we have always known. Such a pity they had to endure these centuries, their race's evolution locked in stasis until we broke from the prison the Sisters locked us within."

Despite re-creating the destroyed flesh and bone, an ache lingered inside Janus's chest and shoulder. Magical wounds were always significantly harder for him to recover from, and the pain combined with the frustration of losing the fight added to the bite of his words.

"Yes, let us pity them and not we who were imprisoned for centuries. Truly they are the ones who suffered the worst."

"Suffering is not a competition," the demigod said. "Tame your tongue or I shall render it useless."

Janus bowed low, quick to apologize after Viciss's earlier threats at the Hive-Tree.

"Forgive my frustrations. I have come to inform you that the process completed as you desired, though the damage to the chamber afterward will require time to repair before it can be used again."

It seemed the swirling galaxies that made up Viciss's form shone just a little bit brighter as he gestured to Janus.

"Then follow me, child. There are others who must know."

The mind of the dragon walked west. Janus fell into step behind him and silently followed. They slowly circumvented the mountainous physical representation of the dragon, which had steadily sunk into the soft earth with each passing day. Janus marveled at its intricate construction. The outer skin was gray rock weathered by the ages, but the interior was a mixture of flesh, metal, and stone. Otherworldly magic pulsed like blood in tunnel-veins. Cascades of muscles stronger than the hardest steel flexed and shifted for hundreds of feet whenever the dragon wished to move one of its legs.

Such a shame Viciss did not desire Londheim's destruction. Watching the crawling mountain smash through its walls and lay waste to its buildings would be a spectacle grander than anything the Cradle had witnessed in all its history.

Hours passed. Sometimes they followed the man-made road, sometimes they skirted the edge of the miles-long crevice that marked the dragon's progress as it had crawled from its prison within Alma's Crown to the edge of Londheim. The two traveled in silence. There was a strange mystery to the air. The world was holding its breath. Enormous owls passed overhead, on their way for another nightly hunt upon Londheim's streets. Other times fog elementals danced runes across the stars, conveying messages of praise and glory to the demigod who passed underneath.

Several families of foxkin had built their homes in the tremendous crevice miles out from Londheim, and they wordlessly hurried out of their mud-and-stick huts to climb up to the grass. They pushed their red-furred faces to the ground and lifted their arms above their heads in praise. All two dozen or so howled in the same deep tone. Janus had not been among foxkin often, but he had heard that growl before, and it was their deepest offering of love and obedience, usually reserved between mates in their private quarters.

Viciss stopped for only a single step so he might bow his head their way in appreciation. The gesture put a worm of ill content inside Janus's stomach. Not once in his existence had the demigod shown him that modicum of adoration. Created to destroy, yet hated for the destruction. If only Viciss had denied him sentience. If he had been as indifferent as a meteor or a hurricane perhaps then he'd be spared the deep-seated resentment for the damage he caused.

The land became rolling hills as another hour passed, and though nothing appeared to mark this one hill as different from the others, Viciss shifted their path and led them toward its top. The demigod ascended, but Janus could not bring himself to follow. He dropped to his knees halfway there upon seeing who awaited their arrival. His heart thundered in his chest. His breath caught in his throat. With trembling arms, he raised his open palms high above his head and bowed in supplication to the five Dragons of Creation.

Human eyes would see them likewise as human, but Janus perceived their deeper truth. Viciss, a shifting darkness of ever-flowing black water. Chyron, a silver scar of light surrounded by an orange whirlwind of ethereal sand that winked in and out of existence. Gloam, composed of one hundred fluttering fireflies, little streaks of electricity arcing between them as they blinked in and out of view. Aethos, a black cloud filled with a maelstrom of pure energy that somehow manifested as ice, lightning, and fire simultaneously. Nihil was a humanoid distortion, as if all light and noise about him were pulled inside and warped in strange, unknowable ways. The grass at his feet slid upward and streaked amid his legs like liquid. The night wind became tangible strings that weaved through Nihil's chest and exited as the sound of falling rain.

All of Janus's bitterness and resentment disintegrated. Such a meeting between all five dragons was rare even in the earliest days of creation. To bear witness here, now, was a tremendous gift. Tears fell from his eyes. He felt blessed to bask in their presence. He felt privileged to witness a gathering that would shape the course of history.

"Greetings, brethren," Viciss said. The other four nodded deeply.

"Is it done?" Aethos asked.

Viciss lifted his arms to the heavens. His voice echoed for miles in all directions, his message not just for the dragons but for all their children. When the Keeping Church collapsed, and a new religion was built upon the ruins, it would be these words that began its holy text.

"It is done," Viciss decreed. "The Chainbreaker lives."

A NOTE FROM
THE AUTHOR

So here we are, perhaps for the first time for some of you, and yet again for a whole lot of you. I make no promises that the following ramble will be interesting, but it's fun to finally sit back and unwind at the very end of a project and just…talk about it. I wrote the first chapter all the way back in September 2016, so it's been a lengthy journey here.

So this entire novel came from a rather odd spot of inspiration. I was taking a walk while listening to music (generally my preferred way to brainstorm) and a song by the band Clutch was playing, "The Swollen Goat." The chorus line in particular struck me with its imagery:

> *Bury your treasure, burn your crops,*
> *Black water rising and it ain't gonna stop.*

Now, the song is about pirates, but when I first heard it I imagined it quite literally: people hiding their valuables, burning their fields, and fleeing a rising tide of black water. But why burn the fields, I wondered. Well, the black water must do something horrible to them, something worse than becoming mere ash.

And that's where the very first inspiration for this massive book came from. The idea that somewhere, in some small town, a sudden flood of black water arrives, destroying even the grass itself and turning it into a dangerous corruption. If it corrupted the grass, what then must it do to buildings? Humans? The dead? Side note, there's also a bit about swollen goats in the song, and sadly I ended up cutting the encounter where Devin fought a bunch of mutated zombie goats with swollen stomachs. Odds are pretty high I'll be bringing them into book two, though. They were too fun and disgusting to abandon entirely.

Now as fun as the initial idea is, I was missing a rather key part of the story, that is, everything else. The biggest, though, was what caused the black water? I tossed around ideas until I settled on something I'd been itching to do for a while: dragons. Not mere drakes that humans could ride. Not even big ancient ones like Smaug. No, I wanted *huge* dragons. Impossibly sized dragons. Years ago on a walk (seriously, music plus lots of time doing nothing are so important to writing) I saw a cloud that stretched across the horizon shaped, I thought, like a dragon. It looked like it floated there, the size of a city and visible for hundreds of miles, awesome and incredible. Perhaps this novel could be my chance to do something remotely resembling it in terms of scale.

All right. So a dragon wakes up, so big that people mistake it for a mountain. It's pissed, and it unleashes the black water. Nice. Got it. I can work with this. But... why is it pissed? Why was it asleep? How does it command the black water? Is it its breath weapon? If so, what does the dragon represent?

Hopefully this gives you a glimpse, at least for this writer, of the thought process for building a story and a world. It starts as neat little ideas or themes, which result in questions, whose answers lead to more possibilities and even more questions. When people ask, "Where do you get your ideas from?" this is basically it. There's no sudden individual *Eureka!* moment where the entire story emerges fully formed within my brain. I'm building everything out of Lego blocks, and the Legos come from movies I see, books I read, and games I play.

As for this story, it was very close to being drastically different. When I first was plotting everything out, and then pitched it to the wonderful people at Orbit, I originally planned for there to be a two-to-three-year gap between Viciss arriving at Londheim and the rest of the book. Just...try to imagine that for a moment. At the time, I'd only written the first five chapters, so my editor responded with what basically boiled down to "We love this beginning, but um, what's with the time skip? It's dumb. We're going to miss all the fun stuff."

Dear reader, you have no idea how happy I am I had only written the first five chapters and not the entire bloody novel following my original outline, because she was so very right. I'm often in a hurry to get to the fun stuff, but what the hell was I thinking building a storyline on the sudden reappearance of magical spells and creatures only to instantly leap ahead in time to where people have (mostly) acclimated to it all? This is why you need a good editor/reader you trust. When your head's been lost in an entire world for over a year, it's hard to remember how the story looks to someone exposed to it for the very first time.

Before I write the traditional thanks, I'm going to do something a little different, and that's talk about the dedication. For five years my brother and I operated a game store focused on card games, board games, *Magic: The Gathering, Dungeons & Dragons,* and stuff like that. One of our first customers was a kid named Devin. We befriended his whole family, who became regulars at our board game nights where we insulted one another over rounds of Spyfall, Drawful, and Sheriff of Nottingham. Four years later, Devin passed away from a rare medical condition. He'd just started his first year of college.

We were devastated. Perhaps this is too personal, but this is my book, and my little section dedicated to rambling at the back of it, so screw it. His family doesn't know it yet, but this book is dedicated to him, and the main character is named after him. In fact, his family is likely finding out by reading this note. I know I'm not offering much, but I hope this put a smile on your faces.

Okay. Where was I? Thanks so much to my editor, Brit Hvide, who endured long, long phone calls where I rambled ideas and scattershot thoughts much like I rambled here in this note. Without her, this book isn't anywhere near as good. Thanks to my agent, Michael Carr, who keeps me sane. Thanks to the awesome art department at Orbit, who gave me yet another cover to be jealous of. Thanks to my new little critique group (Kat, Fiona, and Elaine in particular). Also thanks to my lovely wife, who helped immensely with developing Jacaranda into the fully fledged character that she is. The same goes to my friend Ryan, my real-life inspiration for the wonderful goofball that is Tommy.

Last, but certainly not least, thank you, dear reader. It's your continued support that allows me to live this dream, and so long as you're willing to stick with me, I hope I give you characters you love and stories that entertain for many years to come. I'll see you at the end of *Ravencaller*.

DAVID DALGLISH

JUNE 21, 2018

The story continues in...

RAVENCALLER

extras

orbit

www.orbitbooks.net

about the author

David Dalglish currently lives in Myrtle Beach with his wife Samantha and his daughters Morgan, Katherine, and Alyssa. He graduated from Missouri Southern State University in 2006 with a degree in mathematics and currently spends his free time helping his oldest on her runs of *Darkest Dungeon*.

Find out more about David Dalglish and other Orbit authors by registering online for the free monthly newsletter at www.orbitbooks.net.

if you enjoyed
SOULKEEPER

look out for

THE THOUSAND DEATHS OF ARDOR BENN
Kingdom of Grit: Book One

by

Tyler Whitesides

Ardor Benn is no ordinary thief – a master of wildly complex heists, he styles himself a Ruse Artist Extraordinaire.

When a mysterious priest hires him for the most daring ruse yet, Ardor knows he'll need more than quick wit and sleight of hand. Assembling a dream team of forgers, disguisers, schemers and thieves, he sets out to steal from the most powerful king the realm has ever known.

But it soon becomes clear there's more at stake than fame and glory – Ard and his team might just be the last hope for human civilisation.

CHAPTER

1

Ardor Benn was running late. Or was he? Ard preferred to think that everyone else in the Greater Chain was consistently early—with unreasonable expectations for him to be the same.

Regardless, this time it was all right to keep his appointment waiting. It was a stew tactic. And stew tasted better the longer it cooked.

Ard skipped up the final stairs and onto the third floor. Remaught Azel clearly wasn't the big fish he purported. Rickety wooden tri-story in the slums of Marow? Ard found the whole thing rather distasteful. Especially after Lord Yunis. Now, that was something! Proper stone mansion with a Heat Grit hearth in every room. Servants. Cooks. Light Grit lanterns that ignited with the pull of a chain. Ard half suspected that Lord Yunis wiped his backside with lace.

Different island. Different ruse. Today was about Remaught Azel, no matter how unaccommodating his hideout appeared.

Ard shifted the Grit keg from one arm to the other as he reached the closed door at the end of the hallway. The creaking floorboards would have already notified Remaught that someone was coming. *Interesting*, Ard thought. *Maybe there is something useful about holing up in a joint like this. Floorboard sentries.*

The door swung open, but before Ard could step through, a hairy, blue-skinned arm pressed into his chest, barring entrance.

"Take it easy," Ard said to the Trothian man. This would be

Remaught's bodyguard. His dark, vibrating eyes glared at Ard. Classic. This guy seemed like a tough son of a gun, although he was obviously past due for one of those Agrodite saltwater soaks. The skin on his arm looked like it might start flaking off.

"I'm a legitimate businessman," Ard continued, "here to do... legitimate businessy things."

He glanced past the large bodyguard to the table where Remaught sat, bathed in sunlight from the western window. The mobster wore a maroon velvet vest, a tricornered hat, and a shoulder cape, currently fashionable among the rich folk. Remaught seemed tense, watching his bodyguard detain Ard at the doorway.

"Search him."

"Really?" Ard protested, holding the Grit keg above his head so the bodyguard could pat his sides. "I left my belt and guns at home," he said. "And if I hadn't, I could easily shoot you from where I'm standing, so I find this whole pat down a little unnecessary, and frankly uncomfortable."

The bodyguard paused, one hand on Ard's hip pocket. "What's this?" he asked, his voice marked by a thick Trothian accent.

"Rocks," Ard answered.

"Rocks?" Like the bodyguard had never heard of such things. "Take them out—slow."

Ard reached casually into his pocket and scooped out a handful of small stones that he'd collected on the roadside before entering the building. "I'll need these for the transaction."

In response, the Trothian bodyguard swatted Ard's hand, sending the dusty pebbles scattering across the room.

"Now, that was quite uncalled-for," Ard said to the mobster at the table. "I find your man to be unnecessarily rough."

"Suno?" replied Remaught. "Three cycles ago, he would have fed you those rocks—through your nose. Going soft, I fear. Fatherhood has a tendency to do that."

Ard wondered what kind of father a mobster's bodyguard would be. Some fathers made a living at the market or the factories. This guy made a living by stringing people up by their toes at the whim of his boss.

The Trothian moved down, feeling around Ard's thighs with both hands.

"At the very least, you should consider hiring a good-looking woman for this step," Ard continued. "Wouldn't hurt business, you know."

The bodyguard stepped back and nodded to Remaught, who gestured for Ard to enter the room.

"Were you followed?" Remaught asked.

Ard laughed as he set the Grit keg gently on the table, stirring a bit of dust that danced in the sun rays. "I am never followed." He adjusted the gaudy ring on his index finger and sat down across from the mobster. "Except occasionally by a bevy of beautiful maidens."

Ard smiled, but Remaught Azel did not return the gesture. Instead, the mobster reached out for the Grit keg. Ard was faster, whisking the keg away before Remaught could touch it.

Ard clicked his tongue. "How about we see some payment before I go handing over the Grit in a room where I'm unarmed and outnumbered?"

Remaught pushed backward in his chair, the wooden legs buzzing against the floor. The mobster crossed the room and retrieved a locked safe box from the window seat. It was no longer than his forearm, with convenient metal handles fastened on both sides. The Regulation seal was clearly displayed on the front beside the keyhole.

"That looks mighty official," Ard said as Remaught placed it on the table. "Regulation issue, isn't it?"

"I recently came by the box," replied Remaught, dusting his hands. "I like to keep my transactions secure. There are crooked folk in these parts."

"So I hear," answered Ard. "And how do I know the safe box isn't full of sand?"

"How do I know that Grit keg isn't empty?"

Ard shrugged, a smirk on his face. They had reached the part of the exchange that Ard called the Final Distrust. One last chance to back out. For both of them.

Remaught broke the tension by reaching into his velvet vest and producing a key. He slipped it into the lock, turned it sharply, and lifted the lid.

Ard squinted at the coinlike items. They looked real enough in this lighting. Most were stamped with seven small indentations, identifying them as seven-mark Ashings, the highest denomination of currency.

"May I?" Ard plucked out a coin before Remaught granted permission. Ard lifted the Ashing to his mouth and bit down on the edge of it.

"Taste real enough for you?" Remaught asked. Ard's relaxed nature seemed to be driving the man continuously more tense.

Ard studied the spot where his teeth had pressed against the coin, angling it in the sunlight to check for any kind of indentation. He preferred to gouge suspicious coins with a knifepoint, but, well, Remaught had made it pretty clear that weapons were not allowed at this meeting.

The Ashing seemed genuine. And if Remaught wasn't planning to slight him, there would be 493 more in that safe box.

"You ever been to the Coinery on Talumon?" Ard flicked the coin back into the open box. "I was there a few years back. On legitimate business, of course."

Remaught closed the lid and turned the key.

"Coining," Ard went on. "Sparks, that's an elaborate process. Just the effort it takes to grind those raw scales into perfect circles...And you know they follow up with a series of chemical washes. They say it's for curing and hardening. I hardly think a dragon scale needs hardening..."

Across the table, Remaught was fidgeting. Ard suppressed a grin.

"Is something wrong, Rem? Can I call you Rem?" Ard pressed. "I thought this information would be of particular interest to a man in your line of work."

"Perhaps you can save the details for some other time," Remaught said. "You're not my only appointment today."

Ard leaned back in his chair, pretending that the mobster's words had really put him out.

"I'd prefer if we just get along with the transaction." Remaught gestured to the Grit keg. "What do you have for me there?"

"One full panweight of Void Grit," said Ard. "My source says the batch is top quality. Came from a good-sized block of indigestible granite. Passed through the dragon in less than five days. Properly fired, and processed to the finest of powder." He unlatched the cap on the Grit keg and tilted it toward Remaught. "The amount we agreed upon. And at an unbeatable price. I'm a man of my word."

"It would seem that you are," answered the mobster. "But of course you understand that I'll need a demonstration of the product."

Ard nodded slowly. Not all Grit could be demonstrated, especially indoors. But he had been expecting such a demand for this transaction.

Ard turned to the Trothian bodyguard, who leaned in the doorway like he was holding up the frame. "I'll be needing those rocks now."

Remaught grunted, then snapped at his bodyguard. "Suno! Pick up the blazing stones."

Wordlessly, the man hunted across the floor for the stones he had slapped away. As he searched, Ard quickly picked up the safe box, causing Remaught to jump.

"Relax," Ard said, crossing the room and carefully setting the valuable box on the wooden window seat. "I'll need the table cleared for the demonstration."

A moment later, Suno handed the rocks to Ard and lumbered back to the doorway, folding his dry, cracking arms.

There were nine little rocks, and Ard spread them into a loose ring on the tabletop. He unclasped the Grit keg and was about to reach inside, when Remaught grabbed his arm.

"I pick the Grit," the mobster demanded. "No tricks."

Ard shrugged, offering the container to Remaught. The man slipped his hand inside and withdrew a pinch of grayish powder. Ard pointed to the center of the stone ring and Remaught deposited the Grit in a tiny mound.

"That enough?" Remaught asked, as Ard brushed the pinch of powder into a tidier pile.

"More than enough," Ard said. "You trying to clear the whole room?" He clasped the lid on the Grit keg and set it on the floor behind him. "I assume you have a Slagstone ignitor?"

From his vest, Remaught produced the device Ard had asked for. It was a small steel rod, slightly flattened at one end. Affixed at the center point along the rod was a spring, and attached to the end of the spring was a small piece of Slagstone.

Remaught handed the ignitor to Ard, the tiny fragment of Slagstone wobbling on its spring. "With the amount of Void Grit you've laid down, I'd expect the blast radius to be about two feet." Ard said it as a warning. Remaught caught the hint and took a large step backward.

Ard also positioned himself as far from the table as he could, while still able to reach the tiny pile of gray Grit. He took aim and knocked the flat end of the steel rod against the table. The impact brought the spring down and the small piece of attached Slagstone struck the metal rod.

A respectable spark leapt off the Slagstone. It flashed across the wooden table and vanished instantly, with no effect.

"Ha!" Remaught shouted, as though he'd been waiting to make an accusation. "I should have known no one would sell a panweight of Void Grit at that price."

Ard looked up. "The Grit is legitimate, I assure you. This Slagstone ignitor, on the other hand…" He held up the device, gently shaking the spring as though it were a child's toy. "Honestly, I didn't even know they sold something this cheap. I couldn't ignite a *mountain* of Grit with this thing, let alone convince the spark to fall on that pinhead target. Allow me to throw a few more sparks before you let Suno rip my ears off."

The truth was, the tiny pile of powdered granite hadn't lit for two reasons. First, Remaught's Slagstone ignitor really was terribly inaccurate. And second, the Void Grit was definitely fake.

Ard leaned closer to the table, pretending to give the ignitor a close inspection. With his right hand hovering just above the pile of gray powder, he wriggled his fingers, spinning his heavy ring around so he could slip his thumbnail into a small groove and slide the face of the ring aside.

The gesture was subtle, and Ard was drawing Remaught's attention to the ignitor. He was sure the mobster hadn't noticed the fresh deposit of genuine Void Grit from the ring's secret cavity.

"Let's see if this does the trick." Ard repositioned himself, bringing the ignitor down, Slagstone sparking on impact.

The genuine Void Grit detonated instantly, the powder from Ard's ring creating a blast radius just over a foot. It wasn't at all like a deadly Blast Grit explosion of fire and sparks. This was Specialty Grit, and the particular demonstrated effect was far less dangerous.

A rush of energy emanated from the pinch of Void Grit, like a tremendous wind blasting outward in every direction from the center.

It happened much faster than Ard could withdraw his hand. Caught in the detonation, his arm was shoved backward, the Slagstone ignitor flying from his grasp. The stones on the table flew in every direction, the Grit pushing them to the perimeter of the blast, their momentum sending them bouncing across the floor.

The Void Grit was spent, but hovering around the table where the detonation occurred was a dome of discolored air. It would have been a spherical cloud if it had detonated midair, but the tabletop had been strong enough to contain the underside of the blast.

Remaught stumbled a step closer. "How did you do that?"

Ard wrinkled his forehead. "What do you mean? It's Void Grit. Digested granite. That's what it does." He bent down and retrieved a fallen pebble. "It voids a space within the blast radius. Clears everything out to the perimeter. The effect should last about ten minutes before the blast cloud burns out."

To prove his point, Ard tossed the pebble into the dome of discolored air. The little stone barely touched the perimeter before the effect of the Grit pushed it forcefully away.

Remaught nodded absently, his hand drifting to his vest pocket. For a brief moment, Ard thought the mobster might pull a Singler, but he relaxed when Remaught withdrew the key to the safe box. Remaught stepped forward and set the key on the edge of the table, just outside the hazy Void cloud.

"I'm ready to close the deal," he said, producing a few papers for Ard's inspection. Detonation licenses—or at least forgeries—which would allow him to purchase Grit.

But Ard wasn't interested in the legalities of the transaction. He dismissed the paperwork, picking up the keg of false Void Grit and holding it out to Remaught.

"Of course, I'll need a receipt," said the mobster, tucking his licenses back into his vest.

"A receipt?" That sounded frightfully legitimate to Ardor Benn.

"For my records," said Remaught. In a moment, the man had

produced a small square of paper, and a charcoal scribing stick. "Go ahead and notate the details of the transaction. And sign your name at the bottom."

Ard handed the Grit keg to Remaught and accepted the paper and charcoal. Remaught stepped away, and it took only moments for Ard to write what was needed, autographing the bottom as requested.

"I hope we can do business again in the future," Ard said, looking up from his scrawling. But Remaught Azel didn't seem to share his sentiment.

"I'm afraid that will not be the case." The mobster was standing near the open doorway, his Trothian bodyguard off to one side. Remaught had removed the cap from the Grit keg and was holding the cheap Slagstone ignitor.

"Whoa!" Ard shouted. "What are you—"

Remaught brought the ignitor down. A cluster of sparks danced from the impact, showering onto the gray powder housed in the open keg.

"Did you really think I wouldn't recognize an entire keg of counterfeit Grit?" Remaught asked.

Ard crumpled the receipt and dropped it to the floor, lunging for the key on the edge of the table. He scooped it up, but before Ard could reach the safe box, the Trothian bodyguard was upon him. In the blink of an eye, Ard found himself in a headlock, forced to his knees before a smug Remaught.

"I believe I mentioned that I had another appointment today?" Remaught said. "What I didn't tell you was that the appointment is happening now. With an officer of the Regulation."

A man appeared in the doorway behind Remaught. Not just a man—a veritable mountain. He had dark skin, and his nose was somewhat flat, the side of his face marked with a thin scar. The Regulator ducked his shiny, bald head under the door frame as he entered the room.

He wore the standard long wool coat of the Regulation, a crossbow slung over one shoulder and a sash of bolts across his broad chest. Beneath the coat, Ard thought he could see the bulge of a holstered gun.

"Delivered as promised," Remaught said, his tension at an all-new high. The Regulator seized Ard's upper arm with an iron grip, prompting Remaught's bodyguard to release the headlock.

"What is this, Remaught?" Ard asked between gasps for air. "You're selling me out? Don't you know who I am?"

"That's just it," said Remaught. "I know exactly who you are. Ardor Benn, ruse artist."

"Extraordinaire," said Ard.

"Excuse me?" Remaught asked.

"Ardor Benn, ruse artist extraordinaire," Ard corrected.

The giant Regulator yanked Ard to his feet. Prying Ard's fingers open, the man easily removed the key to the safe box before slapping a pair of shackles around Ard's wrists.

"Now wait a minute, big fella," Ard stalled. "You can arrest *me*, an amicable ruse artist trying to eke out a humble living. Or you can take in Remaught Azel. Think it through. Remaught Azel. *He's* the mobster."

The bald Regulator didn't even falter. He stepped forward and handed the key to Remaught with a curt nod.

"The Regulator and I have an understanding," answered Remaught. "He came to me three weeks ago. Said there was a ruse artist in town selling counterfeit Grit. Said that if I came across anyone trying to hock large quantities of Specialty Grit, that I should set up a meet and reach out to him."

"Flames, Remaught! You've gone clean?" Ard asked. "A mobster of your standing, working with a Reggie like him? You disgust me."

"Clean? No," Remaught replied. "And neither is my Regulator friend."

Ard craned his neck to shoot an incredulous stare at the Regulator holding him. "Unbelievable! A dirty Reggie and a petty mobster make a deal—and I'm the victim!"

Remaught addressed the big official. "We're good, then?"

The large man nodded. "We're good. I was never here."

The Regulator pushed Ard past Remaught, through the doorway, and into the creaky hallway, pausing to say one last thing to the mobster. "You got him to sign a receipt like I told you?"

Remaught scanned the room and gestured to the crumpled piece of paper on the floor. "You need it for evidence?"

"Nah," said the Regulator. "This lowlife's wanted on every island in the Greater Chain. The receipt was for your own protection. Proves you had every intention of making a legal transaction. Buying Grit isn't a crime, providing you have the proper licensure." He gave Ard a shove in the back, causing him to stumble across the rickety floorboards. "Give me plenty of time to distance myself before you leave this building," the Regulator instructed. "Understood?"

Ard glanced back in time to see Remaught nodding as the door swung shut. Ard and the Regulator descended the stairs in silence, the huge man never removing his iron grip from Ard's shoulder. It wasn't until they stepped outside into the warm afternoon that Ard spoke.

"Lowlife?" he said. "Really, Raek? That seemed a bit much. Like you were enjoying it."

"Don't lecture me on 'a bit much,'" answered the Regulator. "What was that whole 'ruse artist extraordinaire' slag?"

"You know I like that line. I saw an opportunity and I took it," Ard answered.

Raek grunted, tugging at the collar of his uniform. "This coat itches. No wonder we can always outrun the blazing Reggies. They're practically choking themselves on the job."

"You almost look convincing," Ard said. "But where's the Reggie helmet?"

"I couldn't find one that fit," answered Raek. "And besides, I figure I'm tall enough no one can see the top of my head. Maybe I'm wearing a tiny Reggie helmet. No one would know."

"Sound logic," Ard said as they turned the corner to the west side of Remaught's building. "You swapped the key?"

"Child's play," Raek answered. "You leave the note?"

"I even drew a little smiling face after my name."

Raek led them to a sturdy hay wagon hitched to a waiting horse.

"Straw this time?" Ard asked, finding it difficult to climb onto the bench with his hands still shackled.

"Should pad the landing," Raek replied.

"Look at you! Good idea."

"You're not the only person who can have one, you know." Raek pulled himself onto the bench beside Ard and stooped to grab the reins. "You're getting bored, Ard."

"Hmm?" He glanced at his friend.

"This little stunt." Raek gestured up to the third-story window directly above them. "It's showy, even for you."

Ard dismissed the comment. Was there a simpler way to steal the safe box? Probably. But surely there wasn't a more clever way.

Remaught had to be feeling pretty smug. In his mind, the exchange had gone off without a hitch. The mobster had been gifted a Regulation-issue safe box, partnered with a crooked Reggie, and taken some competition off the streets by having the ruse artist arrested.

By now, Remaught was probably reading Ard's note on the receipt—a simple message thanking the mobster for the Ashings and informing him that the Reggie was as fake as the Grit. This would undoubtedly send Remaught scurrying to the safe box to check its valuable contents. All he needed to do was thrust Raek's replacement key into the lock, and ... *boom*.

Any moment now.

The idle horse stamped its hooves, awaiting Raek's directions.

"We're sparked if he moves the safe box," Raek muttered after a moment's silence.

"He won't," Ard reassured. "Remaught's lazy."

"He could have the bodyguard do it."

"Suno was going soft," Ard repeated what he'd heard from Remaught. "Something about fatherhood. I'm more worried that the window won't break..."

Three stories above, the glass window shattered. The safe box came hurtling out on a perfect trajectory, landing in the back of the hay-stuffed wagon with a thud.

Remaught Azel was blazing predictable. Classic mobster. Maybe Ard *was* getting bored.

"I'm actually surprised that worked," Ard admitted, as Raek snapped the reins and sent the horse galloping down the street.

"That doesn't give me much confidence. Tampering with the safe box was *your* idea."

"I knew *that* would work," Ard said. They'd tipped the replacement key with a tiny fragment of Slagstone and filled the inside of the lock with Void Grit. The detonation would have cleared everything within the blast radius, undoubtedly throwing Remaught backward. The box of Ashings, still latched shut, was hurtled outward by the force of the Grit, smashing through the glass panes and falling three stories to the hay wagon waiting on the street below.

"I had full trust in the Grit." Ard gestured behind him. "I'm just surprised the box actually landed where it was supposed to!"

"Physics," Raek said. "You trust the Grit, but you don't trust physics?"

"Not if I'm doing the math."

"Oh, come on," said the large man. "Two and a half granules of Void Grit detonated against a safe box weighing twenty-eight pan-weights falling from a third-story window..."

Ard held up his still-shackled hands. "It physically hurts me to hear you talk like that. Actual pain in my actual brain."

Behind them, from the shattered window of Remaught's hide-out, three gunshots pealed out, breaking the lazy silence of the afternoon.

"Remaught? He's shooting at us?" Raek asked.

"He can't hope to hit us at this distance," answered Ard. "Even with a Fielder, that shot is hopeless."

Another gunshot resounded, and this time a lead ball struck the side of the wagon with a violent crack. Ard flinched and Raek cursed. The shot had not come from Remaught's distant window. This gunman was closer, but Ard couldn't tell from what direction he was firing.

"Remaught's shots were a signal," Ard assumed. "He must have had his goons in position in case things went wrong with his new Reggie soulmate."

"We're not soulmates," Raek muttered.

A man on horseback emerged from an alleyway behind them, his dark cloak flapping, hood up. The mob goon stretched out one hand and Ard saw the glint of a gun. He barely had time to shout a warning to Raek, both men ducking before the goon fired.

The ball went high. Ard heard it whizzing overhead. It was a Singler. Ard recognized the timbre of the shot. As its name implied, the small gun could shoot only one ball before needing to be reloaded. The six-shot Rollers used by the Regulators were far more deadly. Not to mention ridiculously expensive and illegal for use by the common citizen.

The goon had wasted his single ball, too eager to fire on the escaping ruse artists. He could reload, of course, but the process was nearly impossible on the back of a galloping horse. Instead, the goon holstered his Singler and drew a thin-bladed rapier.

"Give me the key," Ard said as another horseman appeared behind the first.

"What key?" replied Raek. "The one I swapped from Remaught?"

"Not that one." Ard held up his chained wrists and jangled them next to Raek's ear. "The key to the shackles."

"Oh." Raek spit off the side of the wagon. "I don't have it."

"You lost the key?" Ard shouted.

"I didn't lose it," answered Raek. "Never had it. I stole the shackles from a Reggie outpost. I didn't really have time to hunt around for keys."

Ard threw his chained hands in the air. "You locked me up without a way to get me out?"

Raek shrugged. "Figured we'd deal with that problem later."

A cloaked figure on foot suddenly ducked out of a shanty, the butt of a long-barreled Fielder tucked against his shoulder.

Raek transferred the reins to his left hand, reached into his Regulator coat, and drew a Roller. He pointed the gun at the goon with the Fielder, used his thumb to pull back the Slagstone hammer, and pulled the trigger.

The Slagstone snapped down, throwing a spark into the first chamber to ignite a pinch of powdered Blast Grit in a paper cartridge. It detonated with a deafening crack, the metal gun chamber containing the explosion and throwing a lead ball out the barrel.

The ball splintered through the wall of the shanty behind the goon. Before he could take proper aim at the passing wagon, Raek pulled back the Slagstone hammer and fired again.

Another miss, but it was enough to put the goon behind them. Raek handed the smoking Roller to Ard. "Here," the big man said. "I stole this for you."

"Wow." Ard awkwardly accepted the gun with both wrists chained. "It looks just like the one I left holstered in *my* gun belt at the boat."

"Oh, this gun belt?" Raek brushed aside the wool Reggie coat to reveal a second holstered gun. "You shouldn't leave valuable things lying around."

"It was in a locked compartment," Ard said, sighting down his Roller. "I gave you the key."

"That was your mistake."

Behind them, the Fielder goon finally got his shot off. The resounding pop of the big gun was deep and powerful. Straw exploded in the back of the wagon, and one of the side boards snapped clean off as the Fielder ball clawed its way through.

"Why don't you try to make something of that Reggie crossbow?" Ard said. "I'll handle the respectable firearms."

"There's nothing disrespectful about a crossbow," Raek answered. "It's a gentleman's weapon."

Ard glanced over his shoulder to find the swordsman riding dangerously close. He used his thumb to set the Slagstone hammer, the action spinning the chambers and moving a fresh cartridge and ball into position. But with both hands shackled together, he found it incredibly awkward to aim over his shoulder.

"Flames," Ard muttered. He'd have to reposition himself if he had any hope of making a decent shot. Pushing off the footboard, Ard cleared the low backboard and tumbled headfirst into the hay.

"I hope you did that on purpose!" Raek shouted, giving the reins another flick.

Ard rolled onto his knees as the mounted goon brought his sword down in a deadly arc. Ard reacted instinctively, catching the thin blade against the chains of his shackles.

For a brief moment, Ard knelt, keeping the sword above his head. Then he twisted his right hand around, aimed the barrel of his Roller, and pulled the trigger. In a puff of Blast smoke, the lead ball tore through the goon, instantly throwing him from the saddle.

Ard shook his head, pieces of loosely clinging straw falling from his short dark hair. He turned his attention to the street behind, where more than half a dozen of Remaught's men were riding to catch up. The nearest one fired, a Singler whose ball might have taken him if Raek hadn't turned a corner so sharply.

The wagon wheels drifted across the compact dirt, and Ard heard a few of the wooden spokes snapping under the strain. They were almost out of the slums, but still a fair distance from the docks. Raek's stolen hay wagon was not going to see them to their journey's end. Unless the journey ended with a gut full of lead.

Ard gripped the Roller in both hands. Not his preferred way of aiming, but his best alternative since his wrists were hooked together. Squinting one eye, he tried to steady his aim, waiting for the first goon to round the corner.

The rider appeared, hunched low on his horse. Ard fired once. The man dropped from the saddle, but six more appeared right behind him. And Ard's Roller only packed two more shots.

"We need something heavier to stop these goons!" Ard shouted. "You got any Grit bolts on that sash?"

Raek glanced down at the ammunition sash across his chest. "Looks like an assortment. Anything specific you're after?"

"I don't know... I was hoping for some Visitant Grit," Ard joked as he reached over and pulled the crossbow off Raek's shoulder.

Raek chuckled. "Like you'd be worthy to summon a Paladin Visitant."

"Hey, I can be downright righteous if I need to be," he answered.

Ard didn't favor the crossbow. He preferred the jarring recoil of a Roller, the heat from the flames that licked out the end of the barrel. The lingering smell of smoke.

"Barrier Grit." Raek carefully reached back to hand Ard a bolt from his sash. The projectile was like a stout arrow, black fletchings fixed to the shaft. The Grit bolt had a clay ball serving as an arrowhead, the tip dyed bright blue.

The bolt was an expensive shot, even though Barrier Grit was one of the five common Grit types. Inside the clay arrowhead, a chip of Slagstone was nestled into a measurement of glittering dust: digested shards of metal that had been dragon-fired and processed to powder.

Ard slipped the bolt into the groove on the crossbow, fitting the nock against the string he had already pulled into place—a difficult task with chained wrists. The goons were gaining fast now. Definitely within range.

"What's the blast radius on this bolt?" Ard pulled the crossbow to his shoulder and sighted down the length.

"The bolts were already on the sash when I stole it," answered Raek. "I'm guessing it'll be standard issue. Fifteen feet or so. You'd know these things if you bothered to keep up your Grit licenses."

Ard sighted down the crossbow. "Seriously? We're riding in a stolen wagon, you're impersonating a Reggie, we're hauling five hundred Ashings we just swindled from a mobster…and you're lecturing me about licensure?"

"I'm a fan of the Grit licenses," Raek said. "If anyone could purchase Grit whenever and wherever they wanted, the islands would be a mess of anarchy."

"I'm not just anybody," Ard replied. "I'm Ardor Benn…"

"Yeah, yeah. I got it," Raek cut him off. "Ruse artist extraordinaire. Just shoot the blazing bolt already."

Ard barely had to aim, the goons were riding so close now. He leveled the crossbow and pulled the trigger. The bolt released with a twang, finding its mark at the foot of the leading horse. The clay ball shattered on impact, and the Slagstone chip sparked, igniting the powdered metallic Grit.

The blast was nearly large enough to span the road. The discolored cloud made an instant dome, a hardened shell trapping two of the horsemen inside it. Their momentum carried them forward, striking the inside perimeter of the Barrier cloud.

The two horses went down, throwing their riders and crumpling as though they had galloped directly into a brick wall. A third rider also collided with the outside of the barrier dome, unable to stop his horse in time to avoid the obstacle suddenly blocking the road.

The two men within the Barrier cloud wouldn't be going anywhere until the Grit's effect burned out. They were trapped, as though a giant overturned bowl had suddenly enclosed them. Although the Barrier cloud seemed like it had a tangible shell, it couldn't be moved. And this dirt road was compact, so they wouldn't have a prayer at burrowing under the edge of the dome.

Ard grinned at the successful shot. "Haha! That'll buy us some time to reach the docks. Teach those goons not to mess with Ardor Benn and the Short Fuse."

"Come on, Ard," Raek muttered. "You know how I feel about that name."

"It's a solid name for a criminal Mixer like you." Ard understood why Raek thought it was unfitting. Raekon Dorrel was neither short nor impatient. Several years ago, during a particularly sticky ruse, Ard had referred to his partner as the Short Fuse. It was meant as little more than a joke, but somehow, the Regulation ended up circulating it through the streets until it stuck.

"Still don't think that's a respectable weapon?" Raek changed the subject, pushing the exhausted horse as they moved out of the slums.

"I'll leave the Grit shots to you." Ard handed the crossbow back to the driver. "I'll stick with lead and smoke."

Here, the road opened to a few grassy knolls that led right up to the cliff-like shoreline. The steep path down to the harbor was just ahead, where the *Double Take* was moored and waiting. Ard could see flags waving atop several ship masts, but with the high shoreline, it was impossible to see the harbor clearly.

"Clear ride to the docks today," Raek said. Now that he mentioned it, Ard thought the thoroughfare, usually bustling with pedestrians and the occasional cart or carriage, seemed abnormally still for a summer's afternoon.

"Something doesn't feel right," Ard muttered.

"Now, that's what you get for eating oysters for breakfast."

"I think we should stop," Ard whispered.

"Definitely," Raek replied. "We wouldn't want to outdistance those goons..." Raek was cut off as the wagon wheels hit a shallow trench across the dirt road.

Ard saw the sparks as the wheels struck a buried piece of Slagstone. He didn't even have time to grip the side of the wagon as the mine detonated.

Drift Grit.

A lot of it.

The blast radius must have been at least twenty yards, the center of the detonation occurring directly beneath the wagon. The discolored air hung in a hazy dome as the Grit took effect.

Ard felt his stomach churn as a bizarre weightlessness overtook him. The jolt from hitting the mine sent the wagon floating lazily upward, straw drifting in every direction. The horse's hooves left the road, and the poor animal bucked and whinnied, legs continuing to gallop in the sudden weightless environment.

"What was that?" Raek shouted. He still held the horse's reins, though his body had drifted off the wagon bench, his long wool coattails floating around his huge form.

"We hit a mine!" Ard answered. And the fact that it was Drift Grit didn't give him much hope. Barrier Grit would have been an inescapable trap, but at least they would have been safe inside the detonation. Adrift as they were now, he and Raek would be easy targets to anyone with a firearm. "They were waiting for us."

"Remaught?" Raek asked. "Sparks, we didn't give that guy enough credit!"

They were probably ten feet off the ground, Ard's legs pumping as though trying to swim through the air. He'd forgotten how disorienting and frustrating it was to hang suspended without any hint of gravity.

Now upside down, facing west toward the harbor, Ard saw more than a dozen mounted figures cresting the steep trail and riding out to meet them. He didn't need to see them upright to recognize the wool uniforms and helmets.

"Remaught didn't plant the mine," Ard shouted to Raek. "The Regulators did it. They knew we were coming."

"Flames!" Raek twisted in the air to see the horsemen Ard had just announced.

A gunshot pealed, and Ard saw the ball enter the Drift cloud. The shot went wide, exiting the detonated area just above their heads.

"We're sitting ducks!" Raek called, sun beating down on his bald head, dark skin glistening. "We've got to get our feet back on the ground."

Even if they could, exiting the Drift cloud now would put them face-to-face with an armed Regulation patrol. Perhaps they could flee back into the slums. Nope. From his spot hovering above the road, Ard saw four of Remaught's goons riding toward them.

"I thought you said this ruse was going to be low risk," Raek said, also noticing the two groups closing on their position.

"Did I? You're putting words in my mouth," Ard said. "How long until this detonation burns out?" He knew there was no way to know exactly. A standard Drift Grit blast could last up to ten minutes, depending on the quality of the bones that the dragon had digested. Raek would make a more educated guess than him.

Raek sniffed the discolored air. "There was Prolonging Grit mixed in with that detonation," he said. "We could be adrift for a while."

There was another gunshot, this one passing below their feet. Ard didn't know which side had fired.

"What else have you got on that sash?" Ard asked.

"More Barrier Grit." Raek studied his chest to take stock. "And a couple of bolts of Drift Grit." He chuckled. Probably at the irony of being armed with the very type of detonation they were trying to escape.

More gunshots. One of the lead balls grazed the side of the bucking horse. Blood sprayed from the wound, the red liquid forming into spherical droplets as it drifted away from the panicking animal.

Raek drew a dagger from his belt. Using the reins to draw himself closer, he slashed through the leather straps that yoked the animal to the wagon. Placing one heavy boot against the horse's backside, he kicked. The action sent the horse drifting one direction, and Raek the other. The horse bucked hysterically, hooves contacting the wagon and sending it careening into Raek.

Ard caught Raek's foot as he spiraled past, but it barely slowed the big man, tugging Ard along instead.

Their trajectory was going to put them out of the cloud's perimeter about thirty feet aboveground. They would plummet to the road, a crippling landing even if they didn't manage to get shot.

"Any thoughts on how to get out of here?" Ard shouted.

"I think momentum is going to do that for us in a second or two!"

They were spinning quite rapidly and the view was making Ard sick. Road. Sky. Road. Sky. He looked at Raek's ammunition sash and made an impulsive decision. Reaching out, Ard seized one of the bolts whose clay head bore the blue marking of Barrier Grit. Ripping the bolt free, he gripped the shaft and brought the stout projectile against Raek's chest like a stabbing knife.

The clay arrowhead shattered, Slagstone sparking against Raek's broad torso. The Barrier Grit detonated, throwing a new cloud around them midflight.

The bolt contained far less Grit than the road mine, resulting in a cloud that was only a fraction of the size. Detonated midair, it formed a perfect sphere. It enveloped Ard, Raek, and the wagon, just as all three slammed against the hard Barrier perimeter. The impenetrable wall stopped their momentum, though they still floated weightlessly, pressed against the stationary Barrier.

"You detonated on my chest?" Raek cried.

"I needed a solid surface. You were available."

"What about the wagon? It was available!"

A lead ball pinged against the invisible Barrier. Without the protective Grit cloud, the shot would have taken Ard in the neck. But nothing could pass through the perimeter of a Barrier cloud.

"Would you look at that?" Raek muttered, glancing down.

The Regulators had momentarily turned their attention on Remaught's goons. Apparently, the Reggies had decided that an enemy of their enemy was not their friend.

"We've got about ten minutes before our Barrier cloud closes," Raek said.

Ard pushed off the invisible perimeter and drifted across the protected sphere. Since Prolonging Grit had been mixed into the mine detonation, their smaller Barrier cloud would fail before the Drift cloud.

"How do we survive this?" Raek pressed.

"Maybe the Reggies and goons will shoot each other and we'll have a free walk to the docks."

"We both know that's not happening," Raek said. "So we've got to be prepared to escape once these two clouds burn out on us."

"I plan to deliver you as a sacrifice," Ard announced. "Maybe I'll go clean. Become a Holy Isle."

"Right," Raek scoffed. "But they won't be able to call themselves 'holy' anymore."

"Just so we're clear, this isn't my fault," said Ard. "Nobody could have predicted that Suno would sell out his boss."

"Suno?" Raek asked. "Who the blazes is Suno?"

"Remaught's bodyguard," he answered. "The Trothian in need of a soak."

"How does he figure into this?"

Ard had worked the entire thing out as they drifted aimlessly in the cloud. That was his thing. Raek figured weights, trajectories, detonations. Ard figured people.

"Remaught wouldn't have double-crossed us like this," Ard began. "It would put too many of his goons in danger, sending them head-to-head with an armed Regulation patrol. Our ruse was solid. Remaught thought he got exactly what he wanted out of the transaction—a dirty Reggie in his pocket.

"Suno, on the other hand, wasn't getting what he wanted. The bodyguard recently had a kid. Must have decided to go clean—looking for a way to get off Dronodan and get his new child back to the Trothian islets. So Suno sold out Remaught for safe passage. He must have told the real Reggies that one of their own was meeting with his mob boss. Only, the Regulators checked their staffing, saw that everyone was accounted for, and determined..."

"That I was a fake." Raek finished the sentence.

Ard nodded. "And if you weren't an actual Reggie, then you wouldn't be heading back to the outpost. You'd be headed off the island as quickly as possible. Hence..." Ard motioned toward the patrol of Regulators just outside the Drift cloud.

"Flames, Ard," Raek muttered. "I wanted to wring somebody's neck for this setup. Now you tell me it's a brand-new dad? You know I've got a soft spot for babies. Can't be leaving fatherless children scattered throughout the Greater Chain. Guess I'll have to wring your neck instead."

"You already killed me once, Raek," Ard said. "Look how that turned out." He gestured at himself.

Ard knew Raek didn't really blame him for their current predicament. No more than Ard blamed Raek when one of his detonations misfired.

Every ruse presented a series of variables. It was Ard's job to control as many as possible, but sometimes things fell into the mix that Ard had no way of foreseeing. Ard couldn't have known that Suno would be the bodyguard present at the transaction. And even if he had known, he couldn't have predicted that Suno would turn against his boss.

Maybe it was time to close shop if they survived the day. Maybe seven years of successful rusing was more than he could ask for.

"There's no way we're walking out of this one, Ard," said Raek.

"Oh, come on," Ard answered. "We've been in worse situations before. Remember the Garin ruse, two years back? Nobody thought we could stay underwater that long."

"If I remember correctly, that wasn't really our choice. Someone was *holding* us underwater. Anyway, I said we aren't *walking* out of this one." Raek emphasized the word, gesturing down below. Their Drift cloud was surrounded. Goons on one side, Reggies on the other. But Raek had a conniving look on his face. "Take off your belt."

Ard tilted his head in question. "I don't think that's such a good idea, on account of us being in a Drift cloud and all. Unless your plan is to give the boys below a Moon Passing. You see, this belt happens to be the only thing currently holding up my trousers. Take it off, and my pants might just drift right off my hips. You know I've lost weight over this job, Raek."

"Oh really?" Raek scoffed. "And how much do you think you weigh?"

Ard scratched behind his ear. "Not a panweight over one sixty-five."

"Ha!" Raek replied. "Maybe back on Pekal. When you were with Tanalin."

"Do you have to bring her up right now?" Ard said. "These might be my final moments, Raek."

"Would you rather think about *me* in your final moments?" Raek asked.

"Ah! Homeland, no!" cried Ard. "I'd rather think about cream-filled pastries."

"Like the ones you used to eat whenever we came ashore from Pekal...with Tanalin."

"Raek!"

The big man chuckled. "Well, Ard, you're not usually the type to let go of things." He let out a fake cough, saying Tanalin's name at the same time. "But I have to say, you've really let yourself go. You're a hundred and seventy-eight panweights. Pushing closer to one eighty with every raspberry tart."

Raek had a gift for that. The man could size up a person, or heft an object and tell you exactly how much it weighed. Useful skill for a detonation Mixer.

"Still less than you," Ard muttered.

"Actually, given our current gravity-free surrounding, we both weigh exactly the same—*nothing*."

Ard rolled his eyes. "And you wonder why you don't have any friends."

"Don't mock the science," said Raek. "It's about to save our skins. Now give me your blazing belt!"

Ard had no idea what the man was planning, but nearly two decades of friendship had taught him that this was one of those moments when he should shut up and do whatever Raekon Dorrel said.

In a few moments, Ard's belt was off, a surprisingly awkward task to perform while floating with both hands shackled. A gentle toss sent the belt floating to where Raek caught it. He held the thin strap of leather between his teeth while digging inside his Reggie coat for the gun belt.

"How many balls do you have?" Raek asked.

Ard made a face. "I'd think someone so good at mathematics wouldn't have to ask that question."

Raek sighed heavily, his developing plan obviously stifling his sense of humor. "Lead firing balls. In your Roller."

"Oh, right." Ard checked the chambers. "Coincidentally, I have two."

"Reload." Raek sent four cartridges drifting over to Ard, who caught them one at a time. The cartridges housed a premeasured amount of explosive Blast Grit in a thin papery material. At the top of the cartridge was the lead ball, held to the cylindrical cartridge with an adhesive.

Ard set the first cartridge, ball downward, into an open chamber. Twisting the Roller, he used a hinged ramrod on the underside of the barrel to tamp the ball and cartridge tightly into place.

It took him only a moment to reload, a practiced skill that couldn't even be hindered by his shackles. When he looked up, Raek was floating sideways next to the wagon, holding Ard's other Roller and making use of the belt he'd borrowed.

"What kind of arts and crafts are you up to?" Ard asked, seeing his friend's handiwork.

Raek had taken every spare cartridge from Ard's gun belt, a total of more than sixty rounds, and used the belt to lash them into a tight bundle. The barrel of the Roller was also tied down so the Slagstone hammer would make contact with the bundle of cartridges. The whole thing looked ridiculous. Not to mention incredibly dangerous.

"Our Barrier cloud is going to close any second," Raek said. "I'll get everything in position." He shut his eyes the way he often did when required to do complicated mathematics under stressful circumstances. "You should probably get the safe box."

Ard felt a sudden jolt of panic, remembering the whole purpose of the ruse. Glancing down, he was relieved to see that their stolen prize was still floating within the confines of their Barrier cloud, not adrift and unprotected like the poor horse.

Ard judged the distance, reaching out to feel the Barrier wall; solid and impenetrable. He shoved off, a little harder than intended, his body spinning and coming in at the wrong angle.

Ard's forehead struck the safe box. A painful way to be reunited, but it gave Ard the chance to reach out and grab it. For a moment he expected the box to feel heavy in his arms, but weight didn't exist in a Drift cloud.

Ard was just bracing himself to hit the bottom of the Barrier cloud when it burned out. He passed the spot where the invisible perimeter should have stopped him, momentum carrying him downward through the weightlessness of the lingering Drift cloud.

Ard slammed into the road, a clod of dirt floating up from his impact. A gunshot cracked and a lead ball zipped past. Normally, Ard enjoyed having his feet on solid ground. But with the goons and Reggies standing off on the road, he suddenly found himself directly in the line of fire.

"Ardor!" Raek shouted from above. "Get back up here!"

Lying on his back on the road at the bottom of the Drift cloud, Ard saw Raek and the wagon sinking almost imperceptibly toward him. The full strength of the Drift cloud had expired. Prolonging Grit kept it from collapsing entirely, but the effect of pure weightlessness would continue to diminish until both types of Grit fizzled out.

Gripping the safe box against his chest, Ard kicked off the road and sprang upward, the Drift cloud allowing him to float effortlessly upward.

"Gotcha!" Raek grabbed Ard's sleeve, pulling him against the flat bed of the empty wagon.

Raek carefully reached out, taking hold of a thin string. It looked strange, lying flat in the air like a stiff wire. "What we're about to do is among the more experimental methods of escaping."

"You mean, you don't know if it's going to work?" Ard said.

"I did the math in my head. Twice. It should…" He dwindled off. "I have no idea."

"Do I want to know what's tied to the other end of that string?" Ard asked.

"Remember how I lashed your other Roller onto that bundle of Blast Grit cartridges?"

Ard's eyes went wide. "Flames, Raek! That's going to blow us both to…"

Raek pulled the string. Ard heard the click of the gun's trigger on the other side of the wagon. The Slagstone hammer threw sparks, instantly accompanied by one of the loudest explosions Ard had ever heard.

The two men slammed against the wagon as it grew hot, fire belching around them on all sides. The energy from the explosion hurtled the broken wagon on an upward angle, a trajectory Ard hoped was in line with whatever blazing plan Raek had just committed them to.

They exited the top of the Drift cloud, and Ard felt gravity return around him. It didn't seem to matter much, however, since both men were sailing through the air at breakneck velocity. The burning wagon started to fall away behind them, like a comet soaring over the heads of the Reggies.

Raek reached out, grasping Ard's coat at the neck to keep the two of them from separating in the air. Ard had a lot of questions for his big friend. Namely, *How the blazing sparks are we going to get down?* But Ard couldn't breathe, let alone speak.

They were at the apex of their flight, any moment to begin the death-sentence descent, when Raek reached up with his free hand and ripped something off his ammunition sash. It was a Grit bolt, but the clay arrowhead was a different color from the Barrier bolts Ard had used earlier.

Raek gripped the shaft in one hand. Reaching back, he smashed the clay tip against Ard's left shoulder. The Grit detonated, throwing a fresh Drift cloud around them.

Ard felt the weightlessness return, along with a throb on his shoulder from where Raek had detonated the bolt. Guess he had that coming.

In this smaller, new Drift cloud, high over the road, the two men were no longer falling. They were shooting straight through the air, their velocity and trajectory maintained in the weightless environment.

In a flash, they had passed out the other side of the cloud. But before gravity could begin pulling them down, Raek detonated a second Drift bolt, this time shattering the clay tip on Ard's other shoulder.

They were flying. Sparks! Actually *flying*! High over the heads of their enemies, leaving both Regulators and goons behind. A few lead balls were fired in their direction, but there was little chance of getting hit, moving at the rate they were, spinning dizzying circles through the air.

One after another, Raek detonated the Drift bolts, the discolored clouds slightly overlapping as the two men shot horizontally through the air.

The concept of propelling an object over long distances through a series of detonated Drift clouds was not unheard-of. It was the basis for moving heavy materials used in the construction of tall buildings. But for a person to fly like this, unsheltered, the only calculations done impromptu and under gunfire. This was madness and genius, mixed and detonated on the spot.

The two flying men cleared the cliff shoreline, and Ard saw the harbor and docks just below. They exited the latest Drift cloud, the eighth, as Ard was made painfully aware from the welts on his back, and finally began to descend. Gravity ruled over them once more, and Ard judged that they'd slam down right against the first wooden dock.

"Two more!" Raek shouted. He crushed another Drift bolt on Ard's back, maintaining the angle of their fall and buying them a little more distance. As soon as they exited, Raek detonated the last bolt. They soared downward, past the docks and moored ships. Ard saw the *Double Take* below, docked in the farthest spot, a tactical location to speed their getaway.

They exited the final cloud and Ard watched the rapidly approaching water. He had hoped for a more elegant ending to their haphazard flight. Instead, he'd be hitting the bay at tremendous speeds, shackles locked around both wrists, holding a terribly heavy safe box.

Well, I'm certainly not bored, thought Ardor Benn. He took a deep breath.

~

It begins here. Although, for me, I suppose this is something of an ending.

Enter the monthly
Orbit sweepstakes at
www.orbitloot.com

With a different prize every month,
from advance copies of books by
your favourite authors to exclusive
merchandise packs,
we think you'll find something
you love.